THE WOUNDED HAWK

THE CRUCIBLE: BOOK TWO

Sara Douglass

A TOM DOHERTY ASSOCIATES BOOK
NEW YORK

THE WOUNDED HAWK: THE CRUCIBLE: BOOK TWO

Originally published in 2000 by *Voyager,* an imprint of HarperCollinsPublishers, Sydney

A Tor Book
Published by Tom Doherty Associates, LLC
175 Fifth Avenue
New York, NY 10010

www.tor.com

ISBN 0-765-34283-9
EAN 978-0-765-34283-6

First U. S. edition: January 2005
First mass market edition: September 2005

Printed in the United States of America

0 9 8 7 6 5 4 3 2 1

The Wounded Hawk *is for Diana Harrison, who first opened the way into parallel worlds across my kitchen table one damp afternoon in Bendigo (our way aided, as always, by a few good glasses of wine).*

Well ought I to weep
When I see on the Rode,
Jesu, my lover,
And beside him standing
Mary and Johan,
And his back is ascourged,
And his side is atorn,
For the love of man;
Well ought I to weep,
And sins to forgo,
If I of love know,
If I of love know,
If I of love know.

—Early fourteenth century

CONTENTS

The Wounded Hawk

PART ONE

Margaret of the Angels

Ill father no gift,
No knowledge no thrift.

—Thomas Tusser,
Five Hundred Points of Good Husbandrie

Chapter I

The Feast of the Beheading of St. John the Baptist
In the first year of the reign of Richard II
(Monday 29th August 1379)

✠

MARGARET STOOD in the most northern of the newly harvested fields of Halstow Hall, a warm wind gently lifting her skirts and hair and blowing a halo of fine wheat dust about her head. The sun blazed down, and while she knew that she should return inside as soon as possible if she were to avoid burning her cheeks and nose, for the moment she remained where she was, quiet and reflective, her eyes drifting across the landscape.

She turned a little, catching sight of the walls of Halstow Hall rising in the distance. There lay Rosalind, asleep in her crib, watched over by her nurse, Agnes. Margaret's eyes moved to the high walls of the courtyard. In its spaces Thomas would be at his afternoon swordplay with his newly acquired squire, Robert Courtenay, a likable fair-faced young man of commendable quietness and courtesy.

Margaret's expression hardened as she thought of the banter the two men shared during their weapon practice. Courtenay received nothing but respect and friendship from Thomas—would that she received the same respect and friendship!

"How can I hope for love," she whispered, still staring at the courtyard walls, "when he begrudges me even his friendship?"

Margaret might be Thomas' wife, but, as he had told her on their wedding night, she was not his lover.

Margaret had never imagined that it could hurt this much, but then she'd never realized how desperately she would need his love; to be the one thought constantly before all others in his mind.

To be sure, this was what they all strove for—to force Thomas to put thought of her before his allegiance to the Church and the angels—but Margaret knew her need was more than that. She wanted a home and a family, and above all, she wanted a husband who respected her and loved her.

She wanted *Thomas* to love her, and yet he would not.

She turned her head away from Halstow Hall, and regarded the land and the far distant wheeling gulls over the Thames estuary.

These had been pleasant months spent at Halstow Hall despite Thomas' coolness, and despite his impatience to return to London and resume his search for Wynkyn de Worde's ever-damned casket. The angels had told Thomas that the casket held the key that would see the demons who thronged earth cursed back into hell. As an ex-friar and a cold, heartless man of God, Thomas was devoted to the archangel's cause, and he was determined to discover the casket and work the angels' will. Margaret needed, desperately, to crack the cold hard shell Thomas had built about himself when he'd turned to the Church after the dreadful suicide of his lover, Alice. She needed, desperately, to have Thomas love her before he found that casket.

And she had no idea how she could ever achieve it. Sweet Jesu knew how she had tried these past months.

There had been mornings spent wading in clear streams, and noon-days spent riding wildly along the marshy banks of the estuary as the herons rose crying about them. There had been afternoons spent in the hectic fields as the harvest drew to a close, and evenings spent dancing about the celebratory harvest fires with the estate men and their families. There had been laughter and even the occasional sweetness, and long, warm nights spent sprawling beneath Thomas' body in their bed.

And there had been dawns when, half-asleep, Margaret had thought that maybe this was all there ever would be, and the summer would never draw to a close.

Yet this was a hiatus only, the drawing of a breath between screams, and Margaret knew that it would soon end. Even now hoofbeats thudded on the roads and laneways leading to Halstow Hall. Two sets of hoofbeats, drumming out the inevitable march of two ambitions, reaching out to ensnare her once again in the deadly machinations of the looming battle between the angels of heaven and the demons escaped from their imprisoning hell.

Margaret's eyes filled with tears, then she forced them away as she caught a glimpse of the distant figure striding through one of the fields. She smiled, gaining courage from the sight of Halstow's steward, and then began to walk toward the Hall.

Visitors would soon be here, and she should be present to greet them.

MASTER THOMAS Tusser, steward to the Neville estates, walked though the stubbled fields at a brisk pace, hands clasped firmly behind his straight back. He was well pleased. The harvest had gone excellently: all the harvesters, bondsmen as well as hired hands, had arrived each day, and each had put in a fair day's work; the weather had remained fine but not overly hot; the ravens and crows had devastated neighbors' fields, but not his; and little had been wasted—like their menfolk, the village women and girls had worked their due, gleaning the fields of every last grain.

There would be enough to eat for the next year, and enough left over to store against the inevitable poor years.

The fields were empty of laborers now, but the work had not ceased. The threshers would be sweating and aching in Halstow Hall's barns, separating precious grain from hollow stalk, while their wives and daughters swept and piled grain into mounds, before carting the grain from threshing court to storage bins.

Tusser's footsteps slowed, and he frowned and muttered under his breath for a few minutes until his face suddenly cleared. He grinned, and spoke aloud.

> "Reap well, scatter not, gather clean that is shorne,
> Bind fast, shock apace, have an eye to thy corn,
> Load safe, carry home, follow time being fair,
> Give just in the barn, life is far from despair."

Tusser might well be a steward with a good reputation, but that reputation had not been easy to achieve. He had made more than his fair share of mistakes in his youth: leaving the sowing of the spring crops too late, allowing the weeds to grow too high in the fields, and forgetting to mix the goose grease with the tar to daub on the wounds on sheep's backs after shearing. He had found that the only way he could remember to do the myriad estate tasks on time, and in the right order, was to commit every chore to rhyme. Over the years—he was a middle-aged man now—Tusser had scribbled his rhymes down. Perhaps he would present them to his lord one day as a testament of his goodwill.

Well . . . that time was far off, God willing, and there would be many years yet to rearrange his rhymes into decent verse.

Tusser reached the edge of the field and nimbly leaped the drainage ditch separating the field from the laneway. Once on the dusty surface of the lane, he looked quickly about him to ensure no one was present to observe, then danced a little jig of sheer merriment.

Harvest was home! Harvest was home!

Tusser resumed a sedate walk and sighed in relief. Harvest *was* home, praise be to God, even though it had not been an easy year. No year was ever easy, but if a steward had to cope with a new lord descending upon his lands in the middle of summer . . .

When he'd commenced his stewardship of Halstow Hall eleven years ago, Tusser had been proud to serve as a servant of the mighty Duke of Lancaster . . . even if the duke had never visited Halstow Hall and Tusser had not once enjoyed the opportunity to meet his lord. But the duke had received Tusser's quarterly reports and had read them well, writing on more than one occasion to thank Tusser for his care and to congratulate him on the estate's productivity.

But in March preceding, Tusser received word that Lancaster had deeded Halstow Hall to Lord Thomas Neville as a wedding gift. Tusser was personally offended: had the duke thought so little of Tusser's efforts on his behalf that he thoughtlessly handed the estate to someone else? Was the duke secretly angry with Tusser, and thought to punish him with a new lord who was to actually *live* on the estate? A lord in residence? The very idea! Tusser had read the duke's news with a dismay that increased with every breath. No longer would Tusser have virtual autonomy in his fields . . . nay, there would be some chivalric fool leaning over his shoulder at every moment mouthing absurdities . . . either that or riding his warhorse at full gallop through the emerging crops.

> Good Lord who findeth, is blessed of God,
> A cumbersome lord is husbandman's rod:
> He noiseth, destroyeth, and all to this drift,
> To strip his poor tenants of farm and of thrift.

Thus it was, that when Lord Thomas Neville had arrived with his lady wife and newly born daughter, Tusser had stood in the Hall's court to greet them with scuffling feet and a scowl as bad as one found on a pimply faced lad caught with his hand on the dairymaid's breast.

Within the hour he had been straight-backed and beaming with pride and joy.

Not only had Lord Neville leaped off his horse and greeted him with such high words of praise that Tusser had blinked in astonishment, Neville had then led him inside and informed him that Tusser's responsibilities would widen to take in Neville's other estates as well.

He was to be a High Steward! As Tusser strode along the lane back toward the group of buildings surrounding Halstow Hall, he grinned yet again at the memory. As well as Halstow, Tusser now oversaw the stewards who ran Neville's northern estates, and the second estate in Devon that Lancaster had deeded Neville. Admittedly, this necessitated much extra work—Tusser had to communicate Neville's wishes and orders to the northern and Devon stewards, as well as review their estate books quarterly—but it was work that admitted and made full use of his talents.

Why, Tusser now had the opportunity to send his verses to his under-stewards! Thus, every Saturday fortnight, Tusser sat down, ordered his thoughts, and carefully composed and edited his versified directions. He was certain that his under-stewards must appreciate his timely verses and homilies.

Tusser tried not to be prideful of his new responsibilities, but he had to admit before God and the Holy Virgin that he was not completely successful.

Not only had Neville praised Tusser's abilities, and handed him his new responsibilities, but Neville had also proved to be no fool meddling with Tusser's handling of the estate. He had a deep interest in what happened to the estate, and kept an eye on it, but he allowed Tusser to run it in the manner he chose and did not interfere with his steward's authority.

Neville was a good lord, and surely blessed of God. And his wife! Tusser sighed yet again. The Lady Margaret had an agreeable manner that exceeded her great beauty, and Tusser rose each morning to pray that this day he would be graced with the sweetness of her smile.

Aye, the goodness and grace of God had indeed embraced Halstow Hall and all who lived within its estates.

TUSSER TURNED a corner in the lane and Halstow Hall rose before him. It was a good building, built of stone and brick, and some two or three generations old. Originally, it had consisted only of the great hammer-beamed hall and minstrel gallery, kitchens, pantries and larders, and a vaulted storage chamber that ran under the entire length of the hall, but over the years Lancaster had caused numerous additions to be made, even though he had never lived here. Now a suite of private chambers ran off the back of the hall, allowing a resident lord and his family some seclusion from the public life of the hall, and new stables and barns graced the courtyards.

The sound of horses behind him startled Tusser from this reverie, and he whipped about.

A party of four horsemen approached. Tusser squinted, trying to make them out through the cursed sun . . . then he started, and frowned as he realized three of the four riders were clothed in clerical robes.

Priests! Cursed priests! Doubtless come to eat Halstow Hall bare in the name of charity before moving on again.

Priests they might be, but Tusser had to admit to himself that their habits were poor, and they showed no glint of jewels or gold about their person. The lead priest was an old man, so thin he was almost skeletal, with long and scraggly hair and beard.

His expression was fierce, almost fanatical, and he glared at Tusser as if trying to scry out the man's secret sins.

Evening prayers will be no cause for lightness and joy this *night*, Tusser thought, then shifted his eyes to the fourth rider, whose appearance gave him cause for thought.

This rider was a soldier. Sandy hair fell over a lined, tanned and knife-scarred face, and over his chain mail he wore a tunic emblazoned with the livery of the Duke of Lancaster. As the group rode closer to Tusser, still standing in the center of the laneway, the soldier pushed his horse to the fore of his group, pulled it to a halt a few paces distant from the steward, and grinned amiably at him.

"Good man," said the soldier to the still-frowning Tusser. "Would you be the oft-praised Master Tusser, of whom the entire court whispers admiration?"

Tusser's frown disappeared instantly and his face lit up with pride.

"I am," he said, "and I see that you, at least, are of the Duke of Lancaster's household. Who may I welcome on Lord Neville's behalf to Halstow Hall?"

"My name is Wat Tyler," said the rider, "and, as you can see, I am a sergeant-at-arms within good Lancaster's household. I ride as escort to my revered companions," Tyler turned and indicated the three priests, "who know your master well, and have decided to pass the night in his house." Tyler grinned even more as he said the last few sentences. "Perhaps you have heard of Master John Wycliffe," he nodded at the fierce-faced old priest, "while his two godly companions," now Tyler could scarcely contain his amusement, "are named John Ball and Jack Trueman."

Tusser bowed slightly to the priests, narrowing his eyes a little. He was well aware of John Wycliffe's reputation, and of the renegade priest's teachings that the entire hierarchy of the Church was a sinful abomination whose worldly goods and properties ought to be seized and distributed among the poor. Many of Wycliffe's disciples, popularly called Lollards for their habit of mumbling, now spread Wycliffe's message far and wide, and Tusser occasionally saw one or two of them at the larger market fairs of Kent.

The steward stared a moment longer, then he smiled warmly. "Master Wycliffe. You are indeed most welcome here to Halstow Hall, as are your companions. I am sure that my master and mistress will be pleased to greet you."

"The mistress, at least," said a voice behind Tusser, and

he glanced over his shoulder to see Margaret walking down the laneway to join him. He bowed, and stepped aside.

Margaret halted, and looked carefully at each of the four men. "I do greet you well," she said, "and am most happy to see you. My husband I cannot speak for."

Wycliffe and Tyler smiled a little at that.

Margaret hesitated, then indicated with her hand that they should ride forward. "Welcome to my happy home," she said.

THOMAS NEVILLE was anything but happy to welcome John Wycliffe and his two companion priests into his home. He had just finished at his weapons practice with Courtenay when he heard the sound of hoof fall entering the courtyard.

Turning, Neville had been appalled to see the black figure of John Wycliffe walking beside Margaret, two other priests (Lollards, no doubt) close behind him, and Wat Tyler leading the four horses. As he watched, Tusser, who'd been walking at the rear of the group, took the horses from Tyler and led them toward some stable boys.

Margaret said nothing, only halting as Neville strode forward.

"What do *you* here?" Neville snapped at Wycliffe.

Wycliffe inclined his head. "I and my companions are riding from London to Canterbury, my lord," he said, "and thought to spend the night nestled within your hospitality."

"My 'hospitality' does not lie on the direct road to Canterbury," Neville said. "I say again, what do you here?"

"Come to enjoy your charity," Wycliffe said, his voice now low and almost as menacing as his eyes, "as my Lord of Lancaster suggested I do. I bear greetings and messages from John of Gaunt, Neville. It is your choice whether you decide to accept Lancaster's goodwill or not." Wycliffe paused. "It is for a night only, Neville. I and mine will be gone by the morning."

Furious at being trapped—he could not refuse Lancaster's request to give Wycliffe lodging and entertainment—Neville nodded tightly, and indicated the door into the main building. Then, as Margaret led Wycliffe and the two other priests inside, Neville directed a hard glare toward Tyler.

"And you?" he said.

Tyler shrugged. "I am escort at Lancaster's request, Tom. There's no need to glower at me so."

Neville's face did not relax, but neither did he say any more as they walked inside. Wat Tyler and he had a long, if sometimes uncomfortable, history together. Tyler had taught Neville his war craft, and had protected his back in battle more times than Neville cared to remember. But Tyler also kept the most extraordinary company—his escort of the demon Wycliffe was but one example, and Neville felt sure he knew one of the other priests from somewhere—and Neville simply did not know if he trusted Tyler any longer.

In this age of demons who could shape-shift at will, taking on whatever form they needed in order to deceive, whom *could* he trust? Neville had trusted the Frenchman Etienne Marcel—and yet he had been a demon, intent on destroying God's order on earth and distracting Neville from working the angels' will. Tyler kept the company of demons; Neville knew he could not trust him.

MARGARET VERY carefully washed her fingers in the bowl the servant held out for her, then dried them on her napkin. Finally, she folded her hands in her lap, cast down her eyes, and prayed to sweet Jesu for patience to get through this dreadful meal.

Thomas was not the sweetest companion at the best of times, but when goaded by John Wycliffe, as well as two of his disciples . . . Margaret shuddered and looked up.

Normally, she ate only with Thomas, Robert Courtenay, and Thomas Tusser in the hall of Halstow. Meals were always tolerable, and often cheerful, especially when Courtenay gently teased Tusser, who always good-humoredly responded with a versified homily or two. Tonight their visitors had doubled the table, if not its joy.

They had eaten before the unlit hearth in the hall, and now that the platters had been cleared, and the crumbs brushed aside, the men were free to lean their elbows on the snowy linen tablecloth and indulge the more fiercely in both wine and conversation.

Margaret sighed. Under current circumstances, and with current company, religion was most assuredly not going to make the best of conversational topics.

Neville toyed with his wine goblet, not looking at Wycliffe, who ignored his own wine to sit stiff and straight-backed as he stared at his host.

Margaret suspected that Wycliffe, as well his companions, John Ball and Jack Trueman, were enjoying themselves immensely. During her time spent at Lancaster's court before her marriage to Neville, she'd heard tales of how Wycliffe liked to goad more conservative companions into red-faced anger with his revolutionary ideas, and Margaret was certain Wycliffe wouldn't miss this opportunity to torment Thomas, who so clearly disliked the renegade priest.

"So," Wycliffe was saying in a clipped voice, "you do not disagree that those who exist in a state of sin should not be allowed to hold riches or excessive property?"

"The idea has merit," Neville replied, still looking at his goblet rather than his antagonist, "but who should determine if someone was existing in a state of—"

"And you do not disagree that many of the higher clerics within the Church are the worst sinners of all?"

Neville thought of the corruption he'd witnessed when he was in Rome, and the sordid behavior of cardinals and popes. He did not reply, taking the time instead to refill his goblet.

Further down the table, Courtenay exchanged glances with Tusser.

"Over the years many men have spoken out about the corruption among the higher clergy," Margaret said. "Why, even some of the saintlier popes have tried to reform the worst abuses of—"

"When did you become so learned so suddenly?" Neville said.

"It does not require learning to perceive the depravity rife among so many bishops and abbots," Tusser said, his eyes bright, and all three priests present nodded their heads vigorously.

Neville sent Tusser a sharp look, but the steward preferred instead to see his lady's smile of gratitude. He nodded, satisfied that he'd made his stand known, and resolved to say no more.

"You can be no defender of the Church, Lord Neville," said one of the priests, John Ball, "when you have so clearly abandoned your own clerical vows to enjoy a secular lordship."

"I am more able to work the Lord's will as a nobleman than as a priest," Neville snapped.

Ball gave a soft, disbelieving laugh. "Such a convenient answer, my lord."

Neville repressed a surge of guilt. It *had* been best that he leave the Dominican order. As a nobleman, he had far better access to those who worked their demonry within the English court than ever he would have had as a friar. He tried to find the words for to justify his decision to this self-righteous priest, but instead satisfied himself with a hostile look sent Ball's way. He remembered where he had seen the man previously—at Chauvigny in France, where the priest had openly mouthed treasonous policies. The man was in the company of Wat Tyler then, too.

"Perhaps," Ball said, easily holding Neville's stare, "you found your vows of poverty too difficult? Your vows of obedience too chafing? You certainly live a far more luxurious life now than you did as a Dominican friar, do you not?"

"My husband followed his conscience," Margaret said, hoping she could deflect Thomas' anger before he exploded. She sent Wycliffe a warning look.

"We cannot chastise Lord Neville for leaving a Church so riddled with corruption," Wycliffe said mildly, catching Margaret's glance. "We can only commend him."

"Then why do *you* not discard your robes, renegade?" Neville said.

"I can do more good in them than out of them," Wycliffe said, "while you do better at the Lady Margaret's side than not."

Neville looked back to his goblet again, then drank deeply from it. *Why did he feel as though he were being played like a hooked fish?*

"My lord," said Jack Trueman, who had remained silent through this exchange, "may I voice a comment?" He carried on without waiting for an answer. "As many about this table have observed, the dissolution and immorality among the higher clerics must surely be addressed, and their ill-gotten wealth distributed among the needy. Jesus Himself teaches that it is better to distribute one's wealth among the poor rather than to hoard it."

There were nods about the table, even, most reluctantly, from Neville, who wondered where Trueman was heading. For a Lollard, he was being far too reasonable.

"But," Trueman said, "perhaps there is more that we can do to alleviate the suffering of the poor, and of those who till the fields and harvest the grain."

"I did not realize those who tilled the fields and harvested the grain were 'suffering,' " Neville said.

"Yet you have never lived the life of our peasant brothers," Trueman said gently. "You cannot know if they weep in pain in their beds at night."

"Perhaps," Wat Tyler said, also speaking for the first

time, "Tom thinks they work so hard in the fields that they can do nothing at night but sleep the sleep of the righteous."

"Our peasant brothers sleep," Wycliffe put in before Neville could respond, "and they dream. And of what do they dream? Freedom!"

"Freedom?" Neville said. "Freedom from what? They have land, they have homes, they have their families. They lack for nothing—"

"But the right to choose their destiny," Wycliffe said. "The dignity to determine their own paths in life. What can you know, Lord Neville, of the struggles and horrors that the bondsmen and women of this country endure?"

Neville went cold. He'd heard virtually the same words from the mouth of Etienne Marcel, the Provost of Paris, just before the provost had led the Parisians into an ill-fated uprising against both their Church and their nobles. Many thousands had died. Not only the misguided who had thought to revolt against their betters, but many innocents, as well. Neville remembered the terrible scene of butchery he'd come across on his journey toward Paris, the slaughtered and tormented bodies of the Lescolopier family. Marcel, and now Wycliffe, mouthed words that brought only suffering and death, never betterment.

"Be careful, Master Wycliffe," he said in a low voice, "for I will not have the words of chaos spoken in *my* household!"

Courtenay, very uncomfortable, looked about the table. "The structure of society is God-ordained, surely," he said. "How can we wish it different? How could we better it?"

"There are murmurings," Jack Trueman said, "that as do many within the Church enjoy their bloated wealth at the expense of the poor, so, too, do many secular lords enjoy wealth and comfort from the sufferings of their bondsmen."

"Do you have men bonded to the soil and lordship of Halstow Hall, Lord Neville?" Wycliffe asked. "Have you never thought to set them free from the chains of their serfdom?"

"Enough!" Neville rose to his feet. "Wycliffe, I know you, and I know what you are. I offer you a bed for the night begrudgingly, and only because my Duke of Lancaster keeps you under his protection. But I would thank you to be gone at first light on the morrow."

Wycliffe also rose. "The world is changing, Thomas," he said. "Do not stand in its way."

He turned to Margaret, and bowed very deeply. "Good lady," he said, "I thank you for your hospitality. As your lord wishes, I and mine shall be gone by first light in the morning, and that will be too early for me to bid you farewell. So I must do it now." He paused.

"Farewell, beloved lady. Walk with Christ."

"And you," Margaret said softly.

Wycliffe nodded, held Margaret's eyes an instant longer, then swept away, his black robes fluttering behind him.

John Ball and Jack Trueman bowed to Margaret and Neville, then hurried after their master.

Furious that he could not speak his mind in front of Courtenay and Tusser, Neville turned on Tyler.

"And I suppose you walk with Wycliffe in this madness?"

Tyler held Neville's eyes easily. "I work also for the betterment of our poor brothers, so," he said, "yes, Tom, I walk with Wycliffe in this 'madness.' "

"How dare you talk as if Wycliffe works the will of Jesus Christ!"

"Wycliffe devotes his life to freeing the poor and downtrodden from the enslavement of their social and clerical 'betters.' Is that not what Jesus Christ gave his life for?"

"You will bring death and disaster to this realm, Wat," Neville said in a quiet voice, "as Marcel did to Paris."

Tyler's face twisted, almost as if he wanted to say something but found the words too difficult.

Then, as had Wycliffe, he turned and bowed to Margaret, thanking her in a warm and elegant fashion, and bid her farewell. "Go with Christ, my lady."

"And you, Wat." Margaret turned her head slightly as

soon as she had said the words, fearful that Thomas should see the gleam of tears within their depths.

Would this be the last time she ever saw Wat?

Wat Tyler stared at Margaret one more moment, then he, too, turned and left the hall.

Chapter II

The Tuesday before the Feast of SS. Egidius and Priscus
In the first year of the reign of Richard II
(30th August 1379)

✠

WYCLIFFE, TYLER and the other two priests were gone by the time Neville arose at dawn. Although Neville was grateful they had departed, he felt useless as well. He would, by far, have preferred to put Wycliffe under some form of detention before he caused any mischief . . . but to do so might well be to anger Lancaster, and that Neville did not want to do.

So he'd had to let the demon—as he had no doubt Wycliffe was—escape.

Neville set about his morning tasks, hoping they would consume his mind, but instead, his temper became shorter as the day wore on. He was useless stuck here in the wilds of Kent! When would Hal call him back to court? Hal Bolingbroke, the son of the Duke of Lancaster, was not merely one of England's highest noblemen, as well as Neville's oldest friend, but now also Neville's benefactor. Lancaster had asked Neville to serve as Hal's secretary, a powerful position that would aid Neville's search for Wynkyn de Worde's casket and protect Neville from those demons who had infiltrated the court . . . but Neville could do nothing to further his quest for the casket and against the demons until Hal actually recalled him to court.

The only thing that calmed his mood was when, in the early afternoon, he joined Margaret and Rosalind in their solar. Neville loved his daughter, and always made the time to spend an hour at least playing with her each day.

He strode into the room, greeting Margaret perfunctorily—not noticing her wince—and lifted Rosalind from her arms.

Neville grinned and ruffled the black, curly hair that Rosalind had inherited from him. She was strong now, and of good weight and size for her almost six months of age. She had recovered well from the trauma of her birth . . . perhaps it was her good Neville blood, Neville thought, for his entire family was of hearty stock and robust determination.

Margaret watched him with sadness. Her husband looked to Courtenay for friendship, and to his daughter for love, but to her for . . . what? She took a deep breath, controlling her emotions, and then tilted her head as she heard a noise outside the door.

Neville glanced at her, irritated by the solemnity of her expression, then turned to the door as Courtenay strode through.

"My lord!" Courtenay said. "We have yet more company!"

He got no further, for a handsome man dressed in Hal Bolingbroke's new livery as the Duke of Hereford pushed past Courtenay.

Neville's eyes widened, for he recognized the man as Roger Salisbury, a young knight of noble family who had worked in Hal's entourage for some time.

Roger Salisbury stopped several steps into the solar, and bowed.

"My Lord Neville," he said, and was interrupted from further speech by Neville.

"Bolingbroke wants me," he said.

"Aye, my lord. I bear greetings from my Lord of Hereford, and am to inform you of his wish that you return to his side in London within the week."

Neville turned back to Margaret. "At last! I thought Bolingbroke had forgotten me!"

He stepped over to her and gently lowered Rosalind into her care. "I shall miss her," he said, and did not notice the sudden humiliation in Margaret's eyes.

Salisbury cleared his throat. "My Lord of Hereford also wishes that the Lady Margaret and your daughter ride with you."

Neville's eyes narrowed suspiciously. "Margaret is to ride with me?"

"Indeed, my lord," Salisbury said. "Bolingbroke"—he lapsed into informality, for although Hal was now Duke of Hereford, he was familiarly known as Bolingbroke— "is to take the Lady Mary Bohun to wife within the month, and it is her wish that your lady wife serve at her side."

Neville's mouth twisted. "Mary Bohun does not know the Lady Margaret exists," he said. "The wish is Bolingbroke's alone."

He paused, and in that pause allowed his suspicions their full malevolent flood. *Why did Hal want Margaret within his household? Surely it would be better if she and Rosalind stayed within the safety of Halstow Hall? There was no need for Hal to want Margaret back, as well as him, unless . . . no, no. It could not be . . . And then there was Richard . . . in London, Margaret would be so close to Richard's animal lusts . . . too close . . .*

"Richard . . ." he said without meaning to put voice to his thoughts.

Salisbury looked at Neville. Bolingbroke had told him that Neville would fear for Margaret's chastity around a king who had already made clear his desire for her.

"Bolingbroke," Salisbury said carefully, "has stated that the Lady Margaret will enjoy the full protection of his household. She will come to no harm under my lord's roof."

Maybe not from Richard, Neville thought. *But from Hal?*

Hal has made it plain enough to me that he wants Mary only for her lands. Does he now want the woman he does *desire back under his roof?* Neville suspected there was more to Hal and Margaret's relationship than just that of mere traveling companions during the time both had spent within the Black Prince's entourage in France. Margaret had then been the mistress of Baron Raby, Neville's uncle, but had her relationship with Hal merely been one of superficial acquaintance? Neville had occasionally come across them together when they had no true reason to be sequestered alone, and he remembered Hal's deep care for Margaret when she had been pregnant and unwell. Was that just Hal's natural care for the weak . . . or was it indicative of deeper emotion?

Then Neville mentally shook himself. What was he doing, acting like a desperate husband?

"My lord husband," Margaret said, rising. "You have told me previously that Lancaster thought I could do well to serve his wife, the Lady Katherine. But now that you have taken service with Bolingbroke, instead of his father, it is natural that I should serve Bolingbroke's wife instead."

Neville looked at her closely, but finally nodded his agreement to something he fully realized he had no choice in.

"Very well," he said, silently vowing that he would ensure Margaret came to, or caused, no harm.

Chapter III

The Feast of the Translation of SS. Egidius and Priscus
In the first year of the reign of Richard II
(Thursday 1st September 1379)

✢

RICHARD THORSEBY, Prior General of the Dominican Order in England, sat at his desk in the dark heart of Blackfriars in London, slowly turning a letter over and over in his hand. His eyes were unfocused, his sharp-angled face devoid of expression, and his equally sharp mind fixed on a memory of the previous Lent rather than on the contents of the letter . . .

The Dominican friary in the northern English city of Lincoln. The Lady Margaret Rivers, tearfully confessing that Brother Thomas Neville was the father of the bastard child in her belly. Neville himself, his behavior, dress and conduct advertising to the world his blatant abuse of every one of his vows. And John of Gaunt, Duke of Lancaster, humiliating Thorseby and allowing Neville to escape Dominican discipline.

In the months since, Thorseby had never forgotten his affront, nor had he relaxed from his intention of bringing Neville to Dominican justice. Indeed, what had once been intention had now become obsession. Thorseby would move heaven and earth, if need be, to bring Neville to penitent knees.

Or worse.

But how to do so? Lancaster and his son, Bolingbroke, were powerful men, and Neville enjoyed their full support.

If the arch-heretic, John Wycliffe, could escape the Church's justice through Lancaster's protection, then there was little Thorseby could do about the less-heretical problem of Thomas Neville. (Thorseby's personal sense of insult would sway no one to attack the Lancastrian faction on his behalf.) For a time, Thorseby had thought he might be able to use the long-ago deaths of Neville's paramour, Alice, and her three daughters, to his advantage. Surely Alice had well-connected family who would be pleased to see Neville brought to account for her death? Even her cuckolded husband could be useful.

But Alice's family and husband proved disappointing. They were all dead: her parents, her sister, and even her husband, who had succumbed to a wasting fever while on a diplomatic mission to Venice four years previously. The family who were left—distant cousins—simply did not care overmuch . . . and certainly didn't care enough to take on Lancaster and Bolingbroke.

"I will see you humbled yet, Neville," Thorseby murmured, then blinked, and looked down at the letter in his hands.

It had arrived an hour ago, and was a summons to Rome where there was to be an Advent convocation of the Dominican Prior Generals. Normally, such a summons would irritate Thorseby; travel through Europe in November and December was never the most pleasant of pastimes, especially when the Advent and Christmas season was so busy here in England. But now such travel would give Thorseby the perfect opportunity to meet with those who had known Neville in the months when he had apparently decided to abandon completely his Dominican vows.

Somewhere in Europe lay the evidence that would enable Thorseby to extract Neville from Lancaster's protection. *Someone* must have seen *something* that would damn Neville for all time; witnesses to a foul heresy, perhaps.

If there was one thing that Thorseby had learned from his Inquisitor brothers, it was that disobedience never goes totally unnoticed and unremarked upon.

Thorseby very carefully refolded the letter and put it to one side. He paused, briefly drummed his fingers on the desk, then leaned forward, picked up a pen, and began to compose the first of several letters he would send out later that evening.

WHATEVER HE'D said to Neville, neither Wycliffe nor his companions had any intention of traveling to Canterbury in the near future. Tired and, on Wycliffe's and Tyler's parts, saddened by their inadequate farewells to a woman both loved in different ways, they'd moved directly from Halstow Hall south to the port city of Rochester.

There, as arranged, they met with several other men—two craftsmen and another Lollard priest—in a quiet room in an inn.

"Well?" Wycliffe said as he entered the room.

"Ready," said one of the craftsmen. He indicated a stack of bundled papers. "Several hundred, as you requested."

"Show me."

The craftsman took a single large sheet of thick paper from the top of one of the piles and handed it to Wycliffe. Tyler, Ball and Trueman crowded about him, trying to read over his shoulder.

Wycliffe relaxed, then smiled at the three men he'd come to meet. "Very good. Wat?"

Wat was already shrugging off his distinctive livery, changing into the clothes one of the craftsmen handed him. Within minutes, he'd lost all appearance of a hardened sergeant-at-arms (save for his face) and looked more the prosperous farmer.

"You have mules for these men?" Wycliffe said.

"Yes," the priest replied.

"Good." Wycliffe turned to Tyler, Trueman and Ball. "My friends. You shall have the most troublesome of days ahead of you. Be careful."

Then he smiled, the expression lightening his normally harsh face. "Remember, when Adam delved, and Eve span—"

"Then," Wat finished for him, "there were no gentlemen!"

All the men broke into laughter, and, with that laughter, so were the seeds of revolution watered.

Chapter IV

The Feast of the Translation of St. Cuthbert
In the first year of the reign of Richard II
(Monday 5th September 1379)

— I —

✠

THE THAMES WAS QUIET—most ships and boats had put into harbor so their crews could devoutly mark the feast day—and its gray-blue waters lapped gently at the side of the small sailing vessel as it passed Wolwych on the southern bank. One more turn in the river and the great, smoky skyline of London would rise above the cornfields and orchards spreading beyond the marshy banks.

Neville sat impatiently on a wooden bench in the stern of the vessel.

They had ridden from Halstow two days past and had taken ship in Gravesend at dawn today, leaving several men from Roger Salisbury's escort with the horses to follow more slowly by road. The roads leading toward London from Kent and the other southern counties were crowded with merchant and grain traffic at this time of year, and the wheels and hooves of this traffic churned up the soft surface of the roads until they were nigh impassable in places. The Thames provided the faster and smoother course, and Salisbury had offered no objection when, the previous evening, Neville had suggested they complete their journey via the river; not only was it faster and more commodious, the river was safer and they could dock directly at the river gate of the Savoy rather than ride through the dust-choked London streets.

Margaret sat by Neville's side, Rosalind asleep in her arms. She was content and fearful in equal amounts: content because the river wind was cool and soothing as it whispered across her face and through her hair; fearful because of the inevitable travails and treacheries ahead. She glanced at her husband. He was fidgeting with a length of rope, his body leaning forward slightly, his eyes fixed on the river ahead.

Margaret shuddered and looked to where Rosalind's nurse slouched, dozing against a woolsack. Agnes Ballard was a homely woman in her late thirties who, three months previously, had in the same week lost her infant son to a fever and her husband to the savagery of a boar. Struggling to cope with her tragic loss, Agnes had been weepy-eyed with gratefulness when Margaret had suggested she wet-nurse Rosalind, replacing the nurse who had originally accompanied Margaret and Neville from London and who had wanted to return to her home. Agnes also acted as maid to Margaret herself, and Margaret enjoyed Agnes' motherly attentions almost as much as she believed Rosalind did. Agnes was a simple woman (but not so simple that she did not harbor her own strange secrets), but she was honest and giving, and she allowed Neville's occasional impatient or ill-meaning remarks to pass straight over her head.

Beyond Agnes, toward the prow of the vessel, sat Robert Courtenay with Roger Salisbury, who was laughing quietly with the remaining men of his escort and the three crew.

They were rolling dice, and sharing a flask of wine between them.

Margaret shifted slightly, adjusting Rosalind's sleeping weight in her arms, and hoped the flask contained only weak drink. This boat held those two people most important to the forthcoming battle between the angels and the demons—Thomas and herself—and Margaret's mouth quirked a little as she imagined the stratagems of angels and demons alike drowning uselessly in the mud of the Thames if the drunken crew lost control of the sails and tipped everyone out.

Who would arrive to save us, she thought, as we flailed about? Would both the minions of heaven and hell shriek in a horrified chorus at the careless ruin of their conspiracies?

"At what do you smile?"

Margaret jerked out of her reverie and looked at her husband. "I was hoping Roger will not let the crew get too drunk, for it would be a disaster if the boat overturned."

Her arms tightened slightly about Rosalind as she spoke, and Neville did not miss the movement.

He laid his hand on her arm. "There is no danger, Margaret. Nothing can—"

Margaret gave a low cry of terror, and gathered Rosalind so tightly against her breast that the baby awoke and cried out with protest.

Neville frowned, opening his mouth to speak, and then realized that Margaret was staring at something in the water on her side of the vessel.

He looked, and his breath caught so violently in his own chest that it felt as if his heart had stopped.

Beneath the rolling surface of the river spread a great golden glow.

Neville jerked his head around to look across the deck. The glow spread underneath the vessel to radiate an equal distance beyond on its other side.

"Tom!" Margaret said.

"Hush!" he said, and his hand gripped her arm tighter. *"Hush!"*

He looked toward Agnes, and to Courtenay Roger and their companions beyond her.

Agnes continued asleep, and the men were still engaged in their dicing as if nothing at all supernatural was gathering beneath the boards of the boat.

"Saint Michael!" Neville whispered, and Margaret whimpered and twisted about as if she wanted to jump overboard.

"Be still!" Neville said, moving his hand to her shoulder. Then he twisted a little himself so that he could stare directly into her terrified eyes.

"If, you are as innocent as you have always claimed yourself to be," he said, very slowly and carefully, "then why now do you fear?"

Sweet Jesu, why did he make it so easy to hate him? "I can have no innocence," she hissed, a spark of anger stirring within her, "when you allow me none!"

As Margaret spoke the glow coalesced, first directly under the keel of the vessel, and then seething up through the timber to form a fiery column not two paces away. The column assumed the spectral shape of the archangel, and then his voice thundered around them.

You are corruption made flesh, Margaret. An abomination which should never have been allowed breath.

Agnes and the men continued their respective activities—only Margaret and Neville were blessed with the angelic presence.

Margaret's lips curled at the archangel's words. If the archangel had whispered sympathies to Margaret, he would have destroyed her, but his hatred only served to transform Margaret's terror into fury.

Her face twisted in loathing. "If I am corruption made flesh," she said, "then I am truly my father's daughter!"

The archangel's face took on a terrible aspect and his arms spread wide—impossibly wide, for it seemed to Margaret and Neville that they stretched from bank to bank. He hissed, and the sound was that of the wind of divine retribution.

Filth!

"I may be the *daughter* of filth," Margaret said, her eyes locked onto the archangel's face, "but I choose not to tread the path of filth!"

"Margaret!" Neville was unsure of the meaning of the exchange between St. Michael and Margaret—*did Saint Michael accuse Margaret of demonry, or merely of the charge of being the daughter of Eve, the burden that condemned all women?*—but he was appalled at Margaret's words and the anger she displayed toward the archangel.

"Divine saint," Neville said, finally letting go of Margaret's shoulder and sinking to his knees before the archangel. "Forgive her words, for—"

Do you not know what she is, Thomas?

Neville did not reply.

Do you not know? She is that which you seek to destroy, Thomas.

Still Neville did not reply, and he lowered his gaze to the planking before him.

What does she here at your side, Thomas? Why have you not killed her, as her issue?

Finally, Neville raised his eyes back to St. Michael. "She is useful to me."

Useful?

"She will draw out other corruption so that I may see it for what it truly is, and so that I might destroy it." Neville stopped his words abruptly, wondering if that sounded as pitiful to the archangel as it did to himself.

Corruption is drawn to you anyway, Thomas. You know the foulness seeks to destroy you, before you destroy it.

"She is useful. She is a woman, after all." There, that was better.

Then make sure you do use her, Thomas, but do not allow her to use you. Remember the price if you fail.

Neville gave a low, confident laugh—and, in that instant, Margaret truly did hate him. How could she ever have wanted him to love her?

"They think to trap all mankind into eternal damnation," Neville said to the archangel, "by forcing me to hand her my soul on a platter, blessed saint. But there is no danger. I cannot possibly love her."

She breathes, Thomas, therefore she is a danger.

"She is *no* danger," Neville said, with such horrifying confidence that Margaret had to shut her eyes and force away her hatred of him. *If she allowed herself to hate him, then the angels had won here and now . . . and was that why Michael had chosen to show himself before both her and Thomas? To force her into hatred of her husband?*

The archangel's vision swept over Margaret, and what he saw on her face seemed to satisfy him.

Good, he said. *Thomas, Joan has taken her place, and soon you will take yours. Danger surrounds both of you, but you must endure.*

"The casket . . ." Neville said.

Is in London. It cries for you, it screams to you . . . do you not hear it in your dreams?

"Aye," Neville whispered.

It shall be in your hands soon, but beware, Thomas, for the only truth that matters lies inside its bounds. Listen not to what demons whisper in your ears.

"Aye," Neville said again, his voice stronger.

Blessed Thomas, the archangel said, and then he was gone.

NEVILLE STARED at the place where the archangel had stood, then he turned to look at Margaret.

She quailed at what she saw in his eyes, but she forced herself to speak before he did, and she used every ounce of her willpower to keep her voice steady.

"All truth matters," she said, "whether it lies inside Wynkyn's damned casket or not."

"Demon," he said. His voice was shockingly expressionless.

Her eyes filled with tears. "No, I am not, and have never been. But only when you hear the truth will you understand that."

There was an instant's hesitancy in his eyes at her words, and it gave her the strength to continue.

"If you love your daughter," she said, "then you cannot believe her mother a demon . . . for what does that make Rosalind?"

Neville blinked, and dropped his eyes from hers. "You plan my destruction. You would say anything to further your plan."

"No," she whispered, and the sadness in her voice made Neville lift his eyes back to her face. "No, I plan only for your infinite joy."

Then the sails cracked and filled with wind as they rounded the bend in the river, and Roger Salisbury jumped to his feet and shouted as London hove into view.

"TOM! TOM!" Graceful and certain, Bolingbroke leaped down the steps at the Savoy's river gate, laughing and waving. Light glimmered about his fair hair and in the brilliance of the sun it seemed that his gray eyes had turned to silver. "Ah, Tom, I have so missed you!"

Neville jumped from the side of the boat onto the wharf and embraced Bolingbroke as fiercely as Bolingbroke did him. "You affect the happy face well, my lord, for one who is shortly to be married."

"Ah, Tom, those are not the words to speak when your own wife is so close."

Bolingbroke turned away from Neville and held out his hand for Margaret who, with Rosalind now in Agnes' arms, was proceeding from boat to wharf with caution.

"My Lady Margaret," Bolingbroke said softly, and kissed her gently on the mouth.

Neville, who had taken a step forward, now halted, transfixed by the look on Margaret's face as she stared into Bolingbroke's.

It was an expression of the most immense and intimate love.

And it was the more horrifying because, although Neville could not see Bolingbroke's face, the expression on Margaret's made it apparent that the love was returned in full measure.

Terror swept through Neville, and this terror was the more frightful because he could not place the reason for its existence.

She thinks to use Hal against me, he thought, frantically trying to justify his fear. *She thinks to use her arts as a whore to lure him into her—*

"Tom," Bolingbroke said, turning back to him, "you look as if you have all the fishes of the Thames roiling about in your belly."

"We have had a difficult voyage," Neville said, finally, managing to twist his mouth in a tight, unconvincing smile.

"Oh, aye, we have that," Margaret muttered, and Bolingbroke shot her a sharp look.

Chapter V

Vespers, the Feast of the Translation of St. Cuthbert
In the first year of the reign of Richard II
(early evening Monday 5th September 1379)

— II —

✠

"MARGARET?" Bolingbroke closed the door to the storeroom quietly behind him, and stood, allowing his eyes to adjust to the dimness. The soft, warm glow of the autumn twilight filtered in through the half-closed shutters of the high windows, but all Bolingbroke could see, initially, were the bulging outlines of sacks of grain stacked against the back wall, and kegs of ale cached under the windows.

Then she moved from the safety of a shadow, and the golden twilight swirled about her, and Bolingbroke made a soft sound and stepped forward and gathered her in his arms. They had spent so much of their lives apart, and while circumstance dictated that for the moment they could not reveal to Neville the true nature of their relationship, Bolingbroke was not going to deny himself this small moment of closeness with a woman he loved deeply and who was so important to their cause.

"Meg! Sweet Jesu, I did not know if my message had come safely to you!"

She shuddered, her face still pressed into his shoulder, and he realized she had sobbed, silently.

He pushed her back so that he could see her face. "Meg? *What happened?*"

Margaret managed a small smile. "What, Hal? Do I not even receive a kiss of greeting?"

Exasperated and frightened for her in equal amounts, Bolingbroke planted a quick kiss on her forehead. *"What happened?"*

"The great archangel appeared to us as we sailed down the Thames."

"Michael dared . . . ?"

"Oh, aye, he dared." Margaret's face twisted in remembered anger and loathing. "He called me filth, and said I was an abomination."

Bolingbroke drew her to him again and tried as best he could to give her comfort. "And Tom?" he whispered, and felt her stiffen.

"The archangel told him to beware of me, as I was that which he had to destroy."

"We have always known that Tom would suspect you—"

"Aye, but Tom said that I was more useful alive than dead, and that I was no danger to him."

Bolingbroke hugged her tight. "He does not love you?"

"No. I do not think he ever will."

Bolingbroke was silent a long moment. "We cannot have that," he eventually said, very low. "Thomas must love you. He *must*."

Margaret sighed and drew back. "If he knew I was here now . . ."

"He will not know. I sent him riding to Cheapside, to the goldsmith crafting Mary's wedding finery, and to supervise its return here to the Savoy. He will be gone an hour or more yet. Margaret, events move more swiftly than any of us had thought."

"This Jeannette . . . this Joan of Arc."

"We never planned for her existence, nor for her intrusions. Sweet Jesu help us if she manages to rally the French . . . ah! but I cannot speak of her now. This is one of the only times we will have together, Meg, and I must use it well."

He let her go, and started to pace the narrow confines of the storeroom. "I had thought we would have two or three years yet, but now I think we shall have only a few months. A year at most."

He stopped, and stared at Margaret. "He *must* love you before a year is out."

"How? How? He thinks me filth! Lord Jesu, Tom will do whatever his beloved archangel tells him to do!"

Bolingbroke slowly shook his head. "Nay, I do not think so. Not completely. He has already denied the archangel's wishes once when it came to your death—you *know* Wat told us that, when he brought the physician to your side in Lincoln, they interrupted the archangel's fury over Tom not immediately sliding the sword into your body."

Margaret almost smiled remembering Wat Tyler's too brief visit to Halstow Hall. "Not immediately," she said, "but one day, when it comes to the choice, then Thomas *will* slide it in."

"Not if we can help it," Bolingbroke said. "Sweet Meg, he is capable of love, great love, but he needs to be pushed."

She made a dismissive sound. "I cannot believe that. He is too cold . . . too arrogant. Too sure of himself and his damned, cursed God."

"Meg, I have known Tom for many, many years. I knew him as a boy—even before his parents died. Once he was softer and kinder, with a truly gentle soul, but then God's hand descended . . . and Tom's life became a living hell. First with the death of his mother and father, then with the horrific tragedy of Alice. That happy, gentle boy is still there, *somewhere*, and it is you, Meg, who will draw him out. He must trust enough to love again."

"And how am I to accomplish the impossible?"

Bolingbroke drew in a very deep breath, took both Margaret's hands in his, and spoke low and soft for many minutes.

When he'd finished, Margaret stared at him, her eyes wide. "I cannot!"

"We must move quickly," Bolingbroke said. "Margaret, I am sorry that it must be with such abominable trickery—"

"Trickery? Trickery of *whom*, Hal? Tom . . . or *me*?"

"Margaret—"

"And how can you ask such a thing of *me*? Have I not already suffered enough?"

"Meg—"

She jerked her hands out of his. "You'll tread anyone to the ground to achieve your ambition, won't you? Me . . . Tom . . . and now," her voice rose, became shrill, "this Mary Bohun! Why marry her when you know your heart is pledged to another?"

Bolingbroke tensed, his eyes narrowing.

"Our entire cause is tied to you marrying another," she said. "Will you tread Mary Bohun into the ground when she has outlived her usefulness?"

"You know why I need to wed Mary," Bolingbroke said. "She is the sole heir to the Hereford family's vast estates and her lands shall strengthen my position. I need that strength *now*, Margaret. The inheritance she brings will bolster my position against Richard—"

"And what if Mary gives you an heir? Do you truly want to dilute your blood with that of—"

Bolingbroke sighed. "She won't."

Margaret arched an eyebrow. "You will leave her a virgin? But won't that compromise your claim to her lands?"

"I will make a true wife of Mary—I can do that for her, at least." Bolingbroke paused. "Margaret, when you come to Mary, when you attend her, look deep into her eyes, and see the shadows there. You will know what I mean."

"She is ill?"

Bolingbroke nodded.

"How fortunate for you," Margaret said.

"It is not of *my* doing!" Bolingbroke said.

"Be sure to tell her of your ambitions and needs on your wedding night, Hal. Be sure to tell her that you expect her affliction to be of the most deadly nature. And timely, no less."

"You have no right to speak to me thus!"

"I have every right!" Margaret said, close to tears. This had already been an appalling day, and Hal had made it so much worse than he needed to have done.

He reached out a hand, his fingers grazing her cheek. "Margaret, be strong for me. I do not need your womanly weeping, or your reminders of what is right and what is not. We've come too far for that."

His hand lifted, lingering a moment at her hairline, then it dropped. He hesitated, as if he would speak more, but then he brushed abruptly past her and left the room.

Margaret put a trembling hand to her mouth, fought back her tears and leaned against the door, giving Bolingbroke the time he needed to get back to his apartments.

Finally she, too, left.

LADY MARY Bohun was also staying in the Savoy, chaperoned by her mother, Cecilia, and later that evening, in the hour before a quiet supper was held in the hall, Bolingbroke introduced his betrothed to her new attending lady.

Margaret, composed and courteous, curtsied gracefully before the Lady Mary, who stared at her a little uncertainly, then patted the stool beside her chair, indicating Margaret should sit.

Margaret fought the urge to glance at Hal, and did as Mary requested.

Mary gave an uncertain smile—*this Margaret was so beautiful . . . what was she to Hal?*—then leaned forward and spoke quietly of some of the lighter matters at court.

Margaret responded easily enough, but kept her eyes downcast, as she should when in the presence of such a noble lady.

Bolingbroke watched carefully for a minute, then turned and grinned boyishly at Neville, who had returned from the goldsmith's in the past hour.

"And now that we have disposed of the ladies," Bolingbroke said, "perhaps you and I can have a quiet word before we sup."

BOLINGBROKE HAD a suite of eight or nine chambers set aside for his personal use in the Savoy, and the chamber he now led Neville into was part of his office accommodation. Its furniture—two tables, two wooden chairs, three stools, several large chests and innumerable smaller ones, and a great cabinet standing against a far wall—was almost smothered in vellum rolls containing legal records, and several large volumes opened to reveal columns of figures written in the new Arabic numerals, and half-folded papers drawn with everything from maps to diagrams of the inner workings of clocks.

From the ceiling joists hung a variety of strange mechanical contraptions. Neville would later learn that two of them were the fused skeletons and internal organs of clocks, one was the result of the strange and unsuccessful mating of a clock and a crossbow, one was something Bolingbroke had been told could predict thunderstorms by measuring the degree of anger within the air, one was a strange hybrid abacus, and one sparkling collection of brass and copper cogs and wheels and shafts did nothing but bob and tinkle pleasantly whenever there was movement within the air.

Bolingbroke looked apologetic as he gestured about the room. "I have several clerks who try to keep my affairs in order . . . but as you can see, Tom, I need you badly."

Neville ducked as he almost hit his head on the hybrid abacus. "Lord Savior, Hal. What lies buried amid this mess?"

For an instant, amusement glinted in Bolingbroke's eyes, only to be replaced with a look of abstracted and irritated worry. "What lies here? Bills, receipts, reports, petitions, memorandums from at least four working committees of Commons in which, apparently, I am to take an interest, lists of passports issued in the past five months, accounts of lambing and harvest from sundry of my stewards, digests of legal debates from the Inns of Courts, summaries of—"

"Enough!" Neville threw up his hands, then he turned to Bolingbroke and laughed. "What sin have I committed, my friend, that you so burden me with minutiae?"

"Minutiae is the oil which smooths the English bureaucracy, Tom, surely you know that, and the bureaucracy is determined to see to it that every nobleman in England is to be kept out of mischief with an excess of the mundane. A memorandum is as vicious a weapon as has ever been invented. Far better than the axe."

Neville shook his head, then let the amusement drain from his face. "It is good to be back, Hal."

Bolingbroke grasped Neville's hand briefly. "And it is good to have you back. Tom, we need to talk, and it has nothing to do with this mess."

"Aye, Richard."

"Richard, indeed." Bolingbroke moved to a table, swept a portion of it free of papers, and perched on a corner. "He moves fast to consolidate his horrid hold on England."

"Hal, the archangel Saint Michael appeared to me as we sailed toward London."

Bolingbroke's face tightened with shock. "What did he say?"

"That the casket is in London, and that it screams to me. That I am to be surrounded by lies, but that all lies will be as naught once I read the truths that the casket contains."

"It is *certain* that Richard holds the casket," Bolingbroke said.

"Have you learned anything?"

"About the casket? No."

"About Richard, then."

Bolingbroke grimaced in distaste. "Do you remember,

years back, when you were still at court, that the boy Richard scurried about with Oxford's son?"

"Robert de Vere? Yes . . . he was a lad some few years older than Richard." Neville idly scratched at his short beard, remembering some of the gossip that had spread about the two boys. "De Vere was probably the one who first taught Richard how to piss standing up."

"Undoubtedly 'dear Robbie' taught Richard to do a great many things with his manly poker other than to piss with it. Well, now de Vere struts about as the Earl of Oxford . . . his father died some two years past," Bolingbroke grinned slightly, "while you were ensconced in your friary. He also managed to wed Philippa, Hotspur's sister."

Neville raised his brows—that wedding and bedding marked an important (and potentially dangerous) alliance between the houses of Oxford and Northumberland.

"De Vere has left his wife at home in his drafty castle and is now back at court and in the king's great favor." Bolingbroke's grin faded, replaced with a look of contempt. "Rather, de Vere gifts the king with the benevolence of his patronage. It is said that not only will Richard not make a single decision without consulting de Vere—sweet Jesu, Tom, if de Vere said that black was white then Richard would believe him!—but that the two men share an . . . unnatural . . . relationship."

Neville stared at Bolingbroke. "You cannot mean that they still practice their boyhood follies!"

"Oh, aye, I do mean that. Their hands are all over each other in those hours that they're not all over some poor woman they've had dragged in from the alleys behind St. Paul's."

Neville was so appalled he had to momentarily close his eyes. *Saint Michael had been right to say that the English court was corrupted with evil. Soon Richard would have the entire court—nay! the entire country!—dancing to his depraved tune.*

"I *must* find that casket!" Neville said. The casket held

Wynkyn de Worde's book, and that book held the key to sealing the demons back into hell, where they belonged.

"Aye," Bolingbroke said. "And it must be in Westminster. Where else?"

"And how can I—"

"Patience, my friend. I called you back not merely to witness my forthcoming nuptials and to take care of this mess"—Bolingbroke waved his hand laconically about the tumbled muddle of papers and reports around them—"but because Richard himself will shortly present me—and thus you—with the excuse to haunt the halls of Westminster."

Neville, who had turned to stare in frustration out a small window looking over the river wall of the Savoy, now looked back to Bolingbroke. "And that excuse is . . . ?"

"Do you remember the terms the Black Prince—may sweet Jesu watch over his soul—set for John's repatriation back to France?"

A year earlier, the Black Prince had seized the French king during the battle of Poitiers. Ever since then, the English had been trying to exact the greatest ransom they could from the French for the return of their king. "Aye," Neville said. "Charles was to pay . . . what? Seven hundred thousand English pounds for his grandfather's ransom?"

Bolingbroke nodded.

"And, as well, both John and Charles had to be signatories to a treaty of peace that recognized the Black Prince as heir to the French throne . . . disinheriting Charles completely."

"Exactly." A small pile of papers on the table next to Bolingbroke toppled over with a gentle sigh, scattering about his feet, and Bolingbroke kicked them aside impatiently, ignoring Neville's exasperated look.

"But," Bolingbroke continued, folding his arms and watching Neville carefully, "circumstances have changed. Edward is dead. The Black Prince is dead. A young and untried man now sits on the throne. We may have trod the French into the mud of Poitiers, but now we have no tried war leader to press home the advantage."

"Not even you?" Neville said very quietly.

Bolingbroke ignored him. "My father has no taste for spending what time remains to him leading rows of horsed steel against the French, and, in any case, his talents have always been in the field of diplomacy rather than the field of battle. Northumberland is also aging," Bolingbroke's mouth quirked, "although I hear Hotspur is keen enough to take his own place in the vanguard of England's hopes in France."

And you? Neville thought, keeping silent this time. *Where do your ambitions lie, Hal?*

"So Richard must needs rethink the terms of treaty," Bolingbroke said. "This he has done—doubtless with de Vere's advice—and his new terms meet with John's approval. Or, more to the point, John has grown old and addled enough not to truly care what he signs anymore."

"What are the terms?"

"The demand for seven hundred thousand pounds has gone. Instead, Richard has settled for secure access to the Flemish wool ports for our wool merchantmen—John will agree to remove whatever naval blockade he still has in place."

Neville shook his head slightly. The Black Prince would simply have smashed his way through the French blockades. . . . Richard had, in effect, paid the French seven hundred thousand pounds to remove them.

Bolingbroke watched Neville's reaction carefully. "But Richard has not backed down on his claim to the French throne. In two days' time King John will sign at Westminster a treaty that recognizes Richard as the true heir to the French throne."

Neville raised his eyebrows. Maybe the seven hundred thousand pounds had been worth it, after all.

"And," Bolingbroke continued very softly, "Richard no longer demands that Charles co-sign. Instead, he has a more powerful French signatory, someone who he hopes will virtually guarantee him an ironclad claim to France."

"Who?"

"Isabeau de Bavière."

"What? Charles' whore mother?"

Bolingbroke laughed. "Aye. Dame Isabeau will formally declare Charles a bastard. Her memory has become clearer, it seems, and she is now certain that it was the Master of Hawks who put Charles in her."

"And what price did Richard pay for the return of her memory?"

"A castle here, a castle there, a stableful of willing lads . . . who truly knows? But enough to ensure that Isabeau will swear on the Holy Scriptures, and whatever splinters of the True Cross the Abbot of Westminster scrapes up, that Charles is a bastard, and that leaves Richard, as John's great grand-nephew, the nearest male relative."

Neville grimaced. "John must rue the day his father gave his sister to be Edward II's wife."

"I swear that he has spent his entire life ruing it. And the inevitable has come to pass. John must sign away the French throne to a distant English relative."

"What of Catherine?"

"Catherine?"

"Aye, Catherine . . . Charles' sister." Neville wasn't sure why Hal was looking so surprised—he must surely have considered her claim. "Is Catherine a bastard as well? Or did John's witless son Louis actually manage to father her on Isabeau? If Catherine is legitimate, then, while she is not allowed to sit on the throne herself according to Salic Law, her bed and womb will become a treasure booty for any French noble who thinks to lay claim to the throne."

"I am sure that Louis never fathered that girl," Bolingbroke said. "No doubt her father was some stable lad Isabeau thoughtlessly bedded one warm, lazy afternoon."

"And if she's *not* bastard-bred?" Neville said, watching Bolingbroke as carefully as Bolingbroke had been watching him earlier. "We all know who will be the first to climb into Catherine's bed."

Bolingbroke stared stone-faced at Neville, then raised his eyebrows in query.

"Philip is with Charles' camp, Hal." Philip, King of Navarre, known as Philip the Bad for his mischief making and constant designs on the French throne, to which he claimed a right. "You know he is stuck to Charles' side to gain whatever advantage he can. And you also know that Philip's lifelong ambition has been to reach beyond Navarre to the French throne. You're wrong to suggest that Richard is the *only* close male relative to John—Philip thinks he has the better blood claim. The instant word reaches France of the treaty, Philip will be lifting back Catherine's bedcovers with a grin of sheer triumph stretching across his handsome face."

"Catherine would not allow it."

"Why not? She has ambition herself and she will need to assure her future. Philip would be one of the few men in Christendom who could guarantee her a place beside the throne."

Bolingbroke abruptly stood up. "Whatever. I thought you more interested in de Worde's casket than a young girl's bedding." He walked to the door. "In three days' time I will be called to Westminster as witness to the signing of the treaty. You will come with me, and together we can spend our spare hours haunting the cellars and corridors of the palace complex . . . the casket *must* be there somewhere! Now"—Bolingbroke grabbed the door latch and pulled the door open—"we shall collect our women and we will join my father and his lady wife for supper in the hall . . . they will surely be wondering where we are."

"Hal, wait! There is one other thing!"

Visibly impatient, Bolingbroke raised his eyebrows.

"A few days before we left Halstow Hall, Wycliffe, Wat Tyler and two Lollard priests, Jack Trueman and John Ball, came to visit."

All impatience on Bolingbroke's face had now been replaced with stunned surprise. "What? Why?"

"To irritate me, no doubt." Neville paused. "Wycliffe said he was on his way to Canterbury, intimating it was with the leave of your father. Thus, Wat Tyler as escort."

Bolingbroke slowly shook his head. "As far as we knew, Wycliffe had gone back to Oxford. But he is in Kent?"

Neville nodded, and Bolingbroke frowned, apparently genuinely concerned.

"I must tell my father Wycliffe has been misusing his name," he said, then corrected himself. "No. I will make the inquiries. There is no need to disturb my father."

Then, with a forced gaiety on his face, Bolingbroke once more indicated the door. "And now, we *must* return to our women, Tom!"

And with that Bolingbroke disappeared into the corridor as Neville, thoughtful, stared after him.

CECILIA BOHUN, dowager Countess of Hereford, gasped, and her face flushed.

"Madam?" Mary said, leaning over to lay her hand on her mother's arm.

Cecilia took a deep breath and tried to smile for her daughter. "I fear you must pardon me, Mary. I—"

She suddenly got to her feet, and took three quick steps toward the door. Collecting herself with an extreme effort, she half-turned back to her still-seated daughter.

"Before we sup . . . I must . . . the garderobe . . ." she said, and then made as dignified a dash to the door as she could.

Margaret did not know what to do: what words should she say? *Should* she say anything? Did the Lady Mary expect her to go after her mother? Would the Lady Mary hate her for witnessing her mother's discomposure?

"Margaret," Mary Bohun said, "pray do not fret. My mother will be well soon enough. It is just that . . . at her age . . ."

Grateful that Mary should not only have recognized her uncertainty, but have then so generously rescued her, Margaret smiled and nodded. "I have heard, my lady, that the time of a woman's life when her courses wither and die is difficult."

"But we must be grateful to God if we survive the travails of childbed to reach that age, Margaret."

Margaret nodded, silently studying Mary. She was a slender girl with thick, honey-colored hair and lustrous hazel eyes. Not beautiful, nor even pretty, but pleasant enough. However, unusually for a woman of her nobility and inheritance, Mary was unassuming far beyond what modesty called for. When Margaret had first sat down, she thought to find Mary a haughty and distant creature, but in the past half hour she had realized that, while reserved, the woman was also prepared to be open and friendly with a new companion who was not only much more lowly ranked than herself, but whose reputation was besmirched by scandal; Mary must certainly have heard that Margaret's daughter was born outside marriage, even if she had not heard of Margaret's liaison with the Earl of Westmorland, Ralph Neville, while in France.

Margaret also realized that Mary was, as Hal had suggested, tainted with a malaise; deep in her eyes were the faint marks of a slippery, sliding phantom, the subterranean footprints of something dark and malignant and hungry.

Margaret shuddered, intuiting from both Hal's words and her own observations—Sweet Lord Jesus, before her marriage to Thomas, she had been wed ten years to a man with constant illness—that an imp of ruin and decay had taken up habitation within Mary. *Giggling, perhaps, as it waited its chance.*

Having seen that shadow, Margaret knew that Mary's slimness might not all be due to abstemious dining habits, or the pallor of her cheeks not completely the result of keeping her face averted from the burning rays of the sun, and that the lustrousness of her eyes might be as much due to an as-yet unconscious fever as to a blitheness of spirit.

Mary's affliction was as yet so subtle, so cunning, that Margaret had no doubt that Mary herself remained totally unaware of it.

Yet how like Hal, she thought, *to have seen this affliction and to have realized its potential. And how sad that this lovely woman was to be so used. Treasured not for her beauty of character, but for the speed of her impending mortality.*

"My lady," Mary said, frowning slightly, "why do you stare so?"

Margaret reddened, dropping her eyes. "I am sorry, my lady. I was . . . merely remembering my own doubts on the eve of my marriage, and pitying your own inevitable uncertainties."

As soon as she'd said those words, Margaret's blush deepened. *What if Mary had no uncertainties? What if she chose to view Margaret's words, as well as her staring, with offense?*

"My lady," Margaret added hastily, "perhaps I have spoken ill-considered words! I had not thought to imply that—"

"No, shush," Mary said. "You have not spoken out of turn."

She hesitated, biting her lip slightly. "My Lady Margaret . . . I am glad that you are to be my companion. I shall be grateful to have a woman close to my own age to confide in."

Mary's eyes flitted about the chamber to make sure that the several servants about were not within hearing distance. "You have been a maid, and now are married with a child. You have undertaken the journey that I am soon to embark upon."

Margaret inclined her head, understanding that Mary was

uncertain about her forthcoming marriage. Well, there was nothing surprising about that.

"My lady," she said, "it is a journey that most women embark upon. Most survive it."

If not unscarred, she thought, but knew she must never say such to Mary.

"My Lord of Hereford," Margaret continued, "will no doubt be a generous and loving husband."

Again Mary glanced about the chamber. "Margaret, may I confide most intimately in you, and be safe in that confidence?"

Oh, Mary, Mary, be wary of whom you confide in!

"My lady, you may be sure that you shall be safe with me."

Even as she spoke the words she initially thought would be lies, Margaret realized that they were true. Whatever Mary told her would be repeated for no other ears.

Mary took a deep breath. "Margaret . . . the thought of marriage with Bolingbroke unsettles me greatly. He is a strange man, and sometimes I know not what to make of him. I wonder, sometimes, what kind of husband he shall prove to be."

Margaret briefly closed her eyes and sent a silent prayer to Jesus Christ for forgiveness for the lie she knew she now must speak. Christ was her master, and Hal's, and He knew better than anyone how twisted was the path toward salvation.

"My lady," she said, smiling as reassuringly as she could, "your fears are but those of every maid approaching her marriage bed and who fears the unknown. Rest assured that my Lord of Hereford will surely prove the most loving of husbands and one that most women would be more than glad to have in their beds."

Mary's eyes searched Margaret's face, and she began to say more, but was interrupted by the opening of the far door.

"Mary! Margaret!" Bolingbroke strode into the chamber, Neville at his shoulder. "Supper awaits! Come, cease your girlish gossiping and take our arms so that we may make our stately way to the hall where my Lord and Lady of Lancaster await us."

When Margaret gave her arm to Mary to aid her to rise, she was shocked at the tightness of Mary's grip.

Chapter VI

After Compline, the Feast of the Translation of St. Cuthbert
In the first year of the reign of Richard II
(deep night Monday 5th September 1379)

— III —

✠

NEVILLE WAS LATE BACK to the chamber he shared with Margaret. Lancaster and Bolingbroke had kept him for several hours after supper had ended, discussing and debating the treaty about to be signed in Westminster. Neville had been disturbed by Lancaster's appearance: he seemed tired and listless, as if trying to advise and guide Richard had brought him years closer to his grave.

And what was surprising about that? Lancaster, the godly man that he was, was doubtless worn down trying to deal with Richard's demonries. Neville knew from his conversations with both the Archangel Michael and Joan of Arc that the demons had their own king, and that king was none other than Richard.

When Katherine had interrupted their talk, gently insisting that Lancaster needed his bed, Neville had not been sorry—for his own sake as much as Lancaster's. It had been a long day, full of emotion and surprises, and Neville badly needed sleep. His head ached abominably and his limbs were heavy and cumbersome with weariness.

He halted outside the closed door to his chamber, resting his head gently on its wood as his hand lightly grasped its handle. As much as he needed to lie down and close his eyes, he knew even that would be denied him for an hour or so.

As yet, Margaret and he had not had a chance to talk privately . . . and, after this afternoon's confrontation with the archangel, Neville needed to talk with his wife.

He did not know what he wanted to say to her, nor even what he wanted to hear from her, but something needed to be said, for Neville did not think he could lie down by her side this night with the afternoon lying between them.

With what the archangel had said.

An abomination . . .

He straightened, then opened the door, closing it softly behind him as he entered.

Hal had made sure they received a good chamber, light and airy. There were several chests for their belongings (and yet not that one casket Neville so desperately sought), a wide bed generously spread with linens and blankets, clean, woven rush matting spread across the timber floor, and oil lamps that burned steadily from several wall sconces. In the far walls the wide windows were shuttered close—the river night was chill, even in this early autumn—and, into the side wall close by the bed, a fire flickered brightly in the grate.

Margaret sat on her knees by the hearth. She was dressed simply, in a loose wrap of a finely woven ivory wool, her bronze-colored hair undressed and left to flow freely over her shoulders.

Rosalind lay asleep in her lap, and as Neville entered Margaret raised her face and gave him an uncertain smile.

Then she looked to Agnes, folding clothes into one of the chests. "Leave us for the moment, Agnes. You may return for Rosalind later."

Agnes nodded, bobbed a curtsey to both Margaret and Neville, and left via a door which opened into a smaller chamber where she and Rosalind would sleep.

Neville pinched at the bridge of his nose tiredly, not knowing where to start, or even what to do.

Margaret inclined her head to a chair standing across the hearth from her. "Tom, sit down and take off your boots. You have borne the weight of the world long enough for one day."

"Aye." Neville sank down into the chair, sliding his boots off with a grateful sigh. "And yet the day still weighs heavily on me, Margaret."

Margaret dropped her face to her daughter, running a finger very lightly over the sleeping girl's forehead. "As it does me, my lord."

"Margaret . . ."

She raised her face and looked at him directly. "Why hate me so much? What have I done to deserve that?"

"Margaret, I do not know what to make of you—how *can* I interpret this afternoon? Saint Michael tells me to kill you; he says you are filth, an abomination which should never have been allowed to draw breath. He says you are that which I must destroy."

"And yet you do not kill me, nor our daughter. You do not because you think to use me, to draw demons to your side through my presence. At least," Margaret held his gaze steadily, "that is the excuse you make to Saint Michael."

He was silent.

"What demons *have* I drawn to your side, Tom?"

Still he was silent, and she could not know that his mind had flickered back to Wycliffe's brief visit, and to the priest's patent respect for Margaret.

"Or have I," she continued very quietly, "drawn to you only those who are best able to aid you in your fight against evil? Without me you would be still trapped inside the Church. Without me you would not have Lancaster and

Bolingbroke as your strongest allies. Without me you would not have the means you now enjoy to fight against demonry."

"And what is the demonry that now surrounds me, my love?"

Her face set hard at the sarcastic use of the endearment. "Who else but Richard? Richard is demonry personified. Doubtless Richard now holds this casket you search for so desperately."

Neville leaned forward. "You trap yourself, Margaret. You have always known more than you should. My dear, to-night I *will* hear the truth or, before Jesus I swear that I will take Rosalind from your arms and dash her from the window, and then you after her!"

"You would not harm your daughter!" Margaret's arms tightened about Rosalind, but to no avail, for Neville sprang from the chair and snatched the child away.

Rosalind shrieked, but Neville took no notice. "Unless you convince me, *now*, that Rosalind does not bear the blood of demons in her, then yes, I will so murder her! And you after her!"

Margaret tried to take Rosalind back from Neville, but could not force his arms away from the child. "You *love* your daughter! You *cannot* do her to death!"

"Did you not say yourself this afternoon," Neville whispered with such malevolence that all the blood drained from Margaret's face, and she ceased, for the moment, her efforts to rescue her daughter, "that I could not think you a demon, for what would that make Rosalind? Demon you are, Margaret, I know that now, and demon-spawn I would rather kill than allow myself to love!"

"No! Stop!" Desperate, Margaret tried another argument. "Bolingbroke would not allow you—"

"Hal will believe whatever I tell him!"

Rosalind was now screaming and twisting in Neville's arms and Margaret, standing frantic before them, realized that Neville meant—and believed—every word he said. *Oh, why had she spoken so rashly this afternoon?*

And Hal. *Hal would murder Thomas if he laid a hand to either Rosalind or herself, but Thomas did not know that, and would never believe it until the moment he saw Hal's sword coming for its revenge.*

"My lord? My lady?" Agnes had come from the inner chamber at the sound of Rosalind's screams, and now stood in the middle of the room, wringing her hands helplessly.

"Get out!" Neville snarled at her, and Agnes fled.

"Please . . ." Margaret tried yet again to take Rosalind from Neville's arms, but he had the girl tighter than ever. "Please, Thomas, you fought so hard for Rosalind's life the night she was born—"

"And how would you know that, witch, for I thought you unconscious?"

"Thomas—"

"I want the *truth*, for I am tired of living wondering if your lies will kill me."

"And will you recognize the truth if I say it?" Margaret said, frightened and desperate for Rosalind's life well before her own.

"Aye," Neville said, staring steadily at Margaret. "I will."

Margaret fought to calm herself. "Well, then, I will speak of truth to you, but only if you give Rosalind into Agnes's care. I will not speak to you until she is safe."

Neville hesitated, then nodded. "Agnes!" he called, and the woman walked hesitantly through the doorway.

Margaret tried to smile reassuringly at her, although she knew that her face must still be frozen in a rictus of fear, then reached for the child.

Neville let Rosalind go, although he kept his eyes intent on Margaret as she took the girl, soothed her for a moment, then handed her to Agnes.

"Our thoughtless cross words have disturbed her, as they

have you," Margaret said to her maid, "and for that I apologize to you both. Please, take her, and keep her safe."

And, please Jesus, keep her safe from her father should he come storming into that room!

Agnes, hesitant and still afraid, took Rosalind, now considerably quieter after Margaret's soothing, and walked as quickly as she dared into her own chamber.

The door closed with a bang behind her, and Margaret allowed herself some measure of hope.

She would tell Tom as much truth as she dared, but would that be enough? Would he believe it?

If he did not, and carried through his threat, then all would be lost.

If he did believe her, then she and hers would be almost certain of victory.

But why did victory always come at such cost? What was so "victorious" about the suffering that must necessarily be expended along the way?

Then she gasped in pain, for Neville had taken her wrist in a tight grip. He pulled her closer to him, and twisted her arm again until she cried a little louder.

"The truth," he said.

"And what truth does pain buy you, Thomas?" she said, her face contorted with the agony now shooting up her arm. "Truth is only of value when it is given freely."

"Ah!" He let her go and Margaret lurched away, tears in her eyes as she massaged her bruised wrist.

She stopped before the fire, gathering her courage, then turned back to Neville. "Ask what you will."

"Are you a demon?"

"No," she said in a clear tone, holding his stare without falter.

He narrowed his eyes. "Are you a mere woman, as all other women?"

"No," she said.

"Then if you are not demon, and you are not mere woman, then what are you?"

"I am of the angels."

"What?" Neville took a step backward, his mind almost unable to recognize the meaning of the words she had spoken. *"What do you mean?"*

"I can explain no more—"

Neville's shocked look dissolved instantly into one of murderous anger, and he turned and strode toward the door to Agnes' chamber.

"No!" Margaret ran after him, grabbed his arms with both her hands and twisted him about. "You want the truth? *Then listen to it!*"

Now she was angry, and more than anything else that persuaded Neville she might indeed be speaking truth: fear would have only mouthed desperate lies.

"Saint Michael said that the only truth that matters lies locked in Wynkyn de Worde's casket, and in that the angel himself spoke truth. *The truth of what I am telling you lies in that casket!* But, Thomas, the truth within the casket also encompasses such a vast horror that for me to boldly throw the words of it in your face now would be to destroy you. Saint Michael once told you that you had to experience for yourself, rather than be told, did he not?"

Neville found himself momentarily unable to speak. He stared at Margaret, seeing in her eyes the exact same light he'd seen shining from St. Michael's on every occasion the archangel had graced him with his presence. *The exact same light!* Sweet Lord Christ, she *was* speaking the truth!

"Did he not?" Margaret repeated, her eyes still blazing with angelic fury.

"Aye," Neville managed to say, "he did."

"And thus," her voice was quieter now, and her grip not so painful about his arms, "whatever answers I give to your questions will be 'proved' only when you read for yourself the contents of the casket. But you," she lifted her right hand and laid it flat against his chest, "can freely choose whether or not to believe me here, tonight, in this chamber."

"Then I place not only my life in your hands, but also the fate of Christendom."

Yes, Thomas, you do.

"Yes, Tom, that you do. Into the hands of . . . what was it you have called me? Ah yes, into the hands of a whore."

She walked back to the fire, and stood with her back to him as she stared into its flames.

"Margaret, those were the words of a foolish man." *All he could see, even though her face was now averted, was the rage of the angels in her eyes. He could not deny that angel rage, nor disbelieve it.* It was not only Neville's awe of the angels that made him give credence to her words, but something buried deep within him, so deep he could not see it or admit it, made him desperate to believe that she was anything *but* a demon.

"Oh, aye, they were that." Still she did not turn about.

Neville remembered how the Roman prostitute had cursed him.

"Margaret, is it true what I have been told, by angels and demons alike . . . that the fate of Christendom will hang on whether or not I hand my soul on a platter to a woman?"

She turned back to face him so that he could clearly see her face. "Yes."

"And are you that woman?"

"Yes." She paused, frowning a little. "Who else?"

"If you are of the angels, then how is it that Saint Michael has not told me of you?"

"Tom, hush, you will set Rosalind to a-crying all over again, even through these walls."

"Answer me!"

"You cannot understand until you have the contents of the casket laid out before you."

"You said to me earlier this afternoon that there was truth outside the casket as well . . . can you not tell me of that, at least?"

Margaret shook her head. "Tom, I am sorry, but there is

further for you to travel, and more for you to understand before I can—"

"Then I can never love you."

"I know that, and it is of no matter."

Angry now because he had wanted to hurt her with those words and had not succeeded, Neville strode over to a pile of linens which sat on a flat-lidded chest, fiddled with them for a moment, then looked back at Margaret.

"How is it, when you say that you are of the angels, that Saint Michael so reviles you?"

"As there is dissension within God's Church on earth, then so also there is dissension within the ranks of heaven."

"The angels are divided? But that means that . . ."

"Evil has worked its vile way everywhere, Tom. Saint Michael has also said this to you. Now, this time, this age, will be the final battleground."

"And your role in this?"

"You know my role, Tom. We spoke of it only moments past. My role is to tempt you. To test you."

He stared, and then walked slowly over to her, holding her eyes the entire way. When he reached Margaret, he gently cupped her chin in his hand, then bent down and kissed her.

"Then you play your role well," he said finally, shocked to find himself, as her also, shaking with the desire unleashed by that one kiss.

"It is what I am here for," she whispered.

Neville momentarily closed his eyes, then drew away from her. He sat down in the chair, suddenly remembering that his head had been aching horribly for hours; now the pain in his temples flared beyond his ability to deal with it.

Margaret saw him drop his head into his hands. Silently she walked behind the chair, and placed her hands about his head.

He jumped, but allowed her to draw his head and shoulders back until they rested against the high back of the chair.

Her fingers rubbed at his temples, and he drew in a breath of amazement and gratefulness as the pain ebbed away.

She lifted her hands away, and sat down on the carpet before him.

"Thank you," he said, and she inclined her head, but remained silent.

Neville hesitated, but could not put out of his mind the way Margaret had looked at Bolingbroke this afternoon when they'd disembarked. "There is one more question I have for you."

She raised her face back to him, and he drew in his breath at her beauty.

"Do you love Hal?"

"Yes," she replied without hesitation. "But not as you think. When I first went to Raby's bed in the English camp, Bolingbroke befriended me as much as so great a noble lord could befriend a minor lady. Raby treated me well, but not over-kindly. Bolingbroke saw that lack, and supplied the kindness. He is a compassionate man."

Neville stared at her with an expressionless face, not willing to believe her.

"I have never bedded with Bolingbroke," Margaret continued. "You and Raby only. Tom, if Bolingbroke had wanted me, if he had desired me, do you think he would have let Raby stand in his way?"

Neville finally allowed his shoulders to slump in relief. "No."

"I needed to find my way to you, Tom," Margaret whispered. "No one else."

Neville slid off the chair to the carpet beside her. He buried a hand in her hair, and kissed her deeply, finally giving his desire for her free rein through his body.

If she had lied to him this night—and he did not believe she had, not with that rage of the angels he had seen in her eyes—then she had merely delayed her death. When he found the casket he would know all.

"I will never love you," he said, "and I will not sacrifice

the fate of the world for you, but that does not mean I cannot treat you as well as Raby, nor as kindly as Hal."

And with that he drew her down to the carpet, sliding the woolen wrap from her body.

Margaret sighed, and wrapped her arms about him, mouthing a silent prayer of gratitude to Christ Jesus that both she and Rosalind were still alive, and that Tom had believed her.

All would be well . . . and perhaps Hal's vile plan would not be needed. Perhaps Tom *would* love her without Hal's hateful treachery.

Neville was lost in his passion now, his whole universe consisting only of their entwining bodies, and she moaned and held him tightly to her as their bodies joined.

And as Neville drowned in his lust, Margaret raised her head very slightly so she could see over his shoulder, and she sent a smile composed of equal parts triumph and implacable hatred at the archangel St. Michael standing silent and furious in a golden column on the far side of the room.

The archangel screamed, a sound that reverberated through heaven and hell only, and vanished just as Neville cried out and collapsed across Margaret's body.

"Sweet Tom," she whispered, patting his back gently with one hand.

Chapter VII

The Feast of the Nativity of the Blessed Virgin Mary
In the first year of the reign of Richard II
(Thursday 8th September 1379)

— I —

✠

IT WAS A WARM blustery autumn day this feast of the birth of the Virgin, and the Londoners and their cousins from nearby villages and towns thronged the streets and marketplaces of the city. Priests stood on the porches of London's parish churches, shouting reminders that this day all good Christians should be in the cold deep shadows of their churches' bellies, praying for forgiveness for their too-numerous transgressions and pleading with God, Jesus and every saint in heaven that they might have even the remotest chance of salvation.

The people ignored them. Sweet Jesu, this was a *feast* day, and no one was going to waste it mumbling unintelligible prayers inside a frigid church. The autumn markets and fairs were in full swing: stalls groaned with the fruits of the summer harvest, flocks of geese and pigs squawked and squealed from their pens, landless laborers stood on boxes and shouted their availability to any landlord looking for cheap hired hands, and pedlars and quacksalvers sung the praises of their wares and cure-alls.

Buy my physick! Buy my physick! 'Tis a most excellent and rare drink, pleasant and profitable for young and old, and of most benefit to the hysterical woman with child. Use day and night, without danger, as the occasion and level of hysteria demandeth. This most wonderful of potions will also purge the body, cleanse the kidneys of the stone and gravel, free the body from itch and scabbedness, as well as all chilblains. It shall abate the raging pain of the gout, and assuage the raging pains of the teeth. It will expel all wind and torment in the guts, noises in the head or ears, destroy all manner of worms, and free the body from the rickets and scurvy. And that is not all! Why, this most wondrous of physicks also increases the quantity and sweetness of milk in the breasts of nurses!

"I swear to sweet Jesu," Bolingbroke muttered as they turned their horses south onto the Strand from the gates of the Savoy, "that if I thought that most wondrous of physicks would also purge England of its most vile king I would swoop down on that abominable quack and purchase his entire stock!"

Neville laughed, even though the matter was serious. "I am sure," he murmured, kneeing his horse close to Bolingbroke's so that only he might hear, "that most of the dungeon keepers in this fair land will know the ingredients of a swift and certain poison. I would counsel a purchase from them, my friend, rather than from that pedlar of honey-water."

Bolingbroke shot Neville a speculative glance. "You would condone murder to rid us of this demon, Tom?"

Before Neville could answer the crowds of people swarming along the Strand toward Westminster caught sight of Bolingbroke and his escort.

"Prince Hal! Fair Prince Hal!"

"Hal! Hal!"

A cry that turned into a roar swept along the Strand.

Hal! Hal! Fair Prince Hal!

Neville reined in his horse to come alongside the eight

men-at-arms who rode as escort, allowing Bolingbroke to ride ahead and receive the acclamation of the crowds.

Bolingbroke had left his silver-gilt hair bare to the sunshine, and his pale gray eyes sparkled in his beautiful face as he stood high in the stirrups and waved to the crowds. If his head was bare, then the rest of Bolingbroke was resplendent in sky-blue velvets, creamy linens and silks, and jewels of every hue. From his hips swung a great ceremonial sword and a baselard dagger, both similarly sheathed in gold- and jewel-banded scarlet leather scabbards. As the roar of the crowd intensified, Bolingbroke's snowy war destrier snorted and plunged, but Bolingbroke held him easily, and the roar and adulation of the crowds increased yet further with every plunge forward of the stallion.

In pagan days he would have been worshipped as a god, Neville thought, unable to keep a smile of sheer joy and pride off his face. *Now they merely adore him.*

A woman with a child in her arms stumbled a little at the edge of the crowd, and Bolingbroke kneed his stallion closer to her. He leaned down, taking her arm so that she might catch her balance, and the crowd roared approvingly.

The woman, flush-faced with joy that Bolingbroke should so care for her safety, held up her child, a girl of perhaps two years age.

Bolingbroke dropped the reins of his stallion, controlling the beast with his knees and calves only, and gathered the child into his arms.

Neville thought it a pretty trick, something to further strengthen the crowd's approval, but he caught a glimpse of Bolingbroke's face—the man was staring at the child with such love that Neville instantly thought that the girl might actually be his get from some casual affair.

He looked to the woman again. No, surely not . . . she was plain, and approaching middle age. She was not a woman who would catch Bolingbroke's eye or fancy.

Neville gazed back at Bolingbroke, now planting a kiss

in the child's hair, and remembered how he enjoyed playing with Rosalind. *Perhaps he merely loves children,* Neville thought. *Well, Mary shall give him some soon enough, pray God.*

Bolingbroke now hefted the child, showing her to the crowd. "Is she not beautiful?" he cried. "Has she not the face of England?"

Now that *was pure showmanship*, Neville thought, grinning wryly.

Again the crowd roared and clapped, and Bolingbroke, with apparent reluctance, handed the girl back to her mother and took up the reins of his stallion, urging the horse into a slow, prancing trot down the street.

"Whither goest thou?" shouted a man in a rich country burr, and the question—and the burr—was taken up by the throng.

Whither goest thou, fair Prince Hal?

Bolingbroke waved for silence, and the close-pressing crowd consented to dull its adoration to a low rumble.

"I go to Westminster," shouted Bolingbroke, "to receive the surrender of the French bastard king!"

The crowd erupted, and Neville burst into admiring laughter. *Why, Hal would have them believe that he alone had taken King John on the battlefield, and then negotiated a treaty to see all of France quiver on its knees before even the lowliest of English peasants!*

Bolingbroke swiveled in his saddle, sending Neville a quick grin, then he turned forward again, and spurred his stallion through the crowds who parted for him as if he were Moses.

Neville eventually managed to ride to Bolingbroke's side as they cantered past Charing Cross and Westminster rose before their eyes.

"They would have you king!" he shouted above the continuing roar.

"Do you believe so?" Bolingbroke said, his eyes fixed

on Neville. "Should we indeed reach for that vial of poison, Tom?"

And then he was gone again, spurring forward and waving to the crowds. Neville was left staring after him and wondering, as others already had, how high Bolingbroke's ambition leaped.

If they did manage to destroy Richard—and wasn't that what they truly planned?—then who else could take the throne? Who else? Who else was there to lead England to safety but Bolingbroke?

RICHARD HAD caused a table to be set under the clear skies beyond the porch leading into Westminster Hall. The Hall was closed, undergoing renovations to its roof (Richard would have a greater roof put on, so he might be the more gloriously framed), and so the treaty would be signed in the courtyard, where not only the noblest peers of the realm could witness, but also (suitably restrained behind barriers) the commons themselves of England.

Bolingbroke and Neville dismounted when they reached the courtyard's perimeter, and monks from Westminster Abbey led them to their places in the ranks to the right of the table. Here stood the greatest of nobles and their closest of confidants, and Bolingbroke led Neville directly to his father's side.

"My Lord of Lancaster," Bolingbroke said formally, greeting his father with an equally formal bow. Katherine, Lancaster's duchess, was not present: no wives were here, only the holders of titles and the wielders of power.

Neville also murmured Lancaster a greeting, bowing even deeper than Bolingbroke, but Lancaster gave him only a cursory glance before turning to his son.

"I wish Richard had taken my advice and had this cursed treaty signed under roof." Lancaster, who looked even more tired and gray in the noonday sun than he had in the candlelit dimness of the Savoy, gestured at the table several paces away: it was strewn with damasks and weighted down with gold and silver candlesticks and a great golden salt cellar. "If the crowd doesn't become unruly and upset everything, then no doubt a raven will fly overhead and shit on the treaty. John is being difficult enough about the signing . . . if his pen must perforce thread its way through a pile of bird shit then doubtless he will call the odoriferous mess a bad omen and refuse to sign."

"At least a treaty *is* to be signed," Bolingbroke said.

Lancaster sighed, his eyes still on the table. "Aye. But a treaty declaring Charles a bastard and Richard the heir to the French throne is worth even less than a pile of bird shit in real terms."

"How so, my lord?" Neville said.

Lancaster turned and gave Neville the full benefit of his cold gray stare. "Do you think that even with this treaty in Richard's possession the French will lie down and surrender a thousand years of proud history into his hands? Richard can wave it about all he likes, but unless he can enforce it with sword and spilled French blood then it becomes worthless in practical terms."

"No Frenchman will accept it unless he be forced to do so," Bolingbroke said.

"Aye," said a new voice behind them, "and do not think, my bright young Lord of Hereford, that English swords will *not* force French pride to its knees in the near future."

All three men turned and stared at the newcomer.

"My Lord of Oxford," Lancaster said, with no bow and no respect in his voice, "how pleasing to see you here. But also how passing strange, for I thought that surely you would have been at Richard's side."

Robert de Vere, Earl of Oxford, lifted a corner of his mouth in a well-practiced sneer. He was a man of some twenty-five or twenty-six years, of the broad chested and shouldered physique that often softened to fat in later years. His face, however, did not suit his body: it was narrow and suspicious, with a sallow complexion and scarred along cheeks and nose by a childhood pox. Yet this was an arresting face, for his dark eyes and full-lipped mouth were of startling beauty, and invariably made any who met him for the first time wonder if perhaps he had stolen both eyes and mouth from some poor beauteous corpse and somehow incorporated them into his otherwise fox-like features.

"And will *you* lead our fine English knights and archers to so humiliate the French?" Bolingbroke said.

De Vere simpered, the expression challenging rather than coquettish. "Why, dear Hal, I much prefer the comforts of home fires and the sweet meat of our home-bred wenches. Perhaps," and his face suddenly, violently, darkened into outright threat, "*you* might like to lead the charge? Unless your father cannot bear the thought of you spitted on some French count's lance, of course. Well? What say you, oh brave one?"

Neville suddenly realized that the crowd's cheers for Bolingbroke must surely have been heard by de Vere . . . as most surely also by Richard, and he wondered if the same thoughts had occurred to them as had to him.

How high did *Bolingbroke's ambition fly?*

And how much danger did that place Bolingbroke in?

"Richard must surely be pleased that the treaty is finally to be signed," Neville said, succeeding in deflecting de Vere's attention from Bolingbroke to himself.

"Ah . . . Neville, is it not?" Some of the threat died from de Vere's face. "I have heard from Richard that you have recently gained yourself a most beautiful and alluring wife. She has brought you no dowry or riches, to be sure, but then," now nastiness filled de Vere's face, "sometimes the heat of the bedsport can compensate for almost anything, is it not true?"

"Enough!" Lancaster said. "De Vere, you speak with the utmost vileness on occasion, thinking yourself high above those who outrank you both in birth and in manners. You have favor only because you are Richard's current pet. Be wary you do not discover a dagger in your back the day that favor dies!"

"And you," de Vere said, "should watch out for the dagger in *your* back, for I think it not long in the coming!"

And with that he was gone, shoving his way through the assembled nobles as they found their way to their seats.

"Father!" Bolingbroke said, making as if to go after the Earl of Oxford.

"No!" Lancaster grabbed his son's arm. "Leave him! He is obnoxious, but of no account."

"How can you say that?" Bolingbroke said. "How dare he so threaten you!"

Lancaster smiled sadly. "The world has changed," he said. "My father and brother are dead, and nothing is as once it was. Perhaps we should just accept it."

Bolingbroke opened his mouth again, but Lancaster waved it shut. "No. Say it not, Hal. Not today, for I am too weary. Come, let us find our seats . . . Tom, I believe there is a place for you to stand behind us. Come, come, leave de Vere's unpleasantness behind us."

ONCE THE nobles were seated, their retainers and men-at-arms ranked behind them, and the crowds who had rumbled out of London to witness the public humiliation of the French restrained as best could be behind wooden barriers and sharp spears and pikes, a clarion of trumpets sounded, and the monarchs of England and France appeared in magnificent procession from behind a row of screens masking the entrance to the palace complex.

Or, rather, Richard, with Isabeau de Bavière on his arm, proceeded in magnificent procession. King John of France sulked and shuffled his way toward the table, his eyes occasionally darting to the sky, almost as if he were waiting for a sympathetic raven to deposit an excuse not to sign the treaty now spread out on the table before them.

The crowd roared and every bird atop the spires of Westminster Hall, Abbey and Palace fled into the sun to finally alight far away on the banks of the Thames.

John descended into a black fugue; his last chance to avoid signing the treaty was fluttering away.

Traitor birds!

If John had slipped further toward his dotage, then Richard had moved from youth to man in the few months since Neville had seen him last.

Kingship sat upon him well. He still affected his cloth of green, almost as if he never wanted (or wanted no one else) to forget that gay May Day of his coronation, but now it had been augmented with enough jewels and chains of gold that he seemed to outrival the sun itself for power and glory. His face was more mature, harder . . . more knowing and far more cunning, if that were possible.

Every step of his green-clad legs radiated confidence, every slight movement of his crown-topped head bespoke the power that he commanded.

Richard was king, and no one would ever be allowed to forget it.

On his arm Isabeau de Bavière walked straight-backed and proud. She was aging now, but Neville thought he had never seen a more beautiful or desirable woman. She was gray-haired and wrinkled, and her delicate form very slightly stooped, but her eyes were of the clearest sapphire, sparkling in the light, and her face . . . her face was so exquisitely fragile that Neville thought a man would lust to bed her simply so he could prove to himself (as to his fellows) that he could do so without breaking every bone in her body.

The English crowd, both men and women, instinctively loathed her on sight. Women catcalled, and men roared lusty words, exposing themselves until guards struck them where it was most likely to sting and forced them to cover up again.

Isabeau cared not. She had endured insults all her life and yet, with her wealth and power and influence, none could touch her. Men and women alike loathed her, but were too afraid of her retribution to move against her. She lived out her days manipulating kings and popes alike, and not even they could curb her independence. She was a woman of her own mind, and free to indulge her ambitions with the wealth of a husband she had managed to drive beyond the bounds of sanity (Isabeau had never been slow to recognize the potential of the well-trained-and-aimed lust of a peacock). Isabeau de Bavière was a woman both beyond and out of her time.

She lifted her free hand and elegantly waved to the spitting, roaring crowd.

Lancaster groaned, and cast his eyes heavenward.

Only a few paces away now, Isabeau de Bavière turned her eyes to Lancaster and sent him a swift, conniving look that had Neville wondering if Lancaster himself had ever succumbed to her charms. *Why was it that Lancaster had called off the proposed marriage between Catherine of France and Bolingbroke . . . had Isabeau sent him a carefully worded warning about possible incestuous complications?*

Suddenly Neville had to repress a laugh. He had an image of all the highest nobles and princes of Europe furtively counting dates on their fingers and wondering if *they* were possibly responsible for Charles or Catherine.

Had all Europe shared in the making of King John's soon-to-be-declared-bastard heir?

The laugh finally escaped, and of all who shot Neville looks, Isabeau de Bavière's was the only one that included a glint of amusement.

And so, with the sun shining, the wind gusting and the crowd roaring, Isabeau de Bavière leaned over the creamy parchment that contained the words which made the Treaty of Westminster and signed away her son's self-respect.

Then she leaned back, held out the quill for the frowning, pouting King John, and laughed for sheer joy at the beauty of life.

Chapter VIII

Compline, the Feast of the Nativity of the Blessed Virgin Mary
In the first year of the reign of Richard II
(evening Thursday 8th September 1379)

— II —

✠

IN THE EVENING, Richard hosted a celebratory banquet in the Painted Chamber to which all the nobles who had witnessed the signing of the treaty were invited together with their womenfolk who had been excluded from the more serious business.

Neville and Margaret both attended the evening, not as invited guests, but in their capacity as attendants to great nobles.

The evening was a splendid affair: Richard proved the most generous of hosts, de Vere behaved with the utmost gentility, Isabeau de Bavière shone with the brilliance of the evening star at Richard's side, and no one minded that King John had refused to attend.

The talk among the guests was of many things, although most topics were generally concerned with the treaty and the current situation in France. Could Richard enforce the treaty? And what was the now-formally-declared-bastard Charles doing? The latest intelligence had him still ensconced in la Roche-Guyon, dithering about what to do and how to take advantage of the sudden deaths of Edward III and the Black Prince. Once the Black Prince had abandoned Chauvigny, Philip the Bad had left Chatellerault and rejoined Charles at la Roche-Guyon, no doubt to keep a closer eye on the Dauphin and see what advantage he could wrest from the situation. Rumor also spoke of this Joan of Arc, and her spine-strengthening effect on the Dauphin. What if Charles did rally the French behind his banner, and did manage to retake all English holdings in France? Would Richard counter such a move, or sit fuming on his throne in Westminster waving about his useless scrap of a treaty?

The Abbot of Westminster had been sharing Bolingbroke's plate and cup during the banquet, but when the dishes were removed, he excused himself saying he had matters within the abbey to attend to.

As soon as he'd gone, Bolingbroke waved Neville to take his place.

Bolingbroke checked to make sure that the man seated to his left was engaged in conversation elsewhere, then leaned close to Neville and spoke quietly.

"Richard is to send Isabeau de Bavière to Charles with a copy of the treaty. It is a good plan, for it may further demoralize Charles . . . and Isabeau's black witchcraft may act to counter this saintly"—Bolingbroke spoke the word with utter loathing—"Joan we hear so much prattle of."

Neville glanced at the High Table. Isabeau de Bavière was leaning back in her chair, her brilliant eyes glancing about the hall, her mouth curled in a small smile . . . perhaps in contemplation of the pleasures of deceit.

"Isabeau is merely a woman rather than a witch," Neville said, "and one who has been clever enough to make her weakness a powerful weapon for her ambition."

"Tom! Are these admiring words for a *woman* I hear you speak? This is not like you at all. Ah, I think marriage has mellowed you."

Neville's face took on a reflective aspect at the indirect reference to his wife. "Hal . . . you know I have suspected Margaret of demonry."

Bolingbroke's own face became very careful. "Aye."

Neville's eyes lost focus as he remembered what had passed between him and Margaret several nights previously.

"She is not what she seems," Neville said slowly, "and she has lied to me on many occasions."

Bolingbroke was now very, very still, his eyes fixed solely on Neville's face. *What had happened?*

"I could bear it no longer. I confronted her the night we first arrived in London. Sweet Jesu, Hal, Saint Michael told me she had to be destroyed!"

"What happened, Tom?"

Neville gave a small humorless laugh, and, focusing his attention on Bolingbroke, suddenly realized how tense the man was.

"I threatened to kill both her and Rosalind," he said, "if Margaret did not replace all her lies with truths. Lord Savior, Hal, I think I would have done it, too, I was so beside myself with anger and doubt."

He shook his head. "I cannot believe that I was so out of my mind that I would threaten Rosalind's life."

Bolingbroke was pale. "You threatened to kill a child? Tom, tell me what happened!"

Neville met Bolingbroke's eyes. "I was angry with Margaret, not only because I thought her a demon, but because I thought she might be your lover."

Bolingbroke stared incredulously, then erupted in loud and completely unfeigned laughter, surprising Neville, who had expected any of a hundred different responses but not this.

People glanced at them, and Bolingbroke managed to bring his laughter under control, although tears of mirth slipped down his cheeks and his face went stiff with the effort to keep his chortling muted. "I cannot believe you thought . . . I . . . and *her*? Nay, nay, Tom, never fear that!"

Although Neville's doubts regarding Margaret and Bolingbroke were finally and completely laid to rest, he now felt slighted on her behalf that Bolingbroke should prove so immune to her charms.

"Margaret is a very beautiful woman," he said.

"Oh, aye, aye!" Bolingbroke continued to chortle, wiping away the tears from his face with a hand. "But . . . I . . .

she . . ." He stopped, took a deep breath, and finally managed to gain complete control of himself. "Tom, I do beg your indulgence and forgiveness for any slight you felt I delivered to your wife. Margaret is truly an utterly desirable woman, but she is your wife, as she was once Raby's woman, and I have too much love and respect for you, as I did for Raby, to even consider her a possible companion for bedsport. But tell me, what did she say to your other charge? That she was a demon."

"She spoke strangely," Neville said, "but with such a heavenly anger in her eyes that I was forced to believe every word she spoke."

"And . . . ?"

Again Neville focused his gaze on Bolingbroke's face. "She told me she was not a demon, but was also not a mere woman. She said she was of the angels."

Any merriment still remaining in Bolingbroke's eyes and face vanished completely. "And what else did she tell you?" he said softly.

Neville told Bolingbroke what had passed between them, and also detailed for Bolingbroke, as he had not done previously, the curse that Neville had heard from both Roman prostitute and demon. "Hal," he finished, "she had such a look in her eyes that I was forced to believe her."

"Such a look?"

"A look that I have seen only in one other being's eyes—Saint Michael's. She spoke truly when she said she was of the angels."

Bolingbroke considered a long while before he spoke again. "Then Margaret is a remarkable woman indeed. Tom, even though she has told you she has been sent to provide the temptation to test you, can you truly resist her?"

"I must," Neville said, "and I will. I shall regard her and treat her with the respect and pity she deserves, but I will not love her. She understands this." They were strong words, and strongly said, but even as they fell from his mouth, Neville wondered how true they could be. He'd seen a strength in Margaret that night he'd confronted her—not just her angelic strength, but something else, something deeper—and a part of Neville had responded to it very powerfully. It had been a strength deserving of . . . respect, yes, most certainly of that, but perhaps of something even more. It unsettled Neville, for he was not used to recognizing such strength and determination within a woman.

Bolingbroke saw the indecision within Neville, but he did not comment on it. He reached out a hand and placed it directly on Neville's shoulder, forcing Neville to look into his eyes.

"And when the pyre is lit, Tom, will you truly be able to throw her on it? Will you? *Will you?*"

Neville held Bolingbroke's gaze a mere moment before he slid his eyes away. "Can I sacrifice her? I must, Hal. I cannot lose sight of what it is I fight for—the angels, and their quest to doom all demons back to hell."

"But you couldn't allow her to die the night she gave birth to Rosalind, though, could you? How easy will it be for you to sacrifice her to heaven's cause?"

"That was different! She needed to live so that she might fill her proper"—*her sacrificial*—"role later!" *And that was why I prayed so hard for her that night,* Neville told himself. *It was!*

Bolingbroke drew back with shock and sorrow in his eyes. "Then God has a magnificent champion in you, Tom. No wonder the heavens rejoice in your very name."

Neville nodded, although his heart felt heavy. "But the casket . . . the casket." He shot a glance to the High Table, where Richard was now leaning toward Isabeau de Bavière, engaging her in a conversation that had both their faces lit with amusement and their eyes dusky with lust.

Well, and it was surely no surprise that Isabeau de Bavière would tempt the boy-king into her bed. Or was it Richard who seduced Isabeau?

"We can do nothing until Richard summons us to his presence," Bolingbroke said, barely restrained frustration and anger evident in his tone. "And at the present, the Demon-King is amusing himself by withholding that summons."

Neville nodded once more, watching Isabeau and Richard, his mind full of nothing but Margaret. He'd thought her just a woman he could disdain and use, yet over the past few days—over the past few months, if he were honest with himself—he'd been forced to reassess how he felt about his wife. Yes, that angelic light in her eyes had shocked him—and had awed him, if truth be told—but since their marriage, Margaret had conducted herself with nothing but gentleness and nobility, and had been nothing but a true and gracious wife to him. If Neville had been harsh and distant with her, then it was because he'd felt he'd had to keep himself at a distance from her.

Neville had always admired women of gentleness and nobility, and during these early months of his marriage, he had found himself wondering on more than one occasion if Margaret was such a woman by nature, if not by birth.

And a woman of the angels . . . Neville shuddered. With each passing day, and with every night he spent at her side, Neville was finding it just that much harder to maintain both disdain and distance.

Margaret was eating her way deep into Neville's soul, and he didn't know what to do about it.

ISABEAU STRETCHED out her arm and admired both its firmness and the brilliance of the gems in its armbands and finger rings. In the candlelight the gems glittered and sparkled, and their glow lent further sheen to her ivory skin.

Apart from her jewels, Isabeau de Bavière was utterly naked.

Women moved with silken whispers in the shadows about her, folding her clothes, pouring rosewater into a tub so that she might bathe away the sweat of both banquet and Richard. Isabeau's mouth curled in silent memory: Richard had not even pretended decorous behavior, escorting her behind the curtain that separated his bed from the High Table on the dais in the Painted Chamber and forcing her to its mattress even as diners were still exiting the hall.

Isabeau lowered her arm and sighed. Perhaps age was finally claiming its own, for she had found her bedsport with Richard a nauseating affair, and had risen and pulled down her skirts as soon as he'd rolled off her.

"I shall present my son with your kindest felicitations," she had said, and then left him to return to her own chambers in Westminster's palace.

"Madam?" one of the women said, sinking into a deep curtsey before her.

Isabeau sighed again and peered at the woman—girl, really. Who was she? Richard sent her new ladies every few days so that she might not form a close bond with any of them and perhaps subvert them to her own interests, and Isabeau found it difficult to recall names and faces. Ah yes, now she remembered . . .

"Mary, is it not?" she said. Her voice was deep and melodious and heavily accented with the dulcet cadences of her native country.

"Mary Bohun," the girl said, finally looking up at Isabeau. She flushed, as if Isabeau's nakedness disconcerted her.

"And I would hazard a guess," Isabeau said, smiling, "that this Mary Bohun is a virgin."

"But soon to be wed," said another woman, now stepping from the shadows into the circle of candlelight that surrounded Isabeau.

"Who is this?" Isabeau said, not liking to be so interrupted.

Mary Bohun's flush darkened, but she maintained her composure. "This is Lady Margaret Neville," she said of Margaret, who had now sunk into her own curtsey before Isabeau. "She is one of my attendants, sent to serve with me this night, and also one of my closest confidantes."

Isabeau studiously ignored Margaret, who had a beauty that was, disconcertingly, almost as great as her own.

"And so you are to be wedded and bedded, my dear," Isabeau said to Mary. "And to which noble will fall the pleasure of inducting you into womanhood?"

"My Lord of Hereford," Mary said. "Hal Bolingbroke."

Isabeau's face went still, then she affected disinterest with some considerable effort that did not escape Margaret's attention.

"I have seen this Bolingbroke from afar," Isabeau said, now reaching for a vial of cream on the chest beside her and fiddling with its stopper. "He is fair of face, and struts as if he has the virility of a bull. If I were you, my dear, I should eat well at your wedding feast, for I believe you shall need the energy for the night ahead."

Isabeau put the vial of cream back on top of the chest with a loud crack and leaned close to Mary. "No doubt he'll bruise you, and make you weep, but at least you shall have the blood-stained sheets in the morning to prove to your maids and, subsequently, to court gossip, that you are now truly the obedient wife and that you are well on your way to proving yourself yet another willing brood mare for the Plantagenet stallions."

Isabeau sat back, a look of utter malice on her face as she stared down at the shocked Mary. "You are not a particularly desirable woman, Mary, and doubtless poor Bolingbroke shall have to call other faces to mind in order to rouse himself enough to accomplish your bedding. Never mind, Bolingbroke shall be happy enough the next morning, knowing that for his efforts he has won himself untold wealth with all the lands that fell under his control the instant he smeared your virgin blood across the sheets."

Mary continued to stare at Isabeau's face a moment longer, then she rose silently, her face ashen, and walked away.

"That was a cruel and unnecessary thing to say, madam," Margaret said to Isabeau. "And spoken out of nothing but maliciousness!"

She, too, rose, but instead of immediately leaving Isabeau

to her circle of candlelight and spiteful thoughts, leaned close and spoke so low that no one but Isabeau could hear.

"If you return to Charles' camp, *then tell Catherine that Bolingbroke takes Mary to wife. Tell Catherine!*"

Margaret turned to go, but Isabeau's hand whipped out and seized her sleeve with tight fingers. "And who are you to so issue me orders?"

"I am Catherine's friend and soulmate," Margaret said. "And you know, as well as I, that Catherine needs to know of Bolingbroke's plans."

Something in Margaret's gaze, perhaps contempt, perhaps even pity, made Isabeau drop her hand.

"Send the girl Mary back to me," she said, and sighed. "She is but a child, and I may have misled her. Perhaps it is not too late to undo the damage I have wrought."

Chapter IX

Ember Saturday in September
In the first year of the reign of Richard II
(17th September 1379)

✣

EMBER SATURDAY IN SEPTEMBER was Feversham's most important market day of the year. Men and women from all around the Kentish countryside made their way to the town, not only to market their wares, but their labor as well. The autumn agricultural markets were the best time for itinerant laborers to try to garner themselves a year-long work contract with one of the wealthier landlords or free farmers.

By Terce, a huge throng of people crowded the marketplace. Goods spilled over trestle tables and hastily erected stalls. Pigs, cows, horses and sheep jostled in small pens or tugged at their tie lines; dogs barked; geese, chickens and ducks squawked and honked; and the mass of people shouted, laughed, argued and prodded at the goods for sale.

A goodly proportion of the crowd, however, was edging away from the marketplace toward the church set at one boundary of the square.

There, a dusty, ragged priest with long, tousled hair was nailing a broadsheet to the church door. A sheaf of duplicate broadsheets ruffled in the light breeze at his feet.

As he nailed, the priest shouted out an abbreviated version of the contents of the broadsheet:

"Did God create both lords *and* bondsmen? Nay! He created all men equal! Why should you be the ones to live in drafty hovels and eat coarse bread while your lords live in castles and eat white bread, and rich clerics live in corrupt luxury? How is it they claim our lot is in the dirt and the freezing rain, while they wear fine furs and drink good Gascony wine? Truth is kept under a lock, my friends, and it is time to set it free!"

The priest had finished nailing the broadsheet to the door, and now picked up the pile of loose copies at his feet, turning to hand them out to the crowd jostling for position. He knew that few of them could read, but on a busy market day like this, the few that could would, within a short space of time, share the contents of the sheet with thousands of people.

"We all know how corrupt the Church is," the priest continued to shout, "for have we not for generations witnessed the sins of the abbots and bishops? Has not good England labored under the yoke of the *Roman*—"

"Or French!" someone in the crowd yelled, and there was general laughter.

"—Church for centuries? Why should we listen to fat bishops and foreign popes who say that unless we pay another penny, and yet another penny again, we shall not achieve salvation? Is salvation something to be *purchased*, my friends?"

The crowd mumbled, and then roared. "No! No!"

"Salvation is yours through the sacrifice of sweet Jesus Christ," the priest yelled, his arms waving about emphatically now that he'd handed out all the broadsheets. "It is His *gift!* There is no need to pay the Church for salvation!"

The roar swelled again—the priest had touched a raw nerve.

"And what of your lords? Do they also not wallow in wealth while you grovel in the dirt? Do they not tax you until you cannot feed your children so that *they* can have their pretty tournaments and wars?"

There was a movement on the edge of the crowd, and the priest saw it. Soldiers, on horses.

"Who wears the face of Christ in this unhappy world of pain? Not the fat clerics, no! Nor the greedy lords. *You* wear the face of Christ, my friends, every one of you, through your hard work and poverty!"

The soldiers had pushed their horses very close, and the priest's face began to gleam with sweat. Not through fear of being apprehended—he had always expected this—but through a desperation to preach to the crowd as much as he could before the soldiers reached him.

"The goods of both Church and lords belong to *you*, the face of Christ on earth! Not to bishops and dukes who care more for silks than for the thin cheeks of your children!"

People began to shout, some to voice their agreement with what the priest said, others to yell their anger at the now close soldiers.

"My name is John Ball," the priest screamed, now directing his voice toward the soldiers, a few paces distant. "John Ball! I am not afraid that the corrupt lords and bishops should know it! My name is John Ball and *I am the voice of the people, and of Christ, who weeps for the people!*"

There was a huge surge of sound, and the soldiers pounced, seizing John Ball by the back of his robe and hauling him kicking and screaming atop one of their horses.

One of the soldiers rode his horse close to the church door, and tore down the broadsheet.

"Let him go! Let him go!" the crowd shouted, and the twenty soldiers had to lash about with their swords and push their horses forward to fight their way free.

"It is the Archbishop of Canterbury's men!" someone in the crowd shouted, and the throng screamed and pushed and pummeled. "Christ damn the Archbishop of Canterbury! Christ damn the Archbishop of Canterbury!"

John Ball, now held firmly across the saddle of one of the men, nevertheless managed to raise his head and yell one last defiant message to the crowd. "When Adam delved, and Eve span—who then was the gentleman?"

And then the soldiers were free, pushing their horses into a hard canter, and there was left only the swelling, murmuring crowd, passing the broadsheets to those who could read out loud.

"WHAT DID you know of this?" Lancaster said, throwing the broadsheet down on the table before Bolingbroke.

"My lord," Bolingbroke said, then hesitated, picking the broadsheet up as gingerly as if it were gunpowder.

Lancaster's furious eyes swung toward Neville, who stood just behind Bolingbroke's shoulder. Neither of the two younger men were sitting. They had been summoned into Lancaster's presence just a few minutes before.

"My lord," Bolingbroke said again. "I had known that Master Wycliffe and several of his men were traveling through Kent—"

"And you had not informed me? Sweet Jesu, Hal, why not? And why not stop them? Do you think I would be pleased to have men known to be of my household engaged in such seditious activities? Ah! Wycliffe has gone too far this time."

Neville knew he was going to earn Lancaster's anger for

not informing him personally of Wycliffe's visit to Halstow Hall, but all he felt for the moment was relief. Lancaster had finally seen the danger in nurturing the demon Wycliffe, and now, perhaps, would go to the lengths necessary to stop him.

"I only found out myself a few days ago," Bolingbroke said. "I had thought to gather greater intelligence before informing you."

"My lord," Neville said. "This is my error, not my Lord of Hereford's. The day before Salisbury came to Halstow Hall to summon me back to London, I received a visit from Wycliffe, accompanied by Wat Tyler—"

Lancaster sprang out of his chair. "What?"

"—and two Lollard priests, John Ball and Jack Trueman. My lord, I do beg your forgiveness, but they told me they traveled at your pleasure toward Canterbury. I had not thought to comment further on it to you."

Lancaster muttered an obscenity, moving to stare out a window before turning back to the other two men. "And now Wycliffe and Tyler and the other two are roaming about the southeast, tacking sedition to every wall they can find? No, do not answer that, I do not want to hear the affirmative!

"Well," he sighed, and rubbed at his beard, thinking, "at least Ball is incarcerated in my Lord of Canterbury's prison and is, for the moment, the lesser problem . . . unless he decides to implicate my entire household in treason."

"My lord," Bolingbroke said, stepping forward, "he surely will not do that!"

"Does anyone know where the other three are?" Neville said.

"Wycliffe, yes," Lancaster said. "Tyler and Trueman, no. Good Master Wycliffe is in Rochester, where he has been some few days. I have sent men—forty trusted men-at-arms—to fetch him away."

"You will not bring him back here, my lord!" Neville said.

Lancaster glanced at him. "No, I won't have him within

shouting distance of London, Tom. He goes to my manor of Lutterworth in Leicestershire where he can contemplate the sins of the world in its walled herb garden. As for Tyler—what has gotten into the man?—and Trueman . . . they have vanished into the laboring population of Kent. Word is out for their apprehension, but I know Wat better than most men, and if he doesn't want to be found . . ."

"And Richard?" Bolingbroke asked softly.

Lancaster actually looked relieved. "The three of us in the room are the only ones who know of Wycliffe's involvement, and that of Wat Tyler. Those two are the only ones publicly associated with my household. The broadsheets, thank God, are unsigned, and do not mention Wycliffe's name, or the name of any of my house. As far as John Ball is concerned, my Lord of Canterbury has agreed to hold him without public comment for the moment."

Neville relaxed a little. Simon Sudbury, the Archbishop of Canterbury, was heavily indebted to Lancaster for supporting Sudbury's election to the archbishopric some years ago.

"So we must hope Tyler and Trueman cause no disturbance that might come to the king's ear," Bolingbroke said.

"Aye," Lancaster said. "That we must."

JOHN BALL huddled a little deeper into his thin robe, closed his eyes against his dreary, dirty cell and prayed to Jesus Christ for strength.

Then footsteps sounded outside the door, and Ball's eyes flew open.

A key rattled in the lock, and the door opened.

One of the guards stood there, carrying a bundle of warm clothing and a bag of food.

"From a friend," the guard said, tossing both clothing and the bag of food to Ball. "A good man, a former sergeant-of-arms of mine. He said to tell you to be strong and of good cheer, for when the time comes, yours shall be the voice to strike the match."

Ball nodded, then, as the door closed and locked, once again closed his eyes, this time to thank Christ for the love of a man known as Wat Tyler.

Chapter X

Vigil of the Feast of St. Michael
In the first year of the reign of Richard II
(Wednesday 28th September 1379)

✠

THE BLACK PRINCE'S VICTORY at Poitiers had crippled French pride and determination. Not only had the cursed English ground French pride into the mud, but King John had been captured, and the flower of French nobility had been lost to either the arrows of English longbowmen or the ransom demands of English nobles.

And then, out of all of this calamity, God in His boundless goodness sent hope to the virtuous French in the sweet form of the miraculous virgin, Joan, and judgment to the vile English in the simultaneous deaths of both Edward III and his warrior son, the Black Prince.

At the darkest day, when the French were stricken with defeat, God had opened the door for a Gallic triumph.

Now, Isabeau de Bavière was determined to slam it shut in His face.

"AND SO, my darling boy," Isabeau said, enjoying every moment, "I did so sign away your heritage and your throne.

It was but truth, and I was bound to speak it some day. Here," and she held out the copy of the Treaty of Westminster to Charles, who stared at it pallid-faced and tormented.

Isabeau stood there with her arm extended just long enough to make the moment intensely uncomfortable, then she let the treaty flutter to the floor.

"Well," she said, "no matter."

She stepped past her son and smiled maliciously at the gathering standing behind Charles in the hall of la Roche-Guyon. "Why the surprise over all your faces? Have you not called me the harlot and whore behind my back for decades? Well, now I confess it." Isabeau threw apart her arms in a dramatic gesture. "I am *so* the whore and harlot! 'Twas indeed the Master of Hawks—oh, how I wish I could remember his name!—who put Charles inside me with his peasantish vigor and odious onion breath. And . . . see!"

Isabeau clasped her hands together before her face, and turned back to Charles as if enthralled by the very sight of him. "Has my son not inherited his father's penchant for the stables? I swear before God he'd be far more comfortable atop a dung heap than standing in this grand hall. And . . . see!"

Now Isabeau whipped about and stared at the girl, Joan, standing thick and dark in men's clothing to one side.

"Has he not also inherited his father's taste for peasant company? His companion betrays him, for my son prefers the stench of peasants to the sweet spice of nobility."

Charles' face was now so white that he looked as if he might faint. In contrast to his bloodless cheeks, his pale blue eyes were brilliant, brimming with tears of mortification.

His mother, his *hateful* mother, had never so publicly nor so successfully humiliated him. All those whispered rumors, now being flung into his face with a devastating, ruthless candor. Isabeau was a powerful woman in her own right, with independent wealth and estates—and thus with her own armed forces—and surrounded herself at court with her own influential coterie of supporters. Despite the hatefulness of her words, no one would think to move against her, or disbelieve her. Charles certainly could not.

He was the son of a peasant—how could anyone now gainsay it?

His eyes jerked to the treaty lying on the floor. *All France—and England!—must be laughing at him.* He trembled, and started to wring his hands. Every argument Joan had used to sustain his courage was lying on the floor along with that treaty . . . lying on the floor with his whore dam's laughter washing over it!

"Madam," Joan said, glancing at Charles as she stepped forth. Her face was serene, but her demeanor was that of the stern judge. "It is you, not your noble son, who produces the stench in this hall. You lie for profit, and to further your own ambitions. Before God, you know it was Louis who fathered Charles on you. Admit it, or damn your soul."

Isabeau's haughty expression froze on her face. Her eyes widened, her mouth pinched, and her hands clenched at her sides.

She tried to stare Joan down, but the girl's serene, confident gaze did not waver, and eventually it was Isabeau who looked away.

She saw that Charles was gazing at Joan with an expression almost of fear.

Useless, hopeless man, Isabeau thought. *He wants nothing less than to believe me, not Joan. To believe Joan would mean be might actually have to do something about regaining his realm. No doubt he thought it would never go this far.*

"Look at him," said Isabeau softly. "How can anyone here believe he was sired by a noble father? He is the very image of wretchedness. How can you want him as your king?"

Having regained some of her courage, Isabeau looked back to Joan, who she saw was still wrapped in her damned self-righteous serenity.

"I swear to God, Joan," Isabeau said, "that he must give

you good satisfaction in your bedsport, for I cannot imagine why else you champion the cause of such a dullard."

Joan smiled very slightly, very derisively, but it was Charles who finally found some voice.

"I have not touched her, madam!" he said, his voice horribly shrill. "Her flesh is sacred . . . I . . . I would not dare to touch her."

"Are you telling me you *haven't* slept with her?" Isabeau said, arching one of her eyebrows. "What ails you, boy?"

Charles' hitherto wan cheeks now mottled with color, his flush deepening as he saw every eye in the hall upon him.

His mother's mouth curled mockingly.

"You must surely be weary after your journey," Charles stammered, too intimidated by years of his mother's vicious tongue to stand up to her, and desperate to get her out of his presence. "Perhaps you should rest before our evening meal. Philip!"

Philip, King of Navarre, stepped forth from the huddle of nobles who had stood and watched open-mouthed through the entire scene. His dark, handsome face was reflective, but he smiled and bowed before Isabeau with the utmost courtesy.

"Perhaps you could provide my mother with escort to her chamber," Charles said, and Philip smiled, and offered Isabeau his arm.

"Gladly," he said.

As they left the hall Joan turned to Charles. "My very good lord," she whispered urgently, "you must not believe what she says."

"I am the get of a peasant," he mumbled miserably, then looked around. "See? They all believe it!"

"The Lord our God says that you are the get of *kings*!" Joan said, exasperated with the witless man.

"I am worthless . . . worthless . . ."

Joan laid her hand on his arm—an unheard of familiarity, and not missed by some who watched—and leaned close. "You are the man who will lead France to victory against the cursed English," she said, her tone low and compelling. *"Believe it."*

Charles sniffed, staring at her, then looked about the hall.

One of the nobles stepped forth—Gilles de Noyes. "You are our very dear lord," he said, and made a sweeping bow, "and we will follow you wherever you go. We know that your mother lies, for does not the saint by your side tell us so?"

One by one the others stepped forward and made similar assurances, and Charles finally managed to regain some little composure.

Joan smiled again at him, relaxing a little herself, and nodded her thanks to de Noyes.

De Noyes had, by now, thoroughly warmed to his theme. "My sweet prince," he said, "you will be the one to lead us through fields of blood and pain and into victory!"

Fields of blood and pain? Charles swallowed, and then started as Joan leaned down, seized the Treaty of Westminster, and tore it to shreds.

WEARY AND sad at heart, Isabeau lay upon her bed and tried to dull her thoughts so that she could, indeed, sleep.

But this afternoon's events kept sleep a long, long way distant.

Isabeau had thought that Charles would quiver and wail when presented with the treaty which formally bastardized him. Then, having seized the proffered escape, Charles would scurry away to whatever hidey-hole he found comfortable in order to avoid the laughter of his fellow Frenchmen.

True, Charles had quivered and quavered and flushed and wailed at the sight of the treaty and the sound of his mother's derision . . . but he had not scurried away. And why not? Because that damned saintly whore had not *allowed* him to escape! He danced to her tune now . . . and that made Isabeau almost incandescent with rage.

How dare that peasant bitch control *her* son!

If it hadn't been for Joan's presence, Isabeau knew she

could have persuaded Charles to stand aside from his pathetic fumble for the throne.

But, no, that damned saintly whore had shoved her Godly righteousness so far up his spine that Charles had actually managed to remain on his feet . . .

Sweet Christ Savior. If Joan hadn't been there, Isabeau *knew* Charles would have bolted for the door.

Whore! Isabeau had a great deal to lose if this treaty did not bring Richard the French throne, and she had the feeling that Richard would prove the most appalling of enemies should he be crossed.

And what of Philip? In the short while she had had to speak with him, Philip had appeared almost as seduced by the whore's aura of saintliness as Charles was. But was that merely Philip's wiliness, or was it *true* awe? Isabeau had known Philip a very long time, knew how he lusted for the throne of France as much as did the English king, and knew him for the conniving, treacherous bastard that he was.

Isabeau de Bavière had always liked Philip.

She sighed and then turned over, angry with herself that she could not sleep.

How could she convince Charles that he was, indeed, the son of a Master of Hawks? How could she undo him, and further her own cause?

Suddenly, all thoughts of Charles and Joan flew from her mind as, panicked, she lurched into a sitting position.

Someone had entered the room.

Isabeau squinted, damning the maid for closing the shutters against the afternoon light, and cursing her thudding heart for fearing the entrance of an assassin.

"Madam?"

Isabeau rocked with relief. "Catherine."

Catherine walked into the chamber, and Isabeau slid from the bed, tying a woolen wrap about her linen shift. There was a fire burning in the hearth, and Isabeau indicated that they should sit on a chest placed to one side of its warmth.

For a minute or so she sat and studied her enigmatic daughter, knowing that Catherine was also using the time to study her.

Catherine. Isabeau had never quite known what to make of her . . . especially given the unusual circumstances of her conception. Catherine was not a beautiful woman in the same manner that Isabeau was, but she was striking nevertheless with her pale skin, dark hair and the blue eyes she'd inherited from her mother, and she had a form that most men would be more than happy to caress.

But, form and face aside, Catherine was an enigma, although Isabeau suspected her daughter had the same depths of ambition and strength that she had.

What was she now? Eighteen? Nineteen?

"Nineteen," said Catherine, and Isabeau jumped slightly, and smiled slightly.

"I had forgot your disconcerting habit of reading my thoughts," she said.

"I was not reading your thoughts at all, madam, but whenever you screw up your brows in that manner I know you are trying to recall either my name or my age and, as you have already spoken my name, then you must have been wondering about my age."

"Ah." Isabeau was not in the slightest bit put out at the implied criticism in Catherine's words. Then, because Isabeau had never been one to waste time on womanly gossip, she went straight to the heart of the matter. "I am wondering what you do here at la Roche-Guyon, Catherine. There must surely be more comfortable palaces to wait out the current troubles. You are, perhaps, another of this peasant girl's sycophants?"

Catherine gave a wry smile. "I am here, madam, because I have nowhere else to go and because for the time being my fate is linked to that of Charles—"

Isabeau made an irritable gesture. "Don't be a fool, take charge of your own fate."

Catherine ignored the interruption. "And as to what I think of Joan . . ." She gave a bitter laugh. "She shall ruin all our lives should Charles let her prattle on for much longer."

"But surely," Isabeau said with some care, "she should be commended for her devotion to Charles' cause?"

Catherine looked her mother directly in the eye. "You and I both know, madam, that France will be ruined if Charles ever takes the throne. He is truly his father's son."

Isabeau hesitated, then nodded. "Aye, he is that. I regret the day I ever let that breathing lump of insanity get him on me."

"Ah, the truth of the matter. Not the Master of the Hawks, then?"

Isabeau waved her hand dismissively. "A subterfuge only. Over the years I have made good use of my reputation for harlotry."

"And so you sold Charles to Richard for . . . how much, madam?"

"A castle here, a castle there, a stableful of lusty lads . . . you know the kind of bargain I drive, Catherine."

Isabeau stood up, pacing to and fro in front of the fire before she stopped and looked at Catherine.

"My dear," she said, in a voice so gentle Catherine could hardly believe it was her mother speaking. "You and I have never been close and we have never talked as we do now. You were always so much the child."

"I have grown in the year since last we spoke." Isabeau had never taken much interest in her children, and Catherine had been raised in a succession of castles and palaces far from her mother's side.

"Oh, aye, that you have. Catherine, I have sold Charles because I want France to live. I—as you do, I suspect—want France to have a king who can lead it to glory, not some pimple-faced toad afraid of his own shadow."

"And so you want to hand it to *Richard*? I have heard but poor reports of him."

Isabeau sank down to a pile of cushions on the floor before Catherine. The firelight flickered over her face, lighting her eyes and silvering her hair.

"I have opened the door, my dear, for the right man to fight his way through to the throne," she said very quietly. "And I do not think that man will be Richard."

Catherine stared at her mother for what seemed a very long time.

"You have come from the English court," she said eventually. "What news?"

Isabeau dropped her eyes and fiddled with a tassel on her wrap. "I have a message for you from a Margaret Neville," she said.

Catherine leaned forward. "Margaret? What message?"

Isabeau raised her head and looked her daughter directly in the eye. "She told me to make certain that I passed on to you the latest gossip."

"Yes?"

"Hal Bolingbroke is to take Mary Bohun, the flush-faced virgin heiress to the Hereford titles and lands, as his wife on . . . why, on Michaelmas. Tomorrow."

Catherine reacted as if she'd been struck. She reeled back, her face paling save for two unnaturally bright spots in her cheeks. "I cannot believe it!" she whispered.

"But you must," Isabeau said, "for I spoke with the little Mary-child myself." She grinned. "Poor Mary. She dreads her wedding night whereas you would have lusted for it more than Bolingbroke."

Catherine's eyes had filled with tears, and Isabeau regarded her with suspicion. "I did not know you *had* lusted for him, Catherine. Why so shocked?"

"There had been talk . . . some time ago . . . of a marriage between us."

"There is always talk and there are always negotiations that never eventuate into actuality. You know that as much as any other noble-bred girl. And, truth to tell, Bolingbroke did not fight very hard to ensure the success of the negotiations. He was somewhat indifferent. But I can see that you managed to take a fancy to him, at the least. A shame, for you shall never have him."

Catherine's face tightened in anger, and Isabeau smiled, well pleased.

"You shall never have him," she said again, "unless you fight for him, and make him want you."

"What do you mean?"

"I mean that I know the Plantagenet princes very well." She smiled. "Very, very well. Well, at least the older generation of them. But, come what may, all the Plantagenet princes are the same—they lust for power—and for the women they cannot have. I do not think Bolingbroke any different."

"And . . ."

Isabeau shrugged elegantly. "Mary will not suit him. All can see that. She has not the fire to earn his respect. One day, Catherine, he will regret very, very much not having fought for you.

"My dear," Isabeau leaned forward and took her daughter's hands in hers, "*make* him fight for you now!"

"But he will soon have a wife!"

"Ah! You tie yourself down with such pettinesses! God above, Catherine, *you* can bring him France!"

"But with Mary as wife—"

"A wife? Of what matter is that? Wives come and go . . . and I have a feeling that Mary Bohun is so vapid she will catch a chill and die with the first touch of an autumn fog. Mary can be disposed of when the time comes, but in the meantime, she will provide a good power base so that eventually Hal's lusts and ambitions can straddle the Narrow Seas."

Isabeau's teeth glinted momentarily. "And while you wait, there is no reason why you can't make him sweat . . . and further our own cause to dispose of this Joan."

Catherine, who had been fighting despair and hope in equal amounts in the last minutes, now eyed her mother warily. "Explain."

"You said that Joan will ruin all our lives should she be allowed to prattle on for much longer. But I do not think myself wrong to say that most in this castle think her a mouthpiece of God?"

Catherine made a wry face. "I think most follow her about sweeping up the discarded skin she scratches off her neck and ears to keep as holy relics. Men flock to this castle as news of its saint spreads. And of all within this house of fools, Charles is the greatest fool of them all!"

"But what of Philip?"

"What *of* Philip?"

"What does he think? Does he have a collection of sacred dandruff tucked away under his pillow?"

"Who knows what he thinks?"

"I think we must learn what he thinks," Isabeau said carefully, "for he might yet prove our greatest ally. And I think you the perfect woman to secure his secrets."

"No," Catherine whispered, trying to pull her hands out of her mother's grip.

But Isabeau was surprisingly strong for her seeming fragility, and she kept tight hold of Catherine. "Don't be such a fool! I said before that you should control your own destiny. Don't let others do it for you! Bolingbroke uses people as he wants for his own devices, Catherine. Don't let your womanhood stop you from doing the same."

"Philip will think to use me to gain the throne for himself."

"Of course! I would expect no less from him. But, Catherine, don't you see? If Philip thinks he might have a chance at the throne through you *then he will turn against Joan*! One day, somehow, we can use him to destroy her, and once she is gone . . ."

"Then Charles fails."

"Aye. He will never have the strength to fight for his inheritance on his own."

Catherine took a deep breath. "I would have liked to have saved myself for—"

"Oh, stop prattling on about saving yourself!" Isabeau

laughed in genuine amusement. "You've been listening to those pious priests and dimwitted nursery maids again. Enjoy Philip, for he will be good for you and to you."

"Are you sure this is not a task you want to take on yourself, mother?"

"I think it is time for *you* to take wing and fly, child. Besides, yours is the body and womb that will gift a strong man the throne of France, not mine. Not anymore. I have bequeathed you that power, Catherine. Use it."

WHEN CATHERINE had gone, Isabeau sat back and let her thoughts drift.

In many ways Catherine disconcerted her, but most of all Catherine disconcerted Isabeau because she should not exist.

Catherine was conceived one winter when Isabeau was being held captive in a stronghold of the Duke of Burgundy's—the duke had thought to ransom her back to King John until he'd realized after four months that John would not pay a single gold piece to have his daughter-in-law returned. Finally, the duke had been forced to release Isabeau with much grumbling and cursing.

Catherine was not Louis' daughter. Indeed, everyone assumed that Isabeau had consoled herself during her capture with a guard, or perhaps a cook.

But only Isabeau knew the truth. During those four months she had bedded *no* man. When, some two weeks before the Duke had finally released her, Isabeau had realized she was pregnant she was beside herself with fear.

What sprite had fathered this child on her? What imp would she give birth to?

Not wanting to know the answer to either question, Isabeau had taken every potion and herb she knew of to try and rid herself of the child in her womb. But it would not be shifted. Isabeau had gone into her birthing chamber terrified, thinking the child would kill her in its release from the womb.

But the birth had been easy, surprisingly painless, and Isabeau had recovered quickly. The child, Catherine, had been as any human child, and gradually Isabeau had convinced herself that perchance she had imbibed too much wine one night and *had* consoled herself with a foul-smelling guard after all.

And yet sometimes, as she did this day, Isabeau felt strong enough to admit to herself the truth.

Catherine was not the child of any mortal man, and she had not been put in her womb through any mortal means.

Chapter XI

The Feast of St. Michael
In the first year of the reign of Richard II
(Thursday 29th September 1379)

— MICHAELMAS —

— I —

✠

NEITHER MARY'S MOTHER, Cecilia, nor Bolingbroke, had spared any expense to adorn Mary in the finest garments possible.

And yet what a shame, Margaret thought as she carefully buttoned Mary into her wedding dress, *that they did not pick something more suitable for Mary's shy and subtle attraction.*

The dress was of heavy damask, deep red in color, and weighted down with pearls and gems that encrusted its bodice and cascaded down its full skirts and fancy sleeves. Its color and decoration was too overwhelming for the modest Mary, and its cut too close and too cruel, for it served only to further flatten Mary's small breasts and boyish hips.

The costume was too *alive* for her. Margaret could almost hear the sly whisperings of that sickening imp deep within Mary's being. Surely the blood-red vitality of this gown would tempt it forth the sooner?

Margaret shuddered, then regretted her lapse instantly.

"Is something wrong?" Mary asked, trying to twist her head about to see what Margaret was doing.

"No. There, you are fastened in. Now, let me see that your hair is properly secured."

Margaret sat Mary down on a stool and busied herself with the woman's elaborate hairstyle; that it had taken Cecilia, Margaret and two other women half the morning to fix properly. Mary's long, thick honey hair had been bound in two plaits which had been wound above her forehead. A veil, of the same rich color as her dress, had then been laid over the crown of Mary's head, and painstakingly pinned in place with jeweled hairpins. Then a broad circlet woven of gold and silver wires, with beautiful pale-green peridot stones gleaming within its twists and turns, was placed over both plaits, dropping low about Mary's head to cover both her ears and holding the veil in place. The lower length of the veil was left to flow freely to halfway down Mary's back.

The effect of both dress and headdress was stunning—or, at least, it would have been had Mary both the coloring and the regal bearing to set it off.

But Catherine would have worn it perfectly . . .

Margaret forced all thought of Catherine from her mind. Isabeau would have told Catherine by now—*but what could Catherine do? Nothing . . . nothing.*

And Hal. Margaret could understand the *why* of this marriage. It would serve him well in terms of power. *But could he truly afford to alienate Catherine in this manner?* All of them needed to remain strong, *and* united. They could not afford to have Catherine so affronted, she might fail to aid them when the time came.

Poor Mary, Margaret thought, *to have been so caught up in such a desperate battle. She will never survive it.*

"My ladies?" A page appeared in the doorway. "It is time."

BOLINGBROKE HAD chosen to be married not in the Savoy's chapel, nor in either the abbey or St. Stephen's chapel in Westminster, but in St. Paul's in the west of London. It was a calculated choice, for Bolingbroke meant this to be a marriage in which the people of London could participate. The marriage would be a union between Mary Bohun and Hal Bolingbroke, and a cementing of the already strong marriage between Bolingbroke and the English commoners.

In that the Londoners loved Bolingbroke all the more for choosing St. Paul's, it was a fortunate choice. In another aspect, however, it was an appalling one.

Richard (accompanied as always by Robert de Vere, Earl of Oxford) would also be attending.

At noon a great procession started from the Savoy; leading the way were Bolingbroke and Mary, Bolingbroke seated astride his great, prancing snowy destrier, Mary seated far more demurely on a chestnut palfrey mare led by a page.

Behind them rode, side by side, John, Duke of Lancaster, and Richard, who had arrived at the Savoy from Westminster by barge some hours earlier that morning. Behind them rode several peers of the realm, the Earl of Westmorland, Ralph Raby (who had made the trip from Sheriff Hutton the week previously), and Robert de Vere, Earl of Oxford, among them. In the group behind the great nobles rode Thomas Neville with several other of the noble attendants of the leading dukes, earls and barons.

It would be a relatively short ride from the Savoy to St. Paul's, taking perhaps fifteen or twenty minutes at a walk. From the Savoy's gates the procession turned northeast on the Strand. A cheer went up from bystanders, for the Strand was a busy highway, and Bolingbroke smiled and inclined his head, acknowledging the cheers of the crowd.

From his vantage point just behind the leading riders, Neville could see Richard's back stiffen.

They proceeded slowly along the Strand, passing the Inns of Court on the right. These, the great legal schools and courts of England, occupied the old buildings of the Knights Templar.

Then another, greater building arose like a great black crow hunched over its piteous prey: Blackfriars, the home of the Dominicans in London. Indeed, the analogy with the ravening crow was apt, because Blackfriars had grown so large that it had actually consumed that part of London's wall which stretched from Ludgate down to the Thames.

Neville had to repress a shiver. *Was the Prior General of England, Richard Thorseby, in there somewhere, still plotting his downfall?*

A shadow fell over Neville, and he started before realizing that it was the gloom cast by the height and breadth of Ludgate. He looked up at it looming above him and imagined he could hear the cries for mercy from the prisoners held within its dank dungeons.

He shook himself. *What was he doing? This was a joyous day!*

The instant he'd thought that, Bolingbroke and Mary, leading the procession, passed from under Ludgate's shadow onto the wide street that led to St. Paul's, directly ahead.

The cathedral's courtyard was crowded with Londoners, and as Bolingbroke and Mary appeared a great roar went up.

Hal! Hal! Fair Prince Hal!

And Neville, watching closely, saw Richard tense even further before shooting de Vere a dark glance over his shoulder.

Hal! Hal! Fair Prince Hal!

The crowd parted to allow the procession through, and as Bolingbroke and Mary halted, attendants rushed forward to hold their horses' heads.

Neville himself dismounted, throwing the reins of his horse to a boy who stepped forward, and moved quickly to Bolingbroke's side.

Margaret, who had been riding a gentle palfrey in a group a little farther back from Neville, also dismounted with the aid of a page and walked to attend Mary.

As Bolingbroke dismounted, Neville made sure that Bolingbroke's tunic—the same rich bejeweled red as Mary's gown, although his hose and cloak were of the purest white—was straight and that his ceremonial sword and dagger had not snagged his cloak.

"Be wary, my lord," he whispered, "for the crowd's acclaim has Richard glowering at your back."

Bolingbroke turned, smiled and bowed slightly to Richard, then turned back to face the cathedral while all about him tumbled the thunder of the crowd and the pealing of what sounded like the bells of most of the churches of London.

"Do you think Richard would dare stick the dagger in my back *here?*" Bolingbroke said.

"I think he merely makes note of the need to hone it," Neville said, and then fell silent with the rest of the crowd as the Archbishop of Canterbury, Simon Sudbury, appeared at the top of the steps leading into St. Paul's and held up his hand for quiet.

Bolingbroke and Mary moved forward, Mary on Bolingbroke's left. Mary stumbled very slightly, and Bolingbroke smiled gently at her, and held out his hand. She took it, and together they mounted the steps to kneel before the archbishop.

"Brethren!" Sudbury said in a loud voice that carried over the entire courtyard. "We are gathered here, in the sight of God, and His angels, and all the saints, and in the face of the Church, to join together two bodies, to wit, those of this man and this woman—"

Sudbury looked down on Bolingbroke and Mary, then continued, "—that henceforth they may be one body; and that they may be two souls in the faith and the law of God, to the end, that they may earn together eternal life; and whatsoever they may have done before this."

Now Sudbury lifted his gaze and addressed the crowd. "I charge you all by the Father, and the Son, and the Holy Ghost, that if any of you know any cause why these persons may not be lawfully joined together in matrimony, he do now confess it."

There was a silence. Margaret, thinking of Catherine, bit her tongue lest she should betray herself (*and everything she and her brethren had worked toward*), but even as she felt the words must explode from her there was a voice raised from the crowd.

"I do declare that the wrong bridegroom kneels before you, my Lord Archbishop."

Richard.

"I swear that it would be best that *I* wed the lovely Mary so that Bolingbroke will not gain the strength with which to topple me from the throne."

An utterly horrified silence fell over the crowd. Bolingbroke, half rising from his knees, turned and stared down at Richard, who was grinning insolently up at him.

Neville made to step forward, as did several other men, Lancaster and Raby among them, but just then Richard held up his hand.

"A jest only," he said, and laughed. "I thought to bring some levity into this most somber of occasions."

Another silence, then de Vere giggled, and a soft swell of forced laughter ran through the crowd.

"Continue, my good archbishop," Richard said, waving his hand. "Let us see Bolingbroke happily wedded to all this lady has to offer."

Neville closed his eyes momentarily and took a deep breath. *Sweet Jesu, what else would this demon do to ruin the day?*

Bolingbroke sank slowly to his knees again, his face stiff and expressionless, then turned back to face Sudbury, murmuring a quick word to Mary, who looked shocked and distressed.

Sudbury himself was flushed, and had to take several breaths before he was ready to continue.

Richard, meanwhile, happily grinned to any who happened to meet his eye.

Few did.

"Henry," Sudbury said, "wilt thou have this woman to be thy wedded wife . . ."

The speaking of the vows continued without further interruption, although most eyes, at some point or other, darted to Richard's grinning face, wondering what he might do next.

Once Bolingbroke had made his vows, Mary spoke hers in a clear voice, and then Sudbury blessed the ring—a great ruby set in heavy twisted gold.

Another error, thought Margaret, *for that ring will never sit well on Mary's tiny hand.*

Bolingbroke then took the ring and looked Mary in the eye. "With this ring I thee wed, and this gold and silver I thee give: and with my body I thee worship, and with all my worldly chattels I thee honor."

Then he slipped the ring on the thumb of Mary's left hand, saying, "In the name of the Father—"

A great flock of pigeons rose from the buildings surrounding St. Paul's, the roar of their wings filling the air.

Bolingbroke moved the ring to Mary's index finger, saying, "—and of the Son—"

Margaret looked up to the sky, and the sun broke through the shifting gray and black cloud of pigeons, sending a shaft of light upon Mary.

Bolingbroke now moved the ring to Mary's middle finger, saying, "—and of the Holy Ghost—"

There were people present there, that day, who swore ever afterward that a tremor ran through the ground beneath their feet as Bolingbroke spoke those words.

Finally, Bolingbroke slipped the ring onto Mary's fourth finger, sliding it firmly into position.

"Amen," he said, and the pigeons screamed, for at that moment a hawk flew into their midst, seizing a large snowy-white bird, and rose skyward shrieking in triumph.

And as the hawk shrieked, Bolingbroke glanced again at Richard, and this time his face was as full of triumph as was the hawk's cry.

MARGARET BRUSHED out Mary's hair, and hoped that this night would go as well for her as the rest of the wedding ceremony and feast had gone. After Bolingbroke had slipped the ring onto Mary's finger, Sudbury had blessed them, and the archbishop, bridegroom and bride and all the invited guests had then moved into St. Paul's to hear the nuptial mass. Once that was done (and it had been a tedious two hours, indeed), the procession had wound its way back to the Savoy, the cheers of the crowd even louder this time, if possible, and sat down to a sumptuous wedding feast in the great hall.

Now was beginning the last rite that would see Mary move legally from girl to woman, and ensure Bolingbroke could cement his claim to the lands and wealth she brought as dowry: the consummation.

Mary was withdrawn and clearly apprehensive, but Margaret (and Mary, come to that) knew she was fortunate that the ancient custom whereby six lords of the Privy Council would stay within the bedchamber to witness the consummation had finally lapsed into abeyance. Bolingbroke and Mary would be allowed privacy for their sexual union, but they had yet to endure the formal blessing of the bedchamber—with a naked Bolingbroke and Mary lying patiently beneath snowy bedsheets pulled up to their shoulders—and then, in the morning, an inspection of the sheets by three privy lords to ensure that, firstly, a sexual union had taken place and, secondly, that Mary had been a virgin when she'd come to Bolingbroke's bed.

Bolingbroke was a powerful peer of the realm, an heir to the throne, at least until Richard could get himself one of his own body, and the Privy Council would want to be certain that any child that slipped from Mary's womb had been fathered by Bolingbroke.

Margaret had spent a great deal of the evening blessing the fact that she'd married a minor noble and hadn't had to endure some of the more intrusive aspects of the marriage rites tolerated by the peers of the realm.

There, Mary's hair was done, and Margaret could tell from the movements and murmurs behind the screen where Bolingbroke was being assisted by Neville and two valets, that it was time to put Mary to bed.

"Come," she whispered, bending down to where Mary sat before her. "Do not be afraid. Bolingbroke is a glorious man, and there is many a woman in London tonight who will be envying you."

"Look," Mary said, and held out her hands. They were shaking slightly.

"Well then, when you and Bolingbroke are finally left in peace, tell him that you fear, and he will be kind. Come, my lady, the archbishop and guests await outside."

Mary rose hesitantly, just as Bolingbroke emerged from behind the screen, Neville at his shoulder.

Margaret's and Neville's eyes met, then they each removed the light robes that covered the shoulders of Bolingbroke and Mary and held back the sheets as they slid naked beneath.

One of the valets moved to the door of the bedchamber, and the archbishop, Richard, de Vere, Lancaster and Katherine, and some fifteen other great nobles filed in. There were grins and winks and a few whispered ribald words, but the gathering generally behaved itself as Sudbury raised his hand and blessed the marriage bed.

Margaret thought that Richard might say something more to disturb the mood of the day, and looked over to him.

Richard, as de Vere who stood by his side, was paying the ceremony no attention at all.

Instead, both men were staring at Margaret.

Chapter XII

The Feast of St. Michael
In the first year of the reign of Richard II
(Thursday 29th September 1379)

— MICHAELMAS —

— II —

✢

CATHERINE HESITATED IN front of the door, then opened it boldly without knocking.

Philip, as naked as the day he'd slid from his mother's womb, was just lowering himself to the similarly naked body of the woman he had pinned to his bed.

"Sweet Jesu in heaven!" Philip said, and leaped to the

floor on the far side of the bed, leaving the woman, abandoned, to cover her nakedness as well as she could with the bed coverings.

Catherine grinned, then composed her face and spoke to the woman, whom she vaguely recognized as a laundress attending la Roche-Guyon.

"You may dress yourself and leave," she said. "His grace will not require your return."

Disconcerted, the woman looked to Philip who had donned a loose shirt and was now struggling into a pair of hose. "Do as she says," he said, and the woman scrambled from the bed, hiding her breasts with her hands, and ran over to a far corner where her dress lay puddled.

Philip finally managed to get his hose on and stood up straight, looking at Catherine, still standing just inside the doorway.

"Sweet Jesu, Catherine, what do you here?"

Catherine remained silent, inclining her head toward the hurriedly dressing laundress, and then stepped aside as the woman sidled past her and out the door.

Catherine closed the door, and then bolted it. "I have come to speak with you," she said.

Philip had walked over to a table and poured himself some wine from a ewer. Now he held the ewer up to Catherine, his eyebrows raised.

She nodded, and he poured her a cup of wine and passed it to her as she joined him.

"Talk could have waited until morning," he said softly, his gaze intent on her face as he sipped his wine.

"It suited me to come tonight." She drank her wine, then handed the cup back to Philip, making sure that their fingers touched as he took it from her.

"Beware, Catherine," he said, even more softly than previously, "for you play a dangerous game."

His words disconcerted Catherine, not for their meaning, but for the tone of concern which underpinned them.

She had the strangest feeling that the concern was genuine.

"We all play a dangerous game," she said, turning her back to him and walking toward where the embers of a fire glowed in a hearth. "France is in turmoil, and Isabeau has once again cast doubt on Charles' legitimacy."

"Who will listen to the words of a woman whose memory changes according to the price offered?" Philip walked up behind Catherine, and placed his hand gently on the small of her back.

It was a test. *Move away from me now and I will know you do not have the heart for the game.*

Catherine tensed very slightly—which could have meant anything—and then leaned back against his hand, which meant only one thing.

Philip drew in a deep breath. *So.*

"Perhaps," Catherine said, then briefly closed her eyes as Philip's hand slowly caressed her back. "But France needs a strong man on the throne, and whether fathered by Louis, the Master of the Hawks or the ever-cursed peacock, Charles does not have that strength."

"And you do?"

Catherine turned within the semi-circle of his arm so that she faced him. "I am a woman, and you know Salic Law—I cannot take the throne."

Philip's hand was harder now, and pulled her closer toward him. "But . . ."

"But I can do my best to make sure that a strong man *does* sit on the throne."

Philip's hand, as his entire being, stilled. "What are you here for, Catherine?"

"I am here to propose an alliance between us," she said, "cemented with the sweat of our bodies."

"Sweet Jesu!" Philip said, then abruptly spun away, moving back to the table where stood the wine ewer. "What is your price?" he said over his shoulder.

"That you be loyal to me, that you cleave only unto me, that you protect me, that you respect me."

Philip toyed with the wine ewer a while, then put it down

and walked back to Catherine. He lifted a hand and took her chin between gentle fingers; his face, so dark and handsome, was unreadable. "Then be my wife."

"No," she said, and his fingers tightened very slightly. "I will bed with you, and walk by your side. I will be your partner in your ambitions, and I will support you." Her voice softened, and became very quiet. "I will give you any child that comes of my body from our union. But I will not be your wife."

His eyes narrowed, deeply suspicious. She wanted to use him for some greater plan that she would not yet elucidate. Yet, in her own way, she was also being honest with him . . . and with what she *would* give him—her partnership in his ambitions, and any child that came of her body—she would give him everything he needed to seize the throne.

Perhaps, in time, she would attempt to betray him, but for the moment . . .

His hand dropped from her chin, and as it did so, Catherine turned around and lifted the thick plait of her hair over her shoulder, exposing the line of fastenings down the back of her gown.

She did not speak.

Philip hesitated, then lifted his hands to her neck and slowly began to undo the hooks. When he reached the last one, just above the swell of her buttocks, he gently folded back the now-loosened fabric of her gown.

She was wearing no garments beneath.

He slid his hands around her waist and over her belly, and gently pulled her back against him. Her skin was warm and very, very soft.

"From this point," he said, "there can be no going back. Leave now if there remains the slightest doubt."

In answer, Catherine lifted her own hands and placed them over his beneath the material of her gown. She slid them up until they cupped her breasts, and then jumped very slightly, surprised at the sensations that flooded through her as he caressed them.

"I have no experience," she said. "I do not know what to do."

Philip repressed a smile, sure that these words were something Isabeau had taught her: *they will inspire him to greater heat, my dear, for what man can resist being the one to induct a girl into the experience she lacks?*

Then his smile died. *Isabeau was a very wise woman.*

"Then let me show you," he whispered, and slid the gown completely from her body.

IT WAS a night of discoveries, and of unthought of marvels. Catherine had expected many things of Philip the Bad, but not the tenderness and respect and patience he showed her. They talked and laughed and were silent in turns as first he explored her body, and then encouraged her to explore his. Everything was new and wondrous for Catherine. She adored Philip's body, surprised not only by the manner and degree in which his flesh reacted to hers, but how, in turn, hers responded to his. There was no discomfort, no pain, only the discovery of new planes of sensation and of existence; no sense of loss, only the indescribable sense of how two bodies, two souls, could merge into one.

There was one moment, one moment that she thought she would remember all her life. Philip was over her, and deep inside her. He lifted his head and shoulders back from her a little distance, his face gleaming with sweat, his dark hair falling over his forehead.

"There is only you," he said, and somehow that touched Catherine so deeply that she began to cry, and Philip leaned back down to her again, and kissed away her tears, and cried himself.

SHE WOKE very slowly from a deep sleep. It was a dark, dark night, but Philip's gently breathing body was curled against hers and she was not alone anymore.

She was not alone anymore.

So much of her life had been spent alone, always fatherless, and often motherless as Isabeau abandoned her time and time again.

Bolingbroke had not fought for her . . . but Philip—treacherous, untrustworthy Philip—had given her this night honesty and something that was so close to love that there might be no difference at all.

She sighed and stretched slightly so that she might feel Philip's body rub against hers. She was filled with immeasurable content. Tonight, Bolingbroke lay with Mary Bohun, and Catherine could have spent this night weeping in her bed, but she had done what Isabeau had suggested and taken her fate in her own hands.

In doing so, Catherine had discovered in Philip something of infinite value . . . and perhaps, of infinite danger.

Could Hal ever compete? How strong was *he?*

Her movement had wakened Philip, and now he stirred.

"Catherine." A hand cupped one of her breasts, and she gave a low laugh and rolled close against him. "Of what do you think?"

Catherine grinned in the dark and leaned over to kiss his mouth. "I was considering my fortune in this past night. Few women, whether peasant or noble lady, are ever conducted so sweetly over the threshold from maidenhood into womanhood. You did not have to act so tenderly, and yet you chose to do so. For that I thank you."

"I could not act otherwise with you, Catrine."

The unexpected endearment drew fresh tears to her eyes, and she drew in a shaky breath.

He touched his fingers to her cheek. "And I had not thought to spend the entire night wiping your tears away. Perhaps I have not been as gentle as you imagine."

She smiled. "Then you must distract me from my pain, your grace."

"And how may I do that?"

She laughed as his hand stroked down her flank. "May I ask you a question?"

He gave a mock groan. "I you must."

"I was wondering, my King of Navarre, if you have ever bedded my mother."

His hand abruptly stilled, and after a moment he propped himself up on one elbow. "Why do you ask?"

"I was curious only, Philip, for I know how well she regards you. I do not mind if you answer with a yea."

Philip was silent, thinking, then decided to answer honestly. "No, I have never lain with her."

He gave a short laugh, remembering. "When I was a young lad, perhaps thirteen or fourteen years, I lusted after her madly, and put her face to every one of the peasant girls I managed to persuade to lie down in the grass. When I grew older, and had occasion to know her better, I grew to like and respect her too much to become one of the tally marks on her tapestry frame."

Catherine reached up a hand and cupped his cheek in its palm.

"Then my mother has suffered a great loss, because I think she has been looking for you all her life."

"And I think," he said softly, gazing down at the planes of her face now that his eyes had become accustomed to the faint light in the room, "that both you and I, my sweet maid, have gained a great deal more than we thought this night."

"Aye," she whispered.

And Hal has lost a great deal, she thought, as Philip's mouth closed gently and sweetly over hers.

THREE OTHER people lay awake that night of Michaelmas. Three other people who shared Catherine's night of wonder.

* * *

WAT TYLER, deep in the southeastern counties of England where he worked his secret business, paced the streets of the small village where he'd put up for the night.

He was furious both with Catherine and with Bolingbroke.

Subtlety would never work, not now that Catherine had lain down with Philip. Etienne had been right all along—the thunder of revolution in the streets was a sounder means to accomplish their ends than Bolingbroke's pretty subtleties.

MARGARET LAY next to her sleeping Tom, tears of joy and envy sliding down her cheeks. She had not thought Catherine would do this—and what she had done would threaten everything they had fought so hard for—but Margaret was glad Catherine had found some measure of happiness at last . . . *and what happiness she had found!*

BOLINGBROKE ALSO lay awake, Mary silent and still beside him.

He was beyond fury. An awareness of what Catherine was doing had come to him as he had turned to Mary when the door closed behind the last of their well-wishers.

As Philip had laid hand to Catherine, so Bolingbroke had laid hand to Mary.

As Philip's mouth had claimed Catherine's, so Bolingbroke's had claimed Mary's.

As Philip had entered Catherine's body, so Bolingbroke had entered Mary's.

As Catherine cried out in laughter and wonder, so Mary had screamed in pain and fear.

And as Catherine had caught Philip more closely to her, so Mary had fought, unsuccessfully, to push Bolingbroke from her.

Bolingbroke had known Mary was fearful, and had meant to be kind and patient with her. But, as awareness of

Catherine's actions came over Bolingbroke, blind fury, and an even worse jealousy, had swept through him and his hands and body became hard and unforgiving, and every one of Mary's fears had been realized.

He had tried to comfort her, afterward, but what could he say?

What could he say?

And so they lay there, Bolingbroke and his wife, through that long night of Michaelmas, each wondering what lay ahead for their loveless marriage.

And that deep-buried imp chuckled, and peeped into the future, and saw the merry mischief it could make.

Chapter XIII

The Feast of St. Jerome
In the first year of the reign of Richard II
(Friday 30th September 1379)

✢

BOLINGBROKE HAD WAITED only for the first stain of dawn in the east before he rose from his marital bed. As soon as he had dressed there came a tentative knock at the door and Margaret entered, her eyes studiously averted from Bolingbroke.

"My Lady Neville," Bolingbroke said in a harsh voice, as Margaret gathered up a robe for Mary.

She finally looked at him.

He could say nothing about Catherine in front of Mary, but he needed to lock eyes with Margaret, if only to share his silent anguish and anger.

She returned his stare evenly. *What did you expect? Did you think she would sit on her hands and weep and wait?*

The skin about Bolingbroke's eyes tightened. "My lady wife requires your comfort, Lady Neville," he said. "It seems that I have discomforted her during the night."

And with that he was gone.

As soon as the door closed behind him Mary put a trembling hand to her mouth, and Margaret sat down on the edge of the bed and gathered her into her arms.

NEVILLE FOUND Bolingbroke in the courtyard of the Savoy at weapons practice just as the bells of Prime rang out over London. The city was waking into life: barges plied the river, the cries of the fishermen and coal merchants drifting soulfully over the palace walls; carts and hooves rattled down the Strand moving produce into the markets; whores drifted into shadowy rooms to sleep off their night's labors just as priests flung open the doors of London's parish churches to face the sins of the city.

Neville halted in the shadows of an archway and watched.

Bolingbroke was dressed in a fortified leather tunic that hung down over his thighs, and thick studded gloves. A chain mail hood hung over his head, flowing over his shoulders and upper chest. In his hands he had a great sword, and with this sword he was trading blows with a sergeant-at-arms. Or rather, he seemed intent on murdering his sergeant-at-arms, who was clearly tiring.

Even as Neville moved forward from the shadows, the man slipped to the ground, and Bolingbroke stepped forward and raised his sword in both hands.

His face was twisted, his eyes blank.

"Bolingbroke," Neville said softly, seizing Bolingbroke's wrists in both his hands. "Cease. This man is not your enemy."

Bolingbroke tore himself free, the sword clattering to the ground, and whipped about to face Neville.

His eyes were furious. He began to say something, then he visibly fought for control, finally forcing the fury from his gaze.

Bolingbroke took a deep breath. "William," he said, half turning to face the sergeant-at-arms, "I do apologize to you. I meant no harm."

The man managed a half smile, but his hands were shaking as he sheathed his sword. "If you one day direct that anger at the French, my lord, then I do not mind being the near-murdered target of your practice."

"Well, one day, please Jesus, maybe I will," Bolingbroke said, and nodded a dismissal at the man.

"And that day may be closer than you think," Neville said as William walked away.

"What? What news?"

"Hal, your father sent me to find you. Richard has called a council of the great lords currently in London. We have an hour."

Bolingbroke stared at Neville, then muttered a curse and ran for the door.

THE COURTYARD of the palace of Westminster was clogged with horses, men-at-arms, pages, horse-boys, valets, squires, and ill-tempered nobles shouting for their attendants.

What could Richard want?

Although the Lords of the Privy Council were to be present at Richard's hastily called meeting, this was not a gathering of the Privy Council itself, for many more lords were to attend.

Bolingbroke and Neville dismounted from their horses, throwing their reins to the men of their escort. As they shouldered their way through the throng they saw Simon

Sudbury, Archbishop of Canterbury, disappearing through the palace entrance way and, directly behind him, Thomas Brantingham, Bishop of Exeter.

They vanished inside in a flurry of scarlet and blue cloaks.

"Sudbury and Brantingham?" Bolingbroke muttered. "What is happening. Ah, look, there is my father!"

John of Gaunt, Duke of Lancaster, had emerged from a side entrance and was now only a few paces from Bolingbroke and Neville.

"Father?" Bolingbroke said.

Lancaster's face was gray—but gray with anger and frustration rather than illness. "Richard has decided to take personal control of government," he said, and held up his hand for silence as Bolingbroke spluttered. "He is eighteen, and his grandfather had taken personal control at the same age. He has a right . . . and the Privy Council has nodded their collective age-addled heads."

"But why?" Bolingbroke said.

Lancaster gave his son a bleak look. "Why not? Hal, Richard has the *right* to rule on his own. My regency would not last forever."

"He is to keep you as a councillor, surely."

Now Lancaster's look was even bleaker. "Nay, Hal. Richard is determined to cast off the chains of past monarchs . . . and apparently I am the greatest weight of them all."

Bolingbroke and Neville shared a look, but Lancaster interrupted before either could speak. "There is no good to be done idling about here with our questions. Come, let us hear what our king has to say."

RICHARD WAS to meet with his lords in the Painted Chamber. When Bolingbroke and Neville entered, they both noted that the hall had been somewhat modified since they'd last seen it. Richard's bed had gone from the dais at the top of the hall—he had apparently moved to one of the apartments adjoining the Painted Chamber, possibly the queen's apartments which were empty of a queen—and the space was now occupied by several trestle tables cluttered with boxes, maps, small chests and several score documents. Neville instantly thought the scene bore a remarkable resemblance to Bolingbroke's disordered office, which Neville still had to succeed in bringing under some degree of control.

Several large tables had been placed end to end in the center of the hall to form one long table, chairs drawn up about it. To each side stood groups of nobles, murmuring between themselves, some sipping from cups of wine.

Some faces were apprehensive, others confident.

A loud laugh sounded, and Bolingbroke's and Neville's eyes jerked to a group of three men standing close to the dais.

Robert de Vere, Henry Percy the Earl of Northumberland, and his son Hotspur.

All three were huddled companionably close, and de Vere had his arm about Hotspur's shoulders.

The laugh had come from both de Vere and Hotspur, and they were staring straight at Bolingbroke.

"This is a bad business," said a voice, and Lancaster, Bolingbroke and Neville turned about.

Ralph Neville—Thomas' uncle and Baron of Raby and Earl of Westmorland—had joined them, and now he nodded to the three men standing before the dais. "Those three have an uncommon bond today. Why, I wonder?"

"De Vere *is* married to Northumberland's daughter, Philippa," Neville said. "Perhaps . . ."

Raby's eyes had not left the three men, who were returning his stare with more than a little insolence. "There is more," he said. "I think those men have traded something of greater value than a little woman-flesh."

Neville looked back to the group, wondering what their alliance could mean for his uncle. Raby and Northumberland were rivals for power in the north of England . . . and now that Richard was apparently freeing himself of Lancaster's influence, and Raby was so closely allied to Lancaster's house and star, it boded nothing but evil that Northumberland and Hotspur now stood so smoothly with Richard's favorite.

Of course it boded nothing but evil! Richard was freeing himself from all influences who could stay his hand, and allying himself with all those who, for the sake of their ambitions, would condone any devilry he chose to mouth.

"Ah," Lancaster said. "There's Gloucester. Hal, Ralph, we should join him."

They walked over to where Thomas of Woodstock, Duke of Gloucester, and Lancaster's youngest brother, stood with several of his attendants. Gloucester greeted his brother, nephew and Raby warmly, and even nodded civilly enough to Neville, apparently forgetting that Neville had once spoken harsh words to him when Gloucester had blamed Margaret for his wife's death in childbirth.

"The little imp has won himself some new friends," Gloucester said, nodding over to the Percys and de Vere, all still watching Bolingbroke and Lancaster.

"De Vere?" Lancaster said. "Aye, that he has, and I believe that it bodes—"

"My lords!" cried an attendant by the side entrance. "I give you your king!"

And there was Richard, striding into the hall and smiling at the assembled lords. His lean body was clad in tightfitting black—a color he now apparently preferred to green—and he wore no jewels or insignia of office save for a small circlet of gold.

Richard has dressed appropriately for whatever grim tidings he bears, Neville thought.

As the lords bowed, Richard walked to the throne set at the head of the tables and sat down, indicating that the lords, too, should take their places.

Neville moved slightly back as Lancaster, his brother Raby and Bolingbroke all sat midway down the table—

They should have been close to the king's right hand, Neville thought.

—while their noble attendants, Neville among them, stood two or three paces behind the backs of their chairs.

"My lords," Richard said, slowly raising his head and staring about the table, "it has now been some months since my beloved grandfather and father died—"

Why not state the truth, demon? Neville thought. *They were murdered.* He stared at Richard with hard eyes, and for one heartbeat Richard's own gaze flickered his way and met his stare.

"—and, as is right and fitting, there has been a period of mourning and stillness as we honor their passing.

"But now my father and grandfather's age has passed, and a new and fresh king sits upon the throne of England. I have been content to stay my hand during these months of transition, but now I must lift it—"

There was a collective drawing of breaths in the hall. *What did he mean? Who were to lose their heads, and who to have preferments added to their purses?*

"—and break free from the governorship of tutors and regents," Richard looked directly at Lancaster, "who thought to keep me restrained within the bounds of childhood."

"Your grace," Lancaster said in a tight voice, "there was never 'restraint' intended. You came too suddenly to the throne without the training and consulship that we thought would be yours during the years of your father's reign. We—"

"I *was* nevertheless restrained," Richard said. "Furthermore, in past weeks I have well noted that some men," and still his eyes were on Lancaster and his immediate companions, "have thought to gain for themselves a public notoriety and fame that they could well use against me."

Here it comes, Neville thought, *the dagger in Bolingbroke's back. Nay, the dagger in the back of all associated with Bolingbroke and his father.*

Again Richard's eyes flickered Neville's way before casting themselves restlessly about the assembled lords.

"I have thought myself in some danger," he said softly. "Moreover, I have thought England in some danger. Therefore, listen you to these my decisions.

"Lancaster, you are removed as regent. I wish you good health and long life, but I have thought to surround myself with counselors I can the more easily trust."

Now the sharp intakes of breath about the table were clearly audible. Some men may have silently applauded, for Lancaster's fall in favor would surely see the rise of their own influence, but all wondered at Richard's arrogance that he so easily cast aside, and so publicly humiliated, the most powerful man in England.

"As with regents, so with all the major officers of government," Richard continued. "My Lord Archbishop of Canterbury," he nodded at Sudbury, "shall be my new Chancellor, and my Lord Bishop of Exeter," now he nodded at Brantingham, "shall hold the office of Treasurer."

Sweet Jesu, Neville thought, *the imp has such confidence that he surrounds himself with the great men of the Church.* Then his eyes fell on both Sudbury and Brantingham. *Or* are *they great men of the Church? Is it possible they be demons, too?*

Almost as if in reply, Sudbury shot Lancaster an apologetic, almost embarrassed, look—the two had been close allies for years. Neville revised his suspicions of Sudbury; if nothing else the man had obviously not yet told Richard about the subversive John Ball within the dungeons of Canterbury prison. If he had, Lancaster would be in the Tower.

"And to replace Lancaster at my side, as dearest friend and most trusted confidant, I appoint Robert de Vere my Chamberlain and," Richard paused, and looked about the table with amused eyes, "also gift to him the castles and lands of Oakham and Queenborough—"

The sound of murmuring could clearly be heard about the table.

"—as well as the castle of Berkhamsted, and create him the Chief Justice of Chester and North Wales—"

The table fell silent as many of the lords stared at Richard with horror.

"*—and* create him, as token of my love and trust, Duke of Ireland."

The table erupted. *Duke of Ireland?* Many men spoke harshly—others, thinking to ally themselves with the new favorite, spoke words of congratulation—but no one spoke more volubly than Gloucester.

He sprang to his feet and slammed his fist down on the table.

There was instant silence.

"Your grace," Gloucester seethed, "this preferment is beyond reasoning! You have created a man—"

"Who can counter the ill will of my uncle Lancaster!" Now Richard also was on his feet, and all Neville could think of was that Gloucester had very probably signed his own death warrant here this day.

"Lancaster bears you no ill will!" Gloucester said. "None! Had he done so, do you think he would have allowed you to so easily gain the throne? Don't you realize, you silly pasty-faced youth—"

"Gloucester!" Now Lancaster was on his feet, trying to get Gloucester back into his chair, preferably with his mouth shut.

"Do you not think that I haven't seen what my uncle and his beloved son are doing?" Richard yelled. "Did you not hear the screams of the crowds for their beloved 'fair Prince Hal' yesterday?" Now Richard's face was twisted with hatred. *"I will not nurture rivals at my court!"*

He stopped, breathing deeply to regain control of himself.

The entire table was still and tense. Lancaster had finally managed to get Gloucester back into his chair, while Neville had moved forward very slightly toward Bolingbroke, who sat stunned and disbelieving, staring at Richard.

Who could have thought that the demon would move so quickly to consolidate his power?

"You are fortunate, my fair Prince Hal," Richard said, "that I do not commit you to the Tower for your treasonous thoughts."

"Your grace," Bolingbroke said, and all listening marveled at the calmness of his face and voice, "I nurture no treasonous thoughts, nor ambitions that do not include you as my king and lord. I pray you believe me."

"Then you must endeavor to earn my trust, Bolingbroke, for I cannot think but that you secretly yearn for my title and honors, and plan to use both Lancaster's and Hereford's lands and riches to seize them."

The hush about the table was now extraordinary both in its depth and in its anticipation.

"Sire," Bolingbroke said in a very quiet voice, "I went down on bended knee before you last May Day and pledged you my homage and allegiance. What have I done since that you now think me a traitor?"

Richard held Bolingbroke's stare a long moment before he answered. "I move only so that you may never become a traitor, Bolingbroke," he said. "Thank the sweet lord that you still have both your lands and life."

Bolingbroke leaned back in his chair and looked away. He was pale with fury, and a muscle twitched in one cheek.

And had Richard thought he could do it, Neville realized, *then he would indeed have deprived Bolingbroke of both lands and life. But Lancaster and his faction are still too powerful, and Richard must bide his time like a hunchbacked spider lurking in the shadows behind his web. Thank sweet Jesu Richard does not know of John Ball, and that Wycliffe is now safely silenced within the walls of Lutterworth!*

Richard tore his gaze away from Bolingbroke and spoke for a few minutes of some other, minor, administrative appointments. Then . . .

"I have received a request for aid," he said, and rose from his chair and ascended the dais, searching for a parchment which he finally located. He made a great show of perusing it, then spoke again, raising his voice so that he could clearly be heard around the table.

"This request I am disposed to regard kindly, for it could well rebound in England's favor. Count Pedro of Catalonia has requested my assistance in some small domestic dispute he has with his bastard half-brother, Henry."

Here Richard shot Bolingbroke another smoldering look, as if to imply that all relatives named Henry were bound to act treasonably sooner or later.

"Henry has apparently seized control of Pedro's lands and revenues. Pedro needs help to get them back. I, and my chief advisers," Richard indicated de Vere, Northumberland, Hotspur, as also Sudbury and Brantingham, "have decided to send a force into Catalonia in order to—"

"Your grace, this is madness!" Now Raby was standing, and Neville had to suppress a small groan and a desire to tackle his uncle to the floor. *Was everyone he needed to aid him in his quest for the casket about to alienate themselves completely from influence?*

"Any action in Catalonia," Raby said, "is bound to remove forces from the south of France, where we need them most—"

"Westmorland, you will sit down!" Richard snapped. "Your advice on this matter is not sought."

"More to the point," Lancaster said, "Catalonia is under the overlordship of the King of Aragon. He will not be amused to think that England is sending an armed force into what he considers his own—"

"And *your* advice is most certainly not sought!" Richard said. "Pedro has the potential to be a good ally if handled correctly—"

At that remark a number of men about the table had to avert their eyes and bite their lips to keep the smiles at bay.

"—and if handed aid when he requires it." Richard paused. "My Lord of Northumberland's son, Hotspur, will lead the Catalonian expedition."

Neville's gaze shot to Hotspur. *No wonder he had been so free and friendly with de Vere! But Hotspur? To lead such an expedition? He was brave, true, but young for a campaign that was going to need the delicate skills of a diplomat as much as the sword skills of the warrior.*

"Your grace, England can ill afford the cost of such a venture." Now Sir Richard Sturry, a trusted councillor of the dead King Edward, rose to his feet. "Already we are in considerable debt from our continued war with France—"

"All solved with the Treaty of Westminster," Richard said, and waved Sturry back into his seat. "We can . . . and we *will* . . . afford this mission. It is time I make my mark, not only on England, but on Europe.

"My lords." Richard now looked about the hall, and managed a small smile. "I think I have concluded my business for this day."

Many of the Lords rose slowly to their feet as a sound of murmuring filled the hall.

But Neville was unable to tear his eyes away from Richard.

The king was standing behind one of the trestle tables on the dais, his eyes on Neville, a sly grin on his face . . .

. . . and his left hand resting on a small, brass-bound casket atop the table!

"Sweet Jesu," Bolingbroke whispered as he joined Neville. "There it is!"

PART TWO

The Wounded Wife

Thus, dear sister, as I have said before that it behooves you to be obedient to him that shall be your husband, and that by good obedience a wise woman gains her husband's love and at the end hath what she would of him.

—The Goodman of Paris to his wife, 1392

Chapter I

Before Matins, the Feast of St. Melorius
In the first year of the reign of Richard II
(1 a.m. Saturday 1st October 1379)

✠

FOR THE PAST TWO HOURS small boats had slipped silently through the waters of the Thames, sliding to a brief halt at the wharf of the Savoy and depositing their cloaked and hooded cargo before continuing into the night. The men who jumped from the boats and then ran as quietly as they could up the steps to the river gate muttered their names urgently to the man standing there, before taking his murmured directions to dart into an underground storage chamber.

In all, Neville greeted some sixteen men, among them some of the mightiest nobles in England. When the last man arrived, Neville walked with him down to the storage chamber dimly lit with flickering torches.

As Neville closed the door behind him, and sat down on a keg, a deep silence fell over the shadowy room.

This was sheer danger. More than dangerous, for all the men gathered in this room knew that their alliance was as fragile and ephemeral as a spider's web.

The betrayal might as easily come from within as without.

John of Gaunt, Duke of Lancaster, stood by a stack of ale kegs, his brother Gloucester to one side, Bolingbroke to the other. Close to him sat Ralph Neville, Baron of Raby and Earl of Westmorland. These men trusted each other, but were desperately unsure of the others.

And yet had not the others sought them out?

Gathered about in the rest of the room were some of the greatest lords in England. Richard, Earl of Arundel and Surrey and, Lancaster and his brethren had thought, one of Richard's most trusted Privy Councillors. What was he doing here?

Less surprising was the presence of Thomas Mowbray, Earl of Nottingham and Duke of Norfolk. He had once been a close friend of Richard's—they were of an age, and had grown up together. But now Nottingham had been rejected in favor of de Vere, and Nottingham's resentment was widely known among the flower of England's knighthood.

Thomas Beauchamp, Earl of Warwick, was no surprise at all: he had never been close to Richard, and, as with Sir Richard Sturry who sat close by him, had been publicly vocal in expressing some reservations regarding Richard's actions. Both these men had spoken brief words of support to Lancaster and Bolingbroke as they'd stalked from the Painted Chamber yesterday afternoon.

There were others, too, earls and dukes, as well as ordinary knights, men who were profoundly disturbed by Richard's actions of the past day, just as they had been disturbed by de Vere's rapid rise to favor in the past few months.

"My lord." Sturry broke the silence, and rose and gave Lancaster a slight bow as he spoke. "You are in mortal danger. You should—"

Lancaster halted him with a wave of his hand. "Richard would not dare to physically move against me."

"My lord, your very power is enough to make him move," Sturry said. "Perhaps not this week, or even this year, but once Richard feels he has consolidated his hold . . ."

Another brief silence, then Neville spoke: "My lords, I agree with Sir Richard that my Lord of Lancaster must beware of Richard's ire, but I think my Lord of Gloucester in the more immediate danger. As," he paused very briefly, "my Lord of Bolingbroke."

There was a murmur of agreement about the room, and heads nodded.

"It *would* be better if both my brother Gloucester and my son Bolingbroke removed themselves from Richard's immediate vicinity," Lancaster said. "Perhaps my entire family should, for a time. Christmastide is approaching, and it will be easy to remove myself and mine to Kenilworth, citing the holy celebrations as cause enough."

"And while we are all busy saving ourselves," Mowbray said, "what do we do about de Vere? Well? Richard has made this man powerful beyond belief! Who knows what else he will give him in the next few months. My lords," Mowbray leaned forward, his hands on his knees, his angry eyes scanning the room, "I have heard rumor the 'Duke' of Ireland will not be enough for Richard's toy. Our king plans to invade Ireland and create de Vere *King* of Ireland!"

"He wouldn't dare!" Gloucester said.

"Nay?" Mowbray said softly. "And who among us thought two days ago that de Vere would be greeting Saint Melorius' Day as Duke of Ireland? Not to mention his other preferments."

"Richard will move against Lancaster and all his allies," Neville said. "He must if he wants to establish his own power as king. To do that he needs to build a coterie of powerful men who owe him their livings. De Vere is the first, but we all know there are many other men who will be willing to turn against Lancaster."

Again, silence, as men nodded their heads. Lancaster was the most powerful man in England, and he had long been resented. Now that the new king had so publicly turned against him, those men who had long nurtured their jealousy would flock to Richard's cause.

"It may have helped, 'fair Prince Hal,' " Arundel said to Bolingbroke, "if you had not so successfully whipped up the London mob's adulation on your wedding day. Lancaster is threat enough to Richard, but you are worse. You stand to inherit all your father's power . . . and the common's adoration as well. You are a threat beyond imagining."

"My Lord Arundel," said Bolingbroke, stepping forward so that his face was lit by a nearby torch. "I confess myself surprised to see you here, and to hear you speak such words of concern for me. You are one of Richard's most trusted councillors. Why have you allowed yourself to stand closeted so deep with some of Richard's worst enemies?"

Arundel nodded, acknowledging Bolingbroke's distrust. "Richard is driving England into the ground. His expedition to Catalonia will be more ruinous than you know. Richard has no intentions of confining the expedition's field of action to Catalonia—he intends to launch a new drive into the heart of France."

"But that would be madness!" Lancaster said. "We still have to rebuild our strength and resources, and replenish the coffers, after my elder brother's fateful death."

"Exactly," Arundel said, "and Richard has determined the perfect way of raising finances for this folly. When Parliament meets in January, Richard intends to push for a new poll tax to raise the funds and repay the crown's debts."

"But the commons cannot afford a *new* tax," Bolingbroke said. "Sweet Jesu, they are taxed enough as it is. There will be unrest as we have never seen." He paused, and Neville knew that both Bolingbroke and Lancaster must be thinking of the still-at-large Wat Tyler and Jack Trueman, both of whom would surely use the bitterness caused by a new tax to create havoc. "Richard will be busy enough contending with war at home just as much as war abroad. And to send Hotspur abroad to lead this expedition . . . Lord Christ, Richard invites failure!"

And that, thought Neville, *was nothing but resentment and jealousy speaking. Bolingbroke does not want Hotspur basking in the glory he will achieve if the expedition* is *successful.*

"My heart is with England," Arundel said, locking eyes with Bolingbroke, "and Richard will tread England into the dust. God in heaven, potentially he has another fifty years of life ahead of him. Bolingbroke, if you are for England, then I am for you and yours."

Bolingbroke's mouth quirked. "I am a wounded hawk, Arundel, fluttering defenseless about the ground. Richard will see to it that my wings be permanently crippled."

Now Arundel rose to his feet and moved to Bolingbroke. Stunningly, he dropped to one knee before him. "I am your man, Bolingbroke. Test me with what you will." He raised his face and stared into Bolingbroke's. "But be assured that there are men, not only in this room, but across England, who will offer their own lives to ensure that one day you will soar again."

For Neville, as for every other man present, Arundel's actions and words drove home the realization that Lancaster was a finished man. Powerful he might be in terms of lands and wealth and the ability to raise arms, but Bolingbroke was the man who was going to inherit all that wealth and power *and* the love of men besides.

If the opposition to Richard grew so great that it coalesced about one man, then that one man was Bolingbroke.

It was in that single moment that Neville realized Bolingbroke's life would follow one of only two paths: one path led to the executioner's block, the other to the throne of England. It was total annihilation, or total victory.

And every other man in the room knew it, too.

Bolingbroke nodded, accepting Arundel's words—

He has known this all along, thought Neville.

—and addressed the room.

"Your advice? What do we do now?"

"Wait," said Sturry. "As Richard does not have the ability to move against you, so you do not have the ability to—"

"No!" Lancaster put his hand on Bolingbroke's shoulder and pulled him back. "This talk is of treason and I will *not* have it in my house. Richard is young, and misguided. He still has my loyalty—"

Bolingbroke whipped about and faced his father. "Then

you are a fool, father. Richard is not 'misguided,' he is England's *death*!"

Gloucester and Raby exchanged glances. "These are hot and hasty words thrown about the room," Gloucester said, "and tempers need to cool before we commit to any action. My brother Lancaster is right to say that our family should repair to Kenilworth for the winter. The castle is well fortified, and even if Richard should be hasty enough to lay siege to it, we shall be safe."

"And Parliament may not grant Richard's request for a new poll tax," Raby said. "Do we speak hot words for nothing? Does Richard merely need a year or two to settle down?"

Bolingbroke shot Raby a black look, but Raby ignored it. "We wait out Christmastide," he said, "and for the moment we do nothing to further aggravate Richard. In fact," and now it was Raby who shot Bolingbroke the black look, "it might not be the worst of actions to publicly pledge your loyalty to him, Hal. Richard needs to be appeased . . . and that will work as much to your favor as it does to his."

Bolingbroke made as if to object, then a thoughtful look came over his face, and he nodded. "You speak wisdom, Ralph, as does my uncle Thomas."

"Then let us finish," Lancaster said. "It will not be long before dawn tints the sky, and *none* of you dares be seen leaving the Savoy. Neville? Will you escort my lords one by one back to the wharf?"

IT WASN'T until well after dawn that Neville had a chance to have a quiet word with Bolingbroke. They needed to plan to recover the casket.

"It must be soon," Bolingbroke said, "for father is planning our removal to Kenilworth within the next week." He shuddered. "I confess, Tom, it will be good to leave London for the moment."

"I *must* have the casket—"

"Yes, yes, but, Christ Savior, Tom, it is in *Westminster*.

But do not fret, Raby's words have given me cause for thought."

Bolingbroke lapsed into silence. "And Arundel's offer to be tested can be used to your advantage," he said finally. "Tom, I have a plan, but it will require the utmost courage—"

Neville nodded and began to speak, but Bolingbroke hushed him.

"—*and* it will require the courage of our wives. Are you prepared to risk that?"

"*You* are?" Neville said.

"Aye."

Still Neville hesitated, then finally he nodded. "Then, yes, I am prepared to risk them. I must, if it will mean I finally achieve possession of the casket."

Something flared in Bolingbroke's eyes, and Neville was not sure whether it was triumph or extraordinary pain.

"Then let me explain . . . ," Bolingbroke said.

Chapter II

Sext, the Vigil of the Feast of St. Francis
In the first year of the reign of Richard II
(late morning Monday 3rd October 1379)

— I —

✠

THEY CAME TO WESTMINSTER by small barge, rather than on horseback, because it would be less awkward spiriting the casket away.

It would also be faster.

And safer.

Robert Courtenay, subdued because Neville had ordered him to remain behind, had waved them farewell from the Savoy's river gate, and now they slipped silently, almost secretively, round the great bend in the river which would bring them to Westminster. Several men-at-arms sat in the stern of the barge with the two men who poled it through the choppy river waters. Bolingbroke, Mary, Neville and Margaret sat close to the bow, on wooden benches made comfortable with soft cushions and draperies.

Everyone was tense. Bolingbroke sat with his head steadfastly down, as if fascinated with the planking of the barge. Margaret sat white-faced, her hands clasped tight in her lap, terrified of an encounter with Richard.

Neville glanced at her from time to time, torn between his desperate need to achieve the casket and an almost equally desperate worry about what Richard might do to Margaret. *Would she be safe? With* Richard? *Hal had said it would not take long to get the casket—not with the aid they had waiting for them in Westminster—and Mary and Margaret would not be placed in danger for long.*

For an instant, Bolingbroke raised his head and locked eyes with Neville, then looked away.

We need Mary and Margaret to distract Richard, Neville reasoned with himself, even as he fretted over his concern for Margaret. *Why waste time on disquiet? Margaret knows the stakes . . . she knows the risks.*

But each time Neville closed his eyes he thought he could see a gigantic spider scurrying across a shadowed chamber, wrapping Margaret in its loathsome legs as it bore her to the floor.

No! Cease such fancifying! Bolingbroke was right . . . they would take but a few minutes to seize the casket, and Margaret would be in no real danger. All would be well. This afternoon he would have the casket, and the truth would be in his hands. Richard would have a day or two more of life only.

Neville leaned back against the side of the barge, and finally admitted to himself his worry for Margaret. He could no longer deny that she was a good wife to him, and that she was not the whore he'd first thought her. She had far more honor, and far more courage and innate nobility than ever he'd first credited her. *Sweet Jesu, let her be safe. Let Margaret not come to harm. Let Margaret not come to harm. . . .*

The prayer rattled over and over in Neville's mind, and, in his present state of anxiety and edginess, it did not occur to him for a moment that this was a strange prayer to be uttering about a woman he had once been so sure he could deny, a woman he had once been so sure he could sacrifice to the angels' cause.

A woman he was once so sure he could not possibly love.

Mary, although she recognized the tension in the others, did not realize the full extent of the deception of the day. All she knew was that Richard had turned against her husband, who had done no wrong, save that he was more golden and glorious than the king. As Richard would not see Bolingbroke, Mary understood Bolingbroke's request that she entreat an audience with her sovereign so that she might beg Richard to allow her husband to pledge his steadfast loyalty. It was a shame her husband's pledge could not be more public, but there would be no public opportunity before the entire Lancastrian household moved to Kenilworth. Private must do, and there would surely be witnesses enough.

Margaret accompanied her in her capacity as her attendant gentlewoman, and Mary was heartily glad she had Margaret's support.

She had no idea of Margaret's terror.

WHEN THEY docked at Westminster's pier, Bolingbroke stepped out, aiding first Mary and then Margaret from the barge. There was no time for speech, hardly time even for thought, but Bolingbroke gave Margaret's hand a brief squeeze as she stepped from barge to pier: a futile, hopelessly inadequate gesture of support.

She turned her head and would not acknowledge him, and Bolingbroke wondered if she would ever speak to him again.

This is such a pivotal, critical day, he thought, *and from it we hope to achieve victory. But is victory worth the pain that will be visited on Margaret?*

And then Bolingbroke thought of the torments of hell everlasting that awaited them if this day failed, if his plan to turn Neville's heart to Margaret did not succeed, and so he hardened his heart and turned away from Margaret.

He did not see Neville send Margaret a look of such anxiety that, *had* Bolingbroke seen it, would have eased much of his own worry about what this day might bring.

Arundel was waiting for them by the water gate leading into the Westminster complex, and as they approached he spoke quietly to the guards, who raised their pikes and allowed Bolingbroke's party through.

Bolingbroke raised his eyebrows at Arundel, and the earl nodded.

"We have done all we can. Come, if we delay longer the king will depart for his afternoon's hunting."

They walked briskly along a westerly path before turning south along the west wall of the great hall. Most of the old roof had gone, and the hall was now exposed to the elements. Craftsmen and others scampered over the great ribs of the new roof, working desperately against the inevitable onset of the autumn and winter rains.

No one, save one or two of the men-at-arms, spared the activity a glance.

Arundel led them to the doorway of a small atrium in the southernmost part of the palace complex. Inside the atrium, three doors led, in turn, to the lesser hall, the Painted Chamber, and the complex of private apartments known collectively as the Queen's Chambers.

Where, now, Richard had made his nest.

The atrium was cold and comfortless. Guards stood at each of the three doors; all stared with hard eyes at the newcomers.

Arundel walked over to the two guards standing by the door leading to the Queen's Chambers.

"The Countess of Hereford and her lady companion wish an audience with the king." Arundel grinned easily. "I can assure you they carry no weapons save for their feminine charms."

Mary squared her shoulders and held the guards' stare; a wan and tight-faced Margaret kept her eyes averted.

One of the guards disappeared, reappearing in a few moments.

"My ladies," he said, and stood back so that they might pass through the door.

As Margaret followed Mary through she turned and sent Neville a look of such stark terror that he took a half-step forward, stopping awkwardly as Bolingbroke caught at his arm.

And on that look, the fate of the world turned.

THE DOOR closed behind them, and Neville was left staring at its blank, wooden face.

"Tom!" Bolingbroke whispered. "Tom!"

Neville took a deep breath and forced himself to turn away from the door.

It would be all right. Margaret would be safe. They would not be long.

Then the door which led to the Painted Chamber opened, and Sir Richard Sturry walked into the atrium.

"My lords!" he said, as if surprised. "Sweet Jesu smiles upon me indeed. His Grace has asked me to transfer back to the abbey some of the registers he has been studying, and I have been wringing my hands at the thought of finding someone—or four or five someones—to aid me in this endeavor."

He beamed, and threw out his hands. "And here stand my Lords of Hereford and Arundel, and Lord Neville, complete with an able-bodied contingent of men-at-arms. My Lords, may I . . ."

Bolingbroke smiled. "My men are yours for the asking, Sturry. I cool my heels in this frigid chamber awaiting my sovereign's pleasure, but there is no reason why they should suffer along with me. Take them if you will, that they may keep warm with some godly work."

Sturry positively beamed. "This chamber *is* cold and heartless, is it not? Why not await Richard's pleasure in the Painted Chamber? I am sure his men," he half bowed at the sergeant-at-arms, "can fetch you from there if need arise."

The sergeant opened his mouth to protest, but Arundel spoke first.

"I will vouch for my Lord of Hereford and Lord Neville," he said. "There shall come no harm from their waiting in the Painted Chamber."

The sergeant closed his mouth, thinking it over. Arundel and Sturry were trusted confidants of the king, and Arundel a privy councillor besides.

"Very well," he said.

Bolingbroke thanked him politely, and motioned his men to follow as he joined Arundel and Sturry.

Neville fell in behind, but not after one more glance at the door through which Margaret had vanished.

"MY LADY of Hereford," Richard said, rising from his chair before the fire. He had been drinking heavily, for his mouth was moist, and the wine cup he put on a table to one side wobbled alarmingly as his hand shook and almost dropped it to the floor.

Mary, Margaret a pace behind her, sank into a deep curtsey before Richard.

"*And* my Lady Neville," said Robert de Vere from where he sat on the side of a heavily draped bed. "How fortuitous."

"What do you here, Mary?" Richard asked, his eyes on Margaret as both women rose to their feet.

"Your grace," Mary said, "I come to speak on behalf of my husband. If you have heard that he plans your destruction, then you have heard lies. No, pray allow me to speak my piece!"

Richard inclined his head, his eyes darting once more to Margaret.

"My Lord of Hereford is your true subject, your grace. His ambitions are only for your rise in glory and majesty. Please, your grace, my husband begs that he be allowed to sink to his knees before you and pledge again his loyalty and homage. He waits outside, in hope that you will acquiesce."

Richard was silent, toying with a broad ribbon dangling from one of his sleeves. He shifted his weight from one leg to the other, his eyes now intent on Mary.

"Please, your grace," Mary said. "I beg you as a woman who wants only to see her husband reconciled with our sovereign. My Lord of Hereford will do *anything* to prove to you his loyalty."

"Anything?" de Vere said, now rising from the bed and walking forward to join them.

Mary jerked her eyes to de Vere, then looked back to Richard.

"There is nothing he would deny you," she said. "Nothing."

Richard smiled. "Nothing?"

And from the expression on his face Mary suddenly realized that she and Margaret were in horrifying danger. There was no one in the room save for them and the two men. There was no aid, and no hope of aid, for the stone walls were thick, and the solid oak door tightly closed.

"Nothing?" Richard said again, this time spitting the word out with no attempt to conceal his malevolence.

Mary opened her mouth, but could not speak.

"Nothing?" Richard said, and seized her arm.

Mary gave a small shriek, but as Margaret stepped forward Richard twisted Mary's arm, forcing her aside and almost to her knees.

"Nothing," Richard said, and threw Mary completely to the floor as he grabbed hold of Margaret.

"No!" she cried, but it was too late.

STURRY LED them into the Painted Chamber and directly up to the dais.

"See!" he said to a somewhat harried-looking clerk. "I have found some men to help us."

The clerk blinked at him.

"To help us move the chests his grace has indicated back to the abbey library," Sturry said.

The clerk frowned. "I was not aware that—"

"Ah," Sturry said. "I think you were not here when his grace spoke of this. My Lord of Arundel . . . when was it precisely?"

"Yesterday," Arundel said to the clerk. "While you and your helpers were at Vespers service."

"Oh." The clerk shrugged, then sighed. "As if my life was not difficult enough already. Well, then, what needs to go?"

Sturry ummed and ahhed, moving along the trestle tables covered with chests and piles of documents and rolls of registers.

Once he had moved out of the clerk's direct line of vision he raised inquiring eyebrows in Bolingbroke's direction.

"*Where?*" Bolingbroke whispered to Neville.

Neville cast frantic eyes along the table closest to the edge of the dais. It was on this one, *somewhere,* but had Richard caused it to be moved . . . ?

No! No! There it was!

He nodded very slightly in its direction, and Sturry moved along and placed a hand on it, raising his eyebrows yet again.

Neville nodded.

Sweet Christ, he could hear it singing out to him—

"NO!" MARY struggled to her feet, so aghast at what was happening she had almost managed to convince herself that she was trapped in some nightmare, and that all she needed to do to stop this abomination was to wake up.

"No!" Mary said again, but Richard turned aside from Margaret for an instant and struck Mary a stinging blow to her face.

"If you interfere, you mewling child, then I shall ensure that all your husband kneels before is the executioner's block!"

"Mary!" Margaret said, her voice full of her pain and fright. "Don't—"

"Good girl," de Vere said from behind her, and then both he and Richard had Margaret in their strong hands, and they hauled her over to the table.

"You're wasted on that dour-faced friar you married," Richard said, sweeping away the ewer and wine cups that stood on the table. "Wasted."

He slammed her across the table's surface, and then laughed as she cried out in fear.

"THIS ONE," Sturry said, patting the top of the casket, "and . . . this"—he touched another directly beside it, then turned to the table immediately behind him—"and these three."

"Good," said Arundel, and clicked his fingers at the men-at-arms.

They came forward, and Neville tensed as one of the men lifted the casket—*his* casket—and walked down the steps to the floor of the chamber.

Neville hurried after him, unable to tear his eyes from the casket. Finally . . . finally . . .

"IT IS a good day," Richard said in gasps between bouts of thrusting, "when I shall not only see Bolingbroke on his knees before me, but finally manage," he paused, moaned, then resumed his dialogue with an effort, "to ride Neville's beauteous wife."

Margaret hardly heard his words. Her eyes were tightly closed, her hands balled into tight fists at her sides, and her body so rigid that her back was arched almost completely off the table. Her entire universe consisted only of Richard's repugnant, agonizing rape; like Richard's gasping, her breath rattled harshly in her throat, but for very different reasons from his.

Somewhere . . . somewhere far distant in her chaotic mind . . . she thought she could hear Mary's useless cries, and she *knew* she could hear de Vere's laughter, and then his urgent words to Richard to *make haste, sire, for I must have my turn as well,* and then Richard's plunging became even more torturous, more hurtful than she thought she could bear, and worse . . . worse was knowing that any moment his semen would issue forth inside her, and she did not think she would be able to endure the years ahead knowing such vileness had left its stain so deep within her flesh.

And then Richard's loathsomeness did issue forth, and Margaret almost lost her mind, and writhed and screamed, and beat her fists upon the table, and all to no avail.

NOW THE other men-at-arms had gathered up their loads and were moving in a group across the floor of the Painted Chamber, some three or four paces behind Neville and the man carrying the precious casket.

Neville was hardly aware of them. His entire being was

focused on that casket, and the need to get it to safety so he could—

He jerked to a halt and turned to the side wall that abutted the Queen's Chambers.

There had been no sound, but Neville had suddenly been struck with such a sense of horror that he was now unable to move.

Bolingbroke stepped up behind him. "Tom?"

Neville turned a stricken face to him. "It's Margaret, sweet Jesu, Hal, it's—"

"Be quiet!" Bolingbroke said, looking about to ensure no one had heard. "We can do nothing, damn it. We need to get this casket to safety before—"

"My lords?" a guard appeared from a side door. "His grace will see you now."

•

RICHARD HAD stood back from her for a full minute watching her try to scrabble across the table to safety, a smirk stretching across his face as he slowly adjusted himself back inside his clothing. He'd looked to de Vere, nodded, then walked away toward the door, opening it and speaking quietly to a guard outside even as de Vere seized Margaret and dragged her back to the edge of the table so that he, too, could take his pleasure with Neville's wife.

He was a larger man, far more powerful than Richard, and his rape of Margaret's now torn and bleeding flesh went beyond the agonizing.

The only thing that saved Margaret, the only thing that allowed her to keep hold of her sanity, was that Mary had crept across the floor to the side of the table and had taken hold of her hand where it had fallen across the table's edge. As Margaret seized her hand, Mary whispered, very gently, very sweetly, a nothingness of words that, nevertheless, provided Margaret with an anchor strong enough to prevent her losing her mind completely.

Margaret, Margaret, Margaret, she thought she heard Mary whisper, *come home, Margaret, come back Margaret, don't fret Margaret, I am here, I am here . . . Margaret, sweet Meg, hold my hand, Margaret, hold my hand, don't be afraid, Margaret . . .*

Of all the people who could have saved her, of all the people in the palace that day who had the *power* to save her, it was the woman Margaret had the most cause to resent who was there at her side.

"QUICK!" NEVILLE said, and, grasping Bolingbroke's arm, almost propelled him toward the side door that the guard indicated.

"And the casket?" Bolingbroke hissed.

"Go!" Arundel said in a soft voice beside them. "Sturry and I will see to the casket. Now . . . go!"

Neville and Bolingbroke walked after the guard, and, once they were in the corridor leading to Richard's chambers, Neville pulled Bolingbroke back a few paces.

"If he has harmed Margaret—"

"Then *what*?" Bolingbroke said. "What? You knew the risks, and have they not been worth it?"

Neville did not answer.

"If either Margaret or Mary has been harmed then *we can do nothing*, not now," Bolingbroke continued. "We need to get that casket out of here and back to the Savoy. We will both go down on bended knee before Richard and swear our loyalty and love, and we will leave our revenge until we can afford its risks. Do you understand? At the moment we can do no else."

He snapped his mouth shut as the guard drew to a halt before a door. As Bolingbroke and Neville joined him, the guard raised his hand and rapped on the wood.

The door opened immediately.

Richard stood there, his face carefully composed into a

contemptuous expression, but neither Bolingbroke nor Neville saw him.

All they could see was a table against the far wall, and Robert de Vere slowly withdrawing himself from Margaret's half-naked and battered body sprawled across its top.

Even as they watched, de Vere pulled himself completely free from Margaret, and she scrabbled away from him, sliding over the side of the table to slump on the floor next to Mary.

Mary still held her hand in a tight grip.

Chapter III

Nones, the Vigil of the Feast of St. Francis
In the first year of the reign of Richard II
(noon Monday 3rd October 1379)

— II —

✠

NEVILLE SAID SOMETHING, he did not know what, and would have moved forward had not Bolingbroke's hand held his arm in a viciously tight grip.

"Your grace," Bolingbroke said, and bowed.

Neville was still staring over Richard's shoulder and did not move.

"Your wives have been most accommodating," Richard said softly, threateningly, "and it would truly suit your purposes, my lords, were you to appreciate their efforts on your behalf."

Neville jerked his eyes to Richard's face. "You—"

Bolingbroke reached out a hand and clamped it on Neville's shoulder. *"Tom!"*

Neville battled with his intense desire to take the dagger from his belt and plunge it into Richard's belly—and some distant part of his mind admired the way Richard stood there, as if oblivious to the danger—and then he jerked his head and body in as close an approximation of a bow as he could manage—every one of his muscles screamed at this insult to his person that he was forced to perform.

Richard nodded. It was enough. He stepped aside and motioned Bolingbroke and Neville into the room.

"Your wife states that you have something to say to me," he said to Bolingbroke as he closed the door behind them.

On the far side of the room Mary had managed to persuade Margaret to her feet, and was now calmly pulling down the woman's skirts and rearranging her bodice, as if there were no others present.

Margaret was trembling, and her face was tear-stained, but she made no sound, and neither would she look at Bolingbroke or Neville.

Mary lifted a hand to Margaret's cheek, and whispered something in her ear, and Margaret briefly closed her eyes and nodded very slightly.

"Then I thank my wife for her well-chosen words," Bolingbroke said.

"And?" Richard said.

Bolingbroke dropped to his knees before Richard, somehow managing to drag Neville down with him, and bowed his head. Neville kept his head raised, staring to where Margaret and Mary stood.

Margaret avoided his gaze. Her chest was rising and falling rapidly, and she gripped Mary's hand tightly. Neville realized she was very close to the breaking point.

"Your grace," Bolingbroke said. "I would not have you doubt my love and loyalty for your body and your cause."

There was a soft, sarcastic laugh—de Vere, now reclining on Richard's bed.

"And so I offer to you again the pledge that I gave to you on your coronation day," Bolingbroke continued. "That I am your liege man, and obliged to serve you in war and peace—"

"Oh, cease your lies," Richard said, growing bored. "I will have none of this pretense! Get to your feet and get you gone from my sight. I have instructed Lancaster that he is to hold you and be responsible for you, and that I wish to see neither you nor him until Parliament in the New Year."

Bolingbroke rose slowly to his feet. "The house of Lancaster is a bad one to alienate, your grace."

"Are you threatening me? Are you in loss of your senses? Get you *gone*!"

"Hal," Mary said softly.

Neville finally managed to move. He strode over to where Mary and Margaret stood, and reached for his wife, but Margaret recoiled as soon as she felt his hand on her.

"Don't touch me!" she said, and Neville flinched back.

But at least we have the casket . . . at least we have the casket.

Strange how that thought imparted no comfort. Strange how guilt and horror coiled about his belly as if his very soul had been torn apart.

Strange how he felt, in the face of Margaret's rejection of his hand, as if his life had been wrenched to an abrupt halt.

Mary urged Margaret toward the door—as they passed Richard he reached out and ran his fingers softly across Margaret's face.

She whimpered, and recoiled so violently she would have fallen had not Mary had her in firm hands.

As the women left the room Neville walked back to where Bolingbroke still stood staring at Richard.

Neville gave Richard a half-bow, his face twisted with hatred. "On this earth," he said to Richard, "you are my monarch, and you control the fate of my earthly body, as that of my wife's. But there is another life waiting, and in that one you will burn for an eternity for the suffering you have caused here this day."

For the first time Richard allowed a small measure of discomposure to filter across his face.

Bolingbroke spoke, quiet and full of menace, "I have heard, Richard, that the gates of hell have lain open for many a year, and that Satan's imps now crowd the face of this earth. Beware they do not reach out and snatch you before your time is due."

And with that he was gone, Neville at his shoulder.

WHEN THEY stepped outside, and the doors were closed behind them, Neville turned to Bolingbroke.

"Why threaten Richard with the armies of hell," he said, "when he commands them?"

But Bolingbroke only shot Neville an unreadable look, and did not answer, and both men turned to where Mary had Margaret huddled against a wall and escorted them back to the pier where Arundel was pacing up and down with worry.

Margaret clung to Mary the entire way, stumbling occasionally as she wept silently, and she would not let either Neville or Bolingbroke touch her.

Chapter IV

After Nones, the Vigil of the Feast of St. Francis
In the first year of the reign of Richard II
(afternoon Monday 3rd October 1379)

— III —

✠

CLOUDS HAD SCUDDED in over London and Westminster in the hour they'd been in the palace, and now the sky was heavy and ominous. Mary, murmuring nonsense words in a repetitive, soothing monotone, encouraged a stiff and unresponsive Margaret to take the step from pier into barge, and then the few extra steps to a bench. Once there, Mary snatched at a spare cloak draped over the bench and draped it about Margaret, pulling a heavy fold of the material over the woman's face.

Then Mary wrapped her arms about Margaret and held her close, never ceasing her soothing murmurs.

Neville jumped into the barge after them. He hesitated, staring at Mary and Margaret, then wrenched his head to look along the barge.

There!

The casket lay half concealed under one of the benches, and Neville sat down above it. He leaned down, touched it as if to reassure himself, then glanced back to Margaret.

It was worth it. It was. Margaret would heal. After all, surely women were aware that sometimes their fleshly enticements would tempt men too far and that they must pay the price for their beauty . . .

"Oh, sweet Jesu," Neville whispered, and rubbed a shaking hand over his face, disgusted at his attempts to justify away what Richard had done to Margaret. *What* he *had* allowed *Richard to do to Margaret*. "Sweet Jesu!" he whispered. "Sweet Jesu, sweet Jesu, sweet Jesu . . ."

He jerked one of his feet back against the casket, but this time contact with the casket imparted no reassurance, no easy remedy for the guilt that threatened to overwhelm him.

Surely there could have been another way to get the casket?

No. No, there hadn't. This had been the only way, and the prize—man's salvation from the armies of evil threatening to inundate Christendom—was worth one woman's pain. It was . . . it was . . . it was . . .

"It was," he whispered. "It was . . . oh sweet Jesu, surely it was!"

Wasn't it?

BOLINGBROKE HAD remained on the pier for a brief word with Arundel.

"My friend," Bolingbroke said, grasping Arundel's arm, "I do thank you. You and Sturry have surely proved your loyalty here today."

Arundel nodded. "I must get back."

"Aye. Arundel . . . take care of what lurks in the shadows. I cannot think what Richard will do once he discovers that casket is gone."

"And you also. You are not staying long in the Savoy?"

"We leave in the morning. Sooner, if danger looms."

They stared at each other, a silent reinforcing of their new bonds, then Arundel turned abruptly away and strode back along the pier toward the water gate.

After a moment Bolingbroke jumped down into the barge and spoke quick orders to the bargemen who picked up their poles and pushed the barge away from the pier.

Bolingbroke walked over to where Tom sat, ignoring the angry look Mary sent him.

"Well?" he said.

Neville took a deep breath, trying to will himself to believe that once he opened the casket and discovered its secrets his guilt would subside and Margaret would prove herself happy to have been of such service in heaven's quest, then reached down and hauled the casket from under the bench.

It was not overly heavy, and slid easily enough.

Bolingbroke sat down on the bench and looked at the casket that stood between himself and Neville.

"It looks so innocent to hold such secrets, and such power," he said.

"Aye," Neville said. He reached down a hand, shocked to find it trembling, and placed it quickly on the rounded lid of the casket before Bolingbroke should notice.

Why did he not feel more joy, more sense of accomplishment and purpose now that he had the casket in his possession?

He studied it carefully, focusing all his attention on it.

Why did not the angels sing?

Mary's soft, soothing murmuring was driving Neville to distraction . . .

The casket . . . the casket . . .

As Bolingbroke had said, it seemed innocuous enough. Made of what appeared to be well-mellowed elm wood and banded with brass, it would have been unremarkable save for what Neville knew it contained.

The secrets of the angels. Truth.

The means to drive every demon scampering about Christendom back into hell.

Bolingbroke laid his own hand over Neville's.

"We'll open it in the Savoy," he said. "It is too dangerous here."

Neville nodded, and spent the rest of the barge voyage

concentrating on the casket in a useless attempt to keep Margaret's misery pushed to the back of his thoughts.

THEY DISEMBARKED quietly enough at the Savoy's water pier, but Katherine, Lancaster's wife, was in the herb garden to one side of the palace's courtyard when they passed through the gate in the Savoy's riverside wall.

Katherine, abused in her first marriage to Hugh Swynford, knew abuse in others the instant she saw it.

"Get my Lord of Lancaster!" she hissed to her husband's chamberlain who had been conferring with her on some household matters. *"Now!"*

As the chamberlain ran off, Katherine hurried over to Mary and Margaret. She took one look under the flap of material that still covered Margaret's face, then locked eyes with Mary.

"Richard," Mary said, "and de Vere."

Katherine's face lost all its beautiful color—even her extraordinary burnished hair seemed suddenly to dull.

Very slowly she turned her eyes to where Bolingbroke and Neville, the casket carried between them, stood a pace or so behind the women.

There was nothing gentle in that look.

Footsteps sounded behind her, and Lancaster, with Raby and Gloucester at his side, emerged at a run from the outer door of the Savoy. Courtenay ran a few steps behind them.

Suddenly Neville's world collapsed around him.

No! Not Raby! What would his uncle say seeing Margaret so ravaged?

Raby would never have done this to Margaret.

And Gloucester? What would he *say?*

Excuses tumbled through Neville's mind, and he desperately grasped at every one of them, only to discard them in turn, knowing that in a very few moments his self-righteous preaching to Gloucester on the occasion of his duchess' death was going to be thrown back into his face with a furious, condemning force.

Katherine turned to her husband. "Richard, and de Vere," she said, and, as with Mary's simple words to her, so hers needed to further explanation. Then she turned to Courtenay, and asked him quietly to leave. "Your mistress will be well," she whispered, "but this moment is not for you."

Courtenay looked between Katherine and Margaret, then saw Mary mouth the words, *go, please*. He bowed stiffly, and walked away, his face a mask of misery.

Lancaster, Raby and Gloucester looked at Margaret as they waited for Courtenay to disappear, and then, as Katherine had, slowly turned stony eyes to Bolingbroke and Neville.

"Whatever excuse you have can never be enough—" Lancaster began.

"Father. *We have the casket!*"

Lancaster's stare, if possible, hardened into an even deeper fury, but for the moment he kept his rage unspoken, turning to speak quietly to Katherine and Mary. "Take her inside. Now."

Katherine nodded, and she and Mary guided Margaret toward the doorway across the courtyard.

Lancaster waited until he could no longer hear their footsteps.

"Was it worth your wife's rape?" he said to Neville, his voice very, very quiet.

"My lord," Neville began, then had to clear his throat and begin again. "My lord, this casket contains what I—and the angels—need to drive evil back into hell—"

"And in order to obtain that casket you have created hell on earth for your wife, Neville. Having knowingly made use of evil to achieve your ends, you have become evil incarnate yourself."

Neville's mouth opened, but he could say no words. Lancaster's face was so full of accusation that Neville jerked his eyes elsewhere, only to meet Raby's stare.

As his eyes locked into Neville's, Raby deliberately turned his face away.

"Uncle, we *had* to obtain the casket—"

"And the best plan you could formulate was to have Margaret raped?" Gloucester said, and his voice was as viciously judgmental as Lancaster's had been. "Neville, who was it once preached to me that a husband's first care was to protect his wife? To *respect* his wife?"

Neville dropped his eyes from Gloucester and Lancaster, then abruptly let his grip on the casket go, making Bolingbroke stagger as the falling casket pulled him off balance.

Neville closed his eyes, and tried for a brief moment to pretend that he was alone in this black, black world. But it didn't work, because he could still feel the combined weight of Lancaster's, Raby's and Gloucester's stares on him.

He looked up again. "We have to open it," he said. "Once it is open—"

"Even *when* it is open," Raby said, "*nothing* shall remove the stain of shame from your soul for your actions this day."

Chapter V

After Nones, the Vigil of the Feast of St. Francis
In the first year of the reign of Richard II
(afternoon Monday 3rd October 1379)

— IV —

✠

KATHERINE AT FIRST steered Margaret toward the chamber she shared with Neville, but Margaret wailed the instant she understood Katherine's intentions.

"Perhaps my chamber—" Mary began.

"No!" Margaret said, speaking her first coherent word since the rape. "No. Not where you and Hal sleep."

"Then you will come to *my* chamber," Katherine said firmly and to that Margaret made no objection.

BETWEEN THEM, Bolingbroke and Neville carried the casket to Lancaster's private solar.

Behind them rang the heavy footsteps of the three other men.

Once they were all inside the solar, Lancaster closed the door and bolted it.

"Explain," he said.

Bolingbroke briefly began to tell them what had transpired, but before he was too far into his tale Lancaster interrupted him.

"You exposed Sturry and Arundel? My God, Hal, what possessed you?"

Bolingbroke had no time to explain, for Raby stepped forward, and wrenched Bolingbroke about by the shoulder to face him.

"You fool boy!" he said. "Think you to aspire to your father's greatness? Think you to play the great peer of the realm? *Where are your senses?* You have not only endangered Sturry and Arundel, good men who will surely pay for their loyalty, but you have also endangered your father. God in heaven, Hal, Richard will send a man to the executioner's block for stealing a slice of beef from his kitchens, let alone a casket as important as you say this one is!"

Raby took a furious breath. "You have likely destroyed the entire Lancastrian house with this foolish thoughtlessness! And you," he turned to face Neville, "have in like manner destroyed a precious woman."

Neville's guilt found some relief in angry accusation; Raby had been quick enough to push Margaret away when a marriage with Lancaster's daughter beckoned. "She was not so precious that *you* could not bear to abandon her, Uncle!"

"Enough!" Lancaster roared. "I have had *enough.* Neville, open that accursed casket *now*. Let us see if what it contains is justification enough for destroying both Margaret and this entire house."

Bolingbroke and Neville had set the casket to one side when they entered the room; now Neville hefted it himself and placed it atop a table. It was locked, and Neville had no key, but he had no pity for this object which had caused so much misery, and so he took the knife from his belt and slid it underneath the lock and jerked upward with all the force of his guilt and anger and frustration.

The lock clattered to the floor, and everyone jumped.

Neville took a deep breath, then flung back the lid.

AGNES HAD met Courtenay on her way down to the gardens to let Rosalind play freely in the fresh air, and his face had told her that something was terribly, terribly wrong. "What?" she'd said. "The Lady Margaret," he'd whispered, and it was enough to send Agnes running.

Now she met the three women at the door to Katherine's chamber, Rosalind still clutched in her arms.

As had Katherine, Agnes needed only to look upon Margaret's face to know what distressed her. Again, looks were exchanged between the women supporting Margaret.

"She will need to be bathed," Katherine said as she opened the door. "Nay, she shall need to be scrubbed clean, body and, then, pray to sweet Jesu, spirit as well. Agnes . . . it is Agnes, is it not? . . . good. Agnes, will you see to the water? Rosewater, I think. Come, let us lay Margaret on the bed, so, and put her sweet girl in the corner on the pillow there, and thus we may set about our task."

Agnes left the room to organize hot water from the kitchens—she requested that the pages leave the urns outside the door—then returned as quickly as she might with a small urn of warmed rosewater that they might use in the meantime.

Mary and Katherine had stripped Margaret—Margaret was moaning and attempting to cover herself with the linens with which they meant to wash her—and Katherine turned as Agnes re-entered with her urn of rosewater.

"Good," she said, then turned back to the weakly writhing and moaning woman before her. "Margaret, my sweet, we are women only. Cease your wriggling and we can—*sweet Jesu*!"

Mary had pulled the last remnants of Margaret's undershift from her, and Katherine had caught sight of the extent of Margaret's bruises and abrasions.

She stared, then looked across to Mary. "What happened?"

Mary took a deep shuddering breath, and spoke in curt, quiet words.

As she did so, Rosalind began to wail.

* * *

NEVILLE STARED. The casket was filled with creamy parchments.

At last! At last!

"Well?" said Lancaster and Bolingbroke together. They had stepped up to Neville's back.

"Wait," Neville said in a tight voice, reaching trembling hands for the top parchment.

It was so quiet. It shouldn't be quiet. There should be the triumphal chorus of angels . . . There should be joy in my heart . . . why is there no joy in my heart?

Neville lifted the first roll—Wynkyn de Worde's book must be under this initial flurry of rolls—and gently hefted it in his hands.

It was light for the weight of secrets that it carried.

"Open it!" said Bolingbroke, and Neville could almost have turned about and struck him for his impatience.

"Wait," he said again.

The trembling in his hands had increased to such an extent that Neville almost dropped the parchment roll as he turned it over and started to unroll it. He had to stop, consciously force some calm into his hands (*and belly and heart and thoughts*), before he could continue.

Finally, he unrolled it a few turns and spread it out so that he, Lancaster and Bolingbroke could see what it contained.

They stared, then . . .

"What is that?" Lancaster said.

MARGARET SAT up and grabbed the washcloth from Mary's hands. She pushed Katherine's hands to one side and began to scrub savagely at the injured and stained flesh of her inner thighs and groin.

"Margaret!" Mary cried, and reached her hands out to snatch the cloth away from Margaret, but Katherine pulled her back.

"No," she said. "Let her do this. It is something she needs to do."

"But she will further injure herself!"

"Perhaps," Katherine said. "But it is something that she needs to do!"

Agnes had picked up Rosalind and was rocking her to and fro, her eyes fixed on Margaret's frantic cleansing of herself.

Tears ran down Agnes' cheeks.

Margaret's scrubbing became even more frenetic, then she suddenly burst into deep, agonized sobs, lifted the now torn and bloody washcloth, and hurled it as far away from her as possible.

Mary dropped onto the bed beside Margaret, hugging her as tightly as she could, and Margaret clung to her, her entire body now racked with the strength of her humiliation and pain.

Like Agnes, Katherine had tears streaming down her cheeks, and she ineffectually wiped them away.

There was the sound of footsteps outside, and a discreet knock at the door.

"The water—" Agnes said, looking for somewhere to put Rosalind down.

"No," Katherine said. "Keep her in your arms. I can see to the urns."

And she turned and walked to the door. Margaret would be the better for a soak in a tub of warm rosewater.

At least her flesh would, and perchance it might even help her spirit.

NEVILLE STARED, his eyes and mind trying to make sense of what he saw. The parchment was filled with strange lines and symbols . . . He stared, shaking his head slightly, wondering if this was some arcane angelic language that he must master in order to—

Lancaster roared, and snatched the parchment from Neville's hands. He ripped it into shreds, tossing them away, then pushed Neville to one side and reached deep into the casket, pulling out scores more rolls and scattering them across the floor.

There was no book.

Bolingbroke had stepped back, and he now looked at Lancaster and Neville, his eyes veiled, his face expressionless.

Neville, confused and dazed, picked up one of the rolls Lancaster had scattered and opened it.

The same perplexing lines . . .

"Damn you to *hell*," Lancaster roared, and threw one of the rolls into Bolingbroke's face. "Look what you have stolen!"

Bolingbroke grabbed at the parchment, and unrolled it a little.

His face twitched, then assumed an expression of deep puzzlement. "But . . . but this is . . ."

"The entire accursed casket is filled with the plans for the re-roofing of Westminster Hall," Lancaster said. "No angelic incantations. No heavenly secrets. No justification for you claiming Richard is a demon from hell! *What have you and Neville done?*"

Neville blinked, and his vision miraculously seemed to clear. The roll he held was covered in intricate drawings of hammerbeams and trusses, spires and—

He screamed, and that scream stilled the entire room.

Lancaster turned back to Neville, reaching out a hand, but in one sudden, violent movement, Neville sprang to his feet, grabbed the now-empty casket, and hurled it through the leaded windows of the solar with an almighty swing of his shoulders.

Glass exploded, and everyone save Neville spun around and covered their faces.

"What have I done?" Neville whispered, blood running down his face from where a splinter of glass had lodged in his hairline. "*What have I done?*"

A cold wind swept through the shattered windows, and the blood and glass-spattered parchment rolls at Neville's feet shifted and whispered, and Neville began to laugh—a harsh, grating, despairing noise that sounded to Bolingbroke like the rustling of angels' wings across the ice-field of heaven.

Chapter VI

Vespers, the Vigil of the Feast of St. Francis
In the first year of the reign of Richard II
(early evening Monday 3rd October 1379)

— V —

✠

HE WENT TO HER, but she turned her head, and would not speak.

She lay on her side, curled about Rosalind as if the little girl was the only thing which could save her from the wickedness of this day.

"Margaret—"

Still she would not answer.

"Tom . . ."

He turned around from where he sat by the bed. Mary stood behind him, and Agnes sat yet further away by a brazier.

"Get out!" Neville said.

Mary's normally sweet and docile face contorted with anger. "Get out? Get out? Dare you speak *that* to me? What are you that you think it better you be here and I not? What right have *you* to stay by Margaret's side and I not?"

"Mary—"

"My *lady* to you, Neville! I may not be important or dear enough for my husband to confide his darker thoughts to, but anyone could see the care and consideration you and he lavished on that casket you carried from Westminster. Even *I* can now understand that the mission you sent myself and Margaret on was a mere ruse so that you might the more secretively work your mischief while your wife was being raped."

She paused to take a deep breath, and Neville flinched at the expression on her face.

"It was not Richard and de Vere who raped Margaret," Mary said, now very quiet, "but you . . . you, and my husband."

Neville wrenched his eyes away, for he could not bear the accusation and revulsion in Mary's.

"Ah! I will leave you," she said, "for I cannot bear to remain in the same space as that which you inhabit. Agnes will stay here to watch over Margaret, and you will *not* ask her to leave."

Neville glanced at Agnes and saw on her face an expression very much like that which now darkened Mary's face.

He jerked his head in agreement, and Mary stared a moment longer before she turned and left.

•

HE REACHED out to touch her face, but halted at the sound of her voice.

"Do not lay a hand to me."

"Margaret . . . Meg—"

"Was the casket worth it, Tom? Are you now filled with the secrets of angels? Is my suffering to be put to one side as a painful but necessary subterfuge to gain your precious *casket?*"

Neville found it very hard to speak. He looked at Rosalind, the girl so peaceful and yet surrounded by so much anger and pain.

He raised his eyes, and met Margaret's stare, and suddenly, horrifically, understood that she *knew.*

"It was not the right casket," he whispered.

Margaret began to laugh, a sound as twisted and bitter as Neville's had been in Lancaster's solar.

"Not the right casket? Ah well, then, my beloved husband, perhaps I should offer myself to be raped once again—or two or three times if that is what it takes—so that you and Hal can scurry about Richard's apartments looking in dusty corners for the *right* cursed casket!"

"I will not ask this of you again!"

"That you asked it of me once is damning enough, Tom."

He dropped his head and began to weep. "Margaret, I am sorry—"

"No, you are not, for isn't this what the angels chose you for? The great pious priest, cold enough to cast even the most innocent into the flames for God's great cause."

Now he raised his head again. "Margaret, I am more penitent that you can know!"

She looked at the tears streaking his cheeks, and wondered, and then realized that she did not care. Not tonight. Tonight all she wanted to do was to lie back and grieve for what might have been and to wallow in hate for him.

"What now?" she asked softly.

He reached out a tentative hand and placed it over hers where it cradled Rosalind's head.

She did not pull her hand away, although Neville felt her flesh stiffen under his.

"Tomorrow we embark for Kenilworth," he said. "Margaret, it is a beautiful place, and you will be surrounded by those who love you."

"Will Mary and Katherine be there? Rosalind? May I bring Agnes?"

"Aye, of course."

"Then I *will* be among those who love me."

Again Neville flinched.

"I wish this was a world of women," Margaret said in a toneless voice, "for then there would be no hurt, and there would be no pain."

And to that, Neville had nothing to say.

* * *

BOLINGBROKE CAME to her very late that night. She opened her eyes to find him standing by the bed.

She twisted her head a little. Katherine, who had come to sit with her through the night, was slumped sound asleep in a chair a few paces away.

It was a very sound, magical sleep, and Margaret understood that no matter what happened Katherine would not wake. She also knew that the woman's enchantment would have cost Bolingbroke considerable effort.

She looked to what she could see of his face in the shadows: there were lines of weariness stretching from nose to mouth and circling his eyes.

There was also deep sorrow in his eyes.

"And has the day gone well for you, my lord?" she said.

His mouth thinned. "It has gone well for both of us," he said. "Our purpose has been achieved."

"I don't think I want his love," she said. "Not now."

"We cannot stop what we have begun, Margaret. You know this. Besides, you agreed to the plan. You wanted Neville to love you."

Her face tightened. "I 'agreed'? More like I was forced by your ambitions, Hal. I called it abominable trickery then, and I still call it thus now."

He did not respond with words, but merely held her eyes with his own steady gaze.

She sighed, then looked down to Rosalind still curled asleep in her arms. Very carefully she shifted the girl to one side, then lifted the bedcovers and slid painfully out of bed.

She was naked.

Bolingbroke drew in a sharp breath, but Margaret ignored him. There was a small oil lamp burning on a table close by and Margaret picked it up, holding it so that its light shone down the length of her body.

"Can you see what they did to me, Hal?"

She walked closer to him, and with her free hand she

lifted one of his and placed it first on one of her torn breasts, then ran it down over the swollen abrasions littering her belly to the scabs only barely forming over the wounds further below.

"Can you *feel* them?" she whispered, then abruptly lifted his hand and placed it over his own heart. "Can you feel them in *there?*"

"Margaret—" His voice choked, and he began again. "Margaret, they will pay. Dearly."

"That will not take away the hurt, beloved."

"It was necessary—"

"You are growing more and more into an image of your father, Hal! I wonder how you can bear it!"

"Lancaster is—"

"I am not speaking of Lancaster. I am speaking of your *father,* that beast who put you inside Blanche's belly."

"You go too far!"

"And you went too far today, Hal. I was hurt, and so was Mary. Have you spoken to her yet, Hal? Have you offered your wife an explanation for what happened?"

"Mary . . .," Bolingbroke said as if he had only just remembered her.

"Mary was there, Hal, and my rape has scarred her as it has me. And yet she put aside her own horror in order to soothe me. Hal, your wife cannot be ignored. She is a great woman, and it is a shame that you have so corrupted her in taking her to be your wife. Whatever you plan for her, Hal, I will not be a part of it. Not after today."

Chapter VII

Matins, the Feast of St. Francis
In the first year of the reign of Richard II
(early morning Tuesday 4th October 1379)

✢

THE CHAPEL WAS COLD and still, and Neville's breath frosted around his bowed head.

He was on his knees before the altar, hands clasped tightly before him, eyes clamped tightly shut, shoulders and back stiff. Every so often a soft moan escaped his lips, followed by hurried, desperate, whispered prayers that, after a few minutes, stuttered into silence.

Neville was trying with every fiber of his being to hate, to loathe, and to despise Richard . . . but all he could do was to hate, to loathe and to despise himself.

All he could see behind his closed eyelids were the faces of Lancaster, Raby and Gloucester. Sometimes, horrifically, Neville thought he could see the shadowy forms of Richard and de Vere taking frantic turns at Margaret's body.

And somewhere, he knew, that casket lay waiting, hiding . . . laughing.

His hands clenched by his side, and he thought he must scream, if only to shatter the accusing silence of the chapel.

You did what you thought was right. I cannot ask any more of you.

Neville sprang to his feet, stumbling as his stiff muscles cramped, and turned around.

There, that soft glowing light, and the form of the archangel St. Michael, holding out his hands as if in comfort.

"Is that supposed to console me?" he said. "Is it?"

You must be strong, Thomas. You cannot know the twistings that evil will place before you—

"I sent my wife to be raped . . . for nothing! For nothing!"

She means *nothing! She served her purpose—is it your fault that you seized the wrong casket? At least you tried. You did the right thing.*

"Then why am I so consumed with self-loathing if what I did was *right*?"

Thomas, you must beware of the temptations put in your way—

"Using my wife to secure the casket *was* a temptation! And look what it got me—nothing!" Neville's voice dropped to a whisper. "And look what it got her."

Thomas—

Neville sank to his knees before the archangel, holding out his hands as if in supplication. "Is this why you chose me?" he said, and then Margaret's words tumbled out of his mouth. "Because I am cold enough to cast even the most innocent into the flames for God's great cause?"

God's cause must come first. You know that. Thomas, the casket still waits. You must not doubt now—

Neville's face distorted in frightful agony. "Get away from me. *Get away from me!*"

Thomas—

"I am a *man*, angel. A man! I cannot sit apart and watch the suffering my actions have caused and blink as if such suffering means nothing. Get you gone from me, angel. Go!"

You are a man, *Thomas? Ah, beloved, how you have misunderstood—*

"Get you gone from me. Go!"

Neville did not wait for the archangel to respond. He lurched to his feet, sent the archangel one last, desperate, angry look, then ran from the chapel.

Michael had gone long before the door slammed behind Neville.

* * *

LATER THAT day, the Lancastrian household, including Raby and his wife Joan, and Bolingbroke and his household, departed for Kenilworth in Warwickshire. Gloucester would stay a while longer in London before traveling to Kenilworth via his own estates.

At dawn, Bolingbroke had sent the useless, and now somewhat broken, casket and its contents with two men back to Arundel, so that he might replace it in Westminster.

RICHARD, IF he'd even known of the casket's brief loss, subsequently made no move against any of the men he might have suspected to be involved in its disappearance.

It was, after all, a most useless casket.

Chapter VIII

The Feast of the Translation of St. Edward the Confessor
In the first year of the reign of Richard II
(Thursday 13th October 1379)

✠

AS RUMOR OF Joan and of a possible resurgence of French pride continued to spread among the north and central regions of France, and as the heat and haste of the summer harvest season passed, men in their ones and twos, their tens and twenties, and in their hundreds, quietly laid down their hoes and rakes and picked up swords and pikes. They traveled until the gorge and walls of la Roche-Guyon rose before them, and there they pledged their loyalty to Charles and to his cause. Many of those nobles, and their retainers, who had not been murdered in the mud of Poitiers also came: some because they believed the rumors that Joan spoke with the voice of God; some, like Philip the Bad, came because they believed they could wrest some advantage from the situation.

If there was one thing all had in common, it was their determination to see the English hounded out of their beloved country once and for all.

Men and their weapons were not the only arrivals. The Avignonese pope, Clement VII, sent a deputation headed by the Archbishop of Rheims, Regnault de Chartres. This talk of holy virgins was all very well, but Clement thought it more likely this peasant girl was a witch intent on seducing the Dauphin for her own ends.

The pope in Rome, Urban VI, thought the rumors laughable, and merely called for more wine whenever the silly girl's name was mentioned. If Charles wanted to surround himself with delusional peasant girls then that was his business.

Others, hearing the tales of Joan, merely sat back and watched carefully, waiting for the opportunity they knew welled out of every religious ecstatic movement.

CATHERINE STOOD at the parapets of the castle of la Roche-Guyon, looking at the camp that stretched for almost a mile down the gorge. So many men had now flocked to the Dauphin's cause that the castle could not possibly contain them within its walls.

There was a step behind her, and Catherine turned and smiled. "Philip."

He joined her at the parapets, and together they looked at the encampment.

"With such an army," Philip said, "a man could conquer the earth."

"It is not so great," Catherine said. "Only some seven or eight thousand men. John had far more at Poitiers."

Philip turned from the view and looked at her. "But John does not have what Charles does—the holy maid, Joan. Her presence alone is worth twenty thousand."

"Do you truly believe what she says, Philip? Do you worship her as a saint, or view her as an instrument of whoever has the strength to wield her?"

Philip was not sure quite what to make of Joan. The girl had an unmistakable aura of saintliness about her . . . but was that as a result of delusion, or of the hand of God?

"Do you truly believe Joan," Catherine said softly, watching Philip's face carefully, "when she says that God has chosen *Charles* in this battle?"

Still Philip did not reply. If he was not sure what to make of Joan, then he was absolutely sure that Catherine hated the girl beyond all measure. Why, he was not certain—jealousy, perhaps, that a peasant should so command her brother's heart and mind. As for what Catherine hoped to accomplish with her hatred . . . well, that he did not know, either. All he knew was that Joan had, in a way, sent Catherine to his bed, and for that Philip thought he owed the girl a small amount of gratitude. Only a small amount . . . certainly not enough to sway his ambitions.

"It is difficult to believe that Charles could be God's choice," Philip finally said, "unless circumstance made him the only choice available."

Catherine's mouth twitched, but Philip did not see it.

"Not only are Charles' knees weak and knock," Philip continued, "but so is his entire nature." He let his eyes wander back over the encampment. "It has been almost a year since the English fell into disarray with the deaths of Edward and the Black Prince. In that year, despite the growing numbers of men who flock to his side, Charles has done nothing but prevaricate. *God!*" He hit the stone wall at his side in his frustration. "What are we still doing here locked up in *this* useless fort?"

Catherine laughed. "If I know my brother, Charles takes to his bed at night only to draw the covers up to his chin, and shiver and shake at the thought that some blood-letting must be involved if he is to retake the kingdom."

Philip grimaced. "He was worse than useless when we combined to free Paris from the cursed rebels. I had to do all the work myself."

"Aye," Catherine said, concealing her lingering grief at the mention of the slaughter of the Parisian rebels. She had known Etienne Marcel well, and still grieved for him. "He is worse than useless, and if you are to do all the work for him, then why not take the credit as well? Why not take the throne?"

"Because," Philip said, so soft it was almost a whisper, "the holy maid Joan speaks of Charles as God's beloved . . . not me. How can I rebel against God's word? I would be burned for my troubles."

"And if Joan were to be proved a fraud?" Catherine said. "If it were to be proved that she speaks with the words of evil, not godliness? What then?"

He said nothing, staring at her with dark, unreadable eyes.

"Should Joan be proved a fraud," Catherine continued, "then Charles would collapse completely. He would grab at our mother's contention that he is nothing but a common-bred bastard, and he would be content to crawl away and live a useless life in some frivolous court. The way would then be open for a strong man," Catherine reached out and touched Philip's arm, "to take this force," she now gestured over the wall, "and secure the throne. France needs a strong man . . . it doesn't need Charles. All these men are here for France, my love, not Charles."

"*If* Joan were proved a fraud," Philip said after a moment's silence.

Catherine shrugged slightly. "She claims to be a virgin, yet what healthy peasant girl, living in an army encampment, is a *virgin*?"

Philip sent her a teasing grin, but Catherine ignored it. "Joan claims to speak the words of God and his angels . . . but what peasant girl knows the difference between the words of God and the sweet seductive words that demons whisper in her ear?"

Now Philip turned completely away from Catherine and leaned his arms on the stone parapets, his gaze focused on some far distant object in the landscape.

"Regnault de Chartres arrived three days ago," he said.

Catherine smiled. "And doubtless the good archbishop is full of doubts. He could be a powerful ally."

"Why do you hate Joan so, Catherine?"

"Because she has the power to destroy all my ambitions."

Philip turned back to Catherine, and cupped her chin in his hand. "And what will happen, my love, when you come to believe that *I* have the power to destroy your ambitions? What will happen when you come to believe that *I* stand in the way of whatever it is you hope to achieve?"

Her eyes filled with tears. "I pray to our Lord Jesus Christ that I will never come to believe so."

He bent and kissed her.

"So do I," he whispered. "So do I."

Chapter IX

Vigil of the Feast of SS. Simon and Jude
In the first year of the reign of Richard II
(Thursday 27th October 1379)

✢

IT TOOK FOURTEEN DAYS of whispers and innuendoes, during which time Archbishop Regnault de Chartres and his retinue watched both Charles and Joan closely, before Charles found himself confronted by the doubters.

He did not like it.

Charles sat on a wooden chair on a dais in the hall of the castle, fidgeting nervously at the deputation before him. At their head stood the tall, spare archbishop, his thin hands folded before him, and wrapped serenely in his heavy robes and the weight of his office. Immediately behind him was a collection of clerics—priests, monks and one or two friars—as well as several of Charles' own officials, and some of King John's highest officers who had gravitated to Charles' side at la Roche-Guyon.

All were wearing expressions of the most respectful gravity.

Shifting nervously, Charles let his eyes wander beyond the deputation. Guards lined the back wall, their eyes blank and unhelpful.

Charles' eyes flickered nervously to his left.

There sat his mother in a tortuously carved oaken chair, her face resting in one hand as she leaned on an arm of the chair, her bright eyes alive with laughter.

He knew what she was thinking: *a nobly bred man would know how to deal with these accusations, but a peasant-bred bastard would squirm as greatly as do you . . . as bastard born, so bastard acts.*

Charles visibly twitched and tore his eyes away from Isabeau. Beside his mother stood his sister, Catherine, watching him steadily, her thoughts unknowable, and Charles wished vehemently for some of her composure.

Philip stood halfway between mother and sister and Charles, and as he caught Charles' eye, he gave a little nod of support.

But he did not speak, nor take control of the situation, which is what Charles more than hoped he would do . . . even though he knew he would then hate Philip for so emphasizing his own weakness.

Charles took a deep breath, and managed to keep tears of discomposure from moistening his eyes. *Why did the archbishop have to trouble him so?*

Then, as he knew he would, and as he knew everyone present knew he would, Charles looked to the girl, Joan. She was standing against the left wall of the hall, underneath a hanging depicting the Virgin and Child.

Charles tried to take heart at the symbolism, but in the end it only made him feel more nervous. With every day that passed more men journeyed to la Roche-Guyon, and more and more talk arose about how they would eventually coalesce into an army that could retake southern France from the English.

Why couldn't anyone be content with Paris? Charles thought. *Why do we have to risk body and soul trying to reconquer the ever-damned south as well? Surely we can come to some accommodating arrangement with the English? They can have Aquitaine and Gascony, and we the northern and more pleasant regions. It is a sensible plan, surely . . .*

Joan saw Charles' regard, and she smiled with exquisite

sweetness, and, putting a hand over her heart, bowed ever so slightly toward Charles.

She will get me killed yet! Charles thought, losing his battle to keep the tears from his eyes. Everything was getting way beyond control . . .

He blinked, sending a solitary tear sliding down his cheek, and addressed the archbishop. "My Lord Archbishop of Rheims, how can you express such doubts? Is it not apparent that Joan is beloved of God, and speaks with His words?"

It was not that Charles couldn't see the possibilities for his own peace of mind if Joan was found wanting . . . it was just that, right at the moment, the archbishop and his deputation were making him feel more uncomfortable and nervous than the virginal maid was. He glanced at Philip, relieved to see the Navarrese king wasn't laughing at him.

Regnault de Chartres repressed a sigh, wondering why, if God had decided to intervene and drive the hateful English from this lovely land, he had not sent a more manly prince to do so. More than anything else, the fact that the peasant girl, Joan, had spoken in support of this cowardly grotesque clown made him distrust her.

Surely God had more sense?

"Your grace," de Chartres said, "we do all so hope and pray that Joan is indeed beloved of God, and speaks with His voice. What more could any of us desire," he gestured, not only to those who accompanied him, but to the entire hall, "than to have you confirmed as the true heir to the glorious throne of France . . . as king, if our mighty John succumbs to the cold poisons of his English captors."

"Then why accuse Joan with your doubts?" Charles cried, unsuccessfully trying to lower the high pitch of his tone. "Does she not want what you claim to want?"

"Because we must be sure," de Chartres said, not liking the way Charles had said "claim." "Would it not be better to firmly establish the truth of Joan's words now, so that there might not be doubts later? Would it not be better that I question her, rather than a more antagonistic interrogator? I want only what is best for France, your grace, and it would truly please me to find out that what she says is true beyond doubt. A successful outcome would mean that none of us would have to trouble you again about the matter."

"Really?" Charles said.

"Truly," de Chartres said.

Charles looked to Joan, who now walked forward from the wall to stand close to the dais.

She smiled at him encouragingly. "I have no objections to my Lord Archbishop's questions, sire," she said. "I am but a poor ignorant peasant girl, and if I speak strange words, then those are only the words of God. If the archbishop thinks to question me," now she turned and addressed de Chartres directly, "then he will be answered with God's words, not mine."

Power whispered through Joan's voice, and de Chartres paled, and would have spoken himself, save that he was interrupted by Isabeau de Bavière.

"My lords," Isabeau said, rising from her chair, and walking to stand not an arm's length from Joan's shoulder. She would *not* let this ill-favored semi-woman so dictate matters. "This talk of words is all very well, and I am more than pleased that the archbishop shall have his turn to discover whether or not Joan's words have been occasioned by God Himself or by the seductive whisperings of devils, but I now speak with the voice of a woman and I hold a woman's fears about what this girl has claimed."

As Isabeau spoke, Joan locked eyes with Catherine, then looked to Isabeau. She knew what Charles' whore-mother would say next.

"This ignorant peasant girl says," Isabeau continued, "that she is a virgin, pure and unsullied, and that this enables her to speak with the voice of virtue. But, my lords," Isabeau spread her hands and shrugged her shoulders slightly, "has she not traveled with men, sleeping by their sides unchaperoned through long nights? Does she not now inhabit a fortress which has strong and lusty men lining its very corridors? She is a young girl, and healthy, and it would have been natural for her to have succumbed to the blandishments of at least one or two of the men within these walls."

"She is not *you*, mother!" Charles shouted, jerking to his feet.

Isabeau's face twisted with disgust. "There are many who say," she said, "that she favors you with more than *words*, Charles!"

"Aye!" shouted a voice from further back in the hall. "I have ridden this Joan through more than one night, and I tell you all now, before God, that she had been broken in long before I bedded her!"

Isabeau breathed in relief: the guard had interrupted precisely on cue . . . her money had been well spent.

"You speak lies," Joan said in a quiet voice that, nevertheless, carried throughout the hall. She turned and faced the guard who had stepped forth and shouted. "And for your lies, and your foul, craven heart, God shall call you to judgment before a further day has passed."

The guard froze in the act of making an obscene gesture. Then he remembered how much he had been paid, and thought that he feared Isabeau de Bavière more than he feared God's retribution, and so he completed the gesture with considerably more gusto than he had originally intended.

Joan's calm regard did not falter, and the guard, unsure once more, stumbled back into the ranks.

Joan turned back to face Charles. "I am a virgin," she said. "I swear before God that I have lain with no man."

"I believe you!" Charles said.

"But it is best to be *sure*," the archbishop said. "Don't you think?"

He looked to Isabeau. "Madam, as this is a duty not befitting either myself or those of my deputation, perhaps you might . . ."

"I and my ladies agree to examine the girl," Isabeau said.

"No!" Charles cried.

"Do not fear for me, your grace," Joan said, extending a hand to stop Charles. "I have nothing to hide. God and his mighty archangel Saint Michael have been my only companions, my only intimates."

To one side Catherine smiled ironically. *Angelic intimacy can oftimes be a curse, Joan. Do not think that your devoutness endows you with a knowledge of* all *the twisted paths evil can travel.*

Joan's eyes flickered Catherine's way, and she spared a moment to pity the woman whose whoring nature blackened all her thoughts. *I will pray for you,* Joan thought, *but I doubt that even prayer can save a soul cursed from conception.*

Catherine's face tightened, then turned away from Joan. *You know* nothing *of my conception, peasant!*

"Tomorrow, perhaps, my lord and lady?" Joan said, now looking at the archbishop and then Isabeau. "I would prefer to spend a night in prayer, asking for God's strength, before I face this ordeal."

Both inclined their heads, and Charles slumped back into his chair sulking.

AS SHE did every night, Joan knelt before the small altar in the bare room she had taken in preference to the spacious apartments Charles had offered her. A small wooden statue of the Virgin and Child sat on the altar, flanked by two small, fat candles whose guttering flames were barely sufficient to light the Blessed Virgin's serene face. Joan's hands were clasped so tightly before her their knuckles had whitened, and a trickle of blood seeped down her wrists from where her nails dug into the soft flesh of her palms in the ecstasy of her worship.

Joan wore nothing but a simple, sleeveless shift that ended part-way down her calves. Her thick, poorly trimmed and unwashed hair had been pushed haphazardly behind her ears, and there were smudges of dirt on her bare, callused feet.

Goose bumps ridged up and down her limbs, but Joan was so lost in her religious fervor that she did not feel the cold. Her entire body was bowed about her tightly clasped hands. Everything—her expression, her posture, her trembling muscles, even her lank hair and unwashed flesh—bespoke the obsessiveness of her piety. The Archangel Michael was with her.

St. Michael came to Joan almost every night, and usually the archangel comforted Joan with visions of how her strength and piety would enable the French to overcome both demons and English alike.

But tonight was different. Today evil had spoken publicly against Joan, and so, tonight, the vengeance of the archangel must walk the spaces of la Roche-Guyon.

Joan trembled even as she rejoiced in the presence of the archangel, for she found the taste and tenor of his wrath a truly dreadful thing.

Violent images thundered through her mind: battles where men died screaming their defiance on the point of a sword; fires where women burned screaming with joy; tyrannical kings impaled on their sceptres; and men . . . men . . . men taking their hands and making obscene gestures at God's Chosen. Men, speaking words of filth . . . men speaking lies . . . men impaling women on the points of their fleshy spears . . .

Joan shuddered violently, wondering why the archangel thought to put such horrifying images inside her mind.

Instantly the vision changed. She saw a man . . . the man who had spoken filth in her presence this afternoon.

Anger flooded Joan's being, revenge consumed her. Righteous anger, vengeful anger . . . the archangel's anger.

Joan jerked, and hissed.

She was lost.

* * *

THE GUARD walked the walls of the castle, warm with the drink Isabeau's money had purchased. And there was money left over . . . enough for him to purchase some warm flesh to console him once this midnight duty was over.

He smiled, remembering how he'd jested with two of his comrades in the watchtower he had just come from. He had embroidered his tale of the bedding of Joan, telling them how she'd begged him to fuck her, how she'd pleaded, how she'd screamed that God was good for many things, but not for bedsport. His two companions had laughed, and made foul comments, and that had encouraged the guard even more in his tale, and so he had told them that the "virgin" was as practiced a whore as ever he'd had, and he had told them of the tricks she'd performed for him, and the two listeners had gone slack-jawed with lust, and their hands had fallen to their privates to rub and soothe away their envious throbbings.

It had been a good evening.

The guard farted, then belched, then walked a little further along the wall, dreaming now of which castle whore he'd pay to perform such tricks as he'd imagined Joan to be practiced at.

IN HER tiny chamber, Joan's body jerked and a tiny moan escaped her lips.

This man was truly vile.

THE GUARD was almost to the end of his allotted wall space when the golden hand appeared before him.

He halted, blinking in bemused surprise.

Hovering some two paces before him at chest height, the hand flexed, as if measuring its own strength.

The guard blinked again.

The hand lunged, burying itself in the guard's belly.

He jerked into rigidity, the agony of the hand's writhing within his entrails too great for him to scream. His eyes popped, and he drew in a huge, ragged breath.

The hand, so deep within his body, seized a handful of his entrails, and squeezed.

They bulged, then popped.

A thin wail crept from the guard's mouth, and his spear fell to the stone walkway with a strange silence.

His eyes now bulged so far from their sockets that they had begun to bleed.

The golden hand clenched even tighter within its nest of entrails.

The guard lifted from the stone walkway until his feet were well clear of the wall, and then in a sudden, vicious movement, the hand hurled him over.

As he plummeted, the guard finally screamed.

A DULL, sickening thud echoed through Catherine's dreams, and she jerked into instant awareness, her eyes terrified as she frantically searched the chamber.

But there was no one there, save for Philip, murmuring a sleepy protest at her sudden movement.

"Bitch," Catherine whispered.

She did not sleep the rest of that night.

SHOCKED AND horrified by the nature of the archangel's retribution, Joan slumped to the floor. *His words had been foul, yes, but had it been necessary to torment him so?* Her moaning increased, and her stomach heaved with nausea.

Oh, sweet Jesu, if this was God's work, then why did she feel so vile?

Then Joan gagged, for the power of the archangel surged through her with renewed force, and all coherent thought was gone.

* * *

THE GOLDEN hand crept along the stone walkway toward the watchtower where the two foul-mouthed comrades of the guard still talked and jested of Joan's whoring abilities.

It reached the closed door, rose, and knocked.

One of the men opened the door, thinking it to be the guard returning to torment them further with his sexual recollections.

The hand grabbed and clenched and twisted, turning the man's genitals to pulp.

The next instant the other man, also, was screaming, both his hands buried in the bloody mess of his own groin.

Its work accomplished, the golden hand rose high into the air, flicked off the blood and pulp that soiled its fingers, then vanished.

JOAN JERKED and cried out as the power of the archangel left her, then she lay still, her breath heaving.

One man dead, two more impotent.

She burst into sobs, nauseated that the archangel had forced her to partake in his violent retribution.

"It must be a test," Joan whispered, "to ensure my worthiness to serve God in the coming battles."

She rolled over, hugging her legs tight against her body, and lay still a very long time until she regained her composure.

Then she rose, stumbling a little as she did so, and smoothed down her shift.

Tomorrow she would be examined both physically and intellectually, and she hoped that she would be strong enough to prove herself worthy of God's, and the archangel's, faith in her.

There was a subtle change in the chill atmosphere of the room, and Joan realized that St. Michael was back. She tensed slightly, half expecting to feel again the horror he had exhibited during his retributive rage, then relaxed as she felt the familiar loving regard of the archangel.

"Saint Michael?" Joan looked about the chamber for the archangel's golden glow, but he was not visible.

You shall have no need to fear the morrow, Joan.

She relaxed yet further, and smiled.

God has asked me to give you a gift, a miracle, that shall convince all doubters that you are truly the beloved mouthpiece of Heaven.

Joan blinked, thinking to ask St. Michael what he meant, but her mouth gaped as a sudden warmth consumed her lower body.

"God's will be done," she whispered as the warmth finally ebbed away.

Chapter X

The Feast of SS. Simon and Jude
In the first year of the reign of Richard II
(Friday 28th October 1379)

— I —

✠

ISABEAU DE BAVIÈRE stood before the fire, rolling up her sleeves with slow, particular movements. A small smile played about her lips.

Isabeau cared little about what she might or might not find in the course of this morning's examination; she cared only that she might find some means to both humiliate and discredit the upstart peasant girl.

Her smile hardened. Never in her entire life had she

thought to be upstaged by such a pious rustic wench!

A door opened, and Isabeau looked up. "Ah, Catherine. My dear, what's wrong? You look so pale—"

"I look as if I have hardly slept, madam." Catherine nodded a greeting at the three other noblewomen witnesses. Two midwives were also present, and Catherine glanced at them, noting that one was remarkably comely for such a lowly ranked woman. Then Catherine looked about the room. It was bare save for two substantial chests set against a wall, with a bench pushed against them, and a trestle table set close to the window—doubtless for the light afforded. Catherine was mildly surprised that Isabeau had ordered a fire lit in the hearth; Joan was not to be beset by drafts along with the prying fingers and eyes of the women.

Catherine looked back at her mother, who by now had rolled up her sleeves to her satisfaction, and was now ensuring the veil of her headdress was tucked securely behind her neck. "Have you heard that the guard who accused Joan of bawdry in the hall yesterday fell to his death from the castle walls last night?"

Isabeau shrugged. "No. Was it the wine?"

"More like the hand of God," Catherine said, and then walked to the window and stared out, her back precluding any further conversation.

Isabeau stared at her momentarily, then put her daughter's moodiness out of her mind. The fun awaited.

"Marie," Isabeau said to the pretty midwife, "if you would bring in the girl, please."

Catherine turned back into the room as she heard Marie return with Joan. She carefully composed her face into bland neutrality, for she did not want Joan to recognize her fear.

Lord Jesus Christ, if Joan had the power to call down such retribution on three lowly guards who merely insulted her with words, then what would she do to those who attacked her with more substantial weapons?

Joan had arrayed herself in a simple shift of unbleached linen with a high neckline and baggy sleeves. Her feet were bare, her raggedly trimmed hair was uncombed, and her face was suffused with serenity.

Catherine's unease grew.

Isabeau clapped her hands, making Catherine jump.

"There is no need for formality, methinks," Isabeau said, stepping forward and pushing her rolled sleeves yet higher on her arms. "Marie, Belle, please divest the girl Joan of her shift."

The two midwives stepped forward, and Joan—with a small smile sent Catherine's way—lifted her arms obligingly.

Marie and Belle pulled the shift over Joan's head, then stepped back.

Isabeau frowned, her eyes running up and down Joan's body as if she were evaluating a mare for breeding, then made an expression of distaste.

"You are not appealing," she said.

No, thought Catherine, *she is indeed not appealing. Her limbs are too squat and thick, her buttocks too vast, her waist too solid, her breasts too flat, and her body hair is most distastefully copious and dark. She is built not for lust, but for Godliness.*

And Catherine shivered.

Joan made no comment to Isabeau's remark, but walked to the table and lay flat on her back upon it.

"God is with me," she said, and lifted her knees.

Isabeau arched an eyebrow, managing to convey deep disgust, then sniffed, and walked forward, waving the other ladies to walk forward with her. When she stood at the side of the table, Isabeau laid her hands on Joan's thighs, and jerked them cruelly outward.

"Perhaps the midwives can tell us how many men have crawled down this path before this day," she said. "Does she look used, ladies?"

As Isabeau spread Joan's legs even further apart, Joan clasped her hands across her breasts and murmured a prayer.

Isabeau took no notice. She slid her fingers through

Joan's thick black pubic hair and spread her labia apart. "Is her door opened, ladies, or intact?"

And then Isabeau, together with the two midwives and the three noblewomen, bent her head for a look.

Catherine, lagging behind the other women, had barely reached the edge of the table when she heard the other women gasp in shock. A midwife and two of the noblewomen hurriedly crossed themselves and stepped back from the table, affording Catherine room for her own view.

Yet first she looked at her mother.

Isabeau raised her head, and stared incredulously at Catherine. "Mother of God!" Isabeau whispered. "This girl *is* built for saintliness, after all!"

Catherine wrenched her eyes away from Isabeau and looked down to where Isabeau's hands still held Joan's labia wide apart.

Utter coldness seeped through Catherine. Joan had no genitalia at all . . . she did not even have the means whereby to piss and shit! Smooth, unbroken skin ran from the top of her labia right down to where her buttocks began to separate.

Joan was physically unable to be anything *but* a virgin.

"A saint! A saint!" whispered Marie. Religious awe infused her lovely face. "Her flesh is not marked with the evil that stains all other women's flesh. Why, she cannot even produce the odorous waste that ordinary sinners must daily unburden themselves of. She *is* a saint! Her flesh is holiness incarnate!"

Isabeau finally lifted her hands and stepped back. *A true saint?* Isabeau had a frantic desire to wash her hands, but as she had not thought to prepare a bowl and water was left rubbing them up and down her skirts.

Catherine still stared at Joan, unable to comprehend what she had just seen.

Sweet Jesu, she had not thought her such a powerful opponent. How was Bolingbroke going to counter her evil magic? How?

Joan finally spoke, unclasping her hands and raising her head to look at the women still staring at her. "I am God's true instrument, unsullied and pure," she said, and then looked between Isabeau and Catherine. "Now *none* may gainsay it."

Chapter XI

The Feast of SS. Simon and Jude
In the first year of the reign of Richard II
(Friday 28th October 1379)

— II —

✣

THE ARCHBISHOP OF RHEIMS, Regnault de Chartres, assembled his investigatory panel in the hour just after Nones in the hall of la Roche-Guyon. Apart from himself, the panel consisted of five other clerics.

They sat in straight-backed chairs set on the dais. On the floor, immediately below the dais, was a humble bench.

Charles sat on a throne to one side, his legs crossed, now uncrossed. His mouth was thin with worry: *what if Joan were proven a fraud . . . and, worse, what if she were not? What road then would she push him down?*

With Charles were seated Isabeau, Catherine and Philip. All three looked stiff and ill-at-ease: Catherine had told Philip the results of Joan's morning examination, and Philip was now very unwilling to allow himself to be pushed into any move against her. He could not allow Catherine's hatred to undermine his own position.

She is devil-constructed, not God-gifted, Catherine had whispered to him as they'd entered the hall. *Even Jesus Christ had his privates intact.*

But Philip had shaken his head, and gestured to Catherine to be silent. This situation needed to be observed far more closely, and his next move—should there be one at all—taken only after much greater deliberation within himself. Philip was prepared to do many things to gain the French throne for himself, but speaking out against a possible saint incarnate was not one of them.

Not when the maid had God's vengeful anger as her weaponry; Philip—as the entire garrison—had heard what had transpired on the wall during the night.

Around the hall were several score of nobles and knights and, as on the previous day, ranks of guards and soldiers at the back of the hall.

If Isabeau, Catherine and Philip appeared uneasy, then the men in the ranks were even more so. Would their casual ribald words about this maid Joan, so nonchalantly passed among them during previous weeks—*and they meant no ill, indeed not, 'twas just the day-to-day talk of common soldiers, sinners all!*—come back to haunt them in the shape of God's judgmental hand?

None among the common soldiers was now ready to even think of Joan in sexual terms. She was Joan of Arc, Holy Maid of France, and she was apart from any other, male or female, on this mortal realm.

There was a movement at a side door—Joan, still wearing the simple shift she had worn to her examination at Isabeau's hands. She was escorted by the midwife Marie, who now and again glanced adoringly at Joan's face. Joan murmured a word to Marie as they came through the door, and the midwife halted a pace or two inside the chamber, allowing Joan to walk forward on her own.

Joan smiled sweetly at Charles, who returned it tremulously, and then bowed to the assembled clerics.

"My lords," she said, "I greet you well in the name of the Lord our Father."

Archbishop de Chartres waved a hand dismissively. "You invoke God's name easily, Joan. Perhaps too easily. No, do not speak—"

Joan's lips twitched. She had not been about to speak at all.

"—but take your place on the bench. We will address you in due course."

Joan inclined her head and sat down on the bench, folding her hands in her lap.

"Madam de Bavière," said de Chartres, "this morning you performed a great service to this panel in examining the maid Joan to determine if she is truly a virgin as she has claimed. Will you now step forth and tell this assembly of your conclusions?"

Isabeau slowly rose and stepped forth, stopping several feet from the bench on which sat Joan.

She did not look at the girl.

"My Lord Archbishop," Isabeau said, then stopped. She had been steeling herself for this humiliation for several hours now, but several days would never have been enough to enable her to speak her findings with any peace of mind.

"Madam?" de Chartres said.

Isabeau wet her lips, and wished that she'd never left the English court. Even Richard would have been a preferable fate to this.

She turned her head slightly, and caught a glimpse of Catherine. Her daughter's face was suffused with sympathy, and Isabeau grew purposeful. She would not let this dumpy peasant girl get the better of her.

"My Lord Archbishop," Isabeau said again, her voice clear and strong now. "This morning, assisted by my daughter Catherine, several noble ladies, and two midwives, one of whom you see standing by the door, I did so examine the girl Joan to determine if she was the virgin she claimed to be. We viewed her flesh as close as any might, and what we say cannot now be gainsaid by any within or without this hall.

"My lords, the girl Joan is truly a maid. Indeed, she cannot be otherwise."

"What mean you by this?" asked a priest by the name of Seguin, who sat at the Archbishop's right hand.

"Father," Isabeau said, "Joan is a true miracle. Her private parts are completely absent. Where all other women have the clefts which tempt men, and which birth infants, as well as those breaches which enable them to piss and shit, Joan has smooth clear flesh. She is completely untainted, so pure that not only can she never bed with a man, but does not need means to evacuate the foulness that all other sinners need to rid themselves of each day of their lives."

There was silence throughout the hall, all eyes on Isabeau de Bavière as she returned to her chair.

Then, pair by pair, the eyes shifted to Joan, and shocked whisperings began to rustle up and down the assembly.

The archbishop, as the clerics seated with him, stared at the maid, almost unable to come to terms with what de Bavière had said.

Charles had put his shaking hands over his mouth, staring at Joan with eyes wide with awe and fright, and Joan graced him with yet another smile.

As she did so, her eyes flickered triumphantly at Isabeau, then to Catherine, sitting stone-faced by her brother.

Then she turned back to the panel seated on the dais. "I am so blessed," she said. "God has been good to me."

"Have . . . have you always been thus?" said de Chartres.

"Nay," said Joan. "I was born as any girl-child is, and grew as every woman does, but last night Saint Michael approached me, and was with me, and took away from me those parts of me which God has sent to humiliate every daughter of Eve. I am no longer cursed by Eve's sins."

To one side Isabeau rolled her eyes, and leaned toward Catherine.

"God has graced her with everything save the virtue of

humility!" she whispered. "No doubt she hopes to eventually take sweet Jesu's place at our Father's side!"

In her turn, Catherine glanced at Philip to make sure he'd heard Isabeau's remark, then whispered back to her mother: "Her pride betrays her, madam. Perhaps she is more the devil's monster than the saint."

Philip shifted uncomfortably, then shushed them. For the moment he wanted no part of any accusations flung Joan's way. It wouldn't be politic at all.

Although neither Isabeau's nor Catherine's words had reached the clerics seated on the dais, it was clear that several among them entertained their own doubts. Such physical malformation could as easily be a mark of the Devil's favor as of God's.

Who had visited Joan last night? St. Michael . . . or Satan?

One of the investigatory priests, Seguin, whispered to de Chartres. "Perhaps we should have had her examined for a witch's teat. I do not like this absence of natural parts."

"There will always be another day should we need it," de Chartres whispered back, and Seguin nodded slightly.

Now he leaned forward, his eyes sharp. "You say that Saint Michael has spoken to you on numerous occasions. In what tongue did he speak?"

Joan smiled. "In a better tongue than yours, father."

There was a small titter about the hall—Father Seguin spoke with the somewhat rough accents of the Limousin region of France.

Seguin's face hardened. "And what has Saint Michael told you in your visions?"

"That I am come from the King of Heaven to deliver the French from the calamity that is upon them."

"And how shall God's will be accomplished?" de Chartres said.

"By force of arms—"

"If it is God's will that the French be delivered from our current calamity," Seguin said, his voice harsh, "then what need has He of soldiers? Can He not simply will it?"

Joan turned toward him. Her face was serene, and she was apparently undisturbed by his disbelief. "God has sent me word, via the Blessed Saint Michael, that the French must rise up in arms against the hell-bound English, and that I will be the one to lead the nation to victory."

Seguin's expression was now one of outrage—indeed, all of the clerics wore various degrees of scorn and disbelief on their faces.

"You?" said de Chartres. "But you are a mere girl. How can it be that *you* should lead the French armies to victory? How can we believe you?"

"How can you not believe God?" Joan said quietly.

"We need a sign," de Chartres said. "Some proof that you are indeed God's instrument on earth. I ask you again, how can it be that you, a young girl, can lead our nation to victory against the English?"

Joan lowered her face, and closed her eyes. Her hands clasped, as if in prayer.

Seguin made an impatient gesture, but de Chartres laid his hand on the priest's arm and silenced him before he could speak.

Charles stared at Joan, waiting for her to speak. Nothing he had heard thus far had particularly allayed his anxiety about the part God expected *him* to play in this forthcoming battle.

Finally Joan raised her face, and looked first to Charles. "You will be king, and rightfully so," she said. "King John has lost God's favor for disowning you, and he shall not live for much longer. Soon," and yet again she smiled at Charles, who stilled at her expression, "after a great victory which I shall win for you at Orleans, you shall be crowned at Rheims, in the company of the blessed Lord Archbishop who sits before us now."

"This is preposterous!" cried Seguin. "A 'great victory at Orleans'? Orleans is not even in the hands of the English! How can it be that—"

"I continue to speak the words of God," Joan said, turning to face Seguin. "How can you continue to refuse to believe Him?"

Now she looked at the archbishop. "The ways of the Lord our God are sometimes confusing to men, but we should never doubt them."

"My lord," said Philip, who now rose from his chair and stepped forth to Charles' side to address the archbishop. "The maid Joan speaks with great sweetness and persuasion, and yet I am sure"—now he turned to Joan, and smiled at her with the same degree of sweetness she had previously bestowed on Charles—"she understands that we need a sign from God Himself, for we are but humble fighting men, and we find it difficult to understand how such a girl, as saintly as she may be, can lead us to a military victory."

Joan sighed, as if the sins of the world weighed heavily upon her shoulders. "You are unbelievers all," she said. "*I* find it difficult to understand how you can doubt me."

Again she lapsed into silence, her eyes downcast, then she raised her face once more toward the archbishop. "La Roche-Guyon now contains many powerful knights, my lord. Men who have years of experience on both the tourneying and battlefields. If I were to don armor, and then to challenge and subsequently best one of these knights in the tilt, might you not then believe my words?"

Everyone stared at her. Some already believed her a holy maid, a saint who spoke the words that God's messengers gave into her ear, others still held doubts, while yet others had good reason to bear her an implacable hatred . . . but none thought such an untrained peasant girl had any chance against even the poorest of the knights present within the garrison.

Why, she had no skills in controlling a destrier, let alone bearing the weight of armor and the cumbersome lance of the tourney!

Seguin smiled dismissively, and leaned back in his chair, but the archbishop regarded her with more respect.

"If you so ask," he said, "and if the Dauphin agrees—"

"I do! I do!" said Charles. *If she were killed, then perhaps he might not have to go to war . . .*

Joan shot him an irritated glance.

The archbishop shrugged in capitulation. "Then so shall it be. You shall have an hour, Joan, to pray and armor yourself, and then we shall reconvene on the tilting field beyond the walls of this castle."

TO CATHERINE it seemed that the entire day was a nightmare that would stretch into infinity.

After the events of this morning and this afternoon—Catherine had no doubts at all that Joan would best any knight sent against her—Catherine knew she must be very circumspect in moving against Joan. But one day . . . one day . . .

Catherine took a deep breath, taking heart in the knowledge that, however saintly Joan might be, the girl had one potentially crippling flaw . . . and that flaw was St. Michael. God may have chosen Joan, but God had patently forgotten what a frightful encumbrance St. Michael could be.

But then, even God had strayed down the same path of temptation that St. Michael so often took.

Catherine restrained a smile. The seeds of heaven's destruction had been sown long, long before.

She looked about her. The field was lined with rank upon rank of men, whether common soldiers, or knights and their squires. Most of the soldiers, and a goodly number of the knights, were shouting Joan's name with an unquestioning fervor. Pennants fluttered, dogs ran up and down the lines barking as if they chased the demons of hell, and the sky itself seemed to have swollen to greater heights and majesty in Joan's honor.

Catherine gave a mental shrug. She hoped Joan would enjoy it while she could.

There was a sound, a rising murmuring, and Joan appeared from between a gap in the ranks. She had donned a long vest of chain mail which hung to her knees. Over this she wore a breast- and back-plate of white armor, and jointed plates over her arms and legs.

Her head was bare, and her hair, black and unruly, flowed over her shoulders.

Behind Joan walked a man, a common soldier, and in his arms he carried an unvisored helm and a lance, as well as something dangling from his belt that Catherine—who was at some distance—could not immediately make out.

Joan walked to the archbishop, and went down on one knee before him, asking his blessing.

De Chartres hesitated, but gave it, his hand moving in the sign of the cross over her head.

Then Joan rose, and knelt again before Charles, asking for a token of his esteem.

Charles tore a length of silk from one of the tippets hanging from his left sleeve, struggling ungracefully for a moment with the resisting material, then tied the streamer of scarlet material about the plates of Joan's left arm.

The streamer snapped and fluttered in the stiff breeze.

Joan thanked Charles, then stood.

For a moment she hesitated, looking about the field . . . and then she saw Catherine, standing some twenty paces distant.

Motioning to the soldier to follow her, Joan walked over to Catherine, stunning onlookers by going down on her knees before Charles' sister.

"I would that you do something for me," Joan said, looking up to Catherine, and Catherine saw that there was no respect in her regard at all.

Catherine raised her eyebrows.

"My hair flutters about me with impure abandon," Joan said, her eyes steady on Catherine's. "Now that I am a soldier of God I have no womanly need to have it so lengthy, nor to revel in its sheen. I ask you, Catherine, to perform for me a great service. Shear it close to my skull, so that I may not be distracted in the great battle that is to come."

Catherine smiled a little. *That was a pretty speech and gesture, girl, but it will not win you the war.*

I am God's maid, Joan returned into Catherine's mind, *and you are the Devil's handmaiden.*

Catherine closed her eyes and tilted her face so that the sunshine played over it. *I do not know how, Joan, but one day sin shall be your ruin. Believe it.*

She opened her eyes and stared down at Joan's uplifted face.

Joan's eyes were shining with serenity and confidence. *Your words do not frighten me. God is my trust.*

Catherine smiled, and reached out for the shears that the soldier lifted from his belt. She hefted them, then lifted a tress of Joan's hair. *If you trust in your frightful God*, she spoke into Joan's mind, *then you are ours*. Her hand tightened, and the shears sliced viciously through Joan's hair.

A lock fell free, and Catherine tossed it skyward, letting the hair scatter on the wind. Then, none-too-gently, she grasped yet more of Joan's hair, and cut it close to the girl's scalp.

When she had finished, she tossed the shears to the grassy field, turned her back, and walked off.

She had no need to see the outcome of this tilt.

MANY HOURS later Philip joined her in their chamber.

Catherine rose from the stool where she had been working a tapestry. "The only question is, did Joan allow her opponent to live, or did she strike him through the heart?"

Philip gave her a hard look, and walked over to a table where he poured himself a cup of wine. "She is God's maid indeed, Catrine, for not only did Joan mount and ride her stallion as if she had been trained from childhood in the skills of horsemanship, she tilted her opponent out of his saddle at their first pass."

Catherine waited as Philip gulped down the wine.

"She rode over to where he lay," he finally continued, "and threw her lance to the grass, saying that she would never take the life of any man."

Catherine nodded. "I heard the roar of acclaim from here."

"Yet you seem to be of good cheer, Catrine. Why? I thought you loathed the maid."

"Oh, I do, and we shall be rid of her yet." Catherine had spent her hours alone reassuring herself with the certainty that, sooner or later, St. Michael's weakness would cripple Joan's faith.

Sin would always out.

Catherine smiled, and walked over to Philip, laying a hand on his chest. "But not *just* yet. She can be of great benefit to us, and to our goals."

"How so?"

"Were it not better that she do all the hard work in restoring France to French hands?" Catherine said. "Once she is done . . ."

"She *is* of God, Catherine. I am not happy at the thought of doing her wrong."

Catherine paused, her face reflective. "Sooner or later," she said, "I think that Joan will condemn herself, and once she does that, then the world will not hesitate to condemn her." She paused, her eyes distant. "I do not think that day very far away."

Chapter XII

The Vigil of the Conception of the Virgin
In the first year of the reign of Richard II
(Wednesday 7th December 1379)

✠

PRIOR GENERAL RICHARD THORSEBY approached Rome in much the same way as Thomas Neville had done so long ago: on mule, and with his face twisted in discomfort at the cold, poking icy fingers between his sandalled toes. Also, as Neville had, Thorseby stopped at the northern gate of Rome, the Porta del Popolo, to ask of the gatekeeper Gerardo how best to find St. Angelo's friary.

Unlike Neville, Thorseby neither thanked nor paid Gerardo.

Thorseby received a much warmer welcome from Prior Bertrand than had Neville. Bertrand had met Thorseby many years earlier, and while he thought Thorseby a humorless man, also admired his sanctity and devotion to the Order. That evening, once the meal in the refectory was over and Thorseby and Bertrand retired to converse privately in Bertrand's cell, they turned to the subject that most concerned their thoughts—Thomas Neville.

Thorseby had already informed Bertrand by letter of Neville's activities in England since he'd returned from his unauthorized travels through Europe, but now the Prior General expanded on the details.

When he'd finished, Bertrand sat pale-faced on his stool, slowly twisting his hands about in his lap. "Neville's behavior has proved monstrous!" he said.

Thorseby inclined his head in silent agreement.

"I always knew he was trouble," Bertrand continued, "but this . . ."

Thorseby shook his head slowly, further agreeing.

"To fornicate so blatantly . . . and then to discard his robes and act as a secular lord . . . to embrace such *disobedience* to the Rule!"

Thorseby sighed, and cast his eyes down.

"And now the Duke of Lancaster protects him?"

Thorseby nodded, sighing once more. "And Lancaster's son, the Duke of Hereford. Neville is surrounded by powerful friends."

"Monstrous!" Bertrand muttered, regretting that he'd so much as lifted a finger to help Thomas Neville. What had he nurtured here within the friary? Had Neville's appalling behavior left some subtle taint within these walls that might yet reach out to infect the vulnerable minds of novices?

"You can understand why I must find a means to discipline him," Thorseby said.

"Of course! Of course! Such behavior as his cannot be allowed to go unpunished."

"Once this convocation is over," Thorseby said, "I had thought to travel north, perhaps to Nuremberg—"

"Ah!" Bertrand's face brightened. "I have done as you asked, my friend, and I think you shall be more than pleased at the results."

Thorseby raised his eyebrows, almost not daring to allow himself the hope.

Bertrand reached over to a small document pouch on his desk and retrieved from it a letter. "Prior Guillaume in Nuremberg is as anxious as we are that Neville must be forced to account for his actions. He has spared no effort in making inquiries. See?" Bertrand handed Thorseby the letter. "Guillaume has discovered two men who will be of great use to you, and he can arrange to have them meet with you in Nuremberg after the Christmas celebrations are past; a cook, from a tavern in Carlsberg, and a mercenary, who traveled with Neville from Florence to Nuremberg. They have, apparently, some most intriguing information. Guillaume thought it might be best if you spoke to them yourself."

Thorseby scanned Guillaume's letter, his heart beating faster with each line read. Guillaume did not say a great deal, but what he did say . . .

Thorseby looked back to Bertrand with shining eyes. "My friend," he said, "I think I owe you many thanks."

PART THREE

Well Ought I to Love

Take weapon away, of what force is a man?
Take housewife from husband, and what is he then?

—*Thomas Tusser,*
Five Hundred Points of Good Husbandrie

Chapter I

The Feast of St. Thomas the Apostle
In the first year of the reign of Richard II
(Wednesday 21st December 1379)

— I —

✠

KENILWORTH WAS an ancient castle with a somewhat regrettable history. Not only had it served as a base for the thirteenth-century rebel, Simon de Montfort, who had ousted Henry III from his throne, but in more recent times Edward III's father had been imprisoned—and deposed—in the castle by his wife, Isabella, and her paramour, Roger Mortimer. For their temerity, Edward III subsequently executed Mortimer and exiled his mother Isabella, granting the castle and its lands to his fourth son, John of Gaunt, Duke of Lancaster.

The duke had done all in his power to liberate the castle from its ghosts. An impregnable, cold and forbidding fortress when first it had come into his hands, Lancaster had spent vast sums of money and a great deal of effort to turn the castle into a comfortable home—although still an impregnable fortress. Builders had expanded and enlarged the private apartments, adding chimneys and windows so that the duke and his family could enjoy the view in fresh and smokeless air. Along with the private apartments, the duke had caused to be built a great hall, and it was here on the evening of the Feast of St. Thomas the Apostle, in late December, that the household gathered for a quiet celebration of Neville's name-day.

The trestle tables on which the company had supped were now cleared and folded away, and the duke and his family relaxed in informal groups in front of a roaring fire in the enormous hearth. Virtually all of Lancaster's extended family was here. The duke and Katherine's two children, Joan and Henry, were present. Henry was relaxing in a rare visit to Kenilworth and the warmth of his parents' love. Normally his duties as Bishop of Winchester kept him far from their side, but tonight he was laughing with his sister over a game of chess, teasing her at her lack of concentration which had allowed him to checkmate her in less than eight moves.

Joan ruefully rubbed her big belly, laying the blame on it. She was but a few weeks distant from childbed, and Lancaster and Katherine had insisted that Raby allow her to birth their child at Kenilworth, where she would have the love and support of Katherine and her ladies.

Raby, sitting just to Joan's side, had not minded. Indeed, he was more than pleased that, firstly, Joan had bred so quickly after their marriage and, two, Lancaster continued to take such a loving interest in her. Raby's fortunes had risen considerably since he had so closely allied himself with Lancaster (even if they had dulled slightly in past months as both Lancaster and Bolingbroke had fallen into disfavor with Richard), and he was well content with his current domestic arrangements.

As Henry cleared the board so that Joan might have one more chance to wreak revenge on him, Raby's eyes wandered around the gathering of people. Raby's eldest two sons and three daughters were also at Kenilworth for the Christmas season. Both his sons had brought their wives and children, and Raby hoped to arrange marriages for his three daughters present—Lancaster had many noble kinsmen and retainers who would be keen to ally themselves with the rising fortunes of the Neville family.

He glanced back to Joan. Her face was drawn and weary,

and Raby felt a twinge of concern for her. This baby was important—more than important. If it was a son, well, Raby envisaged an illustrious future for him. He would be the great-grandson of a mighty king, and perhaps even the nephew of another . . . Raby looked over at Bolingbroke sitting by the fire with his wife, Mary, then dismissed his thought as mere speculation . . . great-grandson to a king was a powerful enough connection. Raby scratched his chin reflectively, watching his two eldest sons as they gossiped with Lancaster's chamberlain. They were good men, but from a less worthy mother than Joan . . . and now Raby was beginning to wonder if he shouldn't arrange for the titles of Raby and, now, the earldom of Westmorland, to pass to his son by Joan. His sons by his first wife would be disappointed . . . but they could be managed.

Joan laughed, and then coughed in the laughing, and Raby bent to her in concern.

FROM HIS solitary spot at the edge of the group, Neville had been watching Raby with as much speculation as Raby had been observing his children. Neville knew Raby well, perhaps too well, and thought he knew exactly what was going through his uncle's mind. He liked Raby's sons, and hoped that if Raby was going to pass them over for the titles of Raby and Westmorland then he should do so with as much grace and circumspection as possible—the Neville clan was large enough for its own bloody civil war if Raby was less than cautious or conciliatory.

He sighed. Who was he to judge others on their family relations?

As if they had a will of their own, his eyes slid to where Margaret sat with Mary and Katherine, Bolingbroke standing to one side and Rosalind playing with a ball of scarlet wool at their feet. Margaret had a faraway expression on her face, but when she caught Neville's look she hurriedly glanced away.

* * *

MARGARET BENT down and picked up Rosalind, hoping that Neville would not realize she'd seen his look. She held the baby to her, gently kissing the girl's black curly hair, and trying to ignore her husband's continued gaze.

She did not know what to do about Thomas. Once she had wanted his love so badly, but now? While Margaret had healed physically from Richard and de Vere's rape, the emotional and psychological wounds were taking far longer to close over. A very large part of her wanted to continue to punish Thomas, to hurt him as badly as his callousness had hurt her, and so she refused any overtures on his part, refused any of his attempts to beg forgiveness, or to be kind to her.

Margaret smiled grimly into Rosalind's hair, rocking her back and forth and pretending a total absorption in the child while thoughts of her husband dominated her mind. Bolingbroke kept saying that there *was* a loving and gentle man beneath the carefully built layers of chill piousness, but Margaret was not so certain. Thomas' infernal casket was all-important to him, as was his devotion to his hateful, wicked God and archangel.

He would never, *never* give up them for her.

"Margaret." Mary's gentle voice cut into her reverie. "Come back . . . please."

Margaret blinked, and wiped away her tears with a jerky motion of one hand. "I am sorry, Mary."

Mary gave Margaret's hand a brief squeeze. "Here it is almost Christmastide, and you are still lost in melancholy—"

"Wouldn't you be?" Margaret said, and then flinched as she realized what she'd said. Two weeks ago Mary had miscarried of a tiny fetus—if that pulpy lump of black-veined flesh *could* be called a fetus—and Margaret knew that Mary had wept long into many nights over its loss.

She'd also lost considerable weight in the past six weeks,

and Margaret wondered if the seeds of malaise Mary carried within her were finally starting to manifest themselves. Had that imp decided to poke its blackened face into the sunlight?

"My lady," she said softly, "I am sorry. What I just said was—"

Mary laid a hand on Margaret's arm, silencing her. "What I have lost is gone," she said. "But what you think you've lost can be regained." She looked steadily at Margaret. "Let it go. Accept Thomas' contrition. You hurt yourself only by keeping him so distant."

Margaret tightened her arms about Rosalind, rested her chin in the girl's hair, and stared at the floor. "He does not love me," she said.

"You wouldn't know," Mary said, "as you've not given him a chance to show you."

To that, Margaret was not prepared to reply. While Margaret was no longer sure if she wanted Thomas' love, she knew she did not want to have to fight for it. She was too tired of fighting and hoping, and she wasn't sure now if she *could* accept Thomas' love, even if he did offer it. Disturbed by the wretchedness of her thoughts, Margaret twisted her mind away from Thomas, thinking instead of Mary and Katherine. Both women had been extraordinarily good to her in these past months; their warmth and friendship had kept her alive during hours when she'd thought it better she were dead. Raby's wife, Joan, had also become a close companion. Margaret's mouth twisted a little in wry humor . . . no doubt Raby spent some sleepless nights wondering if she would ever prattle to his wife about the time Margaret had spent in Raby's bed during last year's French campaign.

Katherine, Mary, Joan . . . all were good friends, but the world of women wasn't the entire world, and ever since she'd been a child—and certainly ever since she'd become aware of her role in the great battle looming—Margaret had wanted only to be held and loved in a man's arms. Hal loved her, but he didn't count, not in the way she needed to be loved.

Besides, Hal's love didn't stop him using her to further his own ambitions—*our ambitions*, Margaret corrected herself. *This is not only his battle.*

Her time with Roger, her first husband, had been sweet, but endlessly frustrating. An impotent husband withering away *needed* love—he could not give it. Raby? Margaret sighed. Raby was a good man, but more than most nobles he needed titles and power attached to a woman's skirts in order to love her.

And so back to Thomas. Always back to Thomas. How could she trust him when the next time Thomas betrayed her for his casket, God or archangel, Margaret knew he would destroy her completely? After all, wasn't that what God and Michael had planned?

How could she dare to love him, or even allow him to love her, when there lay only death ahead?

NEVILLE FELT sick at heart as he watched Margaret ignore him. Margaret had spoken to him only those words necessary for politeness in the past three months since they'd come north—

In those three months since that terrible night when he'd discovered that he'd sent his wife to be raped for the wrong casket.

—and in the privacy of their chamber had cringed every time he had tried to touch or caress her. All Neville wanted to do was beg her forgiveness, and perhaps hold her and try and ease away some of the hurt he had caused . . . but Margaret would not allow him even that.

Neville had changed greatly in these recent months. He had thought himself prepared to risk his wife—and Bolingbroke's Mary—in order to win that casket . . . and the realization that the price was greater than the reward had come as a horrifying shock to him.

Neville could have blamed Bolingbroke, for the entire endeavor had been Bolingbroke's idea, but he did not. He could have blamed Richard, for surely it was Richard who had made him think he'd discovered the right casket, but he did not. He still loathed Richard as the Demon-King, and despised him for what he had done to Margaret, but he could not blame him.

Instead, Neville blamed himself. Every day, every hour, Neville relived in his mind that horrific moment when he'd realized that the casket was worthless.

Every day, every hour, Neville re-heard those words his battered wife had spoken to him as she lay on her bed: *isn't this what the angels chose you for? The great pious priest, cold enough to cast even the most innocent into the flames for God's great cause.*

Lord Christ! He had sent Alice to the flames, and he'd sent Margaret to the brink of them.

He had once thought not to care for Margaret.

He now knew that he did.

He had once thought it would be easy to sacrifice her.

Now he knew that it wouldn't.

He had once been proud enough, *blind* enough, to think that love didn't matter.

Now he knew that it did.

Tears suddenly filled his eyes, but Neville did not immediately wipe them away—Christ knew he'd got used enough to them in the past months. His continual agonizing self-reproach had become a suppurating wound that not only would not heal, but had turned him from his once single-minded determination to win the casket. Never again would he sacrifice Margaret, nor anyone else, in the effort to gain it. St. Michael had told him that the casket would eventually find him, and, as far as Neville was concerned, that was the way it damn well would have to be from now on.

There was a movement. Raby, walking over to where Bolingbroke, Mary, Katherine and Margaret sat, and leaning down to play with Rosalind—a girl he believed was his child—before looking up and smiling at Margaret.

She smiled back at him with all the warmth she'd denied him—*that I've denied her*, Neville thought—and a raging emotion consumed him.

He'd felt this emotion many times previously when either Raby or Bolingbroke had smiled at Margaret, and yet it was only recently that Neville had recognized it for its true nature—jealousy.

"Sweet Jesu," Neville whispered, "what can I do?" A simple curse that he had been self-proud enough to think so simple to avoid had reached out and ensnared him with shocking ease.

If I allow myself to love her, Neville thought, *does that mean I must also offer her my soul? I don't know . . . I don't know . . .*

"Tom?" Lancaster rose from his chair. "What do you there, lurking in the shadows? It is your name-day, and we have yet to drink to your good fortune. Come man, stand forth."

The other members of the gathering added their voices, and Neville blinked away his tears and walked over to where Lancaster held out a goblet of wine.

He took it, and glanced about the gathering. The faces were friendly without true warmth. Although most did not know the details, all knew that Neville's ill-considered actions had resulted in Margaret's rape. None, save perhaps Bolingbroke, was prepared to totally forgive him until Margaret herself did.

Katherine rose and joined her husband so that they might both raise the toast to Neville's health. As she did so Neville caught the look of utter love that passed between them, and the desolation of his own loveless marriage enveloped him like a choking flurry of wet, icy snow.

* * *

LATER, AS the evening had dragged on, and the women excused themselves to retire to their beds, Bolingbroke approached Neville.

Their friendship had been strained since that dreadful day: not because Neville blamed Bolingbroke for what had happened to Margaret, but because Neville had been so wrapped in his own guilt that he'd not been particularly approachable. Neville had continued with his duties to Bolingbroke in exemplary fashion—overseeing his estates, wards, accounts and correspondence, and keeping at bay the hordes of hopeful petitioners who plagued every great noble—but he had been distant the entire time.

Damn Margaret, Bolingbroke thought as he smiled and began to chat to Neville about some inconsequential matter. *She has carried Tom's punishment far enough. We have too little time left, and so much to accomplish in that time, for her to continue to play the aggrieved maiden.*

They talked for a little while about the problems caused by a steward's illness on one of Bolingbroke's estates, then finally, Bolingbroke broached the subject which had been troubling him so deeply.

"Tom, my friend," Bolingbroke said, glancing about to ensure that those left in the hall were still gathered about the hearth some distance away. "I am troubled at your unhappiness. Is it just that we failed to achieve the casket . . . or is it that Margaret was hurt so badly in the failure?"

Neville dropped his eyes, not replying.

"You said to me before we left London," Bolingbroke continued, his voice soft, "that you would find it easy to sacrifice Margaret, for she knew her role and had accepted it. You said that you would regard her with respect and pity, but you would not love her. Forgive me, Tom, but that is not the man I see standing before me now."

"I had thought it easy to sacrifice Margaret," Neville finally replied, still looking down, "but . . . but now I am not so sure. Hal," Neville lifted his eyes back to Bolingbroke's, "I have come to loathe myself for what I did to Margaret. I knew that Richard would likely ravish her the first chance he got, but I reasoned that assault away with the thought that it would be worth it to get the casket. But it wasn't the right casket, was it? And Margaret's rape was not worth it . . . oh, Lord Jesu, Hal, I thought myself immune to her suffering until I saw her blood!"

"But, Tom, Margaret *must* be sacrificed if mankind is to be saved . . . mustn't she? Didn't you tell me that she is the temptation you must resist if mankind is to be saved? Forgive me, perhaps I misunderstood . . ."

Neville took a deep breath. "No, you understood aright, Hal. She is the temptation, and if I choose her above God's cause then mankind is lost."

"Then what are you to do? Ah, my friend, I do not envy you your choice."

"I know what I am *not* going to do," Neville said. "I will no longer actively hunt out that casket—to do so only causes pain and suffering. Saint Michael said it would eventually find its way to me, and with that I must be content. Hal, Richard had twisted me about his little finger, *and* hurt Margaret in the doing! He manipulated me into thinking that worthless casket was what I sought . . . and I fell into his trap."

"But—"

"That does *not* lessen my commitment to God's cause or my duty as Saint Michael's servant, Hal."

Bolingbroke repressed a smile.

"Saint Michael once told me," Neville said, "that my way would be strange, and I must believe him."

The angelic fool has dug his own doom, Bolingbroke thought.

"My task is to remove the stain of demonry from England's court, Hal. I, as you are, am committed to the removal of Richard. Once he is gone . . ."

"Then all will be well."

"Aye, then all will be well, and the casket and the secrets of the angels will be mine."

"Except that there still awaits the greater battle between God and the demons."

Neville's face lost some of its determination. "Aye."

"Margaret," Bolingbroke reminded him softly. "You must decide what to do, for you cannot go on as you are. Your misery distracts you."

Neville took a long minute to reply. "Hal," he eventually said, "to love her does not mean I must hand her my soul, does it?"

"No, although you must face that choice eventually. To love her will simply make your decision the harder."

Strangely, Neville only felt relief. He must eventually resist her, but to love her in the meantime would give her comfort against her eventual sacrifice . . . wouldn't it?

Chapter II

In the Hour before Midnight on the Feast of St. Thomas the Apostle In the first year of the reign of Richard II (Wednesday 21st December 1379)

— II —

✠

NEVILLE STIRRED, and woke from something which had never been quite a sleep.

It was quiet, but not quite silent, in the chamber. A faint hissing and crackling came from the coals in the hearth, and there was a rattling at the windows as the winter wind scurried past.

He opened his eyes, but did not move.

He was alone in the bed. He could not see the space where

Margaret should be lying sleeping, for he was turned away from her side of the bed and was staring at the blankness of the far wall of the chamber, but he could *feel* the emptiness.

While this had been a bad day for Neville, he realized now that the night was going to be even worse.

He suppressed a sigh, wishing he could suppress the emptiness within him as easily. Twice before he had felt this emptiness: when his parents had died when he was five, and when Alice had murdered herself. *When his lover Alice had killed herself because he refused to acknowledge that the child she carried was his.* When he had abandoned Alice to her fate as he had abandoned Margaret.

Now Margaret was gone from him. She might still walk by his side, but in all things that mattered, Margaret was as dead to him as his parents and Alice.

His coldness had killed her as surely as it had killed Alice.

And had somehow this iciness also managed to infect his parents with pestilence? Had their child been so distant he had murdered the spark of life in them?

After the death of his parents, Neville had sought escape in the harsh world of men; in fighting and battle, in the thrill of dealing death to others, in a frenzy of using women to sate his bodily needs.

When Alice had died Neville sought relief in the embrace of the Church, and the Church, as had God's angels, welcomed him.

After all, was he not one of their own? A Beloved?

Is this what the angels chose you for? The great pious priest, whether in orders or not, cold enough to cast even the most innocent into the flames for God's great cause.

Was this what God's great cause needed? A cold-hearted, self-righteous shell of a man?

Oh, sweet Jesu! He could *feel* the emptiness in his bed.

He could feel the emptiness within himself.

It wouldn't hurt to love her . . . would it? No, surely not. Surely not. He could still make the fateful decision later, when he needed to.

But for now, he needed to fill that emptiness, or die.

Neville clenched his fists, tensing his entire body, fighting to bring his emotions under control, and then rolled over.

Margaret was a huddled shape on the bench set into the great glassed bow window. She was leaning against the glass, looking out across the dark winter landscape.

Neville rolled quietly out of the bed, grabbed a blanket to wrap around his nakedness, and walked over to the window.

It was a magnificent construction, one of the many new and luxurious features Lancaster had built into Kenilworth. Sitting in an alcove fully ten feet long, six deep, and twelve high, the leaded glass window looked over the fields as they rolled away from the castle. The window made this chamber one of the best in Kenilworth, but Neville was fully aware that it had been given to Margaret and himself for her sake, not his.

He sat down on the padded and cushioned window seat and drew the blanket tighter about his shoulders against the chill that radiated off the freezing glass.

He did not sit close to Margaret. Since that night—*that shocking night*—she recoiled every time she thought he might attempt to touch her. Neville had not even held her hand for three months, let alone caressed her face, or kissed her.

The great pious priest, cold enough to cast even the most innocent into the flames for God's great cause.

Cold enough to send a wife to be raped for a worthless cause.

Too cold to love?

Margaret turned her head slightly to look at him—even though she did not speak, at least she was prepared to acknowledge his presence.

Neville held her gaze for a brief moment. She was beautiful in this frosty night: her hair a dark mass save for the faint glimmer of those ethereal golden streaks; her face so pale; her eyes as dark and unreachable as the clouds that chased themselves across the night sky. She was wrapped in a black cloak, wrapped so tightly that not even her hands or neck showed beyond its protective folds.

Neville looked out the window. Far below, the fields of Warwickshire stretched for miles. He caught his breath, for the winter landscape was impossibly beautiful.

The fields were covered in snow, the bare branches of trees cloaked in ice; clouds hurried across the sky, billowing and bulging, sending shadows chasing across this otherworldly countryside; the icy trees swayed and dipped; a lone fox—its ears flattened against the wind—loped across a frozen laneway and disappeared into some black bramble bushes.

The winter beauty reminded him of another wondrous landscape—a wonder he had denied.

"When I traveled through the Alps," Neville said, keeping his eyes on the landscape, "I met a young man called Johan Bierman. I was both puzzled and angered by him, for he used to stare at the black icy mountains and proclaim his admiration for them, exclaim at their beauty. I thought the mountains ugly and ungodly . . . useless mounds of rock that served only to frustrate man's purpose, and which refused to be tamed to his needs.

"Now?" Neville shook his head very slightly. "Now I can understand why Johan believed them so beautiful."

Margaret did not answer. She did not want to get drawn into a conversation with him.

Neville looked back to her. "Once I thought you ungodly, and useful only if you could be manipulated to serve my needs. Now? Now I think you as beautiful and worthy in your own right as is this landscape stretched before us. You said you were of the angels, and tonight, as you sit suspended above this spectral landscape, it has never been more apparent, nor you more lovely."

He hesitated, wanting her to look at him, but she kept her face turned away, her eyes fixed stolidly on the landscape outside.

The chill of the window glass struck him with renewed force, and Neville shivered and pulled his blanket yet further about him.

"I have been the most cold-hearted of men," he said, forcing the words out. "The most unfeeling of men. All that has ever been important to me has been my own path, and I have trodden into the dirt all who have stood in my way. No wonder, as you said, Saint Michael chose me for God's great cause."

The last three words came out harsh and grating, and Margaret looked away from the window and stared at him.

Neville took a deep, shuddering breath and looked at her. "As we relaxed this past evening, I looked and wondered at those who sat with us. Lancaster and Katherine . . . sweet Jesu, Margaret, I have never seen such love in my life as that which exists between those two people! And then my uncle Raby and Joan . . . not the love that Lancaster and Katherine share, but a deep respect and caring that will probably develop into the same depth of love as the years pass.

"And then," Neville said softly, "Hal and Mary. Coolness and fear. No respect. And then," his voice dropped to a whisper, "you and I . . ."

He turned his eyes back to the frozen fields. "Both Hal and myself are lost on a cold, dark sea, Margaret, and I, if not he, want to come home."

Again he turned to face her. "How do I do that?"

"Ask your God, Tom, not me!"

"It is not God I want to come home to."

"Beware, Tom, for you edge too close to the precipice of damnation for comfort."

"Ah," he said softly. "That wicked prophecy. If I hand you my soul then mankind is damned."

He lapsed into silence again, pulling at a thread in the blanket.

Margaret sat stiff, staring at him.

"You know," he said eventually, looking at her with a

strange new expression in his eyes, "I have been sitting here wondering how best to frame your beauty in words. But," he grinned, and its boyish charm took Margaret by surprise, "I am not a poet, and I cannot find the words. I wish we were home at Halstow, for then I would have the redoubtable talents of Master Tusser to aid me."

The grin deepened, and Margaret realized with a jolt that he was teasing her.

"I should command his presence before me," Neville continued, "and I would require him to write me one of his damnable verses to commemorate your beauty.

"Can you imagine what he would present me with to court you? 'Good lady, your face is more seemly than the hay in sunshine, your lips more delicate than the sturdiest hop poles.' "

Margaret gaped at him, wondering if he had gone mad. Then, as his lips twitched, and his eyes danced with merriment, she realized that what he was doing was showing her his true self—a man that no one, save perhaps Bolingbroke, who'd always had the faith that he'd existed, had ever seen. Perhaps even Tom had never seen this man . . . and certainly Tom's God had never seen *this* whimsical fellow.

Neville's smile broadened as he watched Margaret's stunned expression. " 'Your form is more beauteous than a newly plowed field, your grace more exquisite than a newborn calf.' "

Margaret could not help herself, she smiled . . . and as Neville held her gaze, and smiled with her, that smile became a laugh.

For his part, Neville's breath caught in his throat as he realized that this was the very first time he'd ever heard her laugh.

"And then," he said, his smile fading as long-repressed emotion consumed him, "I should ask Master Tusser to compose me some verse that I might the more surely convince my lady that I do most truly love her."

* * *

THE ARCHANGEL strode down the corridor, incandescent with rage. His fiery form glimmered and glowered, his half-raised fists twisted and clenched, sparks crackled and snapped from his hair and face.

He marched toward the chamber where the witch was seducing Thomas—

—and stopped dead as he saw who stood outside the door to Thomas' chamber, his legs apart, both hands leaning on the unsheathed sword whose point rested on the floor between his feet.

Well met, Dark Prince!

"A good night, indeed," Bolingbroke said. As the Archangel Michael's face was suffused with fury, so Bolingbroke's was suffused with triumph . . . and something else . . . love, perhaps.

Let me pass.

"No."

The archangel raised his fists and screamed. *Let me pass!*

"No," whispered Bolingbroke.

The archangel's form blurred as he fought to contain his rage and maintain control of himself. *You cannot think that with this night's work you have won.*

"Nay," said Bolingbroke, "I do not. I do not share your arrogance."

He will recant his words and his love when he knows your and her foul secret.

"I do not think so."

You cannot keep the casket from him for much longer.

"Long enough. Longer perhaps, for methinks he no longer lusts for that casket as once he did."

He cannot keep himself from the casket. It will *find its way to him!*

"Do I detect panic in your voice, Michael? Does love terrify you that greatly?"

The archangel did not answer. His form had now dissipated into a swirling, blinding confusion of light.

"Begone," said Bolingbroke. "You have no place here tonight."

Thomas will recant, the archangel said yet again, *when he learns your foul secret.*

Bolingbroke's face darkened with rage and he hefted the sword, and taking a single pace forward, levelled it at the archangel at shoulder height.

"*My* foul secret, Michael? This is not my secret alone, nor Margaret's, but the dark foul secret of the *angels*!"

Now the archangel was nothing but a throbbing ball of light. *He will recant when he finally faces the ultimate choice: earth's eternal damnation, or the love of a whore. He will sacrifice her for that . . . believe me.*

And then he was gone, and Bolingbroke was left alone in the corridor.

"The love of a whore?" Bolingbroke whispered. "Nay, Michael, he will not do it for the love of a whore, but for the love of all mankind."

"YOU CANNOT say you love me! You cannot!"

"I have run from love all my life, Margaret. I will run no longer."

"You will not stand by it—tonight you will say you love me, but in a month's time, or a year, or whenever it is that the choice is laid before you, you will choose mankind's salvation before you choose me."

Neville dropped his eyes, again playing with the thread in the blanket. "I cannot believe," he said finally, "that God would ask me to sacrifice that which I love—"

"He asked it of Abraham! He asked Abraham to murder his son Isaac in order to prove his love for God."

"And did He not then grant mercy to Abraham?"

"God murdered his own Son."

To that Neville had nothing to say.

"If He was prepared to so crucify His own Son, I do not think that God will grant *me* mercy," Margaret whispered.

"Margaret . . . *I* will not condemn you again. I cannot! Sweet Jesu, Margaret, I have come to loathe the man that sent you into Richard's chamber. I was so fixated by that damned, *cursed* casket that I was prepared to sacrifice you to gain it. And for what? For what?"

She was silent.

Neville took a deep breath. "I let Alice murder herself rather than stand by her, or admit to her that I loved her. I will not allow you to be murdered also."

"You have a greater cause than me, Tom. You cannot love me."

"I have no greater cause than you, Margaret," he said with boundless gentleness.

She began to weep. "You cannot say that—"

"I have the most infinite joy in saying that. Margaret . . . I have fought against loving you for so long. When Hal suggested to me a means whereby we might snatch that—" Neville hesitated, and Margaret could see that he was trying to bring a deep anger under control, "that casket, then I justified the risk to you with the thought that achieving the casket was worth it. But the casket wasn't worth it, was it? No, Margaret, let me finish."

He slid a little way along the bench and reached out to take her hand through the cloak she still had wrapped tight about her. "Margaret, even had that been the right casket it would not have been worth the pain that you, and Mary, endured.

"Do you remember what you said to me later that night? You said that God and the angels had chosen me because I was a cold, pious priest, cold enough to cast the innocent into the flames for God's cause. Margaret," his hand tightened about hers, forcing her to look into his eyes, "that cold, pious man cracked apart that night. He cracked apart when he realized what he had done—that once more he'd sent a woman into the flames to suit his own cause. Mary said it had been me who had raped you that night. She was right. Margaret . . ."

Neville's voice broke, and he had to look away for a moment. "Margaret, you have been gone from my life for three months now, and these months have been so empty . . . so bleak. I want you back, yet I have no right to ask."

She stared, silent.

"Dear God," Neville whispered, desperate to find the right words to reach her, and to find the right manner in which he could atone for what he had done to her. "Margaret, I loved you from the moment I saw your face hovering above the woman that I lay with on that day in July last year, the afternoon we got Rosalind. Yet I clothed that love in hatred, because that was the only way I knew how to deal with it. It was the only way I could feel safe. It was how I dealt with Alice, and with her death. It was how I dealt with the death of my parents. I wrapped myself in the twin cloaks of piousness and coldness, and told myself it made me a great man, God's man.

"But it only made me a foul man. A despicable man—surely ugly in God's sight, as well as in yours."

"And in Saint Michael's sight?"

"Saint Michael will surely understand—"

Margaret's mouth twisted.

"Margaret, Margaret, the attainment of that casket is never, *never* going to compensate me for not having you or your love."

"But one day you will attain that casket," Margaret said brokenly, "and learn its secrets. One day you *will* have to make the choice that, if mankind is to be saved, *must* see me burned. You know that!"

Neville let go her hand and took her face between his hands. "Margaret, I swear before you now, that when that day comes I will allow love to make the choice for me—not cold callousness, not fear, not pious bigotry, and not what some archangel whispers in my ear. This I vow as the *only* way I can atone for what I have done to you, and for what I did to Alice, the child she carried, and the three daughters she took with her. Sweet Jesu, Margaret," now Neville broke down, "what more can I do? What more can I do?"

It was enough, and it was all she could ask. Margaret lifted her arms, throwing back the cloak, and wrapped them about Neville's body, drawing him close to her.

"No more, Tom. You need do no more."

He kissed her eyes, her forehead, and finally her mouth, his every move hesitant and fearful. She tightened her arms about him, and thought his kiss the most wonderful thing that had ever happened to her throughout the desolation of her life, for it was full of love rather than lust or the need to dominate.

"Do you love me?" she said.

"Oh aye, I love you."

She smiled, and put her lips against his, and said, "That is all that matters."

Neville shuddered, then gathered her into his arms and carried her back to the bed, away from the chill of the window.

He laid her down and slowly folded the last of the cloak away from her nakedness.

He had not seen her unclothed—save for a brief flash of pale flesh as she climbed into or out of their bed—in three months, and what he saw now shook him.

Scars, on her breasts and along her inner thigh.

Richard's marks.

She looked at him silently, seeing the tears well in his eyes, allowing him this moment of reflection. Sweet Jesu, he was handsome! Margaret had always known that, but now that his facade of coldness had been stripped away she suddenly realized how strong and seductive his features were.

She reached out a hand, and touched his face.

"Sweet Lord!" Neville muttered. "I had not known they hurt you so badly."

"It is past now, beloved," she said, and drew his hand down. "It is past now."

He kissed her, but then pulled back. "I don't want to hurt

you," he whispered, wanting her so badly, yet terrified that she would only remember Richard and de Vere's rape with every touch of his body.

"Then do only one thing for me," she said, her hand now gently caressing the side of his face.

"What?"

"Be my lover," she said.

He smiled through his tears. "Ah, beloved, that is so easy, for art thou not more beautiful than the newly forged plowshare? More wondrous than the warmth of the sun on the turned earthen clods of the field?"

She burst into laughter, and all was well between them.

ARCHANGEL MICHAEL ascended slowly into the Field of Angels, highly pleased. True, Thomas had capitulated to love this night, but it was a capitulation won by manipulation and lies. When Thomas discovered the extent of his betrayal . . .

Joy suffused the archangel's being. Tonight, Bolingbroke and Margaret had dug *their* own doom! Michael began to laugh, and, as he joined with his brothers in the Field of Angels, the entire angelic assembly began to screech in triumph.

Chapter III

Before Matins, on the Thursday before the Nativity of Our Lord Jesus Christ
In the first year of the reign of Richard II
(2 a.m. Thursday 22nd December 1379)

✠

BOLINGBROKE STOOD, the sword still hanging unsheathed from his hand, his eyes filled with tears.

His supernatural perception had allowed him to be privy to most of what had passed between Neville and Margaret—their emotions at least, if not their precise words.

Slowly, still staring at the door, Bolingbroke lifted the sword and slid it back into its scabbard, and then he lifted his hand and wiped away his tears.

This night had repaid in full the faith he'd held in Neville for all these years.

Damn it, he thought. *I always knew there was a reason to like the man.*

And then he walked away.

WHEN HE opened the door to his own chamber, Bolingbroke was surprised to see the lamps blazing and Mary whipping about from where she'd been pacing back and forth before a brazier.

"Mary? What do you up this late?"

Bolingbroke closed the door behind him, realizing with a further start that Mary's face was pale with fright.

She put a hand to her throat, her hazel eyes wide and staring. "I woke . . . and you were gone. I wondered . . ."

Her eyes dropped, staring at the sword that Bolingbroke wore. "I'm sorry, my lord. I didn't mean to question you."

Bolingbroke took several paces into the chamber, then stopped as Mary's eyes flared yet wider. "Mary . . ."

She took several steps away, moving to her side of their commodious bed. "I will trouble you no further, my lord."

She pulled back the coverlets, and climbed in, forgetting in either her haste or her fright to remove her outer robe.

Bolingbroke stared at her, then turned away, thinking as he unbuckled his sword-belt and laying the weapon on a chest against a wall.

Why was she so frightened?

And then Bolingbroke suddenly realized that Mary's behavior tonight was nothing unusual. She was always tense and apprehensive with him, and it was just that, coming back to their chamber still wrapped in the warmth of what he'd felt between Tom and Margaret, he had just noticed it for the first time.

And no wonder, considering the hatred and force he used to take her on their wedding night. No wonder, considering that he'd sent her into Richard's chamber as coldly as Neville had sent Margaret.

For one horrible instant, Bolingbroke was tempted to reflect on the freedoms of bachelorhood, but he managed to overcome the temptation, and to chide himself for not having seen earlier Mary's discomfort in his presence.

Mary deserved better, not only because her dowry of lands and titles had added greatly to his own power, but because she had that right as his wife, and as an honorable and virtuous woman.

And one who was increasingly ill.

Bolingbroke had wept with Mary when she'd lost that . . . thing . . . that she'd hoped would be a son for him, but he had not been truly distressed. He'd known she would not carry to term any child she conceived of him, had known she would lose the child almost as soon as she conceived it.

Had he not seen the gathering darkness deep in her womb long before they'd married?

He did not love her, nor ever would, but Mary deserved his pity, and she did not deserve to live in fear of him.

Bolingbroke, still turned away from Mary, briefly closed his eyes in self-reproach. How different was he from Richard, or from all those he loathed and wished to destroy? There were those who needed to fear him, and those who deserved his implacable ill-will . . . but Mary was not one of them.

She had lost a child, and of all people Bolingbroke could understand her grief at that.

The silence between them had grown too long, and so Bolingbroke stripped off his tunic and boots, and wandered over to Mary's side of the bed, unlacing his shirt as he did so.

Lord Jesus, see that terror in her eyes as she sees my body.

"Mary," he said, sitting down on the edge of the bed and taking her stiff hand in one of his. "What is wrong?"

"Nothing, my lord!"

He stroked the back of her hand with his thumb, saying to her with a smile what he had once said to Neville. "I am only 'my lord' in public, Mary. In our own private rooms we are Hal and Mary. Now, what is wrong?"

"Nothing—"

He smiled again, taking care that it be light and easy. "No, something *is* wrong. If you insist," he said, making his words as non-threatening as his expression, "I shall command that you tell me, as any good and loyal wife should confide in her husband."

There was a long silence as Mary stared at the coverlet of their bed. When she did speak, it was in the most hesitant and apprehensive manner. "I had wondered," she said, blushing slightly as her eyes now drifted everywhere but Bolingbroke's face, "why you should be out so late, and I thought . . . I thought . . . perhaps you preferred . . ." Her voice dropped to a whisper. "That perhaps you'd found another that you . . ."

"You thought I had gone to a mistress?" Bolingbroke laughed, truly amused, and the genuineness of his merriment relaxed Mary as nothing else could have done. "Nay, sweetheart, I have no mistress. I would not so dishonor you."

And Lord Christ Savior, I do not need the distraction.

She had relaxed, but still avoided his eyes, and so Bolingbroke continued. "Mary, our marriage has not made a good start, and that is through no fault of your own. I have been a distracted husband, and a poor one because of that."

His hand tightened about her own, and his voice became grave. "Worse, I have been a careless husband, involving you in my miserable conspiracies. In doing so, I have injured you sorely. For that I beg your forgiveness—would that I had the consideration to do so earlier."

"That was a bad day, Hal. Many poor decisions were made."

"Aye," Bolingbroke said, and allowed contrition to spread over his face. *And yet it worked its purpose*, he thought, *if even now Margaret and Neville lie entangled in love.*

"Mary," Bolingbroke hesitated, wondering how he could best broach this subject. "Mary, tonight I am aware that Tom has made his peace with Margaret, and it shames me that while he has acted, I have not yet done so."

Now her eyes flew to his. "When I thought that you had gone to your mistress . . . I had thought her Margaret."

Bolingbroke flushed, truly shocked and shamed by what she'd revealed. Mary thought Margaret to be his mistress, and yet Mary had been nothing if not gentle and kind to Margaret in the past months.

He lifted her hand, and kissed it softly. "Your nobleness further shames me, Mary. I do not deserve you."

"Sometimes you frighten me. You are so gallant and so blithe, but sometimes I think I can see a darkness lurking about you that intimidates me. An anger barely quiescent. I fear—"

"Never fear me, Mary!" Bolingbroke said. "Never! Yes, I have cruel thoughts, and angry ones, but they are not directed at you. I am sorry beyond measure that you should have thought so."

She smiled, contented, and looked him full in the face for the first time. "I thought you did not care for me, Hal. Nor need me."

He looked deep into her eyes, and then leaned forward and kissed her slowly, and as tenderly as he could.

The sickness was still there; he could see it in the depths of her eyes, and taste it in the faint taint of her mouth. She had a year, perhaps less, and that suited Bolingbroke's purposes well.

Yes, she deserved his pity, and his care. He could do that for her, at least. He could pretend for a year.

When he leaned back, he hoped that she would misunderstand the relief in his eyes.

"When you sent myself and Margaret to Richard that day," she whispered, laying her hand on his cheek, "I wondered afterward if you had only been using us. I am glad I was wrong about you."

Bolingbroke smiled, easy and loving. "I shall never place you in danger again. Ah, Mary, I have been a bad husband, in bed as well as out. Will you let me remedy that?"

"I have heard that what happens between a husband and a wife can be truly wondrous," she whispered.

He leaned forward and kissed her deeply on the mouth, continuing the kiss until he felt her respond.

Eventually, he pulled back.

"Shall we find out?" he said.

Chapter IV

The Nativity of Our Lord Jesus Christ
In the first year of the reign of Richard II
(Sunday 25th December 1379)

✠

CHRISTMAS WAS celebrated with joy and devotion at Kenilworth; the newfound peace between Neville and Margaret, as between Bolingbroke and Mary, had pleased everyone. The world might yet turn awry beyond the walls of the castle, but within lay only warmth and contentment.

The joy of Christmas deepened when Joan went into labor directly after Shepherd's Mass at daybreak and was delivered of a healthy son as the bells rang out for the noonday mass of the Divine Word. Joan was attended by Katherine, Mary and Margaret, as well as three midwives and two other ladies. Given her own two abysmal experiences with childbirth, Margaret had expected to find this birth trying at best. Instead, she found it delightful. Not only did Joan deliver with astounding ease, Margaret was almost overcome with the atmosphere of love and companionship generated by the women present within the birthing chamber.

"Your son is so blessed," Margaret said to Joan, and she bent down to stroke the child's cheek as it lay on his mother's breast, "to have been born on the day of our Lord Jesus Christ's own nativity."

Joan, her eyes wet with tears of joy and relief, could do nothing but smile. Like most women, she had regarded her childbed with dread . . . but her labor had taken only a few short hours, and the child had slipped out with such grace and brevity she could not, only a half hour since the birth, remember having suffered at all.

And to have a son . . . her husband would be so pleased!

"Thank you," Joan finally whispered, and lifted her hand to take Margaret's. "And for your aid and friendship I wish for you such an ease of birth when you deliver Neville's son next autumn."

Margaret's eyes widened in shock, not only at Joan's words—*were they true? Did she already carry the child that would make or break her and Hal's cause?*—but at the sensation of power that had passed between their linked hands. It was the power of women, she realized, strengthened and reinforced by the shared experience of this birth.

Margaret's eyes misted with tears, and she leaned down to give Joan a brief kiss on the mouth, sealing the covenant. "As you have wished," she said, leaning back, "so shall it be."

Just then the baby stirred and cried, and both women laughed through their tears.

Not only the newborn boy, but this entire day had been blessed.

RABY WAS ecstatic, and the passing about of wine at the Yuletide feast that night was perhaps a little freer than it would normally have been. Although the women had joined their menfolk for the feast (other than Joan, of course), they had departed as soon as the meal was finished to return to Joan's chamber and continue there in more womanly fashion the celebration of both Christ's and the new child's birthday (which womanly celebration also, truth be told, included the passing about of much sweet and good wine).

Now, as Compline came and went, Lancaster and his immediate family and retainers sat around a table set before a roaring fire in the great hall. There were platters of fruit and sugared confectioneries placed up and down its length, but they were hardly touched in preference to the silver ewers of Gascony wine that wound their way about the table. Raby's fortune was toasted over and over with ribald humor (even if the humor was a little stilted on the part of his eldest sons), and with wishes that Bolingbroke would be the next to be so toasted at the birth of a son.

To this Bolingbroke smiled, and winked over the rim of his goblet, and then lowered his wine to remind everyone that Mary had barely recovered from her miscarriage, and that now was not the time to be discussing her future fertility.

The men were enjoying themselves, truly pleased for Raby and Joan, but also using the occasion and the wine to dull the unsettling knowledge that a confrontation with Richard was more than likely with the turning of the old year to the new.

The wine was good, and it worked wonders in dulling thoughts of the trials ahead, but it could do little against the great trouble that suddenly burst in through the twin doors at the far end of the hall.

Thomas of Woodstock, Duke of Gloucester.

Gloucester had remained behind in London when his elder brother, Lancaster, had removed himself and his household to Kenilworth. After several uncomfortable weeks, Gloucester had left London for his estates, sending his brother word that he would join him for the New Year celebrations.

This early arrival, combined with Gloucester's glowering face, was ill news indeed.

Gloucester strode toward the table at the head of the hall, brushing snow from his cloaked shoulders with impatient hands.

Lancaster rose, as did everyone else at the table.

"Brother," Lancaster said, extending his hand to take Gloucester's. Neville noted how ashen Lancaster's color had gone, and shared a quick glance with Bolingbroke: *Richard?*

"What is it?" Lancaster continued. "What news?"

Gloucester unclasped his cloak and flung it across a bench. "Poor news, indeed, John. May I . . . ?"

"Of course, of course!" Lancaster held out his goblet for Gloucester and the man drained it of its contents in three swallows, wiping his lips with the back of a gloved hand.

A sheen of wine gleamed at the corner of his mouth, as if it was a bloodstain waiting to pounce, and Neville felt a chill run down his spine.

"This news has come to me by several messengers," Gloucester said, "and I stinted no effort to bring it to you before you heard it from someone else. But first, sit . . . sit, if only to allow me to do the same. I do not think my legs will hold me upright much longer."

Lancaster motioned everyone down, and poured Gloucester more wine before sitting down also.

"I thank you," said Gloucester, taking the wine and seating himself with evident relief.

He hesitated, looking about the table and then to his brother. "John," he said quietly, "this is heavy news, and I will not speak it lest you give me your word that you trust each and every man about this table."

John stared at him, then looked slowly around. Bolingbroke, Neville and Raby, he nodded at. Likewise Henry, his son by Katherine—bishop or not, Henry's first loyalty would always be to his father. Then he considered Raby's two sons at the end of the table. He stared at them, then raised his eyebrows at Raby.

"They are my blood," Raby said, "and they will betray neither you nor me."

John nodded, accepting Raby's word, then motioned for his brother to continue.

"Ten days ago," Gloucester said, now staring about the table at each man present, "news arrived from Catalonia, as also from Aquitaine. Count Pedro has managed to wrest control back from his bastard half-brother Henry without any aid from Hotspur. Indeed, Hotspur had not yet moved his forces from Bordeaux before Pedro acted on his own. Pedro has sent him word not to bother marching on Catalonia—he's decided he doesn't want any bastard English on his territory, after all."

Bolingbroke laughed. "Poor Hotspur, to be so denied his glory!"

Gloucester shot him a dark look. "Hotspur has no intention of being denied any glory. Can you imagine *Hotspur* contenting himself with an 'Oh, very well,' and then coming home? Nay, Hotspur has decided to clear up another small source of irritation."

Silence.

Then Lancaster spoke. "Well? Speak, man, speak!"

"Hotspur is marching north on Limoges."

"What?" Lancaster exclaimed, along with several others. "Why Limoges, for the Holy Virgin's sake?"

The small city of Limoges was situated on the Vienne River some forty miles south of Chauvigny. After the English victory at Poitiers it had declared its loyalty for the Black Prince and his heirs, and—or so everyone about this table thought—had been a safe English stronghold.

Gloucester gave a wry smile. "As we have all heard of this miraculous Joan of Arc, now known far and wide as the Maid of France, so too has Limoges. Egged on by their bishop, the city has changed its collective mind and declared its loyalty to Charles and France, not to . . . well, not to the accursed English. Hotspur is marching north to 'deal' with the problem, as his communication to Richard said."

"And Richard?" Bolingbroke said.

"Richard is thrilled. He thinks that Limoges is a small enough target not to give Hotspur any trouble and large enough to give everyone a good deal of satisfaction when it is appropriately 'dealt with.' "

"This is perhaps mildly irritating, no more," Lancaster said, "especially if Hotspur does manage to deal effectively with the city."

"Unless either Richard or Hotspur has thoughts beyond Limoges," Neville said quietly.

There was a silence. *Where to from Limoges?* Everyone remembered what Arundel had said that night deep in the Savoy: *Richard has no intentions of confining Hotspur's field of action to Catalonia. He intends to launch a new drive into the heart of France.*

"There is more," Gloucester said eventually. "And closer to home. For the moment France must be the least of our troubles."

"Aye?" Lancaster said.

"Richard has heaped yet more titles upon his pet."

"De Vere?" Lancaster said.

"Aye. Perhaps not 'titles,' but one in particular."

"Yes?" said Lancaster.

Gloucester paused. "King of Ireland."

There was a stunned silence about the table. There had been rumor of this . . . but to hear rumor spoken of as fact was a harsh thing indeed.

"The Irish will never stand for it," Raby said eventually.

"I have heard," Gloucester said, "that Richard thinks he might command an army to invade Ireland and damn well *force* the Irish to accept it. Richard does not mean his lover to be heaped with pretty but useless titles. Ireland is de Vere's."

"If he does that then Richard will destroy England," Neville said. "Our war with France has not been closed out, and if Richard commits the English army to Ireland instead of France . . ."

"Then we are likely to find ourselves invaded by one effeminate Dauphin and his virginal saint," Raby finished for him. "We have all heard how northern France rallies to her cause, and Richard of all people cannot afford to ignore it."

"And then there are the taxes Richard will need to levy to invade Ireland," Bolingbroke said. "Perhaps that might work in our favor. We'll be so damn poor the French might decide we're not worth the effort of an invasion!"

No one smiled, and again there was a silence about the table.

"Richard has called Parliament for January," Gloucester said. "He is committed to his poll tax, and will need Parliament's consent to raise it."

Lancaster, as he had earlier, looked deliberately at each man about the table.

"Then I think it is time we thought about returning to London," he said.

Chapter V

The Feast of the Epiphany of Our Lord
In the first year of the reign of Richard II
(Friday 6th January 1380)

✠

THE COMMONS of the southeastern counties of England had not experienced the same degree of Christmas comfort and cheer enjoyed by the Lancastrian household. Bitter frosts settled over home and fields on the morning of the fourth Sunday in Advent, and had lasted well into the week after Christmas. Not even village elders could remember a winter this cold, or this hard. Ravens dropped frozen from the sky; starving wild boars attacked children and lambs; men and women found themselves sharing their inadequate bedding with rats seeking the warmth of human flesh. In those areas where the lords had limited the autumn gathering of wood to a ridiculous amount each, peasants found themselves forced to burn old thatch for warmth, or to slaughter their breeding stock for sheepskin.

It was a time when entire villages gathered around one or

two fires, conserving wood at the same time as they stole extra warmth from the close-pressed bodies of their neighbors. While they huddled, they talked. They remembered the smoke rising from the halls of their lords, and thought how warm it might be inside the manor houses and castles of their betters. They discussed how best to ration the remaining sacks of moldy grains and legumes from the long-ago summer harvest, and wished that their lords might distribute some of the fine white bread from their well-stocked pantries. They discussed how they would find enough able-bodied men to begin the late-winter plowing and harrowing of the village fields when their lord demanded that they work his land instead.

They thought how they went to church on Sundays to hear a mumbled Latin mass of which they understood not a word, and saw that their priests looked remarkably well-fed and comfortable in their furs and velvets . . . purchased with their parishioners' hard-earned tithes.

As they huddled all the tighter about their fires and their hostile words, the peasants wondered how they would survive the coming year when they needed to eat the seed stock and breeding livestock in order to survive the winter. Would it be better to starve now, or next autumn when there was no harvest, because there had been no grain to sow, and no meat, because there were no cattle to slaughter?

And more than once, and in many more than just one village, a man or a woman muttered the words that John Ball had screamed as he was dragged off to the Archbishop of Canterbury's prison: "When Adam delved and Eve span, who then was the gentleman?"

Across the frozen, resentful wastes of southeastern England, eyes turned to the homes and comforts of the nobles, and minds wondered: What right do they have to call themselves lords, and to eat fine food, and to bask before the warmth of roaring fires, when we all sprang from the same stock? When we are as much sons and daughters of Adam and Eve as they? Why are we not able to control our own destiny, to choose where we will work, and for whom, when once we were all free men together?

On the day that the frosts finally relented, and men and women could breathe without feeling slivers of ice tear through their lungs, word of a possible poll tax filtered through to the villages.

In a world where survival depended on whether a family could afford that one extra sack of grain to see them through the winter months, the rumor of an added tax—to fight a *foreign* war, for sweet Jesu's sake!—was enough to twist resentful thoughts into the mutinous.

Then, as the ice slowly melted from the narrow country laneways and roads, Wycliffe's Lollard priests and Wat Tyler's revolutionaries moved once more into the fertile fields of peasant bitterness. The English peasantry had suffered through generations with hardly a complaint; they had deferred to their lords, and they had paid their tithes to lord and priest alike.

Now, as they listened to the soft-spoken men who moved among them, they realized they'd had enough. Indeed, they should have protested years ago.

If the nobles looked to Parliament to resolve their complaints, then the English commons looked to their axes, and waited for the warmer weather.

No one wanted to start a revolution while it was still cold outside.

Chapter VI

Plough Monday
In the first year of the reign of Richard II
(9th January 1380)

✠

PRIOR GENERAL RICHARD THORSEBY glanced down at his bandaged feet, and once again wondered if his decision to travel north to Nuremberg would prove to be worth the frostbite in his toes.

The journey from Rome had been horrendous. Thorseby had joined with a party of pilgrims and merchants, but whatever illusion of safety the group gave him was destroyed when bandits savagely attacked them on three separate occasions. Four pilgrims and one of the mercenaries attached to the merchants had died in the bandit attacks, while the journey through the frozen Brenner Pass claimed a further five lives. Only merciful God Himself had enabled Thorseby to survive. On the second day's journey through the pass Thorseby's mule had slipped, tumbling into the abyss to its death and leaving Thorseby desperately gripping an icy rock at the very edge of the precipice. He had screamed for help from his fellow travelers, but they had been concentrating so intently on their own survival they ignored his cries, and Thorseby had been forced to plead with God to send him the strength and fortitude to crawl back onto the track.

He had managed it, just, but at the expense of the skin on his fingers and the loss of his sandals. The final half day's stumbling, barefooted journey through the Brenner along the ice-coated footpaths, and with winter sleet beating down, had caused Thorseby's feet to turn black.

He had prayed long and hard to God in the days since then that his traveling companions be called to a hellish account for their uncharitable refusal to allow him to claim one of their mounts to ride. That *they* had ridden and *he*, a Dominican, had been forced to walk until he could purchase a new mount the other side of the pass . . . unbelievable!

In the end, however, Thorseby placed the final blame for his sufferings on Thomas Neville's shoulders rather than those of his fellow travelers. If it hadn't been for Neville, Thorseby would be back home in the comfort of Blackfriars rather than rotting away in this damp, frigid and gloomy corner of Christendom.

Thorseby frowned, and hoped today's interviews would make his travails worthwhile.

There was a knock at the door, and the prior of the Nuremberg friary, Brother Guillaume, entered. He was so enormously fat that he wheezed and gasped for breath as he walked over to his chair and squeezed himself in. He nodded a greeting to Thorseby, and to the two clerics who sat at a desk in a corner of the room, pens to the ready.

"They are here," Guillaume finally managed to say in Latin, the universal tongue of all clerics.

Thank God, Thorseby thought, *for once these interviews are done then I can go home.*

"Then may we delay no longer?" he said, as pleasantly as his painful feet would allow.

Guillaume nodded, and motioned to one of the clerics, who rose and went to the door.

"First," Guillaume said, "the cook."

Thorseby composed himself, settling his face into a bland expression, and folding his hands in his lap and tucking his feet out of sight beneath the trailing hem of his robe. This cook claimed to have been working in the kitchens of a tavern in Carlsberg, a small town a day's journey south of

Nuremberg, when he'd overheard a conversation between Thomas Neville and one of his traveling companions. Apparently, this conversation had proved so interesting it had remained in the cook's head.

Thorseby looked forward to its recounting.

The cook entered, a swarthy middle-aged man with a strange left-shouldered droop and a shock of fine, dark hair sprouting from underneath an ill-stitched and tight-fitting cap. He looked both apprehensive—an interview before Dominicans was nothing to feel relaxed about—and sly, as if he knew the worth of what he was about to say.

Prior Guillaume greeted him tersely, then indicated he should sit in the chair that faced those of the prior and Thorseby.

The cook sat, removing his cap as he did so, allowing his abundant hair to spill over his shoulders.

Thorseby's mouth thinned as if the man's profusion of hair was a direct insult to his own tonsured scalp.

Guillaume spoke to the man in German, receiving a muttered few words in reply, and Guillaume leaned a little closer to Thorseby. "He says his name is Fermond, and that he has lived in Carlsberg his entire life."

Thorseby grunted. "What does he know of Neville?"

Guillaume turned back to Fermond, and spoke again, translating the cook's replies to Thorseby.

Within moments, Thorseby was leaning forward, his eyes glittering. This man, Fermond, had been working in the kitchens when Thomas Neville sat down to eat with a Frenchman called Etienne Marcel. The conversation that had then transpired between them was incriminating in the extreme. *Thomas Neville had been associated with the leader of the Parisian revolt, Etienne Marcel? Marcel had given Neville money, and a ring as token?*

As Guillaume continued with his muttered translation of the conversation that had occurred between Marcel and Neville, Thorseby finally sat back in his chair. He knew that, whatever the other witness had to say, at this point,

Thorseby had enough to interest Richard in indicting Neville on suspicion of treason. The passing of money and a ring between Marcel and Neville, and, more importantly, Neville's acceptance of both money and ring, indicated a contract between them. A contract to what? To incite rebellion in France, yes, but perhaps also in England? No king liked to have the lieutenants of dangerous rebels in their realm.

Ah, Neville, Thorseby thought as the cook was finally escorted away, *you have earned yourself a traitor's death with this man's testimony alone. What will you earn for yourself with the testimony of my next witness, the German mercenary?*

A heretic's death by burning, as it happened. The German mercenary, a hulking, brutish man, patently had no love of the Dominicans—Thorseby saw him fingering his dagger on several occasions as he testified—but he also had no love for Thomas Neville. What he said was brutal, and to the point.

"I traveled with the English friar from Florence to Nuremberg," Guillaume muttered to Thorseby, translating in almost perfect time with the mercenary's grunting words, "and, during this time, I came to understand that the friar was not a man of God at all, but a demon lurking in the guise of a man."

Thorseby's eyes widened, and his hands clenched into fists.

"We traveled through the Brenner Pass," the mercenary continued, "spending the night wrapped in its dangers."

"Yes? Yes?" Thorseby said, and the mercenary needed no translation to realize the Prior General's eagerness.

"I woke during that night," said the German, "and saw a most frightening thing. Brother Thomas lay wrapped in his blanket some distance from me, but I could easily see what manner of creature he entertained that night."

"Yes? Yes?"

The German grinned, and leaned forward very slightly. "A demon, my lords. Horned and horrible, and with evil, silvery eyes, crouching in conversation with the English friar. I did not need to be any closer to understand their devilish intimacy . . . if you know to what I refer . . ."

Thorseby's mouth gaped, and for a moment or two he literally forgot to breathe.

The German's grin widened. "Would you like to hear more detail, my lords?"

Thorseby's head jerked in assent, and every regret he had harbored about his own trip north to Nuremberg vanished as Neville's doom spilled forth from the German's inventive mouth.

Chapter VII

The Feast of St. Hilary
In the first year of the reign of Richard II
(Friday 13th January 1380)

✠

KING JOHN OF FRANCE lifted his velvet-clad arm and tried to wipe the red wine from the corners of his mouth. He missed with his first pass, his arm bumping into his nose and forehead, and the aged monarch giggled and snorted. He made another more determined and successful effort, and sighed in contentment.

When he laid his arm, now trembling with the effort of its master's will, back on the armrest of his chair, his two companions saw that the sleeve's sky-blue cloth was soiled and filthy, and the fibers of the velvet clotted into ragged spikes.

Robert de Vere caught Richard's eye, and the two men shared a conspiratorial smile. *Feeble old man.*

John did not see their contempt. Indeed, he was so befuddled with the wine his rheumy eyes were having trouble focusing. All he knew was that he was warm, he had a constantly refilled goblet of spiced wine in his hand, and that the two men who sat on the opposite side of the hearth from him were fine and hearty companions.

John knew that he should be unhappy and concerned about something—wasn't there a battle that he had, perchance, lost? Wasn't he being held against his will while his realm disintegrated without him? Hadn't he been forced to sign something humiliating within the recent past?—but John's mind had been slipping in and out of coherency for many months, and now he lived only for and within the moment.

And this moment was fine and comfortable and was here to be enjoyed, not spent fretting over the shadows that lurked in the corners of his mind.

He raised his goblet at Richard and de Vere, burped, then drained his wine with several slurping gulps.

Now the neckline of John's velvet tunic was spotted with the thick red wine.

De Vere grimaced, and rose from his chair to refill the French king's goblet.

There were no serving men present within the chamber and the men-at-arms who constantly provided protection to Richard were standing outside the tightly bolted shutters and doors. What happened in this chamber was going to remain secret between those who inhabited its spaces.

"You are fine companions," John slurred. "Fine men all."

He took another swallow of wine.

"You do us honor to allow us to keep you company," said Richard.

All three men were conversing in the polite French of John's court, and John could almost imagine that he *was* home, chatting amiably with the courtiers who came to fawn at the foot of his throne.

Except that now King John presided over no court save these two handsome men who sat sprawled and contemptuous in chairs opposite him. Both were clad only in black and close-fitted tunics and hose that showed off their fine forms—de Vere also wore a sword—and sported little jewelry, save a great ruby ring on Richard's right hand and a similarly sized emerald on de Vere's hand.

After all, was not de Vere now a king in his own right as well?

John gibbered something unintelligible, and shifted in his chair so he could scratch in the crack of his buttocks.

More wine spilled down his arm and, now, over the floor.

Again de Vere rose and replenished John's goblet. But this time he did not return to his chair. He stood behind John, and looked to Richard, raising his eyebrows.

Richard's mouth curved in a sly, secret smile, and he gave a slight nod.

Then, as de Vere moved to the door, Richard spoke again to John. "Your grace, Rob and I wonder if we might offer you something a little softer than the wine to slake your needs?"

"What?" John said, struggling to sit a little higher in the chair.

De Vere had opened the door, and motioned to the men-at-arms outside to allow someone through.

"This," said Richard, and looked toward the door.

"What?" John said again, turning his head to look at the door.

His mouth gaped open, his eyes refocusing rapidly. "Oooh," he whispered.

A young girl, not more than fourteen or fifteen, came in through the door which de Vere closed behind her.

She was very pretty, with blue eyes and fair curly hair that fell down the full length of her back. She wore a cloak, but as she passed de Vere, she stopped at his murmur, and shrugged the cloak off, letting it fall to the floor.

Underneath she wore nothing but a loose and diaphanous shift. Its skirt was split from hem to hip on either side, and the front was slashed almost to her waist.

At each step, one or other of her breasts slipped free from its confines to enjoy a brief exposure to the warm air and John's lustful eyes.

Again Richard and de Vere exchanged glances, smiling. De Vere had found the young girl plying her flesh down the alleys behind St. Paul's. She was perfect for their needs: pretty, sexually experienced—de Vere had ridden her personally to make sure she could perform to the full extent of her boasts—and young enough not only to pander to John's old-man lusts, but also naive enough not to understand immediately all that went on around her.

De Vere had caused her to be brought to Westminster this afternoon, stripped down, given a good wash and a close inspection for fleas and lice by one of the laundresses, and some new and fresh clothes: the privy purse could surely stand a simple shift . . . and when all was done the cloak could be brushed and returned to the man-at-arms who currently stood shivering at his post.

Neither de Vere nor Richard had any doubt that the girl would perform her function adequately.

John was still gape-mouthed as the girl walked slowly toward him. He began to draw in harsh, deep breaths as she approached, and his hands trembled alarmingly on the armrests.

De Vere moved quickly forward and slid John's goblet from his hand, taking it to a side table where stood several earthenware ewers. He put the goblet down, but did not, for the moment, refill it.

John wet his lips, and glanced at Richard.

"A gift," Richard said. "Take her. Or rather," he laughed shrilly, "let her take you!"

De Vere also laughed softly, turning to face the back of King John's chair. He rested his buttocks on the edge of the table, stretched out his legs comfortably, and crossed his arms.

Watching would be almost as much pleasure as partaking.

The girl moved to within a pace of King John. She smiled, slow and seductive—the expression a grimace on her young, corrupted face—and took the neckline of her shift in both hands.

John blinked, his tongue protruding slightly over his top lip.

The girl's smile hardened, then with an abrupt motion she tore the shift down its center seam, letting the now useless garment puddle about her ankles.

All three men stared.

Her form was one which drove most men who saw it into thoughts of wantonness. Her breasts were full, high and firm, their pale pink nipples puckered by her determined pinching as she'd waited outside the chamber. Her waist was slim; small enough to be spanned by a man's clasped hands, and, as it had never been swollen and disfigured by pregnancy, it gave the girl an aura of virginity. From her waist her hips flared out, round and infinitely agreeable. She had plucked away her pubic hair so that her cleft stood exposed . . . smooth and inviting.

John moaned, his hands fumbling at the front of his tunic.

Richard's hand had also crept down to his own groin, but de Vere remained still, his eyes hard on the girl. He could sate his lust later, when she was gone.

"Oh," the girl whispered to King John, as de Vere had instructed her, "let me do that for you, sire." She moved forward to John, and bent over his lap, lifting up his tunic and undershirt so that they folded over his round, wrinkled belly, and then undid and pulled apart his hose.

John's eyes were almost popping out of his head, and his breath came even faster and harsher. He grabbed at the girl's breasts, pinching and kneading.

She winced, then quickly replaced her grimace with a smile of pleasure.

She moaned also, practiced, and wriggled her hips, then took the French king's semi-engorged penis between her hands and massaged it, rousing it until it stood fully erect before her.

"Thus shall the great king of France conquer all that lies before him!" Richard said, but John was way beyond conversational niceties.

He had slid halfway down his chair, and now lolled back, his face slack, his eyes clouded as they continued to stare at the girl before him. His blood pounded in his ears, and his hands now trembled so badly they kept slipping off the girl's breasts.

She murmured to him, soothing him, then lifted a leg and straddled the king, allowing his penis to finally slip into her cleft until her body had absorbed its entire length.

John's eyes closed, and the pounding of his blood and lust now obscured everything else that might be happening around him.

The girl's expression flattened into contempt, but at Vere's gesture she dutifully pumped her hips up and down.

John began to wheeze violently, and his hands clamped viciously about the girl's breasts until she cried out in pain.

But her eyes were on de Vere, and she put her hands on the armrests so that she could increase the rhythm and strength of her pumping, squeezing her flesh about John's penis until the old man shrieked and writhed beneath her.

The girl's face was sweating—with sheer effort rather than lust—and she muttered a curse, wondering if this ancient French prick would ever manage to spurt forth his seminal muck.

And then, to everyone's surprise, it did, and the French king dropped his hands from the girl's breasts and collapsed slack in the chair, gasping for air.

The girl, her face wrinkled in disgust, made as if to rise, but de Vere motioned her to stay put.

"Best to keep him warm for the moment," he said, and

swiveled back to the table. He lifted John's goblet and filled it once more—but not from the ewer he'd used previously.

When he turned around, de Vere's eyes met Richard's, and both men's expressions were hard.

De Vere walked over to John's chair, stared for a moment at the king slumped muddled and half-senseless from the effort of his orgasm, and handed the goblet to the girl. "He needs to drink," de Vere said, and then wandered slowly over to the door of the chamber.

The girl sighed—was not her work yet done?—and leaned forward and tilted the goblet into John's mouth so the king could suck and slurp at its contents. As she did so de Vere leaned down to the cloak lying on the floor and slipped a small vial into one of its inside pockets.

John gulped the wine down, and felt sufficiently revived to once more ogle the girl's body above him.

This had been a most happy night, indeed.

Then he gasped, his eyes more wide and starting than they had been at his orgasmic height, and his body suddenly spasmed violently.

The girl cried out in shock, lifting away from the king's body, but he was now convulsing so severely she found it difficult to disentangle herself from his flesh. At the same moment, Richard jumped to his feet and de Vere threw open the door, surprising the men-at-arms outside.

"A murder!" de Vere cried. "A murder most foul!"

And he pointed at the now screaming girl, trying desperately to clamber off the dying king's body.

Several men-at-arms rushed inside just as the girl managed to finally free herself, tripping and falling to the floor as she did so.

John's violent convulsions stopped as she fell away, although his entire body continued to quiver. His eyes stared unblinking at the ceiling of the chamber.

Although his muscles still spasmed, King John was already very, very dead.

The girl had sprawled across the floor when she fell. Now she scrabbled about, trying to get to her feet, but she was not fast enough.

Richard leaned down, seized her by an upper arm, and hauled her up.

"Murderess!" he cried.

The girl's eyes were wide and horrified, her mind numb, and she could do nothing but whimper as several men-at-arms strode across the chamber and seized her shoulders and arms.

Richard stood back.

"No!" the girl whispered, staring at de Vere. "It was not I—"

She got no further. Even as she began to speak, de Vere was closing the space between them with huge, angry strides, drawing his sword.

"Murderess!" he shouted, and drove the blade so hard into her belly that there was a horrifying ripping sound as the blade exited through her back.

The men-at-arms jumped aside, as much to avoid being splattered with blood as to avoid any further sword thrusts.

The girl made a sound that was half groan, half shriek, and her hands fluttered as if they wanted to catch at the sword . . . or perhaps as if she thought to beg de Vere's mercy.

De Vere's face twisted, and he put a hand to the girl's shoulder and wrenched the sword free from her body.

For an instant, she remained on her feet, the blood from her belly wound streaming down over her plucked pubis and mingling with the dead king's semen that had trickled down her inner thighs, then she toppled forward and crashed to the floor. She writhed about feebly, her hands clutching uselessly at the blood that now pumped from her belly, her breath ruckling in and out with her suffering.

Richard caught de Vere's eye, and the older man leaned down, grabbed the girl's hair to pull back her head, then cut her throat with two quick, economical slices of his sword.

He straightened, and looked at the men-at-arms. "She poisoned the French king with something she put in his wine," he said.

"Perhaps she carried a pot of the vile poison in the clothes she wore," Richard added.

One of the men-at-arms bent down to the flimsy shift, shook it out, then discarded it as he walked to where the cloak lay. He searched about in its folds for only an instant before he turned back to the others, flushed with triumph as he waved about the small vial he'd found.

"A murderess true!" he said, and Richard and de Vere hid their grins and nodded soberly.

LATER, WHEN both corpses had been removed—John's to be washed and laid out in the state which befitted a king, and the girl's to be tossed out for the crows to scavenge in the fields beyond Westminster—Richard and de Vere relaxed in the chamber.

As the corpses, so also had the bloodstains been removed.

Both men were in a fine mood. As Richard poured them some of the spiced wine they had been so frugal with earlier, de Vere carefully took the ewer that had contained the poisoned wine and poured its dregs over some of the hot coals in the hearth.

Flames sizzled green and loathsome for an instant, then died away.

De Vere smashed the earthenware ewer on the stones before the fire, then carefully scraped the shards into a chamber-pot. They could be disposed of in the morning.

But for now . . .

He rose and took the wine Richard held out for him. He held it up in a formal toast. "To the King of France," he said.

Richard laughed, profoundly relieved that de Vere's plan had been so successful. *King of France!* Then his smile faded, and his brow furrowed.

"The French *will* accept the terms of the Treaty of Westminster, won't they?" he said.

"Of course," de Vere said. "And if they quibble, why! Hotspur is there to grind their whimperings into the mud."

"Yes, yes," Richard said, and again frowned at another worrisome thought. "But what if Parliament will not grant me the taxes I need to clear the crown's debts and finance Hotspur's expedition . . . as . . ."

"As *our* expedition, my dearest lord, to ensure the Irish accept my rule?"

"Of course, Rob! I will not forget your cause!"

De Vere smiled, and, putting his goblet down, placed his hands about Richard's face. "The Parliament will not dare deny you," de Vere whispered, his fingers gently stroking Richard's smooth cheeks.

"Are you sure?" Richard whispered.

"Very sure," de Vere murmured, and stepped close so he could lovingly kiss Richard's mouth.

It was a very slow and deep kiss, and Richard moaned when de Vere lifted his face away.

"Don't ever leave me, Robbie."

"Never," whispered de Vere, and slid one hand down to Richard's genitals.

JOAN HAD lain awake for many hours listening to the evil as it whispered along the tendrils of wind that tapped outside the closed shutters. She did not know the details of the murder that had been done this night, but its conclusion had been all too clear to her.

St. Michael had said it would be thus.

Joan wept a little, and prayed for the dead king's soul. But she could not be too sad, for she knew that John's vile end meant that Charles could now come into his own.

Surely, once he knew that he was King of France, Charles would accept the responsibility that was his by right.

Joan rolled over and slid off the wooden bed, walking quietly to the door and looking into the outer chamber. There slept the midwife, Marie. Since the day of Joan's examination at the hands of Isabeau de Bavière, Marie had become Joan's companion. The midwife, her lovely face pleading, had begged Joan to accept her as a servant, but Joan had refused, saying she'd no need of servitude. But, Joan had added, she had every need for a womanly companion in this garrison of men, and Marie's face had lit up.

Joan had her doubts about Marie—surely a woman with as lovely a face as Marie had would prove no more than a temptation for lust—but the midwife was as godly and devout a maid as Joan could have ever wished for. She'd become fond of Marie, and the two often prayed together in the mornings.

Joan frowned as she walked into the outer chamber and paused as she made sure Marie had not awoken. Marie was twisting about slightly on her bed. Only slightly, and still apparently remaining in a deep sleep, but with a subtle movement that Joan recognized as wantonness.

Of what did Marie dream?

Then Joan shivered, and looked about, for she thought she felt the Blessed St. Michael's presence . . . but no . . . she must have imagined it. There was nothing in this room but herself and the sleeping, dreaming Marie.

Joan moved toward the outer door, and then hesitated yet again, regarding Marie. The sense that St. Michael was close came over her once more, and then passed as quickly as it had previously.

Marie's sleep quieted, and her breathing became deep and easy.

Joan watched a few more minutes, but Marie now slept peacefully, and she felt no more the faint suggestion of St. Michael's presence.

Finally Joan let go her doubts, and thought of her purpose that night. She slipped into the corridor, closing the door on Marie's dreams.

Charles needed to know that he was now the legitimate king.

IF JOAN had managed to quit her chamber without Marie knowing of it, her passage through the quiet chambers and halls of la Roche-Guyon did not go completely unobserved.

Catherine—who had also lain awake through the evil work of this night—pulled Philip from his slumber, and then led him, grumbling under his breath, to stare from the gallery of the great hall.

There they watched in silence as Joan padded through the hall far below them, walking to where the stairwell to Charles' apartments rose at its far end.

"Why does she go to him?" Philip whispered once Joan had disappeared.

"There are many ways to experience sexual pleasure other than what is normal between a man and a woman," Catherine said.

"As you know?" Philip said, turning to stare at her profile in the dark.

"As you have taught me," she said, and he smiled at the suppressed laughter in her voice.

He looked back down, and his face sobered. "Aye, there are indeed many things which can be done . . . especially to a man by a compliant woman."

There was a silence between them as both imagined what might even now be going on between Charles and Joan.

"To creep to a man's chamber in the dead of night is hardly the action of a virgin," Catherine murmured eventually.

"But you witnessed for yourself the smoothness of her flesh where normally cleaves that cleft all men lust for."

"To creep to a man's chamber in the dead of night is hardly the action of a virginal *soul*," Catherine amended.

Philip thought for a while. "Could it be that she is devil-inspired rather than God-blessed?"

"It is what I have feared all along," Catherine said.

"What should we do?" Philip said. "Throw open the door to Charles' chamber and expose her evilness for what it is? Sweet Jesu, perhaps even now Joan has her mouth clamped about—"

"Nay, sweetheart. For the moment we do nothing. But at least we have seen for ourselves the extent of sweet Joan's lies. One day, Lord Christ willing, we will be able to use this night to our advantage."

"Others should witness this," Philip said. "Not just us."

Catherine nodded, and Philip faded silently away.

THUS IT was that when Joan wended her way back to her own chamber, there were five sets of eyes that watched from the gallery: Catherine, Philip, Regnault de Chartres, and two of his clerics.

"You were right all along," the archbishop said, once Joan had gone. "What shall we do?"

"Wait," said Catherine, "and observe."

Chapter VIII

The Second Sunday after Epiphany
In the first year of the reign of Richard II
(15th January 1380)

✠

LANCASTER AND HIS PARTY, which included his son Bolingbroke, Neville, Raby, and Gloucester, as well as the immediate retainers of all the nobles, left Kenilworth on Plough Monday, traveling hard and fast for London. None of their womenfolk was with them. Raby's wife, Joan, had traveled northward instead, taking their newborn son home to Raby's castle of Sheriff Hutton in Yorkshire. Katherine had accompanied her daughter to make sure both Joan, and Katherine's grandson, were safely settled.

Mary, accompanied by her ladies, whose number included Margaret, would travel to London within a week. Neither Bolingbroke nor Neville was sure they wanted their wives in London where they would be too close to Richard and to any potentially dangerous political maneuvering, but Mary and Margaret had insisted, and neither of their husbands had refused them.

This time, Neville swore, he would take far better care of Margaret.

The Lancastrian party traveled hard and fast, and there was little banter or talk on the journey. Consequently, Neville spent a great deal of time wrapped in his own thoughts.

These thoughts were principally to do with Margaret, and what had taken place between them at Kenilworth.

Now that Neville was physically distant from her—her

soft, warm, sensual body—he began to fret about what he'd done.

Had he gone too far? Had he betrayed St. Michael and God by admitting his love for a woman who he knew was placed here on earth to tempt him away from God's true path? Did it display weakness or strength that he had done so? Would his love for Margaret compromise what he knew he must eventually do?

Everything had been so much simpler when he'd been Brother Thomas and not Husband Thomas.

Everything had been so much simpler when he had kept his love for Margaret at bay.

Sweet Jesu, have I done the wrong thing? Have I perjured my soul, and mankind's salvation, by admitting my love for Margaret?

Neville's doubts became greater the further they traveled from Kenilworth. He became surly, snapping at everyone, including Bolingbroke and Courtenay.

By the fourth night, when they drew into a wayside inn, everyone avoided him as much as possible.

Neville dismounted from his horse, stamping about as he slid off its saddle and cloth, then snapped hard at Courtenay when he finally came to take his master's horse away to the stable.

"You have no call to so bite at Courtenay!" Bolingbroke said behind Neville, who swung about to face him.

"He was slow—"

"He was as fast as he possibly could be, Tom. Sweet Christ, man, what ails you? A tooth? Griping in the guts? A twitch in your ear? Whatever it is, see to it that it's gone by the morning!"

And then he stalked off.

Neville stared after him, bitterly resentful that he'd been so publicly humiliated . . . then he saw Courtenay emerging from the stable.

Sweet Jesu, I have been no more humiliated than has Robert.

He walked over. "Robert, I am sorry. I've been ill-tempered and thoughtless."

Courtenay stared at him, then his face relaxed into a smile. "You have had much on your mind, my lord."

Neville grinned ruefully. "And you are quite the diplomat. I shall keep my bile under better control from now on, Robert, for you are not the man I should be snapping at."

The only man he should *be snapping at,* Neville thought as he entered the inn, *was himself.*

But, sweet Christ above, how was he going to resolve his fears?

THAT NIGHT, as Neville lay awake fretting and worrying in the dormitory he shared with several others of their party, a sudden strange peace swept over him.

For an instant Neville thought that he had slipped unknowing into sleep and dream, then he realized that this was no dream at all. It was as if another power had claimed him, for Neville felt himself being physically lifted from the chill dormitory and pulled into another world.

Strangely, he felt no fright or concern at all.

HE BLINKED, startled by the sudden feel—*the sudden reality*—of ground beneath his feet, and looked about. He was standing on a hill swept by a warm, fragrant wind but clouded by a heavy, depressing sky. In the distance he could see a walled city dressed in pale stone, and a roadway lined with people leading from the city gates to the hill on which he stood.

Neville turned his face from the distant city and looked before him. He was standing in front of a cross.

At its foot a woman crouched, weeping softly, and smearing bloodstained dirt over her face and neck in ritualized grief and mourning. She was young and dark-haired, and, even kneeling as she was, Neville noticed her statuesque build. She moved slightly, her pale linen robe pulling about her body, and Neville saw that she was five or six months pregnant.

Neville's breath caught in his throat, and his heart thudded. For a long minute he could do nothing but stare at the woman weeping and grieving at the foot of the cross, then, very slowly, he raised his eyes.

An almost naked man gazed down at him from the cross. He had been vilely nailed to the wood, through his wrists and ankles, and a crown of thorns hung askew on his bleeding brow. His loincloth was darkly soiled with the blood that had crept down his body.

Yet, even so cruelly pinned, the man smiled down on Neville with such overwhelming love that Neville's breath caught in his throat.

He dropped to his knees, unable to drag his eyes away from the man on the cross. As he did so, the woman crept back a few paces.

"Thomas," Christ whispered, and then coughed, a trickle of blood oozing past his lips. "Why do you doubt?"

Neville could hardly speak, nor hardly knew how to explain what tormented him. Eventually he spoke simply, knowing that Christ already knew what was in his heart. "I love a woman, and I have told her so. Yet I also know that if I love this woman, and that if I hand her my soul for her love, then mankind will be doomed."

Christ groaned, then wept, and Neville wept with him, loathing himself that he should so add to Christ's agony.

"Thomas," Christ said eventually, "am I not sacrificing myself for love? Am I not dying for love of mankind? Am I not handing you *my* soul on a platter for the sake of love?"

From the corner of his eye, Neville could see that the woman looked at him with deep pity. Something about her made Neville take a second, more careful, look. There was something familiar about her face, as if he should know her, but he did not: her face was that of a stranger, and Neville dismissed the woman and looked back to Christ.

"I have loved this woman," Christ said. "And now I die for her. Would I hand her my soul on a platter? Thomas . . . Thomas . . . is that not what I do now?"

Neville's weeping deepened in its intensity, appalled that he had so offended the dying Christ.

"Does *my* love damn mankind?" Christ whispered.

"No! No! Your love is mankind's salvation!"

"Aye," whispered Christ. "Aye. What can I say, Thomas, to make you understand? Why can you not embrace the truth? Love does not doom . . . it only saves. How can you have misunderstood this? How can you have allowed yourself to be so wrapped in lies?"

Neville wept and held out his hands in supplication, and the mingled blood and sweat from Christ's body dripped onto his palms.

Love saves, Thomas. It does not damn. How can you have misunderstood this?

Neville lowered his head, unable to gaze any more upon the suffering Christ. *How could he have misunderstood so badly?*

His sobbing now racked his entire body, and Neville sank down until he lay full length in the dust of Calvary, and let the wind of death sweep over him, knowing Christ's agony was his fault.

As Alice's agony had been his fault.

"Love saves," Christ whispered, and Neville knew no more.

HE WOKE, suddenly, jerking into full awareness, and began to shake as he remembered the vision which had consumed him. He lay for a long while, staring at the ceiling of his chamber, then he lifted his trembling hands.

There on his palms twisted dried trails of mingled sweat and blood. He closed his eyes, clenching his fingers about his palms, and took a slow breath. A deep calmness came over him and he relaxed, allowing the lingering peace and beauty of Christ's love to enfold him.

As they had in his dream, tears filled his eyes and trickled down his cheeks.

How *could* he have allowed himself to be so misled? Christ sacrificed Himself for love of mankind. Love did not damn, it saved.

Neville breathed deeply, pulling in the sweet morning air. He had not felt this relaxed, this certain, for . . . since forever, it seemed. Christ had redeemed him this past night, had allowed him to love without guilt and without fear.

Neville smiled, and the lines of worry and pain that years of hatred had etched into his face softened and then vanished completely.

He *had* done the right thing. Neville thought about St. Michael's strange antagonism toward Margaret, and he felt a flicker of uncomfortable doubt. *Why, if loving Margaret was the right thing, did St. Michael loathe her so greatly?* But then Neville remembered his vision of Christ, and its strength and love. That vision completely overwhelmed his memory of St. Michael's antagonism to Margaret. Christ's benediction was all that mattered, and if Christ Himself blessed his love for Margaret, then Neville needed no higher authority to be convinced he had done the right thing. Besides, had not Margaret said heaven was in disarray? Perhaps even St. Michael had been misled. All knew that angels could be flawed. . . . Was not Satan a fallen angel? Christ had appeared to Neville and had shown him his true path—*to love Margaret*—and Neville understood with every fiber of his being that Christ would never be deceived, could never be tricked.

Although Neville did not yet consciously realize it, his former utter devotion to the archangel St. Michael had suffered a final, fatal blow. Neville's commitment to the archangel had been fractured ever since their meeting on the night of Margaret's rape, when Neville had been racked with pain and guilt and sickened by St. Michael's words of praise for his actions. Now, filled with the memory of Christ's message, as with His love, one of the fundamental pillars of the old, cold Neville crumbled away into nothingness, to be replaced with Christ's message of hope.

Love saves; it does not damn.

He sighed happily, and smiled, and daydreamed about love until Courtenay came and roused him from his bed.

THEY ARRIVED at the Savoy by boat during the early evening of the second Sunday after the Feast of the Epiphany. The horses and the majority of their goods would arrive by road within two days, but Lancaster decided the river approach was not only speedier for the final portion of their journey from Kenilworth, but also much safer.

Everyone in the three boats had held their breath as they'd sailed downriver past Westminster, but they'd passed quietly enough, and none of the faces which undoubtedly watched from the palace windows had raised a hue and cry at their passage.

Lancaster's chamberlain, Simon Kebell, met them at the steps of the Savoy's wharf. His face was drawn, but brightened noticeably as he saw that his lord and companions had arrived safely.

Neville waited until Lancaster, his brother Gloucester, Bolingbroke and Raby had disembarked before he prepared to move to the side of the boat. He had just stood up, and was shaking out his cloak, when he heard Lancaster's voice.

"What?"

Neville looked up. Lancaster—Bolingbroke, Raby and Gloucester about him—was staring at Kebell.

Kebell spoke quietly, too softly for Neville to hear, and even before he'd finished Lancaster and his immediate group were talking furiously among themselves. Raby had gone white, Gloucester flushed—and had moved his hand to his sword—while Bolingbroke, having exchanged a brief word with his father, was now searching the disembarking crowd of retainers and servants for Neville.

Bolingbroke finally caught sight of him, and motioned him forward with an abrupt movement.

"What is it?" Neville asked as he managed to work his way to Bolingbroke's side.

"John is dead," Bolingbroke said.

"Dead? How?"

"It is said one of the street whores so disliked him she fed him poison while she serviced him."

"But—"

A hard-eyed Raby turned from Lancaster and interrupted Neville. "There are men-at-arms who will verify it. They saw the girl atop John's body, saw a goblet in her hand, and found for themselves a vial of poison that she'd secreted in her cloak."

"Was she alone with John?" Neville asked, and Raby and Bolingbroke shared a tight smile.

"Nay," Raby said. "She was not alone with him. Richard and de Vere were also there, jumping up and down and shouting 'Murder!' "

"And what makes me think," Neville said quietly, "that this girl is no longer able to defend herself?"

Now Gloucester joined them as Lancaster strode into the Savoy shouting orders at some servants.

"De Vere killed her even as she began to speak her innocence," Gloucester said.

There was a momentary silence, then Raby spoke. "It is no matter here nor there that John is dead . . ."

"The great matter," Bolingbroke said, "is that Richard and de Vere now commit murder with such impunity. Of a *king*, no less!"

Raby looked between Bolingbroke and Gloucester. "None of us are safe," he said, "but you two are now in the gravest danger. If Richard and de Vere are starting to remove whatever and whoever they see as encumbrances, then your names will surely be close to the top of their list. Perhaps it might be best if . . ."

Gloucester and Bolingbroke shared a look.

"We stay," Bolingbroke said, his face bleak and angry. "I will not run from Richard."

MUCH LATER that night Neville and Bolingbroke stood wrapped in cloaks atop the parapets of the Savoy's river wall. They were staring southeast toward Westminster.

"How can we move against him?" Neville said.

Bolingbroke remained silent.

Neville turned from the distant lights of Westminster and looked at Bolingbroke. The prince's face was strained, his gray eyes angry and frustrated as he gazed southeast.

"We need to talk plain words between us," Neville said quietly, and Bolingbroke blinked and turned himself so he could look at Neville. "We have been too distracted in past months to speak as we need to," Neville continued, "and we must talk now, this night.

"Hal, Richard needs to be removed. He is demonry personified, he is its king, and England will perish if he is allowed to lead it for much longer. But, Christ Jesus, Hal, all we"—Neville's hand swept back over the Savoy, taking in all their allies contained therein—"ever talk of is 'removing,' or of 'moving against.' What do we mean by that, Hal? No one wants to commit themselves to action, nor even to the words that might lead to action. All," Neville's voice tightened in frustration, "people ever talk of is waiting . . . watching . . ."

Bolingbroke turned his eyes back toward Westminster. "We must move against Richard, and it cannot be left for too much longer," he said. "But, Lord Jesus, Tom, you know we must be wary."

"Wary of *what*? Richard's coterie of powerful allies, de Vere and Northumberland and Hotspur at their head?"

"Aye, them most certainly—"

"But it does not take much for a man to sneak into Richard's chamber and slide a dagger into his—"

Bolingbroke whipped about and seized Neville's arm in a tight grip. "You speak the words of a foolish youth. It is easy to see that *you* have had no lessons in statecraft."

Neville's face flushed, but Bolingbroke did not give him a chance to speak.

"Tom, the only way to overthrow Richard is if the entire realm overthrows him. It would be a relatively simple matter to slide that knife between his ribs, or to set fire to his chamber at night, or to cause his stallion to bolt and throw him one fine day. But that would be a disaster."

Neville was still smarting at being called a foolish youth. "In what way?"

"You have seen our instant reaction to the news of John's death—and we were not the only ones to react so. Kebell told us that all London is abuzz with rumor about John's murder . . . and who might or might not have been behind it. If Richard were to die suddenly, and in unusual circumstances, then rumor would envelop his death also.

"Tom, we may know him for what he is, and revile him for it, but the Londoners—all of England's commons—do not! They see him only as the fair young boy elevated by tragic circumstances to the throne. He has their sympathy."

Neville was silent, thinking, and Bolingbroke let his arm go.

"Tom, if Richard were to die suddenly, violently, then all England would believe their fair young king murdered . . . and whoever took the throne after Richard would soon lose it in a baronial uprising riding the surge of popular suspicion and resentment."

"So you say that the commons must be given time enough to come to loathe Richard?" For the moment Neville ignored the implications of 'whoever took the throne after Richard.'

"Aye," Bolingbroke said. "Whoever moves against Richard must do so publicly *and* with the surge of popular opinion behind him, so that other barons will be hesitant to challenge him. It is the only way to succeed."

"If Richard raises this poll tax—"

"—and the commons of England smart under its sting for some months—"

"*Then* will be the time to act."

"Aye," Bolingbroke said again, nodding slowly this time. "When both barons and commons are likely to support a usurper."

Neville watched Bolingbroke very carefully. "And you will be the one to take his place. You plan to be the next King of England, don't you, Hal?"

There was a stiff breeze blowing along the Thames, and it whipped Bolingbroke's silver gilt hair about his forehead and eyes. Apart from the movement of his hair, Bolingbroke was very, very still, and his pale gray eyes steady as they watched Neville.

"Who else?" he said softly.

"Lancaster," Neville said. "Gloucester. They are both in line to the throne before you."

"The commons will never accept my father—they have loathed him for years. And Gloucester . . . Gloucester is not the man to do it. So," Bolingbroke took a deep breath, and Neville realized that this was likely the first time that Bolingbroke had spoken these words aloud, "yes, Tom, I do intend to take the throne of England from Richard."

He hesitated a little. "What say you, Thomas Neville. Are you with me, or against me?"

Neville did not hesitate even for an instant. He dropped to his knee before Bolingbroke, and took one of the prince's hands in his. "I am with you, my Lord of Hereford. I will be your man until death."

Bolingbroke smiled.

Chapter IX

The Monday after Septuagesima
In the first year of the reign of Richard II
(23rd January 1380)

✢

MARGARET HAD a far more relaxed journey south to London than had Neville. Mary (and the other ladies who accompanied them) was pleasant company, the weather was sunny if still bitterly cold, Rosalind was delightful, laughing and crowing at every new sight and, to add to her good temper, Margaret now was almost certain she was pregnant again. She knew this pregnancy would bring difficulties, she knew that Hal would use it eventually to further his (*their*) own cause, but for the moment it simply pleased her. She and Tom had conceived this child amid love and honesty, far from the turmoil and hate of Rosalind's conception.

This time, the birth would also be accomplished amid love and honesty.

Margaret was now so happy, not only with the fact that Neville had openly admitted his love for her, but with the warmth and companionship she'd found within the womanly Lancastrian household, that she no longer truly cared about what machinations Hal might be up to. Margaret knew deep within her that this happiness would not last, knew that, like her time at Halstow Hall, her current contentment was only a breath between screams, but for now that did not matter. There would be some months of happiness ahead of her, months when she could allow the political maneuverings to wash over her, months when she could allow herself only to be contented and loved.

Months when she did not have to think about what would happen when Tom inevitably discovered the truth.

A horrifying, dark depression washed over her, and she drew in a sharp breath and gripped the reins of her palfrey tightly.

"Margaret?" Mary pulled her own mount a little closer to Margaret's. "What ails you?"

Margaret swallowed, and shoved her sudden melancholy back deep within her where it belonged. *It had no right to spoil such a wonderful day, no right to make her sad and afraid when there was no need for it . . . not yet.*

"Ah, my lady, I was thinking of what might be awaiting us in London. Are our husbands safe? What does Richard plan?"

Mary was about to laugh away Margaret's fears when she stopped herself. She couldn't laugh away what was all too real. "I fear for Hal," Mary said softly so that none of the other ladies, or the men-at-arms of their escort, might hear. "He is a man of great ambition."

Grateful to be distracted away from her own fears, Margaret sent Mary a surreptitious glance. She knew something of what had happened between Mary and Hal the past few weeks, and she was glad of it, especially as Mary now seemed so much happier. Even if Hal did not truly love Mary, at least now he seemed to treat her with a gentleness and respect that before he had denied her.

"What has he said to you?" Margaret said. Over the past months Mary and Margaret had become close friends despite the great gap in their social ranks. In private, Margaret now addressed Mary informally, although still respectfully, and felt she could broach most matters with her. Most. Not all. Margaret could not speak of the deep secrets she and Hal shared.

Mary shrugged, and a momentary unhappiness came over

her face. "About his ambitions? Nothing. But I can see and hear, Margaret, and I can think . . . and I know that little stands between Bolingbroke and the throne but Richard."

Now Mary studied Margaret as carefully as Margaret had so recently studied her. "I think I can say this to you, Margaret, for you and Tom have no secrets—"

Margaret's stomach lurched over sickeningly in guilt.

"—and I think Hal is closer to Tom than any other person alive."

Mary had turned her eyes back to the road ahead, and Margaret took the opportunity to briefly close her eyes and try to bring her raging guilt under control.

"I think Hal means to depose Richard," Mary said, whispering now, her eyes darting about to make sure no one else was within hearing range.

"Aye," Margaret said. "I am not surprised to hear those words spoken aloud. My lady . . . you know that Tom and myself have found a peace between ourselves in past weeks, and I know that you and my Lord of Hereford have also. Knowing my own happiness, I am happy for you as well."

There, she had not asked a question, but she had said enough that Mary might respond in kind.

To Margaret's surprise, Mary flushed.

"Margaret, please forgive me for what I now tell you. I have been a fool, and I am so sorry for what I thought—"

"My lady, what is it?"

Mary's flush deepened. "Several nights before Christmastide, my lord came to our chamber very late at night. I was frightened—as you know I have been more than wary of my husband—for I thought that he had been with a mistress."

Now Mary had shocked Margaret. She had known of Mary and Hal's reconciliation, but had no idea that Mary thought Hal kept a mistress. "My lady! My Lord of Hereford surely would not—"

"It is what I *thought*, Margaret! Furthermore, I thought that mistress was you."

Truly shocked, Margaret could only gape at Mary, thinking much the same thing that Bolingbroke had when Mary had told him of her suspicions. *Mary thought I was Hal's mistress, and yet she has never been anything but kind and gentle with me? Sweet Jesu, she is too good for Hal!*

Mary gave a little laugh, and shrugged. "I was wrong, I know, but my accusation opened a door for us, for that night we spent a good deal of time talking—"

"Amid other things, I think," Margaret said.

Now Mary's flush deepened until her cheeks and neck were a bright cherry color. "Aye . . . amid other things. Hal was very forthright with me that night, Margaret, and he eased many of my fears."

"In what way?"

"Well . . . for one, in the manner of the loving that should take place between a man and his wife." Mary gave another little laugh, and laid one of her gloved hands over her stomach. "I do hope that I might soon be with child again, Margaret. This one I *know* I shall carry to term."

Margaret nodded, and smiled, but kept silent. The dark malaise within Mary had strengthened in the past weeks, tightening its grip, and, like Hal, Margaret could now see where it was centered.

No wonder Hal was so sure Mary would never bear him an heir. And no wonder he was now so kind to her in their bed. He could afford it.

"But for the most part," Mary continued, "Hal comforted away the fear that I'd had of him." She laughed a little. "Why, Margaret, I knew he'd harbored cruel thoughts, and I'd thought some of them directed at me. But now I know better."

"I am happy for you," Margaret said, but looked away before Mary could see the sadness in her eyes.

Mary lapsed into silence, presumably contemplating her good fortune in marriage. She stared at the road ahead, all the warmth and joy gone from her day. *Dear Jesus, Mary,* she thought, *what would you do if you knew that one day Hal's thoughts toward you might become worse than cruel if you do not die as promptly as planned?*

As Mary had said, Bolingbroke was indeed an ambitious man.

A DAY later they arrived at the Savoy. Margaret's anxious eyes searched the courtyard for Neville, wondering if the time they'd spent apart had given him the opportunity to regret his admission of love.

But when she saw him striding toward her, his eyes alight with joy, she knew that he did indeed still love her, and she laughed with relief as he swung her down from her palfrey and enclosed her within his arms.

"My lord," she said breathlessly, finally freeing her mouth from his kiss, "you must not be so rough with me!"

"Are you so breakable, my lady?" he said, grinning.

"Not normally," she said, and slid one of his hands between them so it lay sandwiched between their bellies, "but I do think you might want to take a little more care with your son."

Neville's eyes widened, and then he enveloped her in a huge hug. "You are wondrous beyond belief," he whispered.

Across the courtyard, Bolingbroke had turned to watch them as Mary brushed off the travel dust from her cloak, and he did not fail to notice how Margaret had slid Neville's hand to her belly. His eyes narrowed. *So.*

THAT EVENING, after supper, Bolingbroke knocked briefly at the door to Mary's solar, then walked in.

He stopped dead the instant he entered. He couldn't believe his luck: there was no one here save Margaret.

She was sitting close by the fire on a stool, a book of poems dangling in her hand. She was staring at him with the same surprise that he felt, then managed to collect herself and smile. "Hal."

"Where is Mary?" Bolingbroke said, closing the door softly behind him.

"She is gone to chapel with her other ladies."

"And you thought to remain here?"

"You know I would prefer to pray to Christ Jesus anywhere *but* in chapel," she said.

"Aye. And Tom?" Bolingbroke sat down on a bench the other side of the fire. Close, but not too close. No doubt Mary and her ladies would soon return.

Margaret's mouth lifted in a wry smile. "Attending to your household accounts, my lord. They shall make me a widow yet."

Bolingbroke's own mouth lifted in a smile, but it had nothing to do with what Margaret had said. "So, we have a chance for a talk. Finally. It is hard to be alone, you and I."

She inclined her head, but did not speak.

"Tom loves you," Bolingbroke said.

She hesitated, then nodded.

"Good. And, even better, you are with child again."

Again she nodded, her expression far more guarded now.

"When are you due?"

"Michaelmas."

Bolingbroke laughed. "Ah, my dear, I cannot believe it! Did you plan it this way?"

"I am not the manipulator you are, Hal."

"I'm a fighter, Margaret, not a manipulator. And don't forget that I fight for *your* life, as well as for the life of every other one of our brethren!"

"Hal, I am sorry. I spoke poorly."

He inclined his head, accepting her apology.

"Hal . . ."

"Aye?"

"I know that you have fought harder and longer than most . . . save—"

"Do not speak their names, Meg!"

"—well, save those two who come before us. What I wanted to ask you, Hal, was whether you are responsible for Alice."

Bolingbroke frowned. "I cannot understand what you mean."

"Tom's guilt has driven him to admit his love for me, but that guilt has not been occasioned only by what happened to me."

"Ah. Alice. He abandoned Alice, and watched her die, and so now he thinks he cannot do the same to you."

She grimaced. "I hope so, indeed. But, yes, that is what I mean. Alice's fate was very, very convenient for our cause, Hal, for she as much as anyone else has made it possible for Neville to dare to love me. I need to know, Hal. *Did you push Alice into suicide?*"

Bolingbroke looked at her steadily for a long minute before he replied. "Do you think that of me, Margaret?"

She remained silent.

"Sweet Jesu, Margaret, Alice did not only kill herself, she killed her three daughters and her unborn child! *Do you think I would slaughter innocent children?* Do you? Do you?"

"Hal," Margaret said softly and with tears in her eyes, "I have loved you from the moment I first set eyes on you, from the moment I knew you existed in this hell we call life! Do I want to think you murdered Alice to further our cause? No, I do not . . . but in this past year you have become so cold, so calculating . . ."

"Sweet Jesu," Bolingbroke whispered, "the only way we *can* succeed is if I be nothing but cold and calculating! Meg, all I want to do is to take you in my arms and hold you and comfort you and tell you it will all be well. Yet we must be so circumspect—"

At that moment soft laughter sounded outside the door.

"—but believe me, darling woman, *Alice was God's deed, not mine!*"

Margaret took a deep breath, believing him. "Then she was God's great error, my love."

The door opened, and Mary and two of her ladies stepped through.

"Hal!" Mary said.

Bolingbroke swiveled about on the bench and smiled easily at his wife. "I thought to find you here, sweetheart, but found you lost to God instead. Margaret has kept me entertained with some of Chaucer's verses."

Mary returned his smile, accepting his words without doubt. She walked over and sat on the bench beside him, her two ladies taking chairs a little closer to the fire, and soon all five were chatting back and forth about London gossip.

"BLESSED VIRGIN?"

Joan raised her head and looked to the door of her small chamber, keeping her expression sweet. She had hoped to have spent the afternoon in prayer . . .

Her companion, Marie, was in the doorway, her face unsure, her hands twisting before her. "Blessed virgin . . . I am disturbing you. Perhaps—"

"No." Joan rose to her feet and held out a hand. "You do not disturb me, Marie. Come, let us sit on this bench."

They sat down, and Marie hesitated, looking everywhere but at Joan's face.

Joan reached out and took Marie's hands in hers. "Marie? Come, do not be afraid. What is it?"

"Blessed virgin," Marie said in a rush, staring at the floor. "I did not know who else to talk to . . . there is no priest within these walls as holy as you . . . no one else that I may confide in as readily as you."

"You can trust me," Joan said as gently and reassuringly as she could. She no longer minded being disturbed from her prayers. "Marie, come, tell me of what bothers you."

Marie's cheeks flushed, and her eyes jerked from regarding the floor to staring at Joan's face. When she spoke, her words fell over each other in Marie's haste to get them out.

"Blessed virgin, I find this so hard to talk of. I cannot

think of what has happened to me, why I am so afflicted. It is not from want of prayer nor piety—"

"I have never met a maid as holy as you," Joan said, meaning it.

"Not as holy as *you!*" Marie said. "Oh, if only I *were* as holy as you. Then I would never have fallen, never have committed so grievous a sin, never have—"

"Marie, just tell me."

Marie drew in a deep breath. "Holy maid, you know that once I was married, and that my husband died only a few months after our vows?"

Joan nodded.

"I loved and respected him," Marie continued, "I truly did, but I found the intimate nature of the relationship that exists between every husband and wife distasteful."

"This is no sin, Marie. Indeed, your distaste was but an indication of your virtuous soul."

Marie shrugged slightly. "Although I grieved deeply for his death, I was nonetheless relieved that my wifely duties would be no more."

Joan nodded, encouraging Marie to continue.

"But recently, I find that my nights have been disturbed by dreams that are . . . are . . ."

Joan frowned, remembering the night she had gone to tell Charles that his grandfather was dead at the hands of the murderous English. She had seen Marie then, twisting in her sleep as if she lay with a man. "That are what, Marie?"

"That are of a most sensual nature," Marie whispered. Her flush deepened. "Most holy maid, there is worse. What is most abhorrent, most sinful, is that my flesh quivers in delight at these dreams."

Joan looked away, disappointed in Marie. She had hoped that the woman was truly virtuous despite her beauty, but to find she had the wretched soul of a whore was most disappointing. She let go of Marie's hands. "Do you dream of a man, Marie?"

Marie nodded jerkily, tears sliding down her cheeks.

"And whose face does he wear?"

"There is no face, only the weight and the thrusting of his body . . . and . . ."

"And?"

"And sometimes I sense a great golden hand," Marie whispered. "A most beautiful golden hand. It rubs up and down my body. It causes such a great throbbing deep within me that—"

"Enough!" Joan said, appalled at Marie's words. *How could she intimate that St. Michael—*

Joan's thoughts skidded to a horrified halt. Marie had not "intimated" at all. Joan had done that all by herself. She remembered the feeling she had had that night as she watched Marie in her dream, the feeling that St. Michael was close . . .

No! No! It could not be so!

And yet the golden hand . . .

No! No!

"They are but dreams," Joan said very calmly, taking Marie's hands once more in her own. "Perhaps demonic fabrications—"

Yes! That must be it! Catherine, perhaps, sending nightmares to confuse Joan's weak-minded companion in the hope of confusing Joan herself.

"—and we must pray together that you have the strength to resist them."

Yes, these dreams were Catherine's demonry. Nothing else. Nothing else.

Marie's face sagged in relief. "Thank you, blessed virgin, thank you!"

Catherine's demonry . . . nothing else.

ST. MICHAEL came to Joan that night as she prayed. Hesitantly, lest she anger him, Joan told him of her suspicions regarding Catherine.

The demons will throw at you the most devious of impish tricks, Joan. You must be wary always.

A great peace came over Joan. "Yes, blessed saint."

You must trust me, Joan.

"Oh, blessed saint, I do! I do!"

And yet you almost allowed the demon's frightful treachery to trick you.

Joan hung her head. "I shall not do so again, beloved archangel."

You are a good girl, Joan.

IN THE morning Joan asked Marie how she had slept.

Marie smiled. "I slept so soundly, blessed virgin, that I remember not a thing from the moment I laid my head down. I thank you for your aid and concern."

Joan took the woman's face between her hands and kissed it, relieved.

Chapter X

The Thursday within the
Octave of the Conversion of St. Paul
In the first year of the reign of Richard II
(26th January 1380)

— I —

✠

NEVILLE SAT IN the chamber where resided Bolingbroke's official life. The chamber had once been a spacious, light-filled room. Now it was crammed from floor timbers to ceiling plaster with chests, cabinets, stacks of documents, shelves packed with ledgers and accounts, diplomatic correspondence, manuscripts, maps, navigation charts, itineraries, architectural drawings, several engineers' reports, star charts, astrological predictions, medical texts and diagrams, three half-built and two completed clocks, lists of masters and their specialties at the Florentine academies, two newly completed humanist texts and one commentary on the dialogues of Plato, one sack of a newly developed species of wheat grain, a smelly, oily wool fleece, five packets of vegetable seeds and several baskets of sweet apples and pears.

Bolingbroke's interests and responsibilities covered virtually every sphere of human endeavor.

As on most days that Neville spent sorting through Bolingbroke's responsibilities, today he spent as much time cursing Bolingbroke's curiosity as he did sating his own. Bolingbroke had the most extraordinary contacts, especially within the new breed of intellectuals, the humanists and new scientists and mathematicians of northern Italy and Germany, and much of the material they sent into Bolingbroke's household fascinated Neville.

Sometimes, however, Neville could find some of Bolingbroke's attraction for the new slightly uncomfortable. Bolingbroke had, for instance, insisted that all of his household and estate accounts now be managed and written in the new-style Arabic system of numbering which included the recently adopted zero. There was no doubting that the Arabic system was much easier and far less cumbersome than the Roman numeric system . . . but Neville sometimes found himself grinning wryly when he used Arabic numerals himself. His old Dominican Order had been fighting the introduction of the zero for decades, claiming it was the mark of Satan for its representation of "nothingness." Bolingbroke had merely laughed when Neville had reminded him of this, claiming that the Church only railed against the Arabic numeric system because the priests were upset it was the *infidels* who had developed the better and easier system of counting. Bolingbroke was even thinking of extending the use of this new-style numbering system within his household to dating as well, and that Neville found very difficult to accept. Calculating time around the constantly shifting feast days of the annual Christian religious cycle was cumbersome, yes, but it was a familiar and beautiful routine that he wasn't sure should be replaced by cold, heartless numerals.

But worrying whether the days were given saints' names or numbers was not what should be occupying his mind today. There were other numeric computations to set his mind to: Bolingbroke supported as diligently as he received, and this day Neville had to sort out the living expenses of several scholars at the Oxford colleges, one mathematician who worked at one of the Flemish academies and two somewhat eccentric London clockmakers-cum-astrologers-cum-marine-navigators whom Bolingbroke sponsored.

Neville sighed and laid down a report from one of the eccentric London clockmakers, which purported to have found a means to navigate the great western ocean via a mechanical apparatus which could tell both longitude and latitude. Neville thought the entire project highly unlikely—almost as bad as the underwater sailing machine one of Bolingbroke's other pets had come up with last month—but it amused Bolingbroke and presumably kept the clockmaker from developing even more bizarre mechanical oddities which might prove more dangerous than curious. Neville picked up a pen and allocated nine pounds for the eccentric's household expenses in the coming year. That should be plenty enough to keep him warm and fed.

Neville was not alone in the chamber. Two clerks were kept busy at a far desk transcribing the continual correspondence that the life of a great noble generated, another scurried about from shelves to chests to cabinets finding what Neville needed to accomplish his task, while a somewhat nervy Robert Courtenay—turning a dagger over and over in his hand—stood by the door in case Neville required him to fetch anything from beyond the Savoy, and Margaret sat in a chair by the low-burning fire sewing up the seams of one of Neville's shirts and keeping an eye on Rosalind playing at her feet with a large, plump tabby cat that was more than half asleep.

Neville put his pen aside and carefully folded up the report on the navigational aid, slowly running his hand over the creases to make sure it sat as flat as possible for storage, his thoughts far away. The room was warm and comfortable, it was more than pleasant having Margaret and Rosalind here as he worked, and some of these reports and documents he'd sorted through in the hour or two he'd been here had been more than intriguing . . . but, truth be told, Neville would much rather have been somewhere else.

The outcome of the world was being decided somewhere far away from this room—and yet here Neville was, reading of petty things that mattered neither here nor there.

He shifted irritably, and both Courtenay and Margaret glanced at him, but they remained silent, knowing the reason for his exasperation. Indeed, it was why, dagger in hand, Courtenay was shifting from foot to foot himself.

Parliament was even now meeting in the Chapter House of Westminster Abbey. Lancaster, Bolingbroke, Raby and Gloucester had all gone, but there was no room for any of their attendants or retainers, and so Neville had stayed within the Savoy.

Sweet Jesu, but he would give his right arm to know what went on there now.

Richard was attending in order to present to Parliament his request for a new poll tax, so—as he said—he could finance a continued campaign in France. *The last campaign*, he would say, *for surely we will have France on her knees by December!*

But Neville knew that Parliament was not going to accept his explanation at face value. Many suspected that Richard wanted to raise the tax in order to finance a campaign to force the Irish to accept de Vere as their king.

Richard was not going to have an easy task . . . an impossible task, if Gloucester had his way.

Neville reached for another report and unfolded it, his eyes unseeing as they traveled over the closely written lines. Gloucester would hotly oppose the tax as a means of trying to remove de Vere from influence at court, and, moreover, meant to raise the voice of other lords to his cause. Neville was aware that last night Lancaster, Raby and Bolingbroke had spent hours arguing with Gloucester about what would be said and done at Parliament this day. It was not that they didn't agree with Gloucester's opposition, but that they felt a direct attack on Richard, in Parliament, was a more than foolhardy move.

But Gloucester had faith in Parliament, and in its power, as he did in the collective power of the lords there gathered. Parliament had opposed a king and won before. Today, perhaps, it would do so again.

The problem was, Neville thought as he smoothed out the report for the tenth time, *who among the lords were demons, and who were god-fearing men?*

THE DAY passed agonizingly slowly, and it wasn't until the bells rang for Vespers and Neville was reaching for an intriguing unopened casket under his table that he heard horses clatter into the courtyard. The casket forgotten, Neville rose so quickly and violently from his desk that documents scattered across the floor. Margaret and Rosalind had long gone, Margaret to sit with Mary and Rosalind to be put to bed by Agnes, and the three clerks had also left for their residences. Courtenay was the only one left to keep Neville company.

As Neville ran out the door, Courtenay was directly behind him.

The courtyard was filled with horses—far more men had come back to the Savoy than had left it this morning. Besides the Lancastrian party, Neville recognized Warwick and Arundel, both great nobles who had met secretly with Lancaster in the storage chamber of the Savoy that night some three months ago. There were others, too, that Neville did not recognize—some patently lords, others attendants to those lords—sweet Jesu!

Suddenly Neville caught sight of his uncle. He pushed his way through men and horses, grabbing at Raby's arm.

"Uncle? *What happened?*"

Raby turned about to face him, and Neville gasped at the haggard look on Raby's face.

"Gloucester made a stand," he said, wasting no words on pretty narratives. "Many among the lords listened to him. Parliament has adjourned to discuss the poll tax, but the general consensus seems to be that it shall not be allowed. Richard . . . Richard is furious."

Neville could imagine. "What will—" he started, then got no further.

Raby had turned and was now shouting through the throng to Gloucester. "My lord! My lord! This way!"

And Neville suddenly realized what was going on. Richard was so enraged that all now feared for Gloucester's life. Raby, as just about everyone else, it appeared, was endeavoring to remove Gloucester from London as fast as possible. Thus the crowd. Gloucester would surely be safer in a crowd than anywhere else.

Whatever the plans, Gloucester was apparently having none of them. Both Lancaster and Arundel were by his side, but Gloucester was angrily refusing their requests that he make his way to the waiting barge. He thrust aside Lancaster's frantic pleas and Arundel's desperate hand, and started to shove his way through the throng.

Neville could see Lancaster and Arundel move after him, as also Bolingbroke who was several paces distant.

Then, just for an instant, all were lost amid the throng of milling horses and men and—

—and Neville remembered Lancaster and Gloucester try-

ing to make their their way through the dancing carollers to their father that Christmas Day a year past—

—Neville screamed a warning, punching aside two men who blocked his vision, but even as he pushed past he was struck by the shoulder of a plunging horse and he almost fell to the ground. Just as he regained his balance, and was shoving forward again, he heard shouts, frantic shouts, a desperate scuffling of boots, several grunts as men had the breath knocked out of them, and a strange clatter as if of a knife falling to the cobbles . . .

The crowd parted and Neville stumbled into open space. Directly before him lay two still, bloodied bodies on the cobbles.

Gloucester and Arundel.

Lancaster, who was kneeling beside his brother's lifeless body, slowly raised his head, staring with unseeing eyes at Neville who was directly before him.

The duke raised his hands, and they were covered in blood.

"Has Richard this much power," he whispered, "that he can strike into the heart of my family? Is he this confident?"

Chapter XI

The Thursday within the
Octave of the Conversion of St. Paul
In the first year of the reign of Richard II
(26th January 1380)

— II —

✢

FOR A LONG MINUTE no one spoke, no one moved. All stared at the two corpses and Lancaster kneeling above them, looking bewildered at the blood covering his hands.

It was no man who broke the stillness and silence, but Mary.

She had walked unseen from the door leading into the Savoy, pushed unremarked through the throng, and only seemed to enter Neville's field of vision as she knelt down by Lancaster.

Mary laid a hand on his arm. "Father. We can do naught here. We must move them inside, into a state fit for their nobility."

It was not her movement, nor even her manner of addressing Lancaster, but the gentleness with which she spoke that seemed to break the spell binding the courtyard.

Lancaster blinked, lowered his hands, and turned to stare at Mary. The bewildered expression had vanished, replaced by a profound rage—although it was not directed at Mary.

"There is nothing you can do here for them," Mary said, holding her father-in-law's eyes, "but everything you can do for them elsewhere."

Margaret had now materialized behind them, and Mary turned her head slightly to speak to her.

"Have two trestle tables set up in the great hall. We can lay them there."

Margaret nodded, and vanished, and as she did so, Mary helped Lancaster rise to his feet.

Now the courtyard crowd began to murmur and swell. Men shifted and whispered, then some moved to shout accusations and grab at suspects.

But none, thought Neville, *had moved so well nor so quickly as Mary. Why is it always the women who so brilliantly oversee the gateways of birth and death?*

For a moment Neville's thoughts drifted away. There was something about the way Mary had knelt at Lancaster's side, something in her posture . . .

"Tom?"

Bolingbroke. Neville jerked out of his momentary reverie and turned as Hal reached his side. The prince was pale and shaking; shocked not so much at the deaths, Neville thought, but at Richard's audacity in arranging the assassinations, not only in Lancaster's house, but under his very nose.

"Who?" Neville said softly.

Bolingbroke shook his head, obviously fighting for control of himself. "I do not know," he said. "There were so many people about, so many voices, so many bodies . . . I don't know. Oh Lord Christ Savior, Neville. I had not thought Richard would dare to move so quick—"

"Hal, Tom, inside . . . *now!*" Raby walked between them and gave each a none-too-gentle shove toward the courtyard door of the Savoy.

"Ralph—" said Bolingbroke.

"Quick," Neville said, joining his uncle in pulling Bolingbroke toward the door. *The assassins might still be in the vicinity.*

Bolingbroke regained some of his sense just as they stepped over the threshold and he shook off Tom's and Raby's hands.

"The hall," Raby said.

Men-at-arms had carried in the corpses and arranged them on the trestle tables that Margaret had caused to be set up. Mary and Margaret wiped off the worst of the blood from the corpses, and rearranged their clothes neatly.

Once they had done, Lancaster dismissed everyone from the hall save Raby, Thomas Beauchamp—the Earl of Warwick—and Bolingbroke and Neville.

Lancaster still had not wiped the blood from his own hands, and now, as he stood at the head of both the tables, he raised them to chest height and looked at the four men standing about.

"Richard has gone too far," he said in a flat voice. "This," he moved a hand toward the two corpses, "is not the action of a misguided youth, but of a man of evil. Neville, Hal, you warned me against Richard many months ago. I did not listen to you. This . . . this is the result."

He dropped his hands. "I listen now. Nay, I am prepared to do *more* than listen."

Warwick glanced at Bolingbroke, then spoke. "My lord, there are many who will support you, but there are also many who will not. Richard has considerable strength behind him: de Vere, and all that unnatural sycophant's allies and flatterers; Northumberland, who will be glad enough to watch both you and Raby trodden into the gutter, and all *his* allies." Warwick mentioned five or six other names, all great peers of the realm who brought with them scores of lesser nobles. "And Richard has the support of the Church," Warwick finished, "and the Church regards you with suspicion because of your protection of Wycliffe."

Neville glanced at Bolingbroke, but neither said anything.

"And your point is . . . ?" Lancaster said.

"My point, my lord, is that while the support you can muster is greater than can any single man within this kingdom, including Richard, it is not greater than the combined support of those who will stand behind Richard."

"Parliament?" Lancaster said.

"Once they hear of Gloucester and Arundel's deaths," Bolingbroke said, "Parliament will piss itself in order to please Richard. Gloucester was the backbone of its dissent against the poll tax, Arundel his greatest supporter. They are now dead. No one will rush to take their place."

"Richard will further strengthen himself with Gloucester and Arundel's lands," Raby added. "Now, even more will back Richard in the hope that he might pass on those lands and titles to them."

"He wouldn't dare to take Gloucester's lands!" Lancaster said.

No one spoke.

"Oh dear God," Lancaster said tiredly. He sighed, then resumed speaking in a stronger voice. "Richard's strength will wane. It must. Sooner or later he is going to make an error of judgment and alienate half the nobles of England with one stroke. When he does that . . . we must be ready."

"Ready for what, father?" Bolingbroke said.

Lancaster hesitated, decades of loyalty and obedience to both his father and brother screaming at him not to speak these words of treason. He straightened, and something of his old strength came back into his face.

"Ready to depose Richard, should it come to that. If we don't, then he will destroy this realm."

"And you think to take his place?" Warwick said, very carefully.

Lancaster gave a small smile. "Nay, not I, Warwick. I am too old, and too tired." He nodded at Bolingbroke. "England needs my son, not me."

Chapter XII

The Feast of St. Chad
In the first year of the reign of Richard II
(Friday 2nd March 1380)

✠

THEY LAY IN utter silence and stillness in that strange halfway place between the world of waking and the world of sleep. Their limbs were entwined, their bodies heavy and languid. There was no need to move, no need to speak, and barely the need to even breathe, wrapped in the complete realm of each other and the encompassing bed.

Neville could feel the faint beat of Margaret's heart through her ribcage where it pressed against his chest, could feel the faint rise and fall of her breast with each breath. Underneath his right hand, which rested on her belly, he fancied in his dream world that he could feel the heartbeat of the child within, perhaps even the gentle rise and fall of its chest as it breathed in Margaret's goodness.

A son, she said. Neville did not disbelieve her. She was of the angels, a magical, sinless creation of heaven, and she had the power to know of what she carried within her body. Neville had a brief urge to smile, but he was too warm and lazy to complete the movement. Instead he sent a grateful—and somewhat sleep-muddled—prayer to the Lord Jesus Christ for His goodness in sending Margaret to him and for His goodness in making Neville understand that love was nothing to be afraid of.

How many years did I waste, he thought, *in denying myself love? How many cold, dark years did I spend running from it?* These days, when he rose to wakefulness with his body curled about Margaret's, that thought was almost always at the forefront of his mind. His vision of Christ had affected him so deeply, and had moved him so profoundly, that Neville wondered if he'd actually become a different man. He was so changed from the man who had allowed Alice to die, so changed from the cold, heartless man who had affected to abhor love.

He rarely thought about St. Michael, and then only in passing. He was still committed to his mission, but now that mission had become Christ's mission rather than that of St. Michael.

Thank you, Lord Jesus Christ, for your blessing, Neville prayed silently, feeling an overwhelming gratefulness for Christ's care sweep through him. *Thank you, Lord Jesus Christ, thank you . . .*

He snuggled closer to Margaret, wrapping his arms tighter about her, and finally smiling as she murmured sleepily before slipping back into her doze. He could hardly comprehend his fortune in having this beautiful, heaven-sent woman to love and who loved him in return. It was *beyond* fortune that she had already given him one child and now carried another.

"Christ sent you to me," he whispered in her hair, now moving his hand from her belly to her breasts. How could he have believed she was his enemy, and *demon*-sent? How could he have believed those lies that it was mankind's doom if he ever chose her before God's cause? St. Michael must have been muddled, perhaps misled by demonic craftiness. It were better, far better, to listen to what Christ had spoken to him.

His hand massaged Margaret's breasts a little more firmly. They still had time for love before Agnes bustled in with Rosalind for their morning cuddle, still time before Robert Courtenay arrived to help his master wash and dress, still time before the sorrows of the world intruded and reminded Neville that today would be yet another slow step toward his ultimate goal of removing Richard and his demonic conspirators from power.

"Margaret," he whispered into her hair, "wake up."

She murmured again, and very slowly stretched as she turned onto her back.

Neville almost groaned at the feel of her moving against his body, and he leaned over her, bringing her to full wakefulness with a deep kiss.

His hand squeezed her breast, and pinched her nipple.

"Tom," she said, wincing. "Don't."

He was instantly contrite, remembering too late how tender her breasts were now that she was with child. He murmured an apology, kissing her sweetly, and stroking away her hurt.

She relaxed, and then moved so lasciviously against him that Neville wasted no more time on preliminaries. He rolled atop her, smiling and kissing her as she parted her legs, and then slid deep inside her, groaning softly with pleasure as he did so.

"Tom?"

Neville pulled away so violently that Margaret cried out, and clutched the bed covers to her.

"Tom? Margaret? Have I disturbed you?"

Neville sat up in the bed, pulling his own share of the covers over his lap, and silently cursed Bolingbroke. "Yes," he said.

Bolingbroke did not even grin. He walked silently enough into the room, but now closed the door with a thud, and strode across the chamber.

"Then you have my apologies," Bolingbroke said, "but this is news that could not wait for your morning's loving."

Margaret blushed, and lowered her eyes, but Neville forgot his irritation at Bolingbroke's sober face. "News?" he said.

"Aye." Bolingbroke sat on Neville's side of the bed. "News has reached us from France. News of Hotspur."

"Yes?"

"Hotspur has 'dealt' with Limoges in the manner he saw fit."

Bolingbroke paused, and neither Neville nor Margaret, both with their eyes fixed on Bolingbroke's face, spoke.

"He burned it to the ground," Bolingbroke said, and his eyes flickered Margaret's way. "And he slaughtered every man, woman and child within its walls."

"Oh, Hal!" Margaret said. "No! Not the children."

The news was so shocking that it did not even register with Neville that Margaret had addressed Bolingbroke so familiarly. "Why?" Neville said. "Surely Hotspur need not have been so cruel?"

"He had *every* need!" Bolingbroke said, and clenched his right hand into a fist where it lay on his thigh. "Hotspur wanted to impress Richard, he needed a victory to carry home for Richard, and so," Bolingbroke spoke with deliberation, saying each word slowly, and with infinite anger, "he slaughtered every craftsman, every wife, every babe in arms within Limoges."

Margaret, her hand to her mouth, had begun to weep silently. "The children . . ." she whispered. "Why? *Why?*"

"Have I not just said why?" Bolingbroke shouted, and Margaret jumped at his anger.

"Hal—" Neville said, but got no further.

"Lord Christ," Bolingbroke said. "I am sorry, Margaret. I had no cause to shout at you. It's just . . ."

"It is just that these are truly dreadful tidings," she said, accepting his apology, and knowing the pain he would be feeling. Men took their own chances in wars which they too often began, and to some degree so did their wives. But children . . . children were so innocent! To heartlessly slaughter them . . .

"When will it end?" Bolingbroke said softly. "How?"

"Where is Hotspur now?" Neville said.

"Marching north, looking for more"—Bolingbroke's voice hardened into sarcasm—"military glories."

He paused. "He is marching toward Orleans. He thinks to take that in Richard's name."

AS BOLINGBROKE left Neville jumped from the bed and began to pull on his clothes.

For the moment, Margaret stayed where she was, watching with worried eyes as Neville dressed.

"Can't Bolingbroke do something?" she said.

Neville sat down on the bed with a thump and pulled his boots on—*damn? Where was Courtenay when he needed him? The man had picked a fine morning to sleep in!*

"Do what?" he said, then cursed as he caught his thumb under one of the boot hooks.

"Something about Richard," Margaret said.

Neville glanced at her. "What?" he said again, irritably, then sighed. "Ah, my love, you have had every man in creation snap at you this morning, have you not? I am sorry for my ill-temper."

"I thought that Bolingbroke and Lancaster . . ." Margaret drifted off, not wanting to actually voice the words of treason. Neville had confided in her what had been said over Gloucester's and Arundel's corpses, but had said little since.

Neville stopped fussing with his boots and turned to look at his wife. "It takes time, Margaret. Neither Hal nor Lancaster is strong enough—not even combined—to . . . well, to challenge Richard. Richard has many men, and many powerful men, behind him. Now he has Parliament as well."

Parliament had been so shocked—and so frightened—by the ease of Gloucester's death that it had acquiesced to Richard regarding the poll tax. Neville had heard that even now tax collectors were moving through the counties collecting six pence for every household. It was not much—a day's wage, perhaps—but it was enough to cause resentment.

"I cannot believe that all England has cowered before Richard," Margaret said.

"Nay. All England has not. There are many men who believe he should be curtailed, at the least. But Margaret, we are talking of raising a coalition against the throne, and that is never easy to do. Good men always hesitate before they can be persuaded to act against the established order. Richard is the anointed king, and opposition will take weeks, perhaps months, to forge into an effective weapon."

"Months," Margaret whispered, and Neville saw that she slid her hand beneath the covers to cover her belly.

He leaned over the bed, and kissed her. "We will be safe," he said. "Do not fear."

" 'We will be safe,' " she echoed. " 'Do not fear.' Is that something you whispered over Gloucester's and Arundel's bodies, Tom?"

THERE WAS nothing to be done, save to listen as London whispered and gossiped about the news from France. Generally, the whispers were prideful: Hotspur had won a brilliant victory against the French, and was even now marching to the north to slaughter every last breathing man, woman and child of the hateful French race.

The Londoners had never had a great deal of sympathy for their eastern neighbors.

Neville spent an hour or so talking with Bolingbroke and Lancaster, but then somewhat desolately wandered back to his duties. Book work waited for no man, and there was correspondence regarding Bolingbroke's five wards that needed to be attended to before the monies for the wards' education and the upkeep of their households became due on Lady Day.

But Neville had barely bent his head to the first of the wards' financial matters when Courtenay opened the door to the chamber and interrupted him.

"My lord? I am sorry, but—"

He got no further as a man squeezed through the door and walked past Courtenay.

Neville rose to his feet, a grin spreading across his face despite his best efforts. "Master Tusser!"

Tusser bowed, then straightened. His face was knotted up into an expression of utmost urgency; he had no conception that there might be worldly matters more important than the daily running of Lord Neville's estates.

"I have brought the accounts!" Tusser said, and deposited several large volumes on the table before Neville.

Neville looked at them, then raised his face and, most unfortunately, caught Courtenay's look of amusement at Tusser's self-importance before Neville could say something appropriately serious.

His lips twitched, then Neville burst into laughter, stifling it only when he saw the injury in Tusser's eyes.

"I am sorry, Master Tusser," Neville said, and waved for Courtenay to leave them. "It has been a strange day and I have responded to your arrival most inappropriately. I am glad you are here. News of Halstow Hall and its concerns will be welcome indeed after the machinations I must endure in London."

Somewhat mollified, Tusser pulled up a stool to the table and sat down, accepting the goblet of watered wine that Neville offered him.

"I have ridden hard and long to bring you these accounts," Tusser said.

"I know, Master Tusser, and I really am sorry—"

"I should be home, overseeing the barley crop, and making sure the men harrow properly, because if they don't then the crop will be lost to the crows. And there are the hops to be set . . . I should be there for that . . . and the grafting to start . . . but, no, here I am. 'He'll be more than glad to see me personally,' I thought—"

"Tusser—"

" 'and glad to see how well I have looked after the accounts of *all* his estates,' but, no, you only laugh when—"

"Tusser, I am most *truly* sorry!"

Tusser lapsed into a sulky silence, and to fill the quiet Neville slid the first of the heavy books toward him and opened it. He scanned the first three or four folios, feeling guiltier at each entry read, for Tusser had indeed done a fine job with his accounting, and had deserved much better than Neville's laughter.

"I am most well-served in you," Neville said quietly, and closed the book, "and Margaret will be sad indeed to hear how I have repaid your service."

Tusser's mouth lost a little of its sulkiness. "The Lady Margaret is here?"

"Indeed, and close to her quickening with our second child." Neville had shared the news with very few people, but felt that offering Tusser such an intimacy might go some small way to repairing the injury to the man's feelings.

Tusser's face cracked in a broad smile. "My lord, you are so blessed!"

Now Neville's face relaxed into a smile and his eyes into softness. "I am indeed," he said.

"Now," his manner became brisk, "perhaps you could give me a brief overall accounting before the bells ring for Nones. Then Margaret will, I am sure, be happy to fuss over you and provide a fine feast to soothe away your travel weariness."

Having finally decided to forgive Neville, Tusser happily launched into a summary of the noteworthy events on Neville's four estates, and an account of the harvesting of the previous autumn. Neville had known of the harvests from Tusser's communications to him while he'd been at Kenilworth, but now his steward filled in the gaps. They were talking of the need to hire more men to cope with the early summer haying on Halstow Hall's extensive meadowlands when Neville first realized the worry in Tusser's eyes.

"Master Tusser?" Neville said, leaning forward a little over the table. "Why the concern?"

Tusser did not immediately answer. His fingers drummed softly on the open accounting book he had before him, and his brow furrowed.

"It may be nothing," he said eventually.

"But?"

"But . . . my lord, this poll tax has stirred the peasants grievously."

"Has it caused hardship?"

"Only in a few cases, my lord, but that is not what stirs the men to anger."

Neville waited.

"My lord," now Tusser leaned forward, staring anxiously at Neville, "you know how wages have risen ever since the time of the great pestilence."

Neville nodded. So many had died during the pestilence that those laborers who survived had demanded, and received, higher wages along with a reduction in rents and, in some cases, complete freedom from feudal bonds. Many a family had improved its lot in life.

Tusser's air of anxiety deepened. "But for years ordinary men have felt that the nobles and Parliament were only waiting their chance to beat the commons back into the mud of bondage again. Men now fear that this poll tax is the first shot in the war to re-impose feudal dues and conditions."

"It was *Richard* who pushed this tax," said Neville.

Tusser shrugged. "But it is Parliament and the nobles who are being blamed. My lord, I fear this coming summer."

"Why?"

Tusser caught Neville's eyes and held their gaze steadily. "There is talk, my lord, of a rising. Men feel they must make a stand against a Parliament which seeks to reimpose feudal restrictions. They will refuse to pay this poll tax."

"A rising? But they cannot hope to succeed!" Neville thought of Wat Tyler. Was he behind this talk?

"Furthermore, there is a belief," Tusser said, "that if Richard only knew how greatly the commons resented this tax he would rescind it."

Neville almost laughed. Richard? Rescind the poll tax through sympathy for the common man?

"He is as likely to slaughter them," he said, and then wondered why he'd said that.

If Richard was truly the Demon-King, wouldn't he rather they succeed?

Chapter XIII

Passion Sunday
In the first year of the reign of Richard II
(11th March 1380)

✠

FOR MONTHS Joan had wondered how Thomas fared, deep within the demons' camp. Now she wept in sorrow as St. Michael stood before her, telling of Thomas' surrender to the demon Margaret.

"How can he have allowed himself to be so seduced?" she said, clasping her hands before her as she knelt.

Thomas is a man, and weak in the ways of the flesh. He does not have the strength of your virginal flesh. The demon has convinced him that she is pure and good, and Thomas believes her.

"Then we are lost." Joan had no way of understanding that the archangel was not as distraught at Tom's situation as he appeared to be.

Anger seethed out toward her, and Joan quailed. "Forgive my doubts, blessed saint!"

Do not think that we have not planned for this.

Joan was so terrified by the archangel's anger that she could not answer.

Thomas only does what we expected. Soon enough he will

learn of the extent to which he has been betrayed . . . and then . . . then there is always the great Secret, waiting to be revealed.

"Great secret, blessed saint?"

Now amusement radiated toward her, and Joan felt the goodness of the archangel's benevolence.

Thomas is a Beloved. On that day, the day when he learns what that means, and what awaits him, and how he has been betrayed, then Thomas will not fail you nor me. Believe it.

"Most assuredly, Blessed Saint Michael."

It is a most seductive Secret, Joan, and Thomas has already shown himself readily enough seduced.

"Your paths are most wondrously wrought, blessed saint."

St. Michael thought about that last remark, wondering if Joan wasn't trying to pretend a little too much understanding. *Be still, Joan. I must speak to you of a thing other than Thomas' weak flesh.*

"Yes, blessed saint?" Joan said.

I have already spoken to you of the significance of Orleans.

"Yes, blessed saint."

Soon one of the damned Englishmen will lead an army against Orleans. They will attempt to strangle that proud city with a foul siege. It is time to make a first strike. You shall tell Charles that you will lead the French army to Orleans, where you shall raise the English siege. It shall be a magnificent victory.

Joan said nothing, but raised her clasped hands before her face as she stared at the archangel with shining, fanatical eyes.

After Orleans you will ride to Rheims, where you shall crown Charles king of France.

"Blessed saint!"

From that time, your victories shall be legion. You will drive the English from this land, and then . . .

"Yes, blessed archangel?"

Then, once France has roused behind you, you shall lead

the armies of God across the seas and into the den of the Demon-King himself.

Joan was so overcome with awe and humility that God had chosen her for this cause, that she could not speak.

Beware, Joan. There are many who conspire against you.

"They shall not harm me. I have their measure."

Ah, Joan, I pray that it be so. But this Demon-King is cunning beyond our understanding. What seems like trap might be clear path, and what seems like clear path might lead to death.

He paused, and considered the girl before him. There was something else she needed to be told, but it should not be he who would do the telling.

As Joan stared at the archangel she was amazed to realize that two glowing figures stood before her. At one moment there had been just St. Michael, the next . . .

"Blessed Saint Gabriel!" she cried, and bent her forehead to the floor, now almost completely overcome.

Blessed child, said Gabriel, *there is much mischief about, as well you know, but I fear that you may not recognize the worst of it.*

Joan remained silent, waiting for the archangel to finish.

Beware Catherine, Gabriel continued, *for she is evil beyond compare.*

"Most blessed saint," Joan whispered, "I have felt her vileness." She tried to quash the smugness that welled within her, but failed miserably. She resolved to say a prayer for Catherine's sluttish soul.

She is cunning, and will trap you, said Gabriel.

"With your help," Joan whispered, "I will not allow myself to be trapped." She was strong. She would prevail. She knew it.

You are sweetness personified, Gabriel whispered into her mind, and with her head still bowed, Joan could not see that the archangel's hand hovered over her head . . . and now down her back, barely above her body, and now close to the side of her robe where swelled her breast . . .

She moved slightly, and the hand sprang back.

Michael resumed. *You are God's own, Joan, and as you lead the French to victory you shall carry the mark of His favor.*

There was a change in the light, a subtle dappling, and before Joan could even draw a breath of surprise she saw that a massive square of white cloth had appeared on the floor before her.

It was a battle standard.

There was a design embroidered in its center, and Joan had to squint a little in the glow of the archangels to make it out.

At the top-center of the design was a face wearing great and utter fury, and Joan understood this face to be that of the King of Heaven. Underneath this face stood two archangels: St. Michael and St. Gabriel, and in their arms they held the earth. About all were woven fleurs-de-lis—Charles' own emblem.

Carry that standard, said the archangel Michael, *and all shall fall before you.*

"Charles will resist," Joan said. "He is weak."

You must make him strong, said Gabriel. *Tell him that on your march southeast a miracle will take place to further demonstrate that you and he walk in God's grace and that ultimate victory shall come about.*

"Blessed saint, what miracle?"

Bending close, the archangels told her.

Chapter XIV

Maundy Thursday
In the first year of the reign of Richard II
(22nd March 1380)

— I —

✠

HOLY WEEK and the Easter celebrations approached, and London was crowded with pilgrims, pedlars, traders, thieves, prostitutes and every rank of society between peer of the realm and homeless riffraff. Among all the repentant—and unrepentant—sinners who pushed their way through one of London's eight gates was a black-robed, hard-faced Dominican.

Prior General Richard Thorseby, recently arrived from the continent, had a wad of documents under his arm that he dare not entrust to the two friars who now escorted him. Thorseby walked with a pronounced limp, the remaining vestiges of his frostbite, and his cheeks were wan and sweating, a legacy of the rough Channel crossing.

Infirm in body he might be, but there was nothing weak or wan in the determination of his mind, or in the belief in the righteousness of his cause.

Thorseby made his way first to Blackfriars, the London home of the Dominicans. Set into the western wall of London, and bounded at its north by Ludgate prison and at its south by the gray waters of the Thames, Blackfriars was a huge, jumbled mass of dark and forbidding buildings, and Thorseby felt at home here as nowhere else.

But he did not linger.

Having briefly greeted the prior of Blackfriars, and then taken some refreshment, Thorseby made his way to the small pier in the southern wall of the friary and boarded a rowboat.

He sat down, not greeting the oarsman, and carefully wrapped his cloak about him.

The boat moved slowly upriver, the northern bank of the Thames on Thorseby's right hand.

He kept his eyes ahead the entire trip, save for when the boat passed the Savoy. There, Thorseby turned his head and stared at the magnificent palace rising behind its river wall.

Are you there? he thought. *Enjoying your last, lingering days of freedom?*

The oarsman continued to row, and the boat turned south with the bend in the Thames.

Eventually the palace at Westminster hove into view, and Thorseby's grip tightened in its hold on the edge of the boat.

RICHARD ADMITTED the Prior General only with reluctance. The man depressed him, and always looked upon him as if he knew Richard's innermost and most deviant sins . . . and that irritated Richard.

But the Prior General had sent word that he had important information regarding Bolingbroke's household, information the king would most surely appreciate, and so Richard had finally acquiesced.

"Dear Lord," he muttered to de Vere, sitting next to him on the dais in the Painted Chamber on a chair so intricately carved it was almost a throne in its own right, "why couldn't he have picked a less hectic time?"

De Vere smiled, and laid a hand on Richard's where it rested on the arm of his throne. "If he gives us something with which to attack Hal, my dear sweet boy, then there should be *no* time too hectic for us to see him."

"True," Richard said, thinking about admonishing de Vere for calling him a "dear sweet boy" before deciding it wasn't worth the effort. Besides, he rather liked it, and it was far better to think about how he might punish Hal when he finally had him in his power. Richard sighed quietly, wishing he could have moved against Lancaster and Bolingbroke long before, but both men—and their coterie of allies—were still too powerful for him to attack without very good cause.

Bolingbroke was far too popular with the ever-cursed mob, and Lancaster still commanded too much respect among the other nobles for any to move directly against them.

Still, Hal's time would come . . . and Richard did not think it would be much longer in the coming.

He wondered vaguely who it was had done away with Gloucester and Arundel, so saving himself the trouble, then his mind snapped back to Bolingbroke as his eye caught movement at the far end of the chamber.

"I want a charge of treason," Richard said, as Thorseby's black limping figure entered the far door of the Painted Chamber, pausing to bow deeply.

"A charge of picking his nose is going to be enough if it gives us cause to take Bolingbroke," said de Vere. His beautiful dark eyes gleamed even brighter than usual, and he leaned forward very slightly in his chair as Thorseby continued to walk toward them.

"I'd prefer *treason*," said Richard.

"Your grace," de Vere murmured as Thorseby approached, "may I suggest we take whatever he offers?"

Thorseby halted before the dais, and de Vere smiled genially. "Prior General," he said, "your presence, as always, is the greatest of gifts to my dear lord, as to myself."

Thorseby forced a returning smile and inclined his head very slightly in acknowledgment. *Lord Jesu, how he despised these two sodomites.*

He spoke some general pleasantries and flatteries, then

got straight to the point as he saw irritation and impatience spread in equal quantities across Richard's face.

"Your grace," Thorseby said, inclining head and shoulders this time, "I come before you this most holy of days to petition you for a special favor."

Richard almost snarled at the disagreeable man. No charge of treason against Bolingbroke then? He just wanted a *favor?*

"My Lord Bolingbroke, Duke of Hereford, has taken into his household a most evil man."

Richard's face lost some of its anger, and he sat a little straighter on his throne. "Aye?"

"Bolingbroke has, as his personal secretary, a man called—"

"Thomas Neville," said Richard. "Yes, yes, get on with it, man."

Thorseby pursed his lips and sent Richard an irritated look of his own. "Yes, Thomas Neville. As you must know, Neville was once a member of my Order—"

"Until he found he preferred fornicating to praying," de Vere said.

Richard laughed, enjoying the mortification on Thorseby's face.

Thorseby took a deep breath. "Yes, until he found he preferred the sins of fornication. Your grace, it has come to my attention that Neville is a most dangerous man, and I would request your favor in granting me aid to bring him under the disciplinary rule of my Order."

"A most dangerous man?" said de Vere very softly. He, also, was now perched on the very edge of his chair, as if he thought to spring forward at any instant. "In what manner?"

"I suspect Neville of the most profound heresy," Thorseby said. He paused for effect. "As well as treason."

Silence.

"Heresy?" said Richard. "Treason?"

"Indeed, your grace. For many months I have suspected that Neville might well be associated with the Lollards and their arch-heretic leader, John Wycliffe. After all, he does reside in Lancaster's household, and we all know—"

"Get on with it!"

"But what I did not realize until most recently," Thorseby continued, "was that while Neville was in Europe he not only consorted with demons—"

Both Richard and de Vere laughed, if a little uneasily.

"—but also consorted with Etienne Marcel, who I am sure you are aware was—"

"Marcel?" Richard said, glancing at de Vere. "The instigator of the Parisian rebellion?"

"The very same, your grace. The man who suggested that power be taken from the king and be given to the commons."

"And you have proof of Neville's association with Marcel?" de Vere said.

"Aye, my lord. A witness to attest to the contractual bond between them. Your grace and my lord, undoubtedly Neville is committed to furthering the same cause here. He is dangerous in the extreme. It would surely be to your betterment, as well that of my Order, if Neville be taken into custody."

There was a silence as Richard first stared at Thorseby, and then at de Vere.

"Perhaps so," de Vere finally said slowly. "But I think it would be best if, for the moment, Neville be arrested only on a charge of heresy. I do not doubt your charge of treason, Prior General, but if Neville be involved, then what of others within the Lancastrian household? Lancaster? Bolingbroke?"

"And if we take Neville on charges of stirring the masses into treason against their king," Richard continued, "then we forewarn Bolingbroke and Lancaster before we have the evidence to move against them as well. But if, for the moment, we merely aid the good Prior General to extricate Neville from Lancastrian protection into Dominican care on a charge of heresy, then we disguise our moves and meaning."

He smiled at Thorseby, hardly able to contain his excitement. *I have you!* he thought. *I have you, fair Prince Hal!*

"You have done very well, Prior General," he said, deciding he rather liked Thorseby, after all. "Very well. Your favor is granted, with the proviso that during your inquisition of Neville you find evidence to also implicate his master, Hal Bolingbroke. So . . . how may I best assist you?"

BOLINGBROKE AND his household attended evening mass in St. Paul's rather than remaining within the anonymity of the Savoy's chapel. Neville had cautioned him against it, but Bolingbroke believed there would be no trouble. How could Richard move against him when he was cushioned by the adoration of the Londoners?

As they left the cathedral, its bells pealing joyously across London, Bolingbroke—Mary on his arm—turned and saluted the yelling and cheering people on the steps and crowding the courtyard.

"Is this not a merry day?" Bolingbroke said, turning to grin at Neville and Margaret.

"You can be sure that Richard shall hear about it," Neville said.

"Ah," said Bolingbroke, "today I care not about . . . *sweet Jesu, Tom, watch your back*!"

The crowds around them had suddenly parted as if a giant hand had swept them aside. Where there had been a solid cheering mass behind Neville and Margaret, now there were the pikes and reaching hands of at least forty heavily armed soldiers.

Neville's first thought was to push Margaret out of harm's way, his second a stunned realization that these men had come, not for Bolingbroke, but for him.

Chaos exploded about him.

At the same time that Neville had pushed Margaret, Mary had stepped forward and wrenched Margaret into her arms, pulling her well back from the men-at-arms.

Margaret struggled, crying out with fear for her husband, but Mary held her tight.

Bolingbroke had not worn a sword this day, and now he cursed his stupidity. He stepped forward, grabbing at the pike of the first soldier who approached Neville.

Robert Courtenay and Roger Salisbury, who had both been waiting with the horses at the foot of the cathedral steps for their masters, let go the reins and sprang up the steps, drawing the swords that they, at the least, had had enough forethought to wear.

The crowd roared, thinking only that Bolingbroke was being attacked.

The men-at-arms pressed forward, four of them grabbing Neville, the others surrounding him.

"I command you set him free," Bolingbroke shouted, losing his grip on the pike he held and stumbling back.

Courtenay and Salisbury had now reached his side, but stood impotently, unsure what to do.

The sergeant of the men-at-arms stepped forward and bowed deferentially at Bolingbroke.

"My lord," he said, "I do you a favor." Then he raised his face and shouted at the crowd. "I come for Neville, not Bolingbroke! Neville is a traitor to his master, and puts him in great danger."

The crowd retreated slightly, muttering and murmuring in great swells. What cared they about this Neville?

"He lies!" shouted Bolingbroke, incredulous and angry in equal amounts.

"What charge?" Neville said. "*What* charge? And who brings it?"

"A charge of heresy," said the sergeant, no longer deferential. "Brought by Prior General Thorseby." The sergeant paused, assessing the situation and the mood of the onlookers, and decided that some inventiveness was called for. "As well as a charge of plotting the downfall of my Lord of Bolingbroke—"

"He lies!" cried Bolingbroke again, his voice now charged with desperation.

The crowd did not listen to him. Neville? A traitor to their fair Prince Hal? Their murmuring increased, their mood darkened.

"Tom!" Margaret screamed, still struggling with Mary.

"You are to be taken to Blackfriars," the sergeant said, somewhat relieved now that the mood of the crowd had been deflected away from himself and his men. "There to face an inquisitory panel led by—"

"Thorseby," Neville snarled, and met Bolingbroke's eyes across the forest of pikes that surrounded him. *Thorseby, but partnered by Richard's ill-will.*

"Aye," said the sergeant.

"Are we to have a burning?" asked a hopeful voice from somewhere several faces back in the crowd.

"No!" Margaret screamed.

Neville still held Bolingbroke's eyes. "Take care of her," he said, "for me."

And then the pikemen wrenched him away, half dragging him down the steps of St. Paul's.

Margaret finally managed to jerk herself free of Mary and grabbed at Bolingbroke.

He did not look at her, his eyes still on Neville being hauled further and further away.

"Do something!" Margaret said to him.

"What?" Bolingbroke snapped, finally looking at her. "Send Robert and Roger to their deaths at the end of forty pikes?"

"Hal, *save him!*" Margaret whispered.

"For Christ's sake, woman!" Bolingbroke snarled back at her. "Be grateful that he is going to Blackfriars where Thorseby will, at the least, observe the formality of an inquisitory panel and then, perhaps, a trial, rather than the dungeons of the Tower, or Ludgate, where he would be dead before nightfall at the swords of Richard's lackies!"

He looked at Courtenay, standing helpless several paces

away, his sword dangling impotently, and still staring to where Neville had disappeared.

"Robert?" Bolingbroke said. "Come, aid your mistress here. We must return to the Savoy as soon as we may.

"Margaret," he spoke quietly in her ear as Courtenay approached. "Be sure that I will do all that I can to free your husband."

Margaret made a helpless gesture, and began to weep.

Bolingbroke turned away from her and stared at the dark smudge of Blackfriars.

Damn Richard to all the fires of hell!

"YOU CAN do nothing," Lancaster said.

"I cannot leave him there!"

"Hal," Lancaster said as gently, yet as firmly, as he could. "You have no choice."

Bolingbroke looked at his father, then walked away a few paces, staring sightlessly at a book of hours that his father had open on a lectern.

"Richard wants nothing more than that you should make some grand gesture to free Neville," Lancaster continued.

"I *cannot* leave him—"

"He will be in relatively little danger, Hal—"

"Unless Thorseby suddenly finds him guilty of a flammable heresy."

Lancaster looked at his son carefully. "*Should* he find him so guilty, Hal?"

Bolingbroke turned about. "No . . . no. Of course not."

"Thorseby will eventually allow him free. I will have the matter raised in Parliament."

Bolingbroke flashed his father a cynical look, and Lancaster's temper frayed.

"I will raise the matter in Parliament, Hal, and I will speak to the sergeant of the clerks of the King's Bench. I will appeal wherever I can . . . but right now, appeal is *all* we can do. You must resign yourself to the fact that for the moment Tom is under the stewardship of the Dominican Prior General with the backing of the king. There is nothing you can do against such power, Hal. Nothing."

He paused. "Not without giving Richard good reason to throw you in the Tower for flouting the law. Hal, do you understand me? Do you?"

Bolingbroke stared at his father, then jerked his head in assent.

Chapter XV

Maundy Thursday
In the first year of the reign of Richard II
(22nd March 1380)

— II —

✠

JOAN STOOD before Charles, and he slid his eyes this way and that, not wanting to hear again what she had been telling him these past ten days.

Raise an English siege of Orleans?

"We are not strong enough," he said, for what seemed to Joan like the hundred and fiftieth time.

"We will have God and His archangels to fight for us," Joan said, as she always said when he claimed they would not be strong enough.

Charles pouted, trying to hide his fear. He did not want to fight, he did not want to be king (it was just like his grandfather to go and die while enjoying the English king's hospitality), he simply wanted to be left in peace so that he might enjoy those things in life he most appreciated. For one thing, music; the soothing ballads of the ancient troubadours and the stirring phrases of more modern historians.

He most certainly did not want to be God's chosen. Not anymore. It had been exciting when Joan had first appeared . . . but now . . . now it all seemed so dangerous.

Charles envied Philip of Navarre. Philip was a man born to be a king—gallant, handsome, courageous. He was amusing, spending hours allowing Charles to win at chess, and regaling him with the stories of his womanly conquests. And Philip was compliant. When Philip had united with Charles to retake Paris two years previously he had readily agreed to Charles' suggestion that Philip be the one to lead their forces through the gates and into the thick of the fight while Charles guarded the rear from his tent.

Charles liked Philip.

But Charles had a horrible suspicion that Joan was going to want *Charles* to participate in the French action against whoever awaited at Orleans, an action that was going to involve a battle with hardened English warriors rather than disorganized urban craftsmen.

Joan's eyes narrowed as she watched the emotions play over Charles' face. By now she knew well enough what he was thinking: he did not want to fight.

Joan thought that contemptible. Charles needed to be strong. France needed a powerful sovereign, not some weak-kneed fellow who wept when he nicked his chin on the edge of his morning razor.

"*You* lead the army," Charles said. "You're the saint, not I."

Joan almost lost her temper. "I will carry the archangels' standard at the head of the army, yes, but France also needs to know that *you* are there. They need to know that they have a king who will lead them from this cursed English occupation."

Charles dropped his eyes. "I cannot."

"But—"

"I will not." His voice raised to an almost-shout. "After all, I am king, am I not? I can do whatever I like, can I not? I can say and—"

"If you are not there then Philip of Navarre will walk out of Orleans as king—not you!" Joan yelled. "God has chosen you, and you may *not* deny God!"

Charles lapsed into a sulky silence.

Joan took a deep breath, hating to make the concession, but knowing she had to.

"Ride with us," she said in a tone rich with cynicism, "but perhaps it might be best—to protect your gallant self, of course—if, for the battle, you remained in some nearby secure stronghold. Then, once all is won, you may ride forth to receive the cheers of the good folk of Orleans."

Charles brightened, suddenly having a vision of himself riding into Orleans in the guise of savior.

"Are you sure I won't have to fight?" he said.

Joan sighed. "I am sure no one could ever make you fight," she said.

Charles' bowels suddenly clenched. "When do we have to leave?"

This time Joan's sigh was even deeper. "Not yet," she said. "The archangels will tell me when it is best."

And she knew why the archangels waited: *it would be best when the English were at their most dispirited.*

It was not only the French Joan hoped to impress with her victory at Orleans. She would also be sending a powerful message to the English and their dog-cursed Demon-King.

Chapter XVI

Easter Tuesday
In the first year of the reign of Richard II
(27th March 1380)

✠

THREE DAYS AFTER Joan had managed to persuade Charles to at least ride with the French force to a point somewhere vaguely close to Orleans, Hotspur was moving his own force into position around the city.

Like Charles, Hotspur was riven with doubts, but ones that Charles would be barely able to comprehend. Hotspur *wanted* to fight, he *wanted* to feel the sweat of battle about him and to hear the cries of his enemies at the point of his sword . . . but his master, Richard, appeared intent on making it impossible for him to succeed.

This wasn't how it was supposed to be.

Hotspur had grabbed at Richard's offer that he lead an English expedition to aid Count Pedro of Catalonia. It had the potential to not only expand England's influence in the area (where both Richard and the Percys believed that Lancaster held too much influence via his influence in Castile) but to expand Hotspur's reputation twenty-fold. Hitherto, Hotspur's renown had been built entirely on his efforts against the cursed Scots, and while that was good, he would prefer to win wider renown with a continental victory or two.

He'd set off for Bordeaux in high spirits, but continual delays, caused by Richard's parsimonious attitude toward actually releasing the funds needed to pay for the expedition, had meant he'd not even left Bordeaux before Pedro had solved his problems on his own.

Hotspur had been left simmering in port while, he had no doubt, the Lancastrian faction at home had been laughing over the rims of their wine cups.

When Richard had sent word of Limoges, Hotspur had led his force out of Bordeaux within two days, needing to vent his anger and embarrassment in whatever way he could.

Limoges had suffered terribly, and somewhere within him Hotspur knew he had treated the city and its inhabitants too harshly.

But he'd needed something to hit out at, he had needed something to counter the Lancastrian laughter, and so he had murdered the entire population of the small city. Murdered them because they had announced their loyalty to their home prince, and to this saintly virgin, the Maid of France.

Sometimes, at night, Hotspur woke screaming from nightmares that were filled with smoke and the stench of screaming, roasting flesh, nightmares where he did not know if he was standing watching Limoges burn, or standing trapped in hell.

Perhaps there was no difference.

And so, again at Richard's prompting, Hotspur had marched north to take the city of Orleans. Here, perhaps, he could ensure that his name be wrapped in glory rather than the horror of Limoges.

Hotspur *knew* he could take Orleans . . . if not for Richard. The force Hotspur had assembled in Bordeaux and then marched north was relatively small, some eight or nine thousand men—it had, after all, only been meant to aid an insignificant Spanish count. Hotspur did not have the numbers or the equipment or the supplies necessary to establish a successful siege around a city such as Orleans.

Now, this Easter Tuesday, Hotspur sat his horse some

three miles distance from the city, his commanders about him, staring silently toward the city.

Orleans sat on the northern bank of the Loire river. The city had four land gates, and one river gate reached by a substantial (and substantially defended) bridge that stretched from the southern bank of the Loire.

The commander of the French garrison at Orleans had ensured that all the gates were well bolted hours before the first sight of the approaching English.

Well, at that Hotspur was not surprised. On their own the gates did not perturb him overmuch—starving men tended to unbolt gates more quickly than their well-fed counterparts. The trick was to ensure that Orleans starved before any French reinforcements arrived. (Who? The panicky and cowardly Charles? This saintly maid that Hotspur had heard so much about?) Hotspur knew that the city would be well-stocked, perhaps enough to keep hunger at bay for two or three months, but his task would be to ensure that no fresh supplies reached the good folk of the city.

And that Hotspur was not sure he could do.

The walls of Orleans were so well defended by high towers and thousands of men that, for the protection of his own soldiers, Hotspur needed to keep his siege fortifications back half a mile, probably more. That meant he would have to stretch his men in a huge circle about the city . . . and he did not have the men to do that without leaving them dangerously vulnerable.

The upshot of all this meant he would not be able to encircle the city completely. Instead, Hotspur would have to place his men in well-defended garrisons at key placements along the roads (all bloody twelve of them!) approaching the city in order to stop food supplies or reinforcements getting through.

And then there was the river . . .

And he did not have the men to do it!

"Damn it!" Hotspur muttered, and his commanders glanced at him, not envying him his position.

"Is there no word from Richard?" Hotspur asked Lord Thomas Scales, one of his immediate subordinates. In the weeks since Richard had ordered Hotspur to march on Orleans, Hotspur had lost count of the messages he'd sent back to his king requesting—and, finally, pleading—for more men, more supplies, more equipment . . . more aid, *damn it!*

"Nothing, my lord," Scales said.

"Prick," Hotspur muttered, knowing that Scales was aware he didn't refer to him. Somewhere deep inside, Hotspur knew that Orleans was going to turn into a complete disaster.

And he had a feeling all his men knew it, too.

PART FOUR

The Hurtyng Tyme

And in Kyng Richardes regne the commons arose up in diverse places of the realm and did them much harme the which they called the hurtyng tyme.

—Chronicles of England, 1475

Oh miserable men, hateful both to land and sea, unworthy even to live, you ask to be put on an equality with your lords! . . . Serfs you were and serfs you are; you shall remain in bondage, not such as you have hitherto been subject to, but incomparably viler.

—Richard II's response to the rebels' demands

Chapter I

The Monday before Corpus Christi
In the second year of the reign of Richard II
(21st May 1380)

✠

IT WAS A HOT DAY, the last gasp of spring before the sweat and labor of summer fell upon the land. Wat Tyler paused on the small rise, catching his breath and wiping the perspiration from his face and neck with the sleeve of his undershirt.

Flying grubs buzzed about him, and the sun beat down mercilessly. He waved the insects away, and looked at the countryside stretched before him.

Fields and pastures shimmered in the heat, broken up by the twistings of narrow, silvery streams, the broader expanses of fish ponds, straggling stands of woodland, dusty boundary lanes and even dustier roads. Most of the fields were dotted with figures, and carts laden with hay and bound sheaves of grain wound slowly and tortuously along three of the laneways.

Here, in the heart of the garden of England, the home county of Kent, men and women labored from sunrise to sundown to battle the pests and weeds that threatened their ripening crops.

Tyler squinted into the sun, shading his eyes with a hand. Ah, there. The small hamlet of Barming and, several miles further into the distance, the hazy smudge that marked the town of Maidstone.

But Maidstone could wait. For the moment, Barming was

Tyler's destination. He had slipped quietly and secretively through here some time past, laying the seeds of revolution. For long months now, he and Jack Trueman had individually been through scores of other villages in Kent and in the county of Essex which lay just north above the Thames. Others of their kind had been through many more communities. Murmuring, questioning, feeding doubts and stoking fears.

Tyler glanced behind him, even though he knew he would see nothing.

Somewhere behind him, several days' journey distant, were two tax collectors, wending their way through Kent to raise Richard's bastard poll tax.

They would never get past Barming.

Tyler grunted, half smiling at the thought, and turned back to the road before him. He started down the rise, but his thoughts were now removed from the landscape before him.

Instead, they were with Hal Bolingbroke.

For most of their adult lives Bolingbroke and Tyler, as so many others, had been working toward the same goal: the goal that the angels were prepared to move heaven to prevent. But even though they wanted to achieve the same end, Tyler and Bolingbroke were divided as to how best to achieve this goal. Tyler, like Etienne Marcel, advocated outright revolt using the misery of the ordinary people; Bolingbroke preferred the twisting dim alleys of subtlety and falsehood. While Bolingbroke did agree with Tyler that the commonality needed to be freed from the social, economic and clerical shackles that bound them, he scorned Tyler's idea of inciting open violence and rebellion, thinking it would create more problems than it would solve. Instead, Bolingbroke spun delicate webs of intrigue and deception among the powerful nobility; better a slow redirection within the top echelons of society than a catastrophic revolution from below.

Tyler did not think he could wait any longer for Bolingbroke's subtle plans to ripen into full fruition. He had given Bolingbroke long enough. Besides, Tyler was sure that Bolingbroke had missed his chance, that he should have made his move when Edward III and the Black Prince died. Sweet Jesu, even Catherine had turned to another man.

Bolingbroke was running out of time and opportunity, and Tyler knew it. Richard was moving from strength to strength. Despised he might be, but Richard still enjoyed the support of Parliament and many of the nobles, even if that support had been gained through fear. Those who sympathized with Bolingbroke were, as yet, reluctant to move . . . and every day they left it, the move would become harder, more foolhardy, less likely to succeed.

Well, if Bolingbroke's plans lay in tatters, then he, Tyler, must needs take charge.

Rebellion. The masses rising for their rights as human beings: freedom to make the choices that would ensure their family's well-being, freedom to choose their path in life, freedom to shape, not only their own destiny, but the destiny of their country . . . the right to call themselves free men and women . . . the right to throw off the fetters that millennia of lords and priests had draped about them.

Freedom from the crippling chains of the angels.

Sudden tears pricked Tyler's eyes. Freedom for the common man would be so hard to achieve, and Tyler was perfectly aware that the next few weeks could end in his death, as Etienne Marcel's struggle had ended in his death.

Then he sighed, and pushed away his maudlin thoughts. Better to think of John Ball who had spent the past nine months rotting in Canterbury's prison.

Time, soon, to set him and his glorious talents free. Tyler smiled grimly, and stepped out down the road.

JACK STRAW straightened, dropping his weeding hook and rubbing his aching back as he did so. A man was walking down the track between the two fields, waving as he saw Jack rise and look.

Jack frowned, squinting. Who was it? Not any of the men from his village . . . nor any from the neighboring estates.

He was just about to curse, thinking the stranger a wandering friar or priest looking for free board and food, when the stranger lifted the hat from his head and waved it vigorously about.

Jack's suspicious expression vanished, and he laughed. "Wat!" he called, and strode to greet the man.

THAT NIGHT they sat around the fire in the house of one of Barming's most respected husbandmen, John Hales. There were some twelve men present besides Tyler, Straw and Hales: eight of these men were from Barming, one was a craftsman from Maidstone, one a villager from Allington just to the north of Barming, and the last two were men from the village of East Farley which lay a mile or so to the south.

The talk was quiet-toned, but rich-hued with violence and resentment.

These were men who had grown to adulthood raised on the stories of their fathers and grandfathers, stories which told of the ancient, and anciently despised, feudal bonds and dues; bridles and manacles designed to keep men from bettering their lot in life. But these men, raised in the labor shortage and subsequent opportunities created by the ravages of the pestilence, had grown to maturity knowing personal freedom lay within their grasp.

Yet every time their lords—whether of the nobility or Church—tried to reimpose the ancient bonds of serfdom, that tantalizing glimpse drifted farther and farther beyond their reach.

"Parliament wants nothing more than to grind us back into the hell of eternal serfdom," growled one man.

Just as the angels want to tighten the chains of heaven, thought Tyler.

"Aye. They have their townhouses and fat purses," said another, "but what do we have? A lifetime of backbreaking labor to wrap *them* in furs and silks."

"A lifetime of paying heavy taxes to keep them safe and warm more like," said Jack Straw. "A lifetime of taxes so heavy that we have no time nor chance to better ourselves."

"Yet are they not born the same way we are?" said Tyler softly, his eyes shifting from face to face as he fanned the fires of revolution. "Do they not eat and shit and fornicate in the same manner as we? What right do they have to call themselves better men than us? By what right do they hold *us* in servitude?"

There were growls of assent among the men.

"By the right of the damned Church," said one. "Every time we beg for a chance to improve our lot, fat clerics heave themselves into their pulpits and tell us that it is God's will that we work, God's will that we sleep with the grubs, God's fucking *will* that they lord it above us!"

"After all," mocked Hales, "shall that not get us a place in heaven?"

Someone laughed, and it was not a pleasant sound. "Nay," the man said, and spat. "Never! Do not the priests sadly inform us that we are such horrible sinners we shall spend eternity burning in hell?"

"Unless we plan ahead by paying them in heavy gold for an escape, of course," someone said.

"Are we not all useless fools," said Tyler, "for sitting about this fire mouthing empty words but doing nothing else?"

Silence.

"In several days' time two tax collectors will arrive in Barming," said Tyler. "My friends, all around England this night good men like yourselves are sitting about their fires cursing the affliction of the poll tax that Parliament has added to the already onerous burden of labor and dues we carry through life. All they need, all we need, is someone to make a stand."

Again, silence.

"Perhaps if we took our grievances to good King Richard," said Jack Straw. "Perhaps he does not understand the burden good Englishmen labor under. If he knew, perhaps he could set it to rights."

"Aye!" came a chorus of voices. "If only Richard knew!"

"Perhaps it *is* time we made a stand," Hales said.

"We will aid you," said one of the men from East Farley.

"And we!" said the man from Allington.

"The whole country will rise, my friends," said Tyler, "for this is a good and just cause."

"What day did you say those tax collectors would be arriving?" asked Hales.

Chapter II

The Feast of St. Bede
In the second year of the reign of Richard II
(Monday 28th May 1380)

✠

"MY LORD?"

Neville whipped about from the narrow window he'd been staring through. Sweet Jesu, he'd been so wrapped in his thoughts he'd not even heard the door open.

"Robert!" Neville crossed the cold floor of the cell in three strides and embraced Courtenay in a great hug.

Eventually Neville stood back, although he kept his hands locked on Courtenay's shoulders. Neville grinned even as his eyes filled with tears. "My God, Robert," he said, "I had thought never to see you again, nor any other loved face."

Courtenay likewise had tears in his eyes. In past months he had come to love his previously dour master, and these previous two months had seen him become gaunt and haggard with his worry.

"Margaret?" Neville said, his grin fading. "Is she well?"

Courtenay nodded. "Aye, my lord, although she weeps for you daily." He tried to smile, but couldn't.

"And Rosalind? And the new child?" Neville said.

"Safe, my lord. Rosalind wanders the courtyard and stables looking for you—"

"Sweet Jesu, Robert! You do not let her wander among the horses?"

"No, no, my lord. Either Agnes or myself is with her at all times. But she frets for you, and seeks you in every shadowed place."

Neville let Courtenay's shoulders go and turned away, trying to surreptitiously wipe away his tears. "And the new child grows safe?" he said quietly.

"Aye. My lady says that she is well past her early months of sickening, but lies sleepless at night with the kicking of the child and with her worry for you. My lord, she sends you her deepest love, and wishes that she could come to you as I do."

Neville took a deep breath, the worst of his worries eased, and turned to face Courtenay again. "And how is it that my gaolers have let you through?"

"Either myself or Roger Salisbury have come to Blackfriars daily, my lord, demanding entrance and a few minutes spent with you. My Lord Bolingbroke, as Lancaster, has spent countless hours seeking aid and explanations as well. But, until today, to no avail. The Prior General," Courtenay's voice hardened, "had wrapped you in chains so tight that none could get through."

Thorseby and Richard, Neville thought, but, as Hal had said to Margaret, he also knew that his life was safer—for the moment—in Blackfriars than it might be somewhere else where Richard could move against him more freely.

"And today . . . ?" Neville said.

"Today a friar came for me before dawn, saying that I was to bring fresh clothing and a razor." Courtenay indicated a bundle that he'd dropped at the door.

Neville nodded, also observing the shadow lingering outside the open door. Everything said within this chamber would be noted.

He tipped his head to the shadow, catching Courtenay's eye, and his squire gave a single nod. *I will be careful.*

"Well, for the fresh clothes and the razor I am more than grateful," Neville said, his hand rubbing his full beard ruefully. "The friars have thus far thought it best for me to wallow in my own uncleanliness."

As if on cue a lay servant of Blackfriars entered the cell carrying a steaming bucket of water and some cloths. He stood the bucket at the foot of the bed, dropped the cloths, and left.

He did not once look at Neville or Courtenay.

"Thorseby has given me plenty and more time to wallow in my own thoughts as well," Neville said, starting to strip away his filthy clothes.

"They have not questioned you yet, my lord?" Courtenay took Neville's clothes and folded them with a grimace of distaste.

"Nay, although this sudden desire to make me clean also makes me think that a questioning is not far distant. Thorseby has heretofore allowed himself the pleasure of making me wait." He bent and wrung out a cloth in the hot water, and scrubbed at his face. "Ah, Lord Jesus Christ, that is good!"

Courtenay took another cloth in hand, wet it and soaped it well, and washed down Neville's back and legs. "At least you have not succumbed to an infestation of lice, my lord."

"Hush, Robert. If Thorseby hears of my escape he shall send a pailful of them down!"

Courtenay laughed, and for a few minutes neither spoke as they washed away the grime of Neville's two months incarceration. Then Neville sat on a stool and allowed Courtenay to take the razor and cut his hair, and trim his beard back close to his cheeks and chin.

"Robert," he said quietly, catching Courtenay's eye and then looking to where the shadow still shifted beyond the door. "What news? I am as starved of news as I am of fresh air and my wife's love."

"My lord, where to start?"

"At home, Robert, then move outward."

"Aye, my lord. Well . . ." Courtenay paused as he clipped away carefully at Neville's chin, "my Lady Margaret tells me that my Lady of Hereford is with child."

"Mary? Ah, that is news that will gladden Hal's heart."

Courtenay shrugged. Bolingbroke had been smiles and cheer when Courtenay had heard him discuss Mary's pregnancy, but Courtenay had thought there was something artificial about Bolingbroke's cheerfulness. Ah well, who was he, a bachelor, to judge the words of a husband?

"Lancaster has been ill with a late-winter chill," Courtenay said, turning his mind from Bolingbroke, "and with missing his lady wife."

"Katherine still lingers in the north?"

"Aye. Raby also has spent some five weeks in the north seeing to his affairs." Courtenay grinned. "He is back in London now . . . and it is said that his wife Joan again grows big with child."

Neville laughed. "Poor Joan!" Then he sobered. "But Lancaster . . ."

"It is only a chill, my lord, and he recovers well."

"Good. And Bolingbroke?"

"Missing you sorely, my lord, and has been beyond grief that he cannot save you."

Courtenay hesitated, and Neville waited.

"Bolingbroke has spent hours haunting Richard's court," Courtenay finally continued, "begging and threatening whoever he is able to come to your aid."

"He has not put himself in danger with Richard, surely."

"He would have done so, my lord, save that Lancaster

sent Raby to forcibly return Bolingbroke to the Savoy. My lord, be sure that if there was a way you might have been freed, then Bolingbroke would have found it."

Neville nodded, thinking of all that Courtenay was not saying. Bolingbroke would have ranted and raved, and only Lancaster's cautious hand would have kept him from storming Blackfriars to release Neville.

And Richard's ill-will would have stayed Bolingbroke's hand in every other way. Neville sighed. Bolingbroke would be frantic with both worry and frustration, knowing that if he so much as looked at Blackfriars when riding by it might give Richard the excuse he needed to accuse Bolingbroke of treason.

And I must be more than careful what I say when brought before Thorseby, Neville thought as he tilted his head to one side to allow Courtenay to chip away at his left jaw, *for everything that comes from my mouth will be reported to Richard who will try and trap Bolingbroke through my words.*

"There was a great celebration held on May Day," Courtenay continued, "when our blessed king rode in state through the streets."

Neville caught Courtenay's eye and grinned—"our blessed king" indeed!

"I heard," Neville said, "although I could not see. This window overlooks nothing but a bare patch of the Thames."

"There has been news from France," Courtenay said.

"Aye?"

"Hotspur has closed the pincers of his army about Orleans, and some say he will take it for Richard within the month."

"What have the French done?"

"Little, my lord. There have been rumors that the maid Joan has been urging Charles to march south, but that the man has found a thousand different reasons to delay thus far."

Neville grunted. God Himself would have trouble frightening Charles into action.

"And there have been troubling reports from Essex and Kent, my lord."

Neville's eyes jerked upward. "What reports?"

Courtenay's eyes flickered to the doorway, and Neville barely managed to keep his frustration under control. *Damn those listening ears.*

"London is abuzz with rumor," Courtenay said, finally wiping clean the razor and packing it away: he would have to show it to the guards on his way out to prove he hadn't left a potential weapon with Neville.

"Rumors of *what?*"

"Of bands of angry men, talking strange words of freedom from servility."

Neville waited as Courtenay searched for the right and careful combination of words.

"It is said," Courtenay said, handing Neville his clean underclothes, "that these men speak of marching on London to present their grievances to good King Richard."

Neville stared at his squire, understanding the words, but not knowing the deeper meaning that Courtenay wanted to convey.

His squire returned Neville's stare in full measure. "Many good folk are terrified," Courtenay said carefully, "of the inevitable chaos of looting and burning should the mob invade London. My lord Bolingbroke is very concerned about the traitors and the murderers that might be set free."

Neville nodded, slowly drawing on his underclothes while he thought. If this mob did come to London, then the opportunity would be there for every scoundrel to use the ensuing chaos to garner for himself what he would.

And Neville had no doubt that Blackfriars would be one of the first places attacked.

By the most friendly of scoundrels, of course.

He almost smiled, then thought of the greater implications and jerked to his feet. "Sweet Jesus, Robert! Get Margaret and Rosalind out of the city! If this is as bad as you suggest, then—"

"I will do my best, my lord, but your lady wife will probably refuse to leave without you."

Neville grabbed Courtenay by the shoulders. "Robert—"

"I will do my *best*, my lord!"

And with that Neville nodded, trying to put out of his mind a vision of Margaret and Rosalind being trampled under the pounding feet of an out-of-control mob, or burning to death as the rebels set fire to the city.

"Enlist the aid of Bolingbroke," Neville said. "If Bolingbroke can't get Margaret to leave, then no one can."

Now Courtenay nodded, and held out Neville's tunic. "Come, my lord, you cannot go to meet your accusers dressed only in your underpants."

Neville did not manage to raise even the smallest of smiles.

Chapter III

The Tuesday and Wednesday within the Octave of Corpus Christi
In the second year of the reign of Richard II
(29th and 30th May 1380)

✠

THE MOOD OF rural England was grim but still, barely, controllable. Tyler thought it like a dark lake with seething undercurrents—apparently calm, but likely to explode into uncontrollable fury at any moment.

He, as all of his, had been laying the seeds for this uprising for years, but Tyler had never thought the uprising might grow beyond his control . . . and that thought terrified him.

Since he'd arrived in Barming some nine days ago events had moved swiftly. From Barming, men and whispers had spread like twisting carp through the still waters of peasant England. The whispers, the call to action, had rippled out from other villages, too, for many of Tyler's cousins and kin had been waiting for the mind-thought from him, and were ready to agitate the waters.

The two tax collectors who arrived in Barming seven days ago had not left. Their corpses were even now feeding the fishes in their breeding ponds.

They were not the only two to die. Other tax collectors lay rotting in field and furrow across Essex, Surrey, Sussex and Suffolk.

Peasant men began to band together into their tens, then their scores, and then their hundreds. At first they milled about their home fields, then, as their numbers grew, moved more purposefully toward major towns and cities.

Where lay more tax collectors, and the men who directed them.

As men banded together both their sense of resentment and their sense of purpose grew stronger. The poll tax had been the final burden—the indignity that would set the dark waters rolling out of the lake in a great, destructive tidal wave—but it was not the only grievance. The commons of England realized that this might be their only chance to force their overlords to grant them the same rights and freedoms under law that the nobles and clerics enjoyed.

So, as these growing bands of pike- and stave-wielding men murmured and rumbled their ways down the lanes and roads of the home counties, they added other objectives to the initial intention to voice their grievance about the poll tax. They remembered the deeds and documents stored in courts and manor houses by which their overlords claimed the legal right to bond them to the soil. They remembered the weeks and months they had to spend working their lords' lands when they could more profitably have been working their own.

They remembered that the great clerics of England lived in luxury funded by the peasants' sweat and toil. They remembered the pennies they had to pay to the local priests every time they wanted their babies baptised, or their parents buried, and the pennies and taxes they had to pay to ensure their salvation.

And all these pennies went out of England and to the fat, corrupt cow of a *Roman* Church, the laughing stock of all honest men now that two (or was it three, or even five or six?) popes squabbled among themselves for the right to speak the words of God.

And the right to control the massive wealth the Church plundered from honest country men and women who merely wanted a better life in the next world to the one they endured here.

Well, perhaps it was time to ensure that *this* world was the better one, instead of listening to the seductive words of lords and priests who told them that it was God's will they suffer in this life so that they might have a greater chance at salvation in the next.

With these men of the land marched renegade priests and friars, who fed them ideas and visions of a future that inflamed their already raging resentment at the lords and clerics of England. Who needed this great hierarchy of priests when all you needed for salvation was an understanding of the Bible? It was no wonder that the *Roman* Church refused to allow the Holy Scriptures to be translated out of Latin and into the words of the common people! The great Master Wycliffe surely spoke sense when he said that the corrupt Church existed in such a state of sin that it no longer had God's mandate to control so much wealth and land. And so *much* land. The Church of Rome owned fully a third of the land in England. Why did the Church need that if not to feed the corrupt and luxurious lifestyles of the higher clergy?

Perhaps the land and wealth of this foreign, uncaring and dissolute Church could be shared out among the people.

And so, as these groups marched and merged, their anger grew to unprecedented proportions. They had to make a stand—now!—or both the nobles and the higher clergy would grind them back into the dust of slavery forever.

No one stood in their way as they marched. England's army was in France, or in the north to keep the ever-cursed Scots in their misty hills and fens. Local militias were too small to cope with these murderous bands of peasants . . . or too willing to join them.

All that the lords could do was send frantic messages to Westminster pleading for aid—and then run for their lives.

Some didn't make it.

THE ANGER and this willingness to fight for freedom filled Tyler's soul with joy, but at the same time he feared that the rising mass of commons might seethe out of control. This huge, murmuring beast—still split into groups spread over the southeast of England—had to be kept in check in order to be effective . . . and Tyler had not thought it would be so difficult, nor that the beast would prove so savage.

Having murdered the two tax collectors, the men from Barming had picked up whatever might best serve them as weapons—pikes and staves, as also bows and quivers full of arrows and swords to supplement the knives that all men carried at their waist—and merged with men from the villages in their immediate vicinity: East and West Farley, Allington, Aylesforde, Ditton and East Mallyng.

Having collected in a field some two miles from Maidstone, the band—numbering some two hundred men—then marched on the town itself.

It "fell" with nary a struggle. Not only was Maidstone unwalled and largely undefended, the band was welcomed by the majority of the townsmen who had suffered under the burden of taxes and personal restrictions almost as much as their rural cousins.

Maidstone's small prison was attacked, the jailers murdered, and the prisoners set free.

The local court building was burned to the ground, together with all the manorial deeds and documents it held, and the throng shouted with delight as they watched almost five hundred years' worth of feudal records being destroyed.

Having dealt with the props which upheld their landlords' claim to lands and labor, the mob turned its attention to those who laid claim to their souls. The Maidstone priest having fled, the mob marched out of the town half a mile southeast to Milgate Abbey where they ravaged and burned deep into the night, murdering the few monks who were too old and lame to run for their lives.

It was here, finally, that Tyler managed to regain some semblance of control.

"Do you want to waste your energies on burning down *barns*?" Tyler screamed at the mob undulating before him in the torchlight.

"Barns?" called out one man. "This is *filth* that we destroy here!"

There were murmurs of agreement, but Tyler spoke before they could swell and surge into another wave of destruction.

"We have no time for this!" Tyler said. "Do you think we will be left in peace for months so that we might skip about to every abbey and every hermitage in the land? If we want success then we must move *fast*, before the lords can move against us!"

"He's right!" cried Jack Straw, coming to stand by Tyler's shoulder. "Lads, I know your anger, but we cannot run amok like goose-boys! We need a head to direct our body, so that we might best use its strength. Tyler speaks well, and he speaks with hardened years of soldiery behind him."

Murmurs again, but agreeing with what Straw said.

"We need a head and a mouth to speak what is in all our hearts," Straw said. "And I say that Tyler is our man!"

Men shouted, but Tyler's voice overrode them. "Lads! In short time the lords will rise from their shock and assemble against us—if we don't achieve our aims before then we will *never* do so!"

"Richard!" shouted a man. "Richard will aid us!"

"Aye!" cried several more. "*He* will surely aid us against our oppressors."

Fools, thought Tyler, but knew that he needed to foster this illusion to mold the mob to his will.

"We need to make ourselves heard," Tyler said, then paused, his sharp eyes staring about the crowd. "And we will never be heard if we stay mired in the muddy fields of Kent."

"Where?" said a man.

"Canterbury—" Tyler began.

"Where resides the murderous archbishop!" screamed someone from far back in the crowd.

Tyler almost smiled. The genial and good-hearted Simon Sudbury could never be described as "murderous." But he needed the mob to go to Canterbury—there lay his second-in-command, rotting in jail—and the thought that they might get their hands on poor Sudbury in doing so was a good enough excuse to get them marching westward.

"Canterbury," Tyler said. "Then London."

The mob erupted again, now shouting Tyler's name, and Tyler relaxed a little.

LATE THE next night, Canterbury lay under the pall of the rebels, many of its buildings on fire, the archbishop's palace completely destroyed in the mob's rage that the archbishop himself was, apparently, in London.

For the moment, Tyler did not care that Sudbury had avoided the mob's anger. He had better things to do than think about the archbishop's lucky escape, and one of those things consisted of leading a band of some twenty-eight men into the prison that rose outside the walls of the town.

Here lay the one man who could—hopefully—consolidate Tyler's control over the maddened beast that roiled outside.

John Ball.

Tyler found him, eventually, brushing off his shabby robe in one of the lower cells. He was dirty—but then that was largely Ball's natural state anyway—and hungry, but otherwise seemed well, and Tyler embraced him with a brief, fierce hug.

"John!"

Ball grinned. "It has begun then?"

"Can you not hear them?"

"Oh, aye, that I can. Well . . . what now?"

"London," said Tyler, "and whatever fate awaits us there."

Chapter IV

The Vigil of the Feast of St. Nicomedes
In the second year of the reign of Richard II
(Thursday 31st May 1380)

✠

PRIOR GENERAL THORSEBY finally condescended to send for Neville three days after he'd allowed Courtenay permission to visit his lord.

Neville was not surprised Thorseby had made him wait—had not Prior Bertrand done the same to him at St. Angelo's?—and thus was not disconcerted by it. He knew that Thorseby had wanted to make him sweat, and he refused to pander to the Prior General's machinations.

Two friars came for him in the early afternoon. They did not speak, merely opening the door and indicating that Neville should follow them.

As they remained silent, so too did Neville, and he walked forward from his cell without a backward glance.

THE PRIOR General was waiting for him behind an oak table in a chamber in the main building complex of Blackfriars. The stone and brick chamber was lit only from narrow slit windows high in its northern and eastern walls, and its air was cold and merciless. Spring had not yet managed to penetrate into the depths of Blackfriars. Three other Dominicans sat with Thorseby: one Neville recognized as a master at the Oxford colleges, the other two he did not know.

Far more malevolent than the heavy presence of the Dominicans was the figure of Sir Robert Tresilian, Chief Justice of the King's Bench, who sat at Thorseby's right hand. Behind Tresilian were two lay clerks, pens poised to record whatever incriminating words issued forth from Neville's mouth.

"Thomas Neville," Thorseby said as soon as Neville halted before the table, "you have been brought here today—"

"By whose authority?" Neville asked, pleasantly enough.

Thorseby stared at him. "By the authority of the Holy Church—"

"And which pope was it that gave you—"

"—and by the authority of your sovereign, Richard, king of England and France."

"Ah, so I am to be one of Richard's victims." Neville knew he should not goad Thorseby so, and he knew that his interruptions worked only in the Prior General's favor, but he was so infuriated by Tresilian's presence, and by the knowledge that Richard would use him to get at Bolingbroke, that he could not help himself.

"You are here to save your body and your soul," said Tresilian quietly. He was a gray-haired, haggard-faced, spare man with, as Neville knew by reputation, all the mercy of a swinging axe and the warmth of a week-dead snowbound carcass.

"And will I be allowed to so save my body and soul?" Neville said as quietly, holding Tresilian's stare.

"You have been under scrutiny for well over a year," said Thorseby, somewhat ostentatiously shuffling a pile of documents which lay on the table before him. "Your behavior as a subject has been questionable, your behavior as a friar has been abominable, your behavior as a Christian even worse."

"I have served my God as truly as any man might," Neville said.

"You will not speak until you are offered the chance to do so!" Tresilian said.

Neville's face tightened, but he remained silent.

Thorseby stopped shuffling the papers about and looked steadily at Neville. "You doubtless can remember our last conversation, held in Lincoln during Lent of last year."

Neville inclined his head.

"You may answer!" Tresilian said.

"Yes," Neville said.

If Thorseby was irritated by Neville's refusal to grant him his honorific of "Prior General," or even "Father," then he gave no sign. "And do you remember my concerns regarding your behavior at that time?"

Neville's lips curved in a small smile. "You claimed that I had abandoned all my clerical vows and demeanor. As my most good lord, the Duke of Lancaster, summed up, I had been a 'very bad boy.' "

Neville had finally managed to needle Thorseby. The Prior General's cheeks mottled, and he took a deep breath.

"But," Neville continued before Thorseby could speak, "I assume that the current charge of heresy relates to that which you accused me of last year—my claim to have been visited by the archangel Saint Michael."

To Neville's surprise, Thorseby smiled a little at that.

"Ah, yes. Your angelic visitations. Well, Neville, I wish we could rest merely at archangels."

He paused, and Neville kept his face as impassive as he could.

Thorseby's expression suddenly turned into that of the vicious attacker. "Is it not true, Neville, that you have been consorting with demons?"

Neville stared in disbelief at Thorseby. "I—"

"You have been *seen*!" Thorseby yelled, now half standing. He picked up a sheaf of documents and then slammed them down on top of the table again. "I have sworn documents here to prove it. Neville, do you truly mean to *deny* that you consorted with a demon in the Brenner Pass? Would you so damn your own soul?"

Neville was so stunned he could not manage a single word. *How had Thorseby managed to gain that information?* Sweet Jesu, he had totally underestimated the power of Thorseby's maliciousness.

"These statements," Thorseby whispered, now leaning forward over the table, "together with those from others who saw you cavorting with imps outside the village of Asterladen—"

"Lies! Thorseby, I did not 'consort' with that demon—"

"So you admit the demon's presence, Neville?" Tresilian said very quietly to one side.

"—are enough to see you burn, Neville," Thorseby finished with no regard to what either Neville or Tresilian had said. "And you can be sure that I will push the sentence through. I should never have allowed you entry into the Dominican Order. I should have seen your evil ways from the outset in your murder of your paramour—"

"You cannot accuse me of Alice's murder, you blackhearted—"

Now Tresilian leaped to his feet. "Silence!" he roared, and both Thorseby and Neville fell quiet, staring at Tresilian.

"I have had enough talk of demons and angels," the Chief

Justice said, "and I care not for the intricacies of heresy. I accuse you of treason, Neville—"

"What?"

"It is common knowledge," Tresilian said, sitting down, "that you had dealings with the rebel Etienne Marcel in Paris—"

"He kept me a prisoner, for God's sake, my lord! I was not a willing conspirator."

Thorseby retook his seat as well, noting to himself that Neville was prepared to honor Tresilian with a title if not Thorseby.

"Not a willing conspirator?" Tresilian said. "And yet surely you had dealings with him on your journey north from Florence to . . . where was it . . . Carlsberg?"

Neville did not answer, wondering what else Tresilian knew.

"Not a willing conspirator?" Tresilian said yet again, "when you so clearly were his willing comrade?"

"I was not—"

"You did not, while you were with Etienne Marcel in Carlsberg, accept from him payment and a token—a valuable signet ring?"

Again Neville chose to keep silent.

"You know as well as I," Tresilian said, "that acceptance of both money and a valuable item, such as a ring, indicate acceptance of a contract. What was that contract, Neville? To bestir rebellion in England while Marcel tore France apart?"

"I have never agreed with Etienne Marcel," Neville said, "and I do not bestir rebellion here."

"Then why accept the money?" Thorseby put in. "Why take the ring? You do not deny these actions?"

"I did not think—"

"Then such lack of thought may well prove your death, Neville," Tresilian said. "Furthermore, I think it no coincidence that the stirrings of unrest are even now being felt across the English countryside."

For an instant, Neville held his breath in horror, thinking

that Wat Tyler's connection to both the unrest and to Lancaster's household had become known. Then he took a breath and relaxed very slightly—Tresilian had used no names and he had spoken only in the broadest of generalities. The Chief Justice was merely trying to trap Neville into confessing knowledge of the rebellion, and into implicating members of Lancaster's household . . . and he had almost succeeded.

"I put it to you, Neville," Tresilian went on, "that for at least two years you have been surreptitiously working for the destruction of the English throne—even now peasant rebels march on the city—and that your arch-conspirator in this has been Bolingbroke!" Tresilian was standing now, stabbing his finger at Neville as he shouted. "Do you deny that the rebels march to your plan, and that they mean to murder Richard and put Bolingbroke on the throne?"

"No. You mouth only lies." Neville suddenly realized they were going to kill him no matter what he said. The decision had been made. This was merely the playacting that would give them the excuse to sign the death warrant. *Sweet Lord Christ!* Neville thought of Margaret, and a desperate sadness swept over him. Then he thought of how the world would descend into bleakness and chaos if the demons were not defeated, of how all those he loved would be tormented and murdered, and a blackness so profound gripped Neville that he almost swayed on his feet.

"Do you deny that there are some who would depose Richard?"

Neville hesitated just an instant too long. "If Richard is a God-fearing man, then he has nothing to fear," he said, but even as he spoke he knew that he'd not only said the wrong thing, but said it far, far too late.

Tresilian lowered his arm, then spoke to the scribbling clerks. "Note well, sirs, that he did not deny the last question put to him."

He looked at Thorseby, then back at Neville. "You will be taken back to your cell and within the week moved to the dungeons in the Tower," said Tresilian in a flat voice. "There you shall be kept at his grace's pleasure until it is time for you to face a trial of your peers in the matter of treason."

"*And* heresy," Thorseby said.

"He'll die one way or the other," Tresilian said, "and a traitor's death is far, far worse than that meted out to a heretic."

Thorseby thought about arguing the matter, then nodded agreeably. A morning of being drawn and part-quartered, and then having your cock sliced off and forced down your throat—followed, after a lengthy interval, by your balls and bowels—was, in the end, a longer and far nastier way to slide down into hell than facing the flames.

Chapter V

The Feast of St. Nicomedes
In the second year of the reign of Richard II
(Friday 1st June 1380)

— I —

✠

"HE SAID *WHAT*?" said Richard, finally sitting straight in his chair.

Tresilian smirked from where he stood some two paces distant. "Thomas Neville virtually admitted, your grace, that he and Bolingbroke have been working in concert with traitors here and abroad in order to usurp you from your throne."

"I knew it!" Richard said, and sprang from the chair to pace back and forth. *He had him.*

"What do you mean, 'virtually admitted,' Tresilian?" de Vere said.

"Why question it?" Richard said, coming to a halt before de Vere. "We have all we need to—"

"Forgive me, your grace," de Vere said in an obsequious voice, "for perhaps I speak out of turn. But, surely, until we have hard evidence we do not have all we need. Bolingbroke is too great a noble, and way too popular, to attaint on charges of treason without ironclad cause."

Richard shot him a bleak look, then turned aside.

De Vere moved to stand before Tresilian, taking over the interview. "What do you mean, 'virtually admitted'?" de Vere asked again. "Tell me fact, man, not wish, for your life depends on this."

Tresilian's face hardened in barely controlled anger. *Dear God, how much longer must England's nobles submit to the dominion of this ambitious arse-poker?* "My lord," he said, "when I put it to Neville that he did indeed conspire with Bolingbroke, he refused to deny it."

"There!" Richard said, swinging about and staring at de Vere. "You see?"

De Vere still held Tresilian's eyes. "Did he sign a confession? Name his co-conspirators?"

Tresilian turned aside his eyes, wondering *why* it was he'd stopped the interrogation when he had. If he'd pushed . . .

De Vere's lip curled and he looked at Richard. "It is not enough," he said.

Richard's face flushed with frustration. *Curse Robbie. This was perfect!* "Why not?"

"Where is your *sense*, boy?" de Vere said, shocking Tresilian who could not believe that Richard allowed de Vere to speak thus to him. "Lancaster and Bolingbroke carry almost half of the barons of England with them! If you accuse Bolingbroke without sufficient evidence, then *you will cause civil war*!"

De Vere paused, visibly struggling to control his temper, then continued in a more temperate tone. "But then, you would not live long enough to witness it, sweet boy, for if the commons of London heard that you'd arrested their beloved 'fair Prince Hal' they would storm this palace and rip you to pieces."

Tresilian could see that Richard was torn between lashing out at de Vere for this public humiliation and capitulating entirely to what was an obvious truth.

Tresilian hoped that Richard would find the strength to put de Vere in his place. *Come on, Richard!* You *are the king, not your pet, Robbie.*

"But . . ." Richard eventually said, "but I want Hal . . . I want him stopped . . ."

Tresilian suppressed a sigh.

"Shush," de Vere said, and stroked Richard's cheek gently. "We will have him eventually. Do not fret."

Richard leaned his tear-streaked cheek into de Vere's palm and Tresilian had to turn away, sickened at Richard's increasing dependence on this man. He suddenly understood why it was he'd halted Neville's interrogation so precipitously: even then, unconsciously, he must have known England would yet have need of a man of Bolingbroke's caliber.

He was just wondering how best to extricate himself from the repellent scene unfolding before his eyes—de Vere had just leaned down to kiss Richard full on the mouth—when the far door of the chamber opened and Henry Percy, Earl of Northumberland, strode in.

Tresilian thought that, for an instant, just an instant, there was a flash of revulsion in Northumberland's eyes at the tableau before him, but then it vanished as he drew close.

He bowed perfunctorily at Richard, and sent an unreadable glance at de Vere, before speaking.

"Your grace, there is great trouble to hand."

Tresilian, who knew Northumberland well and respected

him as he respected very few men, instantly realized that "great trouble" meant very real, extreme danger. His mind instantly began to run through the armed force Richard had about him at Westminster, and he frowned as he realized how small the number actually was.

Richard was completely unconcerned. "My lord, you are always mouthing about some great trouble or the other. I pray that this is indeed great trouble, for you have disturbed me considerably."

"There is never a need to wish disaster upon yourself, your grace," Tresilian said, if only to let Northumberland know that he had an ally in this corruptly tainted chamber.

"I cannot think—" Richard began but got no further.

"There is a rabble of at least one hundred thousand peasants converging on London as we waste our breath in speech," Northumberland said. "They will have the city surrounded by nightfall."

Richard's eyes widened and his face went ashen. He tried to speak, but couldn't, and his mouth dropped uselessly and foolishly open.

"*What?*" de Vere said. "Intelligence put the peasant uprising at only a manageable few hundred! What mean you, *one hundred thousand?*"

"Would you like me to name them one by one?" Northumberland said. "There are at least one hundred thousand. They come from Essex, and East Anglia and Kent, and from a score of other regions. They scream for a redress to their grievances, and they scream your name, your grace."

Richard whimpered.

"Sweet Jesu," Tresilian said. "We have almost no armed men in either Westminster or London, and the militias of the city are not enough to prevent—"

"Aye," Northumberland cut in. "We cannot repel them."

"You must!" Richard shouted. He had grabbed de Vere's arm for support. "You *must* protect me! *I am your king!*"

De Vere ignored Richard and looked at Tresilian and Northumberland, all animosity gone from his eyes. "The Tower," he said.

"Aye," Northumberland said. "It is the only relatively safe place. Your grace, you must come with us. *Now!*"

THE NEWS of the approaching rebels was spreading throughout London when Northumberland strode into Richard's chamber in Westminster. Even as Northumberland was organizing the king's removal to the Tower, the markets and streets of London were ablaze both with fact and with rumor.

The Londoners greeted the news with a great deal of ambivalence. On the one hand, the majority of the men and women who lived in the city sympathized with the plight of the peasants. Most had relatives in rural villages, or were rural émigrés themselves. Almost without exception, the Londoners loathed the poll tax as much as the peasants did, and hated the Church even more than the peasants did. The prospect of winning even greater freedoms with this rebellion also raised more than a few voices in heated enthusiasm—*now was their chance to seize some independence along with their country cousins!*

On the other hand, few Londoners cheerfully embraced the prospect of being invaded by one hundred thousand fit, angry men armed with iron pikes, shovels and hoes. The rebel mass moving toward London was as likely to riot out of control as it was to peacefully present its grievances to the king. *More* likely to riot, in fact.

And London burned so easily.

Most shopkeepers and craftsmen closed up their shops, bolting tight the shutters across windows and doors. Valuables were moved to safe hidey-holes, generally buried deep in the hidden spaces of cellars, cesspits and the secret walks of London's sewers. Fires were damped down, and ovens left to cool. Children were moved inside, and told firmly to stay there. Some mothers bustled themselves, their children and a picnic supper into the nearest stone church, there to seek sanctuary from both the rebels and any conflagration. Men moved in tight, murmuring groups to join the watches to which they were assigned—the aldermen of most wards ensured that the fire watch was the first to be organized.

Not a few men, mostly wealthy merchants, or nobles who had somewhere to go and the wealth to purchase transport, quietly slipped down to private wharves and shipped themselves and their families out of danger. Foolishly, others thought to wait out the unrest within their London townhouses.

Despite the fact that so many families stayed indoors, the streets remained fairly crowded. Most men, particularly the younger men and youths, sensed the oncoming tempest and preferred to wait out in the open—perhaps even hoping to ride the crest of the storm. After all, did they not have grievances? Their ranks were swelled with the dispossessed and the mischievous, who saw in the night ahead some chance to take for themselves what had been so long denied them.

By late afternoon people thronged the streets, and the working life of the city had ground to a halt. Although the crowds were relatively quiet, the atmosphere was charged with such a heavy expectation that it seemed ready to explode, even without the presence of a single rebel.

BOLINGBROKE WAS frantic, and it showed in every nuance of voice and body. "You must get away from the Savoy, away from London!"

Lancaster turned away from his son and walked slowly to the window that overlooked the Strand.

People seethed up and down its entire length.

"Even had I wished to," he said, turning back to look at his son, "I could not now escape past those below."

"The Thames—"

"Is as crowded now as the Strand," Lancaster said.

"Sweet Jesu," Bolingbroke said, trying one last time. "The mob will shout your name, father. They will take this approaching rabble as an excuse to commit whatever mischief they have dreamed about for years!"

"And my name—or the extinction of it—is at the top of this list?"

Bolingbroke's face worked, and he half raised a hand, but he knew it was no good. Lancaster was right, it was too late to move now. "We can get you to the Tower," he said.

Lancaster laughed. "You would shut me up with Richard? What better way to accomplish my murder, Hal?"

Bolingbroke looked distraught and Lancaster was instantly contrite. "Ah, lad, I am sorry. It is best this way. I would prefer to take my chances with the London mob any day. Besides, all this may blow over. By this time tomorrow, everyone may well be back in their homes and no harm done."

"Not with a hundred thousand marching on the city," Bolingbroke said. *Not with Wat marching at their head.* Damn *him for what he had done!*

"We have men here, Hal, and we are surrounded with good, solid walls." It was Raby, walking forward from the corner where he'd been watching the other two silently. "And unless Richard's advisers have completely lost their heads"—he faltered, nonplussed by his unconscious choice of such unfortunate words—"then they will have sent for aid from the Earl of Surrey, and others within a day or two's march from London. Men who can raise a force sufficient to bring London back to its senses."

"But until aid *does* arrive, London is so vulnerable," Lancaster whispered, looking out the window again. "So vulnerable . . ."

He sighed, suddenly very tired and sad. "The world is turning upside down," he said, "and I confess to not liking the change. Who would have thought the commons could so rise, or demand such freedoms?"

"It is foolish," Bolingbroke said softly, "for they can never win. Change must be seduced, not forced."

Lancaster frowned at Bolingbroke, not understanding him. "Mary?" he said eventually. "And Margaret? What of them?"

Bolingbroke made a gesture of helplessness. "I tried to persuade them to leave when reports of the peasant uprising first came in. Mary refused, as did Margaret. She said that she would not leave Tom."

"Then we must do what we can for them," Lancaster said, and Raby murmured agreement. "Sweet Jesu, Hal," Lancaster continued, "I am so glad that Katherine still resides in the north—but, God, I wish I could see her one last time!"

Completely shocked, Bolingbroke stared at Lancaster. Until this moment he hadn't realized his father was utterly resigned to his death at the hands of the mob.

He glanced at Raby, and saw that he also was staring in horror at the duke.

LATER, WHEN he'd left Lancaster, Bolingbroke spoke quietly to Robert Courtenay in the stables of the Savoy. They passed quick, urgent words before Bolingbroke took a ring from his finger and gave it to Courtenay.

"Show that," he said. "They will let you past."

"Christ Savior, I hope so," Courtenay mumbled, looking at the ring with its distinctive Bolingbroke emblem of the head of a helmeted and visored knight.

"Remember the name," Bolingbroke said.

"Yes. Wat Tyler. I *know* him, my lord. You need not keep reminding me."

"Wat Tyler and his rebels are Tom's only hope, Robert."

"Aye, I know." Courtenay looked at Bolingbroke with sympathy. The man had done everything he could to get Neville freed over these past two months; if he had not succeeded, then it was not through a lack of effort.

Bolingbroke clapped his hand on Courtenay's shoulder. "Then go, man. *Go!*"

"Look after the Lady Margaret," Courtenay said.

"Yes. *Go*!"

Courtenay stared at Bolingbroke for one moment longer, then he turned and vaulted onto the stallion behind him and gathered up the reins.

In the blink of an eye he was gone into the night.

Chapter VI

The Feast of St. Nicomedes
In the second year of the reign of Richard II
(Friday 1st June 1380)

— II —

✠

COURTENAY RODE as fast as he dared through the press of people in the streets; the curfew bells had rung hours ago, but few had heeded them. *The mayor of London would have some explaining to do,* thought Courtenay as he urged his stallion past the crowds milling on Fleet Bridge, *for once all this is done, Richard will surely demand the reasons why Wadsworth hadn't done more the keep the Londoners under control.* He didn't envy William Wadsworth one bit.

His horse's hooves clattered and echoed as he passed under the great archway of Ludgate. Once he was through, Courtenay glanced to his right where Blackfriars rose in a series of dark mounds humped against the night sky. He wondered what Tom was doing, if he had heard any of the news that had swept through London in the past day, or if he was staring out his tiny window across the Thames to the fields of Southwark, wondering at the number of boats plying their way downriver and the groups of people that must even now be congregating on the south bank of the Thames.

Courtenay had heard—along with everyone else—that the peasant bands which had converged on London had consolidated into two huge gatherings. The first group of some forty thousand men, mostly from Essex, had descended on the city from the northeast and were camping in a restless mass in the fields of Mile End beyond Aldgate.

But Mile End was not where Courtenay was headed. He turned off the main streets where the crowds were thickest and rode south to Thames Street, which ran parallel with the river. From here he could find his way to the bridge and—assuming he could cross—to Southwark. From there it was a three mile ride east to where the sixty thousand-strong band of Kentish men had congregated: Blackheath.

And there, Courtenay hoped, he would be able to find Wat Tyler.

The crowds were thick and unruly even on Thames Street. Men and women milled the length of the street, carrying pikes, shovels or whatever other implements had come to hand. Most carried smoking torches, and their sputtering, leaping light shadowing across the high walls of the warehouses and shops gave the street a diabolical air, as if it was only waiting for that one, secret word before it exploded into murderous violence. Courtenay hoped those merchants who lived above their warehouses—mostly foreigners—had already made their escape.

On five or six occasions men reached out to grab at the bridle of Courtenay's horse. Each time, they let his horse go when he shouted out Hal Bolingbroke's name. Courtenay had taken the precaution of riding garbed in Bolingbroke's livery and that, combined with the Bolingbroke name, proved enough to grant him safe passage—he did not have to produce Bolingbroke's ring. The mob might murmur about the nobles in general, but Bolingbroke's name still possessed its magic.

Courtenay knew his life depended on it continuing to do so.

London Bridge was a massive construction: nineteen stone arches resting on massive gravel-filled piers spanned the Thames River and its mudflats. Five- and six-story tenement buildings, warehouses, churches and shops completely covered the bridge's surface, reducing passage across to a narrow tunnel that wound under and between the buildings and that even at noon had to be lit by torches. Courtenay could see now that lights and shouting people dangled from every window and foothold on the bridge and its supporting piers. It could have been a carnival scene had it not been for the dangerous undercurrents which roiled under the words of every man, woman and child.

A well-armed man stopped Courtenay at the entrance to the bridge, taking a firm hold on the bridle of Courtenay's horse. At first glance, Courtenay thought him merely a member of one of the city's watches, but, at second glance, realized he had an air of authority about him that spoke of greater things. Courtenay studied him more closely. The man was big, bulky with muscle, and wore a sword and several knives over his leather tunic. Underneath unruly gray-streaked hair his face was hard-angled and planed, his mouth narrow and uncompromising. The man's eyes slid over Bolingbroke's livery, then up to Courtenay's face.

"Why are you wearing Bolingbroke's badge?" said the watchman.

"I am come on Bolingbroke's business," Courtenay said, and waited for the man's hand to drop from his horse's bridle.

If anything, the hand clenched tighter, and, uneasy, Courtenay's stallion sidled a little.

"A name is an easy thing to bandy about," said the man, and a chill went down Courtenay's spine as he saw the flames from nearby torches reflected in the man's black eyes. "And your pretty tunic and the caparisons of your horse could as easily have been stolen. Tell me your name and your business, and be quick about the telling, for this is a bad night and I am in no mood for men I do not recognize."

"I am Sir Robert Courtenay, attached to Hal Bolingbroke's household."

The watchman stared unblinkingly at Courtenay, who now saw that some score of passersby, mostly well-armed men, had gathered about to listen to the exchange.

"Well, Courtenay, if that truly be your name, tell me what you do here, and why you turn your horse for the bridge?"

Courtenay hesitated, not knowing what he should tell the watchman. Was he in sympathy with the rebels, or their steadfast foe? Depending on what he said, Courtenay could either find himself killed or see Bolingbroke arrested for treason.

"I do not know what to tell you," he said quietly, "for my loyalties lie first with my Lord of Bolingbroke, and I should not want to say anything that would place his life in danger."

The watchman's eyes narrowed. "First prove to me that you *are* Bolingbroke's man," he said, "and then nothing you say to me, or to any about us," he gestured to the crowd of men, "will be used to harm Bolingbroke."

Courtenay reached inside the pocket of his tunic and withdrew Bolingbroke's ring, holding it out for the watchman's inspection.

The man leaned over the ring, as did several of the other armed men crowding about, then he leaned back.

"Either you are Bolingbroke's man," he said, "or you are his murderer. I prefer to believe the former, but should it be shown to me that you are the latter you will die the next time you set foot in London."

Courtenay's look of relief was enough to quell the watchman's final doubts, and the throng of men drew back a little, lowering their torches and swords.

"Where go you?" said the watchman.

"Blackheath," said Courtenay.

A murmuring arose from the crowd.

"And for what reason?" said the watchman.

"Because Bolingbroke loves the commons of England," said Courtenay quietly, his eyes steady on those of the watchman.

"He is in sympathy with the rebels?" the watchman said. Now the crowd was entirely silent, and that was more ominous to Courtenay than anything he'd heard in the past few minutes.

What should he say? He was the last person to whom Bolingbroke had shared his confidences in the past days and weeks, but Courtenay had observed enough of Bolingbroke to be certain that what he was about to say would be a true representation of the prince's thoughts.

"Bolingbroke does not agree with the methods of the rebels," Courtenay said, "nor the violence, but he is in sympathy with their needs and grievances."

"Bolingbroke is a good man," said a man within the crowd.

"Aye," said another. " 'Tis a shame that he is not the king and could listen to our cousins' grievances."

"He will do what he can," said Courtenay, "but the doing cannot be given about publicly. There are many devoted to Bolingbroke's downfall."

The watchman spat. "And doubtless the perverted de Vere is chief among them. Well, Sir Robert, you have my word, as the word of those gathered about—"

There was a chorus of "ayes" and a wave of nodding.

"—that nothing you say, nor your passing, shall be shared among Bolingbroke's enemies."

"Then I thank you," said Courtenay, "for I would not wish my actions or words to be the instrument of Bolingbroke's downfall. Will you give me your name, sir, so that Bolingbroke might know of your aid for his cause?"

The watchman hesitated, then nodded. "I am Dick Whittington, mercer, and alderman of Broad Street ward."

Courtenay raised his eyebrows. This Whittington was an

important man in his own right. It was no wonder he had such an air of authority or that the crowd had deferred to his every word.

An important man . . . and a Bolingbroke man.

Whittington suddenly realized he still held the bridle of Courtenay's horse, and he dropped it with a shame-faced grin. "I apologize for my questioning of you, Sir Robert."

Courtenay shrugged. "It is a night of uncertainties, Master Whittington."

Whittington sighed, suddenly looking tired. "Aye, it is that, and who knows what the morrow will bring? Sir Robert, London is holding its breath, not only because we fear what might happen if these rebels erupt beyond anyone's control, but also because we wait to see how our king will handle them . . . and himself. He is young, and impressionable—"

"And de Vere is making far too great an impression on our king!" said a man to the side amid a chorus of ribald remarks on the exact nature of Richard and de Vere's relationship.

"—and the next few days will be the making or breaking of him, methinks," Whittington finished. "This is a dire event to occur to a young king so early in his reign. What he does will color the tenure of his kingship."

Sweet Jesu! Courtenay thought. *I wonder if Richard realizes that London, perhaps the entire commons of England, will judge him—and his right to hold the throne—on how he copes with this rebellion?*

Whittington was watching Courtenay closely, and understood what he was thinking. "If Richard does not do well, and does not handle these rebels with sympathy," the alderman said softly, "then there are many—a very, very many—who will believe he has no right to sit upon the throne."

"If it were *Bolingbroke* holding the sceptre," said a man, "then I doubt *he* would be cowering in the Tower!"

"Nay," said Courtenay, "he would be on this horse instead of me, riding to parley with those who hold genuine grievances.

"Good men," he continued, looking about. "That Bolingbroke is *not* on this horse speaks of the danger he is in. He has many enemies who would taint him with the corrupt brush of treason . . . men who have laid false charges against Lord Thomas Neville that they might remove his support from Bolingbroke."

"I've heard of this Neville," said Whittington. "And you say he is *not* a traitor to Bolingbroke?"

"Nay," said Courtenay, "he is only the means by which traitors mean to touch Bolingbroke."

He would have said more save that there was a sudden rumble of movement a block further along Thames Street.

"We have no time!" Whittington said. "Quick, Courtenay, ride your horse onto the bridge. I will see that they lower the drawbridge for you."

SOUTHWARK WAS a great deal quieter than London itself. The road that led from the bridge passed several tightly shuttered and barred inns, shops and homes, as well as the deserted palace of the Bishop of Winchester. The bishop had no doubt gathered his skirts and made good his escape many hours ago. A few people wandered the dark road, but they faded into the shadows as Courtenay galloped his stallion past.

The peace and stillness of Southwark lasted only the few minutes it took Courtenay to ride a half-mile along the eastern road toward Blackheath. Groups of men started to congregate in the fields, thickening until it seemed to Courtenay that the entire countryside was seething with people. He was stopped almost as soon as he had ridden past the first few groups, but was allowed passage (together with an escort to see him through) as soon as he produced Bolingbroke's ring.

The crowd became almost impassable as they neared the small village of Blackheath: only the horses of Courtenay and his escort enabled them to push through.

Courtenay thought his escort would take him to one of

the village houses, perhaps to a barn or one of the small warehouses bordering the river, but his escort indicated a small hill just beyond the village.

Courtenay squinted as they neared, trying to make out what was happening. There was a crowd about the hill—so immense that Courtenay could not even comprehend its numbers—but the crest of the hill itself was clear. Several figures stood there, and Courtenay looked inquiringly to his escort.

"Tyler," one of the men said, and with that Courtenay had to be content.

A good quarter of a mile from the hill Courtenay dismounted to shoulder his way through on foot, while his escort stayed behind with the horses. He thought he'd have trouble in the passage, but to his surprise he was met after only a few paces by a man who introduced himself as Jack Straw.

"Tyler said you'd be coming," Straw said.

"How did he know?"

Straw shrugged. "Tyler knows many things that are dark to the rest of us," he said, then turned back the way he'd come, leaving Courtenay to follow him as best he might.

COURTENAY SUDDENLY realized how cold it was as they broke free of the crowd and walked to the space at the top of the hill. He was breathing heavily and sweating slightly—the hill was steeper than it looked from a distance—but even so he wrapped his cloak tighter about him.

Wat Tyler turned from the man he was speaking to, and stopped still, staring as Courtenay approached. He nodded, half to Courtenay as greeting, half to himself as acknowledgment of another marker reached.

"Well met, Robert," Wat Tyler said.

Courtenay nodded his own greeting, remembering the uncomfortable meal shared at Halstow Hall the day Tyler had arrived with John Wycliffe and two Lollard priests.

He suddenly realized that there was a waiting silence, and that the man whom Tyler had been speaking with now stood at Tyler's shoulder, staring at him belligerently. Courtenay blinked, recognizing John Ball.

"Bolingbroke asked me to come to you," Courtenay said, looking back to Tyler. "He has a request."

"What?" Tyler said. "That I go home?"

"Nay." Courtenay stared at Tyler's face, wondering what was in the man that had made him lead the rebel army to almost certain ruin. "It concerns my master, Thomas Neville."

"Aye?"

"Neville is being held in Blackfriars—"

Tyler laughed, a sound of genuine amusement. "What? Did Thorseby manage to catch Tom at last?"

Courtenay fought to stop his jaw from clenching. "—and Thorseby is working in concert with the Chief Justice and Richard to not only hang Neville, but to hang Bolingbroke through Neville."

"And so Bolingbroke wants Tom's life saved in order to save his own?"

"Nay. He told me to tell you that Neville must not be allowed to die for his own sake."

"Then Bolingbroke shouldn't have allowed Tom to be taken in the first instance!"

"Wat, please, listen to what I say! You are Neville's only hope. If you enter London—"

"*If?* You think there's a possibility we might just turn about and go home to our plowshares as soon as dawn lights the sky?"

"*When* you enter London, Bolingbroke asks that you take advantage of your numbers," Courtenay glanced at the crowd beneath them, "to free Neville."

Wat slowly shook his head. "I can't believe that Bolingbroke thinks I will jump to his every wish."

"Bolingbroke told me to tell you," said Courtenay, "that it is better that Neville be the battlefield than the Maid of France."

Wat stared at him, his thoughts in turmoil. It was patently obvious that Courtenay had no idea what the message meant, but Wat knew Bolingbroke's meaning only too well.

If Neville died, then the angels would probably move their battlefield to Joan of Arc, and it was very, very unlikely that Joan would choose any way other than that of the angels.

"He further told me to tell you," Courtenay continued softly, "that you do this for love of Neville, if not for love of Bolingbroke."

Tyler abruptly turned away then, after a moment, looked back to Courtenay, who was stunned to see tears in Wat's eyes.

"I will do this for love of *Bolingbroke*," Wat said. "Not for Neville."

"Neville has changed," Courtenay said, relieved that Wat had agreed to help, but needing to speak on Neville's behalf.

"Changed? How so?"

"He has become a gentler man."

Wat laughed harshly. "Gentler? The word does not marry well with 'Neville.' Tell me, Courtenay, how does he treat his wife, Margaret?"

"With love and respect. When I saw Neville last Tuesday—the first time any of his household or family had seen him in the two months of his imprisonment—his first words were for Margaret, and when I told him of the approach of this," Courtenay waved his hand across the masses below, "his first thoughts were for her."

Wat shrugged. "Whatever, I care little for Neville." His eyes shot to Courtenay's. "But I *do* care for his wife, as also for Bolingbroke, whatever chasms lie between us."

"Then I thank you."

Wat started to say something else, when John Ball, still waiting behind him, made an impatient sound and stepped forward.

"Wat," he said, "we must begin."

Wat nodded. "Aye. Courtenay, do you remember this man?"

Courtenay nodded, regarding Ball with some measure of disrespect, for he was ill-clothed and unmannerly in his appearance. Still, that was hardly unusual behavior for a Lollard.

Wat grinned at Courtenay's appraisal. "Poor looks or not, what John will say tonight shall set the world afire."

Jack Straw, who had hitherto been standing a few paces down the hill to give Tyler and Courtenay some privacy, now indicated that Courtenay should stand with him.

As Courtenay moved to join Straw, Wat suddenly leaned close and whispered in his ear, "Stay close after Ball has finished, for there is something I need to give you."

Then Tyler moved away, and stood on the grass a few feet away from Ball.

THE RAGGED, wild priest held up his arms and the crowd, who had been murmuring and shifting, quieted.

"Ah, good men," John Ball cried, and Courtenay knew that the man's clear voice would carry over most of this crowd.

"Good men! Things have not gone well in England for generations, and they will not go well until the wealth of this wondrous realm is shared among *all* its people!"

The crowd roared, and Ball had to spend long minutes waving them back into silence.

"You are held in thrall by those who call themselves noble," Ball eventually continued, "but by what right do they so hold you in bondage? What have they done, to be called 'great lords'? Why do they deserve their place over us? And how is it that they say they have the right to hold us in servitude?"

Courtenay glanced about him. Everyone was staring at Ball, and in their eyes glowed a strange light . . . the light of *freedom*, Courtenay realized.

"Do we not all come from the same mother and father?" said John Ball. "Are not we all children of Adam and Eve? So how is it these 'lords,' " Ball spat out the word with the utmost contempt, "say that they are better men than us?

They are clad in velvet and silk trimmed with squirrel-fur, and we are clad in poor cloth. They have wines, and spices, and good white bread, and we have rye bread, and remnants, and straw, and we drink water. They have good homes and fine manors, and we have pain and toil, and till the fields in the rain and wind, and it is from us and our labor that must come the wherewithal to maintain their estate. We are called serfs and beaten if we do not, at once, do their service."

Ball halted, breathing deeply, allowing the silence to deepen before he spoke again.

"When Adam delved and Eve span," he whispered, and that whisper carried deep into the heart and soul of every man present, "who then was the gentleman?"

There was a silence, and then . . .

"No one!" screamed a voice from far back in the assembly. "No one was the gentleman!"

"Nay," said John Ball, and Courtenay was as stunned to see tears in the renegade priest's eyes as he had been amazed to see them earlier in Tyler's. "No one was the gentleman then, as no one now should be any more the 'gentleman' above his neighbor. No one should own more than his neighbor, and no one should call his neighbor his servant.

"And *no one* now should ever look at you and call you or your sons bondsmen and serfs!"

My God, thought Courtenay. *There'll be nothing but death awaiting them if they march up to Richard and say that.*

And then his heart felt as if it had stopped, for he remembered his conversation with Whittington and realized the further implications.

If Richard trod these men into the mud whence they had struggled, then he would in turn be dashed down.

MANY HOURS later, when the crowd had dispersed to campfires and a hurried meal, Tyler sought out Courtenay.

"You must leave us," he said, "and return to Bolingbroke."

"No, I—"

"Wait. Hear me out. I will do what I can for Neville, but I need you to go back to Bolingbroke."

Courtenay hesitated, then nodded. "You said you had something to give me."

"Aye." Tyler reached into a pocket and withdrew a key. "Take this. Give it to Bolingbroke and no other. Bolingbroke should have had the key a long time ago."

He grinned wryly. "His subtle plans will be nothing without it."

Courtenay did not ask what the key was for. He pocketed it, hesitated, then spoke. "You will die if you lead that mob into London speaking words of peasants made lords and lords made peasants."

"I know," Tyler said, "but only death can remake the world. Isn't that what Christ's death taught us?"

Chapter VII

Prime on the Saturday within the
Octave of Corpus Christi
In the second year of the reign of Richard II
(daybreak 2nd June 1380)

— I —

✠

IT WAS THE innocuous aroma of fresh baking bread that pushed the rebels' destructive fervor to breaking point. As a faint rose light stained the skies over Stepney Marsh, London's bakers began sliding thousands of fresh-baked loaves of bread from their ovens, sending the mouth-watering scent over the waking city.

And beyond.

The two massive bands of rebels, the Essex men a mile to the east of Aldgate and the Kentish men three miles south-east of the bridge, stirred and murmured and then, with no spoken direction, began to rumble toward the city.

Although their higher purpose was to parley and persuade the king that their grievances were genuine and their wish for more personal freedoms fair and equitable, the majority of the one hundred thousand which surged toward the city also nursed massive and long-standing resentments that needed to be assuaged first. London harbored many of the fat, corrupt oppressors who had made their lives, and those of their parents and grandparents, such a misery. The rebels were not going to miss this opportunity to settle some of their grievances.

The rebels rapidly descended into a rabble.

The Essex men reached London first, and found Aldgate, as also the small gate next to the Tower, laid open. The peasants surged through, shouting incitements to the Londoners to join in their cause.

Far above, Richard watched from the safety of the bolted keep of the Tower. He was pale and wretched with a combination of fear and anger.

The Kentish men were not far behind their Essex comrades. Wat Tyler, John Ball, John Hales and Jack Straw had managed to force themselves to the front of the mob as it surged into Southwark. The passage across the bridge was narrow, and behind the leaders tens of thousands of men milled through the streets of Southwark waiting their turn to set foot on the bridge.

While waiting, they contented themselves with burning down the Bishop of Winchester's palace and murdering the steward whom they found cowering in the buttery.

Jostled and pushed at the front of the pack surging across

the bridge, Wat Tyler was tired, sad and angry in equal amounts. He knew the rabble behind him would ravage out of control once they'd gained entry to London . . . and he knew he needed to let them do it. One day of rioting and their hatred for the despised nobles and fat clerics would have burned back to manageable embers: they would be more amenable to words again.

But what would they manage to do in that single day of rioting?

What would be destroyed? Who murdered?

Amid this mass hatred, would they remember their love for Bolingbroke, or would they see only the rings on his fingers and the sword at his side and think him one of the tyrants committed to their eternal enslavement?

Jesus Christ, what if they murdered Bolingbroke?

Over the past days Tyler had spread the word that many among the nobles would work for them, listen to them, and Bolingbroke was chief among the names he'd mentioned. Then, men had nodded, agreeing.

But who could tell what they would or would not remember in the heat and blood of their rioting?

Dick Whittington stood by the lowered drawbridge a third of the way across the bridge. He spoke brief words of welcome (what else could he say?) but had no chance to say more as the rabble enveloped him and swept him forward.

He fought his way through to Tyler, managing to grab at his arm and shout in his ear.

"I do not like this mood, Tyler!"

Tyler nodded, and managed a half shrug. He and Whittington had been friends and conspirators against the angels for decades but, like Bolingbroke, Whittington believed more in the power of subtlety and gradual change than the fire of revolution.

"Where is Richard?" Tyler shouted.

"In the Tower."

Tyler grunted. Where else? "What militia will we meet?"

"Almost none. Christ, Wat! We shall be trampled in this stampede!"

"No militia?"

"Wadsworth fumbled and dithered, and by the time he thought he should do something it was too late. But I have heard that Richard has sent pleas for aid to the Earl of Surrey and Sir Robert Knolles"—both nobles commanded large private militias within a day of London—"as others."

"How long?" Wat said as they finally crossed the bridge and headed north along Bridge Street.

"You have one day, no more than two."

"That I even have that I should thank the Lord Jesus," Tyler said. He grabbed Whittington's arm and pulled him into the lee of an alley, shouting to Straw and Hales as he did so to lead the mob further into London and then to split up and storm the major prisons.

Neither they, nor the mob, needed any urging.

"Dick," Tyler said softly, gasping as he tried to catch his breath, "you should not be seen with me. My name is death now, and you should know it."

Whittington said nothing, but he reached out and gripped Tyler's shoulder with one hand.

"Where is Bolingbroke?" Tyler said.

"In the Savoy."

Tyler winced. "Jesu!"

"I have left men there—they will deflect the mob's anger."

"Margaret is there too!"

"What? *Christ*, Wat! Why?"

Tyler shrugged. "She probably refused to leave."

Whittington dropped his hand from Tyler's shoulder and shifted from foot to foot, his face worried. "We must get her to safety."

"Aye, but I've heard that there is only one way she will agree—if her husband is with her."

"Tom," Whittington said. "He is in Blackfriars."

"I know. Listen, can you do your best for the Savoy for

the moment? I'll direct a portion of these men toward Blackfriars—"

"The Essex men raged down that way not minutes before you approached the bridge, Wat."

Wat's entire face froze, then he cursed, loudly and foully.

He stopped, looked at Whittington, and gave a nod of leave-taking. "Fare thee well, Dick," he said, and then he was gone, lost amid the raging of the streets.

ALTHOUGH MANY Londoners had been terrified about what might happen when the peasants overran the city, their fears were quickly set aside. The rebels had very specific targets in mind, and none of them included the homes and shops of their city cousins.

The first objectives were the city jails, specifically the Newgate, Fleet and Ludgate jails. The rebels had little work to do in freeing the prisoners, for in most cases the jailers had prudently unlocked the cells as they heard the noise of the approaching riot.

Next, the peasants attacked the Temple complex in the eastern section of the city. Once the home of the Knights Templar, the Temple and its precinct now housed the barristers and lawyers of England.

The lawyers were not so sensible as the jailers had been. They tried first to bar the doors—they were too late—and then to protect the stacks and shelves of legal records.

In most instances, they burned with their precious records—documents that for centuries had enshrined the bondage of the commons in twisting, malevolent legal clauses that no peasant had hitherto been able to dispute.

Both lawyers and documents burned very nicely.

Having disposed of as many records as they could, the various arms of the mob then attacked many of the warehouses along the wharves, burning and looting, and murdering every foreigner and every Jew they could find.

Then it was the time of the Church.

* * *

NEVILLE HAD not slept all night. He'd been able to see little from his cell save distant lights flickering somewhere beyond the south bank of the Thames, but he had heard the footsteps and voices in the streets, their excitement and fear, and he'd listened to the guard outside his locked door pace back and forth through the night until he'd slipped away—perhaps to save his family, perhaps to save himself—just before dawn.

At daybreak, as the familiar and comforting smell of the fresh-baked bread had wafted over the city, Neville had seen the gray tide surging toward London Bridge, and for the next hour had listened to the roars and screams in the streets outside Blackfriars.

The footsteps in the corridor outside his cell had briefly increased, and had then vanished completely, and Neville realized that the friars within his immediate vicinity had fled—whether to protect Blackfriars or to protect themselves he did not know.

For a while, perhaps a score of minutes, perhaps more, it became very quiet. Even the noise on the street all but ceased.

That worried Neville more than anything else. He paced back and forth in his cell, cursing his inability to act.

Was Margaret safe? Sweet Jesu, she and Rosalind must be terrified! Was Courtenay with her? Bolingbroke?

"Damn it!" Neville muttered over and over as he paced. "Damn it! Damn it!"

He tried the door, setting his shoulder to it and pushing with all his might, but it was of solid construction and did not budge.

He took the stool and battered at the door, but the stool splintered and crumpled into useless fragments of wood while the door remained intact.

Then he pounded at the door with his fists, screaming for someone to come to his aid.

But no one replied.

He stepped back, staring at the door, his shoulders heaving with the effort he'd put into his pounding and screaming.

"Curse you," he whispered, and he did not truly know to whom or at what he cursed.

Then, just as he drew breath to renew his shouting, he heard a great crash on the floor above him. Neville's eyes jerked up. The timber ceiling of his cell was still trembling with the force of whatever had been pushed over.

Then his eyes moved back to the door: men, many men, were pounding along the corridor outside. There were shouts and curses, screams and pleas, and Neville took a step backward and armed himself with one of the shattered legs of the stool.

Something banged violently into the door, and then the sounds of a man pleading—*screaming*—for mercy. There were some grunts, and again the man was pounded against the door.

Neville had now backed up to the rear wall of his cell, his eyes riveted on the door.

The man pinned to the door shrieked, a thin animal sound of pure terror, and Neville heard the unmistakable sound of a knife being plunged again and again into flesh.

Every time it plunged through its victim's body it scraped against the door.

Neville's face hardened into the expressionless mask of the battle-hardened warrior. His eyes became flinty, his mouth thinned, and his hand hefted the jagged-edged leg of the stool.

He was not afraid, only angry at his helplessness.

Blood was now seeping under the door . . . and still the man shrieked, if more breathlessly than previously.

Some part of Neville's mind registered that the man had been gut-stuck only: he was going to die, but he would be some time in the doing.

There were more footsteps, then voices—calmer than previously.

A jangling of keys, the sound of the dying, shrieking man being dragged to one side, and then the turning of a lock.

The door slowly swung open, and Neville raised his piece of wood.

And then lowered it, shocked.

Wat Tyler stood there, several men behind him. Tyler was marked with soot, and he had a shallow cut across his forehead.

His blue eyes burned brightly in a face tight with what Neville thought was fanaticism.

"Sweet Jesu, Wat," Neville said in an almost whisper. "What do you here?"

"Saving you," said Tyler, and then turned to take something from one of the men behind him—a peasant, Neville saw.

"Put this on," Tyler said, and he handed Neville a roughly woven peasant's cloak. "If you wander the streets wrapped in those fine clothes I cannot guarantee your life."

Slowly, Neville reached out and took the cloak.

His eyes slid past Tyler to the Dominican friar slumped against the far wall of the corridor, his shrieks now reduced to a horrid wheezing. The man's hands were clutched about his belly—uselessly, for blood was pouring out—and Neville could see the ropes of bowel that bulged between the man's fingers.

Tyler stepped forward and grabbed Neville by the arm, distracting him from the dying Dominican's agony.

"The Savoy," Tyler said.

"Margaret!" Neville said.

IN A distant part of the Blackfriars complex, a man dressed in a peasant's tunic and cloak slipped quietly from a side door and, slowly and carefully, made his way to the outskirts of London and the road north.

Two miles along the road, and at the top of a small hillock, Prior General Thorseby paused to look back on London.

Smoke rose in columns from the city, and even from this distance the glow of the fires showed clearly over the city walls.

"For the moment you might be safe, Neville," Thorseby whispered, "and think yourself escaped from justice . . . but there *is* no escape from the justice of God!"

And with that he turned and strode northward toward safer lodgings.

Chapter VIII

Terce, on the Saturday within the Octave of Corpus Christi
In the second year of the reign of Richard II
(9 a.m. 2nd June 1380)

— II —

✠

"WHAT'S HAPPENING?" Neville asked Tyler as they ran through the corridors of Blackfriars. Men—both rural peasants and Londoners—seethed through the buildings of the friary; Neville counted at least eight bodies of friars before they ran into the courtyard of the complex, and ten or twelve more lying blood-drenched outside. Smoke was wafting through the air, and as Neville glanced over his shoulder at the main huddle of buildings within Blackfriars he could see that many of them were ablaze.

"Judgment Day come early for these carrion," Tyler said. They were now jogging along the lane that led north to Fleet Street.

"Tyler?" Neville said, almost growling. "What is happening?"

"Revolution, rebellion, freedom struggling out of the grave where your precious Church and fellow nobles have had it pinned for too many centuries," Tyler replied. "Call it what you will, for I no longer care."

"This is your fault!"

Tyler halted and whipped about to face Neville. "This is not *my* fault. It is the *fault* of all those who thought the good men and women of England should have been so ground into the mud. My 'fault' has only been to speak the words that have raised men from their servitude in order to fight for their freedom."

"God help you," Neville whispered.

Tyler gave a bitter laugh. "God will never help such as me. Now, come, I want none of your prating about rights and wrongs while the Savoy burns about your wife's ears!"

"Jesu! The Savoy is *burning*?" Neville pushed past Tyler and ran with all his strength toward Fleet Street, Tyler only a step behind him.

The streets were crowded with city-folk and peasants alike, and once Neville and Tyler turned westward along Fleet Street they were reduced to pushing and shoving and cursing in order to make their way through. Smoke and ash from scores of fires—all warehouses, palaces or monasteries—had settled in a gray, choking cloud over the city, and Neville had to pull the hood of his cloak close about his face so he could breathe. Even so, his breath was more a choking and sobbing than anything else.

Every few steps Tyler gave him an impatient shove in his back, and Neville realized that Tyler was as desperate to get to the Savoy as he was himself.

They should have been able to cover the distance along Fleet Street, through Ludgate, and then southwest along the Strand to the Savoy in ten minutes at the longest at a run . . . but they could not run, not in this city choking with rioters and smoke and fire and fear.

"We should have taken the river!" Neville shouted as they battled their way across the Fleet River bridge. Before them, on their left, many of the buildings within the Temple complex were burning fiercely.

Tyler shrugged, and pushed Neville forward yet again.

The sight and smell of the destruction left Neville dry-mouthed with fear for Margaret. The mob was venting its anger on anything and anyone who they thought had hurt them . . . and if there was one noble the commons hated more than any other it was Lancaster, who they mistakenly believed had always conspired against Edward III and the Black Prince.

The Savoy, and any in it, were now about to pay the price for the malicious and ill-founded rumors about Lancaster.

"Why can't you stop them?" Neville screamed as they finally gained the Strand.

"Not even God Himself could have stopped this lot," Tyler said, finally managing to move abreast of Neville.

At that instant, both men caught sight of the Savoy, still some hundred paces away.

It was wreathed in thick, black smoke, and tongues of blue and orange flames flickered out of its windows.

"See the bastard Lancaster burn!" screamed a gap-toothed and filthy man to Neville's right, and without even thinking, Neville smashed his fist into the man's face.

He gave a grunt of surprise and crashed to the ground where he vanished almost instantly among the feet of the mob about him.

No one took any notice of Neville's actions. This was a day to indulge in violence, after all.

Tyler wasted no time in words or recriminations. He grabbed Neville and pulled him down a laneway leading to a narrow path along the riverbank.

The press of bodies, if not of smoke and ash, cleared almost immediately, and both men broke into a run, dashing down the laneway then turning to their right to run along the path beside the Thames.

MARY HAD spent the previous night with Margaret and Agnes while Bolingbroke watched, with Lancaster's men, from the parapets. While all three women had gone to bed concerned about the unrest, none of them had ever imagined that violence would have enveloped them so quickly or with such murderous intent. They'd been drifting out of a fitful sleep in the hour after dawn when there had sounded the sudden noise of voices and feet in the street. The women had barely managed to rise and wrap themselves in shawls and cloaks before the mob had invaded the Savoy.

Terrified, they huddled behind the hangings of the great bed, certain that once the mob had done with their murdering and looting they would return to rape them.

Shouts and clattering footsteps sounded in some distant part of the palace before, horrifyingly, drawing closer to the chamber where the women cowered. There was a scuffle outside the door and then the sound of fighting—a cacophony of clashing steel, shouts, curses and the grunts of the combatants. It went on for what seemed like hours, but which was probably only minutes, before there came a nightmarish scream of splintering wood as, Margaret supposed, the great wooden dresser containing pewter plate and stoneware standing against the outer wall of their chamber crashed to the floor. A man shrieked, his cry dying to a horrifying gargle, which was abruptly cut off, and then the noise of the fighting faded as both intruders and defenders moved further into the palace.

Unsure if Lancaster and his men had managed to repel the mob, or had been repelled themselves, Margaret, Mary and Agnes nevertheless breathed a little easier. At least they were safe for the moment from the savage anger of the invaders.

But as they relaxed away from their fright, a more terrifying ordeal began. Somewhere in the palace a fire had taken hold, and now smoke trickled under the doorway in an ever-increasing thick blanket. Once under the door, the smoke rose, as if under the guidance of some evil enchantment, toward the low ceiling of the chamber. In its own quiet, silent way, the smoke was far more terrifying—and far more lethal—than the previous clash of steel beyond the chamber. No cloth placed against the crack between door and floor was able to prevent its insidious entrance—smoke filtered through every joint and minute crack between the door and its frame, and within minutes the three women and the child were coughing and hacking in the fumes.

There was no escape. More scared of choking to death than of encountering the mob, Margaret and Agnes tried to open the door so they could escape. But it was outward opening, and now would not budge—the ruins of the dresser had clearly fallen directly across the doorway.

They beat against the door with their fists, screaming (amid their choking) for aid . . . but the only reassurance that reached them was the growing sound of crackling flames, and a spreading heat across the wooden panels of the door. They retreated to attack the window, but the glass was heavy and thick and the leading old and rigid, and in any case, the windows had never been designed to be opened.

There was nowhere for the smoke to go, but to roil in ever-crazier eddies about the chamber, and there was no escape for the four trapped within the chamber.

Eventually Margaret and Agnes, coughing and choking, rejoined Mary and Rosalind, huddling in the farthest corner of their chamber in a futile effort to escape the effects of the smoke. Margaret touched Mary's cheek in ineffectual reassurance, and took Rosalind into her arms, hugging the sobbing child tight against her breast.

The sound of the spreading, roaring fire and of the cracking timbers in the massive roof above them deepened their dread with every moment that passed.

How soon before the roof collapsed?

No longer did they fear that the mob might return to rape them—at this point the women would have welcomed the return of *anyone*. All they cared about were their lives, and the lives of their children—Rosalind, and the unborn children that both Margaret and Mary were carrying. All they wanted to do was to escape, to live, but they did not know how they might manage it.

Suddenly there was a massive explosion, and all three of the women cried out. The great window in the chamber had shattered in the heat, discharging shards of glass throughout the room.

Both Agnes and Margaret felt splinters slice into their scalps, but the wounds were flesh-hurt only, and they brushed the glass away with shaking hands, drawing in great gulps of the fresh air that rushed through the broken panes.

"Can we escape—?" Agnes began, coughing a little.

"No," Margaret said. "There is nothing but a drop of thirty feet or more outside that window."

"Then thank Jesu that at least we have air to breathe," Mary said in a low voice.

"Aye," Margaret said, "but that will be of no comfort to us if we cannot escape the flames."

She was about to say more, but at that moment the smoke thickened as it rushed toward the opening in the window, and all the woman found themselves choking anew. Margaret clutched the material of her shawl to her nose and mouth in a futile effort to breathe a little easier, then dropped the material as she realized that Rosalind was coughing badly.

She leaned over her daughter, thinking to lift her up toward the window, when there was a sudden screech beyond the door as someone dragged heavy wood aside. Margaret froze, half sitting, half standing, and Rosalind cried out. Margaret hushed her, then strained her stinging, watering eyes in the direction of the door.

She heard a harsh scraping as someone pushed the door open, and then the sound of a footfall, and of a man coughing as smoke poured through the doorway and into the chamber before rushing toward the shattered window.

"My lady? Margaret?"

Margaret opened her mouth to speak, but she was so relieved to hear Courtenay's familiar, trusted voice in the midst of this nightmare that she found herself crying instead, unable to form words in her throat and mouth.

"My lady?"

It was Rosalind who raised her voice—a desperate, gagging cry that brought Courtenay at a half run across the chamber.

He had a damp linen wrapped about his face, and Margaret sank to her knees in fright, even though she had recognized his voice.

"My lady," Courtenay rasped, and grabbed at Margaret's arm. "You must get out of here, *now!*"

He dragged Margaret to her feet, then reached down for Mary. Agnes was already standing and dragging at Mary by the thin material of her nightgown.

Courtenay cursed, not caring that Mary whimpered at the sound, and aided by Agnes, pushed the other two toward the door. Both Margaret and Mary came to their senses almost immediately, dashing through the dim outline of the door which suddenly loomed before them and into the corridor that led to the main stairwell of the palace and the courtyard.

"Bolingbroke?" Margaret said as she felt Courtenay take her arm and pull her along the corridor.

"I don't know," Courtenay said. "There's been fighting . . . I broke away . . . ran to find you . . ."

Mary whimpered, and Agnes wrapped an arm about the woman's shoulders, urging her forward.

"Outside, away from the fire," she said, "and then we shall see to your husband."

The corridor was empty save for the smoke, and they reached the stairwell relatively easily and fumbled their way down, leaning on the walls for guidance as the smoke thickened.

The walls were almost too hot to touch.

Margaret began to cry. Now that they were close to escape she began to fear that they would not reach it after all; that the smoke would choke them, or the flames would finally consume them. Rosalind was writhing so violently in her arms that she did not think she would be able to hold on to her for much longer. The child within her was wriggling desperately as well, twisting her off-balance as she fought her way down the stairs.

Between the two, and her own terror, Margaret suddenly believed that she was going to die, that everything was in vain, that the entire world was dying, and that the angels even now were reaching out to judge her.

Her foot missed a step, slipped, and suddenly Margaret was falling. She had no time nor breath to scream, merely to register the thought that she was, finally, going to die, and take Rosalind with her into that dying, when a dark shadow rose before her, and she fell, not to dash herself against the flagstones, but into the arms of a man crying out her name.

It was so unexpected that she could not for the moment comprehend what had happened. She thought the man spoke with Tom's voice, but how could that be, for was he not stilled locked up in Thorseby's black house of God?

"Margaret," the man said, and Margaret realized that, indeed, it was Tom, and she collapsed against him, crying and sobbing his name, and thinking that she would never, never again as long as she lived love him as much as she did that moment.

He swept her and their daughter into his arms, and she was safe . . . safe . . . safe and being carried out of this burning hell into the courtyard where the smoke still swirled, but not with the viciousness that it had inside.

"Margaret?" a voice said, and she thought it was Wat's voice, and she blinked, and saw his face hovering over Tom's shoulder.

"Wat?" she whispered, disorientated by his presence.

Then another man spoke to her, and she blinked again, and turned her head, and there was Hal, his face ravaged with pain and anger.

And beyond Hal, several paces away, flat on the cobbles of the courtyard, lay a man all burned and seared down one side of his body, and Margaret blinked again, and thought that this man's devastated face looked strangely like Lancaster's.

Chapter IX

Nones on the Saturday within the Octave of Corpus Christi
In the second year of the reign of Richard II
(noon 2nd June 1380)

— III —

✠

MARGARET MURMURED, and Neville let her down to her feet. She stared at the tableau before her, horrified.

There were men grouped about Lancaster's still-smoking body: Raby, Roger Salisbury, several men-at-arms and a man whom Margaret did not recognize.

As Agnes took Rosalind from her arms, this man now walked to where she stood with Neville and Bolingbroke.

"He is alive," said the man. "Just."

"Sweet Jesu, Whittington," Bolingbroke whispered. A tear had fallen from one eye, leaving a grimy trail down his sooty cheek. "How could they have done this?"

"If they realize that they have not killed him they will be back," Whittington said.

"Hal," Raby said from where he knelt by Lancaster, "we have to move. Now."

"The water," said Tyler. "It is the only way."

Bolingbroke nodded, and roused himself from whatever horrified reverie he'd sunk into. "The water," he said, and looked to Salisbury. "Are there any barges or punts left from this conflagration?"

Salisbury moved to see, but Whittington waved him to a halt.

"I have a barge waiting," he said. "But you must go. Now."

"You have done well for us today," Bolingbroke said to the alderman.

"I wish I could have done more," Whittington said.

"What happened?" said Neville.

"What happened?" Bolingbroke said, turning to stare at him. "What happened? Men stole into my father's house and set it afire. Then they took my father and they threw him into a stable red with flames."

Raby had been directing several of the men-at-arms to find blankets—*anything*—with which to carry Lancaster down to the river pier. Now he joined the group.

"Without Whittington and his men's aid," he said, "it would have been far worse."

"My father lies dying in agony," Bolingbroke shouted, "*and you say it could have been worse?*"

"It could, and it still might," Tyler put in. "For Jesu's sake, Bolingbroke, get everyone *moving*!"

Bolingbroke whipped about and seized Tyler's jerkin in a fist. "If it wasn't for your actions, *bastard*, my father—"

"Don't call me a bastard," Tyler growled, wrenching himself free, "and never, *never* speak to *me* of fathers!"

Neville had been urging Margaret, Agnes and Mary toward the gate leading to the pier, but now Margaret broke away and ran to where Bolingbroke and Tyler faced each other.

"You cannot battle each other," she said, placing a hand

on each man's arm. "You cannot! Wat," she turned to him, "did you free Tom? Yes? Then I do thank you, for you have given me my life back."

Bolingbroke sighed. "And I thank you as well, Wat. Forgive me . . ." His voice drifted off and he looked to where four of the men-at-arms were now carefully rolling Lancaster onto a blanket.

"Did Courtenay give you the—?"

Bolingbroke's eyes flickered first to Margaret and then to Neville, standing a few paces away with a combination of puzzlement and impatience across his face.

"Aye," Bolingbroke said. "Wat . . . I like not what this means. Do you—"

"The key is yours now," Wat hissed. "Use it!"

Suddenly one of the palace walls bordering the courtyard cracked and groaned, and Neville lunged forward, seized Margaret and dragged her toward the river gate.

"Wat!" she cried.

Wat stared at her, a stricken expression on his face as if he wanted above all to say something but could not, not with Neville so close.

"Margaret," he finally called as she and Neville neared the gate. "Farewell!"

She cried something back, but Wat could not hear it. He took a deep breath, then leaned close to Bolingbroke.

"Brother," he said, "the 'you and I' have no more time, methinks. Soon, it will be only you."

"Wat—"

"Tell Richard to meet me this evening at East Smithfield," Wat hissed. "Tell him!"

"Richard will not—"

"Richard *must*, if he wants to regain any semblance of control. Make sure he understands that."

"Wat. Jesus Christ. You cannot hope to succeed."

"I will speak the words, Hal, and then it must be up to you to take the words into the world. Why else should I pass the key into your safekeeping?"

The Savoy was now disintegrating about them, stones crashing from walls, flames roaring through the hammer-beam roof of the great hall, the few remaining intact windows exploding in deadly splinters of glass.

"You *must* get out of here!" Wat shouted about the roar of destruction. "Get to safety in the Tower! The mob will have sated its murderous rage soon enough, and I will lead them to East Smithfield. This evening, Hal. *Make sure Richard attends!*"

"Christ, Wat. You will die!"

Wat smiled, deep and loving. He embraced Bolingbroke. "Christ will watch over me, in this life and the next," he said. "Now you go with Christ, Hal. Go!"

He gave Bolingbroke a shove and Bolingbroke, at first reluctantly and then with greater speed, ran toward the river gate where everyone else had vanished. As he passed through he turned and held up his hand to Wat in a final salute.

Then he was gone.

Wat stared, then dashed for the gates leading to the Strand. There would be much work to do this day.

THE BARGE was dangerously overcrowded, and the two men-at-arms who worked the poles did so with the utmost care.

Margaret sat beside Lancaster lying wrapped in damp blankets on the flat bottom of the barge. She had torn up the cloak of one of the men-at-arms, and wetted the pieces in the river. Now she carefully sponged at the burns on Lancaster's face.

He moaned each time she touched him, and Margaret's heart almost broke. *Why couldn't he lie senseless and unknowing of the pain?*

Neville sat close to her, one arm about her waist, the other holding Rosalind to him. The child was sniffing and hiccupping, but her cries had ceased, and she clung to her father with all her tiny might. Neville was soothing her with soft sounds and nonsense words, and Margaret thought that he was using these words to soothe Lancaster as much as Rosalind.

Mary and Agnes sat on the other side of Lancaster. Mary was shivering, even though she was tightly wrapped in a cloak over her nightgown. Margaret glanced at her with concern—was her face so gray merely from the lingering shock of being trapped in the burning palace, and then seeing the burned body of her father-in-law?

Both of those would have been enough to whiten the complexion of any woman, but Margaret's concern for Mary was fed by a far greater apprehension. Until recently, Mary had enjoyed a smooth pregnancy—too smooth. She had not sickened as most women did in their early months, and neither had she quickened.

Margaret was beginning to believe that what Mary nurtured within her womb was not a child at all, but something far darker and loathsome.

Far more *impish.*

In the past ten days or so Mary had become very listless and quiet. At first Margaret had believed it to be her natural concern at the approach of the rebels . . . but now?

Margaret looked to Agnes, and the two women shared their anxiety silently. But whatever was wrong with Mary would have to wait for the moment. Lancaster was Margaret's first concern, and secondly, the safety of all the people in the barge: as they wended their way downriver they could all see the smoke and flames leaping above London. Most of the riverside warehouses were alight, and many of the buildings within the city walls as well.

The morning had been lost to a twilight of smoke and haze and fear.

Neville leaned closer to Margaret and murmured something in her hair. She didn't hear the sense of it, but she understood the love in his tone, and she looked up and smiled gratefully. His hand slid a little further about her waist and pressed against the hard roundness of her belly.

"He is safe," Margaret whispered, and she felt Neville relax in relief against her at the same time as Mary sent her a look of pure unhappiness.

Her baby was safe . . . but was Mary safe from what lingered within her?

Margaret's sense of unease increased.

Neville kissed Margaret's hair, then looked to where Bolingbroke, Raby, Salisbury and Courtenay huddled with Whittington and some fifteen or sixteen men-at-arms who'd escaped from the Savoy.

"Will we be admitted?" he asked softly.

Bolingbroke gave a short, harsh laugh. "Richard would not dare to keep us out," he said. "We have some twenty fighting men among us. Besides, it will not be Richard manning the gates to the Tower, but some sensible guardsmen. All they will see when they look at us are twenty extra swords. So, aye, we will gain entry."

They were well past Queenshithe Wharf now and were rapidly approaching London Bridge. Neville looked up at the bridge, and at the people leaning from the windows of the tenement buildings and shops and swarming over both the deck of the bridge and its piers.

"We will be safe," said Whittington, and, as the shadow of the bridge spread over them, he stood up, making the vessel rock alarmingly.

He grabbed at Courtenay and Salisbury to stabilize himself, then shouted his name to the men on the piers even now readying pikes and staves to tackle the barge.

As soon as the men recognized Whittington, they lowered their staves and gestured to the people on the bridge and at the windows to put down their stones and chamber pots.

"I escort my Lord of Bolingbroke to the king," Whittington called, trying to inject as much cheerfulness into his voice as possible, "so that he might persuade him to meet with Tyler and his rebels and listen to their grievances!"

A cheer went up, and men lowered their weapons and waved as the barge glided by.

Neville blessed their luck that Lancaster lay in the bottom of the barge, for he had no doubt that had the men on the piers realized who else the barge contained they would have stopped it and dragged the luckless Lancaster free.

But perhaps that would have done the man a kindness, granting him a swift death on the blade of a sword or in the watery embrace of the river rather than the agonizing lingering death that currently awaited him.

Darkness swept over them as they passed under one of the great stone arches of the bridge, then, as they emerged on the other side, and the Tower loomed into view two hundred yards away, the two men-at-arms resumed their poling with renewed vigor.

Chapter X

Afternoon on the Saturday within the
Octave of Corpus Christi
In the second year of the reign of Richard II
(2nd June 1380)

— IV —

✠

THE TOWER FORTRESS and complex occupied the lower southeastern corner of London. It was completely surrounded by water, the Thames flowing along its southern wall, while a deep river-fed moat protected the other three sides. The double walls of the complex enclosed some sixteen acres of gardens, barracks, palaces, galleries, halls and the square whitewashed lime- and rag-stone Norman keep known as the White Tower.

The land entry to the Tower complex was across a bridge that spanned the moat at the southwestern corner of the walls. This bridge led to the Lion's Gate (so called because it housed the royal collection of moth-eaten and half-starved exotic animals), which in turn led to the Outer Ward, the space between the double walls.

There was one other entry: a water gate set into the southern wall where boats on the Thames could pull in. Above the water gate rose a great tower called St. Thomas' which, at sundry times, formed part of the royal lodgings.

Today it seemed cold and soulless.

Their barge bumped into the small wharf by St. Thomas' and Bolingbroke jumped onto its steps, leaning down to give Mary his arm as she rose to disembark.

He frowned as he looked into her face, and he glanced at Margaret.

She nodded slightly, admitting her own worry for Mary at the same time as she wondered how genuine was Bolingbroke's concern. She walked to Mary's side and took her arm, and smiled at her, and Mary returned the smile gratefully.

Margaret murmured something to her, but Mary shook her head, and said something that, for the moment, eased the worry in Margaret's eyes.

As Whittington stepped onto the wharf he turned to Bolingbroke. "My lord, I will leave you here. I can do more good among my fellow citizens."

Bolingbroke nodded. "What is their mood? How will they turn?"

Whittington thought deeply before replying. "This morning's anarchy and violence will have persuaded most of them that they would be happier to see the last of their country cousins," he said finally. "I do not think Wadsworth will have much trouble raising the city militia to a more active role by this evening.

"However," he continued, as Bolingbroke opened his mouth to speak, "my brothers and sisters of the city still greatly sympathize with the rebels' grievances. Indeed, many share them. Richard would be well advised to treat the rebels with magnanimity and a gentle, guiding hand."

Again Bolingbroke opened his mouth to speak, and again Whittington forestalled him.

"And if Richard *doesn't* use magnanimity and gentleness," he said softly, staring into Bolingbroke's eyes, "then I think they will be greatly disappointed in their king."

Bolingbroke took a deep breath, understanding. "I thank you, Whittington," he said. "I think I shall leave Richard to his own devices in this matter."

Whittington snorted. "You are a subtle, cunning man," he said. "You might as well march in there and hand Richard a shovel to dig his own grave."

A strange, hard expression came over Bolingbroke's face. "Isn't that what I just said?"

Whittington nodded. "Aye, my friend. That you did. And one day, when you are king and I am Lord Mayor, we will sit down and remember this day and toast Wat with the best of wines."

Sudden tears glimmered in Bolingbroke's eyes. He reached out, grasped Whittington briefly by the shoulder, and then turned away.

THE MEN manning the portcullis at the Traitor's Gate needed little persuading to raise it as soon as they knew who stood on the other side.

Bolingbroke thanked them, then led his group under the stone arch of the gate and into the Outer Ward. Directly across from them in the inner wall was another tower and gate known as the Garden Gate, also barred with a lowered portcullis.

This, too, was raised as soon as Bolingbroke announced himself and his companions.

Beyond the Garden Gate was an area containing orchards

and herb beds, and beyond the gardens stretched an open gravelled space.

Across this space scurried armed men between the bastions on the double walls, the barely visible barracks against the far wall of the compound and the huddle of buildings against the great White Tower to the right.

Neville moved to Bolingbroke's shoulder, wondering about the numbers and readiness of the garrison within the complex, but more concerned for the moment with Lancaster and the women.

"Your father needs attention," he said.

"Aye," said Bolingbroke, and beckoned to the four men carrying the blankets in which Lancaster lay. "This way."

He led them toward the palace complex that lay a little distance from the southern wall of the White Tower.

"Shouldn't we go to the Keep?" said Neville.

Bolingbroke shook his head. "We're safe enough within the walls without cowering in the White Tower," he said. "Besides, the royal apartments attached to the Hall are more comfortable than the chill of the Keep itself."

And they'll be free of Richard, thought Neville, *who is no doubt locked inside one of the highest chambers within the Keep*.

They were met at the entrance to the palace apartments by a chamberlain who needed no introductions, nor instructions, once he saw Lancaster and the white-faced women.

"This way, my lords," he said.

He led them to several chambers that were easily defensible by virtue of their narrow windows and entrance ways, and sent two of his servants scurrying for a physician.

Bolingbroke nodded his thanks as Margaret directed the men-at-arms to carry Lancaster into one of the inner chambers where they lifted him gently onto a large bed. Neville handed Rosalind to Agnes, who took charge of both her and Mary, who had sunk to a chair under one of the windows, her face lined with exhaustion.

Bolingbroke conferred quietly with Raby. The earl eventually nodded, then took Courtenay and Salisbury with him, together with ten of the men-at-arms, to secure as well as they could the passageways leading to the chambers.

As Raby and the men-at-arms left, Bolingbroke glanced at Mary, hesitated, then turned away to enter the chamber to wait with his father.

Neville watched Bolingbroke, frowned, then walked over to where Mary sat.

"My lady," he said, squatting on his haunches beside her chair, "in all the fright of the past hours we have forgot you. Are you well?"

She lifted her hand to him, and he bent and kissed it.

"I am most grateful for your concern, Tom," she said softly.

"My lady, Bolingbroke has been—"

"I know, I know, you need not make excuses for him, Tom. His father lies burned and dying, and Hal's first thought must be for Lancaster. But to answer your question, I am tired, and frightened, but otherwise you need have no concern for me."

Neville, still holding Mary's hand, was not sure he should believe that. He felt a surge of protective care for the woman: she was with child, and must surely be terrified at what had happened over the past day.

"I do thank you, Tom," Mary said, surprised and overwhelmingly grateful to see the concern in Neville's eyes. "But Agnes is here with me, and Rosalind too, and if I have time and peace enough for an hour's sleep then I shall be the better for it."

Neville nodded, kissed her hand again, and then joined Bolingbroke in Lancaster's death chamber, closing the door behind him. Whatever happened in here, he did not think that Mary should witness it.

BOLINGBROKE AND Neville stood silently at the bedside, staring down at Lancaster. Margaret sat on the far side of the bed, her eyes shifting between the two standing men and Lancaster, who lay moaning and semi-conscious. Every so often she sponged gently, hopelessly, at Lancaster's ruined face. She was about to say something—*anything* to break this silence!—when the chamber door opened, and the physician and his two apprentices bustled in.

But it was not the physician who commanded Bolingbroke's and Neville's attention, for immediately behind the doctor strode Henry Percy, the Earl of Northumberland.

The man was hard-faced and eyed, and spared Bolingbroke and Neville little more than a glance as he strode to Lancaster's bed.

The hardness vanished as soon as Northumberland saw what had happened to Lancaster. "Sweet God," he whispered.

He looked to Margaret, then to the physician who was hiding his uselessness in bustle and self-importance, then to Bolingbroke and Neville.

"The rebels torched the Savoy," Bolingbroke said, his voice harsh.

Northumberland opened his mouth, struggled to speak, then gave up, and Neville realized how deeply affected the man was by Lancaster's plight. Rivals they might be, but there was still respect there, and horror that a comrade should have met such a horrifying fate.

The physician, aided by one of his apprentices, took hold of a burned piece of clothing that clung to one of Lancaster's thighs and tugged it off.

Lancaster screamed, his body arching off the bed in the extremity of his agony.

Bolingbroke moved, but Northumberland was faster. He grabbed the physician by the shoulder, spun him about, and hit him as hard as he could on the jaw.

The physician slumped to the ground, senseless.

"Lady," Northumberland said to Margaret, having taken a deep breath to bring his temper under control, "will you direct these useless apprentices to *soak* Lancaster's clothes from his flesh?"

She nodded, as angry as Bolingbroke and Northumberland at the unthinking cruelty of the physician, and sent the apprentices scrambling to fill bowls with warm, salty water.

Then Northumberland started, for Lancaster had reached up a blackened hand and taken the earl's arm in a fierce grip.

"Where are we?" he rasped.

"In the royal apartments of the Tower," Bolingbroke said in a gentle voice.

Lancaster stared at his son, then looked back at Northumberland. "*Do not let Richard murder him!*" he said.

Northumberland glanced at Bolingbroke, who was staring at him, then down again at Lancaster.

"John—" Northumberland began.

The duke somehow managed to half-raise himself from the bed. "*Do not let Richard murder my son!*"

"If your son is a traitor to his king then there is little I can do," Northumberland said.

Lancaster snarled, the expression a frightful rictus on his ravaged face. "My son is true to his *land*," he said. "Is Richard?"

Then, exhausted, his hand dropped, and Northumberland took a step back.

Margaret, standing with a warm bowl of water the other side of the bed, cloths in hand, looked at the men, then spoke.

"My lords, it were best, perhaps, if you left the chamber."

They hesitated, wanting desperately to be gone before Lancaster's agony began anew, but all three just as desperately concerned for him.

"She's right," Northumberland said roughly. "Hal . . . Richard knows you are here. It is best you attend him now."

Lancaster groaned something, and Northumberland leaned down to him.

"Many things may happen to your son over the next few days," Northumberland said, "but on my word your son's murder shall not be one of them."

Lancaster jerked his head, unable for the moment to

speak, and Northumberland straightened and walked from the chamber.

Bolingbroke leaned over and said something to his father, while Neville looked at Margaret.

"Will you be well?" he asked.

"Aye. I have these two," she gestured to the apprentices standing to one side, "to aid me."

"Good." Neville looked to one of the men-at-arms standing against the wall. "Take this"—his booted foot poked at the still-senseless physician—"and remove it from this chamber."

As they left, Bolingbroke looked at Margaret. "Do what you can, all you can," he said, and she nodded.

WHEN THE men had gone, Margaret shooed the apprentices away for the moment and sat on the bed close to Lancaster and took both his hands in hers.

"I can do too little for you," she whispered, "but I will be glad to do what I can."

She lowered her eyes to his hands, and gently rubbed her thumbs over their charred flesh.

Lancaster groaned, a deep, terrible sound.

"Shush," Margaret said . . . then jabbed her thumbs into his flesh as hard as she could.

Lancaster's eyes widened, and as he opened his mouth to scream the men-at-arms tensed and made ready to move forward. But then Lancaster slowly closed his mouth, realizing that his pain had receded in great, rolling waves.

A great ache and soreness still consumed him, but the agony had gone.

He blinked, stunned. "What are you?" he whispered.

Margaret smiled, a smile as full of sweetness and love as she could manage.

"I speak for Christ," she said, so softly that only he heard, "as if I were his sister."

Lancaster looked at her, his state of near death allowing him to see her for what she was. "I am going to die," he said.

"Aye," she said, "that you are. But there will still be time to say goodbye to Hal."

"Thank you," he whispered, and Margaret smiled again and leaned down and kissed him on the lips.

Then she sat back, rolled up her sleeves, and set to soaking off Lancaster's charred clothing.

RICHARD TURNED from the window as he heard the door open, and glanced at de Vere before he looked at Bolingbroke and Neville who stood to one side of Northumberland.

"Why, my lords," he said, "I did so think you'd be roaming the streets with the traitorous rebels rather than submitting yourself to my tender love."

"It is clear," said de Vere, walking slowly to stand at Richard's side, "that Neville has taken good advantage of the riot."

There were other men in this chamber high within the White Tower: Tresilian; the Archbishop of Canterbury, Simon Sudbury; the Treasurer, Bishop Thomas Brantingham; the earls of Kent and Warwick; several other high-ranking nobles; and William Wadsworth, the Lord Mayor—and a pale-faced, but calm, Joan of Kent, Richard's mother, sitting in a large chair by the hearth.

All had their eyes riveted on the confrontation between Richard and Bolingbroke.

"Your grace," said Northumberland, and Bolingbroke and Neville were surprised to hear the grating undertone of his words, "Bolingbroke brought to the Tower his father, Lancaster, who lies a-dying in the royal apartments."

Richard managed to prevent himself from smiling, but could not quite hide the sudden leap of glee in his eyes.

"Dying, my lord?"

"The rebels burned down the Savoy," Bolingbroke said.

"My father has been burned beyond recognition, and the rest of us barely escaped with our lives."

Richard laughed. "Escaped straight into *my* clutches!"

"Your grace," Northumberland said again, "Bolingbroke can perhaps give us important information."

Richard made a dismissive gesture, but Bolingbroke managed to speak before Richard ignored him completely. "Indeed," he said, "I have a message for your grace from the leader of the rebels."

Now Richard raised an eyebrow. "A 'message'?"

"Wat Tyler, who speaks for those who wish to present you their grievances, requests that you meet with him this evening in East Smithfield."

Richard stared at Bolingbroke, a muscle flickering in his cheek, then the pink, glistening tip of his tongue flickered over his lower lip. He turned to de Vere, and smiled.

De Vere took his lover's cue, smiling incredulously and lacing his voice with cutting sarcasm. "Have you become a messenger boy for the rabble, Bolingbroke?" Then his smile faded. "How dare you so instruct my lord your liege?"

"I only repeat what my lord my liege needs to know!" Bolingbroke said.

Northumberland put a hand on Bolingbroke's shoulder, and Bolingbroke subsided.

Northumberland dropped his hand. "We must consider the request carefully," he said.

"You expect me to dance to the tune of *peasants?*" Richard said. "I am not going to—"

"Your grace," Tresilian said, rising from his seat and joining the group, "we appear safe enough within the Tower . . . but are we truly? Many of the Londoners agree with the rebels' actions. Did they not allow them entry to the city unopposed?"

"But—" Richard said.

"True, the Tower is garrisoned with some thousand men," Northumberland said quietly. "Yet are they not drawn from London's militia? Are they not all London men themselves?"

There was a silence as Richard thought it through.

"They would not *dare* to allow the rebels entry to the Tower," Richard said.

"No!" cried Joan of Kent, rising from her chair.

"No?" Bolingbroke whispered, but no one heard him over Joan's cry.

Northumberland shot an irritated glance at Richard's mother, then shrugged expressively. "Who can tell, your grace?"

"If I do as they ask," Richard said, "and go to East Smithfield, then they will surely murder me."

"For Christ's sake, you simpleton!" Bolingbroke shouted. "Think it through. You will die if you *don't* go." He felt Northumberland's hand on his shoulder again, much heavier this time, and Bolingbroke moderated his voice. "All the rebels want is to present their grievances to you. If you go, and nod and smile and listen, and say you will take it all under due consideration, then you will be safer than . . . safer than you are in this chamber."

"No," said Richard. "No! I will *not* bend my knee before *peasants!*"

Bolingbroke stared at Richard. "Be it on your own head," he said.

Chapter XI

Compline on the Saturday within the
Octave of Corpus Christi
In the second year of the reign of Richard II
(night 2nd June 1380)

— V —

✠

BOLINGBROKE HAD more than half-expected to be thrown into one of the Tower's dungeons, but Richard waved him away before turning back to de Vere.

No doubt one hundred thousand resentful peasants made even the problem of Bolingbroke pale into insignificance.

Before he returned to his father, Bolingbroke, accompanied by Neville and Northumberland, made his way to one of the bastions in the northern inner wall. From here, they had a clear view over Tower Hill to the northwest and East Smithfield to the northeast. The two areas, meadowland save for a few tents and some small storage houses, were swarming with tens of thousands of men, many of them congregating in shadowy, murmuring clusters around the Tower's northern moat and the roadway approaches to the Barbican leading to the land entry of the Lion's Tower.

Bolingbroke shaded his eyes against the setting sun and stared westward into London. He could just make out the crowds along Fenchurch Street, which led to Aldgate and the smaller gate just north of the Tower.

"Richard should have agreed to meet them," he said.

"Aye," said Northumberland. "Richard's decision was not the wisest he has ever made."

Bolingbroke turned and studied Northumberland. "I find you a sudden and most unlikely ally," he said.

Northumberland gave a small shrug, taking his time in replying. "There are men, Bolingbroke, who are perturbed by Richard's 'alliance' with de Vere."

"I should have thought you pleased with such an alliance," Neville put in, "for is not de Vere your son-in-law? Can you not expect great preferments for your family from what Richard's 'Robbie' whispers in his ear?"

Northumberland sent him an irritated look. "De Vere is not proving a good son-in-law."

"Ah," Bolingbroke said. "Now that he has the crown of Ireland within his grasp, if not quite on his head, he thinks he might find a more suitable match among the daughters of Europe's royal families?"

The sudden anger in Northumberland's eyes was all the answer Bolingbroke needed.

Sweet Jesu, Bolingbroke thought. *Richard is not the only one digging his grave—de Vere is in there aiding him!*

He shared a quick glance with Neville, and saw that he, too, understood: *Northumberland, and all who stand behind him, will soon be ours . . . and all because de Vere has preferred other beds to his marriage bed.*

But Bolingbroke did not waste time on savoring his potential triumph—of what use was a future possibility when they might all lie dead by tomorrow?

He looked over the parapets of the bastion at the gathering horde in the fields beyond. "Did you mean what you said in Richard's chamber," he said to Northumberland, "when you said the Tower's guards might well let the peasants in?"

"What would you do," said Northumberland, "faced with such overwhelming numbers?"

"Only one in six of the peasants are well-armed," Neville said.

Northumberland gave a humorless grin. "Well, then, that

brings it down to . . . what . . . fifteen thousand swords waving at a few score guards who more than likely agree in principle with everything the peasants want.

"Besides," he added, "perhaps only one in six are 'well-armed,' but the other five are armed with anything they can lay their hands on, *and* are driven by a murderous temper. I hear that some several hundred foreigners and rich merchants have been murdered on the streets this day. Maybe the guards will hold . . . maybe not."

Lights flickered through the growing peasant army outside the Tower walls as dusk settled over the city.

"Tell me what you think will happen," Bolingbroke asked Northumberland, and Neville was struck by the manner in which he addressed the earl—as a king asking advice from one of his senior counselors.

"They will not wait for Richard to change his mind," Northumberland said quietly, staring at the peasant army rather than at Bolingbroke. "They must know that Richard has sent for reinforcements from militias close to the city, and that those forces are unlikely to be more than two days away. They also know that the city does not have enough to feed them. If they are to succeed, they *must* press their case within the day—"

"And more probably within the night," Bolingbroke completed for him, "for they know that if Richard will grant their wishes—and save their lives—he must do so before reinforcements arrive."

"You know this Wat Tyler," Northumberland said to Bolingbroke. "Tell me, can he control this rabble?"

"I doubt anyone could," Bolingbroke said softly.

"Jesu!" said Neville. "Hal, our *wives* are here. What can we do to—?"

"We can stay calm," said Northumberland, "and we will do all we can to placate the rebels if they manage to gain entry to the Tower. There is little else we *can* do."

* * *

LANCASTER WAS lying comfortably and dozing when Bolingbroke and Neville got back to the royal apartments, but when he heard Bolingbroke enter the chamber his eyes opened, and he smiled.

Margaret, who had been sitting by Lancaster's bed, withdrew as Bolingbroke approached, their eyes meeting briefly, lovingly.

Neville had waited in the outer chamber.

Lancaster lifted one of his hands, blackened but not so crisp now that Margaret had rubbed salve over it.

Bolingbroke took it without hesitation, sitting carefully on the bed beside his father.

"I am dying," Lancaster said in a hoarse voice.

"You have been most grievously injured," Bolingbroke said. There was no point in denying it. "Has Margaret tended your pain?"

"Aye." Lancaster paused. "She is a most remarkable lady."

Bolingbroke smiled, looking briefly to where Margaret sat in a corner. "Oh, aye, that she is."

"She tells me I will live with Christ for eternity. I . . ." Lancaster's voice broke. "I do not deserve it!"

"No one deserves that more than you," Bolingbroke said, leaning closer to Lancaster and repressing the urge to grasp his hand the more firmly for emphasis. "You have been the greatest of fathers, the most loving of men. I am honored that I am of your house."

Lancaster's eyes filled with tears, and his hand tightened about Bolingbroke's. "Look after Katherine," he said. "I am sorry to leave her, but glad she will not have seen me like this."

Bolingbroke nodded, unable for the moment to speak.

"Richard will move against you once I am gone," Lancaster said.

"If he tries to grind me into the mud I will spring up ten times as strong again."

Lancaster nodded, his face grimacing in what was probably a smile. "Let him think he has defeated you, for then he *cannot* defeat you."

"Aye. I shall bite my lip and skulk away into the shadows of whatever punishment he thinks fit for me . . . and from there . . ."

"And from there . . . the throne." Again Lancaster hesitated. "Sweet Jesu, Hal, I never thought I would live to hear that from my lips. How can it be that Richard is so little a man when his father and grandfather were so great?"

"It is often the way," Margaret put in from her stool.

"Then how sad," Lancaster whispered. "How sad."

There was a lengthy pause, and then Lancaster spoke again. "Tell me of what happens in the outside world. Is the Savoy gone?"

"Probably," said Bolingbroke. "When we carried you away the roof of the great hall was collapsing."

"Why do men seek so hard to destroy?" said Lancaster. "Why do they seek to destroy beauty?"

"It is always the way," Bolingbroke said, with an apologetic look at Margaret for stealing her words.

"And the mob?" said Lancaster. "And Richard?"

"The mob," said Bolingbroke, deciding not to tell his father who led them, "are demanding that Richard meet them to hear their grievances. Richard has refused, saying he won't bow before peasants."

Lancaster bared his teeth. "He is a little man *and* a fool. This is no way to start a reign."

Bolingbroke smiled coldly. "Not for him."

What was left of Lancaster's face grew more sad. "I had not thought it would ever come to this . . . that my brother's son should so blacken his father's and grandfather's names—"

"What? Is this treachery you speak?"

Bolingbroke and Lancaster jerked their heads toward the door, Lancaster moaning at the sudden movement.

Richard and de Vere had walked in and now approached the bed.

Bolingbroke stood up slowly, letting go his father's hand. "What do you here?" he said.

"Disturbing your talk of treason," said Richard, his face a mixture of triumph and contempt as he gazed down on Lancaster.

"There is no such thing as treason against fools," said Lancaster, his eyes glittering with hatred.

Richard's face worked. "I should have had you hanged as a common criminal."

Again Lancaster bared his teeth, and then his hands were grabbing at the bed covers. Bolingbroke started forward, for he thought his father was going to try to rise, but Lancaster only threw back the covers, exposing his ravaged naked body.

"I give *this* for your stupid words, sodomite!" One of Lancaster's hands grabbed at his genitals, shaking them at Richard. "And believe it when I say I would piss at you if I had any left in me."

Richard took a step back, his face pale and shocked. De Vere, his face warped with hatred, stepped up behind the king and placed a hand on the young man's shoulder, offering Richard his support.

"What's the matter, Richard?" said Bolingbroke. "I thought you liked the sight of other men's genitals."

Now Richard's face flushed a deep red, and he jerked his head away from Lancaster to Bolingbroke. "You have never loved me!"

Lancaster waggled his genitals once more. "Take it now if you want it. I have not much time left."

"I will destroy you!" Richard shouted at Bolingbroke.

"You wouldn't dare," Bolingbroke said quietly, holding Richard's gaze.

Several other people had by now come into the chamber: Neville, who moved carefully about the group to stand at

Margaret's side; Raby and Salisbury, who had moved to Bolingbroke's side; and Courtenay, who stayed by the door, lest it needed to be shut quickly.

Richard, and de Vere, his hand now down at his side, stared about, suddenly realizing their danger.

Richard opened his mouth to speak, but was forestalled by the entry of Northumberland and some six or seven guards.

Courtenay stepped back from the door with considerable alacrity.

"Your grace!" Northumberland said, hurrying to Richard's side and sharing a very quick glance with Bolingbroke. "The gate in the Lion Tower has given way. Peasants are swarming through the Inner Ward."

If anything, Richard went even whiter. "*What?* Northumberland, you were supposed to protect me!"

"We are *all* dead if you don't do something!" Bolingbroke said. "Sweet Jesu, Richard, if you don't go out and agree to meet with them, *then we are all dead!*"

"I . . . I . . ."

De Vere locked eyes with Northumberland, glanced at Bolingbroke, and then took Richard by the shoulders and shook him. "Richard, get out there now! You have no choice about whether or not to meet them if you want to live."

How quickly de Vere sees sense, thought Bolingbroke, *when it is* his *life threatened.*

"All you have to do," Bolingbroke said, "is to agree to meet with them. At daybreak on the morrow, if you do not wish to venture out in the dark."

Richard sent a simmering glance Bolingbroke's way, but nodded. "You will come out with me," he said.

Bolingbroke nodded. "As your grace desires."

"And Robbie!" Richard said, looking at his lover.

"Your grace, it might be better if I remained—"

"You *will* do as I ask!"

De Vere nodded—with the utmost reluctance.

* * *

IN THE end, Raby and the two squires stayed with Lancaster and the women, while Northumberland accompanied Richard, de Vere, Bolingbroke, Neville and some score of men-at-arms outside into the open gravelled space occupying several acres within the Inner Ward.

When Bolingbroke and Neville had come through here earlier it had been almost empty save for some score of men-at-arms scurrying about.

Now it seemed thousands of torch-carrying and weaponed peasants stood there.

Richard hesitated as he looked at the numbers present, and Bolingbroke seized his chance.

"My friends!" he called, striding toward the peasants. "See who I have persuaded to speak with you!"

A roar went up from the crowd and, as it died and before Richard could say anything, Bolingbroke again spoke.

"He has seen my reason," he said, "and will meet with you at daybreak tomorrow in East Smithfield!"

Lord Christ Savior, Neville thought admiringly. *Hal has just presented himself as the rabble's friend!*

"Is this true?" shouted a voice, and Wat Tyler strode forth from the rabble. "Will you meet with us, sire, and listen to our grievances?"

Slowly, reluctantly, his eyes darting about at the armed men confronting him, Richard walked forward a few paces. "Aye," he said, then cleared his throat and spoke again. "Aye!"

A great cheer went up from the mob, and Tyler locked eyes briefly with Bolingbroke.

Then he looked back to Richard. "Be there," he said, "or I cannot speak for what my brothers' anger will lead them to. Do not rob them of their trust in you, for already they have vented their ire on those who have robbed them of their livelihood."

And he stood back.

Behind him the crowd parted, and in the torchlight

Richard and his companions could see four headless bodies lying on the gravel.

Four of the rebels leaned down and lifted the heads up in the torchlight for their king to see.

Two of the men were legal clerks who had been heavily involved in instituting the poll tax, but Richard could not help the small cry that escaped his lips at the sight of the third head.

It had once belonged to Simon Sudbury, the archbishop of Canterbury.

For his part Bolingbroke smiled, for the fourth head was that of the physician who had so hurt Lancaster.

"My men will wait out the night here," said Tyler, "and in the morning will escort you safely to East Smithfield."

He paused, his hard eyes staring at Richard. "Do not fail us."

Chapter XII

Prime on the Octave of Corpus Christi
In the second year of the reign of Richard II
(Sunday 3rd June 1380)

✠

IT WAS A GRAY and still morning, heavy with the threat of barely quiescent violence. For Bolingbroke, who had sat through the dark unknown hours with his dying father, daybreak appeared no worse than the night which had given it birth.

For Richard, it seemed as if daybreak could well herald the hour of his execution.

He was furious that his glorious kingship had come to

this, furious that Hal was again breathing in the acclaim of the masses, and furious that Hal had so manipulated him the previous night.

Furious that he had been able to do nothing about it.

When I get my chance, pretty boy Hal, he thought, *I shall crucify you!*

And his people—how was it that his people, his subjects, who should have adored him, who were *obliged* to adore him—had now massed in angry, resentful battalions outside the Tower's walls?

This wasn't the way it was supposed to be.

He was king. His word, his very wish, was law. Why couldn't people understand that?

How dare they *refuse* to understand that?

They were as treacherous as their fair Bolingbroke . . .

Richard almost snarled as hateful Northumberland, with his judgmental eyes and bland, severe face, tugged at the fastenings of his cloak, and straightened the sword as it hung at his hip.

How dare he touch him!

"This meeting with a rabble is a mistake," Richard said.

"It will be the greater mistake if you do not go," said Northumberland, "because then they will storm the Tower and murder you." He stood back after giving Richard's cloak a final tweak.

"I should send Bolingbroke," Richard said, his eyes sliding this way and that about the chamber, looking for Robbie. *Where was he?*

"If Bolingbroke went he would come back king," said Northumberland, and Richard knew at that moment that he loathed the earl. His thoughts flew off at a tangent, wondering how best he might destroy Northumberland . . .

"I will see *all* my enemies defeated," Richard finally said in a low, almost sulky, tone.

Northumberland looked at him, then turned away. "The horses await, your grace," he said, pulling on his gloves and striding toward the door of the chamber.

"Northumberland!" Richard called, furious that he had to raise his voice to attract the man's attention.

Northumberland stopped in the doorway and turned about. "Yes?"

"Is there . . . has there been any news of Surrey's militia approaching the city? *Any* militia?"

Northumberland stared a long moment before he replied. "No," he said, and turned and walked through the door.

Richard muttered a foul curse, looking around at the mayor, Wadsworth, and wondering whether *he* was a potential traitor as well.

Wadsworth was fidgeting with a button on his tunic and, as he saw Richard glare, smiled halfheartedly and dropped his hand to the dagger at his waist before deciding that was a bad idea and moving it back to the buttons of his tunic.

There was a movement at the door, and Richard's eyes jerked that way, opening his mouth to shout at whoever had disturbed him.

Instead he whispered, almost pathetically, "Robbie!"

De Vere smiled, bowed, and walked over to Richard. He touched Richard's cheek, whispering soft words that brought a blush to the younger man's cheeks.

"Where is your cloak, Robbie?" Richard said. "The morning is chill, and you must not ride without it."

"I shall not be riding with you—"

"What? What? I *demand* that you ride with me!"

"Your grace," de Vere said, then dropped his voice and whispered an endearment. "I would that the glory be all yours," he continued in a ringing tone. "I would not dare intrude upon the majesty that will undoubtedly be all yours this day!"

Wadsworth made a grimace, turning his face aside lest de Vere or Richard saw it. *"I want the glory to be all yours" indeed! No doubt de Vere had a rowboat awaiting him at the water gate.*

Richard blinked, unsure of how to take de Vere's fine speech. "But . . . but . . ."

De Vere took Richard's shoulders in his hands. "You will ride out there and impose yourself upon your subjects," de Vere said. "Never doubt it."

Richard's eyes cleared and his back straightened. "Yes! I *will* do so!"

"You must not allow the rabble to dictate to you. You are the son and grandson of kings, descended from the great warriors of Troy and the line of David. You will prove the greater in this encounter!"

Wadsworth had to give de Vere credit for bolstering Richard's resolve, but he wondered how long Richard's assurance would last.

What would happen the first time Richard had a pike thrust in his face?

Richard nodded. He waved at Wadsworth. "Come, my Lord Mayor, the horses await. Why do you linger?"

As Wadsworth walked for the door, Richard leaned close to de Vere. "I will tell you all about it when I return triumphant!" he said.

And de Vere nodded, his smile only faltering when Richard had left the chamber.

In the stairwell leading down to the entrance of the Keep, Northumberland was listening to a soldier whispering hastily in his ear.

As Richard stepped down to join them, Northumberland turned and whispered as hastily in the king's ear.

Richard visibly relaxed, then he smiled, a tight, cold expression.

LANCASTER WAS very close to death. All night his breathing had become shallower and harsher, and all in the chamber—Bolingbroke, Neville and Margaret—could hear the death rattle grow stronger.

Yet still Lancaster lingered, with a clarity of mind that must, indeed, have been Christ's gift.

"I must be shriven," Lancaster said as dawn broke. "I must have a priest."

"There are no priests within the Tower," Bolingbroke said. "The rabble murdered the last one a few hours ago."

"I—" Neville said, but Lancaster instead turned his face toward Margaret.

"Will you shrive me, sister?"

Neville's mouth dropped open. *Margaret?* He would have objected—no matter what he felt for his wife, a woman was not the one to take confession from the dying—but he saw the expression on Lancaster's face, saw the need there, saw an understanding there that he, Neville, did not and *could* not share, and so he closed his mouth and made no objection.

Margaret looked taken aback, but after a slight hesitation she moved forward and sat down on the bed beside the duke. She took his hand in hers.

"I will be greatly honored," she said.

WHEN RICHARD, Wadsworth, Northumberland and an escort of some twenty squires and men-at-arms arrived at the gravelled space of the Inner Ward they saw that the majority of the peasant force that had been there the previous night had, in fact, gone. Remaining was a man who introduced himself as Jack Straw and perhaps sixty peasants, armed with pikes and swords and arrayed in surprisingly ordered columns.

Having introduced himself, Jack Straw cast a wary eye over the king's escort.

"You carry weapons," he said.

"You would have us march into a murderous rabble *without* weapons?" Northumberland said.

"We are not murderous—"

Northumberland laughed.

"—and we are a 'rabble' only to those who seek to enslave us," Straw said. "But, very well, if you think that your king's words will require swords, then bring them by all means."

He shifted his eyes back to the king, who looked calm and controlled.

I hope he hears us out, thought Straw, *for we are dead if he decides to despise rather than embrace us.*

True, their numbers might carry this day, but unless they could change Richard's heart they would eventually be beaten back into complete servitude.

"Where is Bolingbroke?" Straw said.

"I meet my subjects on my own," said Richard. "I do not need the advice or company of my more rebellious nobles."

And then he added, without any thought of what the consequences might be, "I will not have Bolingbroke take any of the credit for what happens today."

To one side Northumberland very slightly shook his head in disbelief. *The fool!*

And then he wondered how he might get word to his son Hotspur, still encased about Orleans. Whatever this day might bring, the ponderous shifting of allegiances had already begun.

Every one of the peasants arrayed behind Jack Straw heard their king's words, and every one of them would, by the end of the day, have repeated them to a score of comrades.

"I HAVE sinned," Lancaster began, but Margaret reached forward and placed a finger briefly on his lips.

"Have you tried to do what you thought right?" she said.

"Aye," Lancaster said, "but—"

"Then how can you have sinned?"

"I have left so much undone," Lancaster said.

"Have you loved?" Margaret said.

"Yes, of course. Blanche, and the son she gave me," he turned his head very slightly to smile at Bolingbroke. "Constance, a little, for despite her gravity she could make me laugh, and our two daughters. Katherine, more than anyone, for she is my soulmate, and our son and daughter. My father, my mother, my brothers and sisters, my—"

Margaret laughed. "Then what a blessed life you have had, and what love you have given! Your family, your wives and your children have all had of you what they should: your love and your care. Embrace your passing with joy, John, not with thoughts of sin."

Lancaster lay in silence for a little time, thinking about it.

"Aye," he said, "I have been blessed, and blessed that you should be here now to shrive me, Margaret. You have said better and more potent words than could have any priest."

Watching, Neville turned the scene he had just witnessed over in his mind. Was love all that was important? Not sin and thought of eternal penance? Not retribution and vengeance?

He frowned, perplexed.

STRAW AND his sixty peasants led the king's party through the Garden Gate into the Outer Ward, then through the series of gates that protected the drawbridge across the moat.

The road leading to Tower Hill and then to East Smithfield was lined with thousands of people, Londoners as well as peasants. As they moved through the six-deep ranks of silent watchers, Northumberland thought he could feel death closing in about him. His hand seemed to have its own mind, for it desperately wanted to stray to the hilt of his sword, but the earl clenched his teeth and kept it fastened securely about the reins, for he knew it would be his death if people saw his hand stray to a weapon.

God, how were they to get out of this day?

He glanced upward at the soldiers standing atop the bastions of both inner and outer wards.

They saw his glance, but they made no sign, and Northumberland took a deep breath and tried to quell the growing fear within himself.

Peasants and Londoners swarmed over Tower Hill as the party turned their horses east for the small gate in the city wall that led to East Smithfield.

The field was entirely gone, lost under a seething tide of humanity.

All England must be here! Northumberland thought, wondering what had gone so wrong with God's ordained society that it should rise up against His word like this.

Again he glanced at the bastions of the Tower.

The watch there made no sign.

There was a shout ahead, and Northumberland reined his horse to a halt to one side of Richard and Wadsworth, turning it slightly so that he could still see the men atop the Tower's walls.

If God was with them, surely there would be a sign.

A man spoke, and Northumberland whipped his head about.

"Good King Richard," said Wat Tyler, who had now stepped forth from the ranks of the peasants. "Welcome to this ground, held by the commons of England."

I hold this land and all your souls, thought Richard, but did not let the thought show on his face. He was feeling in control and very, very confident. The words that Northumberland had whispered in his ear before they'd left the Keep had given him strength, while the thought that Robbie was eagerly awaiting him back in the Tower bolstered his arrogance.

Tonight he and Robbie would laugh and caress, and talk of the great triumph that he, Richard, had achieved on this field.

"You have requested to speak with me," Richard said, allowing his voice to resound over the assemblage, and pausing momentarily to admire the very ringing of its tone, "and so I am here!"

A cheer went up, and Richard smiled.

It did not reach his eyes.

"Your grace," Tyler said, wondering what manner his death would take, "the good men of England have come to you to present you with our grievances."

Richard stirred, his eyes flashing ominously.

"They are not grievances against *you*, sire," Tyler went on, "but grievances against the nobles and clerics who misinform you and oppress us."

"Grievances?" Richard said.

"Aye, your grace. We are men who provide England with its food and its wealth through the sweat of our brows and the ache of our backs, and yet we are treated as vile creatures who exist only to be enslaved and taxed beyond the bounds of human endurance. We are *men*, not *creatures*, and we deserve rights and freedoms as men!"

Tyler finished on a shout, and as he finished so the shout rose about him. "Freedom! Freedom!"

"Freedom?" said Richard in a soft voice. "In what manner 'freedom'?"

"We ask that you abolish the chains of serfdom," Tyler said. "We ask that you make us free forever, ourselves and our heirs. We ask that we each have the freedom to own our own fields, as nobles have the right—for are we not born from the same stock as Adam and Eve? We ask, your grace, that you withdraw the poll tax, as all other grievous taxes, for we do not think you know how onerous they are to us."

"You want your own fields?" said Richard. "How may that be so? From whom should I seize the land to give to you?"

"From the damned whore of a Church!" shouted a man who joined Tyler.

Richard only barely stopped his lip from curling. This man was a renegade priest!

"My friend, John Ball," said Tyler, indicating the man at his side, "as many among the commons, wonders why the Roman Church should own almost one acre in three within this fair land. Do we not deserve the land more than these corrupt, foreign pigs? Share among the commons of England the wealth of the Church and we shall all be free!"

Richard opened his mouth to speak, but just then Northumberland caught his eye.

The earl gave a very slight nod, and his eyes moved fractionally toward the soldiers atop the bastions.

Richard smiled, and gazed upon Tyler.

"Master Tyler," he said, "I am sure that there is merit in much of what you say."

LANCASTER HAD closed his eyes now, his breathing ever more difficult, his hand slack in Margaret's.

"It will not be long," said Bolingbroke, and tears slipped down his cheeks.

RICHARD LEANED back a little on his horse, as if considering, and, as he did so, glanced at the soldiers atop the bastion. One of them was waving to the northeast, another to the east.

He looked forward—east. From his vantage point on his horse and the slight rise that Tyler had chosen so that all men might see the meeting, Richard could see the glint of steel in the not too far distance.

Everyone's eyes were on him, not what approached behind.

Richard looked down at Tyler and smiled.

"You are a fool and a heretic," said Richard, "and you have accomplished nothing for your fellows."

Behind Richard one of Wadsworth's squires, John Standish, slipped from his horse and, moving so fast that none could stop him, raced forth and stabbed Tyler in the belly with a sword.

Tyler groaned and slumped, but before he sank to the ground, he looked up at Richard and said, "I have accomplished my fellows' freedom this day. You are merely too foolish to understand it."

* * *

BOLINGBROKE JERKED, and Margaret whimpered, and Neville wondered what had happened.

"He dies!" said Bolingbroke, and Margaret cried out in grief.

AS TYLER fell to the ground, Wadsworth spurred his horse forward and, leaning down, stabbed his sword deep in Tyler's belly and chest, again and again.

The crowd erupted, roaring.

"Hear me!" Richard screamed, circling his horse about so that all might see his face and hear his words. "Hear me! Your traitor leader is dead, and your cause gone. Look! Look to the east, and the northeast. There ride knights and men-at-arms to cut you down. Tear me apart if you will, but know that in doing so you will accomplish your own deaths."

Northumberland, his heart beating wildly, spurred his horse to Richard's side to protect him from any who thought to raise a weapon against him.

But the crowd were milling, unsure what to do, looking this way and that, some shouting of the great force which bore down on them from two directions.

They looked for someone to lead them, but their rebel leaders were gone, for as Tyler had been stabbed to death, so others among the king's escort had ridden forward and clubbed Jack Straw, John Hales and John Ball senseless.

"Get you gone back to your hovels," Richard screamed further, "before I give the word to have you *all* murdered!"

"Your grace," Northumberland said, trying to grab Richard's arm. "That is *enough*, for the love of Christ!"

Richard threw him off, and stood in the stirrups and screamed yet more.

"Miserable men! Hateful to both land and sea! Serfs you are and serfs you will be forever. You shall remain in a bondage incomparably viler than that you have previously been subject to. Get you gone. Filth! Filth that you did so *dare* to speak in my face."

Northumberland looked about at the scene. He was frantic, hardly able to believe that he and Richard were still alive. Christ! They should have been slaughtered, even with the forces riding to their aid.

But the rabble had apparently fallen apart with the death of Tyler, and now they pushed and shoved in their desperation to get away before the militia arrived, or before anyone remembered their faces and names.

"Vile, vile men!" Richard continued to scream, his voice now growing hoarse. "Miserable and hateful wretches! Filth! Dung! Contemptible worms!"

The militia had now reached the outer ranks of the panicked rebels, and steel glinted as it rose and fell, and the blood of England spilled freely over its meadowland.

As he listened and watched, Northumberland was consumed with a frightful coldness.

You are an oaf, Richard, he thought, *for you may have had Tyler killed, and a few peasants slaughtered, but do you not realize there is a greater rebel waiting in the shadows?*

LANCASTER GROANED, then stirred. "My friend?" he said.

He half rose, and looked past Bolingbroke and Neville to the door of the chamber.

It opened, and Wat Tyler walked through. His face was ravaged and careworn, and bloodstained were his tunic and leggings, but despite all that, his expression was one of peace, and merriment danced in his eyes.

"My lord," said Tyler, ignoring Neville and giving Margaret and Bolingbroke only the briefest of nods.

They smiled at him, tears running down their faces.

"My lord," Tyler said again, "we belong in a different world now. You must come with me."

"Gladly," said Lancaster, and rose from the bed as if he had no injury and with the grace of a youth.

Bolingbroke drew back, allowing both Lancaster and Tyler room.

"What's going on?" said Neville.

"We are farewelling our friends," said Bolingbroke softly. "Now be quiet, for we must not disturb them."

Lancaster slipped his arm through Tyler's and grinned into the man's face. "Well, now, Wat, I believe you have been caught up in some mischief!"

Tyler winked at him. "And you should have kept out of the kitchens, by the look of *you*!"

Lancaster guffawed, and let Tyler lead him toward the door.

"Hal—" Neville said.

"Be quiet!" Bolingbroke hissed.

But Lancaster and Tyler did not go through the door. Instead, an opening appeared—almost *rippled*—in the air before them. Beyond it lay a great field of flowers leading to a small hill in the distance—Neville thought there might be an empty cross on its summit, but was not sure. Within a heartbeat the two men had stepped through and the opening had closed.

"Where have they gone?" said Neville, unable to keep quiet.

"To love," said Bolingbroke.

"Home," said Margaret.

And then the door of the chamber—the real door, the door of this vile, contemptible world—opened, and Richard strode through.

His face was terrible with vengeful anger.

He looked to the bed—when Neville turned to follow his eyes he was amazed to see Lancaster's corpse still lying there—then strode up to Bolingbroke and thrust a finger in his face.

"Your time has come, traitor," Richard said. "Your lands and titles, as those of your fathers, are confiscated into my keeping, and you and yours"—his hand swept about the room, but took in all Bolingbroke's extended household wherever they were—"are exiled from this great realm never to return on pain of death."

Richard drew breath, the resolve on his face slipping slightly as he saw that Bolingbroke had not even flinched.

"Never to return!" Richard suddenly screamed. "On pain of death! Do you hear me?"

Bolingbroke smiled, slightly, contemptuously, then held out his hand for Margaret and nodded to Neville.

"Come," he said.

As they left the chamber Richard stared after them, then looked again to Lancaster's corpse.

He began to laugh in triumph.

PART FIVE

The Maid and the Hawk

You, men of England, you have no right in this Kingdom of France. I, Joan the Maid, bear word from the King of Heaven commanding you to abandon your forts and to depart back into your own country. If you do not, then I shall raise such a war-cry against you as shall be remembered forever. I would have sent you word more decently, but [you have imprisoned my heralds].

—Joan of Arc's letter to the English commander at Orleans, shot into the English lines on the shaft of an arrow

Chapter I

The Feast of St. Barnabas
In the second year of the reign of Richard II
(Monday 11th June 1380)

✠

THEY DEPARTED la Roche-Guyon in a great twisting, glinting convoy of horse flesh, steel and religious fervor. At the convoy's head rode Joan on a roan stallion which she controlled merely with the softness of her voice. She was clad in an ivory tunic, embroidered with a golden cross, over chain mail. Her short-cropped head was unhelmeted so that all might see her face. Behind her rode a squire carrying the banner of SS. Michael and Gabriel.

Orleans lay some four or five days to the south.

The majority of the men in the column behind Joan followed her without question. God had sent them a saint to lead them to victory against the despised English, and this fine summer's morning they were to make a start.

Philip and Charles, riding several paces behind Joan and her immediate escort, shared mixed feelings about the adventure.

Charles was regretting that he'd allowed the Maid to persuade him on this dangerous escapade. Surely no one *really* needed him there? Surely *he* didn't need to engage in such rigorous pursuits?

Such *dangerous* pursuits.

He sulked and pouted, not willing to say to Joan, or any others close about him, that he would vastly prefer to spend his days as a well-fed and entertained noble, safe in a cultivated and comfortable court. (Perhaps in Avignon, for who ever waged war there?) So much more civilized.

Who wanted to lead armies into *war*?

Why had God decided that *he* should be the one to wear the crown?

Why, why didn't anyone listen to his whore-mother?

But almost no one did. That cursed Joan with her pious eyes and the Hand of God hovering constantly over her had persuaded every one of these damned nobles and soldiers who'd come to la Roche-Guyon that Charles' was the just and right cause.

Worth *fighting* for.

Charles' shoulders slumped even further as he heard trumpets sound behind him. Somewhere far back in the column a faint voice raised in a triumphal song of praise, and within a heartbeat scores, hundreds, of others had joined in.

God was with the French, and they were marching to victory.

Philip, glancing occasionally at the sullen expression on Charles' face, thought he knew very well what the idiot-sired man was thinking. Philip and Catherine had talked long into the night, discussing the possibilities this campaign might bring.

They were endless.

Philip smiled to himself as he relaxed on his destrier and let the sun wash over his head and shoulders. Joan's greatest weakness was the cause she espoused: Charles. And, in its turn, her weakness was Philip's greatest strength. No matter what Joan did, no matter how heaven-inspired she was, Charles would eventually prove her downfall.

Eventually, Charles would be her downfall . . . and Philip was just now beginning to see the manner in which he could twist the situation to his favor. But it would be a long time before Philip could take advantage of Joan's weakness, a long time before he could twist the simple-minded Charles to his will. A long time before he could safely move against the Maid of France.

Meanwhile, there was no harm in allowing Joan to win him a kingdom.

A sudden movement to his right roused Philip from his reverie: Charles, clinging grimly to his destrier, which had shied at the sudden bolting of a rabbit in the undergrowth.

Philip's grin widened.

Then there was a movement to his left, and he turned to look.

Catherine and Isabeau had ridden their palfreys to join him. Neither woman had wanted to be left behind when the men rode off to war, and Philip, in lighter moments, wondered if this was because both intended to slip into the forthcoming battle dressed as men, the better to slide their slim women's blades between the ribs of whichever enemy they chose—and the enemy might not necessarily be fighting under the English banner.

He wouldn't put it past either of them.

Isabeau glanced past Philip to where Charles had managed to regain control of his destrier (albeit with the help of a squire, who had ridden forward to take the bridle of Charles' mount to prevent it bolting across the fields that stretched away to the west).

"It was such a shame," Isabeau said to her son without any pretense of sweetness, "that I did not bed the Master of the Horse instead. He might have bequeathed you some skill in the art of managing horseflesh."

Charles flushed a mottled red and he sent his mother a glance seething with hatred and resentment.

"Whore," he said.

"At every opportunity," she said, and laughed.

Philip shared a grin with Catherine, who looked stunning in a deep blue cloak and riding dress. "It would be better," he said to both women, "if you rode further back in the column. If we were attacked—"

"I pray that we *are* attacked," Charles put in, "and that my whoring mother and sister are the first to feel the kiss of brigand blades."

"Have more care for what you say," Philip said to Charles.

"No matter," Isabeau said, waving a hand dismissively. "If we were to be attacked by brigands then I'm sure our saintly damsel would see them off in short order."

"God will have your tongue," Charles snapped, his flush growing deeper by the minute.

Isabeau laughed yet again. "I shall offer Him a more tender part of me," she said, winking at Philip, "and see if He accepts."

"Catherine," Philip said, "it *would* be better if you took your mother further back in the column."

"What?" said Catherine. "And miss the miracle that Joan has promised us for this day?"

Philip sighed and gave up. If he'd thought there was any true danger of the column being attacked then he would have insisted they return to a safer spot, but no band of brigands would attack a force this size, and there were no English within fifty miles.

Besides, it would be good to have Catherine and Isabeau on one side so that their merriment and caustic wit could counteract the depressing moodiness of Charles at his other side.

THEY RODE for some five hours until they approached the castle town of Montlhéry which straddled the main road south from Paris to Orleans. Charles brightened somewhat as they approached the ancient castle sitting atop the hill that commanded views of the surrounding countryside. The town which had sprung up around the skirts of the castle walls contained one of France's major markets, but the prospect of purchasing some cut-price silks was not what cheered Charles. The castle had been in royal hands for many generations, and both Charles and Catherine had spent long summers here.

Perhaps, Charles thought, *if I speak the right words, Joan will allow me to wait out the conflict within its walls. Surely she doesn't intend to risk me too close to Orleans. I shall be safe here, and—*

"I've heard," Philip said, screwing up his eyes against the sun as he stared at the hilltop castle rising some two miles ahead of them, "that the English have pledged to raze Montlhéry to the ground if ever they manage to take it."

Charles blinked. "Montlhéry is one of the safest—"

"The Duke of Burgundy took it eighty years ago with little apparent effort," Philip said, and only barely managed to restrain his laughter as Charles' face fell. *No doubt the fool had thought to wait out the war within its walls.*

"Oh," said Charles.

"Well," Isabeau remarked, "it will do to give us shelter for this night. I, for one, will be glad enough to dismount from this horse."

"It must be passing strange for you to be doing the riding for a change," Charles said nastily.

Isabeau's face tightened in anger—more at the fact that her son had finally managed to needle her than at his actual words—but her vicious retort died on her lips as Joan suddenly rode back to join them.

Charles smiled and nodded, glad that she arrived just as he'd managed to best his mother.

"Do we rest here tonight?" he said to Joan.

"Aye, your grace," Joan said, "but we do not ride direct there. Look, good sir, can you see that stand of trees?"

She stood in her stirrups, graceful despite the heavy weight of chain mail she wore, and pointed to a small wood that grew up a small rise to the west.

Charles nodded. "What of it?"

Joan sat back in her saddle, and smiled beatifically. "Nestled within the sheltering trees is a small shrine dedicated to the Blessed Saint Catherine. We shall ride there, you and I, his grace of Navarre, the six great lords who ride immediately behind you and"—she pointed to Isabeau and Catherine—"your mother and sister. There we shall witness the miracle I prophesied."

Charles frowned. "Is it safe?"

"God watches over us," said Joan, and with that Charles had to be content, turning his stallion's head with some difficulty and much bad grace to follow Joan as she rode toward the small wood.

IT WAS cool and dim under the trees, silent save for the crackling of dead leaves and twigs under the hooves of the horses. Joan led them, her roan stallion treading confidently as if he'd known this track all his life. Directly behind Joan came two of the lords she'd asked to accompany her, then Charles, Philip, the two women and the remaining four lords.

No men-at-arms accompanied them.

The shrine to St. Catherine consisted of a tiny chapel, made of rough-hewn stone and a low, slate roof, that crouched under two massive beech trees. It had a door, but no windows and no spire: nothing to indicate its holiness save the flowers strewn on the ground before its step.

With a soft word, Joan halted her stallion a few paces away from the chapel, then slid from the horse's back.

"Come," she said, glancing behind her to make sure the others were also dismounting. "Saint Catherine awaits."

Philip shared a glance with Catherine—*what was going to happen?*—but walked after Joan with as much self-assurance as he could manage.

Once he stepped inside he understood why Joan had insisted so few accompany them.

The chapel's interior was tiny, and their party of eleven only just managed to crowd inside. Set against the far wall was a large block of sandstone that served as an altar. It was draped with a pale linen cloth and was set with several fat, lit candles. On the wall behind it was a rough-hewn cross with an even more crudely worked figure of Jesus.

Fresh flowers were strewn across the altar.

Joan waited until the last man had stepped inside, then pointed to two of the lords.

"My lords," she said, and smiled so sweetly that Philip suddenly thought her the most beautiful woman he'd ever seen, "do you see this slab set in the earth before the altar?"

They nodded. "How may we serve you, blessed virgin?" said one.

"Lift the slab," said Joan, "and we shall see what we may."

The two lords, both in the prime of their lives, stepped forward, each squatting and taking an end of the slab in their hands. They strained, rested, then strained again, and the slab groaned and shifted.

After catching their breath, the two lords managed to tip the slab over—sending everyone (save Joan who had stood to one side and watched with a small smile on her lips) scurrying to get out of the way.

A sickening stench of damp, mouldering earth rose in the air, and everyone—Joan included—coughed and gagged.

Once they'd grown used to the smell, they stared down at the patch of dank earth revealed by the slab's removal.

At first Philip thought there was nothing there save the barely covered, tangled roots of the two beeches that overhung the chapel, then he realized that the earth-covered twistings were not roots, but long-buried cloth.

It was obvious that whatever the cloth concealed had been there for generations, for the earth had the look of something that had not been disturbed in a very, very long time.

Joan leaned down, digging in the dirt with her bare hands, then she grunted, and pulled something forth.

They could see that it was a sword, wrapped in cloth so old and damp it was virtually disintegrating.

No one spoke, all eyes on Joan.

Very carefully she unwrapped the sword, taking such a time about it that Philip felt like screaming and snatching the sword from her to get the task accomplished the quicker.

But he didn't. As with everyone else, Philip could not have moved to save himself.

Eventually, the last fragment of rotting cloth fell away, to fully reveal the unscabbarded sword.

It lay naked in Joan's hands, its hilt covered with slime and fungus, its blade entirely covered in thick rust.

Joan raised shining eyes, extending her hands slightly so all could see clearly. "Behold," she whispered.

"*That* is your miracle?" said Isabeau. "If God can do no better than the production of that rusting carcass then—"

"Reveal thyself," whispered Joan, and everyone gasped.

The rust and slime fell away from the sword in a sudden shower of foulness. In a blink of an eye the sword changed from rusting relic to a gleaming, silvered weapon. Five crosses ran down the length of its blade, and the words "Michael" and "Gabriel" were inscribed in gold at the very top of the blade where it joined the golden-wired hilt.

"With this sword," Joan whispered, staring at the other ten who gazed transfixed back at her, "I shall lead France to victory!"

Several of the lords fell to their knees, their hands clasped before them, and Catherine stirred as they moved.

Her expression changed from one of amazement to one of contempt.

"Swords can be broken," she said, and turned and left the chapel, Joan's eyes boring into her back the entire way.

Chapter II

The Feast of St. Eadburga
In the second year of the reign of Richard II
(Friday 15th June 1380)

✠

HOTSPUR SAT IN THE CHAIR, one leg swinging idly over an armrest, his chin cradled in a hand, and an expression of utter boredom set on his face. Despite the summer sun, outside the stone tower in which Hotspur had his command post was cold and comfortless . . . as it seemed were most things about this damned country.

Hotspur had come to loathe Orleans and everything French.

Before him, as also the five or six other English nobles present within the chamber, played a troupe of French musicians. They were truly excellent, and Hotspur would on any other occasion have enjoyed their music.

They had arrived this morning, on loan from the commander of the garrison within the city of Orleans, and Hotspur was sure that they were less a gift than an insult: *we have fine musicians, and plenty to eat, and you won't be starving us out of here anytime soon.*

The troupe started up a lively carol, and Hotspur sighed. He'd much rather be back home than stuck here in the French countryside with nothing to do but order a daily barrage of stone balls, hurled by the five cannon, against Orleans' walls.

Most of them fell short anyway, and then the English had

to risk arrows and bolts to try and roll them back to the English fortifications to use another day.

As he'd known, the siege was not going well.

Damn Richard for not sending what he needed!

Orleans still sat, safely walled, on the Loire. Its four land gates were still firmly bolted, as was the gate that opened to a (now breached) bridge across the river. Hotspur had managed to establish his siege in some ten fortifications on the northern, western and southern side of the city—including the great four-towered fortification of les Tourelles on the bridge itself—but the eastern side of Orleans lay virtually free of an English presence. Hotspur simply didn't have the men or the weapons to completely encircle the city.

Thus the good folk of Orleans managed to replenish their supplies of food and ammunition through the eastern gate of the city. The English could harry the convoys moving through the gate, but not stop them completely.

The fact was, the people of Orleans were probably eating better than the English.

The troupe finished with a flurry, and Hotspur sat up and waved them away.

"I thank you," he said, his French perfect, "and would that you thank the Comte de Dunois"—the Comte was more generally known as the Bastard of Orleans, but Hotspur thought it more polite to give him his name—"for his generosity."

The leader of the troupe bowed and made some flowery politenesses of his own, and then the troupe packed up and left.

"Well," Hotspur said once they had gone. "Is it time to start the day's bombardment?"

Hotspur's immediate subordinates, Lord John Talbot and Lord Thomas Scales, both shrugged.

"Might as well," said Scales with a distinct lack of enthusiasm. "Nothing much else to do."

"Perhaps that soldier manning the tower near the western gate will put on his usual performance," Talbot said.

Hotspur shot Talbot a dark look. The French were blessed with a sense of humor that Hotspur, as most of his command, had come to loathe.

And they loathed nothing more than the anonymous French ham in the tower by the western gate.

Almost every day, as the English began their regular afternoon bombardment, this clown sprang into action. As soon as a missile had landed within fifty feet of his particular tower he would stumble screaming onto the parapets, clutching at some part of his anatomy, then theatrically collapse onto the stone walkway.

Within minutes, two of his comrades would sally forth from the tower bearing a stretcher—weeping and wailing themselves—load up the still screaming soldier, and transport him back into safety.

After only another minute or two the "wounded" humorist would emerge from the tower jumping up and down and waving his arms as if he were possessed by demons and shouting that the prayers of the Blessed Damsel Joan had saved him and he was whole again.

Despite all the arrows and missiles the English sent his way they'd never managed to truly murder him yet.

Having agreed with his command that there was nothing better to do with their afternoon than commence another lackluster bombardment, Hotspur had taken one step toward the door when a soldier came in.

"My lord," he said, holding forth a small leather satchel. "A letter."

"From Richard, I hope," Hotspur said as he took the satchel and removed the letter.

"And hopefully with orders for us to come home," Talbot said. "I don't fancy sitting here taking pot shots at this overgrown French wart for the next several years of my life."

Hotspur's face went completely devoid of expression as his eyes scanned the letter.

"Not from Richard," he said. "Listen":

You, Henry Percy, who call yourself Hotspur: Do justice to the King of Heaven and surrender to me, the Maid of France, who is sent here from God, King of Heaven, and raise your ungodly siege. Take your archers and men-at-arms and go hence back into your own country in God's name; and if you do not so, expect to hear news of the Maid, who will shortly come to see you, to your very great damage.

If you will not believe this news from God and the Maid, wherever we find you, there we shall strike; and we shall raise such a battle-cry as there has not been in France in a thousand years. And know surely that the King of Heaven will send more strength to the Maid than you can bring against her and her good soldiers in any assault. And when the blow begins, it shall be seen whose right is the better before the God of Heaven.

You, Hotspur: the Maid prays and beseeches you not to bring on your own destruction. If you will do her justice, you may yet come in her company there where the French shall do the fairest deed that ever was done for Christendom. So answer if you will make peace in the city of Orleans.

And if you do not, consider your great danger speedily.

Written this Thursday before the fourth Sunday after Trinity.

Joan, Maid of France.

"Lord God save us!" cried Talbot as Hotspur finished and folded up the letter.

"Be quiet!" Hotspur snapped, then tapped the letter against his chest as he thought. "Where did you get this?" he asked the soldier who had carried the message to him.

"It was carried to the tower by a guard from the Bastille de Augustines," the man said, naming the English fortification tower directly below the bridge. "The messenger who delivered it said that the letter's author was but a few hours away."

Hotspur swore, slapped the letter into Talbot's hands, and strode from the chamber.

JOAN STOOD on the southern bank of the Loire, some two miles upriver from Orleans, and fought against the too-human urge to lose her temper completely.

Behind her, Philip sat his horse and smirked, delighted to see the Maid of France so discomfited.

They'd ridden hard for the south these past few days, making better time than Philip had thought possible.

But then, the column was fed by a fire of religious fervor that few had seen since the Crusades, was it not?

Yesterday they had deposited the Dauphin and all the women save Joan in a small but secure town five miles to the east: the Dauphin had *insisted* he wait out the inevitable conflict from there.

Charles' sulky, cowardly display—even though Joan had expected it—had been the start of her foul temper.

Then she'd resisted the advice of several commanders and decided to cross to the southern bank of the Loire in order to approach Orleans . . . which sat on the northern bank.

Perhaps, Philip thought, *Joan believed it safer to keep a wide river between her and her objective*.

But now here they were, an armed and fervent column of some eight thousand men, stuck on the southern bank with no easy way to cross the river and both Orleans and most of the English fortifications on the northern bank.

Philip's smile stretched a little further. The raising of the siege would be Joan's first great test. On the ride south she'd proclaimed at every chance how she spoke for God and how her angelic voices and apparitions told her that this would be a great victory, and every night she'd encouraged more and more soldiers to make their confessions. Now, she would have to come through on her promises and prophecies.

As Joan stood staring across the Loire, her hands on her hips and her entire stance bespeaking her frustration, it began to rain; a hard, pelting rain that threw up great droplets of mud as high as a man's shoulder.

Philip shrugged deep inside his cloak and urged his horse up to Joan's side.

"Come away, Joan!" he shouted above the roar of the sudden downpour. "You do no good here!"

Stunningly, when she turned her face to him it was shining with ecstasy.

"This is God's work!" she shouted. "Sent to aid us!"

Sweet Jesu, Philip thought, *she's finally lost her senses.*

"Look!" she screamed, gesturing toward the now choppy river. "Look!"

He raised his head, squinting against the rain.

The fury of the storm had forced the river's waters upstream, exposing a stony ford, wide enough for several men to ride abreast.

"Come!" she shouted. "Come!"

Her roan stallion materialized out of nowhere, and Joan sprang to his back, waving the column forward.

"To Orleans and God's will," she cried, and Philip felt a coldness trickle down his spine that was not entirely due to the effects of the storm.

Chapter III

The Saturday before the Fourth Sunday after Trinity
In the second year of the reign of Richard II
(16th June 1380)

✠

THE DAY WAS clear and bright, washed clean by the supernatural storm of yesterday afternoon and evening.

While it had lasted the English had huddled within their fortifications, thinking that every other creature caught in its fury would have so huddled.

When they'd emerged, late at night, it was to discover Orleans ablaze with light and festival, and the damned Maid's name being screamed from every one of its towers and ramparts.

Somehow, Joan and her force had gained entry to Orleans.

Hotspur was angry and frustrated, not merely that Joan had managed to sneak into the city, but at the moody whispers now spreading about the English camp.

God had sent an angel to aid the French.

The English would be razed by holy fire the instant they lifted a single weapon against the Holy Maid.

Their only hope to live was to run . . . now!

Hotspur had lost almost a fourth of his force to the insidious creepings away that had already occurred under the cover of darkness, and he seriously doubted whether he could get the remaining force to put up much of a resistance when Joan levelled her heavenly fury against him.

Damn it, Hotspur didn't know if *he* wanted to fight someone with God's might behind her.

* * *

THE FRENCH exploded out of Orleans just after midday . . . and they did not come the way that Hotspur had expected.

Several weeks ago, the English had breached the bridge that extended from the fort of les Tourelles on the southern bank of the Loire into Orleans on the northern bank.

Just as Sir William Glasdale, commander of the English forces which had captured les Tourelles, finished wiping away the gravy stains from his beard after his midday meal, he heard a great shouting from the bastions.

When he emerged it was to see the Maid herself, horseless, but clad in gleaming white armor and waving a great standard above her head, standing at the far edge of the breach. Beside her were several score men extending a span of hastily nailed timbers across the gap.

Glasdale screamed at his archers to take out both men and Maid, but even though the air was soon thick with arrows, only a few men fell, and they were quickly replaced by others from the city.

Angry—and frightened—beyond reason, Glasdale himself seized a longbow, took careful aim, and sent an arrow speeding into the air.

He thought he had been blessed, for with a sickening *thunk*, the arrow buried itself into the Maid's armor just above her left breast.

She staggered, and a man rushed forward to take the standard from her, but she waved him away when he tried also to assist her. She took the shaft of the arrow in both her hands, then yanked it from her flesh.

Glasdale swore he heard her cry of agony even from the distance at which he stood.

Blood welled momentarily at the point of entry, and the Maid paused to take a deep breath, but the next instant she was screaming encouragement at her men and waving the standard.

Glasdale swallowed.

Suddenly the span bridging the gap fell into place and men swarmed across.

The battle of les Tourelles had begun.

IT LASTED most of the day. Hotspur tried to send men to aid Glasdale, but most of the other English positions were also under attack—not heavy attack, but enough to keep most of them pinned in their foxholes.

Glasdale had to manage on his own.

For many hours he did well, rallying his men who, whatever they might have thought about Joan, knew they were dead if les Tourelles fell. But by late afternoon his men were failing, and one of the gates of the fortress bulged with the force of their attackers.

He shouted wearily again, trying one last time to rally his men, but even as he opened his mouth a soldier screamed, pointing upward.

Glasdale's eyes, as did every English eye in les Tourelles and about Orleans, looked skyward.

There, raging down at them from the heavens, rode the archangel St. Michael on a fiery horse.

Glasdale screamed, dropped his weapon and cowered. Most of his men did the same.

The French screamed also, but with victory and the knowledge that God was indeed on their side. They made one last effort, breached the gate and swarmed through les Tourelles.

Close after them strode Joan. Weak from pain and loss of blood she nevertheless stood and watched, the standard still in her hands, as her compatriots slaughtered every last one of the Englishmen within the fort.

Likewise, Philip watched from his position on the ramparts of Orleans' walls. He had not joined in the battle, but had witnessed its progress from his spot throughout the day.

His brow was furrowed in thought.

WHEN LES Tourelles fell soon after the horrendous vision had appeared in the sky, Hotspur wasted no time in ordering his men to pull back and to make with all possible speed for the nearest coastal port.

He was not going to stay and waste his life against this holy wench.

God give him the Scots any day!

"Damn Richard to hell," he muttered as he mounted his horse and kicked it into a gallop.

WHEN A soldier pointed out to Joan the fleeing English she sighed wearily.

"In God's name," she said, "they go, finally. Let them depart, and let us depart to give thanks to God. We do not follow them, for soon it shall be Sunday. Seek not to harm them. It suffices that they go."

Chapter IV

The fourth Sunday after Trinity
In the second year of the reign of Richard II
(17th June 1380)

✣

THE BOAT ROLLED and pitched in the heavy swell, and Margaret thought she would never be so glad as when she could quit this vessel. The past eleven or twelve days had been a nightmare. On the morning after the day of Lancaster's and Tyler's deaths, Bolingbroke, along with Mary, Neville, herself and some fourteen or fifteen of their squires and immediate servants, had boarded a Flemish vessel at the Tower's water gate. The vessel was already crowded with Flemings desperate to escape the post-revolt turmoil within London, and the addition of Bolingbroke's party (and even with the gold they paid out) did nothing to ease conditions or tempers. The men shared one tiny, airless cabin while Margaret, together with Mary, Agnes and Rosalind, had been crammed into a slightly larger but no less airless cabin with five Flemish wives.

There had been bedding space for three only, and barely enough standing and sitting room for the others. Rosalind had fretted and whimpered every hour that she was awake, and she was joined by the two similarly aged children of the Flemish women. Three, by the time one of the wives had given loud and riotous birth four days out from London.

The stench of the women, of the birthing, of the vomit and of the damp moldy mattresses, combined with the stifling air, the wailings of the children and the continual pitching of the vessel, made existence intolerable. Margaret had to spend most of her hours awake (and that *was* most of her hours) either on her feet hanging grimly on to a leather strap set into one of the bulkheads or cramped onto a stool with either Rosalind or one of the other children squirming on her lap. She hardly ate, and drank only small sips from the cup of ale the women passed around every hour or so. Her nausea never left her, her head ached the entire time, and her bowels alternately cramped and loosened, sending her scuttling for the waste bucket eight or nine times each day.

But if Margaret's condition was pitiable, Mary's was horrendous. She was the only one among the women who had a bed for the entire voyage—and she never left it. Margaret had known Mary was ill before they'd left London but, with the events of the rebellion, Lancaster's death, and Bolingbroke's and their subsequent exile, had not had any time to give Mary the attention she'd needed.

Margaret bitterly regretted it.

When Mary had boarded the vessel she'd been gray and silent, and none of the women had objected to her taking up one of the valuable beds. Her silence had not lasted past their first terrible day at sea.

Mary had begun to retch violently at the first pitching of the vessel as it entered the sea swells. By evening of their first day at sea she'd whispered to Margaret that she thought she might be losing blood. By nightfall, her blood loss was worrying, if not yet serious.

None of the women had known quite what to do.

Margaret had tried to send for Bolingbroke or Neville, but the door to the cabin was locked—one of the Flemish wives told Margaret that the master of the vessel was determined to keep them out of sight as he believed that the presence of women on deck would attract sea monsters—and none of the sailors listened to her pleadings.

For all she knew the men were as locked in their cabin as she was in hers.

Mary's condition had eased a little on the next day. Her bleeding had ceased, and, while she still retched, it was no more violent than the sickness of those women about her.

Salisbury managed to poke his head in the door in the afternoon, inquiring after the women. Margaret had gestured helplessly at Mary—but what could anyone do? Salisbury told her that Bolingbroke and Neville were as sick as most others and that, furthermore, there was no physician on the vessel who might ease their discomfort.

"Tell Bolingbroke that Mary ails," Margaret told Salisbury, and he'd nodded and taken the message away with him, but Margaret knew Bolingbroke would not appear to stand mute witness to his wife's misery.

Birthing and losing a baby was women's work, and men had no place in its presence.

Besides, Margaret thought hopelessly as, on the morning of the third day, Mary began to spot again, *Hal knew this would happen, and Mary's loss will merely be one further step in the attainment of his ambition.*

THEY WERE close to land now, and had been for at least a day. The harsh cries of gulls, as other seabirds, sounded continually through the bulwarks, and the smell of the sea was different. Sometimes Margaret would hear distant voices, as if sailors on passing vessels shouted out to them.

This morning—and she had no idea which day it was, for all time seemed to have halted in this vile world of the cabin—Margaret lay crammed into one of the bunk beds with Mary. They were both thin enough now that, lying on their sides and tight together, they could share the precious mattress. It was just after daybreak: faint light filtered through the planks of the decking, and the boots of the sailors had been tramping above their heads for at least an hour.

Although Margaret could not see her face, she knew Mary was awake.

"Mary?" she whispered, and laid her hand on Mary's rib cage: the woman was taking rapid shallow breaths.

For a long time Mary did not answer. Then she sighed, and shuddered, and said, "I think I am finally losing this child, Margaret."

Margaret held her tightly, and wept. After a while she raised herself and, with one of the other women, did for Mary what she could.

It was not much, for, as with her previous pregnancy, what Mary passed into the salty morning air was hardly human at all. It was a blackened mass of flesh with one or two hairs and what might, or might not, have been a single eye at one end of its pulpy mass.

The woman aiding Margaret made a face at the sight of it but, at Margaret's silent directions, bundled the dead flesh into a large cloth and hustled it out of the way.

As she did so, Margaret made Mary as comfortable as she could—at least the bleeding had stopped with the birth of the horrid thing!—then sat down by her and stroked her cheek, trying to give the woman as much comfort as she could.

"He will be so angry with me!" Mary whispered, staring at Margaret with great, pain-filled eyes.

"He will not be angry." Margaret said, knowing the truth of what she said. Hal would be glad.

He did not want an heir. Not from Mary's body.

"I wanted so much to give him this child," Mary said. "Was it . . . was it . . . ?"

"Yes," Margaret answered, not knowing truly what she was saying "yes" to, but knowing it was what Mary wanted to hear.

Mary's mouth trembled, and she began to cry. "Why can't I be a good wife?" she whispered.

Margaret was suddenly, violently angry with Hal. "You are the best of all wives," she murmured. "Hush now, and rest while you can."

* * *

NEVILLE STOOD with Bolingbroke on the deck of the vessel, thankful beyond belief that their sea journey was soon to end. It should have taken many days less, but the master of the vessel had apparently lost his way and had sailed up and down the coast of Flanders several times until he'd found his home port.

If he hadn't been the only vessel sailing to Flanders on the day they'd had to leave . . .

The fresh wind blowing off the land exhilarated Neville, and he tipped back his head and closed his eyes, allowing it to wash over his face and tug at his hair.

After a moment he looked back at Bolingbroke, staring at the jumble of boats tied up at the wharf of the small port. "How far from here, Hal?"

Bolingbroke pointed to a small headland which curved to the west of the wharf; at its foot was the silvery wash of a river mouth. "See? The city is only a few hours gentle barge ride up that river."

Neville nodded, grateful that at last he could see the final leg of the journey. They were headed for the great city of Ghent, capital of Flanders. There Lancaster had been born—thus the corrupted "Gaunt" of his popular name—during his mother's travels about Europe with Edward III. The Count of Flanders had ever been a friend of the Lancastrian family, and Bolingbroke knew he would receive a friendly welcome there.

It would be the perfect place to wait for the wounded hawk's wings to heal.

"My lord?" It was Salisbury, Courtenay with him. "The master says we may bring the ladies up. It will be only a few minutes until we dock."

"What? He leaves a few minutes where sea monsters can attack?" Bolingbroke said.

Neville shot him a dark look. "I'll take Roger and

Robert," he said. "We should be able to manage a lady apiece."

WHAT NEVILLE found shocked him beyond all imagining. The crowding and stench in the cabin he'd been forced to inhabit had been bad—but nothing compared to the thick, sickening atmosphere of the hellhole these women were crammed into.

For a long minute after he opened the door he simply stared, appalled.

All the women were gray, gaunt-eyed hags, crouching over pails and bowls.

Hardly a one of them looked up as he opened the door.

It took Neville a minute to cope with the stench, and then another to find the Bolingbroke women.

Agnes, Rosalind in her arms, was the first he saw in her place just by the door. Neville reached over, took Agnes by the elbow and helped her to rise. She staggered once she got to her feet, and Neville took Rosalind from her, giving her a quick hug before he handed the child to Courtenay.

Courtenay made a face at the girl's stench, but took her firmly enough before stepping back to give Agnes room to move through the door.

"Take them above," said Neville, and Courtenay nodded, relieved to be able to get back to the fresh air so quickly.

"Tom?"

Margaret! Neville turned back into the cabin, squinted into the dim light, and finally made out Margaret sitting on the edge of a bed.

"Sweet Jesu, Meg!" he said, shocked by the sight of her. "Are you well?"

"Nay," she whispered, "but Mary is even worse."

"Jesu," Neville murmured, for now he had caught sight of Mary lying on the bed. He pushed through the other women, not caring that he stepped on at least two of them to get to Margaret and Mary. He cupped Margaret's face in his hand, looking deep into her eyes.

"Can you walk?" he said.

She nodded. "Mary . . . please . . . she has lost her child, and now I think she wants to lose herself as well. Get her out of here."

Neville helped Margaret to her feet, holding her to him briefly as she rose, then aided her to the cabin door, handing her into the care of Salisbury.

Salisbury took one look at her, and without the slightest hesitation swung her into his arms and turned for the ladder to the deck.

Neville bent down to Mary. He would have thought her dead save for the gentle rise and fall of her breasts, and he winced as she cried out when he lifted her into his arms. He stepped over the other women, telling them that they should follow him into the sunlight, and made for the deck with as much haste as possible without jolting Mary.

"Shush, sweet lady," he whispered as Mary whimpered when they rose up the ladder to the deck. "I will take good care of you." He paused, long enough to give her the very slightest of hugs, then climbed the final steps.

Bolingbroke was waiting for him as soon as he emerged onto the deck.

"Sweet Jesu," Bolingbroke said, taking Mary from Neville.

He sat down on a wool sack, cradling Mary in his arms.

"She has lost the child," Neville said gently, and Bolingbroke averted his face for a moment, and held Mary tightly to him.

"How ill is she?" he said finally, looking to where Margaret sat by the railing of the deck.

"Ill enough," she said, and then Neville sat down and wrapped his arms so tightly about her that she could say no more.

That was as well, for Margaret didn't want Hal to see her tears.

* * *

THEY STOPPED that night at a hostel by the river where a physician saw to the women and Rosalind. He was a good man at his craft, as only the Flemish could be, and Margaret, Agnes and Rosalind soon revived from the tonic he gave them. Now, he said, assuring a worried Neville that Margaret's unborn child seemed well enough, it was only a matter of rest and good food.

But the physician shook his head over Mary, and said that the loss of the child had sapped her of far more than strength. He did what he could for her, and Mary was pathetically grateful for the relief he gave, but later the physician told Bolingbroke privately that Mary had something else wrong with her.

"A grayness," he said, "about her mouth." He hesitated. "And I did not like what I heard described of the child she miscarried. Perhaps there is something wrong with her womb . . ."

"What can I do for her?" said Bolingbroke.

The physician shrugged. "Care for her. Love her. What else can a husband do for a wife?"

Bolingbroke turned away.

News traveled quickly down the waterways of Flanders, and when the party awoke the next morning it was to find that the Count of Flanders had sent a commodious barge to take them upriver to Ghent. It was fitted out with couches and linens and comforts of all degree and had a cool green arbor covering half its length to keep at bay the sun.

Bolingbroke did not want to move Mary so quickly, but she seemed much better after her night's rest, and ate well to break her fast, and professed such a great desire to see Ghent and to absent herself from the hostel, that Bolingbroke gave in, and by mid-morning the party had boarded the barge and cast off.

Bolingbroke so fussed over Mary where she lay on a couch that, finally, she sent him away to where Neville sat with Salisbury and Courtenay in a patch of sun talking to the captain of the count's escort.

Mary watched him move off, then smiled at Margaret who sat amid a pile of cushions at Mary's feet. Further down the barge Agnes and Rosalind lay curled up together, fast asleep.

"He does not care that I lost the child," Mary said, and her smile slipped.

Margaret's heart broke. "He does care for you," she said.

"Oh, aye," said Mary, and Margaret winced at the bitterness in the woman's voice.

"I thought you would be pleased that he was not angry," Margaret said. "Was that not what you feared?"

"Aye," said Mary and relapsed into silence for a minute. "But he wept too little then, and now he fusses too much. He does not know how to hide his indifference. I would prefer anger to indifference, Margaret."

Margaret moved a little closer to Mary and took her hand. "Hush, Mary."

"He has what he needs of me," Mary said, her eyes brimming with tears, "he had that long ago, and I do not think he wants a son of me now. I . . . I do not know what he wants, Margaret, but I know he does not want me."

"Anyone can see that you are the perfect wife for Bolingbroke—"

Mary pulled her hand from Margaret's clasp. "You should become better acquainted with the art of lying, my lady," Mary said, "if you are to be of any consequence in Hal's court."

"I—"

"Ah, Margaret, I am sorry. The loss of the child has made me bitter." Now she reached out and covered Margaret's hand with her own. "But I am very, very glad to see you looking well. I shall laugh with happiness when your child is born and with that I shall make do."

"Bolingbroke has never deserved you," Margaret whispered, and this time Mary knew she did not lie.

Chapter V

The Feast of St. Swithin
In the second year of the reign of Richard II
(Monday 16th July 1380)

✢

RALPH NEVILLE, Baron of Raby and Earl of Westmorland, sat in the hall of his northern stronghold, Sheriff Hutton, and bounced his baby son on his knee. Several paces away sat his wife Joan, already swollen with their next child, threading a needle in and out of the seam of an infant's nightgown.

The child laughed, and Raby smiled, grateful to have this time to spend with his new wife and son, but also chafing at his inactivity. He was a warrior, not a nursemaid, and he longed more than anything to be once more striding shoulder to shoulder with princes and kings across the field of action, or sitting with them in the parleying room, deciding the fate of nations.

But he would not be doing that for a long time . . . not unless Bolingbroke could manage the impossible.

Over the past weeks Raby had done his secretive best to scry out the level of support for Bolingbroke among England's nobles. The support was there, but it was cautious . . . too cautious. While this baron and that earl mumbled angrily about Richard and de Vere, none yet would stand forth and say, "I have men and swords . . . and I am ready to stand at Bolingbroke's side."

No one wanted to be the first.

Raby stared at his son's face, wondering what the future held for him. Would the Neville family's influence—as its land holdings—be gradually whittled down as de Vere's influence grew? Would this son, and any who followed, be reduced to grubbing about in the field behind a plow in order to eat?

He shuddered at the thought, and then castigated himself for his over-vivid imagination. Richard would eventually commit himself to a stupidity so gross that men would die in the trampling rush to ally themselves with Bolingbroke.

It was only a matter of when.

"My lord?"

Raby jumped slightly. He'd been so engrossed in his son and his thoughts that he'd not heard his squire approach.

"Yes, Will?"

"My lord, you have guests." Will stood back, and allowed Raby to see who stood at the far end of the hall.

Raby took a slow, deep breath. *Was this the time? Was this the man?*

AS SOON as he saw Raby hand his child to his wife, dismissing both her and his squire with a curt gesture, Henry Percy, Earl of Northumberland, nodded to his son and walked forward.

Raby met them halfway.

"I greet you well," he said, looking between Northumberland and Hotspur, "if with some degree of surprise."

"These are surprising times," said Northumberland.

"You have ridden far?" Raby said, gesturing to the two men to accompany him back to the small semicircle of chairs set before the hearth.

"From York," Northumberland said.

"And before that from London," said Hotspur.

Raby glanced at the younger man. He appeared composed, but Raby thought he could see the disaster of Orleans lurking amid the shadows of the man's eyes.

Raby handed cups of wine to Northumberland and Hotspur and sat down.

"We have never been the ones for polite conversations," he said. "What do you here?"

"What?" said Northumberland, raising an eyebrow. "Can we not, just for once, be neighbors stopping for a cup of wine and the sharing of news before traveling on to our own home?"

Raby's mouth curled. "You could . . . but I think you are not. I am tainted with treason through my association with Bolingbroke. I had thought Sheriff Hutton the last place you would want to stop for a gossip. So I say to you again, why are you here?"

"Perhaps if I relay to you some of the news from London then you may surmise for yourself why I am here," Northumberland said.

Raby inclined his head, and took a sip of his wine.

"You have surely heard of Orleans," said Northumberland.

Again Raby nodded, unable to resist a glance in Hotspur's direction.

"I was undermined by Richard," Hotspur said in a low, angry voice. "He directed me to Orleans and then refused to reinforce me."

Raby shrugged. "Such is the wont of kings." He hesitated, then decided it prudent to offer Hotspur some measure of support. "But it is too often others whose reputations must bear the burden of their stupidity."

Hotspur nodded, and relaxed a little, slouching into his chair and draining his wine.

"Richard's stupidity is boundless," Northumberland said as Raby rose and refilled all their wine cups. "He has now decided that France is a lost cause for the time being. Instead, he has announced that he will himself lead England's remaining army to Ireland in time to crown de Vere its king for Michaelmas."

Raby halted in the act of putting down the wine ewer. *"What?"*

"Imagine," Hotspur muttered over the rim of his wine cup, "*Richard* leading an army anywhere!"

Both Raby and Northumberland ignored him.

"How can he be so foolish?" Raby said.

"He will do anything to impress de Vere," the earl replied. "Doubtless 'dear Robbie' whined on and on about wanting to rule Ireland in reality instead of in name only and wore Richard down."

"But that would leave England vulnerable to . . ." Raby stopped, not wanting to say it.

Northumberland caught his eye, and nodded. "Indeed," he said.

Raby stared at him for a few long moments. *Why* was Northumberland here? What was his purpose?

"Richard has proved himself monumentally incapable of sitting upon the throne of England," Northumberland said, leaning forward and putting his wine cup down on a table. "If he is allowed to remain on the throne he will drive England to destitution within five years."

Raby put his own cup down. "I ask you yet again," he said in a cold, careful voice, "why are you *here?*"

"Hotspur and myself travel north not only to whisper of Richard's latest escapades," Northumberland said, "but we also escort back to her ancestral home my daughter, Philippa."

Raby frowned. "De Vere's wife?"

Northumberland's face twisted, full of bitterness and anger. "Wife no longer. He has repudiated her, saying that as king of Ireland he can pick and choose among royal wenches to sit beside him."

Raby stared at the older man, realizing that his daughter's—and, indeed, his entire family's—humiliation was what had driven Northumberland into outright revolt.

"And Richard has allowed it?" Raby said.

Northumberland nodded curtly.

"How can he have been so *foolish*?" Raby said.

"Then you know why we are here," Northumberland said.

"Say it!"

"Richard must be removed."

"And . . . ?"

"It is time Bolingbroke took the throne."

Raby sat back in his chair, picking up his empty wine cup and idly swinging it to and fro. "You do not want the throne yourself, Percy? Nor for your son?"

"Neither I, nor Hotspur, could hope to hold it," Northumberland said softly, meeting Raby's eyes candidly.

Raby nodded slowly. No, Northumberland did not have the popular support to be able to stay on the throne once he had gained it . . . and he had the sense to acknowledge it.

He shifted his eyes to Hotspur.

The man was looking everywhere else but at Raby.

So . . . the son does not have as much sense as the father. Well, Bolingbroke would deal with Hotspur when and as he had to. For now, however, the Percys would see Bolingbroke to the throne.

Raby smiled, warm and honest. He stood and leaned down to Northumberland, holding out his hand. "Welcome to Lancastrian England," he said.

After a small hesitation, Northumberland took his hand. "I have many to bring with me," he said.

"Then be sure that Bolingbroke will reward his friends well. But don't," Raby's smile stretched into a mischievous grin, "expect him to marry your daughter!"

Northumberland smiled, then laughed. "She is well rid of de Vere, I think."

THE NEXT day Raby departed Sheriff Hutton with only his squire and a few men-at-arms as escort. For almost five weeks he quietly traversed the back lanes and ridings of England, moving between this ancestral seat and that, speaking whispered words of treason in shadowy corners and against dark walls.

When he finally returned north, Raby had far more than just names behind him—he carried at his back the wind for Bolingbroke's wings.

Chapter VI

The Feast of the Transfiguration
of Our Lord Jesus Christ
In the second year of the reign of Richard II
(Monday 6th August 1380)

— I —

✠

GHENT WAS one of the great cities of northern Europe. Sitting astride the Lieve and Leie rivers in northern Flanders, the city had grown rich on trade, textiles and the patronage of the Count of Flanders. The count's castle, the Gravensteen, dominated the city, and it was to this pale stone, many-turreted castle on the waters of Ghent that Bolingbroke brought his household in the summer of the year of Our Lord 1380.

The count was a gracious host, pleased to see Bolingbroke, whom he'd not talked with for many years, and delighted to welcome, also, Mary and the other members of Bolingbroke's household. The reason behind their visit—Bolingbroke's exile—was passed off with a shrug. Many a nobleman found himself temporarily out of favor with a monarch, and if that disfavor turned into something more permanent, well then, the Gravensteen had room for them all, and most particularly for someone of Bolingbroke's lineage.

A month passed, then another waxed and waned. Margaret grew bigger with her child; Bolingbroke, Neville and the other men of Bolingbroke's retinue hunted or spent hours in the castle courtyard at sword practice; Agnes and Rosalind turned brown in the sun.

Mary's continuing weakness and illness was combined with an indefinable listlessness that no one could cheer her from. She spent many hours staring sightlessly from windows, or playing with Rosalind.

She was very quiet with Bolingbroke when they were alone in their chamber at night. He asked her on several occasions what was wrong, if she would speak to him of her fears as she had that night in Kenilworth, but Mary would not do so.

She was afraid that if she *did* do so, then he would, this time, be truthful with her, and for the moment she did not want that. Mary had lost much of her innocence with her last pregnancy: she was sure now that Bolingbroke did not truly care for her, or need her now that he had her lands. At the same time she understood quite well that most noble marriages were partnerships of business rather than love, and that most of these marriages managed well enough.

It was just that she wanted to be *needed*, if not loved, and she knew with all her being that Bolingbroke did not need her in any sense of that word.

She wondered if her deepening illness was an encumbrance to him, or a relief.

The latter, she thought, knowing that Bolingbroke would make the most cheerful of widowers.

One night, four or five weeks after they'd arrived in Ghent, Bolingbroke caressed her breast when he joined her in their bed, but Mary tensed, and so Bolingbroke withdrew his hand, and turned away with nary a word of good night.

After that he began to spend some nights away from their bed.

Mary did not ask where.

* * *

OCCASIONALLY NEWS arrived from England. Margaret knew little of what this contained, only that it came from Raby, and sometimes one or two other noblemen. Bolingbroke did not appear either overly comforted or depressed by what the tidings relayed, and when Margaret pressed Neville for details he would only say that he did not think they would see out the winter in Gravensteen.

"We'll be home for Christmastide," he would say as they lay in their bed at night, rubbing a hand over her swelling belly, "and we will celebrate the birth of our son together with Christ's birth."

That never cheered Margaret very much, because by the time this Christmastide came and went, her and Hal's cause would either be won or lost. Thomas would need to make his choice, whether for her or for the angels, at the birth of their baby. It would be then that he would know exactly what she was.

At Bolingbroke's instructions, Raby had caused those of Hal's household goods which had been saved from the Savoy—the majority of them, for most had been stored in chambers beneath the palace and had not been touched by fire—to be sent over to the Gravensteen. Neville had groaned when the two barge loads arrived three weeks after their own arrival, for among all the clothes and scarves and candles and jewels was Bolingbroke's entire collection of bureaucratic muddle.

Bolingbroke had laughed when he'd seen Neville's face, and had said that for the moment the clerical details could wait. "We'll never have another summer like this," he'd said, "never so much freedom again."

And so the wounded hawk stretched his wings in the sunshine, and waited his chance to soar.

IN EARLY August, as the summer heat finally gave up its fury and mellowed toward autumn, Gravensteen finally awoke from its stupor.

Bolingbroke had the use of a large, airy chamber with windows looking out on to the river, and here, in the late afternoon, his household was wont to gather. Mary would sit by the windows, her sewing idle in her lap as, chin in hand, she stared across the gently rippling waters. Margaret would sometimes sit with her, or sometimes with Bolingbroke and Neville, if they requested it, playing softly upon a lute.

Agnes always sat by the door, sewing in hand, industrious where Mary was motionless.

Salisbury and Courtenay, and several members of the count's household, would sit at a table in the late afternoon sunshine, playing cards or dicing, always talking and jesting—but softly, so as not to disturb Mary's reverie, or Margaret's music-making.

About Margaret or Neville's feet, and often Mary's, Rosalind would chase woolen balls. Today, caught by the lethargy of the adults, she slept on the seat next to Mary.

Occasionally, the count and his wife would join them, but this particular afternoon they had not, preferring to spend the day watching the executions in the public square abutting the Gravensteen.

And thus it was, on this lazy, warm afternoon, that when the door burst open, and the man sprang through, no one reacted save for looking up in bemused surprise.

Not one hand reached for a weapon, not one voice was raised in protest.

Everyone merely raised their heads—languidly—and looked.

"What?" cried the man. "Is this the den of that arch renegade, Hal Bolingbroke? Is this the haunt of traitors? Is there treason afoot? Is—sweet Jesu, Black Tom, what do you here without your damn robes?"

"Philip?" Bolingbroke said, blinking. He slowly got to his feet.

"Aye, you rascal." Philip of Navarre had by this time crossed the floor between them and enveloped Bolingbroke in a great hug. Then he embraced Neville, who was also standing.

Then he bent to Margaret, and his eyes darkened and his smile slipped, and he took her hand and kissed it. "My lady, I see you wear the ring of marriage, and bear within your body the fruits of it, but should you ever tire of your husband . . ."

She looked at him, knowing who he was even though he'd not been introduced, and then, slowly smiled. *No wonder Catherine had acted as she did.*

"Her name is Margaret," said Neville behind Philip, "and she is *my* wife."

Philip grinned mischievously into Margaret's eyes as he heard the jealousy in Neville's voice, then he winked very slowly at her—again managing to surprise her with the friendliness of the gesture—before turning back to Neville.

"A wife, Tom? And yet you were so attached to your monkish robes when last we met."

"When last we met at Chatellerault," Bolingbroke said, referring back to that time he and the Black Prince had met Philip to determine if the king of Navarre would support the English or the French in their war, "you were shouting insults to my uncle and hurling decapitated heads at us." He walked slowly forward. "What was it you said? Ah yes, we were a 'filthy presence' that you could not wait to rid your beloved land of. You had decided that you preferred the alliance of a sacred damsel to that of old friends."

Philip shrugged and waved a hand dismissively. "It was the atmosphere of that quarry tunnel, Bolingbroke. So dramatic, didn't you think? I got quite carried away."

He swiveled around before Bolingbroke could reply and caught sight of Mary sitting by the window.

"Ah," Philip said softly, "*this* must be your wife, Bolingbroke. France has been quite abuzz with the rumors of your marriage."

He walked over to Mary, who stood as he approached, smoothing down her skirts.

Philip bowed graciously, and took her hand to kiss it. As he did so he looked into her face, and saw there the unmistakable signs of illness, and then looked into her eyes, and saw the unquestionable signs of misery.

He said nothing, but his fingers tightened about Mary's hand, and his own eyes deepened with compassion.

Mary, who had heard so many tales of the various wickednesses of the king of Navarre, had to take a deep breath to steady the sudden emotion that coursed through her.

"I thank you, your grace," she said softly, and Philip gave her hand another brief squeeze before he let it go.

He glanced to Salisbury and Courtenay, as also to the two Flemish squires who had joined the Englishmen over this afternoon's game of chess. All four men now stood with hard faces and hands on knives.

Philip dismissed them without second thought, his eyes flickering to the door of the chamber before he looked to Bolingbroke.

"What do you here?" Bolingbroke said. His eyes were hooded, his stance that of a man ready to spring at any moment.

He did not believe they were in physical danger . . . but who ever trusted Philip?

"I come to talk," Philip said, his voice now serious. "But first—"

"The last time you wanted to 'talk,'" Bolingbroke said, "it was merely to tell us how much you thought us your despised enemy."

"Hal," Mary said, walking forward a little, "I think Philip has brought company with him."

Of everyone in the room, she was the only one who had seen the shadow waiting behind the half open door.

Philip nodded at her. "My Lady of Hereford has quick eyes. Aye, I have brought company."

He moved over to the door but, before opening it farther, placed himself so he could see the faces of most of the people in the room.

Philip had come to the Gravensteen to forge an alliance—but there was one thing he needed to know before he made his proposition, and there would be only one instant when he could learn that one thing.

Now.

"I would have come alone," Philip said, "but there was one who insisted on accompanying me." He shrugged, the action contrived, and looked directly at Bolingbroke. "But you, most apparently, know how difficult it is to be parted from one's wife."

Bolingbroke's face froze, and Philip had all the knowledge he needed.

"My dear," said Philip, and opened the door.

Catherine walked through, her every movement assured and elegant. Her face was flushed and her eyes bright and Margaret, watching, thought that that was more due to her annoyance at being kept waiting outside than anything else.

She also could not help noticing that Catherine was dressed in a gown of precisely the same deep red damask as Mary had worn on her wedding day. *Had Catherine somehow known, or was this just strange fate?*

And as Margaret had thought on that now far-past day, so again she thought: *Catherine wears that color with confidence, whereas Mary was overwhelmed by it.* The gown had a deep square neckline, showing the swell of Catherine's creamy breasts, and was gathered in close to her waist and hips before dropping in heavy drapery over her legs. She wore little jewelery, save some gold earrings and several garnet rings on her right hand.

She was stunning, as much due to the power of character she exuded as to her physical comeliness.

Margaret's eyes looked to Bolingbroke.

He was staring at Catherine with an expression that Margaret instantly knew betrayed every emotion churning about inside him.

She looked to Mary, and saw Mary staring, distraught, at both Bolingbroke and Catherine.

Sweet Jesu, she thought. *Who engineered this disaster? Catherine or Philip?*

"Wife?" said Bolingbroke, hating the way the word rasped out of his mouth.

"Philip has ever been the jester," Catherine said, and looked at Philip with amused eyes. They did not touch, but the air between them was alive with intimacy.

Philip returned Catherine's smile, then stared straight at Hal's eyes. "She refuses to wed me, even though she is not shy about sharing my bed."

Bolingbroke flushed brick-red, and Neville placed a hand on his arm, hoping Bolingbroke wasn't going to explode into violence. *He'd never imagined that Bolingbroke had felt so strongly for Catherine.*

Margaret had eyes only for Mary. The woman's distress was plain enough for anyone who cared to look, and Margaret put aside her lute and rose softly to stand at Mary's side, taking Mary's hand in her own.

Mary's eyes, huge and agonized, were fixed on Catherine.

"That was not well said, Philip," Neville said softly.

Philip affected an expression of surprise.

" 'Was not well said,' Tom? What do you mean? Are there coy virgins among us who cannot bear to hear the truth? Are we not all adults here? Do we not all know of what happens between a man and a woman? Do we—?"

"What do you want, Philip?" Bolingbroke shouted, furious both at Philip and Catherine's actions and at the depth of pain they caused him. "*What in Christ's name are you doing here?*"

"I have come to broker a deal with you, Bolingbroke."

Bolingbroke stared at him, his chest heaving with the depth of his rage and hurt and his embarrassment that all here had witnessed his discomposure.

"If perhaps we could speak," Philip said. "Alone."

Chapter VII

The Feast of the Transfiguration
of Our Lord Jesus Christ
In the second year of the reign of Richard II
(Monday 6th August 1380)

— II —

✠

"WELL NOW," said Philip, "I think I finally understand you."

He and Bolingbroke were sitting at a window in a chamber at the very top of the main keep of Gravensteen. Below them the rivers Leie and Lieve twisted sinuously through the city and the flat country beyond.

Bolingbroke said nothing.

Philip stared out the window, as if entranced by the beauty of the rivers. "I never quite understood why Catherine came to me so freely," he said, sliding his eyes back to Bolingbroke. "For a virgin, she was very eager."

Bolingbroke's face was flat and hostile.

"But then I began to make some inquiries," Philip continued, again looking out the window. "I came to realize that the night she came to me was your wedding night, my friend. And then I remembered that, some years back, there had been some negotiations between you and her."

Philip shrugged. "Of course, what inference could I draw from that? But still I wondered. Why did Catherine refuse to wed me? Was there some deeper purpose within her that

I could not discern? She says that she wants a strong man on the throne of France, and she says that she will be a partner in my ambitions, but I find myself thinking that *I* am not the strong man she wants to take the crown from her knock-kneed brother."

He shifted his eyes back to Bolingbroke, and the vestiges of banter dropped from his voice. "I think, Bolingbroke, that there is—was—some secret pact between you . . . a pact she thought broken when you took Mary to wife. I think that you are the man she wants on the throne. Or at least . . . the man she *once* wanted to sit on the throne of France."

Philip leaned forward on the small table that separated them. "The thing I want you to answer me honestly, my friend, is . . . what do you want more? France . . . or Catherine?"

Bolingbroke's face twisted with anger. "I can have both," he said.

Philip smiled. "No, Bolingbroke, I don't think you can. Not anymore."

NEVILLE HAD taken the other men to guard the door to the chamber where Philip and Bolingbroke parleyed, and Agnes had taken Rosalind to eat in the kitchens, so now there were only Mary, Margaret and Catherine left in the light and airy chamber.

"You must be Margaret Neville," Catherine said, walking over to Margaret once the others had left.

Margaret nodded, and curtsied. She and Catherine well knew who the other was, though this was the first time they'd met.

Catherine took Margaret's hand, raising her back to her feet. "I once spat at your husband," she said.

Despite the gravity of the current situation, Margaret's mouth twitched. "I have been tempted to do the same on many occasions. My lady, may I introduce to you my Lady of Hereford, Bolingbroke's wife."

Margaret held her breath as Catherine turned to Mary but, as Philip had done, Catherine also recognized the illness and misery that consumed Mary.

"My lady," Catherine said, leaning forward to place her hands gently on Mary's shoulder and to kiss her cheek. Catherine was angry with Bolingbroke, but not with this woman. "You have lost a child recently."

"I should think you would be pleased at that loss," Mary said, not attempting to conceal the bitterness in her voice as she drew back from Catherine.

"Then you misjudge me," Catherine said, "for children are blessings, and their loss is tragic."

There was an awkward silence, and Catherine finally walked over to the window and stared out. "This is a beautiful city," she said. "What is that castle next to the cathedral? It has a feel of great subtlety about it."

"That is the castle of Gerald the Devil," said Mary, directly behind Catherine.

Catherine's shoulders stiffened. "And why is he called a devil, Mary?"

"Would you like to refresh yourself with some wine, my Lady Catherine," Margaret said, desperate to distract the other two women from that damned castle.

"He is called a devil," Mary said, "because once he takes one wife, he begins to lust after another. Thus far he has murdered four wives in order to take some other woman who has caught his fancy."

She fell silent, staring at the castle while Catherine stared at her.

"No doubt," Mary finally said, softly, looking back to Catherine, "you cannot understand the terror in which his wives lived, for you are that woman on the outside looking in. How can *you* understand the fear of knowing your husband wants another, and the greater fear of not knowing when that want will grow strong enough to turn his thoughts to murder?"

Again she paused, staring with flat, hard eyes at Catherine. "He has my lands," she said, "and now I am no longer needed. How will you feel, Catherine of France, when he has *your* lands, and you are no longer needed? Will you remember me then?"

"MARY IS in a piteous situation," said Philip, "for she—as everyone else—saw how you looked at Catherine this afternoon. Your secret is out, and she knows she is no longer loved."

"Mary is my wife and I will treat her with all the respect and love that—"

Philip banged his fist on the table. "Don't mouth such pitiful lies to me, Bolingbroke! Mary is expendable—why else marry her?"

"I am not a wife-murderer!"

"You will not take knife or poison to her, I grant you that, but nevertheless you will poison Mary with your neglect. She is a woman who needs to be loved in order to live. Refuse her that love . . ."

"You did not come here to talk to me of my husbandly duties, Philip. What do you here? Did you not tell me and my uncle the Black Prince that you'd decided to ally yourself with Charles and his saintly virgin Joan?"

Philip shrugged expressively. "A temporary measure only—you understand such necessities, surely. But as to what I come to talk to you about, well, I come indeed to discuss Charles and the Holy Maid."

Bolingbroke said nothing, watching Philip with careful eyes.

"The fact is, Bolingbroke, that we both need them dead."

Bolingbroke raised his eyebrows.

"I for one reason. I want the French throne and can't have it until Charles and his saintly damsel are enjoying an eternity with God. And you for two reasons. *You* want the French throne and can't enjoy it until—"

"And the second reason?"

"Even if you didn't want the throne, Bolingbroke, you need to be rid of Joan because she has, it seems, taken a hearty dislike to you. Every evening she leads us in prayers that speak of the destruction of the English throne and the malevolent evil that sits upon it."

Philip laughed. "I, of course, pray for that most fervently, but I have every doubt that you would be so pleased to see it come to pass. You see, my friend, I have the strangest feeling that Joan isn't talking of Richard when she mutters about binding the English king to a pyre and lighting the fires of God's vengeance beneath him. I think she is talking about *you*."

"I am not king," said Bolingbroke. "I am in exile and—"

Philip waved a hand dismissively. "Ah, exile can be such a transitory thing, don't you agree? Frankly, Bolingbroke, I doubt you intend to stay a fugitive forever . . . or for very much longer, come to that."

"You can't think that I would try to—"

"Don't be shy, Bolingbroke, it doesn't become you. You've been as ambitious for the English throne as I am for the French throne. It's just that I have been a trifle more honest about my ambitions than you."

Bolingbroke smiled very slightly, but remained silent, holding Philip's gaze easily.

"I think that you will return to England within . . . oh, shall we say a month or so? You won't want to winter abroad, because that will give Richard too much time to consolidate his position, and if you are going to make a move before winter then you must do so soon, before the rain and sleet set in and the mud makes your task impossible."

Bolingbroke shrugged, as if the matter was of no concern to him.

"Whatever," Philip continued, "I have heard, as no doubt have you, that Richard is feeling so sure of himself that he is about to embark for Ireland, there to bludgeon its heathens into accepting his bottom-boy as their king. I imagine you think this your perfect opportunity."

Philip paused. "And, of course, you would be right. Richard is too stupid to sit on the throne of England . . . the crown shall gleam much more nicely on your scheming head."

He leaned forward and all the banter dropped from his face and voice. "Once you have secured England your eyes shall turn to France—to stop the Holy Maid before she stops you, and then to take the kingdom. But you won't have a chance against Joan, Bolingbroke, unless you ally yourself with me."

"You want an alliance with me against Joan?"

"Once you've managed to secure England . . . yes. We both want her dead and we can work together to achieve that end."

"I can do it without you," said Bolingbroke.

Philip smiled coldly. "No. You can't. I am sure you have heard of Hotspur's small debacle at Orleans."

Bolingbroke's face closed over, and Philip knew that Bolingbroke had indeed heard of the English defeat there.

"True," Philip said, "Hotspur didn't have a strong force, and they were demoralized at that. But I doubt *any* force could have stopped the French that day."

Philip told Bolingbroke what he'd seen—how Joan had rallied Orleans and then, at the battle's height, how the Archangel Michael had appeared in the sky.

"She has God behind her," Philip finished softly. "Can you counter that?"

"She will burn as easily as any mortal flesh."

"But only if you can get your hands on her, Bolingbroke. Ally with me against Joan and Charles, and I can give you Joan."

It was not as simple as that, as Bolingbroke well knew, but on the other hand Philip would be a valuable ally against Joan and Charles . . . and to have Joan delivered to him . . .

"How can I trust you?" Bolingbroke said.

"Because you know I want her dead as much as you."

"And you *can* deliver her to me?"

"Aye. She has a weakness. She can be seized."

Bolingbroke smiled cynically. "Supposing that all this comes to pass. We ally against Joan and Charles, and send both to whatever afterworld awaits them. Then what, Philip? We are left where we began—both wanting the French throne."

Philip nodded. "We don't have to fight it out, though, do we? At least, not on the battlefield."

"What do you mean?"

"The fight between you and me over France will take place in Catherine's bed, Bolingbroke. France will go to whomever Catherine chooses as husband."

Bolingbroke's face was now completely expressionless.

"You love her," said Philip, "and you think she loves you. You think she will conspire with you against me to hand you the crown of France to add to that of England. You think to use me to rid yourself of Joan and then cast me aside.

"But are you still so sure of her, Bolingbroke? Do you truly think that—?"

"I *will* have Catherine," Bolingbroke said.

Philip very slowly shook his head. "You can no longer be so certain of that. For the love of Christ, Bolingbroke, she came to my bed on the night you took Mary Bohun to wife. That was *vengeance*, Bolingbroke, not compliance to whatever intrigue you and she hatched years before!"

"She will not—"

"I offer you a deal, Bolingbroke. Call it a wager if you will. We ally together to destroy Joan. We both need her dead and gone, along with that faint-hearted idiot whose cause she espouses. True?"

Bolingbroke nodded, his eyes locked into Philip's.

"Then," Philip said very softly, "the throne of France. There is no need to fight it out, Bolingbroke. That would be witless. Instead, why don't we agree to allow Catherine to choose for us? Whoever she picks as husband will take the throne. Once Charles is dead, Catherine's marriage bed carries with it the legal right for her husband to be crowned king of France. We let her choose . . . agreed?"

Bolingbroke sat very still for some time, then he jerked his head in assent.

Philip rose, and held out his hand. "Shake on it."

His eyes still locked into Philip's, Bolingbroke also rose, the chair scraping back behind him.

Slowly, he lifted his hand, then grasped Philip's in a viciously tight grip.

"Catherine chooses between us," Bolingbroke said, not loosening his grip. He paused, then said, "You have wagered stupidly, Philip, for she *will* choose me."

"Remember that she came to me on your marriage night," Philip said, his voice both soft and hard at the same time. "In my time with her I have given her nothing but honesty, respect and tenderness. What have you given her?"

Bolingbroke's eyes darkened with anger, and he abruptly let Philip's hand go.

Philip grinned boyishly. "So, we are allies."

He walked to a table and poured them both cups of wine, handing one to Bolingbroke. "To your successful rise to the throne of England, and to Joan's and Charles' untimely deaths!"

Relaxing slightly, Bolingbroke raised his cup in salute, and drained the wine.

CATHERINE AND Margaret watched as Mary turned away and walked toward the door of the chamber. She swayed slightly as she went, and had to grab at the back of a chair for support.

Margaret made as if to move to her, but Mary shot her a look that froze Margaret where she stood.

Then, taking a deep breath and visibly gathering herself,

she straightened her back and walked with sweet dignity through the door.

Catherine and Margaret stared after her for a moment, then Catherine looked at Margaret.

"She is dying."

Unbidden, Margaret's eyes filled with tears. "Aye."

"Hal knows?"

"He knew before he married her. I think . . . I think he thought she'd be dead by now."

"Sweet Jesu!"

"She has a malignant darkness in her womb," Margaret said. "Every so often it appears that she is with child, but she expels only a portion of the mass which has grown too burdensome to bear any longer."

Catherine turned so that she stared out the window rather than at the door where Mary had disappeared. "How can she bear it?" she whispered. "To think yourself with child, and then to discover that—"

"Mary does not know what she bears," Margaret said. "We have told her only that she carried a child that could not live."

Catherine was still staring out the window with faraway eyes. "What is the greater cruelty?" she said. "To continually lose the hope of a child, or to have a husband who is so unheedful?"

"There is no point to asking that, for Mary must bear both of them nonetheless."

Catherine took a deep breath, and looked once more to Margaret. "I am pleased to finally see your face, cousin. For too many years I have had news of you only through our kindred." She looked to Margaret's belly. "And to have a child . . ."

Margaret smiled, although she was still saddened by the effects of Mary's lingering misery in this chamber. She lifted Catherine's hand, and placed it on her belly. "Feel. A boy."

Catherine smiled as well. "A child, and healthy. You are blessed, Margaret."

Margaret looked carefully at Catherine. "And you, Catherine?"

Catherine's smile faded, and her hand slipped from Margaret's belly. "Until I walked into this chamber this afternoon I did not know what I would do. Now . . ." She sighed again, shifting her eyes away from Margaret.

"Hal did much wrong when he married Mary," Margaret said. "He thought her only someone he could use, and who would be of no consequence."

"As I once thought of Philip," Catherine said softly, staring down at the castle of Gerald the Devil.

Margaret also looked down at the forbidding, silent castle. "Do you know what I think?" she said. "I think that between them Mary and Philip have the power to completely undo Hal."

Catherine took a long time to respond. When she did, Margaret could barely hear her words.

"And they shall do so through the love that Hal professes, but which he cannot understand."

Margaret reached out and gripped Catherine's hand, and for a long time the two women stood there, silent, staring at Gerald the Devil's murderous abode.

Chapter VIII

After Compline on the Feast of the Transfiguration
of Our Lord Jesus Christ
In the second year of the reign of Richard II
(late night Monday 6th August 1380)

— III —

✠

THEY SAT together on the bedcovers they had pulled before the hearth.

Both were naked.

Catherine sat slightly in front of Philip and closer to the fire, and as he ran the fingers of one hand softly down her spine he marveled at the beauty of the flame-shadows chasing themselves over her body.

"What did you and Hal speak of?" she said softly.

His hand trailed to a halt, and when he spoke he answered her only with a question.

"Do you know why I brought you to Gravensteen?"

"You came to see Hal—"

"But why did I bring *you*?" His hand resumed its slow tracking up and down her spine.

"You brought me to see Hal," she whispered.

"Yes . . . and no. I brought you so that Hal could see you."

"Philip . . ." She twisted about so she could see his face.

"I needed to know how much he loved you," Philip said, and slid his hand around her body to caress her breast.

Catherine felt sick to her stomach. "How long have you known?"

"Forever," he said, and leaned forward to kiss her deeply.

"I—" she said, when he drew back a little.

"You need say nothing," Philip said, then sat back and dropped his hand from her body. "Hal and I spoke of two things. You . . . and France."

Catherine did not speak, but watched him with frightened eyes. Frightened, not because she thought she might be in physical danger, but because she realized that some secret part of her had always hoped Philip would love her . . . and now the hope of that love was almost certainly gone.

But why hope for Philip's love when she loved Hal?

"I said to Hal," Philip went on, watching Catherine's face carefully, "that I knew you and he had some secret pact that would give him the French crown."

Catherine went rigid.

"Why else will you not wed me?" Philip said. "You have given me everything else . . . but not that. You want someone else as a husband, don't you? And for a wedding gift you would give him France."

"I—"

"No! *Don't* speak," Philip said, furious not with her, but with himself for being so close to tears. *Damn her!*

"You have set out from the first to use me," he continued. "Tempting me with the crown when you meant to give it to someone else."

"I—"

"*I said not to speak!* Yes, I knew you did not love me, and that you used me for your own ends, and I thought that it did not matter, for I meant to use you as much as—"

"Philip—"

This time he stopped her words with a hard, desperate kiss, and at its end both had tears in their eyes.

"But why did you make me love you?" he whispered when finally he lifted his mouth from hers. "Why be that cruel?"

"I did not mean to," she whispered. "I thought this would be merely a meeting of bodies and ambitions."

He should have felt triumph at her words, but he felt only sadness.

"I made your fair Prince Hal an offer," Philip said. "Both he and I lust after the throne, but neither he nor I could achieve it on our own. So I suggested an alliance between him and me, against poor unsure Charles and this saintly Joan—"

Catherine allowed herself a small measure of relief.

"—after which victory he and I would have to fight it out over France itself. But, Catherine, we don't have to fight it out at all, do we? *You* carry the throne on your wedding finger—whichever of us you choose as husband also beds France."

She waited, silent, her eyes watching his face carefully.

"We have wagered," Philip said, "to allow you to decide the fate of the French throne."

"Oh no, Philip, no—"

Gently, he pushed her back until she lay flat.

The firelight scattered over her pale body, and Philip had to take a deep breath. "He thinks he will win."

"Philip—"

He moved over her, leaning down to kiss her once more.

"Have I not been the most foolish of men," he said finally, "to wager a throne on love?"

She reached up a trembling hand and touched his face. She tried to smile, and couldn't.

"In your wisdom," she whispered, "you have become the most dangerous of enemies."

He ran his hand down her body, and she understood how badly he wanted her.

"If, in his turn," he said, "Hal had offered me the choice of either you or the throne, I would have taken you."

"Oh, sweet Jesu," she said, "what have I done?"

"WE MAY not have a marriage of love," Mary said, "but I would that it be a marriage of honesty, and even one of some respect. Tell me of Catherine."

They were in their bedchamber, each as far apart from the bed and each other as they could possibly get: Mary sitting on a small chest under a great Arras tapestry which hung on the far wall of the chamber; Bolingbroke standing, leaning against the doorframe with folded arms.

This was not a conversation he felt like having, not after what he and Philip had talked of earlier, and not while he imagined how Philip might currently be employing his body to further his cause. Nonetheless, Bolingbroke was tired of subterfuge . . . and knew that, having seen his face as he stared at Catherine this afternoon, Mary was tired of it too.

"Catherine and I met many years ago," he said, his eyes steady on Mary's face. "There were some negotiations—mainly pushed by my father—but they did not prosper. King John did not want his granddaughter marrying the son of the *fourth* in line to the English throne . . . and for that matter did not want her marrying an Englishman at all."

"But you loved her. You still do."

"Yes," he said, and Mary looked away.

She thought a long while before she spoke again, but when she did she raised her eyes back to her husband with a clear, steady gaze.

"I do not think that I shall long encumber you, Hal, but while I do I would that you treated me with respect, and with dignity."

Bolingbroke straightened and crossed the floor, dropping down on one knee before her. He kissed her hand.

"I did you wrong this afternoon, Mary," he said, "even though it was unintentional. Respect and dignity is the least I can give you."

She nodded, knowing the words were easy enough to say, and knowing also that his ambition to wrest the throne from Richard meant that he could not yet afford to alienate her. The English commons loved Bolingbroke, and Mary was certain that many of the nobles respected him and were prepared to back him—but that love and respect and support would be severely tried if fair Prince Hal threw over his respected English wife for the sluttish daughter of the French whore Isabeau de Bavière.

For the first time in many, many long months Mary felt an inkling of her own power, and an understanding of how she might use it. She reached out a hand, caressing Bolingbroke's face, thinking how comely it was . . . and thinking of how much he undoubtedly would prefer to be with Catherine this night.

She smiled slowly, thinking of the most effective means to revenge herself for the humiliation he had visited on her earlier.

"Then make love to me," she said. "Gently, and slowly. As any husband should do to his wife."

Chapter IX

Nones on the Assumption of the Blessed Virgin Mary
In the second year of the reign of Richard II
(noon Wednesday 15th August 1380)

✣

TWO DAYS AFTER Philip and Catherine had departed, news arrived for Bolingbroke that brought him to his feet, a tight and hungry gleam in his eyes as he scanned the letter.

He scrunched the letter into a crackling ball in his fist, then flung it on the fire.

"Tom," he said, "you have an uncle who is worth more than his weight in gold."

From that moment, everything became frantic activity.

Almost from the hour of that letter's arrival men and horses had arrived in groups of two or three, ten or tens, crowding the courtyard of the Gravensteen, more and more arriving each day until it appeared that hundreds of men clattered in every hour.

By mid-August they were gone from the Gravensteen.

Bolingbroke had long held plans for this day.

A COLD, gray wind swept across the waterfront of Sluys Harbor in northern Flanders, binding everything in its frigid embrace. Men bustled to and fro, rolling kegs and barrels over the cobbles toward the great ship bobbing at the wharf's edge. Others murmured soft and reassuring words to the skittery and white-eyed warhorses they led toward the gangplank. Others yet counted and then recounted sheaves of arrows and crossbow bolts before piling them into their grim stacks of hate.

Sailors swarmed about the deck and rigging of the ship, readying her for sea. One scrambled up the mast, unfurling the red, gold and white standard of Bolingbroke—a combination of the three lions of the Plantagenet dynasty, the Lancastrian fleurs-de-lis and castle, and Bolingbroke's personal emblem of the head of a visored knight.

It snapped in the wind as if angry, chafing at the delay.

Beyond the ship, bobbing impatiently in the deep sea channel of the harbor, waited five more vessels, already fully laden with men, horses and weapons.

Bolingbroke was striding to and fro, shouting orders and curses in equal amounts. At his shoulder strode Thomas Neville, now and then speaking urgent words in Bolingbroke's ear.

Both men wore thigh-length chain mail, heavy metal-studded gloves and steel greaves above their boots. Over their chain mail, both wore sleeveless tunics: Bolingbroke's white and Neville's scarlet, but both with the Bolingbroke standard sewn across their chests. Cloaks, colored and embroidered to match their tunics, flew back from their shoulders in the cold wind. Both men had swords swinging at their hips, and daggers thrust into their sword-belts.

Their faces were tight and determined, but glowing with purpose and what was probably subdued exuberance.

Bolingbroke stopped to clap a hand on the shoulder of a man-at-arms, sharing a brief smile and jest with him. Then he and Neville were off again, striding to the horse lines, each seeking out his own mount. Raby, the ever-faithful retainer, had managed to ship over to Flanders Bolingbroke's and Neville's favorite stallions when he'd sent Bolingbroke's household goods many months ago.

MARY WATCHED, still and silent to one side, wrapped tightly in a black cloak. Margaret was by her side, similarly wrapped. The ever-vigilant Agnes waited with Rosalind under the eaves of one of the waterfront warehouses, where they could observe the activity but were protected from the wind.

"War," said Mary. "See how they enjoy it!"

Her mouth twitched. *And a war and an ambition heavily funded by the dowry I brought to my marriage bed.*

"If you wish," Margaret said, her eyes following the movement of men about them, "we could wait in the house of the Lieutenant of the Harbor. He has offered us its facilities."

Mary shook her head. "Nay. I prefer that I stand here and watch what my husband does."

Margaret shot her a look, wondering exactly what she meant.

Mary's mouth twitched again, and she smiled, unable to keep the grin back. "Poor Hal. Every night that Catherine and Philip stayed at Gravensteen I demanded that he make love to me."

She saw the look on Margaret's face, and she untangled one of her gloved hands from her coat and briefly touched Margaret's heavily wrapped arm.

"I may not be the woman he wants," Mary said, "but I am the woman he has."

"Catherine is not an evil woman," Margaret said.

"Oh, I know this. She is strong and determined, and I think that under other circumstances I would like her very much. She is also the woman who *should* have been Hal's wife. Nay, do not deny it. I can see it, Margaret, and it has ceased to upset me."

"Do you remember, my most dear lady, on the day after we escaped that hellish ship from London, when I said you were the perfect wife for Bolingbroke?"

Mary nodded.

"Well, then I spoke only to comfort you. Now, I can see it is the truth. You have a greatness and a nobleness about you that I do not think Bolingbroke will ever appreciate."

In the distance Bolingbroke, together with Neville and Roger Salisbury, had supervised the loading of the last of the horses, and now the final few bundles of supplies were being swung aboard.

"He is being kind to me now," Mary said in a soft voice, "because he thinks I shall soon die. He thinks he will have Catherine soon enough."

"Mary!"

"Do not seek to mollycoddle me." Mary slid one of her hands over her belly. "Something grievously heavy lies in my womb, and it drains my strength day by day. At night, sometimes, I can hardly bear the pain that nibbles inside me."

Margaret did not speak, but shifted close so that their bodies touched.

Mary leaned against her, smiling. "You are my greatest strength, Margaret, and knowing that I shall see your child born brings me the happiness that I should otherwise have had in the birth of my own children. But," she straightened, seeing Bolingbroke and Neville turn and walk toward them, "do not think that I shall lie down and breathe my last to the dictates of my husband's ambitions and needs!"

"Bolingbroke has been a fool," Margaret said, but could say no more, for now their husbands were upon them, each one bending to kiss his wife farewell.

Neville kissed Margaret warmly, hungrily; Bolingbroke

touched his mouth to Mary's with more dutifulness than warmth.

"Be careful," Margaret said to Neville.

Neville had the air about him of a small boy engaged in some exciting adventure. His cheeks were ruddy and glowing from helping with the loading, his dark eyes bright, his mouth unable to repress a grin. Even his black hair curled and snapped in the cold sea air as if it were impatient to be off.

"It will not be long," he said, and kissed Margaret again. He laid a hand on her belly. "You shall be home in time for the birth."

At that Bolingbroke turned to look Margaret in the eye. "We will send for you before Michaelmas approaches," he said. "None of us wants your child to be born outside England."

Then Bolingbroke looked again at Mary, and his eyes softened somewhat.

"Mary," he said, "once I am sure it is safe, I will send for you."

He bent down, and this time kissed her on the mouth with far more warmth than he'd done previously.

When he straightened, he was looking at Margaret.

"Richard and de Vere will suffer for what they did to you," he said.

And then he was gone, striding toward the ship.

Neville lingered, kissing Margaret one more time. "Take care," he said.

"And you," Margaret whispered.

"Tom!" Bolingbroke shouted from the edge of the wharf. "England awaits!"

"You are loved," Neville said, kissing Margaret hard on her mouth. He bowed to Mary, and kissed her hand, and then he too was gone in a swirl of cloak and a thud of boots as he jogged over to join Bolingbroke.

Mary and Margaret watched for some minutes as the gangplank was pulled aboard and the ship slowly leaned away from the wharf and into the waves to join the five others at anchor in the channel.

Neville gave one last wave, and then he and Bolingbroke disappeared below decks.

For a long time, the women stood and watched as first Bolingbroke's ship joined the others and then as all six, their sails cracking and billowing in the wind, tacked northeast into the rolling gray waters of treason.

THE NIGHT was cold and dark when, weeping, Marie came to her. She said nothing, merely taking Joan's hand and laying it on her belly.

Joan tensed—the small hard swelling was clear enough to touch if not yet to sight.

"But you said . . ." Joan began, unable to complete the sentence.

"I have lain with no man!"

"Then this child is the get of demons," Joan said.

"Do they have golden hands?" Marie whispered.

Joan flinched, and drew back from Marie. "You must get you gone from here," she said, her tone flat. "Retire from my company."

"Please, no!"

"I cannot have you about me," Joan said, trying to keep her voice calm. "You must be gone."

And so, still weeping, Marie turned and left.

Joan did not sleep again that night.

Chapter X

The Thursday within the Octave
of the Assumption of the Blessed Virgin Mary
In the second year of the reign of Richard II
(16th August 1380)

✠

THE MAGNIFICENT CATHEDRAL NOTRE-DAME dominated the northeastern city of Rheims and the nearby River Vesle. All the kings of France had been crowned here since the late Dark Ages, so it was no surprise to Philip that Joan—or one of her angelic companions—had insisted Charles be crowned here as well.

But, in its own way, thought Philip of Navarre, sitting bored and uncomfortable in his chair, *the Cathedral Notre-Dame could not have been a worse choice for the poor, dithering incompetent that Joan apparently thought was the best choice for the next French king*. The cathedral had been built over a hundred years ago, replacing an earlier cathedral. It stood on the legendary site where the Frankish King Clovis accepted the Christian faith in the fifth century.

Poor Charles, looking lonely and nervous on the throne, was never going to be able to emulate Clovis, nor any one of the scores of warrior-kings who had followed him.

There was a ceremony going on behind the altar screens—Philip had no idea what—and so for the moment he had nothing to do but allow his eyes to flicker about the cathedral. It was a dull day (for a dull king, Philip thought) and there was not enough daylight to set the great, stained glass rose window ablaze with color.

A movement beside him made Philip smile. Catherine. She returned his smile, and then glanced pointedly at Charles. For the moment Joan and her clerical assistants had left Charles marooned on the throne before the altar, and the simpleton had no idea what to do. His eyes were jerking nervously to left and right, his hands clutched about the armrests of the throne one moment, the next clasped nervously in his lap, and yet next pulling at the neckline of his heavy, jewel-encrusted robe.

Catherine rolled her eyes, and Philip grinned.

There was a movement, and the Archbishop of Rheims, Regnault de Chartres, emerged from the screens behind the altar carrying the crown of France. Following de Chartres came a double line of various clerics, murmuring prayers, and after them came Joan herself, arrayed in shining white armor, a chain mail hood covering her short, dark hair.

Philip supposed it was the closest the Maid could come to a womanly veil.

Then his eyes narrowed in surprise, and his hand clasped Catherine's arm.

Joan was looking wan and almost as nervous as Charles.

What was wrong?

JOAN TOOK a deep breath, trying to steady herself.

She must not fail now!

But, oh sweet God, the armor she bore about her body weighed her down as it never before had, and her muscles trembled with weakness. Her heart thudded, her brain ached, and it was only through the most extraordinary effort that Joan managed to keep the expression on her face even vaguely neutral.

Try as she might, Joan could no longer convince herself that Marie's sensual dreams—and now the reality of her child—were the result of Catherine's demonic machinations. Nor could she convince herself that Marie had been secretly whoring with one or two of the soldiers. Whatever else, Joan knew that Marie had been telling the truth when she'd claimed to have slept with no man.

But Joan could not admit to herself the truth of who or what *had* put the child in Marie's body.

To do that would bring her entire world, her beliefs, clattering down in ruins about her.

Joan blinked, and tried to concentrate, knowing that her duty today was one of the most important she had been entrusted with . . . knowing that she could not let her doubts about Marie's child deflect her from her purpose.

Then she saw Catherine's eyes upon her.

CATHERINE GASPED, suddenly realizing the enormity of the emotion and confusion that was consuming Joan. Had the archangel finally exposed himself?

"Catrine?" whispered Philip.

"Saint Michael has betrayed himself," Catherine murmured, "and in so doing, betrayed his Maid."

Philip frowned, but Catherine hushed him before he could ask any more questions.

JOAN BLINKED and twisted her eyes away from Catherine. Her hand strayed momentarily to the miraculous sword at her side—and it gave her the comfort and strength she so desperately needed.

They were before the throne now, and de Chartres was lifting the crown on high, showing it to the assembled masses.

A shout went up.

"Joan! Joan! Joan!"

Catherine smiled.

Then de Chartres turned to Joan, who had walked up to join him, and handed her the crown.

* * *

PHILIP COULD not believe it. *Joan* was going to lay the crown on Charles' head? Sweet Lord, how did de Chartres feel about that?

Philip needed only one glance at the archbishop's tight, angry face to know exactly how he felt. It should have been the Archbishop of Rheims who consecrated and crowned the new king . . . but here, today, he had been usurped by the Holy Maid of France.

Smiling in satisfaction, Philip sat back in his chair, folding his arms. Regnault de Chartres was his.

FOR AN instant, Joan thought she was going to drop the crown, but she gritted her teeth, then walked up the steps to Charles and, avoiding his nervously darting eyes, placed the crown on his head.

It slipped, and both Joan and Charles grabbed at it.

But the crown was heavy and awkward. It slipped through their fingers and, in the stunned silence that filled the cathedral, bounced down the steps to the stone floor.

It rolled over to Philip's feet.

He stared at it, then bent down, picked it up, and stood.

Philip could not help himself. He laughed, and held the crown on high.

Then, as a red-faced Joan walked over, he handed it to her.

"You may have it," he said. "For the moment."

And then he cast his eyes over the cathedral and saw that every eye was on him.

Philip knew then, as he never had before, that he would eventually have France.

PART SIX

Dangerous Treason

King Richard:
Tell Bolingbroke, for yon methinks he stands,
That every stride he makes upon my land
Is dangerous treason; he is come to open
The purple testament of bleeding war.

—William Shakespeare,
Richard the Second, Act III, sc. iii

Chapter I

Prime on the Friday within the Octave
of the Assumption of the Blessed Virgin Mary
In the second year of the reign of Richard II
(daybreak 17th August 1380)

✣

RABY SAT HIS HORSE in the cold pre-dawn, hunching into his cloak and squinting across the waters into the dim light.

There was nothing but the rolling waves.

The jingle of a bit behind him made Raby jump, and he swiveled about in his saddle and cursed the unfortunate man whose horse had shaken its head.

Raby turned back to the empty sea, feeling the better for having vented some of his frustration.

He waited, as behind him a dark twisting column of men and horses waited.

Beneath them spread the tiny village and port of Ravenspur at the very mouth of the Humber estuary in southern Yorkshire. Most of the villagers were huddled in their homes by the embers of their fires; they had not dared to venture outside since the arrival of the horsed warriors late the previous night. Their fishing boats had been moved from the single small pier to an anchorage far out in the estuary. They would not be going anywhere this day.

"Any news?" Raby growled to a soldier standing just to his right.

"No, my lord."

Raby grunted. No man had approached the soldier, and

there had been no signal from the beacons atop the surrounding hills, so Raby *knew* there was no news, but even so, he'd had to ask.

Where were they?

He swiveled about in his saddle again, his eyes searching for the man who sat his horse ten or fifteen paces back.

There, sitting calm and still where Raby fidgeted. Raby nodded, and turned back to the sea.

Where were . . .

A shout sounded, high above, and Raby's eyes shot to the crest of the hill.

A flame flickered in the stacked wood of the beacon, and as Raby watched, it flared into life.

Raby jerked his eyes back to the sea. There! *There!* Six ships, pitching heavily in the waves, the first rays of the sun tangling within their sails.

"Bolingbroke!" Raby shouted, and dug his spurs into his stallion as behind him rose the shout, "Bolingbroke! Bolingbroke! Bolingbroke!"

BOLINGBROKE'S SHIP was the first to draw alongside the wharf, but Bolingbroke was in too much of a hurry to wait for its sailors to slide the boarding planks down to the wharf. He had his white stallion on deck and, as men shouted and milled about him, he swung up to its back and, in a move so foolhardy it took men's breath away, drove the animal toward the deck railing.

It leaped, twisted a little in the air, then sailed down to the wharf, landing with a great clatter of hooves, its snowy mane and tail streaming out behind it like battle standards.

Bolingbroke screamed, a sound half battle-cry, half joyous shout, and drove the horse at a gallop toward Raby, who, his patience at an end, was urging his own horse forward.

"Ralph!" Bolingbroke shouted, reining his stallion to a halt. His fair hair lifted in the wind, and his eyes shone. "Ralph, I am *home*!"

"Aye," said Raby, grinning hugely, "that you are. Welcome home, my lord."

Bolingbroke clasped his hand briefly to Raby's shoulder, then looked past him to the men and horses crowding the streets of Ravenspur and the road and hills beyond.

"Sweet Jesu, Ralph. Tell me."

Raby could not tear his eyes away from Bolingbroke. He was old enough to remember Edward III in his prime, and had fought for many years shoulder to shoulder with the Black Prince, but neither Edward nor his son had ever exuded the presence that this man did, had never inspired the same surge of emotion—

"Tell me!" Bolingbroke said again, swinging his horse against Raby's.

"All England has risen behind you," Raby said. He lifted his arm and gestured to the mass of men waiting in the town and beyond. "Fifteen thousand waiting here to greet you, forty-five thousand waiting above York. All told, sixty thousand—"

"Lord Christ!" Bolingbroke said. "*Sixty thousand?* How did you—?"

Raby indicated the man riding his horse toward them.

Bolingbroke stilled. "Ah, Northumberland."

"Aye," Northumberland said, reining to a halt before Bolingbroke and Raby. "Northumberland indeed."

Bolingbroke kicked his horse forward, then dropped the reins to take Northumberland's hand and forearm in both his hands. "I will reward you well for this."

Northumberland smiled without humor. "I would expect nothing less, my lord."

Bolingbroke picked up his reins again, and glanced behind him to where the ship was now disgorging its load. Neville had now disembarked and was riding toward them.

"Warwick and Nottingham wait for us with the majority of your army above York, my lord," Raby said.

Bolingbroke nodded. "And Richard?"

Raby glanced at Northumberland, and both men shared a smile.

"Richard and de Vere have only just disembarked at Waterford in Ireland, my lord," Raby said. "Where, no doubt, they will soon learn of your arrival."

"If we allow them two days of panic, and then a week to order themselves enough to turn their invading force back to defend England," Northumberland said, "we should have two weeks at least."

"And," Raby said, "they have only twenty-five thousand."

Bolingbroke lifted his face so that the dawning sunlight washed over it, and laughed for sheer joy.

"Good news, my lord?" Neville said, finally joining them.

"The best," said Bolingbroke, "for I have come home to find that England is in my hand."

He looked to where the men lined the road and filled the hill rising above Ravenspur. "This is *my* England," he murmured, then spurred his horse forward toward the men.

"Hear me!" he screamed, standing in his stirrups and swaying lightly with the movement of the horse beneath him. "Hear me! I am Bolingbroke, son of Lancaster, stepped forth once more upon this royal throne of kings, this sceptred isle! But I weep, for I find that this beloved land has been deeply bruised by the hand of a king who laid last summer's dust with the blood of slaughtered Englishmen."

He paused, his gray eyes sweeping over the massed men rising above him, his stallion half-rearing beneath him, then raised his voice once more.

"Some call me a traitor for setting foot once more to this tortured soil, but I step forth for only one reason—my duty! My duty to you, to your wives and to your children, and to this blessed plot, this realm, this England!"

He drew breath once more, and screamed to the very heavens: "Men of England, will you stand at my side?"

And it seemed to Neville that in the roar of acclaim that followed even the waves that girdled the harbor drew back in honor of Bolingbroke's majesty, and in recognition of his right to lay claim to that majesty.

MUCH LATER that night Bolingbroke, Raby and Neville stood on a small hill, staring westward across east Yorkshire. They had ridden hard and fast that day, and were more than ready to lie down wrapped in their blankets before a fire, but there were also matters which needed to be discussed, and those privately.

"Can I trust him?" Bolingbroke asked quietly of Raby.

"Northumberland? For the moment, yes. But I do not know how long that moment will last."

"Why did he change his mind?" Bolingbroke said, tugging his cloak a little tighter about his shoulders—this night air was already sharp with autumn.

"He has entertained doubts long enough, I think, and many a noble brow furrowed in concern when Richard stripped you of your hereditary lands. If Richard took from Bolingbroke, who would he take from next? But," Raby gave a short laugh, "it was the insult to his daughter that tipped Northumberland into your hand, my lord."

Neville noted his uncle's deference. Bolingbroke might have once been a boy that Raby had cuffed about the ears in the stableyard, but tonight, on this hill, he was a man only weeks away from the throne of England.

"And Hotspur?" Neville said.

Raby shot him a sharp glance. "Hotspur does not totally agree with his father's decision."

"He has not joined with my army," Bolingbroke said.

"Nay," Raby said. "He has claimed some minor disturbance on the Scottish border that he must deal with."

"I like this not," Bolingbroke said quietly.

Neither did Neville. The Percys, and Hotspur in particular, could raise from the northern marches an army almost as substantial as the one which now rode behind Bolingbroke.

And Hotspur was an ambitious man. Ambitious enough for the throne if he thought it near enough for the snatching? Bolingbroke might be able to seize the throne from Richard . . . but could he hold it?

"He is more dangerous than Richard," Neville said.

Bolingbroke nodded, his eyes distant. "It is a long time since we walked together as boyhood friends, Tom. A long, long time."

He was about to say more when they heard the sound of hurried footsteps.

It was a sergeant-at-arms, puffing with the exertion of climbing the hill.

He bowed to Bolingbroke, then turned to Raby and murmured something about trouble within the horse lines.

Raby muttered a curse, then waved the man away. He bowed to Bolingbroke. "My lord . . ."

"You have my leave to go," Bolingbroke said, then grinned. "Horses can be more trouble than wives, sometimes."

All three laughed softly, and then Raby was gone, striding down the hill after the sergeant-at-arms.

Bolingbroke turned back to the west. "Somewhere out there lies Richard," he said, and there was something hungry in his voice.

Neville stared at him, trying to make out his features in the dark night. "How soon will he hear?"

"About me? Not long, three or four days at the most, I think." Bolingbroke gave a short laugh. "How can he have been so foolish as to have thought his realm secure enough to embark on his Irish adventure? Ah, but I should not complain, for through his error Richard has handed me my heritage."

Now Neville also looked to the west. There was little to see save the vague outline of distant hills against the starry sky. But somewhere out there, across the Irish sea, lay the Demon-King . . .

"I had thought him to have more cunning," Neville said.

"Richard has been more the silly youth than Satan's emissary of ruin."

"Do you think we should call off the chase then, my friend? Perhaps Richard would do better if he were to have the benefit of some good, fatherly counseling, or perhaps—"

"No! No. Richard must be . . ."

Bolingbroke turned to look at Neville, his eyes almost unnaturally keen in the dark. "Must be *what*, Tom?"

"He must be killed," Neville said. "He is evil."

Bolingbroke had half turned away, hiding the sudden gleam of his teeth as he smiled. "You have not spoken of demons, nor of de Worde's casket, for many months, Tom. I had thought you lost in the pleasures of love."

"Now is the time for war, Hal."

"Aye, that it is. That it is. And when London is ours, my friend, then we will tear it apart searching for your casket. It is more than time that we freed the truth."

Just then the moon floated free of the clouds, and Neville looked at Bolingbroke, standing in a shaft of moonlight. He remembered how on the night he had arrived in Chauvigny, when he had seen Bolingbroke standing under the moonlight, he had thought that Bolingbroke looked like a fairy prince. Now that impression returned to him, stronger than ever. Standing still and straight and strong in glinting chain mail and armored with the weapons of war, Bolingbroke looked nothing less than a king—even his bare head seemed crowned with light as his silver-gilt hair glimmered with the caress of the moon.

"You will be the king that England needs," Neville said softly, and Bolingbroke tilted his head very slightly and smiled at him, making Neville's heart clench in his chest with the sweetness of his love.

Suddenly, stunningly, both men's faces were illuminated with a fiery radiance, and they jerked their eyes upward.

Two falling stars blazed across the heavens, flaring and sizzling in a brilliant cascade of blue and red and white.

Bolingbroke seized Neville's arm in a tight grip. "A sign, Tom! A sign from the heavens."

He dropped his eyes back to Neville's face. "You and I, Tom, against everything that is evil. Do you pledge it? Do you?"

Neville gripped Bolingbroke's forearm with both his hands. "Aye, my lord. I pledge it. You and I against all evil."

Bolingbroke glanced upward at the brilliant firmament again, then stared at Neville. "One day, Tom, one day I swear that I, or the issue of my body, will lead mankind into the stars."

Overcome with emotion, Neville could only nod.

"This wounded hawk," Bolingbroke whispered, "has taken wing into the heavens."

Chapter II

Vespers on the Feast of the
Beheading of St. John the Baptist
In the second year of the reign of Richard II
(evening Wednesday 29th August 1380)

— CONWAY CASTLE, NORTH WALES —

✠

RICHARD STARED out the window of the Keep, his eyes moving slowly over the empty fields of wheat stubble that stretched for miles.

Out there was his enemy . . . outside Chester, according to the latest reports.

Not far. Two days ride, at the most.

Cursed Bolingbroke! Richard grimaced, glad his back

hid his expression from those waiting behind him. Well, this was one lesson he had learned well: magnanimity was all very fine, but not when a crown was at stake.

"I should have killed him when I had the chance," he said softly, turning back into the chamber. "Not sent him into comfortable exile where he could plot at his leisure."

Robert de Vere, leaning against the cold hearth, sent Richard a dark look, but said nothing. They had barely landed in Ireland before the news of Bolingbroke's treason reached them—all hope of a crown on his own head would have to wait until they secured the one on Richard's. They'd had to turn their army about in only a few days, not even waiting to re-provision the ships that had just disembarked them, and then had been forced to endure a nightmare three days stormy crossing of the Irish Sea to reach this godforsaken spot in northern Wales.

Only to hear that Bolingbroke had marched across England in less than two weeks, having met only the barest of resistance along the way.

God, once Richard had put Bolingbroke away there would be hell to pay on the part of those who had rushed to join fair Prince Hal's side.

The door opened, and William Scrope, Earl of Wiltshire and commander of Richard's army of Irish conquest, walked into the room. He bowed to Richard, and gave de Vere only the barest of nods.

"Well?" said Richard.

"The men need five days at the least to recover from the sea crossing," Wiltshire began.

"We don't have five days!" Richard snapped.

Wiltshire flushed slightly, forcing himself to take a deep breath before replying. He was a heavy-set, older man, completely bald above his gray beard, with thirty-five years of battle experience behind him, and a growing suspicion that Richard's idiocy in embarking on this Irish foolishness in the first instance was going to prove the downfall of everyone in this room.

Particularly if Richard didn't take the sensible road now.

"They are weak from seasickness, your grace," Wiltshire said, in what he hoped was a reasonable voice. "They need to rest, and to get some food in them. Dammit"—Wiltshire instantly regretted the curse, but there was little he could do about it now—"their feet are wet, their swords rusted, and their spirits sullen. If you ask them to fight now—"

"If I say they fight, then they fight," Richard said.

"Your grace," Wiltshire said, "the reports say Bolingbroke has as many as sixty thousand at his back—and Northumberland besides! We have only twenty-five thousand, and they are sick and—"

"If I had known you to be such a faint heart," Richard said, "I should never have given you command of this army. Twenty-five thousand is more than enough to counter Bolingbroke. Do you forget that with only a few score of men I defeated one hundred thousand rebels?"

Wiltshire's face was by now a deep red. "They were an untrained rabble of demoralized peasants," he said. "Once their leader was dead—"

"Are you trying to tell me that I should surrender to Bolingbroke?" Richard said, his voice so heavy with menace that Wiltshire took an involuntary step back.

"No, your grace. All I am saying is that if we can find a few days in which to recover our strength, then we will be in a better position to—"

"Bolingbroke *must* be crushed," de Vere said, straightening from his slouch and walking to Richard's side.

"An army of staggering green-gilled soldiers will crush no one," Wiltshire said.

De Vere's face darkened in fury and Richard put a cautionary hand on his lover's arm.

"Having discerned that you have no heart for battle, Wiltshire," Richard said, "I have yet to learn what you do think I *should* do. Well? Why not enlighten us?"

"Your grace," Wiltshire said in as reasonable a tone as he

could manage. "Bolingbroke feels most unjustly dealt with. He believes there was no reason to seize his titles and lands—"

"He has given me reason enough *now*," Richard said in an undertone.

"—and the fact that so many of the great lords and barons of England now flock to his side indicates that they, too, feel he was unjustly treated. They fear that what you did to Bolingbroke you could do to them also. Your grace, you could defuse this entire situation by sitting down to parley with Bolingbroke and listen to his grievances."

"You want me to parley with a *traitor?*"

Wiltshire completely lost his patience. "You could accomplish in one afternoon of reasonableness what you could never manage with an army of two hundred thousand behind you. God curse you, Richard, don't you understand? The nobles want a king who will guarantee them their rights and privileges, not a tyrant who will undermine their freedoms. Bolingbroke's support is based almost entirely on the fact that the nobles think you seized his lands unfairly. Giving him back his pretty titles and lands will undermine that support!"

"I did not parley with a peasant rebel and I will *not* parley with a princely one!" Richard shouted.

Wiltshire began to speak again, but got no further than opening his mouth, for suddenly Richard's dagger was freed from its sheath at his belt and was at Wiltshire's throat. "I think you are in his pay as well, Wiltshire . . . what say you? Answer me or I will bury this blade in your treacherous throat!"

"Your grace," Wiltshire said, but got no further, for at that moment the door opened and a breathless man-at-arms entered.

"My lords," he gasped, too distraught even to bow. "A party of horsemen . . . approaching . . . the gates . . ."

Richard swiveled away from Wiltshire, sliding the dagger back home at his belt. He strode over to the window, staring at the party of some score of horsemen that rode toward the gates.

"Northumberland," he said.

HENRY PERCY, Earl of Northumberland, stopped just inside the door, his eyes darting to left and right as he ascertained who was in the chamber. He wore chain mail and armor plate, but was bare-headed and bore no weapons.

He nodded, first to Wiltshire, then to Richard, but ignored de Vere completely.

"What, Northumberland?" Richard said, walking forward with studied insolence. "You do not bend your knee before me? How dare your joints forget to pay their duty to our presence?"

Northumberland glanced at Wiltshire, noting that the man would not meet his eyes, then looked back to Richard.

"I am come at Bolingbroke's behest," Northumberland said.

"You behead yourself with those words, Northumberland," Richard said. "But I pray you continue."

"My Lord of Bolingbroke feels he was unfairly disgraced," Northumberland said, "when you seized from him his hereditary titles and lands."

"Unfair?" Richard raised his eyebrows. "There was the small matter of treachery . . . treachery which he now flaunts openly."

Northumberland's face tightened. "And yet you did not attaint Bolingbroke of charges of treason, your grace. There has been no formal laying of charges, and no trial before his peers to which Bolingbroke has every right—as laid out by the Magna Carta."

Richard went white with fury at the implied threat in Northumberland's words. Almost two hundred years previously the barons had risen up against the then King John, forcing him to sign a great charter that limited the king's powers and enshrined those of the barons. Ever since then the English barons had only to murmur the words *Magna Carta* to remind the king that he sat his throne only through their goodwill.

Northumberland continued, ignoring the threat in Richard's face. "Many among the nobles feel that in so attacking Bolingbroke you attacked their rights."

There was a silence, then Richard spoke, hissing each word. "How dare he speak of *rights*! Bolingbroke wants my crown, nothing else!"

He stopped momentarily, his face working furiously. "And here you are, Northumberland, come to mouth Bolingbroke's treason, here on his behalf to loose the opening shot in the purple testament of bleeding war."

Northumberland suppressed a small smile. "War? Nay, grace. Bolingbroke has sent me to assure you of his loyalty. Bolingbroke swears by your royal grandsire's bones, and by the buried hand of warlike Gaunt, and by the worth and honor of himself, that his coming hither into England has no intent but to beg you to return to him his lands and titles. His glittering arms he will commend to rust, his barbed steeds to stables, and his heart to faithful service to your grace if you but restore to him his noble heritage."

"And for this he needs sixty thousand behind him?" de Vere said.

Richard turned a little, sending de Vere a smile, then looked back to Northumberland. "Pretty words, Northumberland, no doubt drafted by some equally pretty poet. But they are nothing but ephemeral nonsense, and I am having none of them."

"It will not hurt to speak with Bolingbroke," Wiltshire said, and Northumberland shot him an assessing look. *So.*

"Sire," Northumberland said, "Bolingbroke waits at Chester. He assures you of your safety should you agree to meet him."

Richard laughed. "He even speaks like a king! Has he the tailors at work cutting out his coronation robes, Northumberland? Does he have the minstrels already practicing at their music for his heraldic triumph?"

Richard's face lost all humor, and he stepped close to Northumberland, spitting his next words into the older man's face. "I had not believed that *you* should be the ladder whereby the traitor Bolingbroke thought to ascend my throne, Northumberland! What did he offer you? Well? *What?*"

"He offered me nothing but my honor," Northumberland said quietly.

Richard's face froze, then he wheeled about and spoke to Wiltshire. "Take him and place him in close custody!"

"Your grace, Northumberland has entered this castle under the flag of treaty. I cannot—"

"Do it!" Richard shouted.

WHEN THEY were alone in the chamber, Richard turned to de Vere. He placed a gentle hand on the man's chest, and smiled coquettishly up at him from under his lashes.

"We have two days," he said, "during which Bolingbroke will wait for my answer."

"And during those two days?" de Vere said.

"We move my twenty-five thousand to meet him," Richard said. "Bolingbroke will have scarce woken up on the third day before he finds the tip of my sword at his throat."

He laughed. "Perhaps I shall give him to you, my sweet, to play with a little before he meets his death."

De Vere smiled obediently, but his eyes were uncertain.

Chapter III

The day before the Vigil of the Feast
of SS. Egidius and Priscus
In the second year of the reign of Richard II
(Thursday 30th August 1380)

— I —

✠

THEY LEFT CONWAY CASTLE the next day at dawn, Richard, de Vere, and Wiltshire, leading some twenty-five thousand men. All three men wore light armor—plates over their chest, hips and arms—and had swords at their sides. Their helmets were packed away; Bolingbroke was yet two days' distant. Northumberland came also, unarmored. He and his escort were held under heavy guard at the rear of the column.

It was to Richard's detriment that he placed Northumberland so far back, for it meant he could not see the smile that played about the earl's mouth as they marched forth.

Wiltshire and his immediate command led the column, with Richard and de Vere riding a little further back, a comfortable cushion of sixty or seventy men between themselves and the front ranks. The day was fine and mild, the only measurable discomfort a stiff sea breeze that blew down from the northwest.

Despite Wiltshire's claims about the morale and health of the soldiers, the entire column made good time, approaching the marsh- and sea-encompassed Flint Castle during the late afternoon. Here they would camp for the night—or, at least, Richard and his immediate command would sleep within the comforts of the castle while the majority of the army camped in the fields beyond the castle's marshes—before rising in the dark of the new morning to move forward and position themselves to Bolingbroke's maximum discomfort.

Flint Castle had been built generations earlier by Edward I as a means to cow the northern Welsh. It sat grim and forbidding on the edge of the sandy marshes of the Dee Estuary, protected on three sides by the waters of the river, and on its landward side by the marshes. Rumor had it that the marshes, thick with waving reeds, contained traps of quicksand, designed to snare any who thought to sneak upon the castle unobserved, or escape from its clutches.

"We will be safe enough here," Richard said to de Vere as the castle rose in the distance; it was nothing but a black, forbidding shape against the glowing light of the setting sun. Ahead of them the fields were giving way to the marshes, and they could see that one of Wiltshire's captains was riding back to give the order to the bulk of the army to camp in the fields at the edge of the marsh.

De Vere nodded, feeling more comfortable knowing that shelter lay only a few minutes' ride away. "No one could attack the castle through these marshes."

Richard looked to either side as they turned on to the raised causeway that wound through the marshes, and wrinkled his nose at the stink that came from amid the thick reeds.

"This stench is nigh on unbearable. I hope that—"

Richard got no further, for at that very moment there was a shout from ahead.

"Jesu!" de Vere said, and the fear in his voice sent a jolt of unwelcome terror through Richard. He twisted all about, trying to see what was happening, and unsheathed his sword.

He cursed, for the setting sun across the marshes made everything ahead a morass of such bright light he could hardly make anything out . . . but the ring of steel and shouts of battle carried clearly enough.

"We must get out of here!" de Vere cried, turning his horse about.

Richard swung his own horse's head around—they could not hope to fight on the causeway!—but even as he dug his heels into his horse's flanks the marshes erupted on each side of the causeway.

Scores—no, hundreds!—of archers rose from among the reeds, their longbows trained on the horsemen trapped on the causeway.

Richard tried to push a way through the column that stretched behind him, but could not. Men and horses were milling everywhere with nowhere to go on the narrow roadway but forward or backward. Some men urged their horses forward, trying to reach the sounds of the intensifying battle ahead, others, like Richard and de Vere, trying to turn their horses back and flee from the certain death in the marshes. The result was a milling chaos of men and horses who could move nowhere.

"Sweet Jesu!" de Vere cried, and Richard glanced at him as he heard the panic in the man's voice.

"For Christ's sake, Robbie," he called, "draw your sword. We shall have to fight."

His only response was a panicked look from de Vere. In the next instant, de Vere dug his spurs into his stallion's flanks, sending it straight through a sudden gap in the men and horses about them.

Directly toward a line of archers.

"Robbie!" Richard screamed.

If de Vere heard, he took no heed. Gathering the reins of the horse, he dug his heels yet again and far more viciously into the beast's flanks.

The horse screamed and, as it reached the edge of the

causeway, jumped high into the air in order to avoid the first line of archers.

Richard watched, his mouth dry with horror.

The horse sailed over the archers with more than a yard to spare, but that was not enough to save either him or his rider.

Arrows thudded into the beast's belly, and it twisted midair, throwing de Vere.

De Vere somersaulted through the air, arrows flying about him, before crashing into the marsh some ten or twelve feet past the archers.

He struggled almost immediately to his feet, his right hand clutching at an arrow that had plunged into his left shoulder, and waded desperately deeper into the marsh.

Several of the archers, their bows re-fitted with arrows, took aim, but before they could loose their shafts a voice shouted from further up the causeway.

"Leave him! Leave him!"

BOLINGBROKE HAD been certain of Richard's response to Northumberland's offer of parley, and had moved out some two thousand of his men—a thousand horsed archers and a thousand knights and men-at-arms—within an hour of Northumberland's departure for Conway Castle.

He'd left Raby—fuming and fretting—in command of the major force that remained encamped just outside Chester, shifting his two thousand toward Flint Castle just as Northumberland was approaching Conway to meet with Richard.

Neville rode with him, exhilarated not only to be once more in armor and riding with an army, but to be riding toward the goal he had so long strived for—the elimination of the Demon-King.

They rode side by side at the head of the column, laughing and jesting as only men riding to battle can do.

"I had thought you would bring your entire sixty thousand to bear against Richard," Neville said, as they crossed the Dee some ten miles south of Flint.

"What?" Bolingbroke cried, affecting a surprised look on his face and twisting about in the saddle to peer behind him. "Did you miscount, Tom? I thought I *told* you to rouse the entire sixty thousand."

Neville laughed, and Bolingbroke looked back at him, his own face now merry. "You and I together are worth sixty thousand, my friend. We need this lot behind us only to escort our captives back to the Tower."

"Will he stand and fight, do you think, Hal?"

Bolingbroke rode a few moments in silence, thinking. Then he shook his head. "Nay, I don't think so. Not with what I have in mind. If we met in open field . . . then perhaps, and perhaps even we would lose—"

"Hal!"

Bolingbroke glanced at Neville, and smiled. "You are such the faithful friend—what would I do without you? But whatever the open field would or would not bring, I intend to use trickery to bring Richard to his knees."

"Trickery against the trickster."

Again Bolingbroke glanced at him, but did not smile this time. "Aye. That and a little oratory."

They'd ridden into Flint—its garrison captain conveniently warned about Bolingbroke's imminent arrival by Northumberland, who'd ridden through a day earlier—on the evening that Richard was throwing Northumberland into one of Conway Castle's dungeons, and worked through the night to set the trap.

Virtually all the men, save for those on guard duty or those setting the cooking fires, set to cutting reeds and weaving them into thick mats. Neville and Bolingbroke themselves stripped down to wade through the marsh, shoulder to shoulder with ordinary soldiers, twisting and straining to cut the reeds and lift them back to men who bore them to the causeway.

Then, covered with mud, but laughing and joking with the others, they'd tramped back to the castle, sloshed themselves relatively clean from the courtyard well, eaten a quick meal prepared by the cooks, then sat down with the other ranks of men to weave the sharp-edged reeds into thick mats.

"When I took my spurs," Bolingbroke had said late in the night in his clear, carrying voice, "I swore to spill my blood in defense of England. But in my romantic delusions of grandeur I had thought myself to be skewered by clean, sharp steel . . . not these blades of grass."

The courtyard erupted in laughter, and Neville, smiling, lifted his head from his own blood-spotted hands and looked at Bolingbroke with eyes dark with love.

How could England want other than Bolingbroke?

How could England exist *without such as Bolingbroke?*

By Matins they'd done, and, again with the other men, had helped carry the mats back into the marshes, where they were laid four or five deep on the oozing mud of the surface of the reed banks.

Bolingbroke stood on one of the newly created platforms, jiggling up and down, frowning.

Then he'd nodded. "Good enough," he said. "So long as the archers don't wriggle about too much."

And then, tired, wet, muddy but satisfied, they'd waded back to the causeway, and stared in the direction from which Richard would ride.

"When?" said Neville.

"In the afternoon," Bolingbroke replied. "At sunset."

"You must have elvish prophecy, to know that," Neville said.

Bolingbroke turned and grinned at him. "I know my quarry, and that is all the prophecy I need."

AS BOLINGBROKE had foretold, so it had come to pass. Richard and his twenty-five thousand approached the castle at sunset, and, as the leading unit had neared the castle itself, Bolingbroke gave the signal for the gates to open and the marsh-hidden archers to reveal themselves.

He and Neville, fully armored and helmeted, were at the head of the horsemen who rode out of Flint Castle along the causeway toward the leading ranks of Richard's army, and Neville felt a fierce delight at the prospect of the fight.

True, they would be fighting their own countrymen, but countrymen who bowed their heads at a demon's orders, and who had thus forfeited the right to pity.

Then there was no time for thought or introspection, for Bolingbroke and Neville, their command at their backs, rode straight into Wiltshire's front units.

Despite his surprise at the ambush, Wiltshire put up a spirited defense. Neville found himself trading hard, vicious blows to left and right, parrying here, thrusting there, feeling the sweat of battle trickle underneath his helmet within the opening moments of the engagement.

The heat rose beneath his armor, and he fought with both hands about the hilt of his great sword, controlling his stallion with only the pressure of his knees.

His breath came quicker, harsher, echoing in the metallic confines of his helmet.

There was a man behind him, but Neville somehow knew he was there, and turned, weaving his body to one side as he did so.

The sword stroke meant for his head swept uselessly through the air.

Neville swung his own sword in a great arc, all the strength of his body behind it, and just for a moment he saw its blade catch fire in the setting sun . . . and then saw the fire vanish and felt the jolt through his arms and shoulders as the sword buried itself in his assailant's throat.

The dying man toppled from his horse, and Neville screamed for joy as he wrenched his sword free of the man's flesh.

How had he ever thought to give this up for the Church? This was how he served both God and man best, with his sword in the heat of the battle. *This* is to what his life had directed him, all these years.

Using his voice and knees, he swung his horse about, and buried his sword in the momentarily exposed lower spine of the horseman next to him.

AS NEVILLE fought, consumed with the battle-fury of the berserker, Bolingbroke cut a path through to Wiltshire.

Wiltshire struck at him with his sword, but Bolingbroke parried the blow with ease, sliding his sword down Wiltshire's and thrusting it to one side with the strength of his younger muscles.

As he did so, Bolingbroke dropped the reins of his stallion from his other hand, and lifted the visor of his helmet.

"For Christ's sake, man," he screamed at Wiltshire. "What need is there for us to kill each other? What is the *point*, when this could be solved through talk? Tell your men to lay down their swords . . . now! *There is no need for this slaughter to continue.*"

Wiltshire, his forehead bloodied where someone had caught him a glancing blow, stared at Bolingbroke. Then he hefted his sword, threw it to the ground, and shouted at his men to lay down their weapons, Bolingbroke doing the same to his command an instant later.

"I thank you," Bolingbroke said to him quietly, as the sounds of fighting about them quieted. "Where is Richard?"

Wiltshire jerked his head back down the causeway. "Some fifty or sixty men behind me."

Bolingbroke nodded, then looked about for Neville. "Tom. Tom? Ah, there you are. Come, follow me."

Neville was close by, the visor of his own helmet now raised.

Beneath it his face was flushed and sweat-stained, his brown eyes bright with his remaining battle-lust. He had only lowered his sword with reluctance, and with the greatest of effort, when he'd heard Wiltshire and then Bolingbroke command their men to cease the fight.

He took a deep breath, calming himself, then pushed his horse after Bolingbroke, who was riding down the causeway.

They had gone only a few paces when they saw de Vere's horse leap over the archers, then drop dying into the marsh with its belly bristling with arrows.

De Vere struggled to his feet, but, just as the archers aimed, Bolingbroke shouted, "Leave him! Leave him!"

Neville pushed his horse close to Bolingbroke's. "Leave him? What mean you? *That is the man who raped—*"

"Do you think I don't know that?" Bolingbroke hissed. "Sweet Jesu. Tom, we shall have our revenge, believe me."

They locked eyes, then after a moment Neville looked away, and Bolingbroke nodded. "Good. Now, follow me."

They rode at a slow trot down the causeway. There was a clear space of some twenty or thirty paces dividing the battle that had taken place at the very top of the column, and the section about Richard that had tried to turn and flee.

Now, as Bolingbroke and Neville rode toward them, the men about Richard stilled, not knowing how to act.

Behind them, Richard's army, some on the causeway, some spread about the nearby fields, waited for orders.

Their eyes slid to the man on the white stallion riding toward Richard, and now to Richard himself, sitting his horse in the center of the causeway.

They waited, their breath still in their throats, for someone to tell them what to do.

The men about Richard drew their horses to one side as Bolingbroke approached.

Richard, still pale with shock at de Vere's action, nevertheless managed a sneer as Bolingbroke reined his stallion to a halt two paces away.

He sat at the head of an army twenty-five thousand strong, for the Lord God's sake, and Bolingbroke had nothing but a few hundred pitiful archers.

"You can order your longbowmen to put a score of arrows through my throat," Richard said, his voice low and even, "but you, too, will be dead within the instant. Do you think that England will stand for your treachery?"

Bolingbroke stared at him. "You fool," he said, "I *am* England."

And then he raised his hand, and a peculiar light came into his eyes, and time stilled, and all faded from the marshes and causeway and fields but Bolingbroke, sitting there on his horse, all white and gold in the sunset.

Chapter IV

The day before the Vigil of the
Feast of SS. Egidius and Priscus
In the second year of the reign of Richard II
(Thursday 30th August 1380)

— II —

✠

DE VERE WADED through the marshes, the arm of his wounded shoulder held tightly against his chest. He had broken off the major portion of the shaft of the arrow that had hit him, but the head and a good four inches of the shaft was embedded within the wound, and it gnawed its way deeper into de Vere's flesh with every movement he made.

The pain was agonizing, but de Vere tried to put it out of his mind, concentrating on moving away from the archers as fast as possible. But, even though de Vere was a strong man, his speed was little more than a jerking crawl for there was almost nothing but water and sludge beneath his feet, and in some places de Vere found himself sinking up to mid-thigh in mud.

Behind him the sounds of the battle had stilled, and de Vere struggled the more, believing that at any moment the archers would be following him.

Or at least, sending their arrows plunging after him.

He fell, ten times, perhaps a score of times, and each time he had to lurch and struggle in order to free himself from the marsh's grip his shoulder flared in agony: de Vere had torn free several portions of reed to bite down on to stop himself crying out with the pain.

He struggled on, hardly aware of time passing, until, suddenly, de Vere realized that not only had he completely lost his bearings, but that he could no longer hear any sound but his own harsh breathing. De Vere stopped, trying to orient himself. His strength was draining fast, and he knew that he had to somehow find dry land before he collapsed completely.

He raised his right hand to clutch at his wounded shoulder.

It felt cold, and slimy.

He cursed foully. Then he closed his eyes and breathed deeply, trying to expel the pain with his exhalations.

After a while he blinked, wiped mud from his face, and looked about. Surely he should be almost to dry land by now? Weren't the fields—and Richard's army—in this direction?

But he could see little through the thick, head-high reeds.

He stilled, trying to breathe softly, and listened.

There was nothing but the soft sounds of birds, and the croak of frogs.

Why had no one followed him?

"Didn't want to get their feet wet," de Vere said with as much sarcasm as he could muster.

But his bravado faded almost immediately and, unbidden and unwanted, tales of the imps and demons that haunted these halfway worlds came to his mind.

His lips tightened in a silent snarl, furious that he should let these little-boy tales disturb him, and he began to wade as quietly, but as quickly, as he could in the direction he thought the fields lay.

Fuck Richard—for all he cared Bolingbroke could draw and quarter him.

De Vere began to hope very, very much that Bolingbroke would do exactly that. If it wasn't for Richard and his unnatural lusts he wouldn't be here right now. God, if he ever managed to get his hands on the little prick again he'd—

De Vere stopped, his heart thudding.

Something had made a noise behind him.

Not a bird.

Not a frog.

Not anything *small.*

It sounded again, a strange warbling cry that de Vere instantly knew was not of this world—not of *God's* world.

He drew in a sharp breath, trying not to panic.

Which direction had it come from?

Where?

Again a wet, lilting, warbling cry . . . and it was much, much closer.

And moving.

Fast.

De Vere panicked as he heard reeds being crushed and mangled with the movements of the creature behind him—*no! Now to his left.* He pitched and staggered forward, not caring how much noise he made because now he *knew* that the creature behind him was on his tail, he *knew* it could scent him, he *knew* that at any moment something from the pits of hell would worm its way up behind him and take him by the shoulder, or head, or buttocks—

Something lurched and crashed so close to de Vere he felt reeds pitch forward and slap against the back of his head.

He screamed; then again, and then once more, wanting above anything else for someone, *anyone*, to issue forth across the marsh and rescue him.

Something beneath the water slithered forward and slid about one of de Vere's ankles.

With what seemed the last of his strength he lunged forward, tearing his ankle out of the creature's grip—*Lord God! Now he could smell its fetid breath!*—and, not caring about the agony in his shoulder, used both hands to drag himself forward, forward, *forward* through the marsh as the horror behind him lunged and splashed and roared and gurgled.

Something—something not of this world—raked claws down his back, and he felt skin tear along with the fabric of his tunic and shirt.

His breath now heaving in and out of his throat in short, desperate shrieks, de Vere continued to struggle forward, everything gone from his mind but the need to get away from the creature at his back. He could feel blood mingle with the water and slime of the marsh down his back, but he did not care, his wounds could wait, it was his life that had to be saved—

Suddenly, miraculously, the reeds thinned then vanished. De Vere squinted, and gasped in sheer relief.

There before him, only a few feet away, lay the raised causeway.

Sobbing with relief, uncaring of the further injury he was doing to his shoulder by using his arm, de Vere dragged himself free of the marsh's grip and scrambled on his hands and knees onto the blessedly dry surface of the causeway.

He did not notice that the causeway was strangely deserted.

The marsh lay still and silent behind him. Whatever the creature was, apparently it had slithered away into the marsh world once it realized its quarry had evaded it.

De Vere collapsed to the ground, his breath heaving in and out of his chest, then rolled over onto his back, staring at the cold, starry sky above.

Praise God, praise God, praise God, praise . . .

"Your God shall not save you here. Not here, not in this time. Not in *my* time."

The cold, vicious voice so shocked de Vere that he could not breathe for a long moment.

When finally he managed to rack in a breath, and roll in

the direction of the voice, he refused for another long moment to believe what he saw.

Bolingbroke . . . but not Bolingbroke.

The man stood some three or four paces away between de Vere and the castle, which was itself a good half mile distant.

He was completely naked, his skin glinting in the faint light with the silvery fairness of his body hair.

And even though he *looked* to be a man, de Vere knew instinctively that he was as otherworldly as the creature that had harried him through the marsh . . .

. . . harried him into Bolingbroke's trap . . .

Gasping in agony from his wounds, de Vere managed to roll over and raise himself to his knees.

Bolingbroke snarled, and de Vere saw that his teeth were small, and pointed.

He struggled to his feet, backing away a step or two.

Bolingbroke walked forward two steps with such exquisite grace de Vere could not be completely sure that he hadn't glided instead of stepped.

"Do you remember," the beautiful, silvery thing called Bolingbroke said, "how Margaret lay screaming beneath your body as you raped her?"

De Vere backed away another step.

"Can you imagine her pain as you forced yourself into her?"

De Vere looked over the creature's shoulder toward the castle. He lifted his good arm and screamed, and waved.

The creature laughed. "There is no one there to hear you, nor see you."

Then the laughter vanished from its face. "Did you never think to pity her as you abused her?"

"Please," de Vere said, "please, I'll do anything you want . . . just let me go . . . please . . ."

"Not until I've had *my* satisfaction," the creature said, "as you once had your satisfaction of Margaret."

And then the creature leaned forward, and as it did so its form changed until, by the time its hands had reached the ground, it was no longer man-shaped, but glowed red and gold in the form of one of the Plantagenet lions.

Its form was *exactly* as the lions represented on the Plantagenet standard, not as one of the lions de Vere had seen in the Tower's cages. Its square head was over-large, its mouth a long dark slash. Compared to the size of the head, its thin tawny body was too slight, and its legs far too short and stubby.

Curled, twitching over its back, twice as long as its body, was a tufted tail.

De Vere turned to run, but the lion sprang as he did so, pinning de Vere to the ground.

As the lion's claws tightened in his chest, and the creature's breath washed over his face, de Vere screamed.

Chapter V

The day before the Vigil of the
Feast of SS. Egidius and Priscus
In the second year of the reign of Richard II
(Thursday 30th August 1380)

— III —

✠

BOLINGBROKE DROPPED his hand, and time recommenced. No one had noticed the enchantment that had bound them: it had been merely the blink of an eye from the moment Bolingbroke had lifted his hand and then dropped it.

They only saw what had suddenly appeared beneath the hooves of Richard's horse—de Vere's naked, mutilated body.

Neville, half a pace behind and to one side of Bolingbroke, gasped in shock.

Richard's horse reared in fright, and the youth narrowly avoided being thrown. As the horse thudded back onto all fours, he looked down to see what had startled it, and cried out.

"Robbie!"

Then he cried again, but this time his voice made no words, merely an animalistic utterance of grief and loss.

Bolingbroke turned his head slightly and looked at Neville, who was as shocked as everyone else staring at the mangled mess beneath Richard's horse. Neville dragged his eyes away from what was left of de Vere, then gasped, for he could hardly believe the gray lines of fatigue he saw in Bolingbroke's face, or the desperate weariness he saw in his eyes.

Had that brief battle so tired him, that he should be this close to exhaustion?

"Evil can twist and turn," Bolingbroke said to Neville, his voice a harsh whisper, "but it can never escape justice."

Then he turned back to Richard.

"Richard," he said, his voice a little stronger, "do you admit before the men of England here standing, your malicious tyranny in subverting the law to the detriment of noble and commoner alike?"

"What?" Richard cried, his voice cracking with the continuing shock of de Vere's bloodied corpse. His horse still skittered about nervously, and Richard wrenched at its reins, trying to bring it to a halt.

"What?" he said again. "There is no tyranny here but *yours,* traitor!"

He swiveled about, his eyes jerking from man to man behind him.

"Seize the traitor!" he screamed. "Seize him!"

Before anyone could move, Bolingbroke pushed his horse past Richard and rode deep into the column, its men and horses parting for him, where, earlier, they had milled chaotically.

No one touched him, no one reached out for him.

He rode to where the causeway joined the road through the fields, to where the majority of Richard's twenty-five thousand could see him.

"Men of England!" Bolingbroke cried in his heaven-sent clear voice, standing in his stirrups so that all might see him. "I stand here before you in *England's* name only. If I raise my sword in anger then it is for *England's* sake only. Men of my country, will you murder me, who loves you and who wishes you well with all my heart? Do you wish *me* ill, when it was *he*"—Bolingbroke's sword stabbed back toward Richard—"who thought to lead you into a fruitless bog-dance with the Irish? When it was *he* who thought to tax you until you could no longer feed your wives and children? When it was *he* who soaked East Smithfield with your brothers' blood?

"Men of England! If I raise my sword against the throne, then it is only because the man who sits upon it has turned against you. Will you now turn your swords against me?"

Bolingbroke wheeled his stallion about in a tight circle, lifting his sword on high so that it caught the last rays of the sun.

"Will you turn your backs on *freedom?*"

Then, suddenly, stunningly, he drove the sword down into the soil, leaving only the hilt quivering above the surface.

"Men of England," Bolingbroke screamed, "the choice is yours!"

He relaxed in the saddle, calm now, his stallion still turning around slowly so that Bolingbroke could see the entire assembled mass of men.

There was a long silence, and then a great sigh, as if all twenty-five thousand had let out their breath at once.

"Hal!" someone screamed far distant in the crowd. "Fair Prince Hal!"

"Hal!" another cried. "Hal!"

And then it seemed as if the entire multitude was screaming: *Hal, Hal, fair Prince Hal!*

Neville, watching Bolingbroke with tears in his eyes, saw him sway in the saddle, and for a moment thought he was about to collapse with exhaustion. But then he caught a glimpse of Bolingbroke's face, and he realized that he was consumed with emotion.

The crowd swelled close about Bolingbroke, so close that the prince and his white stallion became an island amid a sea of cheering, screaming men.

The horse was still pirouetting, albeit slowly, and as Bolingbroke came about once more he caught Neville's eyes upon him.

Smiling, tears streaming down his cheeks, Bolingbroke held out a hand, as if including Neville in his triumph.

"*This* is my England," Bolingbroke whispered, and Neville wondered that he could hear that whisper through the roar of the crowd.

"Take wing," Neville whispered back, knowing that somehow Bolingbroke could hear him as well, "and soar!"

Then a movement caught Neville's eyes, distracting him from Bolingbroke.

Richard, his hand groping and grasping about the hilt of his sword.

"What is happening?" he cried. "Why do they turn against me so?"

Neville kicked his horse next to Richard's and levelled his bloody sword at the king's throat.

Richard, his eyes wide and terrified, dropped his sword with a clatter.

"What is happening?" Neville hissed. "What is happening? Why, only that your kingdom now does to you what you once did to my wife."

QUIET WAS restored, but only after some time. Eventually Bolingbroke, Northumberland now by his side, managed to ride back to where Neville still held Richard at sword point.

Bolingbroke nodded at Neville, who lowered his sword.

Richard stared at Bolingbroke, but said nothing.

Bolingbroke sighed wearily. "I arrest you in the name of the people of England," he said, and Richard merely blinked, as if he thought himself trapped in a bad dream that he would soon wake from.

"Northumberland," Bolingbroke said, "take him into custody, and remove him to Chester, and thence to the Tower as soon as can be. What happens to him is now in the hands of Parliament."

Then, as Northumberland relieved Neville, and took Richard's horse by the bridle, Bolingbroke looked back to his friend.

"Sweet Jesu," he whispered, "but I am wearied!"

His face suddenly went gray, and he wavered in the saddle, and Neville only just managed to catch him as he fainted away.

Chapter VI

Vigil of the Feast of the Nativity
of the Blessed Virgin Mary
In the second year of the reign of Richard II
(Friday 7th September 1380)

— LONDON —

✠

THOMAS WHISTLED a catchy tune softly through his teeth as he ran lightly down the steps of Lambeth Palace. The day was soft and beautiful, as only the late autumn could produce, and as Thomas walked through the gate of the palace and onto the path that wound through the gardens toward the pier on the river he began to hum, unable to contain his happiness.

Late the previous week he'd returned with Bolingbroke to a rapturous welcome from the Londoners. Tens of thousands had lined the streets as Bolingbroke, recovered completely from his exhaustion, had ridden his prancing stallion through the city. Although Richard's ascension to the throne had been greeted with cheers and hope, that hope had soon dissipated amid the imposition of new taxes, defeat abroad, the dark, terrible days of the peasant uprising and the exile of Bolingbroke. Now fair Prince Hal was home, and Richard was imprisoned in the Tower, and hope for the future burned bright in everyone's breasts.

Thomas had not seen Bolingbroke so happy for a very long time.

The Savoy was still a gutted ruin, and Westminster held too many dark memories, so Bolingbroke had set up residence with his household in the great and airy palace of Lambeth, directly across the Thames from Westminster. The palace was normally the London residence of the Archbishop of Canterbury, but since Sudbury had been murdered during the peasant uprising, and none of the current two (or was it three?) popes could decide who should succeed him, the palace lay empty.

"Just waiting for laughter," Bolingbroke had said.

Like Bolingbroke, Thomas could not remember when he had ever been so happy. Today Parliament met to decide Richard's fate, and Thomas had every expectation that the judgment would not be a pleasant one. Both the House of Commons and Lords had agreed to a lengthy indictment, the charges including not only the murders of Gloucester and Arundel, and the imposition of harsh and unfair taxes (Parliament had conveniently forgotten that it was they who had voted in the taxes), but also the subversion of justice in matters ranging from the unfair confiscation of lands and titles from Bolingbroke to the unnecessary preferments given to de Vere, as other of Richard's favorites.

The list of indictments numbered more than thirty: Parliament had proved happily inventive when it came to putting away a king they thought would eventually have whittled away at their own privileges and freedoms.

Thomas cared not if some of those indictments were more invention than fact. Richard was finished, and the Demon-King's influence was restricted to the length and breadth of his prison chamber. Thomas could almost feel the tide of evil that had swept over Christendom ebbing further and further away with every new sunrise.

No wonder the day was so glorious!

The cause of justice and good had been so strong in the end that there had been no real battle at all. Richard had given up with nothing more than a whimper, and his easy capitulation had evaporated any immediate hostility toward Bolingbroke.

A sense of peace overwhelmed Thomas. It was a foregone conclusion that Bolingbroke would take the throne, that God's cause would win, and that he would spend his life raising his children and loving Margaret.

He thought of the time when he'd struggled against his love for Margaret, and pitied his blindness. He thought of those uncertain days after he'd declared his love for her, and remembered how Christ had appeared to him, and allowed him to realize he'd done the right thing. He thought, momentarily, of all that St. Michael had once said to him, and meant to him, but that thought Neville put aside. Christ's vision, and His message to Neville, had virtually obliterated Neville's previous dedication to the archangel.

Thomas allowed himself just the tiniest smile of self-satisfaction as he walked onto the pier, wondering, now that the battle against evil had been won, if Joan would have to put aside her armor and go back to her village, there to draw water and breed sons as any other peasant wife did.

For a moment Thomas stared across the river toward Westminster. Bolingbroke had promised that next week they would turn it upside down to look for Wynkyn de Worde's casket, although it would be of little use now that evil had been defeated. Thomas wondered if he would even bother to look inside—every time he thought of that casket he remembered how he'd allowed Margaret to be raped in order to obtain it, and he did not think he could even bear to touch the cursed thing now.

Thomas turned to gaze downriver. This morning a ship would arrive from Sluys containing all of Bolingbroke's household effects, including every one of the damned bundles and chests of correspondence, pleas, petitions and other bureaucratic minutiae that would bog down Thomas' life.

He tried to summon a sigh of resignation, but such was his sense of happiness he could not even do that. If Bolingbroke did take the throne—and who could doubt it?—then he would have halls full of clerks to take care of his bureaucratic cares. Thomas' life would be full of better things.

Thomas wondered vaguely if—when—Bolingbroke would reopen war with France, and his spine tingled at the thought of war. Richard had collapsed with hardly a single arrow being fitted to the bow—God's work, no doubt—and Thomas found himself hungering for the sounds and smells of battle.

Standing on the pier, his hand shading his eyes from the sun, Thomas drifted off into a pleasant reverie about the thrill of the battlefield.

A DISTANT shout jerked him back into an awareness of his surroundings. There . . . the Sluys ship.

Thomas paced back and forth on the pier as the ship drew close, earning himself several curses from the sailor who jumped across to tie the ship down.

"Thomas?"

His head jerked up in astonishment.

Margaret was waving to him from the deck railing. Beside her stood Mary, looking thin and pale, but smiling, and behind the two women stood Agnes, Rosalind in her arms.

Thomas' mouth dropped open, unable to believe his eyes. Margaret and Mary had not been due to arrive for three or four days more yet . . . but here they were.

He couldn't wait for the gangplank to be lowered. Seizing one of the dangling ropes, Thomas hauled himself up hand over hand until he could clamber onto the deck.

And there was Margaret, holding out her arms, her eyes shining with love, and her belly so bulging that Thomas had to step around it in order to enfold her in his arms.

"Margaret," he said, and wondered how Paradise could be any improvement on this glorious day.

NEVILLE LEANED back and smiled at Margaret, then turned to take Rosalind from Agnes' arms, tossing her in the air so that the child laughed delightedly.

Then he turned to Mary, standing back a pace or two.

"My lady," he said, and kissed her hand. "We did not think to have seen you so soon."

She smiled. "We could not wait, Tom. If there was a ship sailing for London, even if it were full of sheep, we would be on it."

Neville looked at Mary with concern. She was very thin, and her skin had a grayish pallor that bespoke a deep sickness.

"My lady needed to come home," Margaret said softly behind Neville, and he looked at her.

The anxiety he felt for Mary was mirrored in Margaret's eyes.

Sweet Jesu! Neville thought. *Mary has come home to die!*

And he remembered the way Bolingbroke had looked at Catherine, and he wondered, and suddenly all the glory of the day was spoiled for him.

There was a shout from one of the sailors, and Neville looked up. A punt was being poled across the Thames from Westminster, a richly robed man seated within.

"Bolingbroke," said Margaret.

Neville smiled again at Mary, and tried to keep his voice light. "Look, my lady, your husband comes to greet you."

Mary looked, but she did not smile.

BOLINGBROKE LEAPED onto the pier from the punt just as Neville had escorted the women down the gangplank.

"Mary!" he cried.

But his eyes went first to Margaret.

"Mary," he said again, striding to stand before her and kiss her hand before planting a dispassionate kiss on her mouth.

"My husband," Mary said, "rumor has it that you have swept all England before you."

"Ah," Bolingbroke said, "England has merely seized its chance and I have only been its pawn."

He finally turned to Margaret, kissing first her hand and then her mouth with considerably more warmth than he'd kissed Mary. None missed it, and Neville frowned, irritated with Bolingbroke that he should so slight Mary.

"I am glad to see you, my lady," Bolingbroke said in a soft voice. "How goes the child?"

Margaret pulled away from him, a slight flush of embarrassment on her cheek. *Why ask after my health, Hal, when your wife stands there so patently ill?*

"Well enough," she said. "Impatient to be born."

He nodded, then finally turned back to Mary, asking after her health, and evidencing as much concern as any proper husband should. Servants had come down to the pier, and for a few minutes there was nothing but bustle as the women and Rosalind were escorted to the palace.

Just as the entourage reached the garden steps leading into the palace itself, Neville pulled Bolingbroke to a stop, allowing everyone else to enter the palace ahead of them. "Well?"

Bolingbroke grinned at him. "Parliament has decided that Richard is an unworthy king, and should stand aside from the throne. They shall send a deputation to him in a week or so, to ask him to resign."

Neville's face flushed with excitement. "*And?*"

"And what, my friend?"

Neville made a gesture of impatience. "Stop toying with me, Hal."

"Well . . . Parliament has further declared the throne vacant, and there must be an election among Lords and Commons to decide who should sit it next."

Now Neville smiled. An "election" was a pretty word that meant little. There was only one man whose name would be called. "And Richard?"

Something of the light in Bolingbroke's face died. "He is to be imprisoned in Pontefract Castle."

"What? He is not to be executed?"

"Execution of a king is a grave matter, Tom."

Neville's mouth did not even twitch at the pun. "If he is allowed to live then he will prove a lodestone for any dissatisfaction at your elevation, Hal."

Bolingbroke did not reply for the moment, looking over the garden and across the Thames, his eyes eventually coming to rest on the great Westminster complex.

"There are many accidents than can befall a man." He looked back to Neville, his eyes dark and shadowy. "I do not think Richard's term of life imprisonment shall be an onerous nor an over-long one."

Neville nodded. "My lord, I would like that I be—"

"Do not speak the words, Tom. But, aye, yours shall be the right. Margaret's revenge shall not have a great time before its execution."

It was a day of puns.

"IT IS over, Margaret," Neville said later that night, snuggling next to her warm, soft body. "We have won." *Sweet Jesu, it was good to have her in his bed again.*

"We have won?" she said.

His hand traveled over the great bulge of her belly, tracing the contours of the child within.

"Aye. The Demon-King will shortly be no more. England—God's cause—has won."

She was silent a long time, thinking what she could say.

"We have all traveled further down the road," Margaret said eventually, very softly, "but the journey is far from over."

Neville did not reply. He was fast asleep.

PART SEVEN

Horn Monday

Seized with an insatiable curiosity, Pandora took the casket into her hands and lifted its lid. Forthwith there escaped a multitude of plagues and sorrows into the world of mankind. Pandora hastened to replace the lid—but, alas! The whole contents of the casket had escaped, one thing only excepted, and that was hope.

—Ancient Greek myth

Chapter I

Horn Monday
In the second year of the reign of Richard II
(10th September 1380)

— I —

✠

NEVILLE HAD SPENT the earlier part of the morning at weapon practice with Bolingbroke in the courtyard of Lambeth Palace, and the latter part playing with his daughter in her nursery chambers. Now, as he strode loose-hipped through the palace gardens, he looked for Margaret; he thought to spend the rest of the day with her as Bolingbroke had said he would be ensconced in Westminster consulting with officials of the Chancery.

Over generations, successive archbishops of Canterbury had built a series of superb interconnecting gardens about their palace on the banks of the Thames. All the gardens, some for herbs, some for flowers, some for fruit, were separated by tall trellises interwoven with climbing vines and flowers—walking through the gardens was at times like walking through a maze. Neville found himself lost on several occasions, but he did not mind, for this was a glorious, warm autumn day, and both the sunshine and the thought of coming across Margaret sitting quiet and still in some secret corner filled his soul with joy.

He almost began whistling again, but decided not to disturb the melodies of the birds who sang in trees and shrubs, nor the peaceful caress of the silent sunshine.

The paths were of shorn meadow grass, rather than the more usual gravel, and Neville's footsteps made no sound as he strode along.

Neville came to an arbor overhung with roses, and he looked within, sure to find Margaret there. He remembered how he had come upon her in a similar arbor in the garden of the Dominican friary in Lincoln, and he smiled in anticipation.

His smile died. The arbor was empty of everything save the hanging roses and some multicolored butterflies.

Ah! Never mind. There were many more arbors to be explored, and Neville had no doubt at all that he would find Margaret somewhere within the gardens. Where else could she be on such a beautiful day?

He walked down another path, and looked inside a small, paved courtyard bordered with lavender.

She was not there.

Now the twinge of disappointment was more extreme, and Neville frowned. *Where was she?*

And then, so soft it was almost inaudible, he heard her laughter.

Neville grinned, relieved. He had her now.

Taking care with his footsteps, he crept down a small brick-lined path that ended in a deeply overhung bower of late-flowering vines.

He heard her laugh again, sweet and joyous, and he wondered at what she laughed.

Or . . . at *whom*?

Something dark clouded Neville's mind, and now he clung to the side of the path, shadowing his approach to the bower with the bordering shrubbery.

He heard her voice—she was speaking to someone.

But who? Mary and Agnes were within the palace, and Rosalind deep asleep in her bed.

And then the deeper timber of a man's voice, and Neville recognized it instantly.

His movements became furtive, and he slid silently to the bower, parting the leaves of the vine with one careful hand.

His entire world disintegrated into dark despair at what he saw.

Margaret was within, and with her, Bolingbroke. They sat close together, too close, for Bolingbroke's entire body pressed against hers.

His hand was on her belly, moving to feel the child in a way that Neville thought only *he* had a right to do.

Bolingbroke said something, his words inaudible, and Margaret smiled.

And then Bolingbroke leaned close, and kissed her.

Neville stared, unbelieving. All he could think of was that Margaret's child had been conceived at Kenilworth—*where Bolingbroke had enjoyed as much time to plant it as he'd had!*

He remembered the way Bolingbroke's eyes always traveled to Margaret before Mary, how his mouth always lingered too long on Margaret's, how his first thought and concern was always for Margaret . . .

. . . and the final thread of Neville's self-control snapped.

He crashed through the greenery of the bower, seeing Bolingbroke and Margaret spring apart, seeing the panic in both their eyes.

He grabbed at the dagger in his belt, and drew it, and realized he was screaming something, although he knew not the words he spoke.

He heard Margaret call his name, desperately, but he paid her no attention. All he wanted to do was to kill the man whom he'd thought his most dear friend, and who had been all the time cuckolding him, and laughing silently at him as he mouthed lie after lie to his face.

Bolingbroke had been so stunned by Neville's intrusion that he reacted a moment too late. Neville crashed into him, sending them both to the brick floor of the bower, and raised the dagger for the killing blow.

Margaret was screaming something, but Neville cared not what it was.

He pulled his arm further back to give his knife blow the greatest force, and found his wrist seized by both of Margaret's hands.

He tried to wrench himself free, but could not . . . *Jesu! How could she have such strength in her womanly hand?*

"Whore!" he hissed. "Let me go!"

Margaret's action had given Bolingbroke enough time to act. As Margaret's hands finally slipped, and Neville twisted his arm free, Bolingbroke hit him a massive blow to the side of his face.

Momentarily stunned, Neville slid to one side, and Bolingbroke rolled away and leaped to his feet.

"You will *never* call Margaret a whore again," Bolingbroke hissed, and hit Neville once more.

Neville slumped to the ground, blackness rolling over his vision, and only vaguely realized that Margaret was now kneeling down beside him, her hands patting frantically at his head and shoulders.

He rolled over and groaned, spitting out a clot of blood from his mouth and blinking to try and clear his vision.

"You are as blind as the angels," Bolingbroke said, now standing over him with Neville's dagger in his hand. "So blind I could almost believe you one of them."

"You didn't have to hit him so violently," Neville heard Margaret say.

"And what would you have had me do, Meg? Allowed him to murder us both?"

Neville managed to clear his vision enough to see Bolingbroke standing over him with the knife held ready and rage in his face.

"You lied to me," Neville said. "You *lied* to me, both of you!" He wiped his mouth with the back of a hand, and glanced angrily at the smear of blood staining it.

"We have never spoken anything to you but the truth," Margaret said.

"Adulteress!"

She flinched. "I have been true to you, Tom."

Neville's mouth curled. "True to me? Then what was this I have just witnessed?"

Margaret looked up to Bolingbroke. "Dearest," she said, "it must be now. This day."

"Dearest?" Neville snarled, and tried to sit up.

Bolingbroke planted his boot in the center of Neville's chest and pushed him flat again.

"Margaret and I love each other as few mortals can," Bolingbroke said, "but not as you think."

Neville gave him a filthy look.

Bolingbroke looked at Margaret, and suddenly smiled. "Yes, you are right. It must be now, this day."

He sheathed Neville's dagger in his own belt, then held out his hand to help Neville rise. Neville took it reluctantly, and scrambled to his feet, Margaret rising cumbersomely beside him.

Neville pulled his hand from Bolingbroke's grasp as soon as he had gained his feet.

Bolingbroke glanced again at Margaret, then looked back to Neville.

"Margaret is my sister," he said.

NEVILLE'S EXPRESSION, if anything, grew more hostile. "That cannot be," he said.

"There is much more than can be on God's earth than you yet realize," Bolingbroke said, "and one of them is the fact that Margaret is my sister . . . well, half-sister."

"Tom," Margaret said, her face strained and worried. "Hal and I share the same father."

"Lancaster was your father?" Neville said, his tone betraying his disbelief.

"Nay," she said gently.

"But . . ."

"Lancaster was everything and more that a father should

be to me," Bolingbroke said, watching Neville very carefully lest he again erupt in violence. "But he was not who planted the seed in my mother, Blanche, nor who planted the seed in Margaret's mother."

"I cannot believe it," Neville whispered. "Are you telling me that *Lancaster was not your father?*"

Bolingbroke's tongue momentarily touched his lower lip, the only sign that he was nervous. "Yes."

"Then who?" Neville said. His mind was reeling . . . *Hal was a pretender? A bastard?*

Again Bolingbroke and Margaret shared a glance.

"Tell him," she whispered.

Bolingbroke reached over and took her hand in his, then looked back to Neville with level gray eyes.

"Our father is the Archangel Michael."

Chapter II

Horn Monday
In the second year of the reign of Richard II
(10th September 1380)

— II —

✠

"NO," Neville muttered to himself, backing away until he stood against the rear wall of the bower. He felt as if he were encased in a frightful coldness that grew tighter and more painful with each breath.

Margaret's mouth lifted in an uncertain, tense smile. "Did I not say to you that I was of the angels, Tom?" she said. "And . . . and did I not also tell you that the truth within the casket encompassed a vast horror. So horrific that I could not be the one to tell it to you?"

He stared at her, not wanting to answer.

"Tom," Bolingbroke said very quietly, "it is time that you knew that truth."

Neville's mouth worked, and it was a long moment before he realized Bolingbroke's meaning. "*You have the casket?*"

Bolingbroke gave a short nod.

"Why . . . why put me through everything you have . . . why put *Margaret* through everything she went through . . . *when all the time you had the casket?*"

"Because you needed to love both of us," Bolingbroke said, "before you could read what is in that casket."

Neville, still against the back wall of the bower, started slowly to shake his head back and forth. His eyes widened as the full import of what Bolingbroke and Margaret were saying sunk in.

"Sweet Lord Savior," he whispered. "Joan knew all along. *You* are the Demon-King, Hal, not Richard. The blithe young man . . . *you*, not Richard. Jesu, Jesu, what have I done? What have I *done*?"

"You have done what has been right," Margaret said. She sent Bolingbroke a worried look.

"You have betrayed me," Neville said. "Both of you!" His shock was now so extreme he found it almost impossible to keep on drawing breath.

"Nay," Bolingbroke said in a voice full of exquisite gentleness and love. "You have been betrayed, aye, but neither by myself nor by Margaret, nor by any of our kind . . . but by the angels."

"Tom," said Margaret, and she risked stepping forward and laying a hand on his trembling arm. "How can we be *demons*, if we be the children of angels?"

He did not throw off her touch. "I don't understand . . . I don't understand . . ."

"You will," said Bolingbroke, "when you read what is

within the casket. Tom, come with us, please. You know we cannot hurt you. You *know* that."

But Neville remained still, his eyes jerking wildly between Bolingbroke and Margaret. "Sweet Jesu, what have I done? What? Have I betrayed mankind to the Devil?"

"Not yet," said Margaret, her tone suddenly impatient. "But you know that you shall eventually have that choice."

Then she turned with as much grace as she could muster, and stalked out of the bower.

"Come with us," Bolingbroke said to Neville, then followed Margaret.

Neville stared as Bolingbroke walked away, then somehow managed to get his legs to work.

He stumbled after the others. "Demon!" he hissed as he caught up with Bolingbroke.

"I dare you to say that to my face after you have read—and fully understood—what lies within the casket," Bolingbroke said with a dark, unreadable look at Neville.

Neville stopped in his tracks, his mind in such a turmoil that he could make no sense of anything. Then, having decided that motionlessness would solve nothing, he slowly followed Bolingbroke and Margaret.

BOLINGBROKE LED them to a small chamber off his own apartments. There he told Neville to wait before he disappeared.

The chamber was bare of almost everything save a small table, several chairs, two large chests used for storing linens and a poky, unlit hearth.

Margaret sat down on one of the chairs, easing her back as she did so and trying to quell her fears. *Sweet Jesu, everything depended on how Tom reacted over the next hour or so.*

Neville stared at her, then sat down himself, turning his eyes into the hearth.

"I had not known that you were a party to your own rape," he said in a harsh voice.

"I knew I would be so violated," she said. "But that does not mean I was willing. It was Hal's idea . . . and one I railed against. Tom, that rape abused me as much as it abused you."

He slid bitter eyes her way. "Why? *Why?*"

She took a deep breath. "Because you needed to love, and yet you had erected such vile barriers of hate against love. Something needed to break them down. Tom, we—"

"You allowed yourself to be raped *to make me feel guilty enough to love you*?"

She flinched, and her cheeks reddened. After a moment she dropped her eyes.

That was all the answer he needed. "Unnatural bitch," he said.

Her flush deepened, with anger now, rather than guilt. "You *needed* to love. Tom—"

"I needed to love *you?* Ha!"

"Love does not doom," Margaret whispered, "it only saves, and you need to understand that."

Neville's head jerked up, not believing he heard aright. *Those were the words Christ had spoken to him.*

"You were wrapped in lies, Tom," Margaret continued, still quoting Christ, "and you needed to be freed. You *needed* to love."

"How do you know—?"

Margaret smiled sadly. "How do I know what our Lord Jesus Christ said to you on your journey from Kenilworth to London, Tom? Because Christ is my Lord, as He is Hal's Lord. We are Christ's servants, Tom."

"You have powers of evil . . . how else could you have known . . ." Neville drifted to a halt, not even convincing himself with those words.

Margaret started to say something, then stopped as a footfall sounded at the door.

"Ah," she said, "here is Hal now."

She rose, leaning heavily on the arms of the chair as she did so, then smiled at Bolingbroke as he entered carrying a small brass-bound oak casket in his arms.

Neville rose also, unable to tear his eyes away from what was in Bolingbroke's arms.

Bolingbroke walked to the table and set the casket down with a thump. His face was red, and trails of sweat ran down his forehead.

"Damn thing," he said.

"I . . . I have seen that casket a hundred times!" Neville said, still staring at it.

"Aye," Bolingbroke said. "It has been rattling about with all the other of my chests and caskets and cabinets. You have worked beside it for many a month at my business, Tom."

Neville could not tear his eyes from the casket. St. Michael had said the demons could not keep the casket away from him, and he had been right. He'd seen this casket every time he'd entered the chamber where rested all of Bolingbroke's bureaucracy. Sometimes it had sat next to the desk he'd worked on, sometimes closer to a window, sometimes under a sheaf of documents or one of the never-ending piles of petitions.

And sometimes he had leaned down to it, curious, but every time—*every single time*—he had done that, something had occurred to disturb him, and to turn his mind from the casket.

"This has traveled everywhere you and I have," Neville said. "From the Savoy to Kenilworth and back again. From the Savoy to Gravensteen, then to Sluys and thence back here."

"It had to follow you, Tom," Bolingbroke said.

Neville looked up, unable to say anything, not knowing *what* to say. He was no longer angry, only consumed with such a sadness that he did not think he could bear it.

Margaret leaned close to him, and kissed him on the cheek. "Know that I love you, Tom," she said, then turned and walked from the chamber.

"You will need this," Bolingbroke said, lifting a key from a purse at his belt.

Neville slowly reached up a hand and took it.

It felt cold and nasty against his flesh.

"Know also that I love you," Bolingbroke said, and Neville looked into his eyes, and knew it for the truth.

He nodded, unable to speak.

Bolingbroke stared a moment longer, then he, too, walked from the chamber, closing the door behind him.

Neville stood there for a long time, looking neither at the casket nor at the key.

Then, slowly, his hand shaking, he lifted the key to the casket's lock, fitted it, and turned it.

The lock gave way without a murmur.

Suddenly trembling too much to stand, Neville sat down with a thump.

He knew that what was inside this casket had the power to destroy his entire life.

Chapter III

Horn Monday
In the second year of the reign of Richard II
(10th September 1380)

— III —

✠

THERE WAS A GREAT, heavy book which took up most of the space within the casket—its pages were curiously inscribed with thick, threatening writing.

Spells . . . incantations.

Neville glanced at them, then shuddered, and closed the book.

He did not want to read such dark magic.

Besides the book, there were some loose pages, and because these appeared to be less threatening than the volume of incantations, Neville chose to read these.

The writing was that of an old man—Wynkyn de Worde—and his words were filled with an old man's impatience and ire. Neville quickly regretted having chosen these pages above the book, but once he'd begun to read, he could not stop.

> Listen you, whoever you are. If you read this then I am dead and have not been able to teach you myself. Fools! Fools! Fools all!
>
> Listen you, whoever you are. You have no time, for if I have been dead longer than one year then evil will already be crawling unhindered over God's good earth.

Sweet Jesus! Wynkyn de Worde had been dead for over thirty *years!* Neville took a deep breath, and continued.

> Ah! But there is evil everywhere, even in heaven, and it angers me that I must speak of it to you in this manner. This evil, these twisting words of depravity, should have been spoken, not written.
>
> Listen you, whoever you are. Listen to the angels' secrets.
>
> Women are the curse of man—and heavenkind, do you understand that? Ah, but you must, if you read this, for the angels would let no one read who did not understand it. Women are filth, whores, their weeping clefts tempting man into corruption and depravity and hell—filth! Filth, all!
>
> Wormy dark temptresses! They are corruption made flesh, bitches burning with diabolical lusts, incubus-suckling sows, and sucklers themselves of Satan's hot poker . . .

Neville skipped over the next page and a half until de Worde managed to tear himself away from his tirade on the frightful corruptions of women.

"Lord Christ," he whispered, "you had the soul of a madman, de Worde."

And then he paused, his stomach twisting in a tight knot as he remembered how he'd treated the prostitutes in Rome.

How he'd treated Alice . . .

> Ah! These devilish temptresses do not stop only at man—they tempt even the angels themselves from heaven! Listen you, and hear this vileness, for this is the vileness you must wipe from the face of this earth.
>
> As with men, so the angels of heaven cannot resist the foul tempting of women. Every so often, screaming with self-loathing, the spirit of an angel descends to earth and lies upon one of these sleeping whores, and puts into her womb what should never have left heaven. And as his spirit ascends from her, the angel weeps with self-loathing, and heaven weeps with him for the manner of his trickery.
>
> These women birth abomination and wickedness, deformed children, demons all! There, did you know that? Did you? Yes, demons only exist and draw breath through the intercourse of angel and foul women—they are not Satan's creation, but they are Satan's servants, and they belong in hell with him, there to burn and scream through eternity.
>
> And if I had the power I would send down into hell every one of their foul temptress mothers as well . . .
>
> Listen you, whoever you are. It was once my task, and now is yours, to remove the angels' spawn into hell. Every year some twenty or thirty of them are conceived and born—is there no end to the vilenesses of women?—and once they have grown into some

manner of strength (but before they have grown too strong), perhaps when they are five or six years old, then is the time they should be thrown into hell.

Listen you, whoever you are. There is a place called the Cleft . . .

Neville scanned the next lines quickly, for de Worde only wrote of what Neville knew, and then read more slowly again.

There you must go every year at the Midsummer Solstice, and there you must open the book you found with these pages. You will find an incantation of Calling, and this you must speak.

The Calling will summon those demons strong enough—those of five or six years of age—from wherever they are across Christendom to the Cleft. They will travel slowly, reluctantly (and why should they not, for they travel toward their doom!), and it will take some six months for them to gather at the Cleft.

Thus, at the time of the Winter Solstice, the Nameless Day, that day when the worlds of earth and hell touch, you will return to the Cleft, and then you will speak an incantation of Opening, and the Cleft will awake, and reveal the gateway to hell.

Then call forth the deformed imps, and then speak the incantation of Incarceration, and they will be forced through the gates into the fiery abyss they deserve . . . thus will you rid Christendom of evil, the foul issue of the angels' temptation.

There was more, but Neville could not read it. His hands began to shake so badly he had to lay the pages down.

He sat a very long time, staring into space.

The spirits of angels descended upon sleeping women, and made them pregnant.

Dark wormy temptresses all . . .

But *were* these women "dark wormy temptresses"?

Neville thought of Blanche, Bolingbroke's mother. He'd never met her, but felt he knew her through reputation—both Lancaster and Katherine had spoken of her often. Blanche had been beautiful, but pious and modest, her behavior proper at all times.

Blanche was no "incubus-suckling sow."

Were any of them?

Neville suddenly felt physically ill, remembering what St. Michael had said to him: *Women exist only for one reason—to bear children. Otherwise they are to be used and discarded with as little thought as the daily sending of excreta on its journey into the cesspool.*

The angels were not the victims here . . . the women were.

These women were violated when asleep.

They were *raped.*

"Rape" was not a word Wynkyn de Worde had ever used, and clearly, the concept had never crossed the old friar's mind. Women tempted angels, and thus women were at fault and not the angels. Was not Wynkyn de Worde the product of the teachings of the Church . . . as Neville had once been?

"Sweet Jesu," Neville whispered, and leaned on the table, one hand covering his mouth as thoughts and images tumbled through his head.

He knew beyond any measure of a doubt that had he read this a year ago he would have accepted de Worde's stance completely.

A year ago he had not loved.

No wonder Hal and Margaret had needed so badly to have him love her.

He lifted Wynkyn de Worde's litany of hatred, carefully folded the pages so he could not see their writing, and pushed them away.

Then he spread his hands on the table, and wondered if they would ever stop shaking.

Angels came upon women, and lay with them—in spirit if not in flesh—and spawned the creatures known as demons.

Satan's servants, if not his creation. Satan's servants, to be pushed into hell.

Then why were they Christ's servants also? Why had Christ exhorted Thomas to love Margaret?

Neville had no doubt whatsoever that he'd been graced with the presence of Jesus Christ Himself in that inn on the way from Kenilworth to London . . . and had no doubts that Christ had meant for Neville to love Margaret.

"Love does not doom," he whispered, "it only saves."

Why had Christ taken the part of demons? Why had He—?

"No! No!" Thomas leaped to his feet, staring with horror at Wynkyn de Worde's pages and the book lying just beyond them.

If the spirits of angels lay with women and created demons, *then what did that make Jesus Christ, the product of a similar union between God and the Holy Virgin?*

"Aye," said a soft voice behind him, and Neville whipped about.

Bolingbroke.

"Christ is our brother and our Lord," he said, "who rests trapped in heaven."

Neville put his hands to his ears, and twisted away, and screamed.

Chapter IV

Horn Monday
In the second year of the reign of Richard II
(10th September 1380)

— IV —

✠

"DEMON IS WHAT our fathers name us," said Bolingbroke, walking farther into the room and watching Neville carefully. "It is a name of hatred. But who are they to say what is good and what is bad? Our only sin is that our fathers have loathed us—and wherefore does that make us 'evil'?"

"Are all unwanted children therefore demons, Tom?" said Margaret, standing in the door. She looked at Bolingbroke, then slowly walked to one of the chairs, and sat down, leaning on Bolingbroke's arm for assistance.

He gave her a small smile, and grasped her hand, briefly reassuringly.

Neville dropped into a chair across the table from Margaret and Bolingbroke. He could not look at them, nor at the book and papers lying on the table before him. Instead, he stared into the cold, unlit hearth as if something in its stonework might save him, or wake him from this monstrous nightmare.

"May we speak further, Tom?" Margaret said softly.

He made a small gesture with his hand, which could have meant anything. He still did not look at her.

"I do not know where to start," Bolingbroke said, sitting down himself. He was careful not to scrape the chair across the floor.

Again Neville jerked his hand in an indeterminate gesture.

Bolingbroke and Margaret exchanged glances again. Where could they start?

"How long . . . ?" Neville said, his voice sounding like that of an old man grating out his last few words of this life. He had begun to rock backward and forward, very slowly, as if he were a lost and unloved child himself.

"How long have the angels been coming upon mortal women?" said Bolingbroke.

Neville jerked his head in a nod.

"As long as there have been women to lust after," Margaret said, "and none of us knows how far distant into the past that stretches."

"As far as we understand," Bolingbroke said, "the children of these matings were for long generations allowed to grow and live naturally among their mothers' peoples. These men and women, like us, grew to fill important roles within their cultures, and led their mothers' peoples into directions they might never have gone."

"What do you mean?" Neville said, in a low voice. He still would not look at them.

Bolingbroke gave a slight shrug. "You know of the giant rings of stones about England? Yes? Well, they were built under the auspices of angel-children. Have you heard of the great mathematical temples of stone built in the lands of Egypt? Well, likewise."

"Paganism," Neville said. "Evil."

"So your Church has taught you to believe," Margaret said. Again she shared a look with her brother, then continued. "But almost fourteen hundred years ago, Tom, everything changed. For millennia God had watched the lusts of his angels, and so He thought to—"

"No . . . no . . . no . . ."

"Yes, Tom," Bolingbroke said. "Yes. Jesus was a God-child, and he was far more powerful than any of the angel-children hitherto born." He paused. "Far more dangerous."

Finally Neville raised his face and looked to Bolingbroke and Margaret. His face was ashen, his dark eyes ringed and haunted. "Why?"

"Because," said Margaret, "he threatened the equilibrium of heaven . . . because he threatened to free mankind from heaven's clutches."

"Christ preached of love and freedom," Bolingbroke said, "not of hatred and bondage. And that, simply, is the path that all angel-children walk in. Abandoned and unloved as children, we ever after seek love, and never deny love to any who need it."

He grinned suddenly, mischievously. "And for that we are labeled 'demon' and mankind is told that we are humped and deformed imps from hell, determined to destroy mankind."

"For virtually your entire life, Tom," Margaret said, "you saw with the eyes that the Church gave you. In the past year you have begun to see with the eyes that we have given you . . . the eyes that love has given you."

"But Jesus . . . ," Neville said.

"Jesus opened heaven's eyes to the danger of continuing to allow angel-children to walk among mankind," Bolingbroke said. "Having set the Jewish priesthood against Jesus, God and the angels snared him into heaven's clutches, and then created the vehicle via which they could ensnare all angel-children ever after. The Church."

Bolingbroke stopped, visibly upset. "A Church created in Christ's name!" he eventually whispered. "What foulness! The angels took Jesus Christ's message, designed to free mankind from heaven's clutches, and twisted it so that instead it would push mankind yet further into heaven's bondage. And the angels called it a message of *salvation!* Foulness? Nay, that went far beyond mere foulness."

"I cannot accept any of this!"

"You *must* accept it, Tom!" Bolingbroke said, then leaned forward and tapped Wynkyn de Worde's pages of hatred. "I do not know the precise words de Worde wrote here, but I know that they corroborate much of what my sister and I have just told you. *I can see that by the horror in your face!*"

"Hal," Margaret said, "perhaps we have said too much. Tom needs time to think, to—"

"No!" Neville yelled, rising to his feet. "I want to hear it all, now! Hal, are you this 'Demon-King'?"

"I am the lord of all angel-children walking the earth, yes, but servant to the great Lord Jesus."

"What is your purpose?"

"The purpose of all angel-children, Tom, is the same as Christ's purpose. To free mankind from the grip of the angels and of the teachings of the Church, and to allow the people of this earth to fulfil their potential in love."

"And that is an almost impossible purpose," Margaret said with a wry look, "for mankind has been so steeped in the grip of hatred that it will take many, many generations to forget it—and who knows if mankind shall *ever* be able to forget?"

Bolingbroke was about to say more, but Neville, now pacing back and forth behind the table, waved him to silence.

Neville thought a few minutes, then said, "Etienne Marcel? Wat Tyler?"

"They fought for mankind's freedom, Tom," Bolingbroke said softly. "You know that."

"They were also Hal's and my brothers," Margaret said. "Both the Archangel Michael's children."

"And you approve of what they did?" Neville said. "Stirring up rebellions that murdered many? How is that *love*?"

"I disapproved heartily of their methods," Bolingbroke said. "Not of their purpose."

"And your 'purpose'?" Neville asked quietly, coming to a halt and staring at Bolingbroke. "Your 'method'?"

"My purpose is to free mankind into his potential. My method is one which involves a much greater gradualness than violent rebellion. As King of England, and perhaps even France, I can guide my subjects gently onto the path of freedom rather than thrust them screaming and protesting through the door."

"We expect our work to take generations, Tom," Margaret said.

"But when *I* soar," Bolingbroke said, "I mean to take mankind with me. Believe it."

Neville turned away, again spending long minutes thinking. When he finally did speak, he did not look at Bolingbroke or Margaret.

"You can shape-shift. This form you now present to me, to the world, is not your true one."

"This form is our most 'usual' one," Bolingbroke said, "and the form we assumed at birth. But it is not our natural form."

"Then you *are* horned imps," Neville said, swinging about to face them. "I have seen your true forms and they are vile!"

"You have seen only what heaven, via the Church's teachings, has taught you to see," Bolingbroke said calmly, holding Neville's furious stare. "After all, heaven *does* need to justify the ongoing murder of scores of angel-children each year, doesn't it? What better way than to present them as vile, deformed hulks who will destroy mankind if given half a chance?"

"Then show me what you are. Now!"

"We *can* shape-shift back to our true forms," Margaret said, "but it costs us dearly."

"Do it! *Now!*"

"I have done it recently, and it would kill me to do so again so soon," Bolingbroke said. "Do you know of what I speak?"

Neville remembered Bolingbroke's exhaustion just after de Vere's body had mysteriously "appeared" under the hooves of Richard's horse. "Devilish imp!" he said.

To his absolute fury, Bolingbroke actually burst into laughter, and even Margaret chuckled.

Neville's face reddened, and the other two quickly dampened their smiles.

"Tom," Margaret said, "all angel-born women must give birth in their true form, or risk death." She patted her belly. "It will not be long before I give birth. Will you sit with me while I birth your son? Will you save your judgment of me and mine until that day?"

"That's why . . ."

"That's why I had to rid myself of Joan and Maude's attentions when I birthed Rosalind," Margaret said quietly. "I could not give birth in my true form with them present. And the fact that I'd had to endure so long a labor in this form," she waved a hand down her body, "was why I was so near death afterward."

The thought of the children he had generated with this . . . this . . . this demon-angel-woman sent Neville's mind spinning in a new and unwanted direction.

"Rosalind?" he said. "Is she—?"

"She is more mortal than angel," Margaret said. "She has no angel-form within her, she cannot shape-shift, she is 'human' in every possible way."

"Tom," Bolingbroke said, rising. He walked to within a pace of Neville. "There is more that you will eventually hear and know, but for now you have heard enough. All I ask of you, Tom, all Margaret asks of you, and all that our kind ask of you, is that you save your judgment of us until you sit through the birth of your son. But watch not with the Church's eyes of hatred, Tom, but rather with the eyes of love."

Now Margaret rose. "I will be taking Rosalind out to enjoy the sunshine in the herb garden, Tom. Join us there if you will."

Neville watched her leave the chamber, then turned away, not wanting to see Bolingbroke's face.

A moment later Neville heard him leave the chamber as well.

Chapter V

Horn Monday
In the second year of the reign of Richard II
(10th September 1380)

— V —

✠

HE STOOD BEHIND a hedge of hawthorn interwoven with honeysuckle and sweet briar and watched them as they sat on a small lawn in the center of the herber.

He could not count the time that he stood there, but it was long enough for his legs to stiffen and begin to ache, and for the afternoon shadows to start their creep across the central open space of the herber.

He watched his wife and his daughter and he wept.

As he could not count the time, neither could he put into coherent thought the reasons why he wept. He watched Rosalind and knew that he loved her unconditionally. He looked to Margaret, and knew that even though she'd manipulated him and used him, he loved her also.

But would that love free him, as the rest of mankind? Or would it trap them forever?

He had been so foolish, and so foolishly arrogant in his self-confidence. He had known that his soul was to be the battleground between "good" and "evil" and he had thought the battle would be so easily won.

How could he have known that his perceptions of good and evil were to be so radically challenged?

The fate of Christendom would hang on whether or not he handed his soul on a platter to a woman.

Somehow Thomas had managed to push that knowledge to the back of his mind in these past few months. He had loved, and had convinced himself that God would not ask him to sacrifice the woman he loved.

But now he knew that God *would* ask it of him, and Neville had no idea what his decision would be. The choice was not whether he chose to hand his soul to Margaret or not . . . but to decide what fate he should hand mankind.

Christ's word, or that of God?

Freedom and love, or hatred and entrapment?

Rosalind was tottering about the garden, laughing and clapping her plump hands as her mother laughed with her. Neville watched as Rosalind stepped close to Margaret and was swept up in her mother's arms to be kissed and cuddled with total abandon.

Rosalind shrieked with joy, and her joy intermingled in the sunshine with Margaret's throaty laughter and with the heavy, honeyed fragrance of the herber.

Neville remembered Bolingbroke's love of children, and thought he understood why. Abandoned and unloved themselves, all demons . . . all angel-children spent their lives compensating every child they encountered.

How was that "evil"?

Rosalind had wrested herself free of Margaret's arms and tottered to within a pace of where Neville stood behind the hedge.

Suddenly she saw him, and crowed with delight, weaving over to him and wrapping her arms about his knees, begging to be lifted up.

Neville hesitated only a heartbeat before he bent down, gathered her into his arms, and slowly walked into the herber's sunshine.

Margaret looked up from where she sat, and her smile faltered a little as she saw her husband with their daughter. He wasn't surprised. No doubt this was a trying time for all her kind . . . waiting for him to speak . . . to act.

He sat down cross-legged on the lawn and Rosalind wriggled out of his arms and sat between her parents, her fingers picking small flowers from the lawn. In an instant she'd forgotten them, as she became totally absorbed in the flowers.

"Tell me about Wynkyn de Worde, and those who went before him," he said softly.

Margaret took a deep breath. "After Christ died, heaven decided it needed to be more careful. It created an antithesis of itself, hell, a jail for all those who threatened it."

"And the priests—"

"The Keepers, we called them."

"The Keepers were the ones who thrust the . . . the angel-children down?"

"Yes."

"Why did the angels not do it?"

"The angels are of heaven, and thus are of the spirit. They can accomplish nothing in this tangible world. Besides, they fear the Cleft greatly."

Neville nodded, but did not reply. For a while he played with Rosalind, running the fingers of a hand through her black curls as she smiled and laughed at him.

"What have you done with the book, and pages?" Margaret eventually said.

He gave a little shrug, as if the subject did not interest him. "I have put the book and de Worde's writings back into the casket, and I have shut it. I left it in the chamber. I do not think anyone will touch it. Margaret . . ."

"Yes?"

He looked up. "If I am Wynkyn de Worde's successor, why can I not simply take up where he left off? Go to the Cleft at Midsummer, speak the incantation of Calling, and then return on the Nameless Day to thrust . . . to thrust you and all yours into hell?"

"Because too long has passed," Margaret said. "We have grown too strong, and we have so badly 'infected' mankind with our ambitions—with the taste of freedom—that heaven well knows that the day of final battle over the souls of mankind beckons. The decision is no longer who to find to thrust us into hell, but to find a choice-maker to decide which path mankind will take. You are that choice-maker."

Again Neville was silent for long minutes.

"After you had been raped in my futile bid for the casket," Neville said, "I spoke with Saint Michael and told him to stay away from me. But," he shrugged a little, "what I have wanted has never influenced the archangel's actions. Margaret, Saint Michael must have known how close I was drawing to you and Hal. Why has he left me alone for so long? Why let me wander deep into a situation that could mean the end of everything he stands for?"

Margaret's smile slipped. "Tom, I don't know."

And that admission frightened her, *terrified* her, because it meant that the angels felt confident enough in Thomas' eventual decision to allow him to wallow in the bed of the angel-children for the time being.

What was it that the angels knew about Thomas that she and her kind didn't?

"Will you be with me for the birth of our child?" Margaret said, needing the reassurance of his answer.

She did not get it.

"I do not know." Neville leaned a hand forward and rested it on her belly, feeling the movements of the child within.

"You said that you allowed yourself to be raped in order

to break through the walls of hate that bound me. But, Margaret," he sat back, lifting his hand from her belly, "why is it that I am the one who feels raped?"

Then he stood, picked up Rosalind, and, turning his back on his wife, walked away.

PART EIGHT

Bolingbroke!

Bishop of Carlisle:
. . . if you crown him, let me prophesy—
The blood of English shall manure the ground,
And future ages groan for this foul act;
Peace shall go sleep with Turks and infidels,
And in this seat of peace tumultuous wars
Shall kin with kin and kind with kind confound;
Disorder, horror, fear and mutiny,
Shall here inhabit, and this land be call'd
The field of Golgotha and dead men's skulls.

—*William Shakespeare,*
Richard the Second, Act IV, sc. i

Chapter I

Monday 24th September 1380

✠

TWO WEEKS PASSED, and for Neville it felt as if he spent much of those weeks drifting from day to day in a strange, dreamlike state. He thought a great deal of what Bolingbroke and Margaret had said to him, and what he had read in Wynkyn de Worde's papers. He went back to the chamber, where sat the casket, on several occasions and lifted out the book of incantations and read through them.

Always they sickened him, for like de Worde's testament, they were constructed of hatreds.

The angels' hatred and fears of their issue.

When Neville did not revisit Bolingbroke and Margaret's shocking revelations, or re-read the contents of the casket, he remembered.

He remembered how Etienne Marcel had taken him to the carpenter's shop in Paris, and shown him how the man and his family suffered under the "blessed patronage" of the Church.

He remembered some of what John Wycliffe had said to him. *There are some who say the world is entering a new age . . . the age of man. An age where salvation and fulfillment can be found in this life rather than the next. An age where a man owes his king and country, even his wife, more loyalty than he does a distant, arrogant God.*

He remembered Gilles de Noyes, standing in that frightful village common with the body of his dead niece in his hands, screaming, "I say fuck to God's will! How can *God* will such as *this*? Eh? Tell me that, friar."

He remembered Bolingbroke, on his way to witness the signing of the Treaty of Westminster, lifting the stranger-child from its mother's arms, and holding her close with such utter love that tears ran down his cheeks.

He remembered how he had felt when Rosalind, so tiny, so bloody, so near death, had been placed in his arms, and oh! sweet Jesu, how desperately he had wanted her to live.

And he remembered how the archangel had appeared to him: *It is better she dies, Thomas. Better for you . . .*

And every night, when he cuddled Rosalind in his arms before he set her down to sleep, and every night when he wrapped himself about Margaret's body and felt the strength and hope of the new child growing within her, Thomas Neville knew how wrong the archangel had been. How could it have been better for him that Rosalind die? How could it? Was a salvation on God's terms worth the life of a child?

And whenever his memories and thoughts grew too troublesome, Neville prayed to Christ. Even though what he had learned about Christ had shocked him deeply, Neville found that his awe and trust and love of Christ had not diminished. It was almost as if there was such a strong bond between them that no revelation, however shattering, could serve to sever it.

Love only saves, Thomas. It does not damn. Remember that.

ON THE second to last Monday in September, on the Feast of In-Gathering, Parliament met again to decide Richard's successor.

Neville attended with Bolingbroke. The two men had talked little in the past two weeks save to pass pleasantries and to exchange those words needed to complete the business of each day. Neville knew that Bolingbroke watched him, but he did not feel threatened, nor did he feel that Bolingbroke exerted any pressure on him.

He simply watched.

This day, the Feast of In-Gathering, Neville and Bolingbroke stepped from the barge onto Westminster's pier, richly robed in velvets and the finest linens, and attended by Raby, the Earl of Westmorland, Roger Salisbury and Robert Courtenay, as well some eight other knights.

There to greet them was a thirty-strong deputation from Parliament. Heading the deputation was Henry Percy, Earl of Northumberland. Standing behind him were Sir Robert Tresilian, Chief Justice of the King's Bench, and the newly appointed Archbishop of Canterbury, William Arundel. Behind them waited a selection of the highest nobles and office holders in England.

Their very presence at the pier bespoke Parliament's decision.

They walked in solemn procession to the Chapter House of Westminster Abbey. Bolingbroke was closely attended by the most senior nobles, but even so, he requested that Neville walk close behind his right shoulder, and just as they reached the cloisters of the abbey leading to the Chapter House, Bolingbroke sent Neville a mischievous glance over his shoulder.

Neville's mouth twitched and then finally grinned. For some reason he was reminded of those faraway days when he and Bolingbroke had been boys, trying to drag their heavy practice swords away from the ground as they dreamed of the future: Bolingbroke that he would somehow succeed to the throne of England, and Neville that he would lead a mighty crusade back to the Holy Lands to wipe the infidels from the streets and holy places of Jerusalem for time ever after.

Well, Neville thought as they stopped just outside the *door* of the Chapter House to be announced to the gathered Parliament therein, *here was Bolingbroke about to succeed in his boyish ambition . . . and himself?*

Who knew now how to define either the crusade or the infidel?

He blinked, for now Bolingbroke was striding into the center of the circular Chapter House, and Parliament—the gathered houses of Lords and Commons both—was on its feet.

Northumberland, holding the white rod of speaking in

his hand, stepped forth, and shouted, "Long live Henry of Lancaster, King of England!"

And then the entire Parliament was shouting, "Henry! Henry! Henry, King of England! Yes. We want Henry for king. No one else. Henry! Henry!"

Bolingbroke raised his arms, his fists clenched, and turned slowly about as he swept his eyes over the assembled Parliament. His gray eyes were shining, his fair face slightly flushed, and Neville thought that Bolingbroke had never looked so beautiful, nor so princely, as at this moment of his triumph.

LATER, MUCH later, when most of the tumult had died down and the wine flowed freely within the great hall of Westminster, Bolingbroke took Neville's arm and pulled him aside.

"Tom," Bolingbroke said, speaking the words close to Neville's face so that no one else amid this gathering might hear, "there is no one now who can stop me taking the throne, but you. Do you understand?"

Neville nodded, and Bolingbroke gave him a small smile.

"I have chosen Michaelmas for my coronation day," Bolingbroke said. "I thought it appropriate."

Neville gave him an unreadable look. Michaelmas was the feast day of the Archangel Michael.

Bolingbroke's smile widened, and he winked, and then pulled Neville back into the celebrations.

Chapter II

Wednesday 26th September 1380

— I —

✢

THERE WAS ONE small matter to be disposed of before Bolingbroke was crowned.

Richard.

In the afternoon of the vigil of Michaelmas, Neville rode through the streets of London with his uncle Raby and the Earl of Northumberland at the head of a small but richly apparelled escort. The mood within the streets was one of an almost overwhelming joy—fair Prince Hal, who had done no wrong and who could never do wrong, would on the morrow be crowned king of England. All the bitterness and disappointments and the bloodiness of the past eighteen months would be put behind them. Beyond lay an age of golden glory. Who could doubt it?

Although the coronation was so close, and even though Bolingbroke's words had haunted him in the past five days, this afternoon. Neville was thinking of everything but the coronation. Margaret had awakened listless and moody in the morning, and had refused to break her fast with anything but a few sips of watered wine.

She had not even wanted to see Rosalind.

Instead, she had wandered back and forth in their chamber, one hand rubbing at her back, the other at her forehead.

Agnes had given Thomas a knowing look.

Richard had been the only thing that had managed to pull Thomas away from Margaret's side—that and her snapped remark that she'd be better without him shadowing her every footstep for the next few hours.

So Neville contented himself with Agnes' whispered consolation that little would transpire before evening save a deepening of Margaret's moodiness, and had joined Bolingbroke's deputation to Richard as already planned.

Many people in the streets shouted his name along with Bolingbroke's, Raby's and Northumberland's, but Neville did little to acknowledge the crowd's approval save offer an occasional nod of his head. He didn't realize that his internal preoccupation with Margaret's well-being and his subsequent terse acknowledgment of the crowd lent him an air of weighty authority.

Raby, who well knew the reason for Neville's preoccupation, smiled to himself now and then, more than relieved that Margaret was finally about to give Thomas a child of his own.

RICHARD STOOD by a window, watching the deputation slowly move through the Lion's Gate and toward the Inner Ward.

He twisted a diamond ring around and about the third finger of his left hand.

Robbie had given him that ring, and now this ring was all Richard had left of his lover.

He blinked as he saw the riders enter the inner ward via the Garden Gate, then drew a deep breath.

Was he to die then?

Richard had heard of Parliament's decision to depose him—*traitors all!*—but of his ultimate fate, Richard was as yet unsure.

All he knew was that Bolingbroke could not afford to allow him to live.

The only question in Richard's mind was how long Bolingbroke would wait before he sent some executioner in the depths of the night . . . long enough for Richard to escape? Long enough for Richard's supporters—and, sweet Jesu, surely there were *some* left—to raise a righteous rebellion to restore him to the throne?

The men had dismounted now, handing the reins of their horses to some men-at-arms, and now they were striding up the steps leading to the entrance of the Keep.

Richard turned to the door and waited, his hands still by his side.

RABY ENTERED first, drawing the gloves from his hands. He looked at Richard standing against the far side of the chamber by its single window, but said nothing to him.

He stepped to one side as Northumberland entered, and then Neville.

Richard drew in a sharp breath as he saw Neville, wondering if Bolingbroke was so confident that he thought not to wait for the deep of the night, nor to cloak the identity of his executioner in secrecy.

But Richard was nothing if not a Plantagenet bred and born, and so the only gesture he made was one of arrogance. He titled his chin very slightly and affected a disdainful air.

"My Lords Traitors," he said. "Do you think to commit your dark work in the afternoon sunshine?"

"We have come, my Lord of Bordeaux," Northumberland said, addressing Richard by the least of his titles, "to inform you of Parliament's decision as to your eventual fate."

"Parliament has *no* right to presume to dictate my fate to me. I am rightful king of England, divinely anointed and consecrated—"

"As you are well aware," said Raby, "Parliament has charged you and found you guilty of breaking your coronation oaths most willfully and with no regard to the rights of your subjects. You are a tyrant damned, Richard, and a most ungracious son to the memory of your father."

"You are not worthy to speak to me!" Richard said, and

now there was a tiny note of panic in his voice. "I am your king and master and so shall I remain."

"You are nothing less than a fool," Northumberland said, drawing a folded parchment from the purse at his belt.

He unfolded it. "Richard, once king of England, it is ordered by the lords and commons of Parliament that you, known as Richard of Bordeaux, shall be carried within the next few days to imprisonment within Pontefract Castle where you shall be confined at the pleasure of Henry of Lancaster. You shall be kept in comfort, with the best bread and meat that money can afford, but know you now that should any attempt be made to rescue you, then they and you shall die in the attempt."

Richard's mouth trembled very slightly. "I ask that I be allowed exile beyond the seas. There is no need to keep me on the king's purse."

Now Neville stepped forth, standing between Northumberland and Raby. "You *are* sentenced to exile, Richard. Exile among those who have reason to hate you most . . . your own people."

"Do you think your beloved Hal will ever sit easy on the throne?" Richard suddenly shouted, spittle flying from his mouth. "Do you think God will sit in silence as Bolingbroke takes my throne through treachery?"

Neville flinched a little, and it was enough to spur Richard on. "Not all the waters in the rough ocean deep," he said, "are enough to wash the balm from the head of an anointed king. For every man that lifts cold steel for Bolingbroke, against my crown, there sits in heaven an angel in God's heavenly pay. *Heaven* guards and protects my right, Neville, whatever Bolingbroke's treachery does to me on this mortal soil!"

Neville opened his mouth to speak, but couldn't, and Raby shot him a concerned glance.

"You will be taken two nights from this," Raby said, turning back to Richard, "to Traitor's Gate, there to be escorted onto ship to commence your journey to Pontefract."

"I wish Bolingbroke well in his treason," Richard said,

very low and angry, "and hope that he can summon sufficient cause in his defense when he must make report to his God."

Northumberland gestured to his companions to leave the room, but just as the three men approached the door, Richard spoke again.

"Tell me, if nothing else, that you gave de Vere a decent burial according to the laws of God."

Northumberland glanced at Raby, but the two earls left it to Neville to answer.

"We fed his corpse to the lions in their Tower cages," Neville said, "but even they refused to touch his corrupted flesh."

And then they were gone, and the door slammed in Richard's distraught face.

Chapter III

Wednesday 26th September 1380

— II —

✠

NEVILLE TOOK THE STEPS of Lambeth Palace three at a time, striding past the guards without acknowledging their greetings and salutes, and running through the interconnected halls and public chambers of the palace to reach the private apartments.

When he turned into the passage leading to the apartment he shared with Margaret he saw that Bolingbroke was slouched in a large chair outside its closed door.

Bolingbroke looked at Neville with unreadable eyes. "It is time," he said.

Neville looked at him, then turned and opened the door.

"See with the eyes of love," he heard Bolingbroke say, then the door swung shut behind him.

NEVILLE WALKED into a small waiting chamber that in turn led into the three other rooms of his apartments. Although Neville intended to stride directly into his and Margaret's bedchamber, he stopped dead the instant the door had fallen shut behind him.

Directly across the chamber, seated on a large carpet-draped chest under a window, was Mary, Bolingbroke's wife. Several of her ladies were grouped about her.

All were staring at him.

Neville glanced at the door that would lead to his bedchamber, fidgeted, hesitated, then looked back to Mary.

She rose, and her frailty made Neville instantly regret his impatient demeanor.

"My lady," he said, walking over to her and kissing the back of her hand softly. "What do you here?"

To his amazement and considerable consternation, Mary began to weep.

"Tom . . . ," she said, then paused to take some control of herself.

Neville was shocked by her appearance. He had hardly seen her in the past weeks—there had been so much else to think about, and he had little enough to do with her in the usual course of events anyway—and these weeks had taken a dreadful toll on her appearance. Her hair seemed stringy and lifeless, her skin was ashen and waxy, and her beautiful eyes were now too large for her thin face.

Her hand trembled slightly in his, and Neville did not think that was due to her current state of emotion.

"Tom," Mary said again, "Margaret's time has come . . . and she waits out that time in her bedchamber . . . with her maid Agnes . . . and my lady Ashbourne . . ."

Neville nodded, trying to encourage her. Lady Elizabeth Ashbourne was one of Mary's attending ladies, and of only minor nobility, but her presence in Margaret's chamber indicated that she had a far higher fatherhood than he had heretofore suspected. Not Michael, for otherwise Bolingbroke or Margaret would have named her as a sister, but one of the other angels. Gabriel, perhaps? Raphael? Azarias?

And *Agnes?* The nurse had hid her secrets well.

Mary took a deep, shaky breath. "But Margaret will not await her birthing time with *me*!"

Oh, sweet Jesu! Neville realized that normally—had Margaret been a "normal" woman—Mary would certainly have been there for the birth. It would be a great honor for any woman to have an all-but-crowned queen attend her lying-in. But of course, Margaret couldn't let in anyone who didn't know her secret . . .

"Tom," Mary whispered, "Hal has shut me out of his life completely. Please don't let Margaret shut me out of hers."

Neville was suddenly very angry, at Bolingbroke and Margaret both. Did they not care whom they hurt with their secrets? He held Mary's hand, and stared into her distraught face, and then he leaned down and kissed her hand again, not taking his eyes from her face.

In this moment he completely changed his mind about what he would do.

Damn Margaret and Hal!

"Women in labor can do strange things," he said, keeping his words light, teasing, and very warm. "Even husbands are most unwelcome. My Lady Mary, this is a cold and disagreeable place to wait out a birth. Will you join me in the gardens? I can lend you my arm for support, and should you grow too weary, I shall swing you into my arms as if you were a child."

Mary's mouth trembled, then firmed. "Ah, Tom," she said, "how I envy Margaret her husband."

Neville straightened, and held out his arm. "The garden, my lady?"

Mary smiled, and Neville was glad to see some of the unhappiness lift from her face. "The garden, my lord."

Her ladies moved as if they would come with her, but Mary waved them back. "My Lord Neville shall keep me well enough," she said. "Stay here, and bring the news of Margaret and her babe to us in the garden."

BOLINGBROKE LEAPED to his feet, his face stunned as they came through the door. "Tom? Mary? What—?"

"My wife has banished your wife from her birthing chamber," Neville said, fixing Bolingbroke in the eye. "I could not bear to think of my Lady Mary's unhappiness and I thought that it would be best if she and I awaited the birth of my child in the gardens."

Bolingbroke narrowed his eyes at Neville. "You must—"

"I *must* do nothing," Neville said very quietly. "I have free choice in this matter."

Bolingbroke fought to keep his panic from his face, knowing that Mary was staring at him strangely. "Tom—"

"The world will not end if I am not there," Neville said. "Imply nothing from my absence, Hal, but that I need the space and quiet of the gardens." He paused. "It might be better if I know Margaret only as I love her, Hal. Not . . . not as she might become in the birthing chamber."

Mary looked between the two of them, puzzled. Hal and Tom were talking as if Tom had been expected to attend the birth—but no man ever entered a birthing chamber.

"Hal?" she said. "Tom?"

"Ah, my lady," Neville said, "we have been prattling on here about matters we understand and you do not. We are thoughtless warriors," he grinned, and kissed her hand again, his eyes sparkling with mischief as they regarded her, "and our manners are as thick as the winter ice that forms on still ponds. Forgive us."

Neville was not feigning his good humor. In denying Bolingbroke and Margaret what they wanted, Neville suddenly found himself back in control. Although he had wished to witness the birth of his son, and although he thought he needed to see what Margaret's true form was, he also now understood that by attending the birth, and watching silently as Margaret assumed her angel-form, he would have given himself one less option. He would have been one step further down the path that led to total alliance with heaven's nemesis.

He also meant very deeply what he'd just said to Bolingbroke—he wanted to always see Margaret as the beautiful woman whom he had come to love . . . did he truly need to see her slither and slide into . . . into . . . something *else*?

Something he might not be able to love?

So, as he lifted his head from Mary, he said to Bolingbroke, "It might be best, Hal, whatever you think, if I not be there. It is the option I prefer to take. My judgment of you and your cause shall have to wait. And"—he smiled back at Mary—"I think I can better spend the next few hours amusing your wife than listening to Margaret curse me for the trial to which my husbandly attentions have brought her. My lord, I wish you a good afternoon."

And without further ado Mary found herself being escorted away from her husband through the palace toward the gardens. She frowned a little, trying to make sense of the scene she had just witnessed. Then she smiled, for although she had not understood the depths of Tom and Hal's conversation, she understood very clearly that Tom had somehow managed to best Hal.

And that suddenly brightened her day considerably.

BOLINGBROKE WATCHED them go, then strode through the doorway into the Neville apartments. He completely ignored the small cries of shock from his wife's ladies, still waiting at one end of the entrance chamber, and strode grim-faced into the birthing chamber.

No doubt this would give the palace something to gossip about for months to come.

The bedchamber had been cleared as much as possible: all chests, chairs and the one low table had been thrust against a far wall, and the bed pushed a little closer to the opposite wall. The window shutters were closed, and five oil lamps burned from wall sconces, bestowing a warm, golden aura on the room. A fire was roaring in the fireplace, and set on the hearthstones before it were two pails of water, a jug, a bowl and a pile of linens.

Three women—Margaret, Agnes and the statuesque blond figure of Elizabeth Ashbourne—stood just to one side of the bed.

Margaret was dressed in a linen shift which clung to her sweat-soaked body in great, wrinkled patches. Her face, staring at Bolingbroke, was flushed and running with sweat as well, with tendrils of hair that clung to forehead and cheeks.

It was also desperate.

"Hal?" she said. "Where is Tom? Has he not returned?"

He opened his mouth to reply, but stopped as Margaret writhed with a contraction.

"My lord," said Agnes. "*Where is Thomas Neville?*"

"He is gone to the gardens," said Bolingbroke. "With my wife. He has decided it best if he does not—"

Margaret wailed, with misery rather than pain. "Where is he? Where? Oh, Jesu, Hal, I want *Tom*—"

"Mary has him," Bolingbroke whispered. "Not you."

And with that he turned on his heel and strode from the room.

"I DO thank you, Tom," Mary said as they sat on a seat at the top of the lawn that swept down to the Thames. "But I do also regret that your consideration for me has kept you from your wife's side."

Their arms were still linked, and now Neville lifted her hand and held it in both of his. He felt profoundly grateful to her for providing him with the perfect excuse to defer his final judgment on Margaret and her kind to a day of his choosing, but at the same time he felt far more than mere gratitude. Mary was a wondrous woman in her own right, and had been as badly used by Bolingbroke in his ambitions as Neville had. "She has her ladies. I doubt she will miss me at all."

"Were you truly going to attend the birth?"

"Aye. Margaret had asked me. But . . . I was having my doubts long before I came upon you in my apartments."

"I so envy Margaret her children," Mary whispered, and Neville looked at her.

"But you and Hal—"

Mary smiled, although her eyes were sad. "No need for pretense, Tom. I am ill. My womb is diseased and thus diseases me. I shall not be giving Hal the heir he needs."

She nodded to where Westminster loomed across the Thames. "Look at it. That is Hal's world, and Hal's towering ambition. Not mine."

"You are his wife," Neville said gently. "The nation adores you."

As if to give proof to his words, a horse dealer leading a string of thin yearlings along the river path looked up, saw Mary and Neville, and doffed his cap before waving it madly in the air. "My Lady Queen!" he called, and the frenzy of his waving doubled.

Mary laughed with pure delight, lifting her free hand to wave back.

The horse dealer made an exaggerated bow, slapped his cap back on his head, and went on his way.

Mary looked at Neville with eyes gleaming with tears. "I do very truly thank you," she said again, "for making me feel a wanted woman this fine day."

Stunningly, tears pricked in the corners of Neville's eyes

as well. "You are most welcome, my lady," he said, and lifted her hand yet again to his mouth.

The press of his lips on her hand lingered just a little longer than courtly politeness required.

She grinned. "My lord, would you have me believe that your only purpose in bringing me to these gardens was to find some privacy in which to ravish me?"

She was teasing, and Neville replied in like manner. "Ah! I have been discovered! And to think that I labored so long to engineer this time alone with you."

Mary laughed, feeling much of the despondency of the past months lift. It felt wonderful just to sit and have this good-looking man enjoy her company . . . *prefer* her company to that of his wife's.

"I feel so much better," she announced, her eyes bright and her cheeks flushed with a color that was not solely due to the sunlight.

In contrast to Mary, Neville's face sobered as he watched her laugh. He found himself astounded and angry—again—in equal amounts. Astounded because now, as Margaret had so long ago, Neville realized what an astonishing woman Mary was; angry because Neville couldn't believe Hal claimed to so love mankind he would lead them into a better (and Godless) world, but at the same time could ignore what was possibly his greatest asset—his wife.

"Hal does not deserve you," he said, and his fingers clasped tightly about her hand.

MARGARET SCREAMED Tom's name, but he did not come.

"It must be now," Elizabeth Ashbourne cried, but Margaret swung her head violently from side to side.

"No! No! Tom needs to be here. We are ruined if he is not here."

Agnes and Elizabeth shared a frightened glance.

"My lady," Agnes said. "It will be *now*, or you will die. You must change. Now!"

Margaret shook her head again, but her two attendants could see her resolve weakening.

"Now," said Agnes, and Margaret whimpered.

Then she tilted her head back against the pillows of the bed, arched her back in agony, and let out a strange, lilting cry, almost like the warbling of a songbird.

"Good girl," said Elizabeth, and she and Agnes exchanged a look of utter relief.

Slowly, Margaret began to assume the form to which she had been born.

As she did so her pain eased, then vanished. But still she wept, crying out her husband's name.

NEVILLE WAS still sitting with Mary on the bench overlooking the Thames when, two hours later, Agnes approached him.

She carried in her arms a tightly wrapped bundle.

"Your son," she said, putting him gently into Neville's arms.

The look she shot him was not so gentle.

"And Margaret?" Neville said.

"Well enough," said Agnes.

Neville nodded. "Thank you, Agnes. You may leave us. Tell my lady wife I shall be with her shortly."

Agnes took a deep breath, then stalked away.

"What a beautiful child," Mary whispered, and Neville looked down at the baby.

He was beautiful, as beautiful as his mother, but with the Nevilles' dark hair scattered in loose, damp curls over his head.

"A son," Mary said, her eyes shining with joy for Neville and Margaret. "What shall you name him?"

Neville looked up at her, seeing not so much Mary's face, but the suffering she'd been forced to endure through Hal's indifference. The choice was not difficult.

"Bohun," he said. "For you."

For an instant Mary did not react, then she lifted two trembling hands to her mouth, and stared at Neville.

He smiled at her, gently, then lifted the baby into her arms.

"TOM?" MARGARET opened her eyes and struggled into a sitting position.

"Hello, Margaret." He sat down on a stool by the bed, their son in his arms.

"Why didn't you come, Tom? Why?"

He looked up from the baby. "Mary needed me more than you—"

"*Mary* needed you? What right has Mary . . . ?" Margaret broke off, hating the strident shrillness of her tone. "What right has Mary to your time when your wife lay in childbed?" she finally finished more moderately.

He studied her, noting that apart from some faint lines of strain about her mouth and eyes she seemed well.

Not like most women who go through prolonged labor.

Well, she'd obviously had an easier time with this birth than the last.

"When I arrived back at this palace this afternoon," Neville said, "I had every intention of witnessing the birth of my son. But when I entered the outer chamber, and there saw my Lady Mary, suffering because she believed that you, like Hal, had now shut her out of your life, I felt her pain, and then I felt angered.

"You have your causes, Margaret, but sometimes I don't think you care whom you hurt to achieve your ends. Mary has never deserved to be hurt, not in the way she has been by Hal, and today by you."

Margaret began to weep silently as Neville spoke, and now she lifted a hand and brushed away her tears. "I had not thought of Mary," she whispered. "Jesus Christ, forgive me."

"In those hours that you spent giving birth," Neville said, looking down and smiling a little at the wrinkled, pink face of his sleeping son, "I talked long and gently with Mary. She spoke to me of Hal . . . and of Hal's love for Catherine."

"Tom—"

"Nay, do not speak. I have had enough of your and Hal's words these past weeks. Mary spoke to me of how she hoped that, once she had died, Hal would find a wife who could be what he needed. A powerful, brilliant queen to match his splendor.

"And I began to think, my love, how convenient it would be for Hal if Mary died. Think of it, a brief, loveless but enormously enriching marriage that would, remarkably, be over in time for Hal to marry his true love . . . if Philip ever lets her go."

"Tom, I know what you must—"

"And think what this new, powerful and brilliant wife would bring as *her* dowry, Margaret. Why, France!"

"Tom, stop it!"

"No! No! I will not 'stop it.' As I wiped away Mary's tears, and made her laugh, I began to *really* think about all that has happened, Margaret, and I realized what a string of convenient deaths there have been in the past two years!"

"Oh, sweet Jesu . . . *no!*" Margaret whispered.

"Edward our king. His son, the Black Prince. Gloucester. *Lancaster*, curse it! And, soon, Richard. Everyone who has stood between Hal and the cursed throne has died before their time, Margaret."

He paused, glaring at her with eyes brilliant with pain. "What hand have you had in that? *What?*"

Margaret lay back against the pillows and closed her eyes.

"What?" Neville hissed once more.

"Lancaster was none of Hal's doing," Margaret said,

looking at him once more. "Hal loved Lancaster. He would not have killed him." She paused. "I am sure of it."

"But the others?"

"Hal," she whispered. "Not me." She touched her smooth belly. "I contain that which generates, not destroys."

"By Christ, woman," he whispered. "Did not Hal love the Black Prince as well?"

She did not, could not, speak.

"Hal wants me to murder Richard," Neville said after a long silence. "But I will not do it. Not now. Not even to revenge you, Margaret. In his own way, Richard has been raped as well."

She nodded, accepting it. Somewhere deep inside her a great dark cave had opened up, and she felt that at any moment now she would fall headlong into it and be smashed to death within its craggy depths.

"I have no doubt that Hal will find someone else soon enough to do the ghastly deed. But it will not be me."

Neville sighed, and stood, and half turned toward the door, and Margaret knew that she had lost him completely.

He would take Rosalind, and the baby, and walk away from her, and then she would die, for there would be nothing left of life but this great, dark, yawning chasm . . .

But after hesitating a long moment, Neville turned back and sat on the bed, close to Margaret. He lifted the baby into the crook of her arm.

"Margaret," he said, "I do love you, but for that which is to come I need you to be my wife, not Hal's sister. Do you understand what I am asking of you?"

She stared at him, not believing he was offering her this chance.

"Well?" he said softly.

"Yes," she whispered.

"Do you love me?"

"Yes."

"Then that is all that matters," he said, and touched her cheek with his fingers. He dropped his eyes to the baby in her arm.

"See the beautiful son we have made between us," he said, and suddenly she was weeping in great, gulping sobs, and Neville leaned forward, and gathered Margaret and their son into his arms.

Chapter IV

Saturday 29th September 1380

— MICHAELMAS —

✠

WESTMINSTER WAS CROWNED in light, and it seemed to Neville that England might never see a winter again. Leaves drifted from trees, and the waters of the Thames lapped cold and gray against the piers and piles of the shoreline, but the surrounds of the abbey and palace were bathed in sunshine and warmth and never-ending happiness.

The abbey forecourt was crowded with tens of thousands of cheering people, come to witness the enthronement of their beloved fair Prince Hal. Neville stood at the top of the steps at the abbey and stared down at the streamer-waving crowd, brilliant with merriment as the sunlight glinted from bright eyes and glanced off flushed cheeks. Neville was more than a little scratchy-eyed and irritable, for he'd had almost no sleep the past night, having stood and witnessed as a crabbed-faced Richard had been quietly removed from the Tower at midnight to commence his journey to Pontefract Castle.

Then, when he'd returned to the apartments he shared with his growing family, he'd sat for hours in the gloom, watching Margaret as she slept, Bohun sleeping cradled in his arms.

He'd looked down at his son from time to time, wondering what kind of a future he would bequeath him.

What choice would he make? Margaret, or mankind's salvation?

But what if Margaret, and her and Hal's cause, was *mankind's salvation.*

Earlier this morning, having shared a brief breakfast with Margaret, Neville had escorted Mary and her ladies to the abbey precinct so that she could take her place with her husband. Mary had been so happy—chattering about Bohun—that she had made Neville smile too. She was also, somewhat surprisingly to Neville, excited about the day's events. Today she would see her husband crowned King of England, and she would become his consort, his queen. As had the horse dealer two days ago, so this morning many people had laughed and waved to Mary as they'd made their way through Westminster, shouting her name with unfeigned joy.

Mary had looked the best she had for a long time, full of life and laughter and goodwill. When Neville had asked after her health, she'd told him quietly that the pain and gripes that had plagued her belly for the past weeks had all but abated.

She turned momentarily from the waving crowds and smiled at him. "It was your care and laughter that chased away my cramps and aches, Tom. You gave me the gift of joy." And then something in the crowd distracted her. "Oh! See? That woman has painted her face completely golden."

And Neville could do nothing but smile at her happiness . . . and hope that Bolingbroke did nothing to destroy it.

To Neville's relief, even Bolingbroke had gone out of his way to make Mary smile. When Neville had escorted Mary into the chambers where Bolingbroke was being robed ready for the ceremony, Bolingbroke had greeted her kindly, and had made her laugh with a small jest. Then Bolingbroke, Mary and Neville had talked a while about Margaret and the child.

Bolingbroke had sent Neville a few unreadable looks through the exchange, and Neville had delighted in the fact that Bolingbroke was no longer sure of him. In refusing to accede to Bolingbroke's wishes to witness the birth of his son, Neville had taken a firmer grip on his eventual freedom of choice. They had tricked him into admitting his love for Margaret, but he would still choose freely.

Now he took a deep breath, flexing his shoulders and neck to relieve their stiffness, then looked into the cloudless sky, wondering if God and His angels were crowded above, looking down.

Neville had no idea what the future held. All he knew was that there would be trials ahead, forks in the path that he could not yet anticipate, much less prepare for . . . and that somewhere in his future rested that final decision on which the fate of the world would twist and turn.

Choose one way and God would triumph, choose another and the world would become a godless place . . .

Choose hate, or choose love?

Whatever else, Neville thought, *it will never be that simple.*

"My lord?"

Courtenay. Neville roused himself from his reverie, and looked about.

Courtenay was walking over to him from where he had been standing with a group of officials. "My lord, they are calling us into the abbey. We must go."

Neville nodded, then looked about, delaying yet one more moment.

Delaying just that one more moment the enthronement of the Demon-King.

But then Neville saw that Raby was beckoning urgently to them from the doorway, and there were signs that the formal procession from the abbot's quarters into the abbey was about to begin.

Neville sighed, smiled at Courtenay, and walked into the abbey.

HE DID not see the black-robed Dominican standing five or six deep back in the crowd, staring with bleak-eyed animosity at Neville's disappearing back, nor did he realize that the obsessive hatred that Thorseby nurtured in his heart for him would shortly help to envelop the realm in civil war.

None of this did Neville see or know, because he had thoughts only for Hal, and his own role in the battles ahead.

Neville had forgotten Thorseby, and did not know that the Prior General was now nothing but a walking winter.

AS WAS the world outside, so also was the abbey bathed in brilliance. Torches and lamps blazed forth from every available space while sunlight shimmered through the stained glass of the abbey windows. From columns and rafters hung huge flags and banners—Bolingbroke's personal standard, the Plantagenet lions, the standards and emblems of the nobles attending—shifting and trembling in the warm updraft caused by the torches.

As Neville strode down the aisle, Raby at his side, Courtenay following some paces farther behind, he saw the faces of the mightiest nobles and greatest clerics of England.

Many a man's face was relaxed and cheerful as he chatted to his neighbors, but many others were still and watchful, their eyes hooded and unreadable even in this brilliant light.

Neville's face remained neutral, but inside he wondered: who was friend, and who foe? Who truth and who falsehood?

And what was *truth, and what falsehood?*

"Tom, if you don't manage a happier face I swear I will march you straight out the door by the choir stalls," Raby hissed.

"Hotspur is not here," Neville said.

"Nay, and neither is Rutland, nor Mortimer. And none of those should be a surprise."

"Nay . . . Hal is not so secure as he would like, methinks." Neville smiled to himself. *Nay, not so secure at all.* "Ah, here are our places, Uncle. Shall we stand?"

Raby shot Neville another glare as they took their places to the right of the throne and chair on the dais before the altar, then turned his eyes to look back down the nave as the horns sounded, and Bolingbroke began his triumphal entry into the abbey.

THE RITUAL of enthroning a new king was one of great antiquity, but this Michaelmas the ceremony was, of necessity, somewhat different.

This was no smooth transition from father to son, but from disgraced king to pretender, and the rite had been altered accordingly.

Bolingbroke was led, not to the throne, but to a wooden chair next to it. There he sat, bareheaded and close-shaved, dressed simply in linen shirt and red hose, his feet naked.

His face was solemn, his eyes downcast, but even so there was a great strength and beauty within it, and when he raised his piercing gaze at the approach of the Abbot of Westminster there was an overwhelming sense that this was a man who not only had vision, but who also carried within himself the strength with which to make his vision reality.

Neville wondered what would happen if he started forth and shouted exactly what vision Bolingbroke had for England and the world beyond. He suddenly remembered what Bolingbroke had said to him atop a hill so many weeks ago—*One day I will lead mankind into the stars*—and Neville shuddered, for he realized now that Bolingbroke had meant that quite literally.

He looked away from Bolingbroke and saw that Mary had quietly taken her place on the dais to her husband's left and slightly behind him. She was seated on a beautifully carved chair, her brow and neck sparkling with jewels. She was wearing an ivory and gold gown, and it suited her soft coloring so much that, for the first time since he'd known her, Neville thought she looked beautiful.

She saw his regard, and inclined her head slightly. One of her eyelids drooped, and Neville thought that had it been anyone else he would have been sure she'd just winked at him.

He inclined his own head to her, and placed his hand on his heart, and bowed very slightly, earning a smile from her and a frown from Raby.

Then a movement caught his eyes, and Neville looked back to the central dais.

There was the Abbot of Westminster, flanked on one side by William Arundel, the new Archbishop of Canterbury, and on the other by Sir Robert Tresilian, Chief Justice of the King's Bench.

Church, and law, standing side by side to consecrate the new king.

Neville saw the abbot's eyes darting nervously about the abbey, and then alight momentarily on the Duke of Exeter, a man who had been conspicuously quiet during these past turbulent weeks.

Exeter was Richard's much older half-brother by Joan of

Kent's first marriage to Sir Thomas Holland, the Earl of Kent (to whom she had borne six children).

Neville tensed, expecting at any moment fully weaponed knights on horseback to violate the abbey . . . but nothing happened, save that the abbot turned to the assembled lords of England and opened his arms as if in supplication.

"The throne of England sits vacant!" shouted the abbot. "What is your will? What is your will?"

"Bolingbroke!" returned a shout, and Neville realized with a start that it had come from Raby at his side.

"Bolingbroke!" shouted someone else, and then the shout rose from thousands of throats: "Bolingbroke! Bolingbroke! Bolingbroke!"

Under the shouting came a strange undertone, and Neville, standing almost bemused at the thunderous acclamation echoing about him, realized that it was the roar of the crowds outside the abbey, and they were shouting "Hal! Hal! Hal!"

The abbot turned to Bolingbroke, and raised him from the chair, and blessed him, and then led him to stand before the throne. Monks came forward, as they had done at Richard's coronation, carrying the robes and sword of state. The abbot, aided by two of the monks, solemnly robed Bolingbroke, and girded the sword about his hips, and then indicated he should take his place on the throne of England.

All this time the shouting continued: *Bolingbroke! Bolingbroke! Bolingbroke!*

Now the abbot turned about and raised his hands for silence.

The shouting murmured to a close.

"You have called for Henry of Bolingbroke, Duke of Lancaster, to take the throne," he called in a clear ringing voice. "Does anyone here know of good reason why Bolingbroke should not accede to your will?"

And as a silence fell like a heavy, stifling curtain across

the abbey, Bolingbroke turned his face slightly and stared directly at Neville with his clear, gray eyes.

Neville could not look away from Bolingbroke. He understood that at this moment he *could* stop Bolingbroke if he wanted. All he had to do was to step forth and shout of what he knew, and, by the indecision he'd seen on the abbot's face, the thinly veiled hostility on Exeter's, and the hooded eyes he'd seen as he'd entered the abbey, he was well aware that there would be people enough within the abbey to stop the ceremony progressing any further.

Enough people to call for a halt, and a questioning.

Bolingbroke's eyes bored into Neville as the silence within the abbey continued.

I could speak and ruin this triumph now, thought Neville, holding Bolingbroke's eyes easily. *What shall I do, Hal? What do you think I will do?*

He thought about what would happen if he *did* step forth and speak his doubts. Harsh words, anger . . . and the vile sound of swords being drawn from scabbards.

If he spoke now, then this abbey would not witness the commencement of a new reign, but the opening thrusts of a long and bloody war as the barons of England fought out the succession between themselves.

Neville's eyes slipped to Mary.

She was still watching him, and again the corners of her mouth lifted. She looked so happy, so happy . . .

His eyes slipped back to Bolingbroke who still regarded him. There was something in his face that made Neville remember that glorious moment when Bolingbroke had ridden his stallion into the heart of an army who could have killed them, and laid his life in their hands.

He had given them the choice: *Freedom, or his death*, and they had chosen freedom . . . freedom and Bolingbroke.

Sweet Jesu, how he had loved Hal at that moment.

Neville suddenly realized that all he wanted was to recapture that love—but to capture it with truth this time.

And so, as the world twisted and waited through the silence of the abbey, and as Bolingbroke stared, waiting, Neville made himself a vow: *If Bolingbroke, whatever his birth blood, worked tirelessly and truthfully for what he had promised those men that day, then Neville would condemn heaven into hell if it might help him. But if Bolingbroke had lied both to England and to Neville . . . well then, hell awaited, and Neville would do everything in his power to see Bolingbroke—*

—and Margaret?—

—thrust down into it.

He shrugged, very slightly—*I will not speak*—and Bolingbroke's shoulders visibly relaxed, and he looked back to the abbot.

The abbot nodded, then spoke, declaring Bolingbroke the true elected king of the English people, and the moment, that one single moment when Neville could have stopped it, was lost forever.

And the abbot turned, and took the heavy jeweled crown, and lowered it upon Henry Bolingbroke's brow.

And time stilled.

THE ARCHANGEL burst through the great arched doorway of the abbey and stood in a pillar of pulsating light, staring up the nave to where the Demon-King sat his throne.

The abbey was crowded, but everyone save the Demon-King had faded into grayness, their eyes staring unseeing ahead, their ears stilled, their consciousness suspended.

Archangel Michael walked slowly down the aisle toward the Demon-King.

The abbey trembled with each of his frightful footfalls, and as his wings dragged behind him a great dry wind of retribution rose to rustle through the frozen assembly.

Hair lifted, and cloaks shifted, but no one saw, no one heard.

No one save the Demon-King.

"What do you here?" said the Demon-King as the archangel stopped at the foot of the dais. "Come to offer your congratulations?"

The archangel smiled, and it was terrible to behold.

"You think to have won," said Michael, and raised his arms above his shoulders, his hands twisted into claws, as if he were about to rain God's wrath down upon the Demon-King's head.

The Demon-King leaned forward, one hand on the hilt of his sword. "I have not won yet," he said, "but I am so close . . . so close . . ."

The archangel dropped his arms, and screamed with thin laughter.

The Demon-King's face flushed with anger. "I wield love as my weapon—what do you have? Hate? Indifference? Your ever-cursed righteousness?"

"You know what my weapon is!" Michael said, and flung an arm toward where Neville stood, gray and unseeing.

Sparks arced from the end of the archangel's fingers and scattered heedlessly over the stone flagging of the abbey.

"But," Michael continued, now leaning forward to the Demon-King, "you have absolutely no idea how I am going to use him, do you? You have absolutely no idea who and what he *is*, do you?"

The Demon-King narrowed his eyes at his angel-father, but he did not speak.

"You pride yourself on your 'royal' blood," the archangel said, "but I spent the least part of myself in your mother. I put my *excrement* into your mother! You are foulness made flesh, imp, and you are *nothing* compared to the forces ranged against you."

"Your rage is merely a measure of your impotence," the Demon-King said.

Michael drew back, and his form collapsed into a raging pillar of fire.

God is working His purpose out, the fire spoke, *and your time is drawing nigh.*

And then it vanished, and King Henry of England was left staring into the cheering nave of the abbey, his right hand clutching at his throne in furious frustration.

God is working His purpose out, as year succeeds to year!

He turned, his eyes ice, and stared at Neville, and wondered what treachery the man's heart hid.

So came the Demon-King to reign over England.

EPILOGUE

— PONTEFRACT CASTLE —

For God's sake let us sit upon the ground
And tell sad stories of the death of kings:
How some have been depos'd, some slain in war,
Some haunted by the ghosts they have depos'd,
Some poison'd by their wives, some sleeping kill'd,
All murder'd—for within the hollow crown
That rounds the mortal temples of a king
Keeps Death his court; and there the antic sits,
Scoffing his state and grinning at his pomp;
Allowing him a breath, a little scene,
To monarchize, be fear'd, and kill with looks;
Infusing him with self and vain conceit,
As if this flesh which walls about our life
Were brass impregnable; and, humour'd thus,
Comes at the last, and with a little pin
Bores through his castle wall, and farewell, king!

—William Shakespeare,
Richard the Second, Act III, sc. ii

Friday and November 1380
Pontefract Castle, Yorkshire

— ALL SOUL'S DAY —

✠

THEY CAME IN the pre-dawn, hooded men slouched within the anonymity of rough woolen cloaks. Richard had barely time enough to jerk out of his sleep before the first two had seized him by his arms and flipped him over onto the mattress, forcing his face into the pillow. He struggled, but the men were too strong, and within a moment they had torn his nightshirt from his body and used it to tie his hands behind his back.

"You have no right," Richard cried, his voice embarrassingly distorted both by the pillow and by his own terror.

"We come on orders of the king," one of the men said. "We have the right of England behind us."

Richard struggled a little more—now that his hands were tied only one of the men had any hold on him—and managed to turn his head to stare about his chamber.

A man was bending over the grate, stirring the coals into life with a poker and tossing on more wood. Light flared as the wood caught fire, and Richard could see that his small chamber was now crowded with five or six men, all hooded and cloaked.

Sweat broke out along his entire body, even though he was naked and the room was still chill. "You come to murder me!"

"We come to assure England's future," said the man who had replied before, and Richard realized it was the man who had stirred the fire to life.

The man had finished stoking the fire, and now he slid the black iron poker deep into the glowing coals.

Richard's eyes bulged in terror, and he tried to throw off the man who had hold of his body.

For an instant the man lost his grip, but then he laughed, and subdued Richard simply by sitting on the small of his back. He bounced up and down slightly, causing Richard to cry out in pain.

"I had thought you would be pleasured by the feel of a man atop you again," the tormentor said in a high, false voice.

Several other men in the room laughed.

"If you murder me," Richard said, his voice now shrill in his terror and panic, "then you murder England!"

"Murder? Murder?" said another of the hooded figures. "We merely thought to come here this day to give you pleasure, my Lord of Bordeaux. We thought you had spent too long grieving for your sweet Robbie de Vere."

Now there was general laughter among the men, and one of them made a foul comment as he stepped forward and caressed one of Richard's buttocks.

It was slimy and cold with sweat and panic.

The man wiped his hand on his cloak, then looked to his companion standing by the fire. "Is it ready?" he said.

The man by the fire leaned down and lifted out the poker, inspecting it carefully. "Soon," he said. "We might as well begin. Hold him."

Richard twisted about with all his might, but now four of the men were holding him firmly, and all Richard managed was to wriggle a little on the bed. He saw the man by the fire reach into the depths of his cloak for something, and he turned his head away, not wanting to see the instrument of his death.

Besides, his panicked, terror-ridden mind already knew what it would be.

The man lifted an object free from one of his inner pockets, smiling a little at Richard's refusal to look, and held it out in the firelight to study it.

It was the funnel-shaped tip of a physician's enema can, a smooth earthenware implement about twice the length of a man's finger, and a little thicker.

A foul smell filled the chamber as Richard's body vented gas.

"Ugh!" one of the men holding him down said. "Be quick about this, my friend, for this boy is more obnoxious than a sewer pit."

The man with the earthenware cylinder wrinkled his own face in disgust, then spat a gob of phlegm onto the narrower portion of the funnel. He rubbed it all around, then, without further ado, strode over to where Richard lay, forced apart his buttocks, and slid the funnel deep into his anus with a single rough thrust.

Richard twisted anew, screaming, but he was held fast now, and nothing he could do managed to dislodge the funnel.

The chief assassin calmly walked back to the fire, lifted out the poker, and held its glowing tip up for the others to see.

"Hurry," one of the men said in a tight voice.

The assassin nodded, then walked back to Richard. "My Lord the King asked me to remind you," he said, "of how Lady Neville screamed when you raped her. He thought that you should know, in your last earthly moments, of the degree of torment that you visited upon her."

Then, carefully, making sure not to mark Richard's outer skin, he slid the poker into the earthenware funnel.

There was a hideous sizzling sound, and a smell so vile that several of the men gagged. Richard shrieked, then shrieked yet higher, his body bucking and twisting even under the weight of the four men holding him.

The assassin slid the poker in six inches, then twelve, all the while stirring and jabbing it about.

Richard's shrieks rose higher, mutating into the unearthly bowling of the damned. His body now convulsed, jittering about in an agonized death dance, and the men had to strain themselves in order to keep him still enough for the poker to complete its work.

His belly now held nothing but a half-pulped mess of destroyed organs and sizzling, clotting blood. The muscles in the assassin's arm bulged, and he pushed the poker in yet further.

Richard's diaphragm burst asunder, and the assassin jerked the poker back into the now-ruined cavity of Richard's belly, lest he burst apart the heart and lungs and cause Richard to bleed from nose and mouth.

The assassin gave one final, vicious twist, then pulled the poker out with some degree of regret.

He made a disgusted face at the slimy mess coating its length.

Watching Richard carefully, his four companions gradually released their hold on him.

But the former king was dead, even if his body still jerked and roiled a little as organs and blood vessels continued to burst and cook within the retained heat of his belly.

The assassin thrust the poker into the coals, burning off the detritus of Richard's internal organs, then carefully replaced it in its spot on the grate. He turned back to Richard's body, and removed the earthenware cylinder from his body, pocketing it.

He ran his eyes up and down Richard, indicating to his companions that they should untie his hands and throw the destroyed nightshirt in the fire. He sighed, satisfied. Richard's body was unmarked. There was nothing to indicate a foul death.

Nothing to indicate murder.

"A natural death," said the assassin, "for a most unnatural man."

The others laughed, then, having tidied up, left the room.

* * *

IT WAS All Souls Day, the day when the souls of the dead most easily walked the earth.

It was that day of the year when a bitter, revengeful soul would have no trouble finding someone within which to smolder.

FAR AWAY to the north, Hotspur stood atop a hill staring at the misty peaks of Scotland plunging and rearing into the distance. On the slopes below his men were cutting the throats of the last of the wounded Scots they'd felled when they'd met in battle earlier this day.

Then, slowly, as the Scots shrieked and died below him, Hotspur turned, and stared south.

His hand slipped to the hilt of the dagger at his side, and his eyes narrowed in thought . . . and ambition. Then his eyes moved, and fell on the Dominican friar walking up the hill toward him.

Prior General Richard Thorseby, black-hearted man of God, come to stir the coals of winter.

GLOSSARY

For more information on characters and places, please visit:
www.saradouglass.com/crucibworld.html.

AQUITAINE: a large and rich province covering much of the southwest of France. Aquitaine was not only independent of France, it was ruled by the English kings after Eleanor of Aquitaine brought the province as part of her dowry to her marriage with Henry II.

ARMOR: the armoring of a knight was a complex affair, done in different ways in different countries and generations. Generally, knights wore either chain mail or plate armor or a combination of both, depending on fashion or the military activity involved. Chain mail was formed of thousands of tiny iron or steel rings riveted together to form a loose tunic (sometimes with arms); plate armor consisted of a series of metal plates fashioned to fit a knight's body and joints—the full suit of armor was rarely seen before the fifteenth century. Helmets (whether BASINETS or the full-visored helms), mail or plate gloves, and weapons, completed the knight's outfitting. See also HAUBERK, PEYTRAL and SHAFFRON.

ARUNDEL, RICHARD: Earl of Arundel and Surrey, one of RICHARD's Privy Councillors.

ARUNDEL, WILLIAM: Archbishop of Canterbury after SIMON SUDBURY.

ASHBOURNE, ELIZABETH: one of MARY BOHUN's attending ladies.

AVIGNON: the French-controlled town which is the seat of the rebel popes.

BALL, JOHN: a renegade priest.

BALLARD, AGNES: maid to MARGARET NEVILLE and nurse to Rosalind.

BARMING: a small village in central Kent.

BASINET: an open-faced helmet (although many knights wore them with a visor attached) that was either rounded (globular) or conical in shape. See also ARMOR.

BAVIERE, ISABEAU DE: wife of LOUIS, mother of CHARLES and CATHERINE.

BEAUCHAMP, THOMAS: Earl of Warwick.

BEAUFORT, HENRY: illegitimate-born son of JOHN OF GAUNT and his third wife KATHERINE SWYNFORD. Henry is the Bishop of Winchester.

BEAUFORT, JOAN: illegitimate-born daughter of JOHN OF GAUNT and his third wife KATHERINE SWYNFORD. Now married to RALPH NEVILLE.

BERTRAND: prior of St. Angelo's friary in Rome.

BIERMAN, JOHAN: a young merchant who accompanied THOMAS NEVILLE on his journey through the Alps in *The Nameless Day*.

BLACK PRINCE: the now deceased first son of EDWARD III and his queen, PHILIPPA. The Black Prince was married to JOAN OF KENT, and was the father of RICHARD II.

BOHUN, CECILIA: Dowager Duchess of Hereford, mother of MARY BOHUN.

BOHUN, MARY: heiress to the dukedom of Hereford, wife to HAL BOLINGBROKE.

BOLINGBROKE, HENRY OF (HAL): Duke of Hereford and Earl of Derby, son of JOHN OF GAUNT and his first wife, Blanche of Lancaster.

BORDEAUX: a port on the Garonne estuary in southwest France and capital of the duchy of AQUITAINE. Bordeaux was the BLACK PRINCE's base in France (and in fact his son, RICHARD, was born there).

BRANTINGHAM, BISHOP THOMAS: bishop of Exeter and Lord High Treasurer of England.

CATHERINE: daughter of Prince LOUIS of France and ISABEAU DE BAVIÈRE, younger sister to the DAUPHIN, CHARLES.

CHARLES, DAUPHIN: grandson of the French King JOHN, son of Prince LOUIS and ISABEAU DE BAVIÈRE, and heir to the French throne. Older brother of CATHERINE.

CHARTRES, REGNAULT DE: Archbishop of Rheims.

CHATELLERAULT: a heavily fortified town some twenty miles north of CHAUVIGNY in central France.

CHAUVIGNY: a town consisting of five interlaced castles situated on a hill overlooking the Vienne River. It is just to the east of POITIERS and some two hundred and twenty miles south of Paris. THOMAS NEVILLE spent some time here in the company of LANCASTER, the BLACK PRINCE and BOLINGBROKE during 1378.

CINQUE PORTS: the five (thus "cinque") important medieval southeastern ports of England: Dover, Hastings, Hythe, Romney and Sandwich. The barons of the Cinque Ports, as the Lord Warden of the Cinque Ports, were very powerful offices.

CLEMENT VII: the man elected by the breakaway cardinals to the papal throne after the election of URBAN VI was declared void because of the interference of the Roman mob. Clement rules from AVIGNON while URBAN, who refuses to resign, continues to rule from Rome.

COURTENAY, SIR ROBERT: squire to THOMAS NEVILLE. See also SQUIRE.

D'ARC, JACQUES: sergeant of the village of Domremy, in the province of Lorraine, France. Father of JEANNETTE D'ARC.

D'ARC, JEANNETTE (JEANNE, OR JOAN): second daughter of JACQUES D'ARC. Known as the Maid of France for her visionary prophecies.

D'ARC, ZABILLET (ISABELLE): wife of JACQUES D'ARC and mother of JEANNETTE D'ARC.

DATING: medieval Europeans almost never used calendar dates; instead they orientated themselves within the year by the religious cycle of Church festivals, holy days and saints' days. Although there were saints' days every day of the year, most regions observed only a few of them; the average number of holy days observed within the English year, for example, was between forty and sixty. In Florence it was as high as 120. Years tended to be dated by the length of a monarch's reign, each successive year starting on the date the monarch was crowned; EDWARD III was crowned on 1 February 1327, so, according to popular use, each new year during his reign would begin on 1st February. The legal year in England was calculated from Lady Day (25th March), so for legal purposes the new year began on 26th March. See also HOURS OF THE DAY, and my web page on medieval time for a full explanation on calculating the medieval year: www.saradouglass.com/medtime.html.

DAUPHIN: the official title of the heir to the French throne, Prince CHARLES, grandson of King JOHN.

DUNOIS, COMTE DE: the commander of the French garrison at Orleans. Better known as the Bastard of Orleans.

EDWARD III: a now-dead king of England. Grandfather of RICHARD II.

GABRIEL, SAINT: an archangel of heaven.

GASCONY: a province in the south of France famed for its wine and horses.

GERARDO: Italian man, keeper of the northern gate (the Porta del Popolo) in Rome.

GLASDALE, SIR WILLIAM: One of HOTSPUR's officers at the siege of Orleans. Commander of the fort of LES TOURELLES.

GLOUCESTER: see WOODSTOCK, THOMAS.

GRAVENSTEEN, THE: the Count of Flanders' castle home in Ghent, capital of Flanders.

HALES, JOHN: a husbandman from the village of BARMING in Kent.

HALSTOW HALL: THOMAS NEVILLE's home estate in Kent on the Hoo Peninsula near the Thames estuary.

HAUBERK: a tunic made of chain mail. Generally, it had sleeves (sometimes of chain mail, sometimes of plate armor) and reached to a knight's knees.

HOTSPUR: see PERCY, HENRY.

HOURS OF THE DAY: although clock time was slowly spreading by the end of the fourteenth century (clock time used an evenly divided twenty-four hour day), most people within hearing of church or monastic bells orientated themselves within the day by the canonical hours. The Church divided the day into seven, according to the seven hours of prayer:

- The day began with *Matins*, usually an hour or two before dawn.
- The second of the hours was *Prime*—daybreak.
- The third hour was *Terce*, set at about 9 a.m.
- The fourth hour was *Sext* (originally midday).
- The fifth hour was *Nones*, set at about 3 in the afternoon, but, in the thirteenth century, it was moved closer to midday.
- The sixth hour was *Vespers*, normally early evening.
- The seventh hour was *Compline*, bedtime.

These hours were irregular both within the day and within the year, because the hours orientated themselves around the rising and setting of the sun, and thus the hours contracted and expanded according to the season.

HUNDRED YEARS' WAR: a period of intense war between France and England that lasted from roughly the mid-fourteenth to fifteenth centuries. It was caused by many factors, but primarily by EDWARD III's insistence that he was the true heir to the French throne. The English and French royal families had intermarried for generations, and EDWARD was, in fact, the closest male heir. However, his claim was through his mother, who was the daughter of a French king, and French law did not recognize claims through the female line. The war was also the result of hundreds of years of tension over the amount of land the English held in France (often over a third of the realm).

ISABEAU DE BAVIÈRE: wife of Prince LOUIS of France, mother of CHARLES and CATHERINE.

JOAN OF KENT: wife of the BLACK PRINCE, and a famed beauty in her youth. Mother of RICHARD II. Before her marriage to the BLACK PRINCE, Joan was married, first, to Sir Thomas Holland, the Earl of Kent, and, secondly, to William Montagu, the Earl of Salisbury. By Holland, Joan had six children. Joan had a complicated marital life. She secretly married both Holland and Montagu in her early teens and managed to keep her bigamous relationship secret from both men for almost ten years.

JOHN, KING: elderly king of France, currently held hostage in England after being captured at the battle of POITIERS by the BLACK PRINCE.

JOHN OF GAUNT, Duke of Lancaster and Aquitaine, Earl of Richmond, King of Castile, and prince of the Plantagenet dynasty. Fourth-born, but second surviving son of EDWARD III (Edward Plantagenet) and his queen, PHILIPPA, John of Gaunt is the most powerful and wealthy English nobleman of the medieval period. The name Gaunt (his popular nickname) derives from Ghent, where he was born. Married first to Blanche of Lancaster, then to Constance of Castile; both dead. By Blanche he had a son, HENRY (HAL) BOLINGBROKE, by Constance two daughters (who became the queens of Castile and Portugal), and by his long-time mistress, KATHERINE SWYNFORD, two illegitimate children, HENRY and JOAN BEAUFORT. Gaunt has now married Katherine.

KENILWORTH: JOHN OF GAUNT's main residence in Warwickshire.

LAMBETH PALACE: the palatial London residence of the archbishops of Canterbury, Lambeth Palace sits on the eastern bank of the Thames almost directly across from WESTMINSTER.

LANCASTER, DUKE OF: See JOHN OF GAUNT.

LA ROCHE-GUYON: a castle to the east of Paris.

LA ROCHELLE: one of the ports on the coast of France, held by the English for many years.

LES TOURELLES: fort sitting over the southern spans of the bridge crossing the River Loire into Orleans. During the siege of Orleans it was seized by the English.

LOLLARDS: the popular name given to followers of JOHN WYCLIFFE. It is a derisory name, taken from the fourteenth-century word "lolling," which means mumbling.

LONDON BRIDGE: for centuries there was only one bridge crossing the Thames. It crossed from Southwark on the southern bank into London itself, linking up with Watling Street, one of the great Roman roads in England. As with most bridges in medieval Europe, it was built over with tenement buildings and shops.

LOUIS: only son of KING JOHN of France. Louis suffered an unfortunate encounter with a peacock which drove him insane, and now his son, CHARLES, is heir to KING JOHN.

MARCEL, ETIENNE: a rich and influential Parisian cloth merchant and Provost of the Merchants of Paris, an office somewhat like that of a Lord Mayor. He died during the French uprising (known as the Jacquerie) some two years before the events of *The Wounded Hawk*.

MICHAEL, SAINT: an archangel of heaven.

MOWBRAY, THOMAS: Earl of Nottingham and Duke of Norfolk and a boyhood friend of RICHARD's.

NARROW SEAS: The French name for the English Channel.

NAVARRE: a rich kingdom in the extreme northwest of Spain, it has been in the control of French nobles and kings for generations. Until the early fourteenth century the king of France had also held the title King of Navarre, but a complicated succession crisis witnessed the separation of the two kingdoms into separate branches of the same family. Currently it is ruled by PHILIP, known as PHILIP THE BAD.

NEVILLE, MARGARET: wife of THOMAS NEVILLE. They have a daughter, Rosalind.

NEVILLE, RALPH, BARON OF RABY AND EARL OF WESTMORLAND: a powerful noble from the north of England. Uncle to THOMAS NEVILLE.

NEVILLE, THOMAS: a senior member of the powerful Neville family. Nephew to RALPH NEVILLE. Married to MARGARET with whom he has a daughter, Rosalind. Neville was once a Dominican friar.

NORTHUMBERLAND, EARL OF: See PERCY, HENRY.

NOTTINGHAM, EARL OF: see MOWBRAY, THOMAS.

NOYES, SIR GILLES DE: a French nobleman.

PEDRO OF CATALONIA: Count of Catalonia in northeastern Spain.

PERCY, HENRY: the Earl of Northumberland and the most powerful nobleman in England behind LANCASTER. Northumberland has long been rivals with the Lancastrian faction which includes RALPH NEVILLE and THOMAS NEVILLE.

PERCY, HENRY (HOTSPUR): son and heir of the Earl of Northumberland, and powerful nobleman in his own right.

PEYTRAL: plate armor covering a horse's chest. See also ARMOR.

PHILIP THE BAD: King of Navarre and Count of Evreux, cousin to King JOHN and a powerful figure in French politics. As well as ruling NAVARRE, Philip holds extensive lands in the west of France.

PHILIPPA: a now-dead queen of England, wife to the deceased EDWARD III, and mother of LANCASTER. She died some years before the events of this book.

PHILIPPA: daughter of HENRY PERCY, Earl of Northumberland, sister to HOTSPUR, and wife of ROBERT DE VERE, Earl of Oxford.

POITIERS: a town in central France, and site of one of the BLACK PRINCE's greatest victories during the HUNDRED YEARS' WAR.

RABY: see NEVILLE, RALPH.

RAVENSPUR: Ravenspur sat on a spur of land jutting out into the sea at the very mouth of the Humber Estuary in medieval Yorkshire. The spit of land vanished in a storm some three hundred years ago: Ravenspur no longer exists.

RICHARD II: King of England, son of the BLACK PRINCE (deceased) and JOAN OF KENT.

SALISBURY, SIR ROGER: HAL BOLINGBROKE's senior squire. See also SQUIRE.

SAVOY PALACE: the Duke of LANCASTER's residence on THE STRAND just outside London's western walls.

SCALES, LORD THOMAS: HOTSPUR's second-in-command at Orleans.

SCROPE, WILLIAM: Earl of Wiltshire and commander of RICHARD's Irish army.

SEGUIN: one of the priests attached to REGNAULT DE CHARTRES, Archbishop of Rheims.

SHAFFRON: plate armor covering a horse's head. See also ARMOR.

SHERIFF HUTTON: the main castle and residence of RALPH NEVILLE, Baron of Raby and Earl of Westmorland, some ten miles northeast of York.

SLUYS (OR SLUIS) HARBOR: a major medieval harbor on the Zwin Estuary which silted up in the seventeenth century. Sluis is now an inland town.

SMITHFIELD (OR SMOOTHFIELD): a large open space or field in London's northern suburbs, just beyond Aldersgate. For many centuries it was the site of games, tournaments, and trading, craft and pleasure fairs. East Smithfield was a similarly large field to the east of London.

SQUIRE: in the late fourteenth century the social status and meaning of "squire" is different to the earlier chivalric perception of a squire as a "knight-in-training." The late-fourteenth-century "squire" is just as likely to be referred to as a valet or even a sergeant. He was generally of noble blood, but he may not be a "knight-in-training" as such.

STANDISH, JOHN: a squire in the employ of WILLIAM WADSWORTH, Lord Mayor of London. See also SQUIRE.

STRAND, THE: an important street running from London along the northern bank of the Thames down to WESTMINSTER, lined by palaces of the nobles.

STRAW, JACK: a husbandman from the village of BARMING in Kent.

STURRY, SIR RICHARD: a councillor of RICHARD's.

SUDBURY, SIMON: Archbishop of Canterbury and Chancellor of England.

SWYNFORD, KATHERINE, LADY: wife of JOHN OF GAUNT, Duke of Lancaster. Her first husband, now dead, was Sir Hugh de Swynford, a member of the retinue of JOHN OF GAUNT. Katherine is sister-in-law to Geoffrey Chaucer. By JOHN OF GAUNT she has two children, HENRY and JOAN BEAUFORT, born out of wedlock but legitimated by Parliament.

TALBOT, LORD JOHN: one of HOTSPUR's commanders at Orleans.

THORSEBY, RICHARD: the Prior General of England, administering all Dominicans and their friaries in the realm of England.

TONSURE: a round, shaved patch on the crown of a cleric's head.

TRESILIAN, SIR ROBERT: Chief Justice of the King's Bench, one of the primary judges in the land.

TRUEMAN, JACK: a LOLLARD priest.

TUSSER, THOMAS: steward to THOMAS NEVILLE.

TYLER, WAT: a sergeant-at-arms in LANCASTER's household.

URBAN VI: the man elected by the College of Cardinals to the papal throne after the death of Gregory XI in 1378.

VERE, ROBERT DE: Earl of Oxford, and close friend of RICHARD's. De Vere is married to PHILIPPA, daughter of HENRY PERCY, the Earl of Northumberland.

WADSWORTH, WILLIAM: Lord Mayor of London.

WARWICK, EARL OF: see BEAUCHAMP, THOMAS.

WESTMINSTER: in medieval England Westminster was an important municipality in its own right, and separate from London, although both were intricately linked. Most of medieval Westminster was destroyed by fire in the early nineteenth century, but it consisted of a large palace complex boasting three halls (only one of which still stands) as well the abbey.

WHITTINGTON, RICHARD (DICK): a mercer and alderman of Broad Street ward in London.

WILTSHIRE, EARL OF: see SCROPE, WILLIAM.

WOODSTOCK, THOMAS OF: Earl of Buckingham and Duke of Gloucester, seventh and youngest son of EDWARD III of England; Constable of England.

WORDE, WYNKYN DE: the last of the Dominican friars who worked the archangels' will on earth. THOMAS NEVILLE now hunts for de Worde's lost casket.

WYCLIFFE, JOHN: an eccentric English cleric and master of Balliol College, Oxford.

[illegible] England; Westminster [illegible] parish/municipality in its own right and separated from London, although both were physically united. Much of original Westminster was destroyed by fire in the early nineteenth century but it consisted of a large palace complex housing three halls (only one of which still stands) as well the abbey.

Whittington, Richard (Dick), a mercer and Alderman of Broad Street ward in London.

[illegible]

Woodstock, Thomas of, Earl of Buckingham and Duke of Gloucester; seventh and youngest son of Edward III of England; Constable of England.

[illegible] one of the last of the Dominican friars who worked [illegible]

Wykeham, William of: an exceptionally [illegible] founder of New College, Oxford.

Prologue

THE LIEUTENANT pushed his fork back and forth across the table, back and forth, back and forth, his eyes vacant, his mind and heart a thousand galaxies away.

Scrape . . . scrape . . . scrape.

"For heaven's sake, Chris, will you stop that? It's driving me crazy!"

The lieutenant gripped the fork in his fist, and his companion tensed, thinking Chris would fling it across the dull, black metal table toward him.

But Chris' hand suddenly relaxed, and he managed a tight, half-apologetic smile. "Sorry. It's just that this . . . this . . ."

"We only have another-two day spans, mate, and then we wake the next shift for their stint at uselessness."

Chris' fingers traced gently over the surface of the table. It vibrated. Everything on the ship vibrated.

"I can't bloody wait for another stretch of deep sleep," he said quietly, his eyes flickering over to Commander Devereaux sitting at a keyboard by the room's only porthole. "Unlike *him*."

His fellow officer nodded. Perhaps thirty-five rotations ago, waking from their allotted span of deep sleep, the retiring crew had reported a strange vibration within the ship. No mechanical or structural problem . . . the ship was just *vibrating*.

And then . . . then they'd found that the ship was becoming a little sluggish in responding to commands, and after five or six day spans it refused to respond to their commands at all.

The other three ships in the fleet had similar problems—at least, that's what their last communiques had reported.

The Ark crew were aware of the faint phosphorescent outlines in the wake of the other ships, but that was all now. So here they were, hurtling through deep space, in ships that responded to no command, and with cargo that the crews preferred not to think about. When they volunteered for this mission, hadn't they been told that once they'd found somewhere to "dispose" of the cargo they could come home?

But now, the crew of *The Ark* wondered, *what* would be disposed of? The cargo? Or them?

It might have helped if the commander had come up with something helpful. But Devereaux seemed peculiarly unconcerned, saying only that the vibrations soothed his soul and that the ships, if they no longer responded to human command, at least seemed to know what they were doing.

And now here he was, tapping at that keyboard as if he actually had a purpose in life. None of them had a purpose any more. They were as good as dead. Everyone knew that. Why not Devereaux?

"What are you doing, sir?" Chris asked. He had picked up the fork again, and it quivered in his over-tight grip.

"I . . ." Devereaux frowned as if listening intently to something, then his fingers rattled over the keys. "I am just writing this down."

"Writing *what* down, sir?" the other officer asked, his voice tight.

Devereaux turned slightly to look at them, his eyes wide. "Don't you hear it? Lovely music . . . enchanted music . . . listen, it vibrates through the ship. Don't you *feel* it?"

"No," Chris said. He paused, uncomfortable. "Why write it down, sir? For *who?* What is the bloody *point* of writing it down?"

Devereaux smiled. "I'm writing it down for Katie, Chris. A song book for Katie."

Chris stared at him, almost hating the man. "Katie is *dead*, sir. She has been dead at least twelve thousand years. I repeat, what is the fucking *point?*"

Devereaux's smile did not falter. He lifted a hand and placed it over his heart. "She lives here, Chris. She always will. And in writing down these melodies, I hope that one day she will live to enjoy the music as much as I do."

IT WAS then that *The Ark*, in silent communion with the others, decided to let Devereaux live.